THE WOMEN OF CHATEAU LAFAYETTE

THE
WOMEN
of
CHATEAU
LAFAYETTE

STEPHANIE DRAY

BERKLEY
NEW YORK

BERKLEY
An imprint of Penguin Random House LLC
penguinrandomhouse.com

Copyright © 2021 by Stephanie Dray

Library of Congress Cataloging-in-Publication Data

Names: Dray, Stephanie, author.
Title: The women of Chateau Lafayette / Stephanie Dray.
Description: First edition. | New York: Berkley, 2021.
Identifiers: LCCN 2020030397 (print) | LCCN 2020030398 (ebook) |
ISBN 9781984802125 (hardcover) | ISBN 9781984802149 (ebook)
Subjects: LCSH: Château de Chavaniac-Lafayette
(Chavaniac-Lafayette, France)—Fiction. | GSAFD: Epic fiction.
Classification: LCC PS3604.R39 W66 2021 (print) |
LCC PS3604.R39 (ebook) | DDC 813/.6—dc23
LC record available at https://lccn.loc.gov/2020030397
LC ebook record available at https://lccn.loc.gov/2020030398

Export Edition ISBN: 9780593335932

Printed in the United States of America
1 3 5 7 9 10 8 6 4 2

Jacket art: landscape © David Noton Photography/Alamy;
mother and child © H. Armstrong Roberts/Retrofile/Getty; archway ©
Маријана Петровић/Getty
Jacket design by Emily Osborne
Maps by David Lindroth
Book design by Kristin del Rosario

To my dad, who patiently critiqued
his teenaged daughter's first novel,
and never told her how bad it really was

ENGLAND

Poperinge
Dunkirk
Ypres
Hazebrouck
English Channel
BELGIUM
GERMANY
Amiens
LUX.
Paris **Drancy**
Versailles
Verdun
Metz

GERMAN OCCUPATION ZONE

F R A N C E

SWITZ.

Bay of Biscay

Riom   Vichy
Clermont-Ferrand
Brioude   Lyon
Paulhaguet
Langeac   Chavaniac-Lafayette
Mont Mouchet   Le Puy-en-Velay

Bordeaux

ITALY

Biarritz
SPAIN
FREE ZONE

Marseilles   Nice
Rivesaltes   Gulf of Lion
Mediterranean Sea

0 MILES 100
0 KM 100

France, World War II
Free Zone

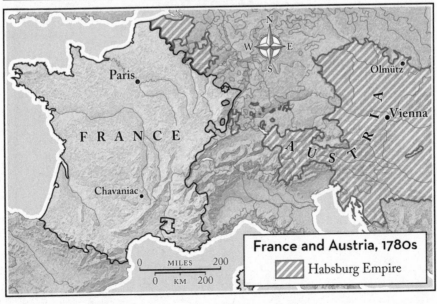

Paris
Olmütz
Vienna

F R A N C E
A U S T R I A

Chavaniac

0 MILES 200
0 KM 200

France and Austria, 1780s
Habsburg Empire

THERE ARE PLACES IN THIS WORLD WHERE THE PAST STILL ECHOES in the stones. The Château de Chavaniac is such a place. There, in the heart of France—where ancient lava once escaped its fiery prison to reach for the sky—was born a knight-errant who fought one revolution and sparked another, breaking the chains of monarchy and transforming the world.

His name was Lafayette, his gleaming white castle a fortress of liberty, and after his death it would be safeguarded by Americans through two world wars, sheltering more than twenty-five thousand sick, orphaned, and refugee children.

Most castles are defended by men.

This one, by women.

IT ALWAYS COMES BACK TO THE CASTLE.

From my perch in the ballroom's window seat, I watch the party latecomers arrive in gleaming coupes, cabriolets, and roadsters, chauffeurs honking to get ahead of the jam. Under the violet haze of the setting sun, a crush of bejeweled women is already storming the entryway and spilling up the spiral staircase in a cloud of Chanel No. 5—all of them hoping to see historical relics of the French general who was born here.

Everybody else is so eager to get into this old pile of rocks, when all I want is to get out . . .

I've lived between these storied walls since infancy, having been rescued from the streets of Paris by the American charity that runs the castle. With other children who lost one or both parents during the Great War, I came of age here—a little French orphan speaking English, playing baseball, chewing gum, and watching Hollywood silent movies. I was lucky enough to get a first-rate education—not to mention hard-won lessons about how to fight bullies on the playground—but I've never been farther away from the castle than the two-hour drive to Clermont-Ferrand, where I took my exam for my teacher's certificate.

Maybe it's selfish to want more from life than an isolated French village in the mountains can provide, but at twenty-three, I'm dying to see more of the world. And that's where a scholarship to the École des Beaux-Arts in Paris comes in.

The first time I applied for the Lafayette Memorial Foundation's scholarship, they said I was too young. The next time, the board reminded me the scholarship was really envisioned only for the *boys* who grew up in the castle's orphanage or attended its prestigious school. The year after that, they hinted I was getting too old for consideration anyway and really ought to be thinking about marriage. But I've never thought of myself as the marrying kind, and tonight's my last chance at a scholarship, so I'm stealing surreptitious glances at my artwork on display, trying to gauge the reactions of the guests and board members to the bust I sculpted of the less famous Lafayette.

Oh, I'd have loved to sculpt something more *avant-garde* than a musty old Revolutionary hero's saintly wife, but an artist has to eat. And the board members aren't going to give me a scholarship unless I press their patriotic buttons. My competition—guys like Samir Bensaïd, a French Algerian wearing a tuxedo and fez tonight—made predictable submissions. Dioramas of General Lafayette's battles, maps of his travels, essays about his philosophies. I wanted to set myself apart, which is why I used a rare portrait of Lafayette's wife to model a sculpture.

I thought it was just the ticket. My ticket out of these mountains, that is. But now I'm worried that I made *La Femme Lafayette*'s eyebrows too prominent and her eighteenth-century hedgehog-style wig too . . . *hedge-hoggy*.

While I'm worrying, Henri Pinton kisses me for good luck. We've been sweethearts of a sort since he was in short pants and I was in pigtails—though *sweet* is really his thing, not mine. Now he's all grown up in tuxedo and tailcoat, looking like he stepped off the set of a Frank Capra movie. "Relax, blondie," he says. "Just breathe."

"I don't know how anybody can breathe in a dress like this," I complain, fiddling with the straps of my glitzy white gown—a purgatorial designer getup that cost more than I can afford on a teacher's salary. Normally, I'm a trousers-and-saddle-shoes kind of girl, but I've got to impress the wealthy patrons who make this establishment possible with fundraising galas like this one.

Though this is more of a good-bye party, truth be told. Glancing down at the courtyard where the tricolor of France and the American Stars and Stripes droop for want of a breeze, I remember that everybody at the castle used to say: *These flags fly together or fall together.* But isn't that a laugh? With all the talk of war, the Americans who bought and renovated this old castle are leaving. The Moffats, who lived here all my life, are long gone, and Madame Beatrice—the colorful founder and president of the institute—left a few weeks ago. She said she helped drag America into the last war, and she'll do it again if she has to.

In the meantime, the preventorium will be left to the supervision of the Baroness de LaGrange, who is currently explaining to a dizzying array of diamond-bedecked middle-aged women sipping at rose-hued vermouth cocktails that this ballroom, the so-called philosopher's salon, has been lovingly restored to its eighteenth-century splendor with tall gilded mirrors and a freshly polished parquet floor. Meanwhile, her husband, the baron, is cloistered with the board's most prominent members—cigar-chomping government officials and pipe-puffing French industrialists, all ranting about the communists and fascists and whether we're ready for a war with Hitler.

All this war talk makes the spirit of the party faintly desperate—people talking too fast, eating too much, and laughing too hard, as if we might never get another chance . . .

"This is over-the-top," says our friend Samir, gesturing at the lavish buffet, buckets of champagne, and rose garlands hanging from the gilt-edged carved doors. "But I guess the moneyed class wouldn't trek into the mountains for a bake sale, so while they're here we'd better soak them for every penny, pound, and franc."

I smirk. "You sound like a communist, Sam. Keep talking like that and I'll tell the baron."

Sam grins. "You're not *that* competitive, are you, Marthe?"

"Orphan's motto," I remind him. "Always look out for *me, myself, and I.*"

He laughs, but I mean it. We're pals, so I know Sam wants this scholarship, but I want it more. I can already hear Parisian professors pronouncing my name with French sophistication instead of in the clumsy American way that sounds like *Marta*. I can already feel the fizz of excitement in visiting the Louvre for the first time, I can almost taste the espresso I'll drink at cafés with a view of the Eiffel Tower, and my fingers are already itching to sketch by the river Seine. My exciting new life starts tonight!

At eight, between bites of crudités, I force myself to listen patiently to speeches about the charitable endeavors here at Lafayette's chateau, where the orphanage I grew up in has been shuttered in favor of an advanced medical preventorium for malnourished and tubercular children.

At nine, Henri tells me I look like Greta Garbo, and dancing with him to "Tomorrow's Another Day," I feel like Cinderella.

Then at ten sharp they announce the winner of the scholarship, and my coach to a better future turns out to be a big fat pumpkin . . .

By eleven I'm drunk and brooding on a bench in the rose garden with a half-empty bottle of champagne, a pilfered tray of hors d'oeuvres, and my bust of Lafayette's wife. Having stolen her off her pedestal display, I now glare at her like a critic. "I admit this isn't your best look . . ." But those fat eyebrows give a little interest to a sculpture. The judges should have appreciated that.

Philistines.

I take another gulp of champagne straight from the bottle because I'm not drunk enough yet to go back inside, where the party roars on without me. I'm feeling sorry for myself. In the blackest of moods. Ungrateful too. "Oh, don't look at me that way," I say to the stone marquise, like her doe eyes can see into my guilty heart. "You had the world handed to you on a silver platter. Title, riches, castles . . ."

I trail off, hearing footsteps. *Merde.* I didn't think anyone noticed when I slipped down the back stairs. The rose garden should be the last place anybody would look for me—anybody but Henri Pinton, who's known my hiding places since childhood. Now he asks, "Who are you talking to?"

"*La Femme Lafayette*," I confess, cradling her stone head. "She's a good listener."

Henri chuckles, fishes a cigarette from his pocket, and lights up. "Listen, I know you're bent about losing the scholarship . . ."

I've always liked his habit of using French-accented American slang, but it annoys me now because I'm more than *bent*. And he should know it. We grew up here together—went to school together, even before the foundation could afford separate classrooms for girls. He's always known that I dreamed about being more than a schoolteacher—a profession to which I'm singularly ill suited, which I prove by stealing the cigarette right out of Henri's mouth.

He lets me do it but asks, "Trying to get fired?"

"Wouldn't that just be another kick in the pants?" I ask, taking a puff.

Teachers here at the preventorium's school are expected to set a good example. That means no smoking or drinking for unmarried young women like me. Even forward-thinking Madame Beatrice expects me to at least *pretend* to be ladylike. Unfortunately, that train left the station a bottle of champagne ago. "Do you think the marquise de Lafayette will rat me out?"

"I think the old hag will keep quiet if you put her back before anybody notices she's missing." Henri takes a bite of pastry, then pops the rest into my mouth, which keeps me from saying that I can throw my sculpture off the castle roof if I want to—and I do. I'm forced to chew, listening to the muted oompah of the bass, the wail of the saxophone, and the sultry song of the chanteuse from the house while Henri says, "At least it wasn't Sam who beat you."

"I wish it *was* Sam," I say in a spray of crumbs.

I could at least feel a little happy for a pal. Instead, the scholarship went to a dull fellow who wants to study engineering, and I overheard one of the board members whisper, "Marthe's talented, but there's no use for artists if there's a war . . ."

Henri clears his throat and says, "I've got an idea that might cheer you up . . ."

I hope he means stealing another bottle of champagne, but he's the wholesome outdoorsy sort who thinks problems can be solved with a camping trip, a hayride, or a midnight swim, so I warn, "I'm in no mood for a jump in the fishpond."

He takes off his tuxedo jacket, slipping it over my bare shoulders. "Let's jump into something else together." I'm too drunk to take his good manners for a tip-off and I sit there like an imbecile as he roots around in his pocket. Then he comes out with something that glints in the moonlight. "How's this for a consolation prize?"

A ring? Grateful for alcohol-numbed emotions, I laugh but give him a little shove. "I'm in no mood for jokes either."

He's not laughing, but he can't be serious. Whereas I'm an orphan without any family at all, Henri's *a ward of the nation,* because his father was killed in the Battle of Verdun. He has a mother and a struggling family farm to support while he finishes his medical studies; it's his dream to work as a physician in the preventorium one day, so marriage isn't in the cards for a long time, if ever, and we've both been frank about that. Nevertheless, now he clears his throat and begins, *"Marthe Simone—"*

I stop him before he can go all the way down on one knee. "Do you want to give your mother a heart attack? God knows she doesn't think I'm good enough for you."

"She doesn't think anyone is good enough for me," he admits, holding the ring up to the moonlight until I recognize it. And I gasp, covering my mouth, because now I know he's serious. It's his mother's ring. When we were young, I'd see that distinctive diamond wreathed in a matte gold halo nearly every month when Madame Pinton came to visit Henri here at the castle . . . visits I used to envy.

Like Henri, some of the kids we grew up with had a surviving parent or grandparent who could take care of them after the war. Most of the others eventually got adopted. But nobody wanted a smart-mouthed rough-and-tumble little girl like me. Oh, some couples expressed interest, one even returned for a second visit, but they never came back. And so I taught myself not to expect anybody to come back for me—taught myself not to need anybody.

Now Henri squints, trying to gauge me. "Maman gave her blessing when I reminded her that I could be called to join a regiment anytime . . ."

I exhale a long ribbon of smoke in frustration that Henri has gotten caught up in the blather of politicians that's come to nothing for four years, and a good thing too, because France still hasn't recovered from the last war. "You probably scared your mother to death with talk like that. You're not going to get called up!"

"Marthe," he says, brows furrowing, "Hitler rolled over Czechoslovakia. Poland is next, and if that happens, France will fight."

He's crazy. Our leaders talk tough to Hitler, but that's all. France isn't going to fight to save Poland—a country most of my students couldn't even point out on a globe. I can see Henri is genuinely frightened, though, so I try to knock the frown off his face. "C'mon. You wouldn't even be thinking of marriage right now if it weren't for your father."

Henri shrugs. "Maybe not. But if I die at war like he did, I'd want to leave something of me behind. If not a baby, then at least a pretty widow . . . So, what do you say? Who needs an art scholarship when you've got a wedding ring?"

I wince because the question cuts me. How did he get the idea that studying art is just something I want to do until a husband comes along? Now I've got two things to brood about. "You're a real romantic . . ."

"You're the one who hates sentiment," he reminds me, stealing the cigarette back. He's right. I do hate sentiment. But I still get a little misty when he holds up his hand and says, "Marthe, I've loved you ever since that math class when Sam dipped your pigtail in an inkwell and you turned to stab him with a pencil in revenge, but missed and stuck me instead. See? I've still got the lead spot on my palm—the prick of Cupid's arrow."

We both laugh, and he glances nostalgically at the castle where it happened. It's lit up beautifully tonight. Even the mismatched square tower—a newer addition the Americans built when they bought this place—looks like less of an architectural abomination with spotlights setting it aglow. The castle has been a sanctuary for both of us, but maybe Henri's always loved it more because he had somewhere else to go.

Though I have no idea who my parents were, Henri used to insist that my father must have also been a soldier and that our heroic patriarchs would have made a marriage match of us, if they'd lived.

I'm sure of it, Henri would say. Henri is very sure of everything, which is his most endearing and irritating trait, because I'm not sure of much.

He means well, but his timing stinks. I *do* love Henri. He can be one of those saccharine saintly sorts, but he's a good kisser, my best pal, and the closest thing to family I've ever known. Now he's offering me a chance to make a real family . . .

I guess I'd have to be crazy to turn my nose up at that, but what would it mean to get married with everything so unsettled? He's not a doctor yet, so how would we afford anything on my teacher's salary? At least now I live in the staff quarters rent-free. I recoil at the sudden thought that he might expect me to get knocked up, move in with him and his mother on the family farm, and spend the rest of my life milking goats, but maybe it's time to face facts and give up unrealistic dreams about living an artist's life in Paris or anywhere else. War seems like a lousy reason to get hitched, but in my drunken state, I can't think of a better one.

Now Henri tosses the ring up and catches it again. "So, what do you think, blondie?"

"I think I need to be sober for this conversation. Give me a little time?"

But as it happens, time is something we don't have.

On the first of September, Germany invades Poland, France declares war, and the call comes for full mobilization even though it's harvesttime and wheat is still bundled in the fields. Henri and Sam are both called up, and I go with them to the train station in Paulhaguet.

To see them off, I've styled my pageboy hair with peekaboo bangs, and I keep up a steady stream of *stiff-upper-lip* chitchat that's supposed to keep spirits high, but I'm almost numb with shock, watching men and their wives embrace in tearful farewells on the platform.

None of this feels real. Like it's all some drunken dream, and I just need to wake up and get on with the hangover . . .

Sam's girl sends him off with a box of his favorite Algerian pastries. I've got only cigarettes for Henri, who tells me, "The war shouldn't last long. A few skirmishes and we'll make the Germans come to their senses, no?"

I nod, though it's difficult to imagine Henri soldiering. Oh, I've seen him with a hunting rifle, but he'd rather be healing creatures than hurting them. Now he kisses the top of my head and looks into my eyes. "Will you keep your nose out of trouble and hold down the fort while I'm gone?"

I'm not sure what that's supposed to mean, but swallowing over the knot in my throat, I promise. I'm trying not to worry as the conductor shouts for passengers to board. I'm also trying to ignore the voice in my head shrieking that when I was a baby, someone left me in the streets of Paris and people have been leaving me ever since. Friends at the orphanage got adopted or grew up and moved away. Teachers and nurses and administrators at the Lafayette Memorial came and went. Even Sam took off for a few years before returning to the castle to work as a valet. Henri's been my only constant, and now he's leaving too . . .

What a prize idiot I've been.

As the train starts whistling, I splutter, "Is it too late to say I'll marry you?"

Henri breaks into a broad grin. "Just in the nick of time!"

Already boarding, Sam calls to Henri, "Pinton, hurry up, will you?"

"I'm getting engaged," Henri shouts back, fishing in his shirt pocket. I can't believe he has the ring, but he does. And he laughs at my surprise. "I knew you'd see it my way, Marthe. I just didn't think you'd wait until the very last minute to say yes."

I want to cry, but I'm not the crying kind. "I'm sorry it's too late to get hitched and get lucky."

Henri laughs. "Gives me something to look forward to." He slides the ring onto my finger, then we kiss as the train starts to move. Reluctantly Henri pulls away, breaks into a run, and hops on the moving train as it chugs out of the station. And I'm left with a lingering kiss and a ring on my finger, feeling alone and aimless. Men hear the drum and march off, but what's a girl like me supposed to do in a world at war?

PART

ONE

Fourteen months later . . .

MARTHE
Chavaniac-Lafayette
The Free Zone
October 1940

I'VE ALMOST MADE IT, I THINK, PEDALING MY BICYCLE FASTER WHEN I see the castle's crenelated tower at the summit. I've ridden past yellowing autumn farmland, past the preventorium's dormitories for boys, and past the terra-cotta-roof-topped houses of the village. And despite blistered feet and scuffed saddle shoes, I'm feeling cocky.

As I near the castle proper, I'm no longer worried anyone is going to take what I've carried all this way, which is probably why I'm so surprised to see Sergeant Travert's old black Citroën parked by the village fountain.

Quelle malchance! What shit luck.

Sergeant Travert patrols our village every evening on his way home. For some reason the gendarme is early today, and having stalled out his jalopy, he's got the hood up to repair it.

I try to ride past, but he notices and waves me over.

My heart sinks as Travert approaches, doffing his policeman's cap, then resting his hand on his holstered pistol. "What have we here, mademoiselle?"

I pretend to be calm while he peers into my bicycle pannier baskets. "Just some supplies from Paulhaguet."

That's the nearest little town, where I bought dried sausage with ration coupons, but I traded on the black market to get sugar, paper for my classroom, and medicine for the doctors at the preventorium.

Black market barters for hard-to-find goods are illegal. I took the risk anyway for a good cause, but I had a selfish motive too. One the snooping constable uncovers with a disapproving arch of his bushy brow. "Cigarettes?"

According to our new leader, Marshal Pétain, Frenchwomen who smoke—not to mention foreigners and unpatriotic schoolteachers—are to blame for France's defeat.

Personally, I think it had more to do with Hitler.

Maybe it even had to do with military leaders like Pétain who believed in fairy tales like the stupid Maginot Line to keep us safe. I can't say something like that, though. I shouldn't even *think* something like that about the Marshal—the man who saved France in the last war, and, as everyone says, the only man who can save us now.

But *merde*, what smug idiots got us into this war?

Hitler's panzer divisions rolled past French defenses five months ago. The Allies fled at Dunkirk, leaving forty thousand French soldiers to cover their retreat and hold the Germans back. All for nothing. Eighteen days later, we surrendered, to the shock of the world. Like almost everyone else, I was relieved; I thought the fighting would stop and that Henri would come home. But now a swastika is flying over the Eiffel Tower, and France—or what's left of her below the line of demarcation—is neutral while Britain fights on, alone.

Almost two million French soldiers are prisoners of war—including Henri. *My* Henri. Given all that, smoking is the only thing keeping me sane, so the lie comes easily. "The cigarettes are for the baron."

The gendarme looks over his shoulder at the castle and says, "I took the Baron de LaGrange more for a man who prefers a pipe."

The baron is now the acting president of the preventorium. The baroness trained as a nurse in the last war and has a knack for organization, but unfortunately, women aren't supposed to run anything now, so her husband got the job. And as the founder of an elite pilots' training school and a senator with connections in the new Vichy government, the baron is too powerful to question about cigarettes.

Travert knows it and knits those bushy brows.

For a moment, I think he'll shrug and walk away. Instead, he sweeps autumn leaves off the low stone wall and leans against it. "It gets lonely around here these days, mademoiselle, does it not? Tell me, what does a schoolteacher with such pretty blue eyes do when class is not in session?"

"I lie about eating chocolates." What does he think? There are four hundred sick children to feed at the preventorium—which means growing vegetables, milking cows in the dairy, and helping to raise and butcher pigs.

Every day since the war started has been a struggle, but I don't think he cares about that. No, I think the gendarme is after something else when he reaches for my wrist and traces it with his thumb. "Your tone is sharp, mademoiselle. You ought to show more respect for an officer of the law."

I probably should, considering he could arrest me or seize my ill-gotten goods, but I'm too angry that he's touching me. I don't think he'd dare if I were wearing my engagement ring. It's tucked under my scarf, hanging from my neck on a chain because it kept slipping off a finger that has become, like the rest of me, thinner than before the war. Thinking about it makes me combative. "You really want to know what I do when I'm lonely? I kiss the picture of my fiancé, praying for his safe return from his prisoner of war camp."

That's enough to shame the gendarme, who shrugs like he was just testing me. "I wish all Frenchwomen were so devoted."

Sure, I was so devoted that I made Henri wait until the very last minute, once it was too late to arrange the wedding he wanted. Feeling miserably guilty, I look away, and the gendarme notices. "You're certain you have nothing to hide, mademoiselle? Your cheeks are pink!"

"The air is chilly," I say, tugging my old red beret down over my ears. "And I exhausted myself standing in line at the shops in Paulhaguet all morning, and on the ride back."

This is a stupid lie, because Travert knows I've been hiking, camping, and hunting in these rugged woods since I was in pigtails. A bicycle ride isn't enough to wind me. Then again, everything is harder when you're hungry.

Travert puffs out his barrel chest. "Exertion is good for you. The Marshal says to stay fit. Get lots of exercise and fresh air."

I could outrun Travert in a footrace any day, but I'd rather not have to, so I settle on sarcasm. "We must fight the rot of *la décadence* and restore the honor of France, no?"

He laughs, and I laugh too, but neither of us is amused.

According to the Marshal, *the honor of France* is so fragile that it was lost to art, accents, women, and wine. Meanwhile, on the BBC, the rogue General de Gaulle says French honor can be restored only by suicidal resistance against the Nazis.

I don't believe either of them.

These days it's hard to believe in anything but self-interest. And it's self-interest that saves me. Tempted by the dried sausage peeking out of its paper, Travert breaks an end off for his lunch and leaves me the rest. *"Au revoir, mademoiselle."*

He knows I'm guilty of black market bargaining or he wouldn't have taken a piece of my sausage, so I don't argue. *"Adieu!"*

Once inside the castle gates, I dodge mud puddles in the drive, where the ambulance has been stranded for a week without fuel. The children are at recess wearing scout uniforms; it seems everyone wears a uniform of some kind these days to *restore our morals.*

A fair-haired eight-year-old who came to us from Lille afflicted with rickets now hops off the swing set, her corkscrew curls bouncing as she runs through fallen leaves to greet me, calling, "Maîtresse! Maîtresse!" She's followed by an asthmatic fifteen-year-old from Toulouse, who is almost cured and ready to go back to her family.

Both girls are curious about my packages, so I scold, "No peeking. It's a surprise for the kitchen."

The littlest's eyes round. "Did you find cat tongue cookies?"

Our Lafayette kids all love the buttery crisps sent to us by Madame Beatrice from New York; they don't know our supplies are dwindling because of the blockade. For the children, the war seems far away, and we want to keep it that way, so I say, "We have to save the cookies for Christmas, but you might get a little sausage in your lentil soup. Now, go play before nap time."

When the girls run off, I stow the bicycle, tuck the cigarettes into my back pocket, and take the parcels to the old feudal guardroom kitchen, which the baroness has all but transformed into a modern canning factory. She's determined to pickle and preserve every last edible thing before winter sets in, assisted by the school's doyenne, Madame LeVerrier, and the foundation's secretary-general, Madame Simon—both of whom are as much a part of the castle as the wooden shutters on the casement windows.

Working beneath old copper pots that hang from the vaulted ceiling, the three women greet me as a heroine for finding even a *little* sugar. But I don't stay to bask in their praise, because the last thing I want is to be pressed into making wild strawberry preserves.

I'm in such a hurry to escape canning duty that I nearly plow over poor Dr. Anglade, who is coming down the castle's winding main staircase with a tray of syringes. When he sees what I've got for him, though, his stern expression melts. "Sulfonamide," he whispers reverently. "Dr. Boulagnon said he didn't expect a shipment in Paulhaguet for a week. Where did you get it?"

"It's better you don't ask too many questions." Or at least, that's what Madame Simon told me when emptying the preventorium's discretionary cashbox to send me on this mission. She also said, *When there's a war on, it's best not to tell anyone anything they don't need to know.*

Now Dr. Anglade eyes me warily through his round, wire-rimmed spectacles. "Can you get more?"

I shake my head. It's somebody else's turn to risk trading on the black market. Doing it once was impulsive. Twice would be stupid. I've always believed that you shouldn't put your neck out for others unless you want it chopped. So, having done my good deed, I trudge to my classroom, a plain chamber featuring rows of wooden desks for little girls and one for me. Over the door hangs a new portrait of the Marshal, white-haired, white-whiskered, and in uniform. Every teacher in France is supposed to enlist children to send drawings and letters and stories to the new head of state as a so-called Christmas Surprise for the Marshal.

I resent this. Our sick kids are with us at the preventorium only between six months and two years, until they're cured. My job is to see they don't fall so far behind in schooling that they can't pass the examinations for their certificate of primary studies. I teach them reading, writing, and basic mathematics. I don't have time to teach them about the Marshal or his so-called new National Revolution. Or maybe I just don't want to, because my feelings about both are mixed. *Not that I have the right to judge.* I'm no war hero, and everyone says the Marshal is doing the best he can. After all, with half the country occupied by the Nazis, we're all held at gunpoint, and it's impossible to know which of the new laws the Marshal is forcing down our throats and which Hitler is forcing down his.

Brooding about this, I make fifteen copies of tomorrow's spelling test, spreading the master copy out onto the hectograph tablet until the ink is ready. Then I carefully press paper to the gel and smooth it until it's a perfect mimic. I'm always particular about making worksheets, because it's about as close to a creative art as I get now that we're short on pens, paper, charcoal, and paint. And while the copies dry, I look over the Christmas Surprise assignments.

One of my students has drawn the Marshal as a lion wearing a French military cap, because I told her he was called the Lion of Verdun—and I laugh because she's given her lion a mustache. I'm less amused by the sycophantic essays written by the older girls about how the Marshal has given France the *gift of his person.* Maybe I'd be feeling more charitable if Henri weren't in a prison camp under the terms of surrender the Marshal negotiated.

I'm still hungry after a few slices of dried sausage at my desk. Here in the countryside we still have eggs and fruit and even butter—but it never seems like enough. Cigarettes take the edge off, so I'll have to find a secret spot in the castle to smoke where I can't be caught by our household management teacher, Faustine Xavier, a prissy little tattletale, who always wears her starched collars too high and her hair pinned too tight. Fortunately, I know all the secret spots. The old hidden feudal passages are too cold this time of year and I'm too claustrophobic to spend much time there anyway, but the attic has sunny windows, which makes it a favorite haunt of the castle cats—and I like it too.

It's where I used to sculpt and sketch, but no one goes up there anymore, so when I push the ancient door open wider on its rusty hinges, I'm startled to see a silhouette in the window seat. And the silhouette is equally startled by me. *"Sacrebleu!"* A dark-haired beauty emerges in statuesque splendor, silk blouse, bright red lipstick, and a cigarette holder between her fingers. "I thought you were my *maman* come to catch me out."

"Your *maman*?" I ask, confused.

The elegant stranger stares. ". . . Marthe?"

I stare back without recognition.

She smirks. "You don't remember me, do you?"

I feel like I should. No artist should forget cheekbones like hers, but lots of people pass in and out of this castle every day, and have every day of my life. Still, I find something familiar about her long dark eyelashes . . .

"About ten years ago," she prompts. "Maman brought me with her for some holiday function. You were one of the only girls at the orphanage, so I knitted you a red beret . . . and you took me sledding."

That jogs my memory. I was thirteen, and she was twelve, sporty and boyish. She's all girl now, which is why I didn't recognize her as the baron's daughter. "Anna de LaGrange?"

Flashing an art deco wedding ring set on her left hand that nearly blinds me with the green sparkle of its big emerald baguettes, she says, "I became the comtesse de Guébriant just before the war . . . not that marriage would stop Maman from scolding me like a child if she caught me smoking near her sacred relics."

She gestures irreverently to the crates filled with old donations to the castle's museum that haven't been sorted yet. Uniforms, maps, flags—tokens of the supposedly unbreakable alliance of Western democracies that helped win the last war. But in *this* war our British allies left us at Dunkirk, and the Americans let Hitler invade us with a neutral shrug. So as far as I'm concerned, these crates contain the detritus of a democratic alliance in decay. And given the current state of affairs, I don't think a little tobacco smoke is going to do it any more harm . . .

"So you're a countess now." I make a whistle that sounds like *la-di-da*. "Should I curtsy?"

She laughs. "Don't you dare. I don't go by the noble title except to irritate Maman with the reminder that I outrank her, but unfortunately she's too American to care."

I grin, stooping to pet the gray cat that circles my ankles. "I actually still wear that red beret. Everyone in the village sees me coming a mile away. And don't worry about your mother. The baroness is too busy pickling everything in reach to come up here."

Anna pats the window seat beside her in invitation to me, the cat, or both. "I'd offer you a cigarette, but it's my last one . . ."

"Thanks, I've got my own." I show her the blue package with its winged helmet, but I don't have a holder like hers and wouldn't use one if I did. "Gauloises."

"Gitanes," Anna says, snapping shut an empty diamond-encrusted cigarette case.

Well, isn't she all sparkle? Taking a long drag, she says, "This summer, when the air sirens in Paris sent me scrambling, this cigarette case was the only thing of my husband's I managed to rescue from our apartment. If I'd been thinking clearly, I'd have grabbed the framed picture from the wall. Now all I've got to remember him by is this . . ."

She pauses, savoring the distinctive sharp smoke as if tasting a lover's tongue. I feel as if I've intruded upon a private memory until she leans forward to light my cigarette with the glowing end of hers—pulling me into the intimate moment.

And I'm caught there.

"Is your husband—is he—"

"A prisoner," she says. "Papa tells me your fiancé is too."

I nod. "Stalag VIII-A, somewhere near Poland."

Her pretty face twists with sympathy. "I'm sorry, Marthe."

I nod, feeling sorry for her too. What a lousy thing for us to have in common. "What brings you to these hinterlands?"

She shrugs. "I fled to Biarritz after the armistice, but Maman wants to breathe down my neck, so here I am with nothing to do."

"Oh, there's plenty to do here—mostly work, though." I wonder if Anna knows how fortunate she is to have a mother to worry after her. I envy her, but I already like Anna more than I envy her, and I don't like many people.

Besides, it's nice to have someone my own age to talk to again.

"Don't worry." She grins. "I'm not expecting a vacation. I have a few tennis and swimming trophies to my name, so come summer I'll give lessons to the kids. Meanwhile, Maman is putting me to work with Madame Simon."

"My condolences."

Anna looks wary. "Simon's that bad to work for?"

I shrug. "She's blunt—but she keeps licorices for the kids in that leather briefcase of hers, so she's not all bad." But her office is in the square tower where we keep all the Lafayette Memorial Foundation's paperwork. Accounting books. Admissions applications. Discharge forms. Medical, academic, and employment records. In short, it's the dullest place in the castle. What I tell Anna is, "It's just chaos in the records office every fifteenth of the month; that's the day kids are admitted to the preventorium."

"Anything else I should know?"

A lot of boring stuff, but I want to impress her, so I say, "There are secret passages in the castle."

Her eyes brighten. "Really? Where do they go?"

"Nowhere now; they've been sealed up at the exit. But as kids we were terrified of getting lost in the walls and turning to a pile of bones."

"So there must be ghosts . . ."

"Doesn't every castle have ghosts in the movies?"

She grins wider. "Which reminds me—do you fancy going to the cinema with me sometime? My treat!"

Blowing a ribbon of smoke, I give her an unfortunate dose of reality. "I'm told there are three cinemas in Clermont-Ferrand, but that's hours away."

Anna sighs, fiddling with the bow of her blouse. "We really *are* in the middle of nowhere. Honestly, Marthe, I was surprised to learn you stayed on as a teacher here. I didn't figure you for the type."

"I'm not," I reply, waving my cigarette as evidence. "This year's letters of instruction say teachers are to serve as a moral example, and are entrusted with *the whole future of the nation*. Well, if that isn't just a bit more than I'm willing to take on . . ."

We both laugh, and it's a real laugh.

Flicking our ashes out the cracked window onto the terra-cotta roof tiles, we fall into easy conversation about books, movies, and art. She remembers that I used to sketch and notices my old easel in the corner. "Oh, no! I've accidentally invaded your sanctum sanctorum, haven't I? Don't tell me you're using this icebox your studio."

"Not since the war." In agreeing to marry Henri, I've given up dreams of a formal education in the fine arts, but that didn't stop the desire to create, and now I'm fighting off a different kind of hunger. "I'm not really working on anything anymore."

"Why not?"

I stare at my scuffed saddle shoes. "What's the point?" We're all too busy trying to get enough food, enough fuel, enough medicine. I can't justify using up paper, pencils, desperately needed supplies on artwork that seems . . . somehow . . . trivial. I'd feel like a pretender anyway.

I don't say any of this to Anna, who finds my bust of Adrienne Lafayette and gasps. "Is this yours?"

I nod, embarrassed, and stub out my cigarette. "It's not any good. It's all wig and eyebrows . . ."

But Anna's interested. She stares a long time, really studying my work. I find myself holding my breath, and I don't exhale until she says, "This piece might be brilliant, actually. It's not the usual shiny marble. It's rougher. You've given a glimpse into the woman's humanity, warts and all . . ."

Pleased, but afraid to look at Anna, I say, "I'm not good enough to work in marble yet, but I left the soapstone unpolished, hoping the texture would give it a modern edge."

"It really does! Where did you learn to sculpt?"

"Madame Beatrice gave me a few lessons."

The somewhat mysterious founder and president of the Lafayette Memorial Foundation is a polymath—actress, sculptress, and author of a book about an obscure desert queen. I was always flattered by the special interest she showed me on her yearly visits to the castle to oversee the charitable venture. I was touched by her warm encouragement too. "Of course, Madame Beatrice studied and mastered the neoclassical style, whereas I'm just sketching and sculpting by instinct."

"Then you have a natural gift, Marthe. You can't let it go to waste just because there's a war on!"

And with these words, I feel like she's shaken me awake from a long slumber.

ANNA CHANGES EVERYTHING AT THE CASTLE. FOR ONE THING, THE baron's daughter is the ginchiest girl around for miles. With her movie-star good looks, bold red lipstick, and formfitting sweaters, she's got men tripping over themselves. Never mind that she's married; Dr. Anglade and the Latin master nearly come to fisticuffs vying to open a door for her. And fourteen-year-old boys in the preventorium are all suddenly devout Catholics, eager for Sunday Mass at the village church, jostling to get close to Anna's pew just for a whiff of her sweet and smoky Tabu perfume.

Anna's also brimming with ideas for the preventorium—which is a shot in the arm, because since the Fall of France we've all existed in a state of suspension, breathing shallowly and waiting for our prisoners to come home. France's defeat has been especially devastating for the older, flag-waving generation, who are teary this Armistice Day, lost in bitter memories of the last war. It's depressing even for somebody like me, and I was never cheerful to begin with, so Anna's spiritedness is a proverbial breath of fresh air.

She hosts Wednesday-night billiard games and Sunday-night socials at which she plays piano for the staff. She teaches the older girls in the preventorium how to roll their hair and walk in heels with books balanced on their heads. She doesn't seem to have any idea of the effect she has on people, but she's a swell distraction. She makes it easier to forget the debacle of our continued national humiliation. At least until the autumn day when officials from Vichy show up at the castle to interrogate us. Then gossip flies up and down the square tower and in and out of the schoolrooms.

"Another political purge?"

"But we don't have any Jews or Freemasons left on the teaching staff!"

"—could they be looking to make arrests?"

We're eventually told the Marshal is considering a visit to the preventorium come springtime. The aging leader of France likes to bask in the adoration of children, but under the pretext of security, he sends advance men to sweep away adult dissenters and so-called undesirables. That's why Sergeant Travert and an officious little inspector from Vichy now sit across from me in the castle library, and the latter asks, "Have you ever been a member of the Communist Party, mademoiselle?"

"I'm not much of a joiner," I say.

From his wing chair, the stately Baron de LaGrange gives me a barely perceptible warning look to let me know that now isn't the time to wisecrack. I rein in my smart mouth, answering a few more questions before the inspector asks me to start snitching. "Tell me, mademoiselle. Are any of your colleagues at the school foreigners or Freemasons?"

All the foreigners are gone, but I'm pretty sure the Latin master used to be a Freemason. He's an insufferable old goat, but now isn't the time to settle scores. "None that I'm aware of . . ."

"Jews?"

"Not on the teaching staff," I say carefully, knowing the administrative offices are another matter. "Again, none that I'm aware of."

"Degenerates?"

Having only a vague idea what he means, I stare at the official—whose lardy complexion no one could ever want to carve in anything but wax.

"Sexual deviants, mademoiselle," he explains. "Women of low morals, corruptors of young people, homosexual men, sapphists, or pederasts . . ."

In my indignation, my mouth falls slack. And as my silence drags on, the baron pointedly clears his throat. This time I don't think his warning is for me, and the inspector moves on. "Any self-avowed champions of the republic?"

"I wouldn't know." *I wouldn't tell you if I did*, I think, plastering on a dim-witted smile. "I'm not political."

At least that much is true. Frenchwomen have never been allowed to vote, so I didn't see the point. Before the war, everybody was so worried about the communists that I never thought to worry about the royalist imbeciles who read *Action Française*—or the fascist crackpots of the Parti

Populaire. Now the imbeciles and crackpots have power—or at least as much as the Nazis let them have. And I wonder which kind of imbecile or crackpot this beady-eyed official is . . .

"I'm told, mademoiselle, that you've lived your whole life here. Perhaps that's why your manner is so . . . American?"

It's true that I grew up surrounded by teachers, soldiers, and doctors from the United States. Still, I snap, "I'm a Frenchwoman."

"You must've been instructed here to revere General Lafayette, no?"

"*Oui.*" Now doesn't seem like the time to admit I paid only half attention to those lessons, but everyone knows the new government's persecutions go against Lafayette's ideals of democracy, political liberty, and religious freedom.

That must be the problem, because the official says, "Individualism and the myth of human equality have brought France to her knees, mademoiselle. We cannot have our schoolteachers wedded to the old revolution, one aimed to appease the evil-minded mob. Revolution in our new age will nourish the people through *discipline*. Discipline teachers like you must provide."

I steal a look at the baron to see if he's on board with this, but he's busy adjusting his expensive silk tie, and Sergeant Travert's expression is like stone. I realize that if I don't go along, I'm going to get the ax. Since I can't afford to be fired from the only job I've ever had and my only means of supporting myself, I keep smiling until my cheeks hurt. "As I said, I'm not political. I just teach neutral subjects."

"There can be no neutrality in the classroom," the official barks. "As Marshal Pétain says, *The teaching of neutrality is the teaching of nothing.* You have to inculcate your students with a love—even worship—of the new order." I nod again, gambling that this guy just likes to hear himself talk. Then he slides a piece of paper in front of me. "Sign this."

He can't be serious. The paper says that I solemnly swear I'm not a member of any secret society. *Should I confess our old orphanage tree house club where Henri and Sam wouldn't let me in without a code word?*

The official says, "Your oath is required under the law for civil servants."

Of which, regrettably, I'm one. Sullenly, I sign the rotten thing.

Meanwhile the baron pinches the bridge of his nose, and I stand, thinking we're finished. That's when the inspector reads my signature aloud. *"Marthe Simone . . .* What type of name is that, mademoiselle?"

I know what he's getting at and I don't want to tell him I was named by and after our secretary-general, who is part Jewish. As the story goes, Madame Simon had to put something down on the forms for orphans with unknown parentage, so she made up some variation of her name. That's why I grew up with an Armenian boy named Simonian. An Italian boy was called Simonetti, and I became Simone.

Before I can say any of that, the baron puts his pipe down, stands to his intimidatingly full height, and says, "Gentlemen, we're running late and I can't have my staff standing in the hall all day. You can go, Marthe."

I don't need to be told twice. Sergeant Travert tries to open the door for me, but I reach it before he can, and I want to slam it on my way out. I'm boiling mad for some reasons I understand and others I don't. I'm in no mood to talk to anybody, but Anna waylays me on the grand staircase. "Maman wants to see you."

Merde. The baroness probably has a whole new list of chores—the annoying ones that always fall to me because everybody else has husbands or families or something better to do.

"It's important," Anna says, so I go. But on my way, I keep trying to remember the exact expression on Anna's pretty face when she said it was *important.* She looked serious . . . but did she look somber?

I worry when the baroness waves me into the parlor. "Ah. *Ma chère mademoiselle.*"

It's not like the matter-of-fact baroness to be solicitous, and my stomach bottoms out when she comes round the front of the desk to greet me, perching on its edge. Her hair used to be dark like Anna's, but in recent months it's gone gray. And she's never looked older than now. Fearing she has news about Henri, I shudder with sudden dread; I've told myself he's too smart to risk an escape attempt from his POW camp, but what if he's tried and got himself shot?

This is it, I think. *Whatever she says next is going to wreck me.*

A memory of Henri in a wild cherry tree flashes through my mind. We were sitting in its branches with our feet dangling when he kissed me the first time. He held his breath like he was afraid I'd pull away. Now I'm the one who can't breathe as I wait for the baroness to tell me he's dead . . .

"I'd like to discuss your employment," she says, and I hiccup with relief, because even if she's going to fire me, the news could've been so much worse. "In light of present political realities, the baron has decided to lock the museum until we can find new homes for the items that invite controversy."

I don't know what this has to do with me. Do they want to get rid of Ben Franklin's ring or Washington's dueling pistols? Maybe Lafayette's copy of the Declaration of the Rights of Man and of the Citizen. Or perhaps the trouble is the tricolor banner emblazoned with *Liberty, Equality, Fraternity* now that the Marshal has replaced our national motto with *Work, Family, and Fatherland.*

I've never cared about slogans or the old trinkets in our museum. In fact, I spent my entire adolescence rolling my eyes at them, so I'm shocked by just how much I hate the idea of locking them away. Maybe the baroness hates it too, because she stares out the window at dormant volcanic mountains and trees now dropping their dried, shriveled leaves. And with real anguish she murmurs, "After all we sacrificed in the last war . . . it was supposed to *end all wars*, yet here we are."

We're both silent until she straightens her smart square-shouldered suit jacket and turns to me. "Marthe, I don't have to tell you the difficulties we operate under here at the castle. The children need food, medicine, and blankets for the winter. Relief ships with supplies from New York can't get through the British blockade. We're going to need the French government's help, and we can't get it if this institution continues to celebrate Lafayette—whose political ideas are, in the current circumstances, considered dangerous."

I'm tempted to ask which of Lafayette's ideas are dangerous, just to see if she has the stomach to name them. But I don't, because I didn't have the courage to argue with the Vichy official when he said more or less the same thing. Now the baroness explains, "My daughter has suggested a way you might be able to help . . . and pursue your art at the same time."

"You want me to paint over the masonic symbols on Lafayette's walls?"

It's a dark joke, but she's serious. "Nothing so dramatic, but your sculpture gave her an idea. Yes, this is the house of Lafayette. Still, here also lived his wife, Adrienne—a good Catholic, a loyal spouse and devoted mother. A woman to whom the new government should raise no objection. If we were to commission you to replace some of Lafayette's portraits with new ones of Adrienne . . ."

I finally understand the direction of this conversation, and why it pains her. I'm shocked by how much it pains *me*. Thanks to Anna, for the first time in my life I'm being offered a commission—my first commission—yet it's for a terrible reason. And I'm being given the opportunity when seemingly every other woman in France is being told her purpose is to get married and breed. I don't like it, but can I turn down a chance like this?

"To start with," begins the baroness, "the foundation would like to purchase from you the sculpture of la femme Lafayette that you made last year. I'm sorry I didn't think to do that sooner. So if you're willing to sell it . . ."

I nod, because of course I'm willing. It'd be hard to find any art collectors interested in Lafayette these days, much less willing to buy a bust of his wife—even if I filed her eyebrows down. So I'll take whatever's on offer. "*Merci*," I say, realizing with a little thrill that it's my first sale. Beyond that, though, I want to tell the baroness I'm not interested in glorifying a dowdy eighteenth-century wife as an example for modern-day Frenchwomen, and I'm not interested in sanitizing this castle for the Marshal's visit either. But after such a long time of feeling purposeless and without an excuse to create anything, I feel my resolve cracking even before she offers me the key.

"Anna tells me you'll need a better workspace," the baroness says, sliding the key onto the desk between us. "This opens the room our Madame President called her own when in residence at the castle. Beatrice used it as a studio at times, and I know she won't mind if you make it yours."

A studio of my own. My first *real* work as an artist. I stare at the tarnished old key like it's an apple in the serpent's garden. And knowing that it's really Anna who rolled it in front of me, I'm not sure if she's an angel or the devil. Like she already knows I'm not going to refuse, the baroness explains, "We'll want a series of sketches portraying Adrienne Lafayette. To really understand her life. Particular emphasis on her devotion as a wife, as a mother, as a persecuted Catholic, and so on."

And so on . . .

The way the baroness says this, I don't think she's a true believer. Oh, she believes in God, but not in Marshal Pétain's so-called National Revolution—which seems like it's aimed to undo the revolutions that came before. No, I think the baroness is a pragmatist like me. So I take that key, knowing it's going to open the door to my future, even though I'm not sure what it's going to unlock . . .

TWO

ADRIENNE
Paris
April 1774

IN THE *ANCIEN RÉGIME* INTO WHICH I WAS BORN, OBEDIENCE WAS the rule. Thus it is strangely gratifying now to remember that when I was *very* young—before deference and duty to my father became the hallmark of my character—it was my nature to question. Indeed, when I was a little child, my long-suffering *maman* once jested that my favorite word was *why*.

But, of course, she was the one who taught me to ask . . .

It was Maman's habit to invite my sisters and me into her sumptuous gold and crimson chambers, where, seated by the fire in her favorite upholstered armchair—the one with gilded arms and embroidered with fleur-de-lis—she instructed us with soft eloquence and a sense of justice to believe that though we were girls, we had a right to our own consciences. We certainly tried her patience in adhering to that principle in matters large and small. Little Rosalie's violent tantrums, pretty Pauline's aloof disdain, Clotilde's refusal of all things feminine, and my persistent doubt in God.

Why must we go to church services?

Why do we not see, feel, and touch God, if he exists?

Why would a good God allow evil things to happen?

Only our eldest sister, the sweet and gentle Louise, was the perfectly pious and biddable sort.

Yet only once do I remember my mother complaining of us. In a fit of exasperation she threw aside the veils that covered her pockmarked face and cried, "You girls are far less obedient than other children your age!"

My sisters cowered, but I argued, "If we are disobedient, it is because you let us question. When we grow older, you will find us more obedient than other daughters because we will have come to understand the reasons for your commands."

Maman liked my answer, and I drank in her approbation like a holy elixir, for my sisters and I loved our mother with passionate devotion—as if, by silent conspiracy, we could somehow compensate for the one unhappy fact of our lives: that our father did not love our mother at all.

Our father, Jean de Noailles, the duc d'Ayen—commander of the king's guard—had little patience for his wife's independence of mind. Thus, they went on as most married nobles in France did then, living separate lives. He with a mistress, court life, and scientific pursuits. She with books, religion, and domestic duties.

I had been given little reason to believe my own marriage would be different. And, on the day of my wedding, my father reminded me, "Marriage, Adrienne, above all, is a duty to your family." My most important duty. So believed my father, a man with five daughters who needed sons. Since he could no longer get sons upon my mother—who had been viciously ravaged by smallpox—he'd set out to procure sons-in-law, entering into negotiations for my marriage before I turned twelve.

I was fourteen now. And on this, my wedding day, I hungered desperately for my father's affection, or even a show of approval. Yet in preparing to give me in marriage, he did not smile like a sentimental patriarch. No, the duc d'Ayen's dark gaze swept over my bridal attire like I was one of his guards on inspection. My gown was a heavy silver brocade that shimmered like moonlight, the sleeves dripping fine lace. Glittering diamonds had been sewn into the bodice, and from my ears dangled more diamonds, these the size of quail eggs, for no expense had been spared.

My stays were pulled tight, my hair perfumed with pomatum, my locks ruthlessly teased and pinned. Then I'd been powdered just short of asphyxiation. All this met my father's standards, but my eager smile must have disconcerted him, for he said, "I bid you again to remember, the purpose of marriage is not romantic love."

Not its *purpose*, perhaps; I knew my groom had been chosen primarily for his immense fortune and presumed virility, yet, quite happily, I was still young enough to believe love could be found under the careful watch of chaperones, in shy blushing smiles, halting conversation, and the agreeable pattern of freckles on my betrothed's nose.

That was enough to make my wedding day welcome to me.

No doubt, my buoyant mood made my father wish to pull me back to earth. "Royals are in attendance and we cannot afford a single misstep."

"Yes, Father," I said, though I knew it was not my manners that worried him, for in our family, the gestures of a courtier were as natural as breathing. I knew how to behave because I was of the Noailles.

But my groom was a Lafayette.

Oh, the Lafayettes boasted distinguished persons in their line, but as provincial nobility with a crumbling castle in the mountains, they had no standing with the king. By contrast, my family was high in favor, filling at least a hundred royal offices. In Versailles, we had a home merely steps from the palace gates, and we boasted that in the city of Paris itself, the Hôtel de Noailles had room enough for the king to stable an entire regiment of his cavalry, then hunt fox without ever leaving the walls of our estate. Hence, in the course of ordinary events, a boy like Gilbert du Motier, the last of the Lafayettes, would never have been considered a worthy candidate for my hand. We would not have been matched but for a calamitous series of tragic deaths in his family that orphaned him and left him wealthy, making him a candidate for my hand, because my father believed the sixteen-year-old could be taken into our family and molded. "Lafayette's edges are rough," my father said. "Still, edges can be filed down. He can be *made* into a Noailles, and it will be your task to shape him."

"Yes, Father," I said again, my head bowed with the weight of the only responsibility ever given to me. A responsibility I took to heart, for I still wished to make my father love me as if I'd been born a boy, capable of bringing glory to our family name.

It was for the same reason I had long ago stopped asking *why*.

Alas, thinking back upon the days of endless social and ceremonial visits leading up to our wedding, I couldn't think of anything about my intended groom that I would shape differently. In young Lafayette, my father saw a timid, bookish provincial lad, seemingly incapable of witty repartee. Yet I saw a freckled boy with wild red hair, whose guileless nature seemed true purity of heart—a heart I wanted for my own.

Thus, I was glad to hear the organ music that finally signaled my wedding in the family chapel. My father led me up the candlelit aisle past rows of bejeweled friends, rivals, and relations. My sisters beamed and Maman wept happy tears, but my eyes were all for Gilbert du Motier, where he stood in blue silk, the braided loop of an officer in the king's musketeers upon one shoulder. My groom took my hands, then the priest recited the words before an altar perfumed by burning incense, and we whispered our vows. At last, the orphaned boy slipped a ring upon my finger and lifted my veil for a kiss so fleeting that I pressed my fingertips to the spot, as if to hold it there.

At the feast, the groom and I sat together in tall gilded chairs upon a festooned dais in the banquet hall whilst liveried servants brought gleaming silver platters with food in endless variety. Sugar-dusted pastries, steaming turtle soup, pureed asparagus, lettuces, snails, pâtés. Heaps of mussels, baked fish, sauced chicken. Sizzling beef, mint-laced mutton, a fat pheasant decorated with its tail feathers, medallions of veal on a bed of greens, and a roasted boar with an apple in its mouth. Then came the parade of pigeon eggs, pigeon bisque, pigeon pie, pigeon au gratin, pigeon in wine, and pigeon stuffed with songbird. All to be followed by silvered cakes and marzipan dusted with gold . . .

It was a display of Noailles wealth, though my father thought it best that the bride and groom peck only at bits of bread and not partake in the excess until later, lest we spill a drop of soup or let a fork clatter in company.

In the roar of boasting lords and flirting ladies, my eyes began to weary, and beside me, my groom's fingers tapped an impatient dance on the arm of his chair. It was unseemly to fidget under the scrutiny of so many guests, any of whom might gossip about irregularity in our conduct. Remembering it was my task to smooth my groom's rough edges, I attempted to still young Lafayette's drumming fingers with my own. And in complaint, he whispered, "Now I have lost count of how many ways pigeon can be served."

I sputtered a laugh, hiding it behind my napkin.

His knee bouncing with pent-up energy, he went on. "We raise pigeons in Chavaniac too. We fatten them up in a dovecote up high, just as we are kept on this dais."

A strange comparison, considering our spare plates. "We are not being fattened . . ."

"Yet I feel as if we are on the menu."

I smothered a smile. "You would rather be a guest than the groom?"

"I would rather steal you away," he said with a rakish lift of his ginger brow.

Steal me away? The thrilling suggestion emboldened me to attempt the courtly arts, sweeping my lashes enticingly low. "But, my lord husband, you cannot steal what is already yours."

I hoped he would reply with flirtation in kind. Instead, his hazel eyes lit with mischief, glance flicking to the door through which servants ferried crystal wineglasses. "We can escape that way."

Realizing he did not jest, I smothered a frisson of panic. My father had worried Lafayette was timid, preferring to read the old Latin political histories, but now seemed hardly the time for him to develop a sense of adventure. "We cannot leave our wedding banquet, sir."

"Cur non?"

I tilted my head, and he smiled at my confusion. "It is my family motto," he explained. "It means: *Why not?*"

What a charming expression! The notion of my groom as a person apt to question the world tugged upon an old forgotten part of me. And it challenged me too. To ask *why* was only to demand justification.

To ask *why not* assumed endless possibility . . .

"Wouldn't you rather be in fresh air?" he asked.

Yes. I would rather be in the garden, the stables, the courtyard—anywhere but here, perspiring, confined by my stays, drowning in leagues of lace and silver brocade. I dared not admit it; still he seemed to know. Gesturing at the feasting tables, he asked, "How long would it take them to notice we were gone? It is our wedding, yet has little to do with us."

Perhaps so. Unlike my older sister, Louise, who had married our cousin the vicomte de Noailles, Gilbert and I were considered too young to have our own household; we would remain, like children, under my mother's protective guidance. Everything had been, and would be, decided for us. We were simply part of the decor; not even like pigeons in a dovecote. More like pretty caged songbirds, without even the dignity of a song.

Fanning myself as hot wax fell from the chandeliers onto the table near my hand, I fretted, "But when they *did* notice, it could be said we ran from our own wedding, and then the duc d'Ayen would be wroth. He told me we must not risk the slightest misstep."

"Do you always do as your lord father commands?"

Everyone did as my lord father commanded—except for my mother, of course, whom he punished with cold indifference. Which is why I had tried so hard, and for so long, to conceal my rebellious heart. "I am a dutiful daughter."

Gilbert's fingers drummed again on the arm of his chair. Then he rolled a shoulder. Tapped a foot. "As your husband, I could *command* you to steal away with me . . ."

This time it was a frisson of excitement I felt, and warmth blossomed on both my cheeks. ". . . and *do* you command it?"

He looked very much as if he wished to, yet said, "No. Wherever you go with me, Adrienne, I want you to go freely."

That wasn't the answer I anticipated. Certainly not an answer any of the swaggering men in my family would give. It seemed my new husband had no talent for courtly flirtation, yet his answer invited trust and emboldened me further. Like all the Noailles, I knew the rules and could, perhaps, turn them to my advantage. "If I felt dizzied, it could be considered nothing short of gallant for the groom to escort me for fresh air to recover myself."

". . . and *are* you feeling dizzied?"

I was. For in the depths of his hazel eyes—a ring of earthy brown wreathed in leafy green—it seemed as if the mysteries of an enchanted forest were awaiting discovery, and so I nodded, a little breathless.

Gilbert needed no more encouragement. A moment later, the boy from Chavaniac rose, sweeping me up and away from our wedding feast. As he hurried me to the courtyard, helping me to turn so my pannier side hoops would fit through the tall glass doors, I teased, "You seem far too practiced at escape for a lord. Have I married a brigand by mistake?"

All too earnestly, he replied, "Never a brigand, but I have been climbing out of tower windows and sneaking through the secret passages at Chavaniac since I was a child."

"Why would you sneak out of your own castle?"

He laughed. "Have you heard of the Beast of Gévaudan?"

I nodded. "A fairy tale."

"*Au contraire.* Quite real. When I was a boy this creature terrorized the peasants. Some said it was a mountain lion, some a wolf. I thought maybe it was a hyena prowling my pine forests. My aunt told me I must keep indoors, but I was the little lord of the castle! Wasn't I meant to protect my villagers? So I escaped to hunt it with my wooden toy sword."

I laughed with delight to discover he was such a precocious child. "Did you find your prey?"

Gilbert smiled. "I am still hunting . . ."

It was then and there in the privacy of the gardens, with petals raining down on us from the almond trees, that he boldly placed a kiss on my lips. A kiss that was nothing like the chaste one he had given in front of the priest and our wedding guests. This kiss—intimate and soft and breathy—was only for us.

Overcome and astonished, I shivered. My first real kiss! My first—

"*Adrienne!*" hissed the governess sent to find us. "Do you wish to cause scandal?"

Our moment of freedom, our gift to each other, had been brief, but I cherished it. It helped sustain our spirits through the hours of the fete, and the humiliation of the bedding ceremony, of which Maman had mercifully insisted upon a truncated version with the bed-curtains drawn and the guests withdrawn, so that we might be alone.

Maman had not kept me ignorant of what happened between man and wife, but now, in a partial state of undress, my groom asked, "When I kissed you before, you shivered. Do I frighten you, Adrienne?"

I shook my head, only a little alarmed by the way my heartbeat fluttered.

"A shiver of revulsion, then?" he asked, half-teasing, half-sincere.

"It is a shiver, I think, of the most peculiar pleasure." My cheeks flamed hotter at this admission.

Yet Gilbert clasped me around my waist with boyish enthusiasm. "It is pleasurable for me too."

"I am happy to know it," I said.

"Then why are you trying to escape me like a cat who does not wish to be stroked?" he asked, glancing down at the palm I had unwittingly planted in the center of his chest.

I did not know the answer until I blurted, "I know that you were told by your surviving relations that you must enter into this marriage agreement."

Gilbert tilted his head. "Were you not also told that you must marry me? Besides, when I saw what a good and gentle heart you have, it was a command I was pleased to obey."

How I wanted to believe it! "You had no choice . . ."

"There is always a choice," he replied. "I could have run away."

"Then you would have been disowned and penniless."

He shrugged. "I have not always had so much money," he said. "I cannot be glad of how I acquired my fortune, nor am I willing to sacrifice much to keep it. Yet I am glad it made you my bride."

I broke into a grin but did not wish to seem prideful. "Surely there are other reasons to be glad of a fortune."

"Yes. At Chavaniac I could barely afford my own horse, much less to repair the castle or provide for the hungry peasants. Now I can afford to make improvements, so when I close my eyes, I build dream castles where all shall be happiness and pleasure."

Happiness and pleasure are what we shared as innocents in the marriage bed, tentative and tender. I did not cry out at the pinch of pain, because I did not wish to do anything that might vex him. I had already decided that no matter what my father said the purpose of marriage might be, I did not want mine to be only a contract to make children and advance family glory. Perhaps I was a silly and selfish girl, but from the boy next to me on the pillow, I wanted so much more . . .

When Lafayette drowsed, his copper eyelashes quivered. And thinking he was asleep, I whispered, *"Je t'aime . . ."*

These words roused him and elicited a grin. "You love me? Do you really?"

"I do," I said, as if making our wedding vow anew, because if I did not love him already, I would make myself love him and make him love me too. I would be somehow so good a wife he would never wish for us to be apart.

And as if he wanted this too, he said, "Many exchange vows, rings, and kisses, but let us exchange hearts. That way you will never be alone; I will always be with you, for you will have, and be, my own dear heart."

Truly touched, I reassured my orphaned husband that he too would never again be alone, for now he was one of us—one of the Noailles. "No," he replied, tucking a tendril of my dark hair behind my ear. "I am a Lafayette and now so are you."

I didn't yet know what it meant to be a Lafayette, for none of us had any idea that the redheaded boy I had married burned for freedom like an ember escaped from the fiery mountains of Auvergne, from whence he had come. Or that his spark would set me ablaze for freedom too. Certainly, I could never have guessed that he would change the world . . . or that I would help him do it.

THREE

MARTHE
Chavaniac-Lafayette
December 1940

"SHE WAS ONLY FOURTEEN WHEN SHE MARRIED?" ANNA ASKS AS she helps me cart a box of research books into the tower chamber with its two sunny windows and recessed crystal chandelier. I've been telling her about what I'm learning for my new series of sketches, and she asks, "Can you imagine being ready for marriage at such a young age?"

I don't even know that I'm ready now, I almost say. I might not have accepted Henri's proposal if not for the war. I certainly wouldn't be taking on a project to make the preventorium over in Adrienne Lafayette's image. And I wouldn't have a fancy studio like this.

I wouldn't want to sculpt stone here—the dust would get into every crevice of the canopied bed and antique furniture—but it's a perfect place to sketch.

It looks like the preventorium's president took most of her belongings with her when she returned to America in the summer of '39—but she left behind some books on the shelf, old hatboxes under the bed, and framed photographs on the wall.

The books are a mix of Shakespeare's plays, Balzac's novels, and Anatole France's poetry. The hatboxes are filled with old letters. And most of the photos are of Madame Beatrice posed in outrageous hats with famous people. There's also a photo of a clean-shaven young legionnaire and a wily-looking game hunter, one or the other of whom I assume must be her late husband. Her empty wardrobe smells like mothballs, but the signature scent of Madame Beatrice's powdery L'Heure Bleue perfume still lingers on her embroidered armchair. And it looks so warm and inviting that I want to curl up in it—especially since outside, hard-packed snowdrifts have smothered the mountains, closing roads, and ice hangs like daggers from every tree.

It's been such a cold winter that the windows are frosted shut. We've got firewood, but not enough coal. And to keep the children in the preventorium warm, we bundle them under the blankets, in sweaters and thick wool socks. As for my own socks these days, they're increasingly threadbare, and I'm not sure how many more times they can be darned. My toes are aching from the cold. Fortunately, my new studio has a big fireplace. Anna helps me pull dust sheets off the furniture and make room for my things.

Besides a little box of scented soaps, our most precious find so far is the old radio cabinet with a windup gramophone that still plays recordings, albeit several decades old. The tower room feels like everything I could ever want, and I'd intended to jealously guard the locked door, treasuring creative solitude, but I like Anna's company.

I like everything about her, actually. She's been everywhere I want to go—Paris, London, New York. She's seen everything I want to see—the Louvre, Buckingham Palace, the Statue of Liberty. She's everything I want to be—rich, worldly, and self-confident.

When we finish moving my easel by the window, we flip through my old drawings—figures in blended charcoal. Hands, faces, torsos . . . other sketches are experimental. Absurd pieces of modernity, dreamlike in quality. As Anna stares at my drawings, I feel so exposed it's like she's staring at *me*. Nobody but Madame Beatrice has ever studied my work with such intense interest before. And when Anna reaches out and traces her fingertip along the jawline of a figure, I feel it on my own face.

"Your style reminds me of Dalí," she says.

And I positively glow at the absurdly overblown comparison. *"Dalí?"* I snort dismissively, but it's hard to keep from preening. "These are just drawings anyway. I'm more of a sculptress."

"Do you prefer to work in clay or something else?" she asks.

"Madame Beatrice liked clay. Shaping something out of nothing. But stone is my favorite because I like carving something down to its essence and finding what no one else knew was there."

I worry she'll laugh at me, but she nods as if she understands. "I'm told stone is the least forgiving. Make one mistake and—"

"You could ruin it," I admit. "That's the miracle of the most beautiful sculptures; one continuous piece. Beautiful and unbroken."

Pretty much the opposite of my life.

When we're finished looking at my old sketches, Anna puts on one of Madame Beatrice's old records and says, "It's been so long since I danced. When I close my eyes, I can still feel the scratch of my husband's beard on my cheek when we did the tango . . ."

I know she misses him even more than I miss Henri. To cheer her up, I say, "You should host a dance at your next Sunday social in the salon. There's not a man in the castle who wouldn't want to partner with you."

She shakes her head, and glossy dark curls frame her wistful brown eyes. "I wish I could oblige them, but I've already heard snide comments about my lipstick from the household management teacher. What would people say if I danced with another man?"

"Oh, don't pay any attention to Faustine Xavier; she's twenty-nine going on sixty," I say to make light of it, but wives of captured soldiers *are* under special scrutiny. Girlfriends too. People already gossip about Anna just because she's so glamorous. But if Anna gave anybody a real reason to think she's stepping out on her husband while he's in a POW camp, they might spit at her in the village square.

Suddenly, Anna tugs my sleeve. "*We* could dance."

I laugh, letting her pull me into a twirl. Then we start dancing a goofy tango, tripping over each other's feet, cracking up because neither of us knows who is supposed to lead. It's a laugh riot until she's laughing warm by my ear, the scent of her perfume making me giddy, and an uncomfortable twist in my belly makes me drop her hands.

"Did I stomp your toes?" she asks, still laughing.

I shake my head, confused. Maybe I'm feeling a little guilty because I'm dancing while Henri's locked in a cage somewhere near Poland. Or because I haven't heard a word from him in so long I've almost forgotten the sound of his voice. "It's just . . . I'd just rather dance to jazz."

Until Anna arrived at the castle, tapping my foot to swing and boogie-woogie blues was the only thing that gave me any hope at all, but jazz is discouraged under the new regime because it supposedly corrupts the soul.

"Maybe we can find some jazz on the radio," Anna says hopefully. And oblivious to my strange mood, she chirps, "Did I tell you I got a letter from my sister in New York? She's planning a wedding to her American beau, Henry Hyde!"

"Shouldn't she wait until after the war?"

"Who knows when it will be over? Papa was sure the British would surrender by winter—he said Churchill couldn't keep fighting alone—but here we are with no end in sight. Anyway, my sister's not one for waiting, and a wedding is a good pretext for my parents to travel to New York. It shouldn't be difficult for Maman, but Papa's another story. If he wants to leave the country, he'll need permission from Vichy."

I imagine he would. If a man as prominent as the Baron de La-Grange somehow diverted his travels to join the rebel General de Gaulle in London, it would be a black eye for the Marshal's regime. Even if the baron simply stayed in America like an exile, he'd likely be condemned and stripped of his French citizenship. All this reminds me that Anna is half-American and doesn't need to be here starving and freezing with the rest of us. "Are you going with them?"

Anna gives a sad shake of her head. "I can't leave France while my husband rots in a prison camp."

Even though her words echo my earlier feelings, I argue, "Just because he's in a cage doesn't mean you need to be."

"I think that's what marriage is. If one of you is stuck, you both are."

Is that what Henri would want because we're engaged? I'm not used to thinking of myself as half of a whole, and while I ponder it, suddenly somber, Anna gives me a little nudge to lighten the mood. "Besides, I can't go to America—what would you do without me here to help manage your art career?"

I grin. "Oh, is that what you're doing?"

Anna grins back. "Just wait until you're done with your first sketches. On Saint Joan's day I'm going to talk you up to every village provincial. Today the Church of Saint-Roch, tomorrow a gallery in Paris!"

I feel the tingle of longing as she resurrects my old dream to go to Paris, the city where I was born, and walk the streets where the family I never knew might have walked. To live the big-city life I might've lived if I hadn't been orphaned. But I beat those thoughts down and blow out an incredulous laugh, because Paris is also the center of the art world. Amateur sketches like mine would elicit nothing but mockery from any honest art critic.

Of course, there isn't any honest art in France right now; just the kind the fascists sanction, and if they sanction mine . . .

Anna hands me a pencil and pretends to crack a whip. "So you'd best get to work—and not just because we need better rations."

We *do* need better rations. We're running out of food. If it weren't for Madame Simon's stealth missions to the black market and all the baroness's pickling and bottling of early autumn, we'd be in real trouble. As it is, we're eating rutabagas every day. If we have meat, it's rabbit from the hutches or pigeon from the dovecotes. We're out of coffee too, forced to make café au lait with a bitter brew of chicory.

I'm not sure that making over the castle in Adrienne Lafayette's image is going to get us real coffee or convince Vichy officials that we're not a hotbed of so-called antinationalist ideas, but if Anna and the baroness are right that my work helps secure government assistance with food and supplies, I'm happy to try.

Not that I have much to work *with*. Just a few dry old books about Lafayette's wife that I took from the castle library. Now I crack them open and flip open my new sketchbook too, cheered for the first time in a while by the sight of a fresh blank page.

Meanwhile, Anna looks for something to read on Madame Beatrice's bookshelf, until her attention is captured by something else. "*Mon Dieu,* Marthe. Is this you as a little girl?"

I tilt my head in confusion. "What?"

"In this photograph," she says, pointing at the wall.

Wondering if I somehow missed an old picture of the first class of orphans, I go over to look, hoping I'll see me and Henri and Sam as kids. But the photo shows a younger Madame Beatrice standing in front of the castle and wearing a nurse's apron, smiling beatifically at a handsome French soldier who holds a little pigtailed girl in his arms.

I squint, because the girl *does* look a bit like me, but I have almost no photographs of me as a child—and none at this age—so I can't be sure. Besides, I don't remember the man or the moment. "I don't think it's me. A lot of kids and a lot of soldiers came through here in those days. Maybe that soldier was someone important, but I can't think of any reason why Madame Beatrice would keep a photograph of me."

Anna laughs. "Why does Aunt Bea do anything?"

"Madame Beatrice is your aunt?"

At my obvious surprise, Anna asks, "Don't we seem like we're related?" They don't look alike, but Anna is certainly more like the colorful preventorium president than she is like her own mother, the militant baroness. And as I squint, Anna laughs. "I'm teasing. She's not my aunt by blood! Just an old family friend, but she says we're so much alike because she practically ushered me into the world during the First World War."

The First World War. Is that what we're calling it now, like there's going to be a series of them? Beyond the fact that it orphaned me, I've never given that war a lot of thought. It's hard enough trying to cope with this one. But now, here in this room, in the trappings of Madame Beatrice's outsized life, I feel a little hope that if people like her survived and thrived, we can too. I just wish she were here to tell us how.

FOUR

BEATRICE
Paris
July 1914

WHEN GOING TO WAR, ONE SHOULD BEGIN WITH A NEW HAT.

For gentlemen, a helmet is best. For ladies, something more magnificent is required. Thus, I had donned a glorious ostrich feather–plumed cartwheel, attracting stares when I swept into the lobby of the American Hospital in Neuilly. There hadn't been time to meet with my personal *vendeuse*, of course, but a stop at the milliner's had been a necessity. I couldn't very well fight for my marriage wearing last season's draped silk toque!

My husband's telegram had said very little. Only that after having hurt his leg in France, he'd require surgery. The newspapers were no help either. Each told a different story about my husband's injury. Fiery automotive crash. Trampled by racehorses. A duel gone horribly wrong. With a man as famously reckless as William Astor Chanler—millionaire soldier-adventurer—nothing beggared belief. And, of course, Willie liked to keep the world guessing, me along with it.

For my part, I took the telegram about his impending surgery as the sign I'd been waiting for to do something about the state of my marriage, so I'd boarded the first steamship for France. Unfortunately, much of New York high society did the same every summer, which is why I was recognized at the hospital reception desk. A rather awestruck American gentleman with a walrus mustache doffed his cap. "Hello, my dear! Why, I haven't seen you since your days on Broadway . . ."

I didn't remember him, but I had many admirers in those days, so I batted my eyelashes in the way that used to make men quiver, and twirled my lace parasol in satisfaction when it had the desired effect. "You were wonderfully funny," the old gent continued. "What was that song? *Rhoda and Her Pagoda* . . . Marvelous musical comedy. You were brilliant in that role."

"Yes, I was, wasn't I?" I leaned in to confide, "But now I'm playing the part of Mrs. William Astor Chanler. My most challenging role to date!"

The gentleman guffawed.

I'd said it only partly in jest. After all, I'd married an *Astor*. As everyone knew, the Astors' grand ballroom had a capacity of four hundred people, and if you weren't one of those four hundred, then you weren't anyone. Thus, transforming myself from ambitious actress into high-society maven fit for a descendant of America's first multimillionaire was my greatest theatrical achievement. And now it was time for a second act. "I'm here to visit my husband in the hospital, you see . . ."

"How is the old chap?" asked the gentleman, his mustache twitching with curiosity. "We've all heard about the accident. Damnable thing. Boxing match, was it?"

I had no choice but to smile mysteriously. "Something like that."

"Well, I wish your mister a speedy recovery." He reached inside his coat pocket for a notebook. "I say, though, would you mind—my granddaughter collects autographs."

I've always found the lure of appreciation irresistible, but then the old gent put a dent in my pride. "I've heard you're dabbling in sculpture these days . . ."

Dabbling. That's what everyone thought women did. Not wishing to make the usual self-deprecating remark, I signed with a flourish, then extricated myself quickly. "So sorry to rush off!"

Truthfully, I *was* in a rush, because I didn't want to give myself time to think better of my decision. I was going to tell Willie that after five years of living separate lives, I missed him. I still loved him. And I meant to take care of him after his surgery until he was well again. After that, well, I'd give up my respectable life in New York and live with him as a vagabond if that's what he wished. From now on, if the boys and I must follow him into the desert sands of Libya or up the snowy summit of Mount Kilimanjaro, well, then that's what we'd do. Because a family ought to be together.

I rehearsed this speech as I marched to my husband's private hospital room, my high-heeled lace-up boots tapping on the tile floor. And my heartbeat quickened in anticipation of how surprised Willie would be by my unexpected visit. I didn't expect him to apologize for his long absence and neglect. William Astor Chanler was not the sort of man to smite his brow and cry, *Forgive me everything, my darling. Let's devote ourselves to marriage and try, this time, for a little girl to add to our growing brood.*

No. That sort of thing happened only in maudlin plays. Not even the good ones. Willie was of that older generation of men who loathed to reveal a weakness; he'd have to be on his deathbed before he uttered the words *forgive me*, so my expectations on that score were low.

But even with well-managed expectations, I was still caught unawares when I pushed open the door to find my supine husband with a young lady, her hands stroking his cheeks.

I froze. The young lady had Gibson girl hair and an hourglass figure perfectly suited to her ridiculously impractical hobble skirt, which forced her to take dainty, mincing steps of retreat. Meanwhile, Willie wore a bashful flush of scarlet upon his neck, obviously trying not to glance at the open doorway, where the young lady lingered far too long before finding the grace to flee.

It might be serious, then, I thought.

A harlot would've made herself instantly scarce. Harlots, like actresses, plied a trade. I might've understood a harlot. I might've forgiven a harlot. A mistress was an altogether different sort. Torn between wanting to stab my husband with my lace parasol and bursting into tears, I did neither. I was, after all, not a naïf. I knew how the world worked. Women of society did not cause scenes over infidelity. That would be considered quite lowborn. And because my husband was quite highborn, he could make my life a misery if he wished to.

I knew the rules of the game. In high society, a husband could keep a mistress while the wife kept his name. And his money too. I should be glad of that, even if it wounded me to think that after being pursued by so many men, I should now be rejected by the only man I ever really wanted. What I did next—what I said next—might ruin everything if I wasn't careful, so I couldn't allow a crack to show. Fortunately, I was still an excellent actress. "How did it happen, darling? I'd like to know how bad it really is."

Willie didn't seem to know if I was asking about the young lady or his elevated leg. Deciding he'd rather talk about the latter, he thumped his thigh just above his knee with the kind of bravado for which he'd earned his fame. "Which story would you like better, Beatrice? An old injury from the Spanish-American War? Maybe a bear trap. Perhaps a mysterious flare-up of a disease I picked up years ago exploring Zanzibar?"

"The unadorned truth will suit me."

"Since when?" Given the twinkle in his dark eyes, I didn't know if he was flirting, trying to bait me into a quarrel, or both. That sort of game used to make for an intoxicating cocktail when we were younger and our tempers sizzled with passion. In the early days of our courtship, we amused each other with the seemingly infinite variety of shapes we could take on at a whim—actress, sculptress, patriot, writer, adventurer, soldier, politician. Oh, the outrageous tales we spun! Both a little reckless and wild, we used to quote from *Much Ado About Nothing*.

Let me be that I am and seek not to alter me . . .

But of course children alter everything. And now, after ten years of marriage, he was using our old game to put a barrier between us.

You left me to gad off on adventures, I wanted to say. *You left me alone with two small children and a flotilla of judgmental in-laws, and now you might've taken a mistress. Surely I have some right to know what the devil you've done to your leg . . .*

I advanced on him, ready to open fire, but then I noticed how shockingly thin he'd become. He had the pasty pallor of morphine—eyes bloodshot with pain—and I began to fear. "Tell me how dangerous this surgery is."

He shrugged. "They hoped to mend the shattered bone, but the doctor today discovered a blood clot, and if they don't take it out, it'll stop my heart."

I sank down onto the chair at his bedside, nearly upending the candlestick telephone there. I was still angry, but this man was the father of my sons. That trumped my jealousy of the Gibson girl, who had hopefully minced off to put the final nail in the coffin of someone else's marriage. "You should've told me how serious your injury was. Thank goodness I took the first steamer."

"There was no point worrying you. You shouldn't have made the trip."

Oh, that stung. "I know you like your independence, Willie, but doesn't a man need his family when he's in poor health? The boys would like to see you."

We exchanged several minutes of conversation about the children, during which he showed a more genuine interest than expected. I sometimes had to remind myself that Willie and his siblings had been orphaned young and left to raise themselves at the family estate, rather like a pack of very rich and spoiled wolf pups. He hadn't any example of parenthood after which to model his fathering. And now he said, "You shouldn't have taken them out of school."

"It's summer, darling," I reminded him. "Besides, I've always loved France. The quaint bistros. The orchards and vineyards made a splendid romantic playground for us, don't you remember?"

It seemed important to maintain a steady flow of chatter and remind him of happier days. To remind myself that I was still his wife. Because if I was no longer that, then who would I be?

Ours, after all, had been a love match.

I'd been onstage playing in *San Toy* when I noticed Willie in the front row. Those intense dark eyes. That boyish face. His gleaming devil-may-care smile. I'd danced that night just for him.

He'd come back the next night. And the next. But despite having the swagger of the big game hunter he was, it took Willie five performances before he worked up the nerve to introduce himself backstage. Then I couldn't get rid of him. Not that I'd wanted to. Remembering it now made my heart squeeze so painfully beneath my lace shirtwaist, it was difficult to breathe, and I did not think it was the pinch of my whalebone corset. The truth was, I had loved William Astor Chanler. I had loved him for himself and not his money, and I loved him still.

The trouble was that at the moment, I no longer wished for him to know it.

I turned, pretending interest in the newspaper, which was opened to an article about the recent assassination of Archduke Franz Ferdinand and his poor wife, for whom I felt enormously sorry. What, after all, had she done to deserve it but marry above her station? Waving at the headlines, Willie said, "That's another reason you shouldn't have come."

I narrowed my eyes in alarm. "Why—you didn't have something to do with it, did you?"

He actually grinned. "I'm a sharpshooter, Beatrice, but even my aim's not so good that I can shoot an archduke in Sarajevo from a hospital bed in Paris."

It really wasn't such an outlandish thing for me to have asked. After all, many men fancy themselves to be of world consequence, but my husband actually *was*. Willie had been funding, arming, and even riding into battle alongside freedom fighters of various nations before I'd ever met him. Like his friend Theodore Roosevelt, Willie had fought heroically in the Spanish-American War. He'd also tried to overthrow a dictatorship in Venezuela, and had personally led cavalry troops in the Italo-Turkish War. He lived by the philosophy that Americans ought to help those who wanted a say in their own governments. *When you have a philosophy like that, you've got to put up or shut up.* That's what he told me when he invited Sun Yat-sen onto our yacht for a chat about overthrowing the Qing dynasty.

Since then, I'd simply come to accept as a matter of course that if a revolution broke out in the world somewhere, Willie might be involved. Now, with mounting anxiety, I said, "I noticed that you didn't actually answer my question. Even if you didn't shoot the archduke yourself . . ."

My husband looked amused. "I had nothing to do with it. I don't even wish I did. It was a damned fool thing to do, one that could cause a war between Austria and Serbia."

His tone carried the additional implication that *I* had been a damned fool for coming to Europe under such circumstances. In my defense, I said, "Well, I couldn't have known someone would be assassinated when I boarded the ship, and I'll be sure not to visit Austria or Serbia until this blows over."

"The danger is wider than that region," Willie said, and I knew that once he started lecturing there was no stopping him. "We're all dancing on a delicate spiderweb of alliances these days. Tug one thread and it could unravel. If either Germany or Russia intervenes, the fight could spread across Europe."

Willie was always thinking ten moves ahead on the international chessboard with a brilliance that bordered on paranoia. It helped him relive his glory days as a congressman and a Rough Rider. Made him forget that he was now nearing fifty and that his glory days were over. In fact, I was beginning to suspect the mystery about his leg was just a ruse to keep anybody from realizing he was *getting old*.

Perhaps he had tripped over a curb like an ordinary mortal and it was to put me off the scent that he finally said, "It isn't anything serious with the girl, you know . . ."

"Oh, well then, I feel so much better!"

In response to my sarcasm, Willie smoothed his bedsheet. "I have vices, but I'm not a fool."

Neither was I. Unlike his famously loony brothers, Willie didn't have a weakness for women, but I doubted he'd been celibate in the years we'd lived apart. Until now, I simply hadn't wanted to know . . .

As if reading my mind, he said, "I'm not bedding that little chippie."

I should've felt more relieved. Why didn't I? Perhaps I didn't believe him. Or perhaps it was simply less painful to think Willie had succumbed to temptations of the flesh than to accept that he found my presence so tiresome that he preferred to keep an ocean between us.

"She was caressing your face," I pointed out.

"She was *studying* my face."

I gave a delicate snort.

"She's an artist," he said. "Mr. McAdams is making a bust of me, and she's his assistant."

At hearing this, a new and more powerful surge of anger sent me shooting to my feet. "You commissioned *someone else* to sculpt you?"

Willie held up a hand to fend off my tirade, but I jabbed a finger into his palm, quaking from the heels of my boots to the tip of my ostrich plume. "See here, Willie Chanler: I studied under Victor Salvatori. My pieces are on display at the National Academy of Design! I carved a four-hundred-foot bas-relief frieze in the lobby of the Vanderbilt Hotel for you—"

"I convinced you to do it!"

"That's not the point. You know how important sculpture has become to me since leaving the stage. When we married, you promised I wouldn't be just one more society lady who plays bridge-whist and attends tango teas."

"You're the Queen of the Social Register, and you love every minute of it."

Again, that damnable smile of his. All confidence and smolder. I simply refused to let it make me soft in the head. "Be that as it may, you posing for some other artist is like taking out an advertisement to denigrate the talent of your own wife."

"Then maybe it's time we let more people know we're separated."

His words were such a slap to the face that I blinked. Years before, we'd come to an amicable arrangement to live apart, but since then we'd enjoyed more than a few reconciliatory trysts. Besides, I'd come to fight for my marriage, and I wasn't ready to surrender. "I'm still your wife," I snapped, wondering why the devil he wanted a bust carved of himself anyway. Busts were for posterity. Busts of *living* people seemed pretentious and—

"Oh, Willie . . . you're frightened about the surgery, aren't you?"

"I'm not frightened of anything."

I used to believe that. Now, staring at his jutted chin, I wasn't sure. I was frightened *for* him and knew I must retreat before I let it show. "Well, you obviously need your rest. I'll bring the boys in the morning."

"I'd rather you didn't. Little boys don't relish hospital visits. Take a trip to Le Touquet and rent a cottage on the beach. Keep them active; toughen them up a bit."

"Ah, the Roman father speaks." This was, after all, an old quarrel. "Shall I leave our boys on a windswept crag and see if they survive?"

His brow furrowed. "Stuff them with pralines and petit fours if you want, but don't bring the boys here tomorrow. Or the next day, or the day after that. It's going to be a difficult surgery, and the recovery will be worse. Do you think I want my sons to see me like this? I don't." I was too dumbstruck by this outburst to interrupt, which may have encouraged him to add, "And tell the Chapmans not to visit me either."

The Chapmans—his sister Elizabeth, her husband, Jack, and our nephew Victor—wouldn't like this news, and I was indignant that Willie expected me to deliver it. "Is there anyone else in the family you'd like me to wound for you?"

His expression softened. "In a month or two when I'm back on my feet, we'll have a family reunion. I'm confident you can enjoy France without me in the meantime. Tell the boys their father loves them."

With that, I understood myself to be dismissed. My husband wished to face this dangerous battle without me. Or perhaps *with* the curvaceous sculptor's assistant. Either way, I wasn't wanted, so I rose, intent upon escape from abject humiliation.

That's when he caught my wrist. "Bea . . ." He stroked the place where my glove gave way to the skin of my arm. "You still have the prettiest, most expressive blue eyes . . . bluer than Capri's grotto on a sunny day . . . astonishing, really."

He hesitated, as if he meant to say more. I hoped he'd changed his mind and would ask me to stay . . . but he only said, "I look forward to seeing those baby blues again when the morphine isn't clouding my head, and then we'll discuss important matters."

"YOUR UNCLE IS IMPOSSIBLE," I SAID, FANNING MYSELF AGAINST both marital outrage and the summer heat of the outdoor café of the Ritz, where ladies in silk hats gossiped and bewhiskered gentlemen hid behind newspapers. "*Absolutely* impossible."

My nephew Victor folded his farm-boy frame into one of the bistro chairs and chuckled indulgently. "I've long wondered how you put up with him."

What choice did I have? I had, after all, *married up*. Even if my married life was an insufferable farce, I'd be expected to put up with everything short of divorce—even by my favorite nephew.

At the age of twenty-four, Victor had the kind of sensitive, artistic nature that meant the world was going to chew him up and spit him out if he didn't have a worldly champion. That had always been me—I'd been the one to steer him to study architecture at the École des Beaux-Arts in Paris when his parents suggested a career in watercolors wasn't the best path for a Harvard graduate.

I simply adored Victor and didn't even count it amongst his faults that he worshipped my husband and tended to take his side. "You must realize Uncle Willie has always been like this. It's family legend that he'd never come home crying with a black eye as a child. He'd just crawl off into a dark corner like a wounded animal."

"Well, I'm happy to let your uncle Willie lick his wounds." Especially since I needed to crawl off somewhere to lick my own. I'd stayed in Paris until my husband was out of surgery. Now that his condition was stable, I was eager to join my little cherubs at the beach, where I'd sent them with their governess. And I intended for Victor to come along.

When he balked, I wiped lipstick I'd left on his cheek when I kissed him in greeting and reminded him, "No one stays in Paris in August. And you're looking so dapper in that gray flannel and boater that you're sure to make a splash with my lady friend."

Victor, who had been perusing the menu, lowered it to peer at me. "What lady friend?"

"The one who will be joining us shortly for tea."

Victor groaned. "You're matchmaking again, aren't you?"

"Of course I am." Until I could do something about my own love life, I might as well meddle in someone else's. A dreamy sort like Victor needed a practical wife to manage things—and I had just the girl in mind. "You're going to adore Miss Sloane. A most charming creature, pretty in a natural way . . . a modern girl, just your age, here in France on business for her father."

I'd met Miss Sloane at a charity gala in New York when some self-important socialite snubbed her. I'd taken her under my wing ever since. As the heiress to the W. & J. Sloane rugs and furniture fortune, Miss Sloane was often spurned in our circles for being *New Money*, but since my nephew was *Old Money*, it would all even out.

Still, Victor looked skeptical. "Why, pray tell, is this paragon still unmarried?"

"Because she was sensible enough to wait for you, darling!"

In truth, the Sloane family name had been tainted by scandal since the sensational divorce of Emily's parents attracted the poisoned pen of Edith Wharton in mockery. In the divorce settlement, Emily's mother had faced a choice between keeping her children or her lover.

She'd chosen the lover.

Poor Emily Sloane—deprived of a mother since the tender age of six—could scarcely have entertained the idea that true love was possible, but I felt confident Victor could change her mind.

Practical-minded girls adore sensitive, poetic young men, after all . . .

Now, through the crowd, Miss Sloane approached, and though her hat was two seasons old, she'd dressed sensibly for the heat in white chiffon. By way of greeting, she waved her newspaper and said, "The world has gone mad!"

Ignoring the bold headlines and the danger of war they portended, I said, "Miss Sloane, I don't believe you've met my nephew."

Having stood to greet her, he now tipped his hat. "Victor Chapman."

"Emily Sloane," she replied, displaying no apparent distress to be seen without a speck of rouge by an eligible bachelor.

Victor cleared his throat. "I hope you don't mind my joining you for tea. My aunt Bea is—"

"Positively dying of thirst." While my nephew held out Miss Sloane's seat and summoned a waiter, I smiled. "Isn't this a magnificent hotel? I adore the classical style. Which reminds me—did I mention that Victor is studying to be an architect?"

"How interesting," said Miss Sloane.

She did not sound at all interested.

And my nephew looked as if he wished to kick me under the table.

Relieved at the arrival of cold lemonade, I took a long drink. Then Victor had the good grace to ask the dark-haired, sloe-eyed Miss Sloane about her visit to Paris. And with an elfin grin she told him, in rather dizzying detail, about her efforts to purchase fine carpeting and antiques for lavishly outfitting a new steamship under budget. When the idiosyncratic young lady began rattling off figures, I interrupted. "Goodness, this lemonade is refreshing in such hot weather. I was just telling Victor he should join us at the beach."

My nephew cleared his throat again. "And I was just about to tell Aunt Bea now might not be the best time for Americans to leave Paris."

Now I wished to kick *him*, but Miss Sloane finally gave him her full attention. "I did hear that Paris troops are confined to barracks . . ."

Victor shrugged. "All I know is Austria has declared war on Serbia, Russia is mobilizing, and France—"

"Oh, not to worry, darlings!" I broke in. "All the powers of Europe can't go to war over the shooting of one measly archduke."

I've never been so wrong about anything in my life.

For by the time we started on strawberry ice cream, the clocks had chimed four, and the bewhiskered gentlemen in the café began clustering together under the string lights, murmuring almost in concert.

I squinted. "What in the blue blazes?"

We didn't have to go far to learn what was happening. Outside, French soldiers tacked up mobilization notices and youths flooded the streets waving the tricolor, yelling, *"Vive la France!"*

"THE AMBASSADOR SAYS THERE'S NO CAUSE FOR ALARM," MY HUSband said without preamble, having rung me up at my hotel straightaway. "The steamship lines are canceling sailings, but Americans will be able to leave at some later date."

At some later date? There were worse places to be stranded than Paris, but I felt a powerful maternal pang. "I need to get the children—or have their governess bring them back from the beach."

"Not possible," Willie said. "There isn't a cab, carriage, or train compartment anywhere in France that isn't ferrying soldiers. Worse, you'll be hard-pressed to find a merchant who will accept a letter of credit. I'll send my man over with some gold coins, but the boys are better off where they are; what you need to do is go directly to the embassy and apply for an emergency passport."

I didn't remember Americans needing a passport in France before. How serious this all was becoming. I might still want to throttle my husband, but there was no one's advice I'd rather have with danger in the air. That Willie had called me straightaway had to mean something, didn't it? Or maybe I was grasping at straws.

In any case, I did as I was told.

The sidewalk was overrun by a shocking number of people watching cavalry officers in shiny crested helmets riding their whinnying chargers down the Champs-Élysées. Then followed men carrying coats folded in the *bandoulière* style. These were sons, husbands, and fathers; their mothers, wives, and daughters trailed after, not wanting to lose sight of them. I knew that if not for Willie's leg, he might've been marching to war with them . . .

By the time I reached the American embassy, I felt swept up in the emotions of it all, nearly weepy, and not just because the line of American tourists was already fifty-deep. Some clutched jewels they hoped to pawn if the embassy couldn't cash their letters of credit, and I began to feel true alarm.

In line, I spotted Miss Sloane, who had stopped at a bakery, and she offered me a pastry from the box. "I'm worried for my lady's maid. She's of German birth."

"For goodness' sake, don't tell anyone else that," I replied, tearing into a croissant. "Should I feel guilty enjoying these? They're a Viennese invention, and since Austrians started all this . . ."

It was my way to make light of bad situations—to make people laugh when I wanted to cry—because I'd learned young that pity has a half-life. That's why hats and humor had become my armor.

Fortunately, Miss Sloane was not put off by my irreverence. "You might as well enjoy the croissants now. The bakers are being regulated to guarantee a bread supply. I suppose we'll only be able to eat *boulot* and *demi-fendu*."

"If we can afford them," I mused.

Emily took a deep breath. "I don't know whether to be terrified or exhilarated. I've never been without money a day in my life. Have you?"

I was nearly upset enough to tell her the truth. Fortunately one of

Willie's friends at the embassy recognized me and waved us to the front. But even when I was at the head of the line, Miss Sloane's question still echoed in my mind, dredging up memories I'd taken care to bury.

"Name?" asked the officious clerk who was typing up information for the emergency passports. The question seemed simple. But names had never been a simple matter for me. I was still *Mrs. William Astor Chanler*—but after my confrontation with Willie in his hospital room, I was more aware than ever that it was yet another name that could be taken from me.

"Beatrice Winthrop Chanler," I said. It still sounded as nice as the day I made it up.

The clerk suspected nothing. He didn't even look up from the typewriter. "Birth date?"

I was tempted to say, *Just see* Who's Who. I'd gotten away with that before, but given the serious circumstances, I chose a date close enough to the truth not to shatter my vanity. "May 7, 1883."

Then the clerk asked, "Occupation?"

And that was the proverbial straw that broke the camel's back. Perspiration pooled between my shoulder blades as I wrestled with an answer. I wasn't a stage actress anymore. And since Willie and I didn't live together, I couldn't say I was a housewife. Perhaps I was simply a mother, but at the moment, my boys were too far away for me to comfort them, and I felt rather a failure at mothering too. Truly, I hadn't expected an emergency passport application to bring about an existential crisis, but how precisely was a woman in my circumstances to answer such a question?

The clerk blinked vapidly. "Most women leave it blank."

"Oh, do they?" I held the brim of my daisy-ornamented picture hat against a growing wind. "I daresay women keep ourselves more *occupied* than most men. I'll have you know that I am a sculptress."

It wasn't the only thing I was, and certainly not the only thing I wished to be, but at the moment it was the only identity to which I could proudly lay claim, so I said this with the greatest hauteur of which I was capable . . . which made it more irritating when the visionless functionary simply granted the emergency passport with a stamp.

That errand complete, I wanted to set out straightaway to get my children. Unfortunately, Willie was right; I couldn't hire a motor or carriage, nor even buy one. Even the bicycles were gone. Everything had been requisitioned. *Everything.* Worse, all the lines to the northern shore had been cut, so I couldn't get a call through. In the space of days, my concerns had gone from marital trouble and idle matchmaking to worrying that my shy, stuttering, ten-year-old Billy and my precocious seven-year-old Ashley might be trapped between advancing armies. The fear was eating me alive.

Barging into my husband's hospital room, I demanded to know, "What's America going to do about this?"

"Nothing," Willie said. "President Wilson just declared neutrality. He could nip German aggression in the bud—make America a real player and save lives—but he's a lickspittle."

I shared his opinion but didn't have the chance to say so, because he fumed, "I told you not to come back until I was on my feet. I was quite explicit with my orders against hovering at my hospital bedside."

My husband's leg was now in a wire cage, and he looked feverish, so I dabbed at his forehead with a cold cloth. "Fortunately for you, I'm not a soldier to be ordered about."

"Wives are also supposed to obey. It was in the vows."

"Oh, are we going to be sticklers about our wedding vows now?"

He flushed, probably thinking I was referencing the *forsaking all others* bit, but I was thinking more about *until death do us part . . .*

"What do you want, Beatrice?"

"I'm worried about the boys."

"Then you shouldn't have brought them into a war zone."

I scowled. "It wasn't a war zone when I brought them here, and you shouldn't have told me to send them to the beach. I'm not leaving until you think of a way to get them back. Because if you can't rescue our boys, William Astor Chanler, then there's really no point in being *you.*"

It took him two weeks. Two weeks in which he pointedly did not wish to discuss our marital situation. Two weeks in which he revealed to me a certain fatalism that he said he'd picked up fighting with Arabs. He spoke of unavoidable destiny—but I'd always made my own fortune. So I took to sketching him in his hospital room, portraying him as two-faced

Janus, one half light and the other dark, until the morning he tossed a letter into my lap. "Here. Take this to the embassy. I've called in a favor to get the boys."

With a cry of relief, I abandoned my sketchbook, leapt up, and threw my arms around his neck, kissing his cheek. He didn't seem to mind. In fact, his smile was wry. "Maybe there's still some point in being me, after all."

The next day the ambassador's town car was put at my disposal—Stars and Stripes fluttering on the front fenders as the driver took me up the coast. I'll never forget my anxiety as we tried to get past the horse-drawn supply wagons that clopped along behind the allied British Expeditionary Force. When we finally pulled up to the cottage where my boys were staying, I called to them frantically, and they came tumbling down the sand-swept stairs, leaping into my embrace. I kissed their little heads, and they tasted like salt from the sea. I stroked their sunburnt cheeks and squeezed them as if I could never get my fill.

We returned to Paris just long enough for the boys to see their father—oh, let Willie rail against me for bringing them to the hospital, there was no time to argue, for the kaiser's forces were now within sixteen miles of Paris, and I meant for us all to leave France as a family. Once the boys had kissed their father, I sent them to wait in the hall and whispered, "This war is a disaster! The Allies are losing."

"Yes, and I don't want you caught in it," Willie said. "I've arranged for the family to take the last civilian train out of Paris."

I nodded gratefully. "Where can we get you some crutches? Or will you have to be carried?"

"I'm not going with you."

I startled. "Are you too ill to be moved?"

Willie sat upright on the hospital bed. "To the contrary. I'm almost good as new. In fact, as soon as this cage is off my leg, I'm going to the front to take a look at the fighting for myself."

"*Willie*, there are rules against civilians doing that."

He grinned. "You know that rules don't apply to me."

I didn't grin, because as usual, my husband did whatever he wanted, and all family responsibilities were left to me. I wanted to break his other leg to keep him from going to play at the front lines while leaving me to get our children to safety, but I didn't argue, because the barbarians were at the gate and our marital problems seemed small in a world at war.

It was my nephew who escorted me and my little entourage onto the crowded train. We were a party of five, including the governess. And I was incredibly relieved to see Miss Sloane waiting on the platform with her lady's maid, a single suitcase between them.

"Thank you for getting word to Miss Sloane," I told Victor. "You've put my mind at ease and increased your romantic prospects."

"I doubt there's going to be anything romantic about this trip," he said. With passengers packed like sardines, it was to be a grueling journey—one made worse when we realized that we were going north. Not away from the fighting, but *toward* it.

When I learned this, I asked, "Good heavens, why?"

"The conductor says it's military reasons," Victor replied. "The train has government officials on board and must make a flying trip to Amiens before returning south again to Bordeaux."

Something about the sight of so many blue-uniformed soldiers and grim public officials put Victor in a melancholy mood. "To think that at school, I frittered away extra hours with no-account pastimes . . . but with the war on, every single one of these Frenchmen seems to have a real sense of purpose."

Miss Sloane nodded sympathetically, though she had the no-nonsense bearing of a woman who had never frittered away an extra hour in her life. "I suppose a terrible clarity must descend when your country and loved ones are in danger."

Terrible clarity indeed, I thought as I fashioned a bed for my exhausted children on a train bench, making a pillow with my traveling coat. This was the first hardship my sleepy little darlings had ever endured, and I felt miserably guilty for having exposed them to it. Much more so when, after many hours, we witnessed a scene straight out of hell.

The train station in Amiens was overrun with wounded soldiers fresh from the battlefield. Some screamed on stretchers; others lay unmoving, possibly dead. And I realized with growing horror that many weren't soldiers at all, but civilians. Our train car had to be swapped out, so we were forced onto the platform, where soldiers rushed past, some limping, some collapsing in a heap of blood-soaked bandages.

The governess and I did our best to shield my boys. I pulled their little faces against me while Victor used our luggage to build them a little fortress that blocked their view. "Now, keep guard, boys, stay at your posts," he said.

How grateful I was for his help, and I wondered where Miss Sloane had gone. I turned to see her giving water to a wounded English soldier. "What happened to you, sir?" she asked.

"Germans came at night into the trenches, miss. My entire regiment was wiped out but for seven of us. They killed even those who surrendered."

I didn't have the words to express my naive shock at such uncivilized behavior, even in war.

"Not even the worst of it," said a bandaged private with a musical Welsh accent. "German troops pushed refugees ahead of 'em on the attack. Imagine hiding behind women and children and still calling yourself a man."

I realized now just how many children were amongst the wounded. I caught a glimpse of a girl in a polka-dot dress that had been stained by her own blood, and as a Red Cross nurse worked over her, I couldn't seem to look away. *My God*, how did these little ones get caught up in the fighting? I didn't want to believe the kaiser's troops were so cruel, but the soldiers all had stories of brutality to tell. What's more, they all insisted they were going back into the fight as soon as they got patched up. "We have to stop the Huns, no matter the cost. These people have no defense but us."

This heroic sentiment made it impossible to complain about thirst or hunger or exhaustion. Not when I saw so many wide-eyed, shivering, and traumatized children. A soot-stained lad in a newsboy cap huddled by the tracks, and another boy with a bloody eye dragged a sack almost as big as he was. Then I saw *her*. I saw Minnie in a tattered dress, clinging to a broken doll, tears streaming down gaunt cheeks. I blinked, startled, but when I opened my eyes again, she was gone . . . and in her place was a little lost French girl.

I was suddenly desperate to take all these children away from this place,

take them with us on the train, but the conductors weren't accepting anyone not on the manifest. This wasn't my war—I wasn't even a citizen of this
country—yet it filled me with an overwhelming sense of *shame* to save my
own skin while abandoning these innocents. One glance at Miss Sloane,
and I knew she felt the same way. Victor, even more so. While he helped
the conductor load our luggage, I called to him, "Don't forget your bag."

That's when he told me, "I'm staying behind."

My heart seemed to stop inside my chest. *"What?"*

There on that ghastly train platform, Victor set his square jaw. "I've
decided to enlist in the French Foreign Legion."

Grabbing his arm, I cried, "Don't be rash! At least talk to your
parents . . ."

Victor slung his bag over one shoulder. "I know what they'll say.
They'll say that as an American I haven't any duty to fight. They'll say I
have my studies—"

"All important points!" I argued.

"Aunt Bea, look around. Some of these children are younger than
your boys. They've just seen their homes blown to smithereens. I don't
think God would wish me to turn a blind eye. Uncle Willie would enlist,
if he could."

"Well, he *can't*," I said sharply. My husband was a hardened adventurer with an even harder head to keep him safe. Victor was a sweet boy,
a student, entirely unprepared for military life. I tried to make him see
reason. "If you're determined to enlist, there isn't any hurry. Why not
make sure your affairs are in order?"

"I only need to make sure that you'll be all right without me. That you
can get the boys to Bordeaux and onto a ship back home."

Never before had I so wished to play the helpless damsel in distress.

Before I could, Miss Sloane replied, "Mrs. Chanler is quite a capable
woman, and I'll help her every step of the way." I saw admiration shining
in Miss Sloane's dark eyes, and much to my dismay, I was sure Victor saw
it too. Now there wasn't any talking him out of it.

Only when the train was whistling did I accept there was nothing to
do but shower my nephew with kisses. Boarding that train without him,
I was beside myself with worry, guilt, and pride.

How was I ever going to explain this to my in-laws? I didn't know if they would understand Victor's decision. But I did. I looked out the train window at these refugee children, frightened and homeless and hungry . . .

I knew what that felt like. I knew all too well. I'd hidden the scars of my childhood away deep, where no one could see. Yet this scene of war had somehow ripped the old wounds open again. I'd clawed my way up from *nothing* so no child of mine might ever suffer. These refugee children weren't mine, but they belonged to someone. I had to do something for these brave young men and these orphaned children, because if I couldn't help them, then what was the point of being *me*?

"WE NEED TO DO SOMETHING," I WAS SAYING TO EMILY SLOANE, MY eyes on the giant funnels pouring a steady stream of smoke overhead.

The war had been our only topic of conversation since our frantic rush to board a vessel leaving France. And as we sailed toward New York's harbor now, our thoughts were still with those we had left behind in the conflict. "If America won't send soldiers to help, we can at least send money. We'll need some manner of charitable foundation."

Miss Sloane delighted me by agreeing enthusiastically.

"And we'll need gentlemen on the board, or no one will take us seriously," I said, removing my gloves as we sat down for coffee together in the stylishly appointed café. It was strictly for passengers traveling first class, and its velvet curtains, wood paneling, and opulent decor—supplied by W. & J. Sloane—gave the impression of a fine hotel. "We'll also need to give our charity a romantic, patriotic name."

"I don't see what could possibly be romantic about war."

"Most people can't," I said. "War is a grim business Americans would like to stay out of, if Wilson's declaration of neutrality is any indication of the public mood. To get them to care, we must appeal to the emotions. Love, hate, patriotism . . ."

I took her notebook and wrote: *The Lafayette Fund.*

Miss Sloane stared uncomprehendingly. "Lafayette? The revolutionary hero?"

"Precisely." I explained, "In the most powerful social circles, the Founding Fathers are revered more than Christ. You can't swing a beaded handbag in Mrs. Astor's grand ballroom without hitting a Daughter of the American Revolution, primed to opine in worshipful ecstasy about Washington, Adams, or Jefferson. They'll open their wallets for the far more romantic figure of Lafayette, French foe of tyrants and kings . . ."

FIVE

ADRIENNE
Paris
May 1774

THE KING WAS DEAD.

And with him went the world as we knew it. Smallpox had carried away the sovereign who signed my wedding contract, and now the king's grandson, the dauphin, was to ascend the throne at only nineteen.

Overnight, the position of favor my family took for granted was at risk. Presiding over a family conclave the following week, my father paced. "Already the old king's mistress has been exiled. We might be next; I blame the dauphine—"

"The new queen," Maman corrected.

"Marie Antoinette is a child!" His shout boomed down the gallery of priceless paintings. Never would he dare speak thus at Versailles, but the Hôtel de Noailles on the Rue Saint-Honoré was a gilded world unto itself, populated by an army of liveried servants beholden to our family. "She banishes the former favorites with no respect for the old order. She wants to change everything. Clothes, jewels, etiquette, courtiers . . ."

Change was not something my father approved unless it benefited the Noailles, and, as we were soon to learn, the new regime did not. The new queen wanted to be surrounded with her own ladies, not those of her predecessor, which left my influential great-aunt—Anne Claude Louise d'Arpajon, the comtesse de Noailles—out in the cold.

Aunt Claude returned from Versailles distraught, weeping into her kerchief, having resigned after being reduced in rank because the new royals prized youth. They had inherited the keys to the kingdom and did not wish to be constrained by or lectured to by my grandfather's generation; they wished to break free. It was an impulse I understood. Even as a married woman, I still remained under my mother's watchful eye—and not long after my wedding, my family secured a promotion for Lafayette as a captain of the dragoons and sent him to Metz for training.

Without Gilbert I was restless, and yearned for a life outside the walls of the Hôtel de Noailles. As it happened, the current royal crisis was to give me that opportunity. "If the new king and queen want youth," my father announced, "we shall oblige. Adrienne, you are to be presented at Versailles."

I inched to the edge of my gilded seat, torn between fear and excitement. To be presented at court meant new adult occasions—possibly a ball. There would be mature responsibilities too, and I was eager to play my part. Indeed, it was the part I had been raised to play by my devoted mother and a bevy of interesting female relations.

By way of social instruction, my freethinking aunt, Madame de Tessé, would always quiz my sisters and me on philosophy and current events and reward correct answers with chocolates. For religious instruction, my addled but devout *grand-mère*—who had such a habit of stealing holy relics that we knew from the youngest age to watch her in any church—gifted us with plumed pens with which she told us we must write the Virgin Mary.

When once I had confessed to Grand-mère my religious doubts, she said, *No matter if you doubt the mother of God, if your penmanship befits a noblewoman, that little bourgeois Nazarene will have no choice but to reply!*

In matters of decorum, we had received instruction from the queen's lady of honor, our aunt Claude, whom Marie Antoinette had mockingly dubbed *Madame Etiquette*. An apt moniker. *No* was Aunt Claude's favorite word. *No! No, Adrienne. You must not plod. You must* glide *if you are to be presented at Versailles.*

She's the one who taught me to delicately fold my fingers, to tilt my head in feminine fashion, to gracefully curtsy. I remember laughing with my older sister, Louise, as we practiced, lowering until our pointed shoes peeked out from beneath our petticoats. And I was excited to finally put our practice to its purpose at Versailles. Yet, at my father's suggestion that I should be presented, Maman put her silver spoon at the edge of her saucer with disapproval. "Do you not think Adrienne still too young?"

"She's married now," my father replied. "Besides, Louise will guide her through the formalities."

Louise, who would turn sixteen in autumn, had already been presented. Still, Maman fretted. "I would prefer to expose *none* of our daughters to the decadent and dissipated creatures of the court."

My father—who some might say was himself a decadent and dissipated creature of the court—rubbed at his eye, which had begun to twitch. "If you wish, you may accompany them to Versailles to ensure they do not fall under the sway of libertines."

He knew my mother seldom strayed from the seclusion of her household, fearing her pockmarks to be gawked at. But his bluff did not work. "It is a sacrifice I shall happily make," said Maman, and silence fell as my father seemed to consider an entire social season during which he could not flaunt his mistress.

With Maman present it would all be very inconvenient, yet he would apparently rather have my mother on hand to manage us than have to do so himself. "We shall all go together, then," he said. "Your task, Adrienne, is to ingratiate yourself with Marie Antoinette. It is not for personal gratification that you give yourself over to the frivolity of court. It is a duty."

Another duty I was happy to perform, for it freed me to give myself over to frivolity with my whole heart! For weeks, Louise and I tried on gowns and shoes. We practiced dancing and the language of fans while eagerly awaiting the return of our husbands from Metz.

The two brothers-in-law were a mismatched pair. Louise's husband, Marc, was considered tall, but my Gilbert was taller. Marc had curly black hair, whereas Gilbert's burned like copper. Marc was elegantly made, his aristocratic good breeding apparent at a glance, whereas Gilbert was big-boned like a peasant. Despite their differences, Marc took it upon himself to befriend Gilbert, for which I was grateful. And I looked forward to the countless amusements the four of us would enjoy together at Versailles.

Despite my excitement, Gilbert groaned when he returned from his garrison and learned that we were going to court. He knew some of the courtiers our age—brash, swaggering boys of perfect pedigrees with rapier wit aimed to slash and cut those they deemed beneath them. It was my brother-in-law who soothed my husband, saying, "Think, Lafayette! Horse races, card games—God knows you don't need more money, but imagine how enjoyable it will be to win some from an arrogant prince of the blood."

In autumn, we all made our way to Versailles, the golden gates to which opened upon indescribable splendor. Atop its verdant gardens, the palace glittered like an ornate gold crown on a pillow of green velvet. The baroque rooftops shone gold, the ancient statuary glowed like polished ivory, and fountains sprayed diamond drops into the air. Even to eyes like mine, accustomed to wealth and opulence, the black-and-white marble court alone—to say nothing of the Hall of Mirrors—was too much to take in.

Yet the duc d'Ayen encouraged me. "You were born for this, Adrienne. A courtier's instinct is in your blood."

I hoped so, for on the fateful autumn day that I was presented at a ceremonial levee to the nineteen-year-old queen Marie Antoinette, I found her so pale and lovely that I wished to reach out and stroke her powdered cheeks. Instead, I curtsied as I had been taught.

"What a tiny girl you are, Madame la marquise," said the queen. "Like a doll. I want to scoop you up and carry you in my *réticule*."

"You needn't abduct me, Your Highness, for I am your most willing follower."

She broke into a bright smile. "Come along, then."

As easily as that, I was swept into the queen's wake, eating chocolates and sipping pink champagne, standing all night on silk heels because only those of certain rank were permitted to have a chair. It ought to have been more difficult a thing to accomplish proximity to the queen, but I did not yet know how capricious Marie Antoinette could be, sometimes pronouncing herself dazzled by a young lady and making her an instant favorite. I was not yet that, but I *was* invited to the queen's next ball. There my sister and I danced, fluttered our fans, and listened to gossip, and by the time we fell giddy into our beds, we felt sure we could report back to my father all he wished to know.

Louise—who saw only the best in everyone—was pleased to tell our father that some of the queen's ladies were pious and sweet, perhaps deserving of the jewels and other gifts the queen bestowed on them. Knowing I had a more critical eye, my father asked me, "And the others?"

The others seemed to be promiscuous carousers, like the beautiful Aglaé d'Hunolstein, whose features were as delicate as a doll's, but it felt wrong to name her. "Others are immodest and occupied with trivial gossip."

"And the men?" my father asked.

I reported that the queen surrounded herself with a cadre of chivalrous young aristocrats who called themselves the Society of the Wooden Sword. Their leader was the twenty-seven-year-old duc de Chartres, who feted the queen with every manner of amusement. Hearing this, my father steepled his fingers beneath his chin, plainly wondering if the queen had taken a lover. "Where is our new king at these fetes?"

"Seldom at the queen's side," I admitted.

Social mingling was not to our new king's taste—something His Majesty seemed to have in common with my husband. Oh, Gilbert dutifully escorted me, but chafed at every silly servile court custom. The king had different reasons. Some said he preferred to hide in his hobby workshop, playing locksmith. Others said he did not care for Marie Antoinette and their childless marriage served as evidence. "Can the king do it or can't he?" Marc jested, then colored when my sister dropped her gaze, for after a year of marriage, Louise had begun to worry she could not conceive.

I wondered if it were not also the case with the queen, but knew better than to whisper such a thing, for queens had been set aside for less. I'd overheard that the queen had never missed her monthly courses—so not even miscarriage could explain her childlessness. Gossip of this nature was precisely the information my father wanted most, but I did not need to believe in God to know it was too cruel to share.

I also declined to tell my father when, at the next ball I attended, the queen approached me to whisper, "Don't look now, but the duc de Chartres is staring at you like a mooncalf in love."

I gave an embarrassed flutter of my fan. "Oh, no, Your Majesty. I'm sure he's looking at you."

The queen let out a throaty laugh, a feather from her wig tickling my ear. "You're blushing, *ma petite marquise!* I see no harm in it. Philippe has certainly admired less worthy ladies."

The duc de Chartres was a well-known libertine, and not knowing how to respond, I said, "I cannot claim to be worthy of his admiration and plead marriage in any case."

"Oh, but you're only a *little bit* married," the queen said with rouged lips. "No one as young as we are can be entirely married. Go, dance with Philippe. Why not enjoy his attentions while you are still a novelty at court?"

The duc de Chartres was ten years my senior and a puckish mischief-maker who often goaded the queen and her ladies into drunken carriage racing in the streets. I did not wish to encourage him. Still, with the queen's prodding, I agreed to dance. When he extended an arm, I rested my fingertips upon it. "Your Serene Highness—"

"You must call me Philippe."

I blushed. "I couldn't."

"Don't you like me, Adrienne?"

Surprised that he knew my given name, I dared a glance into his lupine eyes. "We are scarcely acquainted."

"Give it time, and perhaps we shall become good friends."

"Perhaps." I did not wish to lie.

"Mayhaps more than friends."

I gave a slow wave of my painted fan, meant to warn him off. "What more could you wish?"

"I like your sleepy bedroom eyes," he said, leering. "Though someone should have told you to pluck those brows . . . it makes a man worry the hedges are not trimmed below."

Aghast, I drew back. "Forgive me, but I feel suddenly unwell."

My instinctive horrified reaction seemed to give him the greatest amusement, and he put his hand atop mine, holding fast. "A word of advice, poppet—take care not to be too saintly. Your husband is already an object of mockery at court, and you should not like to join him."

How dizzied I suddenly felt by the musicians and the dancers swirling in lace and brocade. "What has Lafayette done to merit mockery?"

"You're an angel to pretend you don't know your father saddled you with an oaf from the mountains who can't even drink without his knees wobbling."

He laughed at my husband's expense as if he expected me to join in. Then he gestured to where my husband gazed out the window. "Look at him standing at the edge of the dance floor like a dunce. I doubt Lafayette's name is on a single dance card. Perhaps he devotes himself to you. Perhaps to God. Either way he courts resentment, and makes you both seem like children."

Truly, I *felt* like a child trying to fend Philippe off. "Please release me."

His grip tightened. "Only if you promise to be sweeter to me next time we meet. A dull husband need not keep you from blossoming; with my help you could bloom into a rare flower indeed."

I did not promise, but pulled away knowing I could not share this conversation with anyone, lest my husband be humiliated and my father enraged. What's more, there was no escape from my unease in fragrant moonlit gardens, with fireworks overhead, or even watching the card games that went late into the night, for this was a world filled with men just like Chartres. We could be wary of the decadence and corruption of Versailles, but every day, we became more a part of it. And all the while, my husband seemed to lapse more into silence, both at court . . . and at home.

"Is the Lafayette boy mute?" Grand-mère asked at breakfast, tapping her ear trumpet.

"Grand-mère," I said, trying to distract her with a buttered roll, "Monsieur de Lafayette is not yet accustomed to such garrulous society as ours."

We were, after all, an imposing family. But I startled to see my new husband slip marzipan into his pocket like a beggar. Did he grow up hungry as a boy at Chavaniac? "Gilbert," I whispered over the porcelain tea service. "You may call upon servants for marzipan whenever you wish."

He colored. "It's for my horse. An experiment."

This attracted the notice of the duc d'Ayen from the far end of the table, for in addition to his duties at court, my father was an avid scientist, with a laboratory in Paris and a deep interest in chemistry. "What manner of experiment?"

Gilbert's color deepened, as if he feared mockery, and several long moments passed in silence.

"The boy *is* mute!" Grand-mère crossed herself. "Why weren't we informed of this during the wedding negotiations?"

Goaded, Gilbert explained, "At school I was once told to describe a perfect horse. One so well disciplined it would obey at the sight of the whip. I wrote that a *perfect* horse would throw his rider at the sight of a whip. This I still believe."

"Impudence!" cried my aunt, Madame de Tessé, but she grinned, for she read Rousseau and Voltaire and fancied herself quite a philosopher.

Gilbert seemed to fancy himself one too. "No creature should yield easily to cruelty."

My father rolled his eyes heavenward. "You mean to coddle your mount and see how he behaves? You'll ruin a stallion that way."

Gilbert lowered his gaze in apparent deference, but before he did, I saw a storm of defiance in his eyes—a storm that both thrilled and worried me. Later, in the quiet of the bedchamber, where my husband and I shared sweet and gentle intimacies, I broached the subject. "Gilbert, why shy away from conversation at court?"

"Because no one there talks of anything worthy of discussion."

Perhaps this was true, and I could scarcely blame him for disdaining the games of gossip both light and fatal. Still, it seemed unpardonably prideful to hold ourselves above our social betters. "You might raise interesting subjects. You speak to me so knowledgeably about Voltaire and the old Romans . . . about whether God exists, and if he does, in what form . . ."

"That is because you are sincerely interested. Whereas everyone else only wishes to seize upon what I say to ridicule. To them I will always be a *nobody* from Chavaniac."

He was wrong; his marriage to me, his association with the Noailles, made him a somebody. And we were invited to every royal function. By winter my brother-in-law, Marc, had been welcomed into the ranks of the Society of the Wooden Sword, and he obtained an invitation for

Gilbert—an invitation my father said he must accept. Gilbert joined, but soon vexed my father for participating in their antics. "What could he have been thinking?"

"It was only a performance to amuse the queen," I said in my husband's defense. "The king's own brothers took part."

They too had stood upon tavern stools to parody stodgy old nobles. Yet it was Gilbert who had unexpectedly stolen the show with his impersonation of a mean-spirited judge, skewering the judicial system in France that sent peasants to be tortured, broken, or burned alive.

The queen had been as surprised as she was delighted by his audacity, for she thought the performance to be a clever mockery of the Paris Parlement which, in royal opinion, got above themselves. Yet when the word got out, the judges understood my husband to be criticizing the system itself, and now my father ranted, "I cannot rouse my son-in-law to impress important men at court who matter. No, when I need Lafayette to speak, his tongue is tied. Yet he makes a spectacle of himself to amuse the Austrian wench—"

"*Jean*," my mother said sharply, daring to interrupt. "Gilbert is trying."

How grateful I was that Maman took up for my husband. "Father, you have always said there can be no more important opinion than the king's, and when the king heard about this, he laughed."

This my father could not deny. Instead he strode away, and having never got the better of my father in an argument before, I felt the need to make amends. Thereafter, I encouraged my husband to join the sleighing parties, to play billiards in the royal chambers, to drink with the king's courtiers—but to stay silent on matters of politics.

On Christmas Eve, Lafayette had to be carried back to the house by servants. "Tell the vicomte de Noailles how much I drank!" he shouted, then promptly vomited in a washbasin. I knew then how desperate he was to be accepted. Almost as desperate as I was for my father's approval.

Riddled with guilt, I wiped his brow with a cool cloth. And like a dying man yearning for home, Lafayette groaned, "I want to go to Chavaniac."

"I imagine it's dreadfully cold there this time of year," I said.

"Yes, but it's the best time. We slaughter a pig, and on Christmas Eve the family gathers round a loaf of brioche on a pretty table—"

"Only one loaf?" *How poor even the nobles of Auvergne must be!*

"It's our custom. The brioche is more candleholder than bread. From oldest to youngest, everyone takes a turn lighting the candle, making the sign of the cross, then snuffing it out."

I couldn't imagine it. Such a ceremony would last days at court. "Why snuff it out?"

Drifting to a drunken sleep, Lafayette closed his eyes. "Because the world always snuffs out fire, and every generation must bring light from darkness again."

SIX

MARTHE
Chavaniac-Lafayette
December 24, 1940

"IT'S YOUR TURN, MARTHE," THE BARONESS SAYS WITH AN IMPA-
tient glance at her watch. Hovering over her daughter's chair, she's eager
to move our Christmas Eve along. We've already fed the children, tucked
them in bed, and taken midnight mass at the village church.

Now, with hymns playing on the radio, it's finally time for the staff
to eat our modest wartime *réveillon* of rutabagas, mashed Jerusalem arti-
choke, and green lentils with ham. But first, the annual ritual in the
gilded salon under the watchful eyes of philosophers' busts.

The candle is melted down by the time it comes to my hands. For
many years, I was the youngest at the orphanage, so it came to me last,
and I sometimes needed Henri's help to keep from spilling hot wax on
the brioche. The memory of his boyhood hand steadying mine makes my
stomach knot, and I want to pray for him, ask God to keep him warm in
his POW camp. But when I cross myself with the candle, I find only
comfort in the ritual, not faith. Then I hand the candle to Anna, who
crosses herself with what seems like true reverence.

This year our loaf is made with potato flour and filled with chestnut
cream, because the Nazis are taking our food. Of course, everyone knows
you can't make a good brioche without butter, sugar, eggs, milk, or flour,
so the baron calls it Système D Cake as he cuts the abomination into
slices. "Système D?" Anna asks, smoothing a napkin over the green satin
dress she wore to midnight mass.

"*Système débrouiller,*" the baron replies. A system of improvisation.

"*Système* démerder," I whisper, and Anna covers a laugh at my slang
for *improvising our way out of shit.*

The cake is terrible, but we eat every crumb, because it's a bleak winter, bitter cold. Too cold even, on Christmas Day, for sledding or treks on snowshoes. The children are still sleeping in their clothes, because it's impossible to keep the castle and its outbuildings heated; the water pipes are frozen, so bathing the little ones is an ordeal. We're all wearing coats and mittens all day inside. And we're veritable shut-ins.

To pass the time, Anna and I huddle together in front of the fireplace in Madame Beatrice's tower room, where I'm trying to sketch, and she says, "You know, every year since we met, my husband took me to a Paris Christmas market to buy a new decoration for the crèche. We'd visit the vendor stalls for mulled wine and warm crepes . . ." We both groan at the memory of crepes. "How many Christmases did you spend with Henri?"

"All of them." I start to say that holidays here at Chavaniac are nothing special—but I realize how much I've taken for granted, and what a coward I've been, because it's been more than a year since Henri left for war and I haven't visited his mother even once. Before snow blocked the roads, I could've made the half-hour journey by bicycle, but maybe I worried she'd want her ring back or say I never had any right to it in the first place. The truth is that I've never liked Madame Pinton and she's never liked me, but I promise myself I'll go see her after the thaw.

The BBC is jammed, so we're listening to Radio Vichy, which is intolerable. Endless prattle about family, farms, and folktales—as if every advance since serfdom has caused France's doom. We're told our defeat at Hitler's hands was actually a *divine surprise* through which we can now redeem ourselves by returning to our roots in the land. In the Marshal's Christmas Eve address, he said, "*Tonight a New France is born, made by your trials, your remorse, your sacrifice. Take courage and swear to aid this great rebirth so that your children again will know happy Christmases.*"

At hearing it mentioned again, Anna turns the radio off.

I think she must be as disgusted as I am. "Why should we feel *remorse*?" I ask as she pulls out her knitting. "Is it our fault France's soldiers stood in the way of Hitler's plans?"

And if it was, I don't see why we should feel sorry about it.

Anna, who is making a scarf to send to her husband, just shakes her head. "Our men should've been home now. Can you imagine how cold it must be in those POW camps?"

I squeeze the charcoal pencil in my hand, unable to hold my anger in anymore. "I learned in an orphanage full of boys that a bully only stops hitting when you bloody him. So why did we stop fighting? Why agree to an armistice if the Germans are going to starve and freeze us all?"

Anna presses her lips together, as if afraid to say more. Then she does anyway. "Papa says the armistice was necessary to save the young men of France, but he worries the collaboration is a terrible mistake; he blames the ministers."

"No one forced the Marshal to shake Hitler's hand," I say a little heatedly, then regret it because Anna has offered a glimpse into the baron's thinking, and now I've shut her up again.

For a long time, the only sounds in the room are the pop of burning logs, the clack of her knitting needles, and my charcoal pencil scratching on paper. I have to admit, even if I wouldn't have chosen Adrienne Lafayette as a subject again on my own, it's an almost euphoric feeling to have fresh pencils and paper and permission to create once more. Still, I've started over again at least a dozen times, and I'm ready to crumple the latest attempt too, because if I'm going to do this, I want to do it right.

When I sigh, Anna asks, "What's wrong?"

"Your mother wants me to portray Adrienne Lafayette as an icon of motherhood, but I'm not exactly an expert on that."

Anna rolls her eyes. "Neither is Maman."

"What do you mean?"

Anna shrugs, looking a little sorry she said anything. "There was . . . an incident when I was a small child, when she left me for a year. And now she tries to make up for it by smothering me." The idea that the baroness would have *left* Anna is a complete shock, and it must show, because Anna colors. "It was really nothing."

It doesn't sound like nothing, but I see she doesn't want me to pry. I *have* noticed a tendency of the baroness to hover over Anna and supervise her as if she were not a married woman of nearly twenty-four, but I can't imagine complaining about it. "Well, you're lucky to have her now."

Anna bites her lip. "Of course, you're right. If you don't mind my asking . . . what happened to your mother?"

I shrug. "No one knows. They say I'm a veritable foundling left by the faeries in the streets of Paris during the Great War."

As a kid I used to look at picture books of that city and tell myself stories about who my parents might have been. Maybe a young soldier on leave visiting his glamorous wife, both of them dying bravely during church service in a zeppelin attack. Maybe a couple who owned a bakery near the Pont Neuf who died suddenly of the Spanish flu . . .

Since I've so often reached into my imagination for solace, emotions now slip past my mask. "My mother could've been anyone, really. Maybe a prostitute who dumped me in an alley."

This is one of my darkest fears about my parentage, and myself. That not even a mother could love me or want to keep me. That I'm made of sin and vice, and that's why no one ever adopted me or came back for me.

Anna squeezes my shoulder. "I'm sure your mother wasn't a prostitute." Her smile is illuminated by the fire, light dancing on the little gold cross she wears around her neck. Unlike me, she wears hers more in faith than habit. She's the kind of person who believes things without proof. Still, I find her words and her friendship comforting.

"So how did you get your name—why *Marthe*?"

Now *I* roll my eyes. "I was the first girl at the orphanage—so the Americans called me the *First Lady*, like Martha Washington."

Anna laughs. "Well, you see, then? You were practically born to bring bewigged old ladies to life."

"It'd be easier if Adrienne was here in the flesh to model."

Anna turns so I can see her profile in firelight. "Well, *I'm* here in the flesh. I could model for you."

That idea actually sparks something. The faith I saw glimmering in Anna's eyes—that's what the baroness wants me to capture, but I can do it my way with a modern sensibility. I can show Adrienne Lafayette *without* the powdered wigs, portraying her as she might look now, like Anna, the dark-eyed, dark-haired, devoted young wife of a soldier husband . . .

While I'm studying Anna—the point of her eyebrow, the curve of her earlobe, the glossy dark curls, and the downy hair that swirls at her nape . . . she shivers. "I hate this cold. I don't know how you survived growing up in these mountains."

I can't remember it being *this* cold before, but I say, "You get used to it. Take the blanket from the bed if you want it." Instead, she decides to just kick off her oxfords and slide under the covers, so I grouse, "You're fired as my model! You have no work ethic."

Anna fluffs the pillow. "I'm industriously warming up the bed for you! It'll be toasty if you don't give me the bum's rush."

I don't give her the bum's rush. I keep sketching, losing myself in the lines, trying to bring this version—*my* version—of Adrienne to life.

When my hands are stiff, the hour is late, and I'm too tired to go on, I look up to see that Anna has fallen asleep in my bed, bundled in hat, mittens, and sweater. Trying not to disturb her, I slip quietly under the covers, but she stirs, turning to me on the pillow, tucking my red-knitted scarf around my neck. We're nose to nose, her perfume smells wonderful, and I suddenly realize that I can't remember sharing a bed with another person before.

Oh, there were fumblings in the back of Henri's Peugeot. This is a different kind of closeness, one that I don't have a name for. And as I ponder it under the knowing gaze of Madame Beatrice's portraits on the wall, I feel truly *warm* for the first time since the war began.

SEVEN

BEATRICE
New York City
January 1915

"MRS. CHANLER! MRS. CHANLER!" CRIED THE GAGGLE OF REPORT-
ers when I stepped out of the motor in front of the Vanderbilt Hotel.
"What do you say to critics who accuse you of defying the president's
policy of American neutrality?"

In the three cold winter months since returning from France, where
men drowned in the mud of the Marne to halt the German advance, I'd
caused a bit of a stir. And today I was armed with a plan and a new hat.
No more drooping plumes of cowardly ostrich for me. No, the times called
for *mink*—a clever little scrapper.

Festooned with a French tricolor cockade, my mink hat would make
for a glamorous photo. I still knew how to take a picture, thankfully. Thus,
I waited for the cameras to start snapping. Then, in wordless satisfaction,
I sashayed right past the reporters into the hotel, where buttoned-up bell-
hops closed ranks behind me. This was my hotel, after all. Well, my
husband was half owner of the place anyway. Still, I was the one who
chose the fan windows, the stone for the vaulted ceilings, and just a touch
of Italian Renaissance on the facade for posh whimsy.

I considered stopping by Mr. Vanderbilt's office to apologize for the
ruckus outside, but intent upon the leaflet I clutched in gloved hand, I
marched directly to Suite 123—the offices of the Lafayette Fund, the
new war relief charity where I now served as directress. And with each
step, the vile words of the leaflet's accusation poisoned my every thought:

**Do you realize what you're doing, you vociferous criers-out in
the cause of humanity, you members of the Lafayette League**

and other mushy beldames who make themselves party to the murder of mothers and infants?

The outrage of it! I found Miss Sloane already seated at the type-writer, brow furrowed as she clicked away in angry strikes. She was, no doubt, already composing a measured response for the newspaper, but I was in no mood to be measured.

"Oh, dear," said Emily, glancing up in alarm. "A new hat—"

"Beldames?" I waved the leaflet under her nose. "They're calling us ugly old witches!"

I wouldn't let them get away with it. I was, after all, only thirty years old. Or at least close enough to thirty that no reasonable person should quibble over an extra year or four. Thanks to the magic of corsets, rouge, and other hat tricks, men still stumbled over themselves in my presence. I was no beldame. While I seethed, Miss Sloane raised a pointed elfin eyebrow. "I should rather have thought the accusation that we're a party to *murder* would offend you."

I waved a gloved hand. "Well, that goes without saying."

Since Miss Sloane and I had returned from war-torn France, our charity work had forged us in a true friendship; this despite the fact we had very little in common other than a determination that we must do something about this disastrous war. And the audacity to believe that we could.

Our charity had packaged and shipped more than ten thousand kits filled with underwear, socks, and letters of encouragement for French soldiers in the trenches. Soldiers like my nephew Victor. Soldiers who were defending the children I'd seen at the train station in Amiens.

Together Miss Sloane and I had marshaled New York high society such that our offices were overrun most days with Astor ladies in fine lace gloves and Vanderbilt wives in prim shirtwaists, all eager to assemble care packages. We collected donations nationwide, and for our pains, we now stood accused of "equipping" foreign soldiers with dangerous shipments of socks and underpants.

This latest leaflet was the boldest accusation yet. We'd received dire warnings, even from friends, that we must cease, but this was the most like myself I'd felt in years.

Emily pulled the page from her typewriter to show me.

In answer to the criticism that our Lafayette Fund violates neutrality, our purpose is purely humanitarian: We are trying to relieve the intense suffering at the front. We send comfort kits to France because of the debt we, and all other Americans, owe to that country for her assistance, without which we might never have won our independence.

"Very good," I said, flicking the page aside and leaving her to catch it out of the air. "But this attack merits more than another politely worded editorial in the *New York Times.*"

She eyed me—and my hat. "I fear to ask . . ."

"They're trying to intimidate us because we're ladies." Just that morning, women's suffrage had been voted down in the House of Representatives for the second time, and as I peeked out the window in the direction of the Woolworth Building—the tallest building in the world at sixty stories—I felt in a foul enough mood to knock it down. "Do you think they'd fling insults like that at gentlemen? They wouldn't dare. It might provoke a duel, even in these modern times. It's because we're women that they think we're soft."

"Mushy," Emily corrected, which incensed me all over again.

"They think we'll scurry off and hide our heads."

Emily clutched her typewritten words. "Writing an editorial for the *New York Times* is scarcely hiding!"

"No, but some will take your justification for an apology. And we're not sorry, are we, Miss Sloane?"

"Certainly not," she said stoutly.

She was a very stouthearted girl.

With renewed determination, I pulled off my gloves, readying for a fight. "We're going to redouble our efforts. We're going to be brazen, doing what New Yorkers do best. We're going to put on a show!"

"What an engaging idea," she said.

She did not sound engaged.

Because she'd been struggling with the logistical nightmare of how to ship seven thousand more comfort kits to France over an increasingly perilous sea, I forgave her obvious assumption that I was up to something frivolous. I knew what people said about me—what they'd been saying since the first time I had the nerve to take an interest in political matters. *She's just an empty-headed comedic actress who married above herself and should stick to what she knows.*

Well, I was going to take their advice. I was going to entertain . . .

"It'll be a patriotic play about Lafayette," I explained, wedging myself between two stacks of boxes near her desk. "A pageant, in fact, showing harrowing scenes of Valley Forge to remind the public how the French saved us in the darkest hours of the American Revolution. It should remind them that our positions are now reversed and our allies need our help. Ticket sales will fund our work."

Emily's pointed eyebrows inched higher. "If no one comes, we shall be held up to public ridicule."

"Oh, they'll come," I insisted. "There isn't a member of the Social Register who would dare miss it. Do you know why?"

"I feel certain you'll tell me."

"Because I am *Mrs. William Astor Chanler.*" Whatever the troubles in our marriage, and even if we were an ocean apart, I still had Willie's name, and that meant something. Once the old Knickerbocker aristocracy of New York lined up behind my play, everyone else would follow suit, fearing to be left out.

Emily pursed her lips. "Who would headline the play?"

As president of the New York Stage Society, I might recruit any number of celebrities. Douglas Fairbanks. Charlie Chaplin. Lionel and John Barrymore. Still, thinking back to the railway station at Amiens, I remembered seeing a flash of Minnie. Poor little skinny Minnie, who sang and danced for her supper . . . and a better idea came to me. "I want little girls and boys for the lead roles. No one can resist tiny tots in costumes. And we'll call it"—I made a dramatic sweeping motion—"*The Children's Revolution.*"

Miss Sloane blinked, blinded by my brilliance. Or perhaps she thought me mad. In truth, the line between brilliance and madness is very thin, so I felt compelled to add, "You forget how easily I succeed in inspiring others to work. Indeed, this is my real genius; people refuse me nothing and enter with zest into all my plans and games!"

I said it to make her laugh, but Emily shook her head in complete exasperation. "We're being attacked for defying the president of the United States, and you're proposing a pageant for schoolchildren! Am I wrong to think that what we need most is to be taken seriously by powerful men?"

I tilted my head, imperious beneath my mink hat. "My dear, no one is better at getting the attention of powerful men than I am."

"And you think powerful men want to attend a children's play?"

"Heavens no! Their wives will drag them to see it. After all, the only thing society wives love better than showing off their little darlings is boasting of their blue-blooded pedigrees." While Emily gawped, I explained, "By way of example, Mrs. Daiziel takes enormous pride in her familial connection to George Washington. I'll be glad to cast her daughter in the prize role of Martha Washington *if* Mr. Daiziel makes a large donation and joins our committee."

Emily's eyes widened halfway between shock and admiration. "Why, there's something quite wicked about you."

"Oh, I'm really not such a bad creature if humored!"

Emily picked up a pencil and nibbled at the end. Preparing to be vexed, I said, "You think it can't be done." She continued to nibble. "You think it's too outrageous an idea," I accused. "Too whimsical a scheme?"

"I think we're going to need a seamstress," Emily finally said. "The costumes should be authentic."

Oh, I could've kissed her—and not merely for going along with my plans, but for being a true partner in them. For I hadn't felt as if I had a partner in quite some time. "Let's take some notes, shall we?"

I'D LONG BEEN WARY OF REPORTERS, BUT ONE SIMPLY CAN'T DO without them, so at long last, I agreed to an interview. In the airy two-tiered dining room of the Vanderbilt Hotel with its iconic potted palms, I greeted Mitzi Miller, a talented writer and prominent suffragette. None of her cigar-chomping male colleagues took her seriously, which is why she'd been shunted off to edit the society column. But I admired her work and knew, at the very least, she'd spell the name right. (*Chanler*, not *Chandler*. Once a reporter slipped a *d* into the name, the family never forgot or forgave.)

"Thank you for agreeing to this interview, Mrs. Chanler. I am ever so grateful for a reason to write about something other than winter balls and stylish spring weddings."

Well, this was starting off smashingly! "I'm so glad we finally have the chance to talk."

Taking in the hotel's ambience, she gestured toward the frieze. "Is it true you sculpted that?"

"Ah, yes." Playfully, I added, "After years as an actress being blinded by the footlights, I thought I might also ruin my posture with sculpture."

It had been backbreaking work, but I was quite proud of it, so it deflated me a little when Miss Miller laughed and said, "The things society wives do to keep from dying of boredom!"

Hoping she didn't think of me as a mere society wife, I invited her to sit for tea. Francophile though I might be, only the British did tea properly, so a silver tray of scones and sweets awaited us in the English style, but like an ascetic monk, Miss Miller declined both milk and sugar, which put me on my guard. What honest woman doesn't like sugar?

Leather-bound notebook in hand, she said, "Now, tell me all about your little patriotic play."

I reviewed the program, which was to include a reenactment of Washington's inaugural ball. I explained the children would march under a genuine Revolutionary-era flag that I'd procured on loan. I'd also invited children from a nearby Indian reservation to participate, and the play itself would be written by my brother-in-law, John Jay Chapman—a celebrated writer, if a bit mad at times. *Do it for Victor*, I'd said, because my nephew was never far from my mind. *Even if America hasn't chosen a side, your son has, and he deserves our support.*

But the loyalty of a loving father wasn't what impressed Mitzi Miller—it was that Jack Chapman was a direct descendant of Founding Father John Jay. I watched her survey the blue-blooded cast list of nearly two hundred children, and then she declared, "Well, doesn't this promise to be the season's spectacle of high society! The stage mothers will have a veritable reunion of the Daughters of the American Revolution. Speaking of, why aren't you a member? Surely you're eligible . . ."

Had she been digging into my past? I gave a carefully noncommittal shrug. "I understand there's quite a bit of paperwork involved to join the DAR."

"Well, that's true. To qualify, you'd have to submit birth, marriage, and death records for your ancestry, as well as proof of your patriot ancestor's Revolutionary War service." All things I did not have. "I'd be happy to help you get the paperwork together. Where do your people come from again?"

So Mitzi Miller *had* been digging. Fortunately, she wasn't likely to find anything—my husband had seen to that—but I realized my mistake in choosing a female reporter, because I couldn't simply distract her with flirtation. "I'm from Charlottesville."

A lie I'd been telling for quite some time.

"Ah," she said. "Hometown of Thomas Jefferson and some of America's finest families. No wonder you're so knowledgeable about Lafayette."

As if any ordinary person couldn't simply read a book about the French hero! I'm certain that public libraries saved my life when I was a child, but now I changed the subject. "Did I mention we've sold out of our first performance?"

Miss Miller took a long sip from her teacup. "How wonderful. What does Mr. Chanler think about all this?"

Willie had not replied to my letters since we parted in autumn. The harsh reality was that my marriage was still in pieces—half of them on the other side of the ocean—and I didn't know when or how to put them together again. Maybe that was the point of a marriage contract. Like a signed-and-sealed alliance of nations, only a contract held things together when all that remained was financial entanglements and mutual interest.

But of course, one must keep up appearances, so I said, "My husband very much approves of the Lafayette Fund. In fact, he's on the committee."

Or at least he *would* be on the committee once I wrote his name down, which would serve him right. If he'd wished to be consulted, then he should have answered my letters.

Miss Miller closed her notebook. "Mrs. Chanler, may I be frank?" She didn't wait for my answer before adding, "You're *ever* so good at these little fundraising things. Truly, you have a talent for it!"

The word *little* was starting to grate. "You're so kind to say so."

"I just hate to see a woman with your potential fritter away her time."

What a vulnerable place she stabbed! "Oh, but the children's play is a means to an important end. We've just sent seven thousand Lafayette kits to French soldiers, and with ticket proceeds, we'll bring the total number up to an even twenty thousand next shipment."

She leaned back. "Aren't you worried that Germany is threatening to sink neutral ships? All your hard work could sink to the seafloor."

What a miserable lot of people these Germans are! That's what I wanted to say. Discretion being the better part of valor, I said, "Yes, but we can't cower. Kaiser Wilhelm has no right to prevent us from sending humanitarian aid."

"Aid for French soldiers, you mean. You've picked a side."

The right side, I thought. "The side of humanity," I said, wondering how this conversation was going wrong when I should've had her eating out of my palm. Perhaps I'd worn the wrong hat . . .

Miss Miller smiled. "Surely you worry for your nephew in the trenches."

"Yes. Of course." Victor's letters were months out of date, but he wrote of the privations, the lack of ambulances, and the seemingly random ways in which his comrades were blown to bits. We were quite sure that wasn't even the half of it. "But we're very proud of him too."

"Wouldn't you like to bring him home?" she asked. "I must confess, it wasn't only an interview I came for today. By now, you must have heard of the Woman's Peace Party."

I'd read only a little something of it in the papers. Enough to know it had been started by suffragettes I admired. "I'm curious to know more."

"It's all in the name. It's a political party for women and for peace. As we like to say, men brought about this slaughter in Europe. Only women can stop it. We put higher value on human life because we *give* life. And once women have the vote, there will never be another war."

She's obviously never seen a herd of actresses willing to gore each other over a starring role.

"Well, I'd certainly like to see that theory put to the test . . ."

"We should very much like for you to join us. We'd put you in charge of a fundraising committee to produce literature promoting peace."

How flattered I was, although the details sounded vague. "What do you mean by literature *promoting peace?*"

"Pamphlets. Propaganda. Recruitment to the peace movement. You see, in April, distinguished women from all over the world will meet at The Hague for an international conference to demonstrate solidarity! We want our pamphlets to say our feminine bond cannot be divided by the trenches men have dug between us."

I stirred my teacup faster, trying to digest this, then tilted my head, hoping her words would make more sense viewed from a different angle. "A lovely sentiment, but how will this bring an end to the war?"

"Perhaps we women must go, arm in arm, to the trenches and demand the soldiers stop fighting."

I dropped my spoon. "While I love a dramatic gesture, you should know the Germans paid no mind to the demands, nay, even the heartbreaking *pleas*, of the women and children they attacked."

She gave a tragic sigh. "*Of course* we'd insist the protection of women and children must be made the first tenet of civilized warfare."

"The kaiser doesn't give a fig for the rules of war and—"

"You sound like a partisan."

Remembering bleeding, orphaned, homeless children, I asked, "Tell me, did Germany accidentally trip and fall into neutral Belgium? I teach my boys that might doesn't make right, and that there's nothing more American than standing up to a bully."

It was more than I had intended to say, but what a relief to say it even as the reporter's eyes narrowed. "The American public supports neutrality."

"For now." Public opinion could be *shaped*, and I was no bad sculptor. Out of more than 120 countries in the world, only 7 were democracies, and like Willie, I believed we should stand by them. America should be in this fight. "I fear your peace convention will be futile at best, damaging at worst. I cannot be part of it."

"You're making a mistake. I'm sure your heart is in the right place, but you don't seem to understand the complexities of this war."

"Don't I? With all due respect, you weren't in France at the outbreak of the war. I was."

"You didn't stay, though, did you? You fled. Which would be all well and good if you weren't now flouting the president's policies and trading on your husband's name in a self-aggrandizing endeavor to put America's sons in harm's way." She stuffed her notebook back into her handbag, then added a parting shot. "At least we're willing to risk our *own* lives for our beliefs."

"And that would be admirable," I shot back, "were you not also risking the political rights of all women by representing us as a bunch of nincompoops incapable of understanding world affairs."

Sputtering, she rose and took her leave. I lingered, stinging from her rebuke. So she thought me an attention-seeking coward. *Perhaps it was hubris to think the Lafayette Fund could make a difference*, I thought. Perhaps a society wife—and an abandoned one at that—was all I could ever be . . . I had, after all, already risen higher than someone like me had any right to.

While I brooded, slathering my scones with jam and clotted cream with no consideration for my waistline, my eldest moped up to the table and perched on the edge of a chair. "Whatever is the matter, darling?"

Billy stared down glumly, swinging his legs. "I c-can't be Lafayette in the p-play."

"Why not?"

"The other kids don't want to f-f-f—" I waited for him to get the word out. It only made him more self-conscious to have his sentences finished for him—children too have their pride. "F-follow me onstage," he finally managed to say. "They p-poke fun at me."

I bristled like a mother bear. "Which children poke fun at you?"

Billy jutted his chin in a way that reminded me of his stubborn father, and I knew he'd never tattle. Finally, he said, "Lafayette was a h-hero. I'm just a boy."

A shy, awkward boy, he meant, and it hurt to see his confidence shaken. Especially when my own was shaken too. What a sad pair of mopers we were. What would Minnie say?

Nobody gets anywhere being a wet blanket. Even if you've got to dig your nails into your palms, just put on the mask and smile.

I'd given my sons every advantage in life, but maybe I needed to remind them—and myself—that what mattered was a stout heart and a resolution never to bow to low expectations. If only to be a good example, I couldn't let myself sink into the role society set for me and wallow in loneliness and despair. With my work at the Lafayette Fund—however silly it might seem to reporters like Mitzi Miller—I'd found a new sense of purpose that I intended to embrace, with or without a husband. After all, if I'd learned anything as an actress, it was that you can become the role you take on.

I took my son's chin. "Darling, I'm going to let you in on a little secret. No one is born a hero; it's something you have to find inside yourself. Once upon a time, even Lafayette was just a boy like you."

EIGHT

AT COURT, MY SEVENTEEN-YEAR-OLD HUSBAND SHIED AWAY FROM the Hall of Mirrors, afraid that any misstep should be reflected from a hundred angles for all to see. Lafayette worried about making a fool of himself, and he was not a practiced dancer, which is why he did not often join in the queen's quadrilles.

Yet, at her first occasion of the New Year, as a mark of growing favor to me, Marie Antoinette offered her hand to Gilbert to partner with her, and every man turned envious eyes his way. I gave my husband an encouraging nod, despite my irritation that on this occasion, I was left to partner with the lascivious duc de Chartres. "Shall we, my pretty poppet?"

Despite my tender age, I'd grown too accustomed to Philippe's flirtation to blush behind my fan anymore; I had learned to appear indifferent. So I let him guide me to a position across from his lover, Aglaé, whose beautiful emerald eyes gleamed with jealousy—authentic or feigned, I could not guess. And, waiting for my husband to lead the queen in a graceful promenade, I asked, "Are you looking forward to the king's coronation?"

He laughed. "Not as much as the queen, who hopes the ceremony might finally put a little stiffness into the royal rod."

He said this with contempt, which made it a relief that the dance required me to momentarily leave him, crossing the center to clasp hands with the gentleman opposite—the king's portly brother. The king's brother huffed and puffed, but I much preferred this to when Philippe grasped hold of me again. "Not even a smile, Adrienne? Tell me why you refuse to return my love."

I believed Philippe did not mean love, but *lust*. "I have morals, sir."

"Morals, like fashion, can be out of style."

I knew I might rise higher in the royal court—be considered worldlier—if I returned the flirtations of the pleasure-loving young men who made up the queen's coterie, but I was already becoming more Lafayette than Noailles. "Then I am content to be old-fashioned."

Philippe laughed as he made the motions of the dance. "I sense in you and Lafayette a most unchristian vanity. Have you never suspected that refusal to indulge in the vices of others might be construed as self-righteousness? People hate to feel judged."

I felt he was twisting everything, but it has always been part of my character to worry about giving someone else pain. So I said, "We are in no place to judge you, a prince of the blood."

"Exactly so." His voice near my ear was sharp as a knife. "And you must be reminded of that."

What happened next unfolded so swiftly I couldn't trust what I thought I saw—Philippe's foot shooting out just as we circled past the queen, his heel clipping Gilbert's. My husband tripped, landing facedown on the polished wooden floor. The boy who climbed out of castle towers now *sprawled* at the feet of the queen. The musicians stopped playing and the courtiers went silent, waiting for the queen's reaction.

None of us dared move.

Marie Antoinette might've stooped to help Gilbert, or asked if he had taken an injury; she might have said something to soothe his pride. Surely the queen knew—as everyone knew—that whatever she chose to do would be mimicked by all.

What she chose to do was laugh.

Not merely a giggle of nervous impulse, but a tinkling laugh of crystal clear ridicule. Philippe's mistress was first to join in the laughter, Aglaé's porcelain cheeks turning pink with merriment at my husband's expense. Soon every courtier in the room guffawed, until the gilded rafters themselves seemed to shake with laughter. Gilbert leapt to his feet, his skin flushing from red to purple, and we returned to Paris that same night.

My heart bled for my poor husband, for I understood now that the court was every bit the nest of vipers my mother feared. And neither of us truly belonged.

SO SELDOM DID MY FATHER SEND FOR ME WHEN HE VISITED PARIS that I made haste to the duc d'Ayen's laboratory, where he kept a furnace, crucibles, melting pots, and other instruments. I found him hunched over a row of dead goldfinches, studying the different chemical stages of decay, and I stifled the urge to hold a kerchief to my nose against the smell.

My father held some manner of long forceps in one hand and a scalpel in the other, too intent upon his dissection to greet me. "Rumor has it your husband was tripped by Chartres."

"I think so."

"Was he tripped or wasn't he?"

I laced my fingers behind my back to keep them from trembling, for my father's presence always intimidated me. "I cannot swear because it happened so quickly, and yet I believe it to be true."

My father looked up. "What does your husband plan to do about it?"

I lifted my hands in helpless confusion. "What *can* be done about it?"

Thereupon my father startled me by stabbing the dead bird's wing, pinning it to the board. "Adrienne, this creature was singing yesterday. There, yonder, in the tray, rotting and stinking, that bird was alive last month. The desiccated one is slowly crumbling. It's a process inevitable for each and every one of us. Everything ends. Everything becomes dust. Nothing lasts but your name and your legacy."

I could not guess what he meant for me to say. Nor could I hold his gaze, as I felt dissected myself. Did he mean that we should take revenge? Did he wish Gilbert to challenge Philippe to a duel?

At length, my father took up another sharp instrument. "An attack on my son-in-law is an attack on the Noailles. Lafayette cannot simply slink away from the fight."

"What do you wish him to do?"

"Return to Versailles. We have secured him an appointment. He will be the first gentleman to the king's brother."

This was a prestigious hereditary post that the king had somehow been convinced to pass to my husband as if he were, in fact, of Noailles blood. Gilbert's duties would begin each morning in drawing the bed-curtains, providing a dressing gown, and deciding who should or should not be admitted to an audience. It would fall to Gilbert to wait upon the king's brother at supper, to watch and guard his royal person. It was a great honor, and yet one I knew my husband would detest. "Father, you do us a kindness, but neither of us wish to return to court."

My father cut the bird's wing joint. "Untold favors were called to secure this opportunity, and you will both be grateful in time. There is no declining this honor, Adrienne, a thing you will impress upon your husband. A thing you *must* impress upon him."

I nodded grimly, remembering my duty to make my husband conform to the mold of a Noailles, however impossible that might be.

MY HUSBAND RECEIVED THE NEWS OF HIS ROYAL POST WITH AS little pleasure as I expected. "I have my own ambitions," Gilbert said. "That is all I have."

"You have *me*, and I am all yours." I meant this with the deepest sincerity, even though my next words would prove I still also belonged to the Noailles. "To refuse would give offense to the king. Also to my father and grandfather. It would shame the family."

"Would it shame you, as well?"

I wanted to say no. To say that I only wanted us to be happy. Yet no more than my father could I allow the queen's laughter to destroy us.

At my silence, Gilbert buried his head in his hands. "Adrienne, can you not understand that I want to be a soldier like my father and his father before him, going back to the days of Joan of Arc? I am a Lafayette. I am meant to fight for something—not to empty another man's chamber pot!"

"You are proud, I know—"

"Pride does not deter me. Were the king's brother old or infirm, I could serve him in mercy and humility, but he is capable of pissing without my help."

Never had my husband been vulgar in my presence before, and I bit my lip. "We have no choice."

Gilbert shook his head. "There is always a choice."

This time, I thought he was wrong. And I dismissed this quarrel from my mind until the night of the masquerade ball, just before Lent. Hoping to cheer my husband, I chose for him a wolf mask so he could disguise himself as the Beast of Gévaudan.

"I am too tall, and my hair too red, for anyone to be fooled," he complained. Nevertheless, he agreed to wear the mask, because I was to go as Le Petit Chaperon Rouge, the girl in the red hood. Thus, under falling rose petals, to the accompaniment of chamber music, I returned to Versailles, standing by my wolf.

We all pretended to be strangers for the sake of fun, but the king's brother was too rotund for us not to know him behind his harlequin's mask. To amuse the crowd, he quoted lines from a play, boasting of a perfect ability to memorize books. That's when, from behind his mask, Gilbert said, "I have always thought memory to be a fool's intellect. Better to discuss new ideas than recite old ones."

Panic lodged in my throat, and everyone in the nearby crowd tittered. Thankfully, masquerades were called *the world upside down*, and impudence was forgiven—nay, even expected. If the king's brother were a better man, he would have let this pass. Alas, he came upon us the next morning, jowls red with offense. "Lafayette, perhaps you remember insulting a man last night on the subject of his wit; I assume you do not know who that man was."

"That man stands before me," Gilbert replied, placid as ice.

The offer of royal appointment was abruptly withdrawn, which meant Lafayette had not refused; he had been rejected. He had preserved my family's reputation while ruining his own. There was now no place for Gilbert at court; no future for him *but* as a soldier. And my infuriated father sent him directly back to his military garrison at Metz.

My only solace was that Lafayette had left with me some part of himself. I waited until I was certain, then sent a letter. And his reply was everything I could have hoped . . .

*My dear heart, your unexpected news gives me joy. This little
creature will be our creature—proof that we love each other more
than ever. Let us reunite at the coronation; I am told you will go.
And I would go to hell itself to embrace you. I love you madly.*

I treasured this letter, counting down the days until the king's coronation, which was the talk of France and our breakfast table, where
Grand-mère demanded to know, "Who are these upstarts? These so-
called reformers telling the king to cut expenses. Do they mistake him
for some bourgeois shopkeeper who must balance his books?"

My father stabbed at his omelette. "Perhaps if our new queen was not
losing so much money gambling, we could afford to do things properly."

As it happened, things were all done with the greatest pomp and
circumstance, according to tradition, at Rheims, and my family was glad
of this. I was gladder to see Gilbert again, and to be embraced by him
under the colorful stained glass of the cathedral, and to feel him caress
my belly, where our love had borne fruit. And to hear him say, "You have
become more beautiful."

Perhaps not wishing me to become vain, Aunt Claude said,
"Adrienne and the whole city have been made more beautiful for the
coronation."

"The city's beauty is due to France's peasants," Gilbert said. He disap-
proved of the *corvée* in which peasants were forced to labor in repairing
the roads in readiness for the great occasion. He said this prevented them
from planting their crops, and he hoped the king would remember their
sacrifice.

But even Gilbert had little notion of the seeds we sowed that summer
whilst shots rang out across the sea. For as we made ready to coronate our
king, the American colonists at Lexington and Concord took up arms
against theirs. It was a farmers' insurrection that would change our lives,
and yet at the time, the coronation seemed far more important. The
trumpets announced the arrival of the king's magnificent cherub-
ornamented carriage. I gasped to see the jeweled Crown of Charlemagne.
I bore happy witness as our king was crowned as Louis XVI, and I cried,

"Vive le roi!" Bells pealed, cannons boomed, and, imbued with God's blessing, the newly crowned king waded into a crowd of sick persons desperate for his touch. Later, several claimed to have been healed. Both my father and Gilbert were dubious of miracles—the rare thing upon which both could agree.

The other thing they both agreed upon was joy in my pregnancy. Gilbert was the expectant father, but when we returned from the coronation, the duc d'Ayen strutted the black-and-white tiles of the Hôtel de Noailles like a peacock, declaring that I must be denied not even my smallest whim, whether it be asparagus in late summer or raspberries in winter.

Anything to help along the birth of the long-awaited Noailles heir!

I had never known before what it felt like to be in favor with my father—how interesting and charming he could be. How interesting and charming I felt *myself* to be when I had his approval. At long last, I had secured what I craved most: the love of my husband and my father too.

Alas, in the midst of a snowy December, I was delivered of a little girl, pale and frail.

Maman consoled me, telling me what joy daughters could bring. Gilbert pronounced himself smitten with his new daughter and allowed me to name her *Henriette*, after my mother. Meanwhile, my disappointed father called for a carriage and disappeared into the night in search of his mistress, after having mused that if he were not a scientist, he would believe himself cursed.

Yet, with the arrival of my daughter, for the first time in my life, I knew myself to be truly blessed. Before her birth, I had questioned God.

Why does God forgive wicked people?

Why would a loving God bring us into a world where suffering exists?

Why should we have faith?

Now I began to understand. Having made my daughter within my own body, nurtured her, and brought her into being, I loved her fiercely and unconditionally. I would have forgiven her anything. And though I had brought her into a world where suffering existed, I would do all I could to protect the miracle of her being. When she cried, not understanding when I must do something for her own good, I wished her to trust me—to have faith. This must be what God's love truly is. I did not yet know God's purpose for me, and I did not think I would ever stop questioning, but that winter, I had found faith enough to make my first Communion. For what I lacked in an earthly patriarch, I found in my heavenly Father.

BY 1776 EVERYONE WAS TALKING ABOUT THE *BOSTONIANS*— colonists in the New World who demanded of their British king *No taxation without representation*. To make their point, these rebels had, a few years before, dressed as tomahawk-wielding natives and flung crates of tea into the ocean. Thereafter, the panicked British Parliament declared a state of rebellion, much to the glee of every Frenchman.

Some Frenchmen jested that they'd like to go fight alongside the rebels.

For my husband, it was more than a jest. Since the birth of our daughter, it had been a year of restlessness. Gilbert had been forced out of uniform and removed unceremoniously from active duty by the decision of the war minister that French officers should be seasoned fighters— not aristocratic young noblemen. Now, at nineteen, banished both from court and from the army, my husband was in veritable disgrace. Thus, the opportunity to prove himself in America was a powerful temptation, one he confided in me when we were abed. Smiling at the way morning sunlight illuminated his hair like spun copper on my pillow, I accused, "You just want to fight the British."

After all, Gilbert's father had been struck dead by a British bullet.

"*Oui*," he admitted. "I want to avenge my father, but from what I know of the American cause, I believe it to be just. I cannot countenance the notion that people owe blind obedience to a faraway sovereign who cares nothing for their pains. I admire these Bostonians who wish to govern themselves like the Romans of the old republic . . ."

"You countenance insurrection?"

He laughed, only a little sheepish. "I cannot help myself. I'm an Auvergnat; from the home of the ancient king who rebelled against Caesar."

How like him to dredge that up from his Latin books. "I have never heard of a rebel king."

"Vercingetorix was an *elected* king."

It did not, of course, work that way in France now. Our king seemed pious and good-hearted, but relatively disinterested in the matters of state for which he was supposedly born. At times it seemed as if he left these to the queen, thereby frustrating old advisors who found themselves pushed to the sidelines in favor of boys who could dance and flirt. Pretending to entertain the idea of rebellion, I asked, "If you went to fight in America, would you take me and our daughter with you?"

Gilbert sat up and grinned. *"Why not?"*

I was beginning to think he liked his family motto a little too much. ". . . because my father would never allow it, and our daughter is too little and frail to make such a journey."

Gilbert sighed, then fell back against the pillows in defeat. "Very well, since your father believes I am useless for anything else, I shall not yet go to America, but stay longer in your bed."

Despite bitter words, his grin remained playful. He tempted me with a kiss. Yet the carved clock ticktocked on the mantel. "We would scandalize my lady's maid, who is due to help me dress."

Gilbert folded me into his long arms. "Strangely, my dear heart, this does not trouble me . . ."

Alas, before I could melt against him, we were disturbed by the wails of our little Henriette from the nursery. I rose to find her red-faced in her bassinet as her nurse tried to comfort her, all to no avail. Grand-mère always advised, *Just let her cry. Don't ruin her moral character by teaching her to wail for attention!*

It worried me to think I might ruin my baby's moral character before she was out of swaddling—but my urgent instinct was to ease whatever troubled her. If only I knew what it was! We tried feeding her, changing her, carrying her to and fro—until at last Gilbert surprised me by holding his arms out. "Let me try."

When Gilbert hoisted his daughter into his lap, she quieted, which astonished me, because my sisters and I would've shrieked with terror if the duc d'Ayen had ever reached for us when we were babes. Noblemen of my father's generation didn't involve themselves in the care of children, and I suspected that if my father witnessed this, he would have taken it for another sign of Gilbert's weakness. Yet I saw in my husband a man who could not make himself deaf to suffering. There was, in that, a strength my father did not understand. A strength I took pride in.

Gilbert carried our daughter to his chambers so he could read to her from a pamphlet—a reprinted translation of the document with which the Americans had declared themselves independent.

We hold these truths to be self-evident, that all men are created equal, that they are endowed by their Creator with certain unalienable Rights, that among these are Life, Liberty and the pursuit of Happiness. That to secure these rights, Governments are instituted among Men, deriving their just powers from the consent of the governed. That whenever any Form of Government becomes destructive of these ends, it is the Right of the People to alter or to abolish it.

It was the first time I ever heard these words. They sounded to me so pure and simple, intoned with an earnest voice that reached my soul. To some, these words would seem heresy. From my husband's precious mouth, they burned like holy fire, and I too felt illuminated by those flames. These portentous words seemed to reveal the true *purpose* of faith I'd been seeking. Were we not all sinners, noble and peasant alike? Jesus died to redeem us, each and every one. As children of God, was it not our duty to love and defend one another as brother and sister, no matter the circumstance of birth?

Americans wanted to sweep away all the rules of society and start again. In the new society they would build, perhaps it would not matter so much that Henriette had been born a girl. Maybe she would be valued.

"I want to fight for these ideas," Gilbert said. "I have no desire to leave you, Adrienne, yet America is a chance to make my name and do good at the same time. Not often do such opportunities present themselves."

I understood. I half wanted to go to America myself.

Still, I was taken by surprise when, in October, at our lavishly appointed supper table, Lafayette draped his arms over the shoulders of my brother-in-law, the vicomte de Noailles, on one side and their friend the comte de Ségur on the other and announced, "The three of us are going to America to fight!"

If this took me unawares, it shocked my sister Louise, who dropped a napkin in panicked surprise, her voice quavering as she asked, "Fight for America?"

"For a new world," said Gilbert.

My sister and I were accustomed to our husbands' summer absences for military training, but it plainly frightened her to think of them crossing the sea. And I wondered if I too should be more afraid. Meanwhile, my brother-in-law, Marc, said, "These Bostonians are just colonial farmers, but they've got the Brits on the run. Imagine what these Bostonians might do if France was to support them."

Grand-mère twisted her pearls in befuddlement. "I don't understand what you boys are saying. Aren't these peasants traitors to their king?"

Marc diplomatically ignored this. "If the colonies break away, it could be the *ruin* of Britain."

This idea could displease no Frenchman, nor any Frenchwoman, for that matter. Given our humiliation in the Seven Years' War, even Grand-mère wished to see the British suffer a little. Moreover, my aunt, Madame de Tessé, opined that she thought there was something quite *enlightened* about these rebels. Yet I knew it would be my father whose opinion mattered most. Surely the duc d'Ayen could not continue to think my husband timid and bloodless if he undertook such an endeavor. If Lafayette couldn't win military glory in French uniform, doing it in battle with the British was the next best thing. I thought this bold plan was precisely the sort of thing my father would actually admire.

I held my breath as the duc d'Ayen considered, crossing his legs to show his diamond-buckled shoes to great advantage. "Unfortunately, King Louis doesn't want a war, much less for three of his prominent noblemen to go stir one up on foreign shores. The king of France cannot be *seen* to give aid to a rebellion against another anointed king. We must remain neutral."

Gilbert silently stared at his plate as if to disguise his disappointment. My sister, for her part, seemed tremendously relieved, and looked to me to echo her sentiment. I felt only a half measure of relief. I knew my own desire to go to America was a flight of fancy, but Gilbert really could go. It would pain me to be separated, yet it was the lot of every soldier's wife, and there had been few better causes for it.

Marc continued to argue. "We'll go of our own accord. Thus, our actions cannot be blamed on France."

"The Noailles *are* France," my father said. "No one in the world will believe this family would act without the king's blessing. As, indeed, we should not. As we *will not*, do you understand?"

My father intended this to be the end of the conversation, yet my husband insisted, "I must go, for my honor and the glory of France."

The duc d'Ayen's exasperated laughter didn't tinkle like crystal, not like the queen's, still it sent the same flush of shame down my husband's neck, and an answering flush heated my cheeks too when my father said, "Marc might acquit himself well for the Noailles, but, Gilbert, what *you* would find to do in America, I could not guess."

"*Father*," I cried, provoked beyond endurance.

The duc d'Ayen's gaze fell upon me, and fear knotted in my throat, making it difficult to speak. Thus I was forced to watch, helplessly, as the brewing storm in my husband's eyes finally broke. "Do I not have my own family name to uphold?" Gilbert demanded to know. "You wish to prevent me from distinguishing myself with a sacred charge—not only to avenge my father, but to free men from a corrupted system of inequality."

His appeal stirred my blood, but it did not soften my father's heart. "I have something else in mind for you, Gilbert," said the duc d'Ayen. "Given the offense you gave to the king's brother, you cannot go back to Versailles, but perhaps we can find a place for you in a different court as a diplomat."

Gilbert shrank away. "So I can bow and scrape to a king that is not even mine?"

My father growled. "You are such a *boy*, Gilbert. Younger than your years."

He was not a boy. He was a husband and a father. And with the coming of December, I was at least able to give my husband the consolation of knowing he would be a father again. I hoped this news would bring some end to the turmoil in my family, but my father's new plans for my husband were taking shape. "I'm sending you to London, Gilbert. Then to Rome for six months, to keep you out of mischief."

Six months. That would mean my husband would likely be gone for the birth of our child—a thing I immediately protested. I wanted to argue with my father. I was heartbroken Gilbert did not. He claimed he didn't want to be wrenched away from me before the birth of our child, but I came to believe that his spirit, at long last, had been broken. I had fallen in love with my husband's *defiance*. Now, with him completely in my father's power, I worried that defiance was gone and grieved it even more than our forthcoming separation.

On the eve of Gilbert's exile, he gave me and our baby a teary farewell. "Remember, Adrienne, that in whatever country I may find myself, I shall always love you. You know my heart, or at least I hope you believe me when I say it is yours for life."

Alas, soon I would have reason to doubt it.

SEVERAL WEEKS LATER, MY FATHER THUNDERED INTO THE HOUSE on the Rue Saint-Honoré, his spurs scraping the tiles; he made straight for me, where I was sniffling into my kerchief fighting tears, for Maman had already broken the news. Lafayette wasn't in London where he was supposed to be. Nor was he in Italy, where my father had intended to drag him.

Somehow my husband had slipped my father's leash and was attempting to sail away to America.

This would have taken planning—months of planning—and yet Gilbert had kept this secret from me. My sentiments swung wildly among hurt at the betrayal, anger at my own credulity, and fear of my father's wrath, to say nothing of the king's. *Oh, Gilbert, what have you done?*

Now my father stood before me, grim as a reaper. "Did you know what Lafayette was planning?"

In half-numb shock, I murmured, "I knew nothing . . ." Truth was my defense. Surely Gilbert knew I wouldn't have revealed his plan to anyone; so I allowed myself to believe that he had kept his plans from me to protect me. Fortunately, I had another protector too . . .

Maman stepped between us, shielding me from my father's wrath. "Gilbert's farewell letter explains that he pledged himself to the Americans months ago, long before you forbade him to go. He gave his word and kept it." Was that *pride* I heard in her voice? "We all know Lafayette's honorable heart, which has compelled him to answer to a higher cause."

I was too stunned to know whether I believed this. Too devastated at the idea that I had been abandoned. Yet Maman did believe it, perhaps because she too had defied my father when she felt duty-bound to a higher cause. But oh, the price of his fury. "I care not at all about Lafayette's heart. I would give less than a fig for it!" My father snatched up a pen and inkwell from a writing table and slid them to me atop a blank page. "I only care that he does not get far. He is not on that ship yet. Write to him, Adrienne. Tell him you are desperately ill. Make him worry for his heir, and he will return with his tail between his legs."

My father expected my obedience. What is more, I wanted to obey. Infected by sudden fear of what might happen to Gilbert in a war— terrified that he had gone without the king's permission and without boon companions—I wanted to beg my husband to return. I picked up the quill, but my hand stiffened, then stopped.

The duc d'Ayen lowered his voice to coax me. "Poor daughter. You are not to blame. It is my fault for giving you in marriage to a heartless blunderer willing to abandon his pregnant wife and child."

This transparent attempt to manipulate my sentiments produced the opposite effect intended. "That is not true," I whispered. "Lafayette did not abandon me. You were going to take him away for six months."

My father loomed, impatient. "If you do not write this letter, I will put out a warrant for Lafayette's arrest. Is that what you want—for your husband and the father of your children to be dragged back in chains like a criminal?"

This was not an idle threat. I knew my father would do such a thing; that he felt entitled to do it and his position allowed it. As an orphan, my husband had been traded to my family like a prized breeding stallion, and now my father was treating us both like horses in the Noailles stables that must be reined in. In that moment, a fire that had never burned before was kindled in my heart. A fire inspired by my husband's defiance. A fire that would burn for the rest of my life. I would never again allow myself to be used as a whip to command anyone's obedience. My husband, like the American colonies, was in open rebellion.

Now I was too.

I pushed the paper away. "No."

"You will obey me," my father ground out, drawing a hand back to strike.

My mother shrieked, but I did not cower. I thought of all the evils in the world that might be remedied by a victory against the tyranny of kings. I no longer believed that a just God could ordain one man to rule over his brothers and sisters without their consent. I thought of colonists trampled underfoot. French peasants starving in the streets. Enslaved Africans carted in cargo ships. The whole world was an open wound, and my husband, the *nobody from Chavaniac*, wanted to do something to salve it. Even if he failed, it was a noble attempt—*noble* in the truest sense of the word. I had not gone with Gilbert on that ship, but here in my chest beat his very own heart, and I would not betray it.

Thus, I stood—on shaky knees, but still, I stood—to face my father. "There is nothing you can say or do that will make me write this letter, sir. You have taught me the value of a name—and I will not put mine to a lie."

NINE

MARTHE
Chavaniac-Lafayette
February 1941

JUST SIGN IT, I TELL MYSELF, STARING AT THE SLIP OF PAPER ON MY school desk next to the pencil sharpener and the globe of the world. It's another oath for teachers—this time, one of personal loyalty to Marshal Pétain. We'll be dismissed if we don't sign it. It's just a matter of expedience. So why hesitate?

Maybe because rough sketches of Adrienne Lafayette litter my desk, and her big eyes seem to be judging me from more than a century ago . . .

I turn my chair so I don't have to look at her. Now, after all, isn't the time to develop a set of principles that'll land me in the snow without a roof over my head. And for what—the satisfaction of sticking it in the old Marshal's eye?

Our Latin master is talking about quitting, saying he has too much pride to sign. But pride is for suckers, so I slap my inky signature on the line and go up to the records office, where Anna is typing on an old machine that keeps sticking and Madame Simon is peering at a newspaper over the tortoiseshell rims of her cat-eye glasses. "What a disgrace," the secretary-general of the Lafayette Memorial Foundation says, flinging the newspaper into the wastebin, then brushing at her tweed skirt as if the ugly headlines had spattered it with mud. I stoop to fish the pages out for the fireplace, but she stops me. "Leave it, Marthe. I know we can't afford to waste paper, but *Au Pilori* is too poisonous for kindling."

Au Pilori is an anti-Semitic newspaper in which prominent Jews are regularly denounced. We don't often get copies here, but Madame Simon has Jewish blood, and I worry someone sent it to her for reasons other than general interest. I feel ashamed that I've come to turn in my oath of loyalty to the Marshal, who allows these denunciations to continue. I want to tell Madame Simon that I intend to be only as loyal to Marshal Pétain as he is to us, but I find I can't justify myself. And Anna—who is now standing on the toes of her green spectator pumps to file something in a cabinet—shoots me a sympathetic look.

As for Madame Simon, she takes my oath without a word.

After my morning class, I retreat to my studio to blend charcoal lines and lose myself in thoughts about how to bring newer, modern Adrienne sketches to life as a sculpture. Clay is easier, faster, and requires a less expert touch. I can make mistakes in clay. But Adrienne and her saintly perfection seem to call out for stone. I'd love to try some rosy pink marble, with feather-fine chisel work . . .

I'm so consumed by these ideas that when Anna knocks at my door, I react much like I've been caught *en flagrant délit*. I hurriedly dust charcoal from my hands onto my overalls, and I'm disheveled when I fling open the door. "You didn't come down to dinner," Anna points out, a little worriedly. "And you let your fire die out!"

"I—I was distracted," I say, blowing on my fingers, which I realize now are ice-cold. "I can't wait for springtime. At the first thaw, Henri and I used to sneak into the woods at recess to find our favorite wild fruit tree and eat all the cherries even before they were ripe."

"Cherries." Anna moans, biting her lower lip in imagined pleasure. "I love them soaked in brandy and baked in a cherry clafoutis. When Henri returns, you'll have to make him one."

Afraid to think too much about Henri—or food—I cross my arms. "I don't bake."

"Luckily, you've got other talents," she says, admiring my sketches. I hold my breath, wondering if she'll notice the similarities. In portraying Adrienne, I've captured Anna's eyes, the gentle slope of her shoulder, the almond shape of her mouth. If she notices the resemblance, she doesn't say. "This is wonderful, Marthe! Actually . . . beautiful. What are you going to call it?"

"I don't know." I fiddle with my pencils. "Something laughably wholesome."

Anna chuckles. "There's nothing wrong with wholesome, *ma chère.*"

Ma chère. My mind turns the phrase over like a tumbler, smoothing out any rough edge, wondering if I really am dear to her, realizing how much I want to be. "You're right. I guess we can't be cynics about everything or we'd slit our wrists."

She laughs. "Blasphemy!" While I've been sketching portraits and working my way through the dry history books about Lafayette's wife, Anna, it seems, has been to the mayor's office. She pulls two cards out of her pocket. "We just got these—we're allowed to send them to the Occupied Zone and to our prisoners, I think. Even if you don't have a current address for Henri, the Wehrmacht likely does. If nothing else, Germans are good record keepers . . ."

I stare resentfully at the interzone postcards. I see we're supposed to circle or cross out preprinted messages such as *in good health* or *wounded.* And I hate the Nazis even more for treating us like animals without capacity to express ourselves beyond a circle or a strike. After so long without any word from Henri, I have a shaky moment where I wonder if it'd be worse for this damned card to disappear into the abyss of the wartime postal service or to get it back with the word *killed* in a circle.

Anna seems to know what I'm thinking. "It would be better to know, wouldn't it?"

I'm not sure. I might prefer to live with delusions that Henri's in a prison camp, tending to people, making them laugh, rather than to know if Henri's gone—his roguish sense of humor, his dreams of becoming a doctor, just *gone.* "I don't want to find out that I'm all alone, that I don't belong anywhere, and that I don't belong to anybody."

Anna reaches for my hands. "Don't say that."

"It's true. And unlike the cold, you never get used to it."

It's the orphan's lament, but it shames me to complain—I hate myself for it. I can't stand to look her in the eye, so I turn my back on her and the postcard, making it clear that I intend to get back to work . . . but she doesn't let me. "Marthe, you're not alone. You belong here at the castle. You belong to your friends." She smiles. "You belong to me."

You belong to me . . . I don't know what she means by it. I don't know what I want her to mean by it. I only know that her smile is angelic as newly fallen snow, whereas I suddenly feel like I'm boiling inside. If I didn't know better, I'd almost think I had a crush on her—the sort silly girls used to have for boys in the orphanage. Feelings that make girls sigh and spy and write their names in a heart. I mocked them; I laughed at those feelings when they cropped up, telling myself I was too tough to have sappy thoughts like that. Even for Henri. And I *scorned* those feelings, because sometimes I had them for girls too . . .

Now Anna presses her forehead to mine to cheer me up. "You can be the sister I never had."

"You have sisters," I grumble.

"Yes, but I didn't *choose* them." Is she choosing me? That alluring idea is a cliff, and I'll fall if I make one wrong move. At my silence, she gives my hand a squeeze. "If not sisters, then roommates, at least? Your fireplace is nicer than mine . . ."

"An artist likes her solitude," I tease, but when she gives a little shiver, I give in. "I guess you can stay on the really cold nights."

She beams like a girl used to getting what she wants. "I'll be quiet as a mouse! And if you fill out your interzone card for Henri tonight, I'll send it tomorrow with mine to my husband."

At the mention of our men, I get hold of myself. "Thanks."

I scratch the date on the card. Then I circle the words to tell Henri that I'm healthy, still at the chateau, and desperate for news of him. There's no room to write more . . . no way to tell him how afraid I am for him, even if I could find words that I wouldn't mind being seen by the censors. Even if I could understand the jumble of feelings seething inside me, seeming to slip further from my control by the day.

IN MARCH, WE HAVE TWO THINGS TO CELEBRATE.

For one thing, Samir Bensaïd is back. Like Henri, Sam was taken prisoner in the Fall of France. He should be in a stalag somewhere in Germany, but he's somehow *here* sitting in the old guardroom by the fire, hands squeezed between his knees.

"How did you escape, my dear boy?" asks Madame LeVerrier.

Sam explains, "On account of my dark skin, the Nazis didn't know if they should transfer me to a prison camp or shoot me. And while they bickered about it, I grabbed one of their motorcycles and made off with it."

"That took some real nerve!" I say, giving his shoulders a fond squeeze.

"I thought you might approve," Sam replies, explaining that it's taken him months to get back, get his papers in order, and be officially demobilized. "I'm sorry Henri's still a prisoner," he says, smile falling away. "I wish he could've escaped too."

"Oh, you know he'll be thrilled to hear that you got away," I say. "He'll make you tell him every detail when he's released. Which I hope will be soon. The war can't go on much longer, can it?"

"It's over for me," Sam says, taking a deep breath. "Now I just have to find a job."

Fluent in several languages, Sam had wanted to be a diplomat and work in politics before the war. Given the current regime, he wants no part of that now.

"Not to worry, my boy," Madame LeVerrier says, pressing a cup of tea into Sam's hands. "We'll find some work for you here at the castle—we need scouts, teachers, drivers, valets . . ."

We can afford to hire because we're suddenly in the black again, which is our second reason for celebration. From New York, Madame Beatrice sent money and supplies to us via an American ship that was allowed through the British blockade. It's our first shipment in nearly a year. Milk, vitamins, children's clothing, and medicine—all stamped with the Stars and Stripes. Despite the damp weather, it's like a festival day at the castle. Everyone on staff makes a line to relay wooden crates, cardboard boxes, and metal tins from the back of the truck into our storerooms. The only one not on hand to celebrate is the baroness, who went to Marseilles to liaise with the Red Cross to make sure we got this shipment.

When the weather gets warmer, we take our classrooms out into nature.

Dr. Anglade says direct sunlight and fresh air are part of the cure here at the Lafayette Preventorium. There's a scientific explanation having to do with vitamins and ultraviolet rays that I've never understood. But from what Henri told me, infections spread easier inside. The main idea is to get the kids outside as much as possible, even if it's chilly. So I gather my students and take them for a lesson sitting at outdoor picnic tables.

Afterward, Faustine Xavier is supposed to take them to the kitchens, where the students of the household management class often make our Sunday luncheon, but the baroness cancels that plan, because we don't have any food to spare if one of the girls gets inattentive and burns something. As a result, I'm enlisted to take a troop of girls and comb the woods for edible leaves, nettles, roots, and stems now that our long, hungry winter is over.

Faustine should really come with me, since it's her class, but she begs off. "I fear I might be coming down with a little something," she says, exaggerating a cough beneath her tight lace collar. "Besides, why not take the baron's daughter? You two are virtually inseparable these days."

It's true, we are. But something about the way Faustine says it bothers me, and later, when I tell Anna—who tromps along in the forest with me, wearing her best red lipstick, a stylish swing coat, and impractical shoes—she only laughs. "I ran into her on the stairs coming out of your room one morning, and she gave me an evil eye like a filthy-minded biddy."

Anna doesn't seem worried; in fact, she laces her arm in mine and says, "I forgot you were a Girl Guide, Marthe!"

"I've got all the badges," I boast. "Camping. Fishing. First aid. Foraging."

I don't tell her that when I was ten, Henri, Sam, and I learned the hard way that red-capped toadstools are poisonous unless parboiled—and the induced vomiting was only slightly less memorable than the hallucinations.

"Look for wild garlic for our soups." I stoop to show the girls the broad-leafed plant and teach them to rub it for the telltale scent. "Look for rosemary and fennel. If you fill your baskets, I'll show you how to make flower salads."

Little girls love learning they can eat wild pansies, elderflower, bor-age, poppies, and violets, and I watch them fan out while I gather a bou-quet for Anna, who crinkles her nose. "What's this?"

"Lunch. Weren't you listening?" When Anna sniffs at the bouquet, pensive, I worry I've done something wrong. "What's the matter?"

She sighs. "The Marshal isn't coming to visit the kids in the preven-torium after all."

She says this like it's a tragedy, but I'm unexpectedly flooded with relief.

"He's decided to visit a school in Le Puy instead," she explains. "But you mustn't think your work has been wasted. In fact, my father is likely to meet with the Marshal and explain our mission at the preventorium. Papa is even willing to take you—and some of your sketches."

I'm careful not to seem ungrateful. "I don't know . . ."

"I'll loan you my best dress. The one with the indigo stripes. It will really bring out your pretty blue eyes. And just think, maybe the Marshal will like your artwork and want to shake your hand."

Despite blushing at Anna's compliment, I can't help but cringe. I know we need the Vichy government's help to keep the preventorium running. We need more doctors, a new X-ray machine, blankets, soap, and countless other things. And I know I should just keep my mouth shut about it, but I confess the truth. "I don't want to meet Pétain, and I'm glad he's not coming here."

"You shouldn't be," Anna scolds me. "It would've been a great honor! Don't you know how often Maman and Aunt Bea wished to get Pétain's uniform from one of his great battles to put next to the others in our museum?"

She means the uniforms of Generals Foch and Joffre—other heroes of the Great War. I know how loved Pétain used to be by the people who lived in this castle, but that's changing now. "That was before he shook hands with Hitler."

Anna makes a face. "I know. It's terrible that he had to do that. But war makes people do terrible things. We just need to keep people's spirits up and keep our opinions to ourselves. Just think, if the Marshal likes your work, you could be famous too."

I pretend that doesn't matter to me. It does. I always wanted to be a somebody in the world, but I'm starting to think I'd rather be a nobody in *this* world.

GONE WITH WINTER WENT MY LAST EXCUSE NOT TO VISIT HENRI'S mother.

My bicycle needs a new tire, so I start out on foot until a cabbage wagon passes, and I convince the farmer to take me as far as the fountain in Paulhaguet, where the oxen stop to drink. From there I walk to the Pinton farmhouse, a squat structure of black volcanic stone. Given the harsh winter, I expect the farm to be run-down, so I'm surprised to see the old sagging thatched roof has been replaced, and the broken fence Henri's mother was always nagging him to fix has been mended. A skinny brown cow moos from its pen, but no one answers when I knock. Smoke billows from the chimney, so I knock again, but it isn't until I start for the barn that Madame Pinton finally throws open the door of the main house and motions me inside.

In kerchief and black sweater over an old polka-dot peasant dress, she busies herself with a pot of herb tea on the hearth. It's a point of French pride to offer hospitality, and she pours me a bowlful like it's breakfast. I take it, acutely aware of her ring on my finger, with its unique gold wreath. Anna convinced me that for this visit, I should wear it on my finger instead of on a chain around my neck so as not to insult my future mother-in-law.

"You have news of Henri?" she asks brusquely.

"Not yet, madame . . ."

Most everyone in the local villages who has sons, husbands, and fathers in those German prison camps has heard from them by now. Even Anna received a short note back from her husband. But nothing from Henri.

I'm worried sick, and Madame Pinton must be too.

So I say, "Sam escaped, though, and he saw Henri's capture last summer, so at least we know he was alive then."

She shakes her head, the deep lines of a difficult life etched onto her face. "Do you know what I think? I think Henri escaped too. I think he's with General de Gaulle."

Now that's a curveball I didn't see coming. Not that I believe it; it's been nine months since the disaster at Dunkirk, and if Henri is now walking around London with the Free French Forces, sipping Earl Grey during the Blitz, surely he'd have got word to us by now. No, what gives me whiplash is Madame Pinton bringing up *de Gaulle*—and saying the rogue general's name like he's the Second Coming.

Nine months ago, hardly anybody in Auvergne had ever even heard of de Gaulle, and if they had, they spat his name as a troublemaker. Has that changed? Madame Pinton is of good old French peasant stock—one of those rural farmers the Marshal venerates as the salvation of France. In fact, a portrait of Pétain dangles precariously from a nail above her old iron stove. Yet here she is, hoping her son has gone off to fight for the same rogue general the Marshal has tried in absentia and condemned to death.

Not knowing how to make sense of this, I sip the tea. "Is—is there anything I can do to help you get along?"

"*Non*, I have boarders now."

"Boarders?"

"Jews," she says. "French Jews from Paris. The father was in the army; now he helps on the farm. His oldest girl helps cook and sew. I give them a warm bed and soup and they're content."

Not like you, Marthe, she means. *You could never be content as the wife of a country doctor, cooking and sewing and raising livestock on this farm.*

I try not to wonder if she's right; instead, I remind myself that if I'd married Henri before he mobilized, she'd be in the place of a mother to me now. Softening her is probably a lost cause, but I give it a try. "I brought something for you."

I hand her a little sketch of Henri. One I drew on his sixteenth birthday when he still had a gap between his teeth. The drawing is precious to me, but I feel like he'd want his mother to have this one. And, taking it, she almost smiles. "I've heard you're drawing for those rich LaGrange ladies with their big hats now." I start to remind her that it was rich ladies with big hats who saved us both from certain poverty, but before I can get a word in, she grinds out, "I didn't put my husband in the ground so the Boche could steal my country and bring back feudal days with nobles in the castles again!"

I almost laugh at this absurd gripe, because the current situation in France is a dark tragicomedy. Our royalist fringe is propping up the old Marshal, who now has more power than any French king going back for centuries. Still, Anna and her family never act like their noble titles are anything more than honorary. "The LaGranges aren't like you think."

"Fat aristos?" asks Madame Pinton, gulping her tea. "I heard they fled the country like émigrés at the start of the war . . ."

She flings both *aristos* and *émigrés* like the insults they've been ever since the French Revolution, and I have to explain, "They didn't flee at the start of the war. They were in America because the baron was on a mission to get Roosevelt to sell us warplanes."

"And how did that turn out?"

I grind my jaw, wondering if she's just determined to be petty! "My point is, they could've stayed in America. Instead, they came back to keep the preventorium running. We're doing good work there."

"Teaching children to bow and scrape to the Nazis while your baron makes deals with his friends in Vichy . . ."

He's not my baron, and I didn't come here for an argument, but she's asking for one. "That's rich coming from the woman who has a picture of the Marshal over her stove!"

Madame Pinton glowers, leaving me to try to make sense of nonsense. Maybe she thinks the Marshal is playing some kind of double game. That only his advisors in Vichy are wicked. Who knows what she thinks, or what anyone else thinks? Lately public opinion is like a surreal painting, where contradictory beliefs and prejudices melt together like Dalí's clocks.

I think Madame Pinton is ignorant and muleheaded. She grunts as if she thinks the same about me, and would like to be rid of me. Truthfully, I'm just as eager to go, but when I get up to leave, I hear wailing from upstairs in the wood-beamed loft. "Is there—is that a child?"

Madame Pinton folds her arms over herself and calls up, "It's all right. You can come down. Like I said, it's only my son, Henri's, girl."

A family comes down from the loft. The father—a man wearing a tricolor pin on his collar—introduces himself as Uriah Kohn. He's trying to quiet the sobbing, curly-haired kid he's got over one shoulder. There are two older children too, a coltish brunette wearing thick knee socks, whom I judge to be about thirteen, and a boy—only a little younger—who hasn't quite grown into his big ears.

"I'm Marthe Simone," I say.

"*Bonjour, mademoiselle,*" says Monsieur Kohn shamefacedly. "This is my son, Daniel," he says, reaching to give a quick mussing-up of the boy's hair over his too-big ears.

The boy grins at me.

Then the father glances to the coltish teen. "My daughter Josephine."

The crop-haired Josephine does *not* grin; I can tell she hasn't decided if I'm worth knowing, and I like her for that. Then the father presses his lips to the forehead of the crying kid in his arms, who is racked by a worrisome, rattling cough. "This is my little Gabriella. It's her sixth birthday, but she's not so happy today."

I can see that. Her cheeks are rosy from crying, and her wild hair is matted with tears. I notice her skin is also glistening. "She looks feverish."

"It comes and goes," her father replies.

Working with frail children on a daily basis, I know that a cough—even a fever—isn't necessarily anything to panic about, but the scabby lesion on Gabriella's ear sends a prickle down my spine, because I've learned the telltale signs of tuberculosis. "She needs to have that looked at."

Madame Pinton says, "Dr. Boulagnon has been treating her in exchange for eggs and cabbages. He recommends admittance to the Lafayette Preventorium."

I nod. "That's best. We have X-ray and ultraviolet-ray machines and the most advanced pediatric care in Auvergne." When I see the child's father already shaking his head, I add, "The preventorium isn't too far. A short drive; you could walk it in an hour and a half if you had to."

"*No,*" says Monsieur Kohn, very firmly.

"It's a charitable foundation," I stress, because they must be hurting for money if they're paying the doctor in cabbages. "I'm sure something can be worked out." Before he can object, I quickly rattle off the requirements. "All you have to do is have Dr. Boulagnon fill out a medical report, sign an authorization, submit a family history and a school certificate of vaccinations and good conduct. I'll get you the forms; it's easy as pie."

He looks torn, but tells his children, "Go do your chores."

Josephine mopes to the rustic door, but out of the corner of my eye I see Daniel stick out his tongue before he disappears into the yard.

Then Monsieur Kohn addresses me. "I'm sorry, mademoiselle. I know you mean well, but with times being what they are, we can't call attention to ourselves."

"Then it's strange you've come to Auvergne." This is a rural, almost tribal, place where people aren't always friendly to strangers; he wouldn't stand out so much in a city like Marseilles.

"I have a sentimental attachment to the area," he says.

I don't ask what it is. Even so, what does he expect? This isn't occupied Paris; we're still *France*, after all, aren't we? "Trust me, you'd be hard-pressed to find a more isolated spot than Chavaniac. It's a tiny village surrounded by woods."

"I know where it is," he says.

"Then you know there's not a German soldier in sight."

"Not *yet*," Monsieur Kohn says grimly. "I have family in Poland. If you knew what the Nazis are doing there, you'd know how much worse things will get for us here. The detention camps in France are just a start."

A spike of frustration that he's not getting adequate care for his daughter makes me clench my jaw. "You should worry about tuberculosis! French citizens don't have to worry about refugee camps."

"I'm French for now," he says bitterly; he explains that it's bad enough he's been dismissed from the military because he's Jewish. Worse to live with the knowledge that our government has been withdrawing citizenship from naturalized Jews.

The injustice of it—and the fear and uncertainty that it's sowing—is brought home to me, and too obvious for me to argue. "Again," says Monsieur Kohn, "I know you mean well, but we can't have records that make us easy to find. I should put my little girl down to bed now. It was nice to meet you, mademoiselle."

He disappears so swiftly I can't get another word in, and when Madame Pinton walks me to the door, I hiss, "Where is the mother? Someone needs to have some sense. Tuberculosis is contagious, and you're all in close quarters here. It can be deadly."

"The mother is already dead," says Madame Pinton. "Death takes people like her—not disappointed old women like me." She looks down at my drawing of Henri and sighs. "If my son were here, he'd know what to do."

"I know exactly what he'd do. Henri would get that kid admitted to the preventorium *tout de suite*."

She eyes me. "Or he'd talk the doctors into treating the child on the side so no one knows they're Israelites."

I frown at her suggestion; there isn't any *on the side*. There are strict procedures. I couldn't bring a kid into the examination hall or the X-ray lab without paperwork for Dr. Anglade to examine and hand off to Madame Simon for her file cabinets. "I'll send you the forms in case Monsieur Kohn changes his mind. But there's nothing else I can do."

None of this should be my problem—but it *is* my problem, because failing to report being exposed to contagion is grounds for dismissal at the preventorium, ever since a teacher accidentally exposed her students to scarlet fever and we had an epidemic in the village. Dr. Anglade says tuberculosis isn't *that* easy to catch if you're not breathing the same air for a while, but I can't take the chance. I'm brooding about it when I finally get back to the castle and trudge my way up the stairs of the square tower.

Fortunately Madame Simon is still behind the gleaming walnut expanse of her large desk, a stylish pleated turban on her head and a gold pendant dangling from her neckline as she organizes folders.

"I wasn't sure you'd still be in the office," I say, keeping my distance.

"I want to get our staff's paperwork ready for the new law." She means the one that will soon require every French person to carry an identity card. "How can I help you, mademoiselle?"

I see my own file in the stack and absently thumb through it. "I visited Madame Pinton and came into contact with a little girl—she was coughing, feverish, and I noticed a lesion."

Madame Simon looks up sharply, because although she's not a doctor, she's a well-respected expert in public health. "A lesion or a rash?"

She's worried about measles, which by some miracle I've never had, so I'm not immune. "A lesion. I think."

"Well, Dr. Anglade is going to say *Better safe than sorry*. You'll have to take a week off and go into quarantine. I'll ask Madame LeVerrier to take over your classes and have meals sent up for you. Let us know if you get so much as a sniffle."

"Okay."

I'm about to put down my file and go when Madame Simon asks, "What about the child? Has she been seen by a physician?"

"The village doctor in Paulhaguet . . ." I begin, intending to explain, but my words trail off when I see something in my paperwork that makes the world drop beneath my feet.

"Is something wrong?" Madame Simon asks.

Yes, something is wrong. Something so wrong that my knees—and my voice—actually wobble. "Where did this file come from?"

Madame Simon tilts her head. "I pulled it from the record cabinets. Why?"

"I have a birth record," I say, my eyes focusing on the one thing that absolutely shouldn't be on that page.

My mother's name.

TEN

BEATRICE
New York City
February 1915

MY NEPHEW HAD BEEN SHOT.

We learned of it in a letter Victor wrote after the fact, in which he assured us his wound was minor. The bullet passed clean through. Still, the incident terrified his parents, and the strain was evident at rehearsals in the Della Robbia Room, where Miss Sloane attempted to herd a hundred children in hoopskirts and powdered wigs into some semblance of order.

My brother-in-law and playwright was a highly emotional man in the best of circumstances—sensitive to light and sound—and I worried his patience might *snap* when my seven-year-old son Ashley whooped around his table with a toy tomahawk. "Watch my war dance, Uncle Jack!"

"How did I ever let you talk me into this?" Jack groused at me.

"Oh, come now, my dearest," said his wife, Elizabeth, giving me a conspiratorial smile. "You jumped at the chance."

Of all my husband's quarrelsome siblings, his eldest sister, Elizabeth, was my favorite. Having walked with a limp since childhood, she had the air of a tragic heroine from a bygone era who swooned over brooding Victorian poets. Certainly she'd swooned for Jack Chapman—a man who took brooding to a masochistic art form, having once mutilated his own arm to punish himself for committing violence upon another man in jealousy. Long-suffering Elizabeth was patient with her husband's eccentricities, and with mine. She'd been the first to accept me, even when her pearl-clutching sisters exploded in a fit of pique.

For shame, Willie, you've lost your wits!

—to take a chorus girl for a bride. We'll never live it down.

—to thumb your nose at the world by marrying a scandalous woman!

Elizabeth convinced the family that Willie and I were a match made in heaven, and I felt a twinge of regret to have disappointed her. And a little guilt too, over having let my nephew enlist. Jack and Elizabeth had made peace with Victor having signed up to fight, but a thread of tension had pulled between us, and Jack's dark gaze was tortured with anxiety. "We want to get Victor out of the trenches," he said, quite suddenly.

"Out?" I understood; as a mother, of course I did. But Victor wasn't a child and had pledged himself to fight. I feared there was no way out but victory, death, or desertion.

"We hope something can be done," my sister-in-law explained. "He's meant to be more than cannon fodder."

Influential as my husband's family might be, I thought the Chapmans quite naive about their influence over the matter, until my sister-in-law said, "Willie has a plan."

"Is that so?" I asked, trying to hide my irritation that my husband was in communication with his sister while not sparing a line for me. My curiosity was also piqued by the unlikely notion that Willie—who thought war made boys into men—might try to shield his nephew. "What does he have in mind?"

"There's a plan for a volunteer American flying corps," Jack said. "We want Victor transferred into it."

Goodness. An entire unit of American pilots could have the greatest impact on the public mind here in the States while telling the world whose side we were *really* on. I was dubious that aeroplanes were less dangerous than the trenches, but at that point in the war, many people thought so, including my in-laws. "Have you consulted Victor? Young men pride themselves on their independence."

"That's why we're going to France to convince him," Jack said. "We're booking passage on the *Lusitania.*"

I simply could not think of a worse idea. Even if the Chapmans made it without being sunk, they weren't worldly people. They were still suspended in another time, reading Shakespeare to each other by candlelight and occasionally complaining about the innovation of electric lights.

Jack's mental health was fragile, and Elizabeth's physical health was delicate. The last thing either of them should do was attempt a voyage over a war-ravaged sea, much less attempt to navigate a war zone on their own. "Are you sure that's wise?"

Jack said simply, "I can't bear it anymore. My boy being there, me being here . . ."

I felt his pain, and for a moment even wondered if I ought not offer to take the Chapmans back to France myself. A thought still lingering on my mind when, later that afternoon, Miss Sloane asked, "Do you think that reporter, Mitzi Miller, had a point?"

I took umbrage. "A point about how women should go into the trenches to demand soldiers stop fighting?"

"No, that's a harebrained fantasy," Emily replied, restoring my faith in her sanity. "I mean the part about being willing to risk their lives, while we sit here safely performing plays and sending parcels."

Still stung by the reporter's accusations, I argued, "But surely we're more useful here." Between ticket sales for *The Children's Revolution* and weekly fundraising balls, we'd raised a staggering amount of money for the cause. "Besides, I hardly think the French Foreign Legion would accept women in their ranks."

Emily sharpened her pencil. "No, but the American Relief Clearing House needs help distributing the kits in France. So I've come to a decision, quite by impulse."

"Impossible." In the months we'd been working together, I'd never known her to act upon a single impulse. "You decide nothing without a list of pros and cons."

"Of course I made a list! Which is why I can say with complete confidence that we've raised enough to send a fully outfitted ambulance to the front lines. And I want to take it there."

It was not often that buttoned-up Emily Sloane surprised me, but yesterday she'd purchased a tube of lipstick from Elizabeth Arden's Red Door salon, and today she was talking about going across an ocean filled with submarines. Now she said, "We believe America ought to come to the aid of her allies. Whatever else our play is meant to do, it's also meant to drum up support for the idea that America should enter the war. But if you and I aren't brave enough to cross the ocean, how can we convince anyone else to? I'm going back."

"Quite impossible," I said, pointing at her with an imperious index finger. "In the first place, it's too dangerous. In the second place, I need you here. And in the third place, this suggestion does great damage to our friendship, in which hitherto it has been my role to propose outlandish schemes. I refuse to be the sensible one. This is all very upside-down!"

"I *am* being sensible. If one of us must risk our life, I'm the logical choice. I'm a spinster, whereas you're a wife and mother of two."

She made a good argument, though no one ever told a brave husband and father that he must not risk his life. Men like my husband were allowed—nay, encouraged—to do great deeds. No one ever asked Willie, *But who's looking after the children when you're gone?*

As if snatching my thoughts from thin air, Emily straightened her spine. "I am a fit and determined twenty-five-year-old, and if I were a young man, like your nephew, you'd encourage me." I hadn't encouraged Victor. Once he'd made his decision, however, I'd considered him to be the model of gallantry and virtue, the very pride of the family! Perhaps sensing she had the better of me, Emily said, "Excepting my gender, I challenge you to articulate a single reason I should not go back to France and pursue my destiny."

My eyes narrowed as something clicked into place. *Destiny* was a word women seldom embraced except in reference to romance. And I felt a flare of victorious pleasure. "Oh, well done, Emily Sloane. I almost believed you to be driven by pure patriotic gumption. Then I remembered the lipstick." Before she could purse her guilty red lips, I accused, "Far be it from me to say a woman cannot be driven by patriotism alone, but you have a secondary motive, my friend. You're hoping to rendezvous with my nephew."

She puffed up with offense. "Insulting and outrageous!"

"I know you've been exchanging letters with him." I felt smug and self-satisfied that my matchmaking had borne fruit. News of Victor's wound must have pushed her into realizing her true feelings and—

"I *am* fond of your nephew," she said, flushing from red to purple. "But—but if you must know—I've formed an attachment to a French officer."

A French officer? I was at once shocked and deflated. "Do tell . . ."

"You know him. We took tea with his mother and sister before the war."

I felt my eyes bug. "The Baron de LaGrange?"

Drat. The very tall bachelor baron was stiff competition for my nephew, indeed. Miss Sloane already had money, after all; what she didn't have was Old World prestige, and a Frenchman with even a minor noble title could give her that.

"Lieutenant LaGrange is a wonderfully interesting man," she said. "With interesting ideas about technology. He believes France must have an air corps and intends to join."

Only Emily Sloane would find herself enraptured by a man who wrote to her of technology. Thus, I realized my efforts to match her with artistic Victor had always been doomed. Sourly, I complained, "Aeroplanes are diabolical inventions."

"Which is why we need men heroic enough to fly them." Emily's decidedly stiff upper lip quivered on the word *heroic.*

Oh, dear. She was quite gone for the man. I supposed that was all the more reason for us to save the world before this war chewed up a whole generation of gallant young men like my nephew and her French baron.

"PATIENCE, DARLING!" I SAID, PINS BETWEEN MY TEETH, TRYING TO keep Billy from squirming away. "Don't you want to look fetching onstage as Lafayette? I need to fix the button on your uniform."

With the curtains of the Century Theatre set to rise, my son trembled with stage fright. "But I c-can't do it."

I put away the pins and took his shaking hands in mine. "It's only a case of nerves, darling. It happens to everyone."

Miss Sloane was trying to quiet the child performers, and if my son didn't lead them onstage, *The Children's Revolution* would be a catastrophe. *Hell's bells,* what would my husband say to encourage him? Probably he'd regale our son with tales of meeting Butch Cassidy, or tell him how he once charged up San Juan Hill dodging a hail of bullets. Those were the sorts of things that inspired boys. I had nothing comparable to offer.

I could only say something that would have helped me as a child. "If you go out onto that stage tonight, you'll look back with pride to have been of real service at so young an age. And you'll know you're a person of consequence, no matter who your mother and father might be."

Billy looked hopeful. "What if I forget my l-lines?"

"You won't. That's why we practiced. You're going to be marvelous!"

Fortunately my youngest—freckled, precocious Ashley—all but vibrated in eagerness to perform his part . . . which helped his older brother muster his courage. The musicians took up their instruments as the cream of New York society settled in for a show, then Billy blew out a breath and stepped onstage. I watched, heart in my throat, only to realize Miss Sloane was watching *me*.

"It's too late to tell me this was a mistake," I whispered.

"I was going to tell you that I wish I'd had a mother like you."

I leaned my shoulder against hers in fond appreciation—and for support when Billy spoke his first lines. Oh, he stuttered, but it was scarcely noticeable, and the audience loved every minute! I stood in the wings, basking . . . and that's when I saw him.

"He's here," I whispered urgently, tugging Emily's sleeve.

"Who?" she asked.

"The president!"

She gave a dubious little snort, because neither of us esteemed the bespectacled Woodrow Wilson and his feeble administration, but that wasn't the president I meant. I pointed to the colonnaded balcony, where sat our fiery Theodore Roosevelt—the former president and the man who might soon be president again. My heartbeat quickened, knowing his presence at our play would be understood by everybody as a stamp of approval.

At intermission, the crowd jumped up, clapping. And I thought my sons might perish of excitement when Roosevelt came backstage, press agents in his wake. "*Dee-lightful*, Mrs. Chanler," the former president said. "There aren't enough plays for children that teach American history."

"Quite so, sir," I said, flattered but never flattened by the attentions of any man.

An awestruck Emily Sloane, however, babbled incoherently. To put her at ease, Roosevelt continued, "Lafayette's career is a lesson in international morality, which is in short supply these days. You ladies are doing important work at the Lafayette Fund, and I'd like to help."

Emily was so nervous that several pieces of paper slipped from her hands. While she fumbled to retrieve them, I said, "Marvelous, sir! I'll be happy to put you on the committee of your choice."

"Good. Put me to work." Roosevelt gave a grin that was all teeth. "Say, I haven't heard from Willie in ages. How is the old boy? I hear he's going on a trip to Scotland for hunting hounds. Glad to know he's back on his feet after that injury. Fall from a horse, was it?"

Furious that the former president knew more about my husband's health and whereabouts than I did—not to mention being unable to explain the accident—I gave a practiced little laugh that could've meant anything. "You know Willie . . ."

Photographers drew near, flashlamps firing. "Speech, speech!"

The former president pointedly ignored this, turning to the adoring children gathered at his knee. "I want to thank you for your war relief work. I wish adults did as much as you." He patted little heads and started to take his leave, then changed his mind. "There *is* something I wish to impress on you children. That is to never be neutral between right and wrong. Never oppress anybody, or allow anybody to be oppressed. Always stand for what you believe is right, and never flinch in the face of any odds."

Never be neutral between right and wrong. There it was. The quote that would make the papers. Words aimed straight at his rival and my critics. Miss Sloane said we needed the attention of important political men— well, we had it now. So much for Mitzi Miller's biting society column. *This* was going to make the national news *above* the fold.

In the main foyer—after receiving rounds of adulation and bouquets of flowers—as Miss Sloane and I walked the marble halls between rows of elegant hanging lanterns, she asked, "You knew Roosevelt was coming, didn't you?"

"I only *hoped*. It's why I cast Roosevelt's grandnephew as one of the militiamen. I guessed the former president would be champing at the bit to vent his political spleen, so I gave him a stage upon which to do it."

"Why didn't you tell me?"

"I didn't want to disappoint you if I was wrong, and I wanted the pleasure of seeing your astonished expression if I was right."

"Beatrice," she said, "this is going to touch off a *real* discussion in this country about our neutrality policy . . . People underestimate you."

I smiled. "Something we have in common."

Just that moment, my sons came up the stairs, and Billy was beaming. "President Roosevelt shook my hand!"

"I saw that, darling," I said, kissing the top of his head. "And I saw him whisper something to you too."

Billy nodded. "He said: *I hope you will grow up to be as great an American hero as your father and your cousin Victor.*"

Billy actually gulped.

It'd been hard enough for him to walk in Lafayette's shoes. To think my son must also live up to the reputation of an absent father's long-ago battlefield exploits . . . and his cousin in the trenches, well, how could a stuttering boy imagine he might measure up? I never wanted my boys to believe that heroism was only about fighting. I wanted them to know bravery could be found in working to make a difference, whether on a stage or by risking themselves over a mine-laden sea. I wanted them to look for courage not just in their father's example, but also . . . in mine.

I had other reasons, of course—the Lafayette Fund, the Chapmans, Miss Sloane—but it was *this* that decided me.

Damn the torpedoes; I was going back to France.

PART

TWO

ELEVEN

BEATRICE
Bordeaux
April 1915

MISS SLOANE WAS GREEN AS PEA SOUP.

Which may, in fact, have been what she heaved over the rail of the ship as we chugged into the French port. We'd taken an early booking on the SS *Rochambeau*—not as swift as the *Lusitania*, but when we weren't zigzagging to avoid the kaiser's submarines, it'd been full steam ahead. There'd been rough seas, but no torpedoes. Still, my traveling companion was in such a wretched state, I would've suspected morning sickness in any other girl.

While I feasted in the elegant dining saloon on board, partaking of lamb potpie, succotash, and galantines of turkey with aspic jelly, Miss Sloane had been quite unable to keep anything down. Not even her indignation. Looking back over her shoulder, she glared. "Are you *sketching* me while I retch at the rail?"

It was too late to hide my charcoal pencil. "You know I hate to keep idle!"

"You might've kept more usefully employed by reading handbooks on nursing, in case we're asked to render assistance to the soldiers for whom our Lafayette kits are intended."

I ignored this, shading in her jawline. "I'll do my best not to make you look too thin, but we need to get a little food into you."

Miss Sloane groaned. "You must have an iron stomach to talk about food while the sea roils beneath us."

"Oh, but I enjoy tumultuous seas," I said brightly. "It brings back memories of my honeymoon. Did I ever tell you how Willie and I got caught in a storm? We were trapped in that sloop, flinging our sodden bodies against the keel to keep the boat from capsizing. We came ashore on some hellish beach infested with stinging red ants—"

"That sounds *abominable*," she said.

I smiled almost against my will at the memory. "Oh, but it was the time of our lives . . ."

I remembered using gas lamps to flush out alligators. Willie taught me to shoot them right between the eyes and roast them over a fire. We made love to the music of marsh waters against the side of the boat, and what a *man* he was, all hard-bodied, every glorious muscle straining. He made me feel like a wild adventuress, game for anything. Like we were perfectly matched, an unbreakable team. Like we could fight the whole world together and win . . .

How could a fire that had burned so hot now be reduced to such cold ash? This was not, of course, a question to be ruminated upon. Especially not with my in-laws on board. As they approached our sunny spot on deck, Emily said, "Mrs. Chapman, would you inform your sister-in-law that it's ill-mannered to sketch a woman in digestive distress?"

"You poor dear," said my sister-in-law, fluttering over Emily with nurturing concern. "Fortunately, we're nearly ashore."

The Chapmans were eager to see Victor. What's more, they expected my assistance in convincing him to accept a transfer to the air corps, but I doubted I'd remain his favorite aunt if I were to involve myself in this scheme. No, I was neutral in *this* respect, and so I was determined to remain!

"I'm hoping Willie's driver will take us straight to Paris," my sister-in-law was saying.

And my pencil came to a standstill. I glanced up, a little perturbed. "Willie sent his driver?"

"Hasn't he?" my sister-in-law asked. "Why, Beatrice, I assumed you'd cabled ahead."

Though she knew perfectly well that Willie and I lived separate lives, she'd deluded herself into believing otherwise. Now it was my unhappy duty to remind her—and myself—of the truth. "Mr. Chanler is occupied with his own affairs, and I shouldn't like to trouble him."

Jack Chapman growled, "If the railway is clogged, his motor would be useful."

Well, then, perhaps you should have arranged for it, I thought. This was, of course, uncharitable. With a son at the front, the Chapmans had enough on their minds. Had I been selfish not to warn Willie we were coming? But, no, if I'd told my husband I was returning to France, he'd have forbidden it, and that I could not risk. It'd been difficult enough to leave my boys behind with their governess; it would've been so much worse to do so against their father's express command.

Bordeaux was the center of aid shipments from America, and in disembarking, we navigated a veritable maze of wooden crates and iron-banded barrels—most destined for mule-driven carts, because horses had been requisitioned by the military. Since every able-bodied Frenchman was at the front, most of the loading was done by old men and women in clogs—and it was slow going. The American Relief Clearing House—or ARCH, as we called it—wanted us to unload our Lafayette kits for transport to the front lines as soon as possible.

Unfortunately, hours passed before Emily and I finished the necessary paperwork and received the appropriate permissions. Our only consolation was that amongst those on hand to greet us and get us settled into war relief work in Paris were two impressive Frenchwomen who offered to take us, and our ambulance, to Paris.

With a hand on her hip and a foot propped on the running board of a gray military lorry, the elder introduced herself as Marie-Louise LeVerrier, vice president of the Union Française pour le Suffrage des Femmes. In no-nonsense boots and with her hair in a bun, she explained that before the war, she had been both an educator and staunch suffragette. Now, in the cause of helping war refugees, she'd teamed up with the elegant Clara Simon, who had married into a family with ties to the Rothschilds and served as editrix of a women's magazine. Both women shared our sensibilities about the war and had even less patience for the Woman's Peace Party than we did.

"What an honor and pleasure it is to meet you both," I said, having read about their herculean efforts to house refugees and displaced children. Assisting French feminist Valentine Thomson, they had nearly a thousand women and children in their care in Bordeaux alone, to say nothing of their work with the Red Cross and the American Hospital in Neuilly.

Sporting a navy blue suit with a hemline so daring it showed the tops of her white buttoned spats, Clara Simon offered us cigarettes, and when we declined, she said, "How quaint! It's a vice I picked up from my husband's smoke-filled back rooms." She explained that her in-laws were among the first Jews to serve in French government. "But some converted to Christianity. We are a family of mixed religious and political views."

I grinned. "They say love overcomes all . . ."

And Madame Simon replied, "They're idiots who say that."

Meanwhile, Madame LeVerrier was intent on the work at hand. "Your Lafayette kits are in such demand we give them only to the most deserving soldiers. We could use several hundred thousand more."

I nearly deflated. Miss Sloane and I had been so proud of the forty thousand Lafayette kits we'd shipped, but now, to be faced—the very moment our feet touched French soil—with having fallen short of the enormous need might have dispirited lesser ladies. Fortunately, Emily merely scratched in her notebook, *Several hundred thousand more.* And I said, "I'll cable our committee to step up the work in New York. In the meantime, may I introduce my relations, Mr. and Mrs. John Jay Chapman? They have a son at the front."

"Oh, yes!" said Madame LeVerrier, smiling warmly. "Everyone in France is talking of these young Americans who have come to fight for us. Our own men are fighting for their own country, but your boy places himself at our side, against the wishes of his own government, for no other reason than to make right triumph over wrong. That is worthy of a special honor. And it comforts those of us who are in the struggle."

The Chapmans both reddened, overcome with emotion. Perhaps to spare them embarrassment, Madame LeVerrier continued, "I hope you had an uneventful journey without sight of a submarine."

As if she'd not spent nearly two weeks heaving over the side rail, Emily chirped, "It was a perfectly pleasant trip, and danger was the farthest thing from our minds. We're simply happy to do something for France in the name of Lafayette."

"*Lafayette, Lafayette, Lafayette,*" Clara Simon said, lighting her cigarette with amusement. "Perhaps the only French name Americans know except for the fashion houses. *Lafayette, Hermès, Louis Vuitton . . .*"

Clara was witty but biting. *She's not sure she likes us,* I realized. She had, perhaps, seen too many American socialites eager to roll bandages in expectation of a war decoration. Ah, well, we'd simply have to prove ourselves.

ON THE ROAD TO PARIS, I FEARED TO FIND THE CITY IN RUBBLE. A fear made worse when the Eiffel Tower came into view, now armed with antiaircraft guns and encircled with barbed wire—a reminder that the iconic structure was a working communications tower the Germans would dearly love to topple.

When we'd fled the previous autumn, the city had been a somber place, the lamplights extinguished along the Champs-Élysées by curfew to protect against zeppelin attacks, people hiding behind barred doors at the encroachment of both the war and winter. Now the springtime weather was warm and healing, and life was beginning to show itself. The cafés were open, despite the fact the nation was battling for its existence but a few miles away.

That part could not be forgotten, of course. Not with French soldiers on every street corner—bright-eyed boys who'd left home six months ago, now hardened veterans on furlough. Each wore a different shade of blue, as military scientists had yet to determine which hue best disguised them in the muddy trenches. Meanwhile, women strolled in somber dresses in a narrow range of colors between stygian black and mahogany brown.

"The fashion is so disappointing this year," I teased.

"It *is* wartime," said Emily.

"I refuse to think my pink hat ribbon will undermine the war effort! Color boosts morale."

We took lodgings at the St. James & D'Albany. It wasn't the Ritz, but had a few things to recommend it. In the first place, our luxurious lodgings were directly across from the Tuileries gardens, which were now a defiant blooming riot of pink, purple, and yellow blossoms. And in the second place, the St. James was the last extant remnant of the old Hôtel de Noailles, where Lafayette once lived with his wife. "We're walking in the hero's footsteps," I said in the black-and-white-checkered expanse of the lobby.

Sniffing like the scion of a furniture empire that she was, Emily let her gaze fall upon the worn sofas beneath crystal chandeliers. "I imagine it was more luxurious in Lafayette's day . . ."

"Snob!" I cried.

Emily stopped before an architectural drawing on the wall that portrayed the original grounds—a once-palatial structure now reduced to this hotel and an inner courtyard. "I suppose if I squint, I can imagine beautiful ball gowns, powdered wigs . . ."

But my attention was captured by a drawing of a faraway fortress called Chavaniac. "This was Lafayette's birthplace. Quite humble by comparison, isn't it? Can you imagine what he must have felt coming from a place like that to the splendor of Paris?"

Probably out of place, the way Minnie felt when I abandoned her . . .

Not privy to the emotions roiling inside me, Emily chuckled. "Can you imagine what his wife must've thought to discover she was the mistress of that wretched holding?"

"You're not just a snob. You're the snobbiest of snobs."

"I have to be. I'm New Money. You wouldn't understand."

Oh, wouldn't I? "We're American ladies in France. We're *all* New Money here."

This was still on my mind the next morning when I awakened to sunlight streaming in through the tall windows overlooking the courtyard, where birds chirped and hotel guests took their coffee *sans sucre*, for the war rationing had already begun. And I wondered what Lafayette and his wife would've thought to see the bourgeois rabble chattering over breakfast in the remnants of their old home. While I mused on this, Emily—of course, an annoyingly early riser—had already been down to the desk and back again before I finished dressing.

She returned with word from her French lieutenant, whose promised leave had yet to materialize, and I think it was to hide her disappointment that she asked, "Have you called your husband yet?"

"I suppose it cannot be put off any longer."

Perhaps I could send a note. *Dear Willie, I'm back in France. Surprise!* No, he could ignore a note. Better to go directly to his house near the Arc de Triomphe. But what then? My sister-in-law would want to come, and it would be too humiliating to have her see me knock on the black double doors as if I were not, in fact, the lady of the house. Worse, I'd *have* to knock, because we might find another woman ensconced in my place.

I dared not risk it. I'd have to telephone. I decided to invite Willie to luncheon before we visited the hospital to deliver the much-needed ambulance. I thought it a good plan, because my husband would have to be on his best behavior with his sister present. So I made the call—in French, because the censors cut the line if you spoke any other language. Willie's manservant answered. "I am not at liberty to say where Mr. Chanler is or when he's expected back."

"Why not?" I knew how incorrigible Willie could be. "Is my husband standing beside you, telling you to be rid of me?"

"No, madame. He's not standing beside me."

Then he was, no doubt, *sitting* in his wing chair, sipping at a cognac, reading old racing sheets. Or perhaps Willie was supine on the leather sofa, entangled in the arms of a curvaceous . . . no, better not let my imagination run wild. "Please tell Mr. Chanler that his sister wants to see him."

If he couldn't make room for *me* in his busy schedule of dissolute living, surely he could spare an hour for Elizabeth. I hung up in a temper and with an enormous appetite. The Café de Paris—one of my favorite cabarets—was, to my surprise, quite as crowded as in the old days, even if some of the women were of questionable vocation. Then again, soldiers on furlough inevitably attract women of a certain profession . . . It's a perfectly predictable economy.

Seated at a table artfully framed by pillars and crimson drapes, my sister-in-law fretted, "We've heard no word from Victor. I don't know if our messages are getting through."

"I'm sure we'll hear from him soon," I said, patting her hand.

Emily stared forlornly into her cup. "What if something's changed at the front? Lieutenant LaGrange has been refused the leave he was promised . . ."

"It's *gas*," barked Mr. Chapman, slapping down the morning's communiqué. "The Germans are sending clouds of green poison into the breeze. Hundreds of English officers have been asphyxiated. Canadians and French too. It's caused complete panic."

Poison gas was a monstrous violation of the Hague conventions on the rules of civilized warfare. To think of my nephew writhing in a trench, helpless even to fire a shot in self-defense . . . well, it made our work here seem more urgent.

Thus, that afternoon, we delivered the ambulance to the American Hospital in Neuilly, where we learned some manner of defense to poison gas had been devised. Handkerchiefs or cotton gauze dipped in water—or, even better, urine—counteracted the chlorine, explained Mesdames Simon and LeVerrier gave us a tour.

Hearing this, Emily and I decided that we would include cloths in our Lafayette kits from now on. The chief doctor had received us personally, making a fuss over our presence in the wards, which were filled with soldiers who had been ferried back from the front. "We're grateful for the ambulance, and for your company, Mrs. Chanler. We're so well acquainted with your husband, after all."

I gave him a grateful smile. "Yes, well, Mr. Chanler isn't an easy patient. I'm sure he left quite an impression last year."

"Last year?" The physician chuckled. "He's been here nearly every day."

That was a surprise. It lessened my resentment to think Willie was occupying himself with hospital work. The way volunteers from even the wealthiest class of people rushed about, doing every sort of chore, made me wonder if my husband had simply been too *busy* to write.

Certainly the nurses, weary from changing dressings and sheets, had time for only the simplest fare all day. Fruit, war bread, and butter—not even a strong tea to perk them up. Something that, I decided, simply must be remedied. I might not have known how to properly dress a man's face when it had been half blown away, but I could bring tea, soup, and sandwiches for the nurses who did.

And I would learn. It was a fight against nature not to recoil from faces with only gaping nostrils for noses, and with exposed jawbones—

teeth shining like a skeleton in living men. In order to make sense of these ghastly visages, I imagined them as ancient sculptures in some vandalized state. And my sculptor's fingers pined to tenderly add clay to fill in the missing parts so these men would be whole again. "I'll return tomorrow."

"Me too," said Miss Sloane.

It was settled, then. Until the two young soldiers about whom we were most concerned could get their permissions, we'd make ourselves useful. Perhaps we might even run into my husband. But as it happened, Willie wasn't at the hospital the next day when we brought much-appreciated tea trays with dainties. It wasn't until I returned to the hotel that night that I received his curious message, which read like it was sent from a man on the run from the law:

Meet me at noon at Maxim's restaurant, and come alone.

TWELVE

ADRIENNE
Paris
March 1777

I WAS NOW THE WIFE OF A FUGITIVE.

To stop Lafayette from boarding the ship to America that he had secretly commissioned, my father made good on his threat, securing a *lettre de cachet*. By order of the king, my husband was to be arrested on sight. Every seaport in France was on the lookout, as was every patrol at the border. Stopping me on my way to Mass, the duc d'Ayen said, "Pray Lafayette is arrested. If he is caught before he sets sail for America, there may yet be some chance of preserving our family from the king's anger."

Yet the family he wished to preserve went to war with itself, battle lines drawn by generation. To the old men in my family, the idea of British redcoats being driven back by ill-clad rebels was a source of amusement, but they were incensed at my husband's rebellion. They scurried to Versailles to denounce and all but disown Lafayette.

Meanwhile, my mother, my sisters, and my brother-in-law all praised Gilbert's actions.

I knew that if Gilbert were dragged home in chains, he might never recover. And this would hurt my children as well as me. So despite my pain at his leaving, I had to find a way to help him escape France.

I commissioned Marc to send word to his young officer friends to look the other way if they should happen upon my husband at the border. I begged lady friends at court to help Gilbert if he should seek shelter with their families. I was sure to be seen in my carriage riding through Paris, or walking in the public gardens, to put the lie to any rumor of my having fallen ill. Most important—if only for the sake of my unborn child—I *willed* myself to remain calm.

"Drink," Grand-mère said one afternoon, pressing an extraordinary cup into my hands and lowering her scratchy old voice to a conspiratorial whisper. "It's holy water. I mixed it in a sacred chalice and prayed to the Virgin Mary for a boy."

"Oh, Grand-mère, for shame!" I cried, knowing a chalice had recently gone missing after vespers from a nearby church. How had she taken it without any of us noticing?

"You will thank me when you give birth to the long-awaited Noailles heir."

I drank the water—then had a servant return the chalice to the church. Meanwhile, my sister Louise, who was herself finally pregnant, pressed a silk pouch of wet tea leaves to my closed eyes. Maman said tea leaves would leave me looking fresh and cheerful, which I intended to be on the occasion of a family wedding at which I knew everyone would be trying to divine signs of my unhappiness with which to condemn Gilbert as a cruel husband and unfeeling father. "I must make everyone understand that in leaving for America, Lafayette is motivated by only the finest sentiments."

"They will," Maman assured me. "If not now, then one day."

Would it be soon enough? Of the family elders, only Grand-mère tempered her disapproval with begrudging admiration. "Who could've guessed the dullard from Chavaniac had it in him?"

I forgave Grand-mère because she did not have all her faculties, but it was more difficult to forgive Aunt Claude when, at the wedding banquet, she said, "Lafayette will be fortunate if the king forgives the follies of his youth. If not, pray poor Adrienne and her unborn child do not die of shame."

At that utterance, the wedding guests turned, and a dozen pairs of eyes pinned me where I sat. Under a table that glittered with crystal and silver, Louise squeezed my hand, and I waited for the heat of embarrassment. I felt only the prickle of anger. Since my aunt did not worry about propriety in quite nearly wishing me and my child dead, indignant motherhood as much as marital devotion drove me to say, "I am not ashamed of Lafayette. I am proud to call myself the wife of a gallant knight of liberty, gone to fight for the future of humanity."

This was not, for me, merely talk of a loyal wife. I believed that there must be a more enlightened way to exist, where each person had freedom of conscience. I was beginning to embrace a fierce pride in the idea that I might be a part of this experiment in self-government across the sea, even if my only contribution was holding firm against my family's displeasure.

After the wedding festivities, the duc d'Ayen told the young men of the family, "Don't any of you think to follow Lafayette."

He did not know his days of frightening everyone into submission were nearly at an end, but I sensed it when my brother-in-law gave a silky smile. "The wind is blowing against you, sir. It will be difficult for you to find husbands for your other daughters if this is the way you treat heroism in a son-in-law!"

Marc knew the French love a daring hero. Especially one with a fine pedigree.

Thus, stories spread like wildfire, more exaggerated with every telling. How the young marquis de Lafayette disguised himself as a postilion, hiding from the king's soldiers in barns and haystacks, winking at pretty farmers' daughters to keep his secret before making a mad gallop for the border. Lafayette's drama—as it was whispered in Paris back alleys and compiled into official reports in the gilded halls of Versailles—tugged at the sympathies of my countrymen.

Finally, one afternoon, whilst Henriette fussed in my arms, my sister Louise burst into my chamber. "Lafayette is away! He went without noble title—Gilbert du Motier, a mere chevalier de Chavaniac. He made it aboard the *Victoire* and has set sail for America."

I held my baby tighter in silent thanksgiving, knowing the risk was only beginning. Lafayette's ship could still be stopped by a British blockade, and then he'd be thrown into irons. Even if my husband arrived safely in America, he might still be killed in the war there. Yet my heart still welled with joy. "Your papa is free," I whispered to Henriette. "He's free."

And in some sense, so was I.

IN JUNE, WHILE I WAS SO HEAVILY PREGNANT I COULD SCARCELY rise from my canopied bed without the help of my maid, Lafayette came ashore in South Carolina and traversed nine hundred miles under the sweltering sun through mosquito-infested swamps.

In July, while I labored in the dire heat to bring forth a daughter with bright copper curls, my husband reached Philadelphia and received his commission in the Continental army.

In August, while I christened our new baby *Anastasie Louise* after my loyal sister, my husband became a trusted aide to George Washington.

And in September, while Louise was giving birth to a boy, my husband was wounded at the Battle of the Brandywine.

I learned all this only after the fact, as word took weeks, sometimes months, to cross a war-torn sea, and because my mother conspired to keep the more upsetting news from me. In the meantime, I took solace in my own babies. I gave not a fig that another daughter meant another disappointment for my family. Anastasie was so sunny a baby I couldn't wish for her to be anything other than herself, and I hoped she and Henriette would grow up to be good friends.

In any case, my older sister had at last fulfilled my father's long-awaited hope for a male heir, and, guzzling champagne to celebrate the birth of his new son, Marc said, "I wanted to name him after his uncle Gilbert, but to keep the duc d'Ayen from rage, he will be called *Adrien*."

Cradling her infant son, Louise gave me a melting smile. "After *you*, my beloved sister, because you are nearly as courageous as your husband."

There was no truth to this whatsoever, but I embraced her with a full heart anyway.

In the first letter I received from Gilbert, he asked, *Can you forgive me?*

He pleaded with me not to condemn him before hearing him, and I was so overjoyed simply to know he was alive that I softened. His anguish at the thought of losing both my love and my good opinion touched my heart. And to reassure me about the shot he'd taken in battle, he wrote, *I came off lightly. The bullet touched neither bone nor nerve. This is only what I pompously style* my wound, *to give myself airs and render myself interesting.*

Even so, the fright it put in me! He had scarcely begun to fight for the Americans and already had taken a bullet. Though I replied to him straightaway, my missives must have been captured by the British, for his next letter pleaded, *I have received no news of you or the child, Adrienne. I cannot live in such a state of uncertainty. I entreat you, my dear heart, not to forget an unhappy man who pays dearly for the error he committed in parting from you . . . I love you and shall all my life.*

I loved him too.

Despite everything, in my breast beat the heart he had entrusted to me when we wed. I understood why he had gone to America, why he had risked everything. Not only for his own prospects, but because he sincerely believed *the prosperity of America will one day mean the prosperity of all mankind. She will become an asylum of virtue, tolerance, equality, and liberty . . .*

I believed it too. If it could be proved possible in the New World, then it could be done the world over. Which is what I told my visitor, the American minister Dr. Franklin, when he came to the Hôtel de Noailles to deliver felicitations on the birth of my child. Taking the beaver cap from his balding head, he said, "Please forgive the subterfuge in the matter of your husband's leave-taking for our cause, madame. I'm told it couldn't have been avoided, and personally, I have always been of the opinion that three can keep a secret only if two of them are dead."

I should have laughed with the cagey old fellow. I should have granted forgiveness. Instead, I vented my frustration upon the poor man. "You lack faith, sir. For I too am dedicated to this cause, and if I had been entrusted with the secret, I would have taken it to the grave, if need be."

The ruddy-cheeked old ambassador adjusted his spectacles and stared at me. "I begin to believe you would. Perhaps my young friend Lafayette underestimates what he has in you . . ."

My upset at how I had been deceived made me say, "As, perhaps, do you. I could have been of service, and I still could be."

"Is that so?" Franklin asked, instead of reproaching me. He seemed deeply interested. "I always say men and women united are more likely to succeed in this world. Why, the machinations of a man, without a woman, would make him as useless as only half a pair of scissors!"

I explained that I knew American farmers were in rebellion against one of the great world powers and doubted they could win without French help. The king had to be persuaded to join the fight against the British, and in this cause my husband had enlisted me, bidding me to share his reports as I deemed politically wise. Gilbert gave me both the authority and ability to serve as his ambassador, and I intended to do so.

Franklin eyed me carefully. "Yet your august family, and your father in particular, seem to be of an opinion that the king of France will wish to remain neutral."

My father had been an adept courtier under a different king, part of a different generation, whereas I had come of age under *this* king and queen. I wasn't a child-bride anymore, shy and innocent of intrigues. I was nearly eighteen and a mother twice over, having passed four seasons at court. I knew what fired royal imaginations, and what pressures the king and queen submitted to in order to amuse their favorites. How they wished to be seen by the world. As an anointed king believing himself to rule with divine right, King Louis would hesitate to support a rebellion against another king, but it would not deter him if he thought he could both strike a rival and restore the honor and glory of France.

Thus, conspiring with Dr. Franklin, I engaged in my own defiant campaign, sending copies of Lafayette's correspondence and reports directly to the queen. Marie Antoinette loved nothing so much as a good story, and from my letters, she would learn of both Lafayette's tender affections as a husband and father and his bravery as a soldier. More, I knew the queen was not as silly as my father supposed. She would see these reports from America as valuable political intelligence too. I knew she would share these letters with the king.

While in Paris drawing rooms Dr. Franklin told tales of my husband forcing Hessians into retreat, I regaled all the queen's ladies with tales of Lafayette's bravery and chivalry—a kindhearted husband, a fearless fighter, a father who was apart from his children for the betterment of mankind. And before winter, one could not walk down any snowy street without hearing fiery young men arguing with their patriarchs.

"Let me join Lafayette—"

"—why should he get all the glory?"

"I am pledging my sword tomorrow!"

The tide was turning, and I rejoiced to play a part. As barefooted American patriots left a bloody trail in the snow on their way to a place called Valley Forge, I wished to do more. I raised funds for these poor American peasant soldiers who needed boots and shoes and weapons with which to defend themselves. But then, just as triumph was in sight, out of the blue, my duties as a mother came before my duties as a wife.

WHAT AILMENT MADE MY LITTLE ANGELS BURN WITH FEVER? THE physicians couldn't say. Then the illness struck my sister Louise's baby boy. Though we had nurses to help tend our children, we both took turns rocking the babies, our hearts rending with every cry. Then, in the end, clutching each other, soaking each other's hair with tears, both of us were caught in the maw of shared grief when my sweet Henriette and my nephew and namesake both perished within breaths of each other.

I was holding my daughter's fingers as they lost their grip on this world, a moment that loosened my hold on it too . . . *Twenty-two months.* That's all the life Henriette lived. Never again would I feel the weight of her on my chest. Never again would I hear her childish babble or even her sleepless cries. Never again would Gilbert hold her and read to her about the rights of mankind. And never before had I felt such desolation.

The day we buried our children, Louise appealed to God, her eyes on the sky. Mine locked on the direction of the sea. As the graveside wind bit my cheeks, I swallowed my sobs. "I envy him. Monsieur de Lafayette does not know his daughter is gone from this earth. In whatever military encampment he is now, he can still dream of Henriette growing tall, coming out into society, feasting at her wedding . . ."

It would be months before he would hear his daughter was dead—if he would hear at all. An unwelcome bitterness crept into my heart. Knowing me as only a sister could, Louise pressed her rosary beads into my hand. "Turn to God, Adrienne. Pray for strength and rejoice that our children are cherubs in heaven now."

I neither prayed nor rejoiced. I had believed that I was doing God's work in helping Gilbert—in helping the Americans. Now, with this terrible loss, I wondered if God were punishing me for defying my father. Or perhaps he was punishing Gilbert for defying the king.

Had we been idealistic fools? Consumed with grief and doubt, I passed weeks without leaving my rooms. When, in December of 1777, King Louis formally recognized the independence of the American colonies and offered a treaty, it should have been cause for happy celebration. Alas, I couldn't remember why I should care.

"Adrienne," Maman said, stroking my hair. "You must rouse yourself from your bed. The world is looking to you as an example."

Absurd. Why should anyone in France, much less the world, look to me? What was the point of this American war if it kept a young father from his daughter's funeral—or if it should leave me a widow? I had indulged the same vanity at court that I despised, proud of myself merely because my husband was a sensation.

God punishes pride, I thought. That is what was taught in church. That he tested us and took things from us . . .

Trying to put my surviving daughter into my arms, Maman said, "You have Anastasie to think of. She's too little to know how great her misfortune is in losing her older sister, but she suffers without a mother's love!"

I did not wish to hold rosy-cheeked Anastasie, knowing I might lose her too. I nearly thrust her away. But she was the sort of child who simply *expects* to be loved, and insists upon loving in return. She reached for me with chubby little hands, cooing with affection when I finally took her. Even as an infant, Anastasie simply knew—like her father—how to conquer my heart.

It was Anastasie—a gift from God—who saved me from the grief, proving that even in the midst of the greatest trials and misfortune, we are still capable of joy. I would never worship a God who visited cruelty upon his children, in this world or the next. It became, as Gilbert would say, one of my amiable heresies that God *did not* deal in cruelty. Love, connection, goodness, comfort against loss . . . these things *were* God. And there was for me no love so sweetly intimate or comforting as that between a mother and child.

THIRTEEN

MARTHE
Chavaniac-Lafayette
Spring 1941

BUT I DON'T HAVE A MOTHER, I THINK, STARING IN DISBELIEF AT THE
paper. *There's been some sort of mistake; some sort of clerical error . . .*

I'm so disoriented, so transported outside myself, that I have the
sensation of floating above Madame Simon's polished walnut desk, with
its shiny telephone and a lighter embossed with an owl that seems to
blink at me in mockery.

I have to focus my own eyes on the page, where they land each time
on the same words.

Mother: Minerva Furlaud, deceased.

Father: unknown.

So I'm not a veritable foundling left by the faeries? I had a mother—
a real mother—with a name. *Furlaud.* Why isn't it mine? I'm so brittle
with shock that I want to shake myself until the memory of my mother
rattles out of my bones. Failing that, I want to shake anyone who might
remember, so I all but throw the file onto Madame Simon's desk. "I was
told no one knew who my parents were. This says otherwise."

Scowling at my tone, Madame Simon puts on her glasses. As she
reads, her eyes narrow. "Well, that's strange, isn't it?"

"Strange?" Boiling anger bubbles past my confusion. Knowing my
mother's name would've meant everything to me growing up here in the
orphanage. When I was old enough, I could've visited her grave. I
might've felt some sense of solid *connection* to another human being.
Some understanding of who I am . . . and maybe even who I'm meant to
be. *"Mon Dieu*, it's more than *strange* you'd keep this secret."

Madame Simon is somehow impassive in the face of my outburst, unlocking her desk drawer and retrieving a pack of cigarettes. I've never seen her smoke before, and now, impatiently, I watch her flick the old owl lighter. She tries three times before it lights. "What is *strange*," she finally says, "is that I've been keeping records for the Lafayette Memorial for more than twenty-four years and I've never seen this document before in my life."

"You signed it, didn't you?" I snatch the paper back, only to find the signature is Madame Beatrice's.

Then I sit down, hard.

"It was Beatrice who found you when you were a child," she explains. "She must've felt it was her responsibility to file the appropriate papers."

I hadn't known Madame Beatrice found me. Why didn't I know that? I take a deep breath. "I want to know everything. Where I was found, for starters. The street, the time of day, what I was wearing . . ."

Madame Simon exhales, wreathing herself in smoke. "I'm afraid I never knew those details."

A knot of emotion swells in my throat, but I swallow it down, refusing to cry, because I'm not the crying kind.

"I assure you, Marthe, if there was any chance you had surviving family, we would've looked for them."

Surviving family? I'm afraid to hope. Hope, after all, is almost as dangerous as *trust*. "I want to see all my records."

"If there's anything else, it would be at our Paris office, which has been closed since the start of the occupation. With Nazis goose-stepping down the Champs-Élysées, I can't think of any way I could get records from there."

"There has to be a way," I insist. "Even if I have to go to Paris myself."

"You can't even cross the line of demarcation without a travel pass."

This fact pierces my bravado, and my shoulders slump. "Then how am I supposed to find out why this woman's name is on my birth record?"

"You'll have to ask Beatrice."

"Oh, why didn't I think of that?" My sarcasm is sharp, because we're separated from Madame Beatrice by a British blockade, leagues of ocean, and deadly German submarines. Even before the war it was nearly impossible to get a long-distance call through from Chavaniac to New York, and now even the mails aren't reliable, but Madame Simon opens her drawer again and gifts me with several precious tissue-thin airmail sheets.

"Here. You can write her a letter . . . but . . ."

"But?"

She stares a long moment. "Maybe you shouldn't shake this tree just now."

"Why not?"

"Because this record was filed a long time ago in the chaos and desperation of the Great War. Under such circumstances, mistakes can be made."

We're in the middle of a different war now, and our record-keeping is impeccable. "If it is a mistake, I need to know that too."

"Do you? Right now everyone in Europe is trying desperately to get their papers in order. For those in occupied territories, it's literally a matter of life and death. You're fortunate, Marthe. Your papers are *in order*. Just let them stay that way."

"I don't understand."

"Then you're not listening."

"I'm hanging on your every word!"

"You're not *hearing* me, then." An inexplicable pit of dread opens in my belly as she explains, "When Beatrice arranged for the purchase of this chateau, we were trying to find homes for thousands of orphaned and refugee children. We were overrun with sobbing French village girls. Little lost Belgian boys. Abandoned babies. Serbs, Armenians, stateless children. We were determined to save as many as we could, regardless of where they came from, and we didn't know if they'd be allowed to stay. Beatrice never allowed a scruple about official paperwork to get in her way."

I blink. "Are you saying—are you trying to say she might have falsified my birth record?"

"*If* she did, I can only speculate as to her reasons, but remember that at this very moment—right here in France—there are people suffering in lice-infested detention camps because they were born in the wrong place or to the wrong mother."

That pit of dread in my stomach widens into an abyss, and as I absorb the implications of her words, I find myself teetering on the precarious edge. *Mon Dieu.* Is it possible I'm not French? To find that out would be like being orphaned twice over! A smaller, more distant voice wonders . . . could I have Jewish blood?

My panicked silence makes her soften her voice. "Right now, you're Marthe Simone, Catholic, born in Paris, 1916. A relatively safe person to be. Now isn't the time to risk finding out if you're someone else. Certainly not in a phone call or telegram or letter; the censors are monitoring them all."

I swallow. "I can't just pretend I didn't see this file."

"At least keep this to yourself until the baroness gets back; she might be able to answer your questions."

The baroness is in Marseilles, about to leave for America for her daughter's wedding. She won't be back until after summer. The idea of having to wait to learn the truth even one more day, one more hour, one more *minute* makes me want to grab things and hurl them at the tall widows. But fear has also started to sink in.

Now isn't the time to risk finding out if you're someone else . . .

To think how frustrated I was when Monsieur Kohn resisted getting medical care for his daughter because he was scared of a name on a piece of paper. Now *I'm* scared of a name on a piece of paper too.

Fear, it seems, is a contagion as virulent as measles.

I sit there paralyzed with it, staring at the photos on the desk. One shows Madame LeVerrier posing with an Allied soldier from the last war, when she was still young enough to put a boot on a truck ledge and a saucy hand to her hip. She's with another woman, who wears a bright-eyed smile of wry amusement. It takes me a moment to realize it's the baroness because she's so changed . . . it's almost difficult to believe she could have ever smiled that way.

Another photograph features Madame Simon in the backseat of a large touring car amidst a group of orphaned boys—one of whom is Henri. *My* Henri. He's a little gap-toothed child in a side cap that one of the American doughboys must've given him to keep his shaved head warm. Henri had been like me: a child who needed help. And he got help from the women of this castle. I miss him so much; Henri would understand how upsetting all this is. He'd hold me and tell me, *Relax, blondie, just breathe . . .*

But he's in a German prison camp now, and since there's nothing we can do to help each other, maybe I can help another kid . . .

Merde. Some of that claptrap about how I'm a guardian of the nation's youth must have soaked in, because I find myself asking Madame Simon, "Do you ever let a scruple about paperwork get in *your* way?"

I explain the situation of the Jewish boarders at Madame Pinton's farm and ask if we can treat the sick girl *on the side.* "Maybe we could admit her under a *nom de guerre.*" Madame Simon gives me a sharp look, but she doesn't say no, which encourages me to argue, "Dr. Boulagnon could submit her medical records with a more French-sounding name."

"Impossible," she says. "Dr. Boulagnon and the family might go along, but what of the school certificate?"

"How hard could it be to make one?" All we'd need would be an official stamp. *And, with a very fine paintbrush and ink . . .* I think of an easier way. "Just admit her without the certificate. Pretend it was part of the application, but got misplaced. Who's to know?"

Madame Simon scowls, and I see she's had enough of me. "Marthe, I know this has been a difficult day for you, otherwise you wouldn't make such a febrile suggestion."

If I were in my right mind, maybe I wouldn't. But I can't just go back to life as usual. Maybe I can't find out anything about my mother or the name in my file right now. Maybe the smart thing is to just pretend nothing has changed. But I can't. "I don't know how I'm supposed to wake up tomorrow morning like usual and fill inkwells and scrub chalkboards and teach little girls to sing fascist songs like 'Maréchal, nous voilà!' I've been drowning for months as it is. I have to *do* something."

"The only thing you have to do is go into quarantine because you've been exposed to a contagion. And hopefully time alone will bring you back to your senses."

"YOU MUST BE LOVING THIS," ANNA CALLS FROM THE OTHER SIDE OF the door, where she's setting down a tray of soup for me. "The mad artist locked in her castle tower, being waited on hand and foot."

Under other circumstances I'd laugh and shout, *Oh, shut up, will you?*

Instead, I'm grateful for the door between us.

With Henri gone, Anna has become my closest friend. I've shared more with her in these past few months than I've ever shared with almost anybody. I'm pretty sure that one look at my face and she'd know everything I've ever known about myself has been put in doubt. I want to tell Anna everything. On the other hand, what I have to tell can't be shouted through a door.

Mother: Minerva Furlaud, deceased.

Furlaud. Have I heard that name before? And what does Madame Beatrice know about it? I idly wonder if any of her belongings would give me a clue. I look again at the photograph of the French soldier and a pigtailed girl in his arms. And for the first time, I seriously wonder, could it be me?

There's no one to ask, and I feel like I'm going to lose my mind wondering. The only thing that will keep me sane is to finish my portrait of Adrienne Lafayette. Though the Marshal isn't going to visit the chateau, the baroness said it was important to change the castle's image, so the work goes on. Even if I can't figure out who I am, maybe I can figure out Adrienne . . .

The next morning, when Anna brings my breakfast, she calls through the door, "You'd better emerge with a bloody *masterpiece.*"

Later, she's back again to ask, "Are you dying of loneliness yet?"

"Oh, I'm not alone," I say, looking around the room of an absent mistress of the castle who might know more about me than I know about myself, while drawing the mistress of the castle who came before us all. "I'm keeping company with the castle's ghosts."

It's not really a lie. To keep from thinking about my birth record and what Madame Beatrice might have done to it and *why,* I spend every day reading about Adrienne Lafayette. I'm starting to dream about her too. And by the time Dr. Anglade finally comes upstairs to examine me and give me my walking papers, I'm starting to like her a little. Adrienne wasn't the milquetoast dishrag I thought she was.

In fact, I'm no longer sure she was the kind of woman to whom nobody could object . . .

FOURTEEN

ADRIENNE
Paris
February 1779

TWO YEARS HAD PASSED WHILE MY HUSBAND FOUGHT IN THE American war. Years in which much changed for me and inside of me. Perhaps it was the turning tide of public opinion in favor of helping the rebel Americans. Perhaps it was the king's shift in policy with a formal alliance. Perhaps it was the fact that the Noailles—even my father—now supported Lafayette wholeheartedly and basked in the reflected glory of his name. I will always believe, however, that the greatest change came the moment at a house party when the great Voltaire himself, bent with the weight of his eighty-one years, shivering beneath his fur-trimmed pelisse and crimson cap, knelt before me to say, "I have come to make my obeisance to the wife of the Hero of the New World. May I live long enough to salute him as the liberator of the old."

Alas, the great man did not live that long. But Voltaire—one of our ideological heroes and one of the world's greatest minds—had acknowledged that my husband and I were not unworldly or foolish or naive to think we could change the world. Indeed, that the world could not be changed unless we believed it.

And I believed it now like scripture . . .

Unfortunately, Gilbert's temporary leave from duty and his return home remained a most delicate matter. Though my husband was now considered everywhere to be a great war hero, he had defied his king to fulfill his destiny. And though my father was daily negotiating at court to bring about a face-saving reconciliation, Maman warned we must prepare ourselves for the possibility that my husband would be clasped in irons the moment he set foot on French soil.

Thus, I feared I was only dreaming when a candle illuminated my darkened boudoir. Somehow, he was *here*, whispering, "I am sorry to wake you, my dear heart. It is only that after all this time, I couldn't wait to set eyes on you . . ."

Oh, his voice. To hear it again after two years undid me. I rose quickly from my pillow in the same moment he rushed to kneel at my bedside. "Forgive me, Adrienne. I beg you, forgive me!" I threw my arms around him in wordless emotion and he rasped, "I know you were too good to condemn me in letters spies might capture and publish for the world to see, but now that we are alone, I must know the truth. Have I broken everything between us?"

There had been a moment—more than one—where I wondered if he had. Those had been fleeting doubts, and now I had none. "Never. Of course I forgive you. With all my heart."

He bowed his head. "Yet I can never forgive myself for Henriette. I was not here to ease our little girl in her final hours, to console your mother's heart, to mingle my grief with yours. I was not *here*, but in some accursed frozen army camp . . ."

Would it have mattered? He might have helped ease her, he might have consoled me, but Henriette would still be gone, and all our hopes for a better world gone with her. Other fathers, I reminded myself, had been absent for lesser reasons. But in a fresh wave of grief for our first child, Gilbert and I both tried to speak, and faltered. There was so much we had to say, but holding each other seemed the only comfort.

His lips found my hair, my cheeks, my mouth, and we came together in forgiveness and grace. I imagined I felt the changes two years of soldiering had wrought. A new weight. Iron strength in his arms. A width and breadth to his back and shoulders. Only in the aftermath, tangled in linens and bedclothes, was I finally convinced I was neither dreaming him nor imagining the changes. My husband was not just a soldier, but now had experience commanding men, risking life and limb, and if the confidence and mastery of that experience could manifest in a person's body, I felt that change in him too. War had burned away his boyishness, leaving his muscles lean and taut, his stomach flat and hard. A knot of still-angry red scar tissue marred his leg where he had been shot, but there were smaller scars too, and I yearned to know the story of each one.

With half-lidded eyes, the reddish lashes of which glowed in dawn light, he said, "Knowing you still love me, I will sleep easy for the first time in years . . ."

Yet I did not want to share him, even with sleep. "How are you here and not in Versailles?"

He nuzzled my neck with soft amusement. "I have already been to Versailles, interrogated, and judged. I am just now in disgrace with the king, forbidden to appear in public places where my conduct might be applauded. I have been sentenced to ten days of house arrest." He grinned, having gotten away with it all. "You, my dear heart, are to be my jailer . . ."

Light reprimand indeed, if the king should send the hero home to his wife! I sighed happily to think of having him for ten days in my arms. "Whatever shall I do with you?"

He drew my palm up to kiss it. "I shall submit to whatever tortures you devise . . . only allow me the decency of a moment to catch my breath."

I loved his playfulness, yet I felt I must say something earnestly, for this thought had seared my heart during our long separation, when I had desperately wanted him in my arms, all while helping him to flee. "I want your love only freely given, Gilbert."

He sobered and took my face in his hands. "That, my dear heart, makes me love and want you all the more."

AFTER SO LONG A SEPARATION, I WANTED MY HUSBAND TO MYSELF, but I was equally eager to introduce him to his daughter Anastasie—who, at nineteen months old, was a redheaded bundle of vivacity. She toddled straight into his arms without fear, and he held her tight, lavishing her with the love she deserved, and the extra measure owed to our dearly departed Henriette. I bade him tell us everything. Even the stories I already knew. I wanted to live each moment from which I'd been absent. His arrival in America. His first battle. His visits with the Iroquois—savages, some called them, but my husband said they were as noble as the old Romans and had forged true nations. I made him tell me how he had outsmarted the British to save the American army from defeat, but his favorite stories were of George Washington. The stately gentleman farmer was, in my husband's estimation, the wisest and most honorable soldier in the world.

"He draws his sword only against tyrants," Gilbert said. "He has taken me as an adoptive son, and when you meet him, you will love him."

"I already do." After all, I had long harbored admiration for the commander of the ragtag army of the colonies, but real gratitude stole over me at the changes he had brought about in Gilbert, including a confidence he had never had before. It wasn't only a father figure Lafayette had found in America—he had found new brothers-at-arms too. He harbored the greatest fraternal love for all Washington's aides-de-camp, including the loquacious firebrand Alexander Hamilton and the intrepid South Carolinian John Laurens. Gilbert told me too of the dimple-chinned Hero of Trenton, James Monroe, who had nursed him after the Battle of the Brandywine. These were enterprising young people fighting for the right to rule themselves, and yet now he dropped his face into his hands. "The truth is, Adrienne, we are losing. The situation is dire. The conditions of the American soldiers—nearly naked, without blankets, without food, without shoes—make me feel guilty to be here, warm in this feather bed."

I rose to find paper and quill, and said, "Tell me what we can do."

Smiling at my ready willingness to be of service, Gilbert explained, "The Americans need everything. We must commission uniforms, purchase weapons, equip ships . . . even if it must come from my own fortune."

I did not balk. I had already helped him draw heavily upon his accounts in the past two years. But then, what price could one put upon fragile lives?

So great was my husband's glory that I could keep no one away. Maman, who had prayed for my husband and kept up my spirits, kissed him with joy. My adoring sisters gave him tearful embraces. Marc and de Ségur—the faithful friends who had defended him—clapped him on the back, eager to join him on campaign. Even Grand-mère waved her feathered pen and said affectionately, "My dear boy, you have caused quite a sensation!"

It was my father's greeting that meant the most, though the duc d'Ayen merely gave my husband a respectful nod. "I mistook you, Gilbert. It will not happen again." Then, unexpectedly, my father laid a hand upon my shoulder—the most affectionate gesture he ever bestowed upon me—and said, "I mistook my daughter too. Adrienne is like her mother. Prove to her she is wrong, and she submits as meekly as a child. Yet, if she believes she is right, she will *never* give in."

He said this with what seemed like . . . *pride* . . . and my tears overflowed.

All was forgiven, and this grace within our family circle filled me with joy. However, we were not the only ones to rejoice at Lafayette's return. Calling cards arrived from foreign officials, American envoys, and French noblemen. Ladies left perfumed kerchiefs, and I felt my first real pangs of jealousy. I consoled myself in the knowledge that Gilbert had confided in my brother-in-law, who confided in my sister Louise, who in turn confided in me that my husband had no taste for harlots, and had taken no mistress in America either. Perhaps it was because Gilbert so worshipped the Americans, for whom marital infidelity was still a scandal . . .

One evening during his ten days of house arrest, we heard a commotion outside on the Rue Saint-Honoré; we opened the draperies to see a gathering of peasants, fruit sellers, florists, and butchers. Ordinary people in aprons, clogs, and wool caps chanted, *"Lafayette! Lafayette! Lafayette!"*

"Come," Gilbert said, clasping me with one arm, holding Anastasie in the other. Together we went to the Juliet balcony to receive applause. How my husband blossomed in the warmth of public praise. I too felt proud that the common people of Paris understood that we were all brothers and sisters in the same struggle for justice, and that my husband wished to be our champion.

When he had served out his term of house arrest, he was invited to Versailles for a ball to be hosted by the queen, with my husband as the guest of honor. Once I had been the little girl the queen wanted to pick up and put in her *réticule*, and Gilbert was the stumbling dancer she had laughed at.

How different it was now . . .

For this occasion, I wore a *robe à la française* of cerulean blue floral brocade so brightly colored it scarcely needed ornamentation. Nevertheless, all the women of Noailles wore diamonds, because we were again ascendant. Lafayette led our entourage into the opera hall, where thousands of candles glittered and musicians took up a march composed for my husband. And the queen, all in ivory satin, tall plumed wig, and dazzling jewels, welcomed us with a smile. "My dear Lafayette. I should like to send a gift to General Washington, and desire your advice." Thereupon, she listed gifts she had made to other European sovereigns, including figurines, furniture, tapestries, and perfumes.

In reply, Gilbert pondered aloud. "Ah, but those gifts are too humble. Those are gifts for monarchs, whereas Washington is the defender of a free nation." Such a comment would have, in other times, given powerful offense, yet somehow Gilbert turned it into a clever jest. "For Washington, only the gift of an *armada* will do."

The queen laughed, and this time not in mockery. Even the king's chief advisor joined in the jest. "Young man, you are such a zealot, I fear you would strip the jewels from the queen's neck and sell every painting in Versailles to fund your Americans."

Again, the queen laughed. "Let us not make sport of our guest of honor, who shall soon be a colonel in command of a regiment of the King's Dragoons."

My hand tightened with excitement on my husband's arm. He had commanded a peasant army of yeoman farmers across the sea. To rise so high in rank in *France's* professional military was something entirely different. Something he dreamed of.

As the evening progressed from dances to toasts, coquettes giggled behind every fan, batting eyelashes at my husband and casting envious stares my way. Whereas once I had been the object of pity for having been saddled with an Auvergnat, I now caught fragments of whispered jealousy at my good fortune.

To my surprise, one of these whispering women was the doll-faced flirt Aglaé d'Hunolstein.

"Adrienne," she said, sidling up to me in a gown worn without fichu for modesty. "Your tales of how Lafayette conducted himself with distinction in America lifted the stain of his disobedience in going there. How proud you must be now that he has won universal approval!"

"I have always taken pride in him, even when no one else approved." It was a tart reply, but something about Aglaé provoked me. It was not merely that she was the mistress of Philippe, the duc de Chartres—for marital infidelity was so common I should have nary a friend if I condemned a person for that. It was, perhaps, my suspicion that she had conspired with her lover to embarrass Gilbert at the queen's quadrille all those years ago. I would set a better example now that we were in favor at court and Philippe decidedly was not. He had joined the navy looking for military glory, but his failure to follow orders from a superior officer had resulted in a costly defeat.

Still stinging, Philippe said, "Lafayette, your wife told me—and anyone who would listen—that you took a scratch in the Americas . . ."

"She seems to have made a legend of me," Gilbert said.

"I only told the truth, sir," I replied, and we shared a private smile.

"If I had known a bullet would improve your dancing," Philippe cut in with a sneer, "I would have put lead into your leg back in the day."

This taunt was meant to put my husband in his place, which had hitherto been beneath Philippe's boot. Yet Gilbert appeared to take no notice. He behaved as if he was now the man of greater stature, one who could afford to ignore such slights. And indeed, he *was*.

"MADAME," BENJAMIN FRANKLIN SAID, KISSING MY CHEEKS IN greeting, then again in flirtation. "You glow like the fertility of the New World. Dare I say, you are a founding mother of my country, though you have yet to set foot on American soil."

I considered this the most gratifying of compliments, for at nearly twenty years old and in the early months of a new pregnancy, I now stood as representative for my husband at a celebration to mark the anniversary of the Declaration of Independence, during which there was to be a public unveiling of Washington's portrait. But first, Franklin honored me with a little poem he read to his guests:

I've painted a picture for you of the hero, Lafayette;
Now I dare to sketch his charming helpmeet.
Imagine love, virtue, and kindness—
And the portrait is complete.

Of course, there was a more important portrait to reveal that day. "Will you do the honors, Madame la marquise?"

I grinned at Dr. Franklin; then, to the cheers of the assembled guests, I pulled the drape away to reveal a giant painting of George Washington. The great man cut a fine figure in buff and blue uniform, one hand holding a treaty of alliance with France, the discarded rulings of his tyrant beneath his boots.

What a fetching portrait! I knew Gilbert would adore it. However, I was struck by the incongruity of a dark-skinned servant depicted alongside the great man's horse, as I knew the man to be enslaved. Gilbert had promised this war would end slavery—that the Americans believed *all men were created equal.* Could not Washington lead by example in freeing the people he held in bondage? It was not, of course, the last time this question would come to mind, but it was difficult to broach the subject when the war was still unwon.

When next I saw Gilbert, he kissed me and put his hand upon my swelling belly. "You must not think me so ridiculous as to take anything but joy in this new child, whatever sex it might be, but if it would not trouble you too much, I will insist upon a boy."

"You will have to convince the babe . . . I fear he might be too shy to come out, given the burden of carrying your now-famous name."

Gilbert laughed, stooping to plant a kiss on my stomach. "Never fear, little one. I plan to carry the burden of my name for a while longer!"

In the coming months, this reassured me that whatever dangers Lafayette faced returning to battle in America, he meant to come back to me. Perhaps it reassured the little one too, because on Christmas Eve whilst I was visiting relations, out my son came into the world. A precious, perfect little boy who took us all by surprise.

Though it was much past midnight, I sent a messenger to deliver my cheeky note to Gilbert where he was meeting with Franklin. I teased that both America and France should mark the occasion of my son's birth with fireworks. I congratulated myself too for having brought another Lafayette into the world, which was surely a public service!

Gilbert came to me straightaway, and we spent the next week in celebration.

Our son would be named Georges Washington Lafayette.

After fetching her ear trumpet and pretending that she did not hear us the first time, Grand-mère made us repeat the name. Then she complained, "Highly irregular. Disrespectful to the family!"

Fortunately, the duc d'Ayen was so overjoyed at the birth of his long-awaited grandson that he bore the indignity, accepting at long last that my husband was his own master and could name his son as he pleased.

The only thing to darken our joy was a secret missive that came late in the week. "France is finally sending an expedition to America," Gilbert said, throwing the note into the fire.

From childbed, I reeled in confusion, for was this not the news for which he had hoped?

Gilbert put both hands on the mantel and hung his head. "I am being cut out. The king entrusts command to Rochambeau." It was a bitter disappointment. My husband had *earned* this command. He was the only Frenchman for whom there would be no conflict regarding rank when combining with the American army. The Americans had already followed him into battle. For the king to send someone else . . .

"At least . . ." I grasped for something to soothe stung pride. "Rochambeau is experienced; they have not promoted someone unworthy."

"True," Gilbert admitted.

"If you take offense—"

"If I take offense, it will be used as an excuse by the conservatives at court to abandon our hard-won alliance with America." Gilbert sat on the edge of my bed and reached for me. "You see? I have learned something of court politics from you. You are going to say I can help the cause or I can have my pride, but not both."

I nodded. "So which will it be?" Some traitorous part of me wished for him to choose pride and turn away further adventures. Stay here, with his children and me. He had already made his name; did he need to risk himself again?

"I choose the cause," Gilbert said quietly. This was not, after all, the same bristling boy who once insulted the king's brother. "I will congratulate Rochambeau."

I sighed because his willingness to set aside his pride made me love him more. Yet the thought of parting with him again made me so sad I could not let him look into my eyes for fear he would find my sentiments unworthy.

At least this time he would not go alone. France would be with him this time, and my brother-in-law, Marc, too. In March, my husband kissed me and our children farewell. My last sight of him was in his proud American uniform of buff and blue, with its gold buttons and braids. He also wore a white satin sash in honor of our king and the royal house.

To keep up his courage and my dignity, I must not cry, I told myself. Not even when he lifted my chin for a kiss and said, "Adrienne, I love you more than I thought any man capable, and leaving you costs me dearly. Farewell, farewell, my dear heart! The war will be won and I will be with you again by Georges's first birthday."

I managed a brave smile, praying fervently that I would see my husband alive again.

FIFTEEN

BEATRICE
Paris
May 1, 1915

I COULDN'T POSSIBLY FACE MY HUSBAND WITHOUT A NEW HAT.

Shopping the windows on the Champs-Élysées, I spied one in romantic Irish lace that whispered: *Remember how much you once loved me?* A sleek straw panama announced: *I've commenced a new life without you, giving no thought to our past.* But it was the expensive tricorne revival with iridescent pheasant feathers that spoke of my newfound spirit of independence, and that was beyond value.

Especially in light of my husband's cloak-and-dagger note to meet him at noon and to come alone. I could think of no reason Willie would demand to see me alone if it wasn't to scold me and command me back across the ocean. Well, I wasn't going to permit him to be an imperious king. In a marriage such as ours, he hadn't the right. So I paid the extortionist price to the French milliner, clapped the tricorne atop my head, and set out, singing, "*Yankee Doodle dandy.*"

Before the war, the opulent restaurant, with its art nouveau panels, was meant for midnight debauchery. Now my afternoon appearance caused a sensation. I'd hoped the shimmering silk of my dark blue tea gown would remind my husband that he'd married a woman with a *spark* not even his neglect could snuff out, and as I sashayed to the table, an admiring white-aproned waiter nearly dropped a bucket of champagne over the iron rail, while other gentlemen stood in tribute.

Except, of course, for the one man who ought to have.

My husband sat stubbornly puffing a cigar, making not even the most cursory attempt to rise in greeting. It was an appalling breach of protocol meant to either convey fury or embarrass me. Fortunately, this wasn't the

Ritz, where estranged spouses lunched to keep up appearances; no one expected conjugal regard *here*.

Willie was impeccably groomed, graying hair slicked back. He gave off an aura of cool indifference, though his gaze was hot with aggravation. Well, he wasn't the only one.

I put a hand on my hip. "Aren't you going to invite me to sit?"

He blew a ring of smoke. "I wasn't aware you were waiting for invitation; it rather seemed as if, in coming into a war zone without my permission, you've taken it upon yourself to do as you please . . ."

Refusing to let him ruffle my new iridescent feathers, I slid into the bistro chair. "You left me little choice, darling; I could scarcely ask permission from a husband who doesn't answer my letters. But I don't intend to cherish this up against you! Oh, no, I've come in a spirit of goodwill."

He glowered over his starched collar, coat stretched tight over his still-athletic shoulders. "A spirit of folly, I say. Don't you realize the war is just thirty miles away?"

His pretense of husbandly concern seemed laughable and didn't deserve a serious reply. "What safer place could there be than at the side of my husband, a genuine war hero?"

This was, I admit, not very sporting. Given his age and recent injuries, his days as a sharpshooting rough-riding man of action were over, and I knew it nettled him not to be in the fight. Lunching with his wife while other men covered themselves in battlefield glory undoubtedly did not help his mood.

The waiter approached. "Another cognac, Mr. Chanler?"

Willie nodded. "The Furlaud label."

"Excellent choice, sir." The waiter smiled. "Champagne for the lady?"

I nodded. Iced champagne was the drink of choice here, and the only way I'd get through the afternoon would be to drink it by the bucket. Willie ordered for us, then set his cigar on the edge of the ashtray. "You look well, Beatrice. Have you done something with your hair?"

"I chopped it off." Cut in what would become the emerging flapper style, my bobbed hair made me feel lighter—more modern. "Do you like it?"

He paused a moment, then begrudgingly admitted, "Actually, I do."

Well, maybe this conversation was going to go better than I feared.

"The boys are well?" he asked. "I hope you're keeping them active; you've seen the state of the world. We've got to toughen them up if they're going to make their way in it."

"Since you didn't like the idea of leaving them on a windswept crag in the Roman tradition, I'm considering the Spartan example. Shall we send the boys out to murder Helots, or is there enough slaughter happening in the world now?" I removed my gloves as he glowered. "Now, tell me the point of the secrecy of our meeting. I know you and Jack Chapman don't always see eye to eye, but under the circumstances—"

"The Chapmans are going to beg me to get Victor out of the trenches."

"Of course they are."

Willie scowled. "Victor doesn't want the transfer and I can't convince him. My nephew is a grown man and I'm done meddling in his affairs." Just then, steaming bowls of soup came to the table—*printanier* with green leeks, peas, and parsley pureed in a broth, thickened with egg yolk. Given the food shortages, it was the best that could be had.

"They took Olympian, you know," Willie said.

Oh, not Olympian. Willie loved that racehorse, and I did too. We bought the chestnut stallion on the very same day I learned I was pregnant with Ashley all those years ago. We were so happy then that the two occasions were now linked forever in my sentiments. "I'd heard the French were impressing horses," I murmured. "It hadn't occurred to me they'd take Thoroughbreds for the cavalry."

My husband stared at the trail of smoke from his neglected cigar. "Cavalry is proving to be damned useless against artillery fire. They need horses to pull ambulances and mounted guns."

There seemed something tragic about a pampered horse like Olympian being seized by strangers, yoked to a wagon, and forced to slog through mud amidst gunfire. Not that beautiful young men who were born for better things weren't dying in those muddy trenches too. My God, the horrifying waste of it all!

"Willie, your sister is beside herself with worry. Take her to dinner and say something soothing."

"What could I possibly say?"

"At least help arrange a visit with Victor. They've come all this way to see him. Isn't there someone you can—"

"I've already called in all the favors I can. Besides, this unexpected visit of yours is damnable timing, because I'm leaving for Switzerland in the morning."

I stared, confused, as the waiter poured champagne into my flute. "Why are you going to Switzerland?" The rich and famous extolled the amusements of Swiss resorts in peacetime, but this was war. "Now's not the time to enjoy an Alpine spa!"

Willie dug into his soup. "I'm going to get back in fighting trim. The operation on my leg last year took a toll. There's a clinic in Switzerland where I can get my strength back. Roman soldiers used to take the sun cure there and soak in sulfur baths."

"Willie. You're almost fifty years old."

"Forty-eight. There are men my age in the fight."

Men desperate to defend their own homes, I thought. *Not aging adventurers.* "At least see your family before you go!"

His voice was flat, his expression pugnacious. "The trip can't be postponed. The doctor at the clinic is a specialist and in demand."

There was no sense in trying to talk him out of it. When, five years before, he'd insisted on riding off into the desert to fight alongside burnoose-clad tribesmen in Africa, I'd asked that he consider his obligations. His response had been to sign over most of his assets to me and the boys in trust. In the end, Willie always did what Willie wanted to do. And it was about time I started following his example, so now I lifted my champagne glass as if in toast. "I'm happy you're on the road to recovery. Among other things, it means we're both now prepared to talk of serious matters."

"You need more money?"

"No . . ." I screwed up my courage. "Willie, last time I was in Paris, you found every possible way to show your intense dissatisfaction at having me and the boys near. You don't seem any happier to see me now. One wearies of disciplines, even if they're the best medicine. I decided last winter that when a man didn't need his family in sickness, he most certainly didn't need them in days of health and—"

"You have it wrong."

I had it exactly right. If he couldn't make time to see his nephew—a boy facing death in the trenches—he'd never find time for his wife and sons. If he couldn't commit, here and now, to making a go of this marriage, then it couldn't be saved. "Please. Let's be true to ourselves. We're both old and wise."

He drained his glass and set it back down again with a peevish thump. "Then don't make assumptions like a child."

"All of this I say without rancor! You know I'm devoted to you. There's nothing I wouldn't do for you, now or ever. And I've never judged you harshly—be sure of that. I've always hoped you were happy in your easily attained freedom. I *want* you to be happy, but as our marital ties make my presence in the same country or city disagreeable—perhaps it would be better to sever them."

I hadn't intended to put it that baldly. In fact, I hadn't been entirely sure I'd say it at all, and now I half dreaded he'd agree. For months now, I'd been swatting down every rising notion of what it would be like to live a life without being married to Willie—what divorce might mean for the boys, for my work, for my heart. Telling myself that with millions of families being shattered in the midst of a war, I dared not consider breaking mine. But now, pushed to the edge, my thoughts had become words spoken aloud, and it was almost gratifying when Willie blanched as if I'd stuck him with a hot poker.

His horror was absolute. "Are you suggesting a divorce?"

My heart caught with hope. Was he about to reach for my hands, tell me that he loved me, and beg a thousand pardons?

No. Instead, he barked, "Who is he?"

"Who?"

"The other man in your life."

"Besides our sons or the forty thousand soldiers I've sent parcels to?" It was either quip or cry. I'd been fending off lechers from the age of nine and more serious suitors since the age of sixteen; it offended me to think he suspected me capable of succumbing now. "There isn't any other man in the picture."

Willie snorted. "Why else would you need a divorce? I pay your upkeep. I let you do as you please. What could possibly make you risk all that unless some man is promising more?"

Sometimes my husband was a worldly sophisticate and other times he was positively *obtuse*. "Do you think so little of me? Perhaps you'd raise no objection against a discreet extramarital adventure on my part, yet surely divorce is a more honorable course . . ."

Amongst the Chanler brothers, errant wives running off with lovers had become an epidemic. I'd had a front-row seat to the family's private heartbreaks and public humiliations; I didn't wish to subject Willie to such a thing, no matter how richly he deserved it. So I sipped my champagne, fighting tears. "I fear we must accept that our marriage is a failure and—"

"There's nothing wrong with our marriage."

He couldn't believe that, could he? "Willie, we've spent more than five years apart!"

"What's that got to do with the price of tea in China?" He motioned to the waiter to bring him another drink. "You knew who I was when you married me."

How torn I felt between arguing and agreeing. Ours wasn't, after all, an arranged marriage, and I hadn't been a child-bride. I'd known that ours wouldn't be the most conventional sort of marriage, but love made any sacrifice seem worth it. Until Willie, I'd always fought my way through life on my own. But for a few happy years he'd fought for me— and *with* me. When did all that change?

Now he glanced up from his cold soup. "How many years did your precious Lafayette spend away from his wife, do you think?"

At this comparison I almost spit my champagne. "So modest! Why not ask how often Caesar was absent from Calpurnia?"

"You've forgotten the good times."

I sighed. "Marriage should be made of more good times than bad."

"By God, ours *has* been!"

Was that true? I remembered sun-drenched summers yachting off the coast of Spain. Amber-leafed autumn escapades, riding horses and picking apples. Glittering winter parties with politicians at Tammany Hall. Springtime in the South of France to visit his ocher mines. Life with Willie had never been dull for a moment; but one couldn't sustain marriage on moments so few and far between.

The salmon arrived and Willie didn't even pick up his fork. "Have you considered your reputation—the scandal of a divorce?"

My heart ached that scandal was all he seemed to care about. "Times have changed."

"Not as much as you believe." His mouth curved with a touch of callousness. "Society may forgive one divorce, but they won't forgive two."

He'd never done that before. Never raised the specter of my long-forgotten first marriage. I'd been young—a chorus girl blinded by a handsome lead actor. I'd been honest with Willie about it from the start, and he'd said he had no use for virgin brides. He'd promised to erase every other man from my memory, and he'd done it too. So much so that I'd quite nearly convinced myself my first marriage had happened to someone else.

Now he'd shattered my delusion, and I wanted to throw my drink in his face. As if daring me to do it, he went on. "My family doesn't know everything about your past, and what they do know they've forgotten. I made sure everyone else in society forgot it too. A divorce will dredge it up."

"You could stop the gossip for the sake of your children, if you cared to."

"Wishful thinking." He leaned back in his chair, smug. "My sisters tell me it's notoriously difficult to find proper seating arrangements for ex-spouses at social functions. If a hostess must choose between my ex-wife and one of my many Astor family relations, whom do you think they'll invite? Perhaps you've spent so many years at the top where I put you that you've forgotten what it's like to be at the bottom."

The bottom where I'd started, he meant.

No amount of fame or money had made me respectable. Only his name had done that. Even at the height of my celebrity on the stage, flush with cash, I couldn't buy a new house without the town forming a committee to keep me out, saying they didn't wish their neighborhood to be soiled by an actress and divorcée. It was only when I tearfully explained that I was soon to marry *William Astor Chanler* that they relented.

Willie made everyone in that neighborhood pay for their small-mindedness. For years afterward, he rubbed their faces in it, throwing lavish parties for members of the playhouse, forcing snooty society matrons to mingle with my theater friends. I'd loved him for that. Still, it had also been a harsh lesson that no success of my own—no accomplishment, honor, or merit—would ever open as many doors for me as Willie's name.

I knew that if I divorced him, all those doors might slam shut again, but he was breaking my heart. "Even a scandal would be better than continuing this way."

Willie lowered his voice to condescension. "My dear, I'm afraid it simply would not be in your best interests to divorce me at this time."

"Don't ruin my ridiculous faith in your good character," I warned. "You know the boys are best off with me. Moreover, I shall take steps to economize so that you will not resent a divorce agreement."

He waved this away. "Perhaps, in a short time, you'll find that things have changed such that no agreement shall be necessary."

I hadn't the faintest idea what he was hinting at.

He leaned forward. "Be a good girl and do as I say. Go home and content yourself with motherhood, theater projects, and charity dances. If you begin divorce proceedings, I shall contest it."

Never mind throwing a drink in his face; now I had the urge to dump the whole bucket of iced champagne over his head. He wouldn't give me a divorce and yet also wanted me gone? Well, I wasn't budging. "I'm staying in Paris until summer. Someone has to help the Chapmans see Victor. And I have work to do for the war besides."

"I'm sure the war effort can do without tea service at the hospital."

So he was keeping tabs on me and mocking my efforts. Since there was no point in explaining the work we were doing with Marie-Louise LeVerrier and Clara Simon to house refugees and get supplies to the front lines, I drained my champagne, then stood. "Do you know something,

Willie? It would serve you right if there was another man. I could bat my eyelashes and have my pick. American industrialists, British noblemen, French artists. Maybe one of each!"

Only slightly chastened, Willie began, "Listen, I'm going to Switzerland, and then—"

"You can go to hell for all I care."

With that, I stormed away from the table.

And he did not follow.

SIXTEEN

MARTHE
Chavaniac-Lafayette
September 1941

I'M WAITING FOR THE BARONESS DE LAGRANGE, PACING BACK AND forth on the parquet wood floors of the blue salon—part of the suite of rooms that were once Adrienne Lafayette's apartments. The tapestried wall panels, drawings of songbirds, and furnishings of the castle aren't thought to be original, but the restored crystal chandelier and gilt-edged upholstered chairs evoke the Louis XVI style of Adrienne's day. It was the baroness's idea to move her bust up here from the museum room, and as she sweeps in, she says, "I think *La Femme Lafayette* is more at home now, don't you?"

What I think is that a few months in America has done wonders for the baroness's vitality, and she's not so severe-looking with a little plumpness in her cheeks. "I can do better now," I say, more critical of my sculpture than ever. "I could carve a life-sized bust of Adrienne, maybe even in marble . . ."

"Hmm," replies the baroness, a sign she's unsure of my artistic abilities and worried about the expense. "Yes, well, I'll think on it. In the meantime, I'm looking forward to your sketches. We have a lot of walls in this chateau to decorate."

I unveil my best work so far—la femme Lafayette in a series of maternal tableaus, each in lifelike dishabille. Adrienne staring bleakly into the middle distance after her long-absent husband. Adrienne's hair falling in ringlets as she stoops over a cradle, dark eyes lit with faith. Adrienne's anguish over a child in her arms as death separates them forever. It's this last that makes the baroness cover her mouth. "Oh, Marthe . . ."

She looks so distressed that I worry she doesn't like it, and I begin to babble. "I thought . . . I hoped . . . given Vichy's emphasis on motherhood and Catholicism, this might strike the right note." As her silence stretches on, I realize that whatever the reason I started these sketches of Adrienne, they mean something to me now, and my stomach hollows out in anticipation of the baroness's disappointment.

Then she says, "I expected inspiration, but it's a reflection. As if Adrienne could be almost any woman in France today . . ."

"I'm sorry—I—"

"Don't apologize. I think you've captured the truth of the matter. That those who came before us weren't so different. It just serves certain ends to pretend they were. This is marvelous work. A real leap forward for you, Marthe."

Heaving a sigh of relief, I try to brush off the praise, even though this is more attention than I've had for my art since the showing at the castle more than a year ago. *Who were those people at that party?* I suddenly wonder. When I think of that night—jazz, champagne, pastry puffs, Henri's jacket around my shoulders—I don't recognize anyone. Least of all myself. How could so many people—a nation, even—change so much? One night, we were dancing under crystal chandeliers, dreaming of a future. Now we're all afraid of the past.

As proud as I am of the sketches I've shown the baroness, I'm not brave enough to show her my sketch of Voltaire kneeling at Adrienne Lafayette's feet, because it's just the sort of truth we're trying to bury: that however much she might have been like any woman in France—grieving, lonely, trying to find faith—Lafayette's wife was, in her way, a Revolutionary too.

"We'll frame these and put them up in the entryway," the baroness says with satisfaction. "Beatrice would be so very proud . . . I had the chance to see her briefly in New York for my daughter's wedding, you know. Unfortunately, she's landed herself in the hospital with a flare-up of an old medical condition; she's worked herself nearly half to death reviving the old Committee of Mercy to send assistance to France and wants us all to know how it pains her not to be with us in these trying times . . ."

I swallow, unable to imagine a woman as vibrant as Madame Beatrice in a hospital bed. "She'll be all right, won't she?"

"With some rest—if they can get her to rest."

"I've been wanting to write her," I say, remembering those precious airmail sheets Madame Simon offered. "But . . . well . . . I want to talk to you first."

The baroness eyes me with a faint whiff of impatience—she always has so many things to do—but curiosity gets the better of her, and she sits on a damasked sofa, crosses her legs, and pats the seat beside her.

I take the invitation to sit. "I've recently learned Madame Beatrice found me when I was a child."

The baroness nods. "Beatrice brought you to us, anyway. A dreadful winter in the midst of the last war. Nary a chunk of coal to be had, and we were hoping for a Christmas truce."

Screwing up my courage, I show her my file. "I've always been told that no one knew who my parents were, but this record lists my mother's name."

She leans over to look, and then I'm sure I see a flicker of recognition in her eyes. "How curious . . ."

My excitement is palpable. "Did you know my mother? Do you know Minerva Furlaud?"

She seems to hesitate, and my fingers tingle with anticipation, but in the end, she says, "I'm afraid not."

The disappointment is crushing. "You're *sure*?"

"I'm sure I don't know anyone by that name."

"But it seemed—well, it seemed as if this brought back a memory. Maybe even a sad one."

The baroness wraps her arms around herself. "Oh, I'm reminded of that year. How I was pregnant with Anna while nursing soldiers near the front, how the bombs kept falling and I wondered what kind of mother I was to bring a child into such a world. The things I risked in that war . . . it makes me sad that it was all for nothing."

I don't know what she risked in that war, but I want to tell her it wasn't for nothing. I've been taught to thank the men who fought in that war, but I'm starting to realize how many women I have to thank too.

Because of them, my generation grew up in peacetime, as free French people. That's worth something, isn't it?

I try to find the words to say so, but we're interrupted quite suddenly when the door flings open and Madame Simon bursts in, followed closely by the baron, his wingtips shiny in the afternoon light. And at the abrupt intrusion, the baroness stands. "What on earth?"

Madame Simon gives a furious toss of her head and throws the latest copy of *Au Pilori* onto the table. "Your husband has been reading this filthy rag and has suggested I take an extended vacation. Is this your idea?"

The baroness looks taken aback. "Of course not." Then she glances at her husband, unable to hide her aggravation. "But it may not be the worst idea, under the circumstances, Clara."

I shouldn't be here for this, I think. *Whatever* this *is*. I wonder if I can sneak out, but the baroness is blocking one path and her husband is blocking the other. There's nothing to do but fold my hands and sit quietly as the baron's baritone fills the room. "As I was explaining to Madame Simon, certain reports have been sent to Vichy. I was warned by the authorities, and I fear her presence at this institution just now endangers our work."

Madame Simon removes her cat-eye glasses like she's ready for a fight. "The decrees against Jews don't apply to me. I have only two Jewish grandparents. What's more, I was decorated for good service to France in the last war."

"It's ridiculous, of course," says the baroness, her lips pinched. "It goes without saying you shouldn't be put through this."

Madame Simon isn't mollified. "No one should be put through this. And you're right. It goes without saying. That's the problem. The Statut des Juifs is disgusting, and people like you should say so."

"Then I'm saying so," replies the baroness evenly. "Unfortunately, that doesn't change anything. If you go away a few months, the miscreant denouncing you will find someone else to torment. You can stay in our house in Cannes in the meantime. Can't she, darling."

Nothing about her tone suggests that it's a question.

"I'd rather dispense with the fiction of a vacation," Madame Simon says, apparently unmoved by the offer. "I'll tender my resignation, effective immediately."

I inhale sharply.

"Clara," the baroness pleads, reaching for her friend. "Let's not make hasty decisions we might regret."

Madame Simon's voice is strained with so much emotion that an answering lump rises in my throat when she says, "I'm already filled with regrets. How can I stay when your husband would cast me aside after *two decades* of dedication to the Lafayette Memorial?" We all look at the baron, expecting him to deny it. When he doesn't, Madame Simon straightens to her full height. "In light of my long service, I expect either a pension or final compensation in the amount of sixty thousand francs."

The baroness looks heartbroken. "Of course, we can advance the money out of the accounts—"

"I'm not sure we *can* advance the money," her husband interrupts, arms folded, lips thin beneath his mustache. "Certainly not all at once, and probably not until the New Year. Upon our return from America, I reviewed the accounts and found discrepancies. I have to ask, madame, have you taken money from the discretionary cash?"

If it's possible to actually *feel* the blood drain from one's face, I do. And the baroness snaps her husband's name, plainly horrified by the accusation. "Amaury!"

Meanwhile, Madame Simon lets out a bitter laugh. "How disappointing. Someone denounces me as a Jew and your first thought is to check the cashbox?"

The baron remains impassive. "I think only that money is missing and we're owed an explanation."

Madame Simon jabs at the baron's chest. "The only explanation you're owed is this: I took the money to send to my son-in-law in Paris. You cannot begrudge me in times such as these."

I don't know who is more stunned by these words. All three of us— me, the baron, and the baroness—act like we've taken a hammer to the head. "Oh, Clara," the baroness groans, sinking down into the sofa with her head in her hands. "What could you be thinking?"

I'm so shocked I don't even know what the baron is saying now.

Something about how, under the circumstances, they aren't obligated to pay her anything. I'm still standing there dazed after Madame Simon has stormed out, and the baroness murmurs, "Marthe, can we pick this up another day?"

I nod dumbly, taking my folder.

"I'm counting on your discretion about what you just overheard," she says.

I nod again, but the news of Madame Simon's dismissal is already all over the castle. It spreads like wildfire, leaping from tower to tower, when her assistant resigns in solidarity. The overseer of the boys' preventorium also throws her resignation onto the baron's desk. And Sam tells me Madame LeVerrier made such a fuss that the school might soon be without a doyenne.

The staff doesn't want to go to Anna's Wednesday-night billiards game, but it doesn't seem fair to take out our anger at the baron on his daughter. All Anna has ever done is made life livable around here, after all. If it weren't for her, my sketches of Adrienne would never hang in the entryway of the castle. Besides, sometimes I feel halfway smitten with Anna, so I go to keep her company, leaning against the billiards table as she confides, "This is all so unfair . . . everyone is furious with Papa because they think he fired Madame Simon for being a Jew, but he doesn't want to hurt her reputation by explaining she's a thief."

Is she a thief? Now that the shock has started to wear off, I'm thinking about all those times Madame Simon took money from the cashbox to send me or someone else to get supplies from the black market. And I'm starting to wonder . . .

Anna takes my silence for judgment. "The defeat has made people crazy, made them do things they would never otherwise do. I'm sure she'd never steal from the preventorium unless she was desperate."

I tell myself it's none of my business and that I need to remember the orphan's code . . . *Look out for me, myself, and I.* But in the end I go looking for Madame Simon at her stone house in the village. When she's not there, I go back to the castle and find her in the square tower, packing her office.

"I've been thinking about the black market," I say. "I'm not going to ask you who else you sent or how much you spent . . . but did you really take money for your son-in-law?"

Madame Simon stuffs her owl lighter into a crate. "I wish I did. He's been missing since May, when thousands of Jewish men were rounded up by French police in Paris."

My mouth goes dry. "I-I'm so sorry. I didn't know . . ."

"I told my daughter not to stay in Paris, but she didn't believe harm could come to good, respectable people. Now her husband will be put to hard labor in those camps. Or so the authorities say. In truth, I'm terrified it will be worse than that."

What does she believe we're doing to people in those camps? This summer, Churchill announced on the BBC, "*Scores of thousands of executions in cold blood are being perpetrated by the German police troops upon the Russian patriots . . . We are in the presence of a crime without a name.*" But that is Russia . . . this is France. "We should tell all this to the baroness," I say. "Remind her that extra sugar and medicines had to come from somewhere last winter!"

"Don't be foolish, Marthe. The baroness is sympathetic, but the last thing the baron wants to hear is that we've been breaking the law by trading on the black market while he's negotiating with the Vichy government for funding. He'll fire me, you, and everyone else involved."

I bite my lip. "He's that heartless?"

Her nostrils flare as if she wants to say *yes*. Then her shoulders sag. "No. Amaury de LaGrange is arrogant and prejudiced, but he wants to protect this institution. He's right to say my presence endangers the children in the preventorium."

"That's not true."

She says, very sternly, "It is. And I'm not going to let years of hard work go down the drain with me. This castle is too important."

I don't know about that—but I guess there's no point in my moaning about how unfair it all is if she's determined to keep a stiff upper lip, so I swallow, hugging my arms. "Where will you go?"

"To Lisbon, if my daughter will come with me and I can get travel papers. I used to edit a magazine, and now there's a need for someone to tell the world what's happening here in France in no uncertain terms."

I nod numbly, wishing I could go with her.

"But first, I must apologize to you, Marthe," Madame Simon says. "I was wrong to tell you we couldn't help that poor child you found at Madame Pinton's farm. If I'd done as you suggested, little Gabriella Kohn could be safely here now instead of begging medical treatment for the price of a cabbage. I made some inquiries—and as my last official act, I'm going to admit her to the preventorium under a different name, as you suggested. I've already talked to Dr. Boulagnon and Dr. Anglade, and they've agreed to go along, but I dared not involve my successor. She's not likely to overlook missing paperwork, and it wouldn't be fair to ask her to do so. That's where you come in."

"Me?"

"I wish you weren't in this position, but as Madame LeVerrier likes to say, you couldn't have grown up here without the *certainty* that goodness exists and must be defended. So I have to ask it of you . . . if I provide the forms, can you create falsified documents like these?"

She shows me examples of school certificates and other related paperwork. And before I know it, I'm considering it. Filling out the certificates for vaccinations would be easy. Even the letterheads could be mimicked. The tricky part would be the official blue stamp bearing the words *Etat Français*, surrounded by the seal of the town mayor, *but with the right brush and ink . . .*

I should take some time to think about it, but I don't. "I can do it." I'm a better artist than I was two years ago, and I just have to slip these under the nose of whatever overworked, overwhelmed old secretary they hire to replace Madame Simon. "I know I can."

She nods with a fond smile. "Good. Now, we need a false surname for this little Jewish girl . . . something French, something common . . ."

The only inspiration we have is a picture of the castle back when it was white. Henri used to say it was a pretty fortress even then. "What about Beaufort?"

Madame Simon nods. "That will do. Now, I need to ask two more things of you. First, you must promise me that once I'm gone, you won't do anything to get yourself fired. After all, you'll be the only person at the preventorium who knows the real identity of Gabriella Kohn, and you need to take responsibility for her and make sure she gets back to her family when she's cured and released."

I take a deep breath, not really wanting to agree, not wanting responsibility for anybody but myself, but in the end, I nod.

"Second, you must keep this between the two of us. If there's trouble, the only way to protect people is to keep them in the dark."

"I understand. I'll keep quiet."

"Absolutely *silent*, Marthe. You can't tell anyone. Especially not the baron's daughter."

I bristle as she zones in on precisely the one person I most want to tell. "I said I'd keep quiet . . . but why not Anna especially?"

"Because she's going to be my successor and the person you'll have to deceive."

SEVENTEEN

ADRIENNE
Paris
March 1781

THE AMERICAN WAR WAS GOING BADLY, AND I WAS IN NO MOOD TO hear the complaints of the financial agent appointed to manage my husband's finances until he came of age. "*Mon Dieu*, the deficit the marquis de Lafayette runs to equip his soldiers in America is impossibly large!"

"It does not matter." What price could I put on my husband's life and those he fought for? "We must find a way to raise money if the king won't give more."

By necessity, what a merchant I became! I worked with the manager to sell land, collect rents, and find new ways to manage the estates. I was desperately inventive. I could not fight beside Gilbert on a field or carry pitchers of water to his thirsty cannoneers. I could not cook for his soldiers, or tend them in camp in the way of Martha Washington. I could do only *this*, but would it be enough?

In the midst of these worries, I received a letter from my husband.

My dear heart, I am very fond of the man who gives you this message, and wish you to become good friends. He will inform you of what has happened in America, where we republicans rely on the people, our only rulers, to provide aid and comfort in the war.

The man in question was Lieutenant Colonel John Laurens, aide-de-camp to General Washington. This young, soldierly South Carolinian gentleman had been sent by his government to assist the aging

Dr. Franklin, and now he drawled, "Madame Lafayette, what an honor to make your acquaintance."

I returned his greeting in English, and then, with a gallant bow, the American officer explained in French, "It's been a dreadful slog for Lafayette—for all of us. The French fleet is stranded in Rhode Island. We don't know when, or if, the enemy will attack. So your husband bids me to tell you he has been in little danger." I exhaled deeply with relief, and Laurens smiled. "Of course, he also bade me to tell you that he loves you, and to tell you this so often that you will find me tedious . . ."

I laughed. "Oh, I shall never tire of hearing it, sir!"

I invited Laurens for dinner, where he charmed the women of my family—even Anastasie, for whom he drew little pictures of New World songbirds. And Laurens gave us all pleasure when he said, "Lafayette is an essential ingredient to nearly every success we've had against the British. He is, even now, chasing the traitor Benedict Arnold."

An important, if inglorious, assignment.

Laurens, meanwhile, had come as a special envoy with a sobering message—that if France did not send more money, ships, and supplies, the Americans would not only lose their independence, but also be pressed into service on British ships that would ultimately attack France.

"We would have no one but ourselves to blame," I said.

When Gilbert went to America the first time, it was without the king's permission, and if he'd died there, the fault would have been his own. But this time he'd gone at the king's command with other Frenchmen who *deserved* the support of the nation. Whatever debts we might take on now would still be better than the cost of losing this war. My country could not commit to a fight with half measures—we had provoked the British king, and if he emerged victorious, he would visit upon us the worst retaliations. I believed anyone of sense could see this. But would our king?

Laurens needed the ear of important men at court, so I took it upon myself to introduce him into French society. At social functions, Laurens surprised me by speaking openly and with passion about the enslaved persons on his family plantation. "These trampled people are unjustly deprived of liberty and subjected to constant humiliations; they can aspire to a noble existence if only some friend of mankind would open a path for them. Which I am determined to do."

To be a friend of mankind. Could there be a higher aspiration? With renewed determination, I went with him to Versailles—in fact, I was so often in the company of Americans that Dr. Franklin jested I was part of their delegation. I too felt frustrated by the diplomatic roadblocks. Lesser officials told us France could send no more help; the treasury vaults were closed. What folly!

One morning in May as Laurens and I strolled the gardens, discussing strategy, I spotted the foreign minister, quite unaccompanied by his usual retinue. "There is our chance," I said as the minister walked by at a fast clip. "Pray hurry to catch him before he goes into the palace."

Laurens, who apprehended the opportunity, *sprinted* after the minister. I didn't follow, for I would have had to run to keep pace. And because my presence might inhibit the conversation, I lingered in the shade, watching the two men at a distance, until I realized the conversation had taken a decidedly hostile turn. Inching closer, I heard Laurens shout, "If you cannot send aid now, you will condemn liberty itself to death!"

The foreign minister replied testily, "Young man, the sun has addled your senses and made you forget who is friend or foe. Dr. Franklin would remember to whom he is speaking."

"Dr. Franklin has not set foot on the battlefields," Laurens shot back. "I have. The war will end in ignominious defeat for both our nations if—"

"*Young man,*" the minister barked, "you are not on a battlefield now and I am not your junior officer. The king of France has been more than charitable to the cause of your wretched colonies."

On the word *wretched,* Laurens bristled, and I was shocked to see his hand go to his sword. "Not even a minister to the king of France should expect to impugn the honor of my nation in my presence without consequence, sir."

Mon Dieu. What could Laurens be thinking? If he drew that sword, I could not contemplate the catastrophe. The incident would go round the world. "Gentlemen!" I cried, rushing to them with feigned gaiety. "Can you believe this unseasonably oppressive heat?"

Both men, red-faced and furious, stepped back from each other. Laurens let his hand drop from his sword, but then, with a curt bow, he snapped at the minister, "It is not charity that France has given, but an alliance that benefits both partners. Tell the king to expect me. I will take my words directly to him."

The foreign minister was no messenger boy and knew the American officer would never be received by the king. A thing I explained to Laurens as we retreated. "Monsieur, that was folly!"

"Forgive me, madame, but folly is all we have left. I did not wish to put you in fear. Yet you must understand, the British will make a brutal example of all who stood up to them. My father will likely be hanged, and me beside him. As it is, your husband's soldiers are on the verge of mutiny, and every British sharpshooter thinks Lafayette is a prize buck to be mounted on a wall. To stave off tragedy, I *need* to speak to the king."

Having a fuller measure of the danger, I decided folly *was* the order of the day. "The king will never grant you an audience, but there might be another way . . ."

Mine was an imprudent scheme, and only a bold and defiant man would attempt it. Fortunately, John Laurens was that man. The next day, at the king's levee, Laurens wove his way to the front of the crowd. Then, just as the king prepared to make his way to the Hall of Mirrors, Laurens did as I suggested, sliding directly in the sovereign's path, delivering a sealed envelope into the royal hand. This was so unexpected, so breathtakingly improper, that no one said a word. Everyone—even the guards—stood in shock. The king himself didn't seem to know what to do, simply tucking the envelope into his coat pocket before moving on.

A complete breach of etiquette, Aunt Claude screeched when she heard. I myself predicted His Majesty would probably throw the message in the fire, yet the next day, Laurens was summoned to the palace. I waited for news, pacing near the card tables. Would Laurens be censured and banished? Would the Franco-American alliance itself be ruptured? Anything seemed possible, and I would be to blame if it went wrong.

What business had I in inserting myself when lives were at stake?

It seemed like hours before the South Carolinian appeared, striding down the gallery, his face beaming with triumph. He had secured guns, money, ships, and more. And I was so happy that if I were not Lafayette's wife, I would have kissed Laurens, and the king too.

IN THE AUTUMN OF 1782, CHURCH BELLS RANG TO CELEBRATE THE victory at Yorktown. Victory for the French and American allies. Victory for my husband. Upon hearing this, I fell to my knees. *Pray God, let it be the end. Let Gilbert come home.*

Some complained that my husband might've taken more glory for France if he had not insisted that the final battles be led by the Americans. Yet he had known that a free people must have the greater part in liberating themselves. I swelled with true admiration that in the most decisive moments of the war, still young and wishing to prove himself, my lionhearted husband set aside his pride for the good of the cause. And he'd won!

The whole world, I was sure, must change now. Certainly, Paris did. The city was scrubbed clean from muddy street to sooty chimney for the swirl of social occasions, thanksgivings, and galas that continued from crisp autumn into the glitter of icy winter. To celebrate the long-awaited birth of the dauphin, the king and queen opened an opera house in Paris. We now had an heir to the throne, and six thousand guests came to see the debut of Piccinni's *Adèle de Ponthieu* while bottles of wine and baskets of fresh warm loaves were passed to peasants in the streets. Now there was to be a costumed ball at the Hôtel de Ville, and Maman reminded my sisters and me, "Don't forget your masks!" We Noailles ladies were rouged, powdered, feathered, our feet aching in satin shoes because it had already been a very long day. We had already seen the queen purified in Notre-Dame. A banquet had followed, after which we raced home in our carriages to dress for the evening entertainment, which would include a show of illuminations over the Seine.

"*Mon Dieu*, is it possible to have too much gaiety?" I asked wearily, having lain awake half the night with my little Georges, who was teething. Grand-mère always advised that we let him cry, but having lost a daughter, I would never complain over losing sleep for my babies.

Thanks to the queen's discouragement of elaborate poufs and panniers of old, we fit more than one lady in a carriage, and as my sister Louise and I traversed the city in our gilded coach, every building we passed was lit up. A pavilion had been erected for the common citizens to dance, and the royal fete for nobles was even grander.

Never before had I seen the king and queen so happy. King Louis worked the words *my son* into every conversation. The queen, long criticized for failing in her wifely duties, basked in her success. But while I, quite exhausted after so long a day—after so long a war—stared fondly at the queen, I realized everyone was staring at me. A murmur passed like a tray of champagne, excitement following in its wake.

"Lafayette has returned!"

Could it be true? I swayed on my heels as a cheer went up and my sister Louise rushed to embrace me. "Gilbert has gone to the Hôtel de Noailles. He hurried home only to find no one there!"

I sputtered with laughter. After five years of war, my husband and I were in the same city again. Yet still we were apart! I wished to run to him. I wished to sprout wings and *fly*. Alas, none of us could leave before the royals. Sympathetic glances told me the guests understood my difficulty. So too did the queen. Summoning me, Marie Antoinette said, "Go to your husband. Our joy should not keep you from your hero so long absent."

For this gracious gesture, I forgave everything. Her cruel laughter and frivolity—these were the larks of children. We were both women and mothers now, and I wanted, with all my grateful heart, to accept the queen's kindness. Unfortunately, now more than ever, I felt it was important to be worthy of the prominence to which my family had risen. "I would not wish to miss a moment of our national celebration, but if Your Majesties would see fit to stop in front of the Hôtel de Noailles on your return so that my husband might pay respects, I would consider it a great favor."

"Of course!" said the queen. "In fact, you shall ride with me at the head of the procession. It is my wish and command."

I had no right to ride ahead of those much above me in rank, but I said, "Then it is my honor to obey." What a torment it was, every farewell that evening, every last spark of fireworks. Each moment an eternity. As grateful as I was to ride beside the queen in her carriage, the wheels simply could not turn swiftly enough. As the horses clopped down the Rue Saint-Honoré, I saw a crowd gathered at our gates, and when our carriage came to a stop, a tall figure in uniform emerged.

Gilbert! I was blinded by tears. It was everything I could do not to leap out of the carriage. I sat upon my hands, trembling with the effort at self-control until, after the heartfelt meeting of the queen of France and the nation's returning hero, she said, "Go embrace your wife."

A moment later, the carriage door on my side flew open, and there he was. Somehow, impossibly, more dashing and elegant—holding his hand out to me. It had been nearly two years since I'd seen my husband last. Two years of letters. Two years of loneliness and fear. And when I took his hand to exit the coach, our eyes met and a thousand unspoken words passed between us. He had returned to me before in the cloak of darkness, in the privacy of our rooms. This time, all the world was watching, and I understood somehow that he was no longer mine. At least not mine alone.

He belonged to the world.

Thinking this, my step faltered—and I fell, for the first time in my life, into a swoon. Gilbert caught me round the waist, lifting me into his strong arms, cradling my head against his chest as he carried me into the house. And the last things I heard that night were the cheers of the crowd, and my husband's murmurs of love.

EIGHTEEN

BEATRICE
Paris
May 2, 1915

AMIDST BANDAGES AND BROMIDES AT THE AMERICAN HOSPITAL OF Paris, where Miss Sloane and I volunteered, a shockingly tall French officer in leather riding boots strode past the beds, and I recognized him at once as Lieutenant de LaGrange. He stopped before Miss Sloane and offered a bouquet, his hand actually trembling. He seemed, in that moment, so wonderstruck that one might think her white nurse's apron was the most dazzling beaded chiffon. For her part, poor Emily nearly swooned, having not expected her suitor's leave to come through for another two weeks.

They stared as if they'd never met before, which made a strange kind of sense. Miss Sloane was no longer a wealthy heiress on holiday, but an angel of mercy come to deliver relief to his beleaguered country. And LaGrange was no longer a forgettable French nobleman with a possible interest in her father's money, but now a seasoned veteran officer in dark blue coat and red pantaloons.

She blushed when he kissed her hand and held her fingers to his heart. The attraction between them sparked so hot that we were obliged to take some fresh air. Which is how I found myself strolling behind them on the nearby river walk, in the unlikely and entirely unsuitable role of chaperone.

I wondered how swiftly I might abandon my post as guardian of Miss Sloane's chastity, and whether or not she would notice. Since the disastrous luncheon in which I'd asked my husband for a divorce, I was in no mood for romance, even once removed. Thus, I'm afraid I was a little impatient when, on our way back to dress for the opera—which had recently been reopened in defiance of bomb-dropping zeppelins—Emily asked, "Isn't he wonderful?"

At my frown, her expression fell.

"Or am I imagining he's wonderful?" she asked. "Women do that. Women like my mother. They imagine all sorts of fine qualities in a man that don't exist. They lose all sense and become selfish and hurt people. I never want to be like that."

"You're nothing like that," I said, sorry for dampening her spirits. "Besides, your baron does seem rather wonderful."

The baron wasn't as wonderful as my nephew, of course, but he'd fought like a lion in the Battle of the Marne. He had the right to carry himself with a swagger, but he'd adopted an old-fashioned stiffness that bespoke duty and honor. And having spent the better part of his youth in America, where his father had owned a gold mine, he was a forward-thinking young man who listened intently to everything Emily had to say, seeming to treasure her intelligence above all.

Men like that weren't easy to come by.

Despite, or perhaps because of, my own bitterness, I said, "Every girl deserves a grand romance in Paris. Especially you."

My companion's voice softened. "But how can I entertain something so frivolous when so many people are in misery?"

"You won't make anything better by weaving your own misery into the collective shroud. If you find some tendril of happiness, then tug on it. Because a world without happiness isn't worth fighting for. You're worthy of love, Emily Sloane."

Her eyes were teary but grateful. "Oh, I shall be very put out if you turn me into a sentimental girl . . ."

"And I shall be very put out if you attend the opera this evening smelling like hospital liniment—which you do." I insisted we stop at a perfumery nestled on the Rue Saint-Honoré, between a chocolatier and the baroque Church of Saint-Roch, where, I pointed out, Lafayette's wife and family had worshipped; given that we'd named our charity after the man, we'd made a game of spouting historical trivia at the slightest provocation.

At the perfumer, I suggested something sultry, with notes of incense and orange blossom. Something I'd worn for Willie years ago. Without asking its price, Miss Sloane said, "I'll take it. I should also like something for Mrs. Chanler as a gift from me."

I smiled. "Is it my birthday and no one told me?"

She laughed. "You never tell anyone your birthday, so why not?" Well, she had me there. Still, she was too honest a young lady to keep up the ruse. "It *is* almost your birthday. I peeked at your passport."

"Thank goodness I lied on the application like I always do."

She laughed, thinking I was joking. "I want to give you a gift because—well, in spite of the fact that you are unrepentantly wicked, you are also, to me, like a . . ."

She struggled for a word, so I took her hand and said very sincerely, "Beware that if you say *mother*, I'll push you into the Seine."

"I was going to say a *sister*! Consider this a thank-you for agreeing to chaperone tonight."

"I have expensive taste," I warned.

"My father can afford it."

She was right about that, so what to choose? Certainly not the scent Willie enjoyed; that would remind me of him, and I was still furious. Whilst the perfumer was boxing up Emily's purchase, I found a lovely flacon of amber liquid with a heart-shaped stopper and golden tassel. Guerlain's L'Heure Bleue. One sniff and I was enchanted. A soft, mysterious glow of romance at dusk, with notes of powder and pastries. A sweet melancholy of flowers at twilight. In truth, it was like Paris just now—or all of France, really—pushed to the edge of night, but not surrendering to the darkness. And I wanted to bathe in it.

The Chapmans declined to join us at the opera, though Lieutenant de LaGrange tried to convince them. "We're fighting for our way of life. For our *joie de vivre*. The Boche want to steal everything from us, but we sing in defiance."

What a marvelous people, the French! To be able to take up the thread of life in the midst of death and desolation. Still, the Chapmans declined, perhaps because the young baron's gaze did not leave Miss Sloane's face for even a moment, and they feared to be interlopers. I feared it too, but Emily was too prim to venture out without a chaperone, and I never could resist an opera.

The opera house, with its gilded ceilings, murals, and embellished red velvet drapes, evoked an era of luxury well at odds with the untold number of wounded soldiers in the ornate balconies, some of the poor wretches missing eyes, arms, legs . . .

The performance was badly sung, but it was music, and we were hungry for it. Then came the militant French anthem dating back to the Revolution. The singer, Marthe Chenal, swept onto the stage in a white gown of antiquity—the skirt of which was cleverly made to fan out into the red, white, and blue of a Revolutionary cockade. I thought her rendition was not so good as others I'd heard before—I could've sung it better—but it was so heartfelt the audience was in tears and on its feet, even those who had to reach for crutches in order to rise.

After, the baron offered Miss Sloane his arm. "Won't you let me treat you ladies to some refreshments at the Café de la Paix before seeing you to your hotel?"

It was the rare café that had permission to be open at this hour, and I knew Emily wanted to go, for in the baron's presence, she was transported to the paradise reserved for lovers. This was, of course, a paradise from which I had been exiled, but I remembered it well enough to suspect my friend would receive a kiss if only I could absent myself. "I'm afraid, sir, that I wish to retire to write a letter home to my children. I entrust my companion into your care as a true gentleman."

Emily nearly squeaked in panic. "We couldn't leave you to find your way alone!"

"I'll hardly be alone with all these operagoers in the street." The performance had gone past ten, which meant the lights were snuffed and the underground shut down, and all of us were in the same predicament. "Besides, there's nearly a full moon, and it's less than a mile's walk."

Emily and her French lieutenant continued to protest, but I wouldn't hear it. Trailing after them was reminding me that I was loveless, and in any case, as a child I'd learned to make my own way in streets more dangerous than these. So I bade them good evening and let myself be swept away with the crowd.

The walk was at first a veritable fete, with everyone in high spirits, singing the "Marseillaise." After a few blocks, the crowd began to thin.

Still, I didn't regret my hubris until the moon disappeared behind a cloud, plunging the City of Light into stumbling darkness. Then I nearly wished for a zeppelin raid, if only to trigger the searchlights on the sky.

In pitch black, I groped blindly from doorway to doorway, sliding my hand across stone and brick and cold wrought iron. It was slow going, but the hotel could not be far. Just past the Church of Saint-Roch, then another long block. I crossed another wide-open expanse that must have been a boulevard, grateful not to hear the sound of any oncoming motor—for crashes happened nearly every night. I didn't know whether to be comforted or afraid by the sound of footsteps behind me—a man, I guessed, by the crisp confidence and the weight of the echo.

Glancing back the very moment a shimmer of moonlight escaped between the clouds, I caught a glint of a golden statue where it oughtn't have been. Had I gone too far or not far enough?

"Madame, are you lost?" The man's question startled me, coming as it did out of the darkness, and I stumbled. Usually so nimble on my feet, I flailed with one hand and went down hard on the other. The impact of hitting sidewalk reverberated through my bones, and as I struggled to catch my breath, he was upon me, begging leave to help.

You've done quite enough, I thought, uncharitably. I told him I could manage on my own. In my mind's eye, I could see world-wise Minnie, one hand on her hip, the other wagging a finger to warn me away. I knew better, after all, than to give myself over into the clutches of a perfect stranger. He might've been a cutpurse or worse. But when I tried to get up, a bolt of sharp pain in my hand made me cry out.

It wasn't only my pride that was hurt, and he knew it. "Will you let me see your hand, madame? It might be broken."

"You're a physician?" I asked.

"No, but I've seen broken bones before, and enough wounds at the front, so please allow me to reassure myself of your well-being."

The fickle moonlight peeped out to reveal the stranger's silhouette in pale light, and I breathed a sigh of relief. He was a soldier—an officer, by the looks of it. I nodded, and he helped me to a marble bench I hadn't known was there. *"Merci, monsieur."*

When he went to one knee, it felt churlish not to surrender my arm for examination. Gently, inch by inch, he pulled down my torn opera glove. My palm stung when he exposed it to the night air, and I couldn't bite back an audible little *ouch*.

"English or American?" he asked.

"American. And not usually so clumsy."

"The fault was mine," he said, turning my skinned palm up to the light. Little droplets of blood shone. His warm hands gingerly felt at the bones of my wrist, thumb, and fingertips. "I didn't mean to frighten you. It's only that you seemed to have lost your way."

The waxing moon played silver over the rooftops of the Louvre, confirming I had overshot my mark. "How did you guess?"

"Because there are no lodgings here, unless you meant to sleep on a bench in the Tuileries or throw yourself into the river."

"Well, the river does beckon . . ." It was a bleak jest, but because I didn't want him to take it earnestly, I hastened to add, "They say darkness makes other senses more vivid. If I'd relied more on my nose than my eyes—then I'd have known the Tuileries gardens by the scent of the flowers in bloom."

"That is not the garden, madame, but your enchanting perfume . . . topped with notes of anise and bergamot."

His precision surprised me. "You must be a perfumer when you're not soldiering."

"No, but my profession requires a refined nose."

"Does it require you to speak English?"

I saw the shadow of a smile as he cradled my injured hand in his own. "Sometimes. Fortunately, I spent time in Boston."

What a coincidence, I almost said. Instead, I smiled.

He smiled back. "No broken bones, I think, just a scrape to be tended."

"That's good." I started to rise, and he stilled me by producing a flask from the inside of his coat. I thought, at first, he meant to offer me a drink. Instead he poured some out onto his handkerchief. "This will sting."

I bit my lip so as not to hiss when he dabbed the cloth to my rent flesh, tenderly washing my palm, removing the grit of the street. The intimacy was unexpected. How long had it been since any man had touched me—much less in tenderness? How much longer still since anyone had taken care of me? I was an abandoned wife. A mother forever bandaging up little boys from their battles on the playground. I was the president of the Lafayette Fund, packaging up comfort kits for much older boys fighting in much more dangerous battles. Even before I was any of that, I'd learned not to trust strangers. And to let this man tend my wounds elicited a vulnerable silence I couldn't bear. "Don't use up your ration of soldier's wine on me."

He gave an indignant snort. "It's not that swill, it's *cognac*."

"Expensive medicine."

"The best, madame. My family's blend, beyond age."

"You're a distiller," I guessed.

He chuckled. "*Non.* A banker."

This made me sputter. "You—but you said your civilian profession required a refined nose."

"To sniff out good and bad investments." Our soft laughter drifted up into the moonlit sky. At length, he curled my fingers over the kerchief. "Here. You must keep this as a bandage until you can get one better."

Then he stood, and at the withdrawal of his touch, I felt strangely melancholy. "You're too gallant, sir."

"I am a Frenchman, no? Now, let me see you safely home."

"I couldn't trouble you further."

"It is no trouble. It is, after all, to defend my own honor. If I were to leave you alone and something should happen to you . . ."

"You'd be heartbroken?"

"Under suspicion! For the gendarmes would find you with my embroidered kerchief in your hand."

I laughed and took his arm. "For your honor, then."

I let him guide me through the scenic route, down the marble stairs, along the path by the basin, our way lined with the green aroma of lily of the valley. "Does it still hurt?" he asked.

"I can scarcely complain about a little scrape whilst soldiers brave bullets in trenches . . ."

As we passed a statue packed in sandbags, he said, "As if the loss of life wasn't wicked enough, I cannot begin to describe the treasures obliterated, from art to old churches . . . the barbarity of it. The Boche wants to demoralize. Do you know what they do when they come into a town? They seek out the vineyards and burn them to the roots—vines that have sustained families for generations. Unique fruits wiped from this earth."

"You'll stop them," I said as we neared the gate.

"Ah, American optimism!"

"I wouldn't have come to Paris without it," I said.

"Why did you come? Don't you have a safe home across the sea?"

"I came to help France, of course."

He put his palm over his heart. "*Mon Dieu*, you should have said before. Now that I know the wound you took tonight was in the service of France, I shall put you in for a medal."

Again, he was teasing. He had, perhaps, encountered far too many well-to-do American ladies wishing to donate useless items and otherwise getting in the way. I didn't wish for him to believe I was one of them. I was about to tell him about our work, when we stepped into full moonlight, and his breath quickened.

"I had not realized . . ." I expected him to say that he recognized me, but what he said was, "You are so beautiful. I must have your name."

Utterly charmed, I fluttered my lashes. "A name would break the spell, monsieur, as I am only free to flirt as a stranger."

"What, then, will we tell people about our meeting?"

"I shall simply say I met a handsome French lieutenant in the gardens."

Despite the darkness, I was certain he blushed. "Captain, actually."

"Where are you stationed, Captain?"

"At Amiens with the Brits. I was a cavalry officer, but then someone found out I speak English, so now I help coordinate actions between the Allied forces."

"Important work," I said.

"I amuse the Tommies, at any rate. And since you won't tell me your name, I shall amuse them tomorrow by saying that I met Marthe Chenal."

"The opera singer?"

"A good guess, no? Wasn't that you singing the 'Marseillaise' so beautifully? At least I thought so when I heard you singing on the street."

"Well, I *am* a singer," I confessed. "Or at least I was some time ago."

"If you were, you'd be a star."

"Oh, I am."

The stranger chuckled. "Well, you *are* dazzling. What did a humble banker like me do to deserve your company?"

"I used to be a lot humbler than you. Poorer than a peasant." How easy it was to tell the truth to a stranger. "Born on the wrong side of the blanket. Had to support my mother and brother from the time I turned eleven by entertaining those who could pay."

His footsteps came to a halt and I could almost hear him worrying that he'd fallen into the clutches of a prostitute. "Entertaining them?"

"I had a talent for singing and dancing." I squeezed his arm playfully, tugging him along. "I became a star—weren't you listening?"

He grinned, exhaling a relieved breath. "It's unkind to taunt a soldier who returns to duty in the morning . . ."

"Ruminating on the mystery of me will give you something to live for."

He laughed at that, long and hard. We both did. Thus, it was with real regret that when we crossed the street, I stopped under the arcade near the doors to the St. James. "This is my hotel . . ."

He nodded, then took my uninjured hand to kiss. *"Adieu*, Marthe. Be well."

"Adieu, Captain. May fortune protect you."

He tipped his cap. Snapped his coat straight. Turned to walk away.

Then something occurred to me. "Captain!"

He turned back, hands in his pockets.

"Would you care to come inside?" I asked, gratified by the color on his cheeks that was revealed by the light of the hotel lobby. His flush meant that he wasn't the sort of man who ordinarily went into hotels with women he'd just met, but his nod meant he was willing to make an exception for me . . .

I felt almost guilty for giving him false hopes. Inside the lobby, I took a card from the abandoned concierge's desk and began writing. "You said you're going back to Amiens in the morning. I have a nephew in the trenches fighting near there. His parents have crossed an ocean to see him, but their messages aren't getting through. If there's anything you can do to get word to him, I'd be very grateful."

"Grateful enough to exchange names?"

I smiled. "At least that grateful, if not more. You can tell me yours, anyway."

He gave a little bow. "Captain Maxime Furlaud, at your service, madame."

NINETEEN

MARTHE
Chavaniac-Lafayette
December 1941

WHAT A DIFFERENCE A NAME MAKES. IT WAS SURPRISINGLY EASY TO transform a sickly little Jewish girl named Gabriella Kohn into *Gabriella Beaufort*. Just a few pieces of paper. Now I give a reassuring wink to the apple-cheeked girl as she spoons a carrot into her mouth, sitting with the other girls in the dining hall.

The baroness has adorned the tables with red and white cloths and baskets filled with winter flowers. It's important, she says, to give our Lafayette kids as much of a sense of normalcy as we can. I don't know how normal it is to eat thin cabbage soup with withered carrots, then file in orderly fashion back to bed and sleep seventeen hours a day—doctor's orders—but I can't deny the good effect the treatment is having on Gabriella. When she got here she was a mouse of a thing—terrified to meet anyone's eyes—and I don't blame her after the stern warning given by her father: *If anyone finds out you're Jewish, everyone you love might be arrested and killed.*

That's enough to scare the wits out of anybody, but after two months at the preventorium, Gabriella has gained four pounds, her curly hair is taking on a healthy gloss, and her lesions are gone. And I'm feeling entirely justified about what I did to get her admitted, even though it's been hard to keep from Anna.

We're supposed to have lunch together, but when I see her in the corridor, she has a pear and says, "I've got too much work, unless you want to eat with me at my desk . . ."

As angry as I am about what happened with Madame Simon, I give Anna credit for throwing herself into the job instead of complaining about the avalanche of paperwork. So I grab an apple and follow her to the square tower where, two months ago, I slipped a fabricated school certificate into Gabriella's applications file.

Anna filed the admissions paperwork without question. And *voilà*. Gabriella Kohn became *Gabriella Beaufort*, and all I had to do was pull a fast one on a friend . . .

I tell myself Anna would approve if she knew what I was really up to. She might even admire the way I blotted the blue ink to make the fake stamp look more authentic. "So, how's it going up here?" I ask, settling in with my own meager lunch.

"Oh, you know." She looks frazzled as she scurries around file cabinets. "I have no idea what I'm doing. I keep wanting to ask Madame Simon a question—only to realize she's gone." She bites her lower lip. "I don't suppose you've heard from her?"

"Nothing much," I say, but can't help adding a little more, hoping it will get back to the baron and twist in his gut. "She's gone to Marseilles in the hopes she can get a visa from the American consulate."

Anna nods and sighs. "Maybe Aunt Bea can help her."

We don't know yet if Madame Beatrice is out of the hospital, but when she hears about all this, I hope there'll be hell to pay. "So how do you like being in charge?" I ask.

Anna stops what she's doing to say, "Don't tell Maman, but I rather like the feeling of being useful for a change—even if I'm mucking it up. Last admissions day was a nightmare and this one will be worse."

I put my feet up on the desk and take a big bite of apple. "We *do* get more sick kids in winter."

"I've got an idea that might help once the warm weather returns." Anna pauses and taps her lipsticked lips with a pencil. "Half the trouble with admissions day is trying to keep the new arrivals away from the recovering children. We have parents all over the grounds getting lost. Kids crying for their moms. Visitors coming and going. Classes interrupted . . ."

"That about sums it up," I say.

"Well, I'm thinking." I love the way she turns her head, as if to illustrate she's deep in thought. "Dr. Anglade wants the scoutmasters to take the boys on more camping trips to get them out in the air. What if every admissions day in warm weather we sent *all* our Lafayette kids—the ones healthy enough to go—on a camping trip?"

I think about that. But when I don't say anything, she throws herself into a chair next to mine. Her face is near mine, the warmth of her arm against my elbow, and I feel a yearning that all but undoes me. Then she asks, "What's wrong? You're furrowing your brow. Is it a bad idea?"

"It's a brilliant idea, actually." Getting two hundred of our healthiest and most rowdy hooligans out of the dormitories would give the nurses, teachers, and the rest of the staff time to focus on the newest and most needy patients.

You're brilliant, I think. *Brilliant and beautiful and I wish I could tell you all about Gabriella and her secret name and the fact that I might have had a mother and that I'm desperate to find out who she is. That I want us to be as close as we were last winter when we cuddled together in my bed against the cold. But I can't tell you any of my secrets because then I might tell you the one I've been keeping from myself. The fact that I want to kiss you . . .*

I want to press my lips to hers. *Really* kiss her. Like I used to kiss Henri. Even though she's a woman. A married woman, at that. I've been telling myself I like Anna so much because I felt invisible before she came here. But now I know there's something else that I feel; it's something like desire, and I'm confused, and upset, and even a little angry. There's a sound like bees in my brain, and I push my chair back. "I just remembered—I just forgot something—I need to go."

Anna frowns. "What did you forget?"

I forgot that I'm engaged. That there's a man who loves me in a prison camp somewhere near Poland, and I'm sitting here eating an apple and laughing with a beautiful woman and thinking about kissing her. What the hell is wrong with me? "It's nothing," I say. "Just that I need to finish some more sketches for your mother so I can convince her to let me sculpt a better version of Adrienne Lafayette."

With that, I head for the door.

But just as I open it, there's shouting from the staff room, and Sam bursts into the stairwell. When he sees me, he calls, "Marthe, the Japanese attacked the Americans at Pearl Harbor!"

We don't walk but *run* down the stairs to join the staff in the salon, where everyone gathers round the baron's squawking radio in its tall wood console, tuned to a shortwave station to get the news that, at long last, America is in the war.

It's not a cheer that goes up—not exactly. It's a chorus of sympathetic sighs and gasps and worried hiccups. It could mean France will be liberated and we'll get our country back. Or it could mean the war will drag on, without end, across our cities, farms, and villages . . .

That night I'm smoking in the attic, and Anna joins me there. We share my last cigarette; it's stale, but we savor it. "Britain was almost beat," she says. "This is terrible, but I almost *hoped* they'd be beat, because they were supposed to be our allies, but left my husband behind at Dunkirk . . ."

She's not the only one to have the bitter thought that the British seemed willing to fight to the very last Frenchman. It's been hard to think of them as allies since Churchill bombed our fleet to keep it out of German hands. But they've been taking it on the chin ever since, and to hope for their defeat . . . that would mean cheering Hitler.

Anna must see that I'm horrified, because she just shakes her head as if to bring herself back to her senses. "I just miss him."

"I know," I say. *I know.*

"We were practically newlyweds when the war started, and now I can barely remember what it was like to be kissed, or touched, or . . ."

I go hot and cold wondering why she's telling me this, worried that she knows I wanted to kiss her. Wondering if she knows I still do. My stomach clenches because I realize it's been so long since I saw Henri last that I'm starting to forget his voice, his smile, his scent. Maybe the reason I feel the way I do about Anna is just because I'm lonely, so I say, "Me too. I miss Henri, I mean."

Anna stares at me intently, lowering her voice to a slightly scandalized whisper. "Did you and Henri ever . . ."

"Not all the way." Maybe that's another reason I'm drawn to her. She's experienced. She's been married. She's had sex. And I've wanted to ask her about it, but now I don't dare. "I mean, I would have let him, but Henri always had to be a gentleman in the end."

Anna exhales, nodding with less judgment than I had feared. "Sometimes I feel like this war has hijacked my whole life. Do you ever feel that way?"

"Exactly that way." I was twenty-three when it started, an age when you can still be a little wild and adventurous and stupid. I'm almost twenty-six now, and it's long past time to grow up . . .

"And this castle," Anna is saying. "It's like someplace out of time. Like nothing that happens to me here while I'm apart from my husband is real. Everybody is so happy that the Americans are coming into it, but is it so wrong that a part of me just wants this war to be over so I can get my life back and the man I love can come home?"

"No," I admit, getting the message loud and clear. She's not thinking about me. She's thinking about *him*. Worrying about her man the way I should be worrying about mine. I rub my hands together against the cold, dreading the idea of Henri spending another Christmas in a German cage. If the United States stood with France at the start of the war, it would've made a difference, but now I'm not sure they can win. And some of us don't want them to.

Certainly not Faustine Xavier, who over the course of the next week makes a point of reminding us that Japan *destroyed* the fleet at Pearl Harbor. She seems almost as gleeful as the Führer himself, who declared war on the United States before they got a chance to declare war on him. Apparently the Reichstag erupted in thunderous applause, welcoming the fight. Everyone wonders now whose side Vichy—and France—will be on. But I know what side I'm on, even if it means Henri rots another year in that POW camp. Even if it means that I can't tell anyone my secrets.

Because I want to live in a world where I don't have to keep them.

TWENTY

ADRIENNE
Paris
June 1782

THE STACKS OF INVITATIONS WE RECEIVED EVERY DAY SINCE
Lafayette's triumphant return from America astonished our nearly five-
year-old daughter. We were invited to the opera, garden parties, and re-
ceptions of every sort, including one hosted by the graying marshals of
France to pay tribute to my husband. "A busy social life is the price of
your papa's glory," I told auburn-haired Anastasie, as I was too happy to
begrudge my husband a single honor. Anastasie adored the father she had
scarcely known. And now, as we made ready to meet our carriage, which
had been brought round into the drive, Gilbert stood wearing his ceremonial sword of honor with a gilded hilt, which had been presented to
him by Dr. Franklin and was his most prized possession. Anastasie
tugged at it with impunity to get her father to hoist her up into his arms.

Grabbing her up and tapping Anastasie's freckled nose, a delighted
Gilbert asked, "What shall we bring back for you, *ma chère*, to celebrate
the occasion of your fifth birthday?"

Anastasie replied, "I want a white warhorse like yours to ride into
battle!"

"So I have an Amazon for a daughter." Gilbert laughed and did not
sound displeased. "You are not quite big enough for a warhorse yet. Perhaps a pony. I will discuss it with your mother once she has her fill of
being the belle of the ball . . ."

I was hardly a belle, but since Gilbert's return, he made me feel that
way. The occasion on this night was to greet visiting Russian royalty. Our
place at court was born of fame rather than rank. Lafayette had been
promoted to field marshal and made a knight of the Order of Saint Louis.

He looked dashing wearing the prestigious medal affixed to his coat by means of a red ribbon, yet, earlier in the day at prayer, Grand-mère had observed, "All this honor is overmuch for a young man your husband's age. It will go to his head."

I had given a good-humored laugh. "Grand-mère, I begin to think there is nothing whatsoever my husband could do to please you. First he brought too much disgrace. Now he brings too much glory."

On her knees with her rosary, she said, "I do not deny Lafayette's merit, but he is not the same boy you married, Adrienne."

It was true. Gilbert had returned from the war with a relaxed confidence, a quicker wit, and a keen interest in finances. Not his own finances—which, at the age of twenty-four, he was still not considered old enough to administer without a manager—but rather our nation's finances, which he helped bolster with trade in the new American nation.

Having spent several blissful months becoming reacquainted with this worldly new Gilbert, I protested, "I have found every change in him agreeable, and he has returned to me as good and lovable as before."

"Good and lovable, yes," Grand-mère agreed. "Which does little to insulate him against his enemies."

Exasperated, I cried, "Enemies? He is the most beloved man in France!"

"Therein lies the trouble." Grand-mère rapped her cane to emphasize every word. "The *king* should be the most beloved man in France. Only the king is ordained by God to rule over us, his person inviolable, with rules and traditions that hold the envy of others at bay."

"Oh, *Grand-mère.*"

I thought she was hopelessly backward, but she was unchastened. "You young pups prattle on about equality, but heed a woman of experience. In the end, given the opportunity, every man will step upon every other man in a mad scramble to the top. Climb too high too quickly, and the same people who hoisted you up will tear you down. Jealousy, my dear, is the most wicked, and most *certain*, of human impulses."

I gave little credit to this exchange, for what could be done about it, even if it were true? That night, I was introduced to foreign dignitaries out of precedence with my rank, and Aunt Claude complained that we were afforded privileges above our station; but that did not stop the queen from offering my husband a dance—another quadrille—which he performed with such grace as to blot out any memory of his earlier, youthful stumble. The ball also gave us opportunity to press our business. Which is why I conversed with the minister of trade. The American war was expensive for France because we were liberators, not conquerors.

Yet Gilbert believed preferential trade with the resource-rich United States would fill our coffers.

"France has the finest manufactured goods and foodstuffs in the world," I told the trade minister, raising my glass. "After all, what sensible person would not prefer French wine—at least, if it could be bought without crushing regulations?"

I said this because the last time we visited Dr. Franklin, he had complained about both regulations and his painful case of gout. *If American merchants can't sell in French ports without being taxed into oblivion, they'll sail into English ports and sell there after the war is done.* Upon Franklin's advice, my husband set aside his sword to do battle with a pen, composing a study he would entitle "Observations on Commerce Between France and the United States."

Now Gilbert joined me where I had the trade minister cornered and told him all about it. "*Oui, oui,*" said the minister with a dismissive flourish of one hand. "We all know how Americans feel about taxes. They are so spoiled they made war over the price of tea."

Gilbert bristled, and with a flap of my fan, I dared to opine, "Whereas in France we allow ourselves to be robbed with taxes on land, marriage, bridge crossings . . ." I had no business speaking this way—much less characterizing the king's taxes as robbery—but I was drunk on happiness, champagne, and my husband's love.

Before the end of the festivities, we slipped away to a romantic spot where water spilled over jagged rocks into a calm pool. Gilbert did not chastise me for my forwardness with the trade minister, but embraced me in the glow of illuminated Greek statuary. "I begin to despise fame," Gilbert whispered, lips at my nape. "To think I must sneak away for a tryst with my own wife . . ."

I laughed, disbelieving he despised fame even for a moment, but neither did I discourage him. After so many years of painful separation, I wanted to compensate for every absence with pleasure, to balance every privation with indulgence. And privacy *was* an indulgence now.

"Do you think we are grown enough now to have our own house?" he asked. "Nothing too grand. If not beautiful, then gracious. Something with a place to study and entertain, with room for the servants and children. If you are agreeable, I would like to make our family a little larger . . ."

"Oh, would you?" I gave up trying to smother both my smile and a secret. "As it happens, we may expect another by year's end."

"I cannot believe it!" Excitedly, he turned me in his arms. "Or perhaps I do not wish to believe it, so I still have an excuse to ravish you."

I tittered like a coquette. "Fortunately, a husband needs no excuse."

What he did to me in love that night made everything else we had ever done seem like child's play. The mastery of his mouth—the way he used it to taunt and tease—was like nothing I had experienced. His devotion to my rapture was such that I could not catch my breath, and did not want to. Like a wanton, I gave myself over to him fully. It was only in the aftermath, as the candles guttered and the fever dissipated, that my pleasure ebbed away to agony.

Because I knew.

Somehow I *knew* he had learned this from some other woman . . .

TWENTY-ONE

BEATRICE
Paris
May 8, 1915

IT WASN'T EVEN NINE O'CLOCK IN THE MORNING YET, AND GUESTS at the St. James were shouting angrily in the courtyard. Was it too much to ask that news—especially bad news—awaited a civilized hour after coffee and breakfast? Clutching my traveling bag, I asked, "What in the blue blazes is happening?"

Thanks to my moonlit stranger, we'd finally heard from my nephew at the front. Victor had twenty-four hours' leave in Amiens—no more, no less—so we'd come down early to catch the first train, only to find everyone waving newspapers. "They've sunk the *Lusitania*," Jack snarled. "Just yesterday afternoon."

My God. We might've been on that steamer and at the bottom of the ocean now. Gulping at how near we'd come to death, I remembered that my husband's business partner had booked passage on that ship. "Is there news of Mr. Vanderbilt?"

Biting his cigar, Jack shook his head. "Missing and presumed dead."

My eyes misted as I considered this loss so close to home, and how many others might also be at the bottom of the sea. Meanwhile Emily's cheeks went pink with patriotic outrage. "This is as good as a declaration of war! The Germans knew perfectly well there were American civilians on that ship."

My God, Freddy Vanderbilt's poor wife. I needed to send a word of sympathy. What about Willie? As furious as I was with him, I knew he'd grieve. "I should try to send some cables—some words of condolence."

"There's no time." Jack tapped his watch. "Not if we mean to catch the train. We can't miss our only chance to see Victor."

"I'll send the cables for you," Emily said, setting her bag down under the plaque commemorating the spot where Marie Antoinette was said to have greeted Lafayette upon his victorious return from America. "I'll stay behind and take care of it. Just write down what you'd like to say."

I was grateful beyond words. Mrs. Chapman, however, fretted, "You're a sweet girl, Miss Sloane, but it isn't right to leave a young lady behind in Paris to her own devices."

"Oh, Miss Sloane of all people can be trusted to stay out of mischief for twenty-four hours," I said. In any case, Emily had made up her mind, and after a few hastily scribbled lines, we were off.

Khaki-clad Tommies crowded every car of our train to Amiens. Once known as *the Venice of the North*, it was now a veritable encampment of the British Army, who had commandeered hotels and directed a fleet of hospital ambulances to ferry wounded from the front lines. It was, in some ways, even more hellish than when I had passed through last autumn. Rubble heaped in the street in front of a row of what we assumed must have been lovely houses once—now they were faceless chasms of brick in collapse, splinters of lumber jutting out like broken bones. Amid this rubble, soldiers coughed and wheezed into ragged handkerchiefs, victims of the new and terrible chemical warfare.

We met Victor at the city's centerpiece—a magnificent Gothic cathedral that had been spared, thus far, the ravages of war. We found Victor inside, wearing his legionnaire's uniform, staring up at the tympanum with all the wonder of the architect he'd been training to be. In my nephew's reverent gaze, I sensed the hint of a pious crusader sent to fight back forces of darkness. And in that moment, I could believe it to be true.

My sister-in-law rushed to embrace him. "Oh, my dear boy!"

Victor wrapped one arm around her, then slung the other arm over his father's shoulder, and the three pressed their foreheads together in such familial tenderness that I hung back, not wishing to intrude.

From behind me, someone said, "A touching scene."

I turned to the man who had made it possible. "Why, Captain Furlaud, I hoped to see you again."

I enjoyed the look of him in the light of day. I gauged him to be not yet forty, with brown hair and clear blue eyes. I liked his fine Gallic nose and wanted to run my sculptor's thumbs over his jawline, especially now that I knew he'd been too humble by far when we met in the dark. For one thing, I knew the name and the cognac label. What's more, I knew the bank. *Dupont-Furlaud.* Here was the scion of a family fortune, and I felt a little satisfaction that I still attracted men of quality, even by chance.

"Now, madame," he said, "since I've kept up my end of the bargain . . . your name?"

"What if I want to be *Marthe* a little longer?"

"Why the pretense?" He sounded faintly as if he didn't approve.

"Habit. I'm an actress, you see."

"A singer, an actress . . ."

"An artist too," I replied with a grin.

He leaned against one of the pillars. "I have a confession to make."

"Well, a church is the place to confess . . ."

His mouth turned up at one corner. "I already know who you are."

No you don't, I thought, disappointed that the game was already over. *Nobody knows who I am. I've lived in disguise so long I scarcely know myself.*

At my fallen expression, he gave a rueful shrug. "I'm sorry. I had to make inquiries. In wartime a good officer doesn't pass messages from mysterious foreign women he meets on the street."

I sputtered. "You think I'm a spy?"

"I think you're Mrs. William Astor Chanler."

I'd rather he thought me a spy.

I was fairly certain that I no longer wanted to *be* Mrs. William Astor Chanler. Especially when it foreclosed all other options . . . But Furlaud went on, apologetically, "I've read your husband's book about his explorations. I thought he was extraordinarily lucky, and now that I meet his wife, I know it to be true."

"We're separated," I said bluntly.

The frank admission shocked us both into silence. This wasn't something I admitted to new acquaintances. Still, here I was, saying it in public. Saying it to this man, because I wanted him to know. And it was his slow-blooming smile that prompted me to ask, "And is there a Mrs. Furlaud?"

A twinkle came to his eye. "Not yet."

A moment of delicious possibility floated between us.

Then my nephew called, "Aunt Bea!" Victor bounded over and spun me round against my yelps of protest. When he put me down again, I kissed his cheeks, overcome with his transformation. He was still a big overgrown pup with a gleaming smile, but he'd grown into a strong soldier, and I told him so.

"It's from digging trenches all day!" he said.

Years ago, when he was still a boy, I'd glanced up from my chair on the lawn of the family estate to see the shadow of him cavorting on the rooftop with perfect sangfroid in an escape from a nest of hornets he'd discovered. Reminding him of the incident, I said, "Look what a hornet's nest you've stirred up this time. All your family crossing an ocean just to set eyes on you."

Amused, my nephew turned to Furlaud. "Captain, I really must thank you again for getting word to me that my parents were in France."

"Anything for a fellow Frenchman," said Furlaud, and when he saw my American nephew's confusion, he added, "You were wounded in the line of duty, no? That makes you *français par le sang versé*. French by virtue of spilled blood. One of our customs."

Victor grinned wider. "Please allow me to introduce you to my family. This is my mother and father, Mr. and Mrs. John Jay Chapman. And this is my—"

"We're already acquainted," I interrupted. "The captain rescued me from falling into the Seine."

"*Mon Dieu*," Furlaud said. "How is your hand? I should have asked."

I smiled. "Oh, it was just a scrape."

Together the five of us walked the tiled floor of the airy cathedral; the stained glass windows had been removed for fear of damage, but we were able to admire the famous weeping angel, one elbow resting upon a skull, the other upon an hourglass. So realistic was the carving that I wanted to wrench the little marble child away from the horror.

Furlaud asked, "What does it mean, the way the cherub is positioned with an hourglass and skull?"

"The tragedy of mortality, I think," I answered.

Victor added, "The cherub weeps that we have so short a time to make our lives mean anything."

Furlaud nodded. "An anthem to this war, if ever there was one."

Clearing her throat, as if very much not wishing to think about lives being cut short, my sister-in-law asked, "Captain Furlaud, won't you join us for lunch?"

Furlaud gave a rueful shake of his head. "Thank you, but I am expected back soon."

"Of course." I nodded. "We won't keep you from your duty."

We said farewell and parted company, but a few minutes later, the captain doubled back again to speak with me privately. "Madame, my duty takes me to Paris rather frequently, where I liaise with the American Hospital and ambulance corps. When next I am there—if you are still there also—won't you let me take you to dinner?"

I liked this man. I liked myself when I was with him. I'd encouraged this man's attentions. Nevertheless, the reality of my husband's family so near, and my fear of their reaction, was a cold dose of reality. I wasn't free, no matter how much I wanted to be. "I'm afraid dinner would give rise to gossip."

He flushed like a schoolboy. "Of course. I didn't mean—" He straightened, then fixed upon me his clear blue eyes. "No. *En réalité* I did mean it." He pressed a card into my gloved hand with instructions for how to reach him by telephone. "In case you change your mind."

HAVING PARTED WITH CAPTAIN FURLAUD, WE TOOK MY NEPHEW for an elegant meal of lobster in an oyster mushroom sauce, and Victor was grateful to feel civilized for a change. "I've spent so long outdoors exposed to the elements that after this war, if anyone asks me on a picnic, I shall never speak to them again!"

When we asked about his wound, Victor flexed his bicep. "You wouldn't know a bullet went through it now, save for the scar. It was my own fault." He put an elbow on the table, as if he'd been eating with unmannerly soldiers far too long. "In the trenches, the bullets sail harmlessly overhead all day long. *Sing-g-g* and *whap whap*! We go on boards between the trenches so we don't sink in the mud, and I got careless attempting a shortcut. I had my tent cover under my arm, just like this."

He tugged his coat off and bunched it under his arm. "The alcohol lamp and bottle were wrapped inside. All at once, *pop*! The bottle exploded and the bullet went clean through me. I've seen poor chaps shot dead midsentence and drop beside me in a puddle of blood, so I cannot complain."

My sister-in-law paled and dropped her fork, at which my nephew sobered. "I'm sorry. I'm getting too calm and unfeeling. One has to take the horrors lightly, for otherwise life at war would be an unbearable nightmare."

"Well, you're muddling through," I said, determined to keep his spirits up. "You're looking well. Isn't he looking well?"

His shaken parents agreed, and Victor grinned. "That's because I'm clean for a change. The state of filth in the trenches is unbelievable. I only get to wash my face every two days or so. The rest of the time, my head is crusted with mud." At hearing this, I presented him with a Lafayette kit, and Victor nearly cooed over the clean pair of socks, as trench foot was the bane of soldierly existence. "You've no idea how jealous this is going to make my friends, Aunt Bea."

"Tell me if you can think of any other useful items to include," I said.

"The soup cubes Uncle Willie sent have been appreciated and are small enough to ship."

I sat in mute astonishment that my husband had sent his nephew a care package. The same man who couldn't spare a letter for his own sons and was too intent on his trip to Switzerland to even help arrange this visit! Not that I begrudged Victor his uncle's attentions—not at all—but the fact that Willie hadn't mentioned it was yet another reminder of how much a stranger the man I married had become.

After lunch, walking along the canals, the Chapmans made their case, trying to persuade Victor to let them use the family influence to get him into an all-American flying corps. And when he flatly refused, the Chapmans both looked to me in desperation.

"I'm beginning to suspect some plan is afoot to leave us alone together," my nephew said, joining me on a sunny park bench where we watched his parents drift in a gondola amongst floating gardens that blossomed with crimson flowers and succulent vegetables. "Am I due for some manner of scolding? If so, I'm going to need a cigarette."

"Nothing like that."

He lit up anyway. "French tobacco is so bitter. Uncle Willie sent me this American variety, so now I'm happy as a chimney."

"You seem to hear from him often . . ."

Victor nodded. "More than anyone else, actually. I hope you'll thank him for me when you see him."

I was so sore at Willie that I could hope never to see him again, so I merely smiled, which unfortunately didn't seem to fool my nephew. Victor pointed to where his parents floated beneath the weeping willows. "They're so different, you know. My father has hard edges, she has soft ebbs, but they fit like a jigsaw puzzle. Whereas you and Uncle Willie . . ."

"We're both hard edges."

He chuckled. "You're alike. Maybe that's bad in a marriage."

Amused by his newfound worldliness, I felt entitled to pry. "Why is the subject of marriage on your mind—have you met some special girl?"

"No," he murmured, red as a beet.

Ah, *there* was the boy I knew. "Well, I'm sure it's just a matter of time. Girls love a hero."

"I don't feel like much of a hero. I've thrown away ten months of my life, neither helping the French nor injuring the Germans, as far as I can see."

"Surely the stalemate at the front line cannot last."

Victor puffed his cigarette. "What people don't want to understand is that the front is like a chain, pulled tight, nailed at two ends. As long as the nails hold, nothing can change."

"America could change everything."

He snorted. "But what's the betting on America joining the war?"

"Public opinion was already teetering before the sinking of the *Lusitania* . . . now I have to believe President Wilson won't let the murder of innocent Americans go unavenged. But if he can't make up his mind . . ." In spite of my resolution not to interfere, I sensed an opening I couldn't resist. "You might tip the balance a little."

My nephew laughed. "Me?"

"People like a good story. They want heroes. What you're doing here matters, but what if you could do *more* somewhere else?"

Victor's smile was wry. "You want me to join the aviators when it is perfectly obvious that I've been foisted on them by Uncle Willie." He sighed. "Aunt Bea, when I ask myself whether I can do more than vegetate in a mudhole, I think of my comrades. What right have I to take advantage of my connections when they can't?"

"The same right any man has to try to win the war. Piloting can't be characterized as a cushy assignment . . ."

Victor waved this away. "Oh, it's not as dangerous as they say. I've seen aeroplanes nearly every bright day when fifty shells leave white balls in the sky, and not yet have I seen one disabled."

I wished to disagree, but supposed he knew better. "Victor, an all-American flying corps would send a message that our country stands with her allies. A message our president might finally hear."

"I'll think on it. On one condition . . ."

"Name it."

I expected he might ask for a flask of rum, a package of chocolates, or a crate of oranges for his friends, but he said, "Don't give up on Uncle Willie just yet. He has regrets."

"If so, this is the first I'm hearing of it." I knew how a man behaved when he wanted a woman. More particularly, I knew how *Willie* had behaved when he'd wanted me. In our courtship, he'd been relentless; thus, his neglect now told me everything. "Your uncle never regrets."

My nephew stubbed out his cigarette. "He's too proud to admit it."

"Well, I have my pride too."

Victor chuckled. "As I said, you're just alike . . ."

Except one of us gadded off to Switzerland and one of us is here with the family, I thought. "Is there anything else I can do for you?"

Victor lowered his head, and his mask of soldierly bravado finally slipped, his voice thickening. "I've been real cut up about the death of my friend Kohn. Died in my arms. I was wondering if you could see to it that my letter gets to the family?"

"Oh, Victor, I'm so sorry about your friend. Of course, I'll see to it."

He blinked away gathering tears. "Jewish fellow. Brilliant. I'd have liked to show you a picture of him, but Uncle Willie's camera came four days too late. Now I've been taking photographs of all my friends, just in case."

Just in case . . .

We hated to part with Victor that day. We made certain to take his picture. *Just in case.* And I was struck again by the impermanence of life, despairing of all the hours already run out.

"I WAS ONLY GONE ONE DAY!" I CRIED UPON RETURNING TO PARIS.

"It isn't my fault." Emily stood by the tall windows of our suite, sunlight glinting off her new ring.

"Then whose fault is it that you're engaged?"

"Oh, please don't be cross," Emily said, beaming as a spring breeze wafted the white curtains around her like a wedding veil. "Not when I'm so happy! I wasn't expecting a proposal—it came quite out of the blue. If you'd been there in that hospital ward where he dropped to one knee . . . you'd know I couldn't do anything *but* accept."

Had she taken leave of her senses? I could understand Lieutenant LaGrange. A young soldier facing death might throw caution to the wind. But Emily had always seemed to be an eminently sensible young woman. As I stood dumbstruck, she said, "You told me every girl deserves a grand romance in Paris . . ."

"Yes, well!" I unpinned my hat in a fit of temper. "You've rather skipped over the romance and gone straight to matrimony, haven't you?"

Emily's dreamy smile fell away. "Oh, dear, you *are* cross. I thought you liked Lieutenant LaGrange!"

"I did. I *do*. Of course I do. It's just—I despise to be made the voice of reason. This is all so very sudden. Does your father know?"

"Not yet. I have to tell him in person. I have to convince him. Please don't make me convince you too."

I sat on the edge of my bed. "You're certain this is the man you want . . ."

Emily's eyes burned with conviction. "Amaury is the only man I've *ever* wanted."

That's what I thought about Willie, and look where it got me. "Again, I protest this is very topsy-turvy. If one of us was to get into mischief in the twenty-four hours we were apart, it ought to have been me."

She laughed, throwing herself down next to me on the bed to show off the ring. A family heirloom.

"Well, it's beautiful," I said. "And I wish you every happiness." I was delighted for her. Truly I was. And yet, a melancholy stole over me, because here she was at the eager start of a marriage, while I felt trapped in mine. Perhaps that's why, after a celebratory dinner during which I made her tell me every detail of the romantic proposal, I stole down to the concierge's desk to use the telephone.

Captain Furlaud's voice crackled on the other end of the line. "You changed your mind."

And I replied with a grin, "A woman's prerogative."

TWENTY-TWO

ADRIENNE
Paris
July 1782

WHO WAS LAFAYETTE'S LOVER?

Stabbing my needle into my embroidery, I could not stop wondering. From the moment my husband returned from America, the whole nation flung laurels—and ladies—into his lap. I remembered an incident at an opera performed at the Salle du Palais-Royal. Our gilded box with its ornate carved cherubs had the best view of the stage, where we saw unveiled a statue of my husband in the place the Greek hero Achilles ought to have been. While the crowd cheered and the chorus sang about how no beautiful woman could or should resist a hero, the soprano draped my husband's statue in laurel and offered him a flirtatious wave, as if volunteering to become his mistress.

I had easily endured this because she was an actress, but then the crowd's eyes turned, unmistakably, *expectantly*, toward one of the queen's ladies-in-waiting. Some chanted that she should offer the hero a kiss. Fortunately—as he would do again under more perilous circumstances—Gilbert played to the audience and decency, kissing her hand. Still, half the bedroom doors in Paris lay open to my husband, and now I knew he had walked through at least one of them . . .

Who was she?

Not the soprano—my husband was too careful of his reputation to risk bedding a performer or harlot. It must be a lady, then.

Did he love her?

I couldn't imagine so. Not when, on Anastasie's birthday, he presented her with a pristine white pony and me with a pair of pearl earrings. Kissing my lips, he said, "These jewels scarcely compensate you for bringing my daughter safely into this world. Nor for all that you are to me, my dear heart. A wife and partner, precious and rare."

As far as I knew, he had been faithful to our marriage bed for seven years—truly an oddity in France. My father, my grandfather, my brother-in-law . . . nearly every man I knew took a mistress. I had only hoped Lafayette would be an exception in this, as he was in everything else. And, as I have said, I had been encouraged in that hope because the Americans he so admired considered adultery to be a scandal . . .

Alas, my husband was a Frenchman, and as the saying went at court, *Every great man must have a mistress.* Grand-mère sometimes opined, *A man without a mistress is the subject of ridicule!* She also said the benefit of such affairs was that the wife would be credited with her husband's best qualities, while the mistress would be blamed for his faults. I knew I should not consider my husband's taking a mistress to be a comment on my merit. Certainly my father's infidelities did not reflect Maman's worth. Nor did my brother-in-law's adventures tarnish my sister Louise. The women of my family handled these infidelities with grace and delicacy, yet I had conceived of my marriage differently. Thought of it as a fortress against all enemies, one we built together stone by stone. Realizing that he had lowered the drawbridge, my feelings were frightening in intensity, and I feared to dissolve into tears at the slightest provocation. If I should now, whilst Lafayette was in the throes of a new passion, redraw the portrait of myself he kept in his heart as some shrew, fat with child . . . *No.* I would not allow it. So I forced myself to smile, terrified to betray my inner turmoil even though the effort of restraint left me trembling every time Gilbert departed. I never asked the question: *Who is she?*

By the time I learned the answer, the talk was on the lips of every person from dirty cutpurses to bejeweled aristocrats. None other than Aglaé d'Hunolstein was said to receive my husband any hour of day or night at the Palais-Royal, in the home of her more regular lover.

It was a humiliation for Philippe, and in a vain attempt at a fig leaf, he told anyone who would listen, *I had long since tired of her; Lafayette is welcome to my leavings.* I imagined my husband's satisfaction in tasting sweet revenge. Then again, I could scarcely think Gilbert petty enough to seduce a woman *only* for revenge. How long had it been going on?

Perhaps it was a relationship of duration. It hurt to think he might have feelings for a creature like Aglaé. I had loved Gilbert when he was an awkward boy, and she had laughed at him.

How could he forget?

At least in this, Grand-mère agreed. "Lafayette could do better than that brainless trollop. A mistress should at least be the charming sort with whom a wife enjoys taking tea!"

"Please *hush*, Grand-mère," said Louise, alone suspecting the depth of my despair. I dared not ask how many such teas my sister or Grand-mère or Maman had had to endure with women their husbands were bedding. All I wanted was for Gilbert and me to cleave only to each other as God decreed. Yet the world in which I lived decreed this to be unnatural . . .

My mind was filled with spiteful thoughts. Plots of petty revenge upon her . . . upon him . . . truly, I was wretched! Then one day on the way to church, my daughter Anastasie hugged my pregnant belly and asked, "Maman, why are you so sad?"

Her question shamed me. My own sainted mother had kept every manner of distress from me, always restraining her own emotions for my sake. I should do the same. Thus, in confessional I begged God's pardon for my weakness and ingratitude. The lord had, after all, answered so many of my prayers. My life was filled with riches in every conceivable way: wealth, power, family, children, and a husband who—even with a mistress—never missed an opportunity to show his love.

Wasn't it vanity to ask for more?

I left that church with sore knees and a humbled heart, determined to be of good cheer.

Unfortunately, this resolution lasted only until, on a rare outing with my father, after which he would make his way to a meeting of the science academy, we glimpsed the two lovers in passing. I saw Gilbert motion to some trinket in a shop display, and Aglaé stroked his cheek. I reeled back from the carriage window, burying my face against the seat, hoping my father would not realize the cause of my distress. In this effort, I failed.

My father cleared his throat, adjusted his cravat, then cleared his throat again. "You realize this matter of the girl has nothing to do with you."

To my great shame, I crumpled against him, sobbing. And my father seemed not to have the faintest idea what to do. Awkwardly, he patted my back, his mouth a thin, grim line all the while. I took it for censure and tried to dry my eyes. I had not, after all, sobbed when Gilbert left for America, when I was younger and had better excuse.

"Do not put your child at risk," my father finally said.

"I cannot bear it," I sobbed. "I cannot bear it!"

My father glanced down at my pregnant belly, then cupped my chin and made me look at him. "Calm yourself. This is a temporary problem, I promise you. Do you understand?"

I did not—not entirely. Though I should have. How surprised I was, the very next morning, to hear that Aglaé had been abandoned by her husband. It was a catastrophe for her, because an agreeable husband was the polite fiction behind which a mistress was afforded respect; what harm was there in adultery, after all, if the spouse did not object? But how suspicious it all seemed that he suddenly *did* object. Aglaé's husband had not minded his wife's behavior for years. Why, quite suddenly, did he find her affairs intolerable? It almost offended me to think her husband might object to Gilbert as a rival, when he had not minded Philippe. But if she continued without her husband's blessing, she would bring down her whole family.

That evening, Gilbert rolled out over my knees an architectural plan for a new house. A house designed in every way to please me and to get us both out from under my family's thumb.

It is over with Aglaé, then?

I couldn't ask, and distressed beyond measure, I pleaded illness and retreated to my apartment. There, in September, two months early, I gave birth to our third daughter. Like Henriette, she was sickly and small and I despaired for her survival.

We named her Marie Antoinette Virginie in honor of the queen and the Virgin Mary—or at least that is what I told Grand-mère. Lafayette told Dr. Franklin that our new baby was named in honor of the state of Virginia. Franklin sent his congratulations and a wish that I should birth twelve more, naming one after each state. *Miss Carolina and Miss Georgiana will do nicely for the girls*, Franklin suggested. *But Massachusetts and Connecticut may be too harsh for even boys unless you raise them to be savages.*

Alas, there would be no more children for me. The birthing of Virginie left me ravaged, without even milk in my breasts for my infant. The physician said there likely would not—and likely *should* not—be more children. To be all but barren at the age of twenty-two was a new calamity, and I mourned my womanhood as bitterly as I mourned my lost innocence about my marriage.

And I mourned John Laurens too.

The man I had helped secure an audience with the king—and the crucial aid that won the war—had perished in some trifling skirmish. A tragic loss. The news struck both Gilbert and me deeply. Remembering how Laurens and I had worked together at Versailles, I took the little drawing of a songbird he drew for my daughter and framed it upon our mantelpiece, which touched my husband. I was comforted to know that Gilbert still unburdened his grief to me, but was still wretched to think he gave some other part of himself to Aglaé.

I knew the affair must be ongoing despite the growing scandal, for Maman was particularly solicitous, distracting me with charitable projects. It was on my way to giving food for the poor that my carriage stopped at an intersection and the door suddenly opened.

"Aglaé," I said, startled, as the porcelain-skinned beauty stepped inside. This was the sort of laughing trick she might have played to amuse the queen when we were young and Philippe would goad her to dress in breeches like a groom.

She was not laughing now. Eyes bloodshot, a kerchief clutched in hand, she cried, "I am on the verge of ruin! Does that make you happy, Adrienne?"

I had not a single notion how to reply.

"I have tried to break things off with Lafayette," she said, leaning so close I could smell her orange-scented perfume. "Believe me, I have tried. Every time we quarrel, he reaches to comfort me, and then—"

"Mon Dieu." I gasped, wanting to leap out of the carriage. "I don't want to hear it! Have a care for decency."

"Is it decent to spread rumors I'm a prostitute, selling my favors at the Palais-Royal?" she asked hotly. "They say Lafayette is my customer. You may be glad when this rumor destroys me, but must you blacken the name of my children too?"

Indignation rose in my breast. "I have spread no such rumor. How can you believe it of me?"

"How, indeed?" Her cheeks splotched with temper. "Your husband believes you are a veritable angel. A perfect saint, without a speck of sin or jealousy in your heart, but we know better, don't we?"

My heart was, in fact, so black with jealousy I felt the need to say, "I am sorry for these rumors, but they are not my doing. Your husband—"

"You sent your father to poison my husband against me!"

I was so stunned by the accusation that I wanted to deny it at once. Yet the possibility my father had done this for my sake—and the fear Gilbert might suspect as much—mortified me into silence.

"No one will receive me until I reconcile with my husband," Aglaé continued. "Yet your father has made reconciliation impossible. He has my husband doubting even if our children belong to him. And now my family plans to shut me away in a nunnery."

I stared at her agonized painted face and a new and sudden pain throbbed beneath my breast. Despite my distaste for this woman, despite the offenses she had done me, I knew there was, in all this, something unjust. Aglaé was suffering not only for her own actions, but also because of Gilbert's fame. Whilst my husband was away at war, I had played the faithful Penelope to his Odysseus—but the song needed a *Circe*, a seductress, and Aglaé had foolishly taken the role. "I did not send my father, but I am sorry nevertheless."

All traces of hubris gone, she asked, "Do I deserve to be locked away for the crime of loving Lafayette? You have everything, Adrienne. You have Lafayette. He is yours for life. His kisses were mine only for a few moments that have cost me everything. I beg your mercy."

To have her beg my mercy was too much. I was not the angel Gilbert supposed. I wanted to scratch her eyes out. I wanted to throw her out of the carriage and see her land in the mud . . . but I did not wish for her to be locked away for the rest of her life, and even more so, I did not want her children to be deprived of a mother's love. Thus I found myself asking, "What is it you think I can do to help?"

"Call off your father. Prevail upon Lafayette. If he will not give me written proof the affair is over, my husband will never take me back."

Under no circumstances could I bring myself to confront my father, if only because the duc d'Ayen, through this ill-conceived gesture, had finally demonstrated the love for me I had so hungered for when I was a girl. It had been humiliating enough to sob into my father's handkerchief; I could not now tell him I wished to be of service to the very woman who had occasioned those tears.

Gilbert was another matter.

That night I found my husband laboring over his "Observations on Commerce between France and the United States." He wanted to establish free trade with American merchants now, before peace could be concluded with Britain, giving us competition. Taking a breath for courage, I wrapped my arms around his shoulders and adopted a teasing tone. "I have caught you begging favors for your mistress. Fortunately, Mademoiselle America is such a worthy lady I have never resented her!"

Gilbert stopped writing. His eyes met mine, apprehensive.

The sadness he must have seen there made him wince. Yet that is all I gave him in that moment. Only a *glimpse* of my sadness, because I would never lower myself to start a quarrel with him over a woman. And because I was too proud to allow him to see any petty impulse, I merely said, "I remember when you left me for America, I resolved never to show discontent—"

"*Adrienne,*" he rasped.

For a moment I feared that *he* might bring a jealous quarrel into the open. I would not allow him that salve for his conscience either. I would allow no open discussion of this affair, and he would simply have to bear it. As if I did not hear the strained regret in his voice, I went on breezily, forcing a little laugh. "Even if America were not a worthy rival, I could always take pride in your decency in courting her. After all, you have defended her honor, and always done by her what is right, no matter the cost to your pride . . . even when it meant stepping aside. You are far too honorable a man to allow any lady to suffer."

Gilbert put down his pen and reached a trembling hand for mine. He tried to say something, but no words came. They did not need to. He would break with his mistress, this I knew. What I did not suspect was that he would go to Chavaniac to do it.

The next morning his trunks were packed. "I have been gone too long from the place that made me. I have somehow lost my way."

"You are leaving?" These words cut their way out of me; what I really meant to ask was: *Are you leaving me?* It was my greatest fear. To be abandoned as a wife—as my mother had been abandoned—would open a deeper wound than could ever be healed.

Gilbert must have known it, for his gaze softened. "I will send for you and the children as soon as I can show myself to be a decent man."

TWENTY-THREE

BEATRICE
Paris
June 1915

"I'D LIKE YOU TO MEET HIM," I TOLD EMILY. "WITH YOUR KEEN EYE and cool judgment, you'll advise me of your decision on the matter: Is Maxime Furlaud to be taken into our hearts? Are we to fan the flame— or stamp it out?"

I said all this lightly, to prevent causing alarm, but Emily's shock could not have been more complete. "Beatrice, you're a married woman!"

"For the time being," I said, keeping my eyes on the stack of invoices we'd accumulated on Lafayette Fund business.

"For the time being?" Emily's tone forced me to look up.

I took a deep, fortifying breath. "You should know that I've asked Mr. Chanler for a divorce." Emily stared, uncomprehending, shaken as only someone in love for the first time can be to realize that not all love lasts. And I sighed. "That look on your face is precisely why I didn't tell you before now." Also why I didn't explain that Willie apparently planned to fight me. "Divorce isn't the worst thing in the world."

Emily folded her arms, plainly unwilling to accept that view. "What about your boys?"

"Nothing need change for them. Billy and Ashley still have a mother and a father—insofar as Willie is capable of being a father, anyway."

Emily shook her head. "Divorce may not change their daily lives, but trust me when I say it *will* change them. What they'll read about you in the gossip sheets—" She stopped herself, perhaps remembering the barrels of ink spilled when her parents divorced. "Don't tell me you aren't worried."

She made such a very good point that I had no choice but to glare.

"I'm only concerned for you," she added.

"And I'm concerned about your trip north," I replied, for on the heels of her betrothal she'd been invited to visit her future mother-in-law at the castle of Motte-aux-bois. "It's not so far from the trenches."

Emily eyed me shrewdly. "If you're so concerned, you should join me, especially if it will forestall the folly of a luncheon with a French officer."

"Not a luncheon," I protested. "Only tea. Nothing untoward ever happens over tea." I knew this because Captain Furlaud and I had been to tea every afternoon for a week since his return to Paris on some military errand. He'd been the perfect gentleman, picking me up from the hospital, or from my work with Clara Simon and Marie-Louise LeVerrier to help find housing for refugees.

Captain Furlaud and I had exchanged not so much as a kiss, and yet our conversations were emotionally intimate. This I didn't share with Emily, because I knew she'd tell me that if I didn't go with her to meet her mother-in-law, I should at least go with the Chapmans to Switzerland to visit my husband and attempt a reconciliation. I admit, I'd considered it, but Willie hadn't answered my cable of condolence regarding Freddy Vanderbilt's death, and I had no wish to playact the devoted wife while he was getting *in fighting trim*.

Besides, Captain Furlaud had proved to be quite a restorative presence after long hours dedicated to war relief work. So, within a half hour of seeing Emily off at the train station, I was again at the Franco-American restaurant, sipping tea with the earnest blue-eyed French officer, who asked, "What does it mean when President Wilson says Americans are too proud to fight?"

It means Wilson is a craven jackass, I wanted to say, but I worried he'd disapprove of such language. "It means he's not going to avenge the sinking of the *Lusitania*. To hear a real American leader who actually cares about his murdered countrymen, listen to Theodore Roosevelt." The former president had been outraged by Wilson's meek response, saying we couldn't meet the kaiser's policy of blood-and-iron with Wilson's milk-and-water. *There are worse things than war*, Roosevelt had also said, invoking the image of drowning American men, women, and helpless babies.

"Wilson can't hold out much longer," I said, nursing my third cup of tea. "He'll be dragged into this war eventually, so he might as well start getting prepared for it now."

"You speak so confidently and knowledgeably about world affairs," Furlaud said with an admiring smile. "Can I ask where you were educated?"

"The school of hard knocks."

He laughed. "I'm serious."

"So am I." Most people assumed I learned from Willie, and there was some truth to that, but it wasn't the whole truth. I'd taken an interest in political causes before we met. If anything, it was a mutual interest that brought us together, but I didn't want to say any of that to Furlaud.

"So you're self-taught?" he asked.

"In fine American tradition," I replied, remembering the charity school for impoverished children where I first learned my letters. I was lucky to have been able to learn when so many other children were sent to work in factories . . .

The captain's smile faded. "What you said when we first met, that you were a poor girl born on the wrong side of the blanket. Was that true?"

Heat seared down my neck—I'd have never admitted something like that in daylight to a person I could meet again. It would be easy enough to deny it now. Wise to do so, even. Still, for some reason, looking into his calm blue eyes, I found that I couldn't lie. Maybe it was because I was still seeing flashes of Minnie in every refugee child on the streets of Paris.

I lowered my gaze into the swirling depths of my teacup. "My father, well—I'm not entirely sure who he was. I grew up in Boston calling the butcher my mother and I lived with *Papa*. He took me for lemon ices and carried me on his shoulders to better see all the Revolutionary statues on Boston Common. I loved him dearly. Then one day he suddenly dropped dead of a disease that might've been cured if he'd had more money . . ."

"I'm sorry," Furlaud said. "That's terrible."

"It was made worse by the fact that we weren't even allowed at his funeral."

"Why not?"

I cleared my throat. "Because he had a wife in another town."

Furlaud's eyebrow inched up; then he forced it back into place.

"I hadn't known," I explained, my voice thick with dredged-up grief. "It came as a terrible shock. To lose my papa, then our home, then his name, then to learn that I wasn't even his blood . . . Ma confessed that my real father was a man I never met, and that I had half brothers by yet another man."

"I see," replied Furlaud, eyes filling with pity.

But remember that pity has a half-life, Minnie used to say. *So don't cry. Nobody puts a coin in your cup unless you make them smile.*

I forced a shaky laugh. "Here I thought I was the bastard brat of a Boston butcher, but I wasn't even that!"

He didn't seem fooled by my bravado, and put a hand on mine.

It encouraged me to go on.

"It seems that my mother had married young, and her husband died of cholera—a disease easily prevented with clean water. She found herself widowed with two boys to support; she left them with their grandparents and thereafter did what she must . . . which is how I came along."

Furlaud was intent on me, letting his tea go cold. "How old were you when the butcher died and you found all this out?"

"He died four days after my eighth birthday," I said.

He winced. "So young . . ."

"Old enough to learn that life can change with a snap of the fingers. One moment I was a poor but well-fed child living over a butcher's shop, with the occasional opportunity for dance lessons. The next moment I was a cold and hungry urchin in the frozen streets of Boston's Chinatown. I didn't know how long we'd survive; lots of people didn't. So I found a way to sing and dance for my supper . . . and in one way or another I've been singing and dancing for my supper ever since."

I didn't want to tell him more. I wasn't even sure why I'd told him this much. Perhaps he understood, because he squeezed my hand and said, "What a remarkable story it must be. The one about how a girl in those circumstances became *you*. I hope you'll tell it to me sometime."

"I just might," I said softly. But not today. I'd already said more than I wanted to, so I tried to shake off the gloom. "Now, Captain Furlaud, tell me something about you. Something cheerful."

"Only if you call me Max."

"All right, Max. If you could choose any city in which to live, which would it be?"

"New York," he said without hesitation, which seemed akin to heresy for a Frenchman.

I loved New York because it was frenetic and pulsing with life—all-American zest—but Paris . . . why, there was no finer city on earth, and I told him so. "One can't turn a corner in Paris without seeing something older than my whole country or discovering some enchanting piece of art, fashion, or cuisine."

"Speaking of cuisine, in the past week I've drunk enough tea with you to swamp a battleship—now I have an appetite. I wonder if you might let me take you to—"

"A chocolatier?" I asked, ducking the invitation to dinner again. "I thought you were a patriot, sir. *Chocolate* is too important to the war effort to spare; it doesn't spoil, it's easy to ship in large quantities, and it's dense nourishment for the troops!"

Max was good-natured about my taunting. "Well, then, where will you let me take you? I have only Sunday before I return to duty, and I'd like to spend the day together."

I wanted that too. He wasn't like any of the men I'd been attracted to before—he had money, but he wasn't a charismatic star of the stage, not a witty luminary of the social set, or a brooding artist, or a mad adventurer. He spoke of soldiering as a duty, without any relish. His manner was entirely frank, which I found to be a perplexing intoxicant. Perhaps after years of marriage to a complicated man, the straightforward Captain Maxime Furlaud was just the antidote I needed.

Where could we go together? It'd have to be somewhere innocent. "Notre-Dame."

"I begin to suspect you are a secret Catholic."

"No, but I *am* forming a secret passion."

He eyed me with transparent hope. "A passion for . . ."

"Gargoyles. They're brilliantly conceived, providing diversion for both water and evil spirits."

He grinned. "I hope to be equally brilliant in providing diversion for you."

On Sunday he took me to Mass at Notre-Dame. From there, we went to the Church of Saint-Séverin, not so interesting outside but remarkably beautiful inside. From there we visited the old Greek Church of Saint-Julien-le-Pauvre, and I felt full of grace by evening, having passed nearly all my day in the houses of God. I cannot say the spirit descended on me. I was too pagan for that, but I wished to be touched by sanctity at least! Better to fend off the less than saintly urges I was beginning to entertain about the captain as we strolled the streets discussing literature, history, politics, and more personal subjects.

Max told me how, in his youth, he'd yearned to escape the family vineyards. He said he'd founded a bank as much to live in a modern, more cultured world as to make money. "You see, I'm a provincial at heart, but I admire sophisticated marvels. That is why I find you so appealing, madame."

I nearly twirled at this compliment. "I thought it was my new hat."

"That too is a showstopper," he said, leaning one shoulder in a doorway. "Will you write to me at the front?"

I pretended to hesitate. "I'm told the censors read everything."

"Do you have such intimate sentiments to express that you worry about prying eyes? If so, I think you should confide all your secrets now."

I had only one secret I wished to confide. "If you're trying to charm me, you should know that it's working. I'm charmed."

His expression lightened. "Charmed enough to come inside? This is my house. Come up and I'll make you an omelette."

I sputtered a laugh at this tempting offer, but when he opened the door and swept his arm in invitation, I stood there like a wide-eyed ingenue. "Madame," he said with soft reassurance, "my intentions are honorable."

I wasn't sure mine were, but I went with him anyway.

Our first kiss was over a plate of eggs, served with bacon and stale trench cake. A tender first kiss, my side of it curious, his nearly reverent. And I realized I'd never been kissed like that before. I'd been kissed roughly by predatory men. I'd been kissed by Willie in heated passion. But I'd never been kissed by anyone in complete *adoration*.

I lit from within, musing that it was strange to feel a moment of pure joy in the midst of a war.

After that kiss, we couldn't stop smiling, until Max said, "You've rescued me, Beatrice . . ."

Now he looked so serious I had to jest, "From the Huns? Not yet, but I'm trying."

He remained earnest as his thumb caressed my lower lip. "You've rescued me from the despair of this war. You give me hope. I never thought to be caught up in something like this."

I didn't ask precisely what *this* was. A diversion, a wartime romance— or something even more serious? Whatever it was seemed quite outside of the present, but we did linger a little in the future. "When this is over," he said, "I don't want to make cognac."

"Why should you?"

"Because my forefathers have been making cognac for generations. I cannot sell the family business to outsiders. I couldn't do that to my sister."

"Why not sell to her?"

"Sell it to a woman? She doesn't have money."

"Make her a loan. Why not?"

He smiled as he considered it. "What a brilliant creature you are . . . I'd like to write to you when I'm at the front. I'll send letters by way of a friend and tell you of my deep affection for a lady named *Marthe* so the censors cannot gossip."

I grinned and nodded my agreement. "Do me a favor and try not to get shot, won't you?"

Then I planted a kiss on his lips. I'd never initiated a kiss before. With Willie, I'd never had to. I'd never even wondered whether or not I was the kind of girl who liked to kiss first, but now I wanted to find out, and all it took was a man who made me feel admired and adored.

I could get used to this, I thought, not wanting to worry about where it might lead.

TWENTY-FOUR

MARTHE
Chavaniac-Lafayette
February 1942

MADAME BEATRICE HAS SENT WORD FROM NEW YORK THAT SHE hopes to get us another shipment of supplies come spring. Meanwhile, I still haven't had a letter from Henri, and I don't know why. Surely he'd have tried to scribble a postcard from his prison camp. Anna received a long letter from her husband about his winter in Germany. Maybe her husband is allowed to write because he's a well-placed officer and nobleman, whereas Henri is only the son of a French farmer. It's a bitter injustice, but injustice is the theme of our times.

In the Occupied Zone, Germans are executing French boys who pass out leaflets or chalk Churchill's *V for Victory* symbol on park benches or street signs. We hear about more executions every day—for violating curfew, for gun possession, for infractions large and small. Here in Chavaniac, it makes us feel lucky to be in the so-called Free Zone, but we're all on edge when one of those *V* symbols shows up on the side of our church and Sergeant Travert makes a few arrests in our snowy village.

Then he comes to the castle to question the teachers. When he gets to my classroom, he asks, "Can you account for all your chalk, mademoiselle?"

"I use exactly one quarter of a stick every week," I say sarcastically.

Then I snort when the gendarme says, "I'd like to see your records of this regimented chalk use."

"She's joking," Anna says, sweeping into my classroom to wrap her arm around me in an exuberant hug. "Marthe is wonderfully funny that way. She keeps everyone's spirits up with her quirky sense of humor!" I steal a grateful look at her, trying to smother the pleasure I feel at her warmth and the comfort of her touch. Travert stares at us both, a little dumbfounded, but Anna has that effect on men—and on me. She gives him a bat of her eyelashes. "We're ever so glad you're on the case, Sergeant, but I'm sure none of us here at the castle know anything about the graffiti."

And I hope we wouldn't admit it if we did . . .

The gendarme leaves it at that, but the next day, Faustine Xavier suggests one of the kids might have stolen chalk from our classrooms. "Sadly, not all of our boys are upright and honest."

Ever since the supervisor at the boys' dormitory quit in protest over Madame Simon's dismissal last autumn, the boys have been hard to control. Sam is supposed to be keeping them out of trouble, but sometimes he's as bad as they are. They play pranks, leave the property without permission, and listen to both the BBC and the new Voice of America broadcasts on their dormitory radio, from which they've learned an infectious little ditty to the melody of "La Cucaracha."

Radio Paris lies, Radio Paris lies, Radio Paris is German . . .

Fortunately, the little Jewish girl I'm hiding at the preventorium is too smart to sing along with the boys at recess on the playground; Gabriella knows better than to draw attention to herself. And one day, after spelling lessons, I ask, "You don't know about any boys stealing chalk, do you?"

She gives a little squeak of denial. She's my star pupil, but it bothers me how shy she still is. I know it's hard for her being separated from her family and not having anyone to tell her secrets to. I think that's why she clings to me, and why she's adopted Scratch, a black and white piebald with a bent tail who hisses when anybody else pets him—but he's all purrs for her. Maybe he just likes the warmth of her lap now that we're in our fourth winter of the war . . .

The pipes are frozen again, so when I'm not teaching, or sketching Adrienne Lafayette, I'm hauling water. One bright day in February, I'm taking two buckets out to the stream when I notice a few of our boys loitering at the side of the mill. I know they're up to no good because they all scatter when they see me, but they don't know who they're dealing with. Having made my own mischief here back in the day, I know which way they're going to run, so I drop my buckets and nab the ringleader—Oscar, a lanky fourteen-year-old with asthma.

I've got him by the collar when I realize I've also caught him red-handed. Well, white-handed anyway—chalk dust is all over his dark blue mitten, and when I look up at the side of the mill, I see a *V.*

"Have you lost your mind?" I ask, giving him a little shake.

He glares. "I'm only doing what my papa would want."

His father is with de Gaulle in England, trying to save us from the Nazis, but Oscar's just a boy and I want to slap sense into him. "You think he'd want you to get shot? You know the Germans are killing French boys for—"

"You're not going to tell."

"I should! You think it's nice to let other people in the village be arrested because of what you're doing?"

"War isn't nice," he says, but at least he has the grace to look a little ashamed. "The gendarmes let the others go; they couldn't prove anything. I wouldn't let anybody else take the blame."

He promises he won't do it again, but I don't believe him. He *does* carry the buckets of water back to the castle for me, though, where the mood is dark because of the news about the forthcoming spectacle at Riom. At the behest of Hitler, the Marshal is going to put our former political leaders on trial. The idea is to prove that this war—and our defeat—is all their fault. There's a rumor going around the square tower that the Baron de LaGrange will be called to testify against his old colleagues in the cabinet.

Nobody knows what he'll do if that happens. Anna's father is a decorated war hero, but these days bravery—or even decency—is hard to come by, and it's getting harder and harder to wait for a hero to save us. I look down at the chalk in my hand, thinking that I should be doing more. I can't go to London to join de Gaulle, but I know how to draw . . .

TWENTY-FIVE

ADRIENNE
Paris
Spring 1783

CAN A DECENT MAN ADVISE YOU TO RUIN YOUR LIFE?

Lafayette wrote this to his mistress in a letter from Chavaniac that was soon passed round court—as, of course, he knew it would be. It was the written proof Aglaé needed to convince her husband to reconcile. Thus, my husband took all the blame for the affair. He wrote that he had been the pursuer—Aglaé always resisting. He wrote that she never shared his feelings. He wrote that she pleaded with him to release her. He wrote that now all that remained to be seen was whether or not he was an honorable man . . . and he wanted to be.

The letter pained me deeply. Worse, it did Aglaé no good. For Aglaé's mother disowned her to save the family reputation, accusing her daughter of stooping so low as to whore with footmen. It was that last blow—a mother's betrayal—that broke my husband's mistress. Aglaé did not wait for her family to lock her away; instead, she gifted her jewels, shaved her head, and went to the convent in shame.

I felt shame too, for I detested to see my faith used in cruelty. It should be no punishment, no tragedy, to dedicate one's life to God. It should be a joy dictated by conscience. Faith ought never to form the bars of a prison. This was a terrible injustice in which I had played a part. Would my husband's mistress have come to ruin if I had mastered my jealousy—if my father had never seen me lose my composure?

The duc d'Ayen meant well in his way, and I had taken *some* pleasure in my father's defense of me. Perhaps even some small part of me condoned my father's role in my rival's comeuppance. I would not—could not—take all the blame, but on my knees in prayer I acknowledged that

Grand-mère was right to say jealousy was the most certain and wicked of emotions.

Perhaps also the most destructive.

I knew too that even as Gilbert's affair with Aglaé hurt me and destroyed her, it had only enhanced his reputation. Lafayette was now thought worldlier, wiser, a man of more consequence. And I was reputed to be saintly and virtuous. That was the way of it in France.

Very well, then. I would have to make peace with the fact that Lafayette might again take a mistress. If so, let it be someone intelligent and kind, someone not so vulnerable to scandal or to being harmed the way Aglaé had been. Someone who would at least, in the words of Grand-mère, *be the charming sort with whom a wife enjoys taking tea*! However, my indulgence would come with a price; whereas I had given my whole heart to Gilbert as a girl, now I would keep some of it for myself. That was the only way I would be able to prevent jealousy from festering. For I too had lost my way and wanted to start anew.

It was time to go to Chavaniac and see what sort of man, or marriage, I would find waiting for me there. Of course, my family didn't want me to go when Gilbert sent for us. My father warned it would be an arduous journey. Maman fretted about the cold and the possibility of highwaymen. She reminded me that I had never gone anywhere farther than Versailles without her. Only my sister Louise supported my determination to set out by carriage with my children for the unknown. Thus, that spring, I left behind Paris and staked all on a *wilderness adventure*.

As our carriage jostled its way up rough mountain roads, I glimpsed breathtaking gorges of red stone. Volcanic peaks and bubbling hot springs of black water. I pointed out to Anastasie and little Georges the thick pine forest tangled with green vines where their father hunted the Beast of Gévaudan as a boy. I began to fear the place was entirely untamed, but now and again a statue of a saint arose at the lofty top of a stone outcropping, serving as testament that Christian souls resided here.

When at last we reached our destination, I could not quite fathom the squat, utilitarian structure that my husband called home. Why, this so-called castle with its white feudal towers was—by the standards of my family—no more than a hunting house, half falling to shambles.

Yet I already loved it—every crack and stone!

Alighting from the carriage, I set three-year-old Georges down, and he ran through the garden as fast as his little legs would carry him. His dog—and his older sister, Anastasie—chased after him. Meanwhile, baby Virginie was polite enough to gurgle a smile at her father, who bounded out to greet us, and Aunt Charlotte was not far behind. "Madame la marquise," said the woman who had been all but mother to my husband. She kissed my cheeks, and I was charmed to learn she was not a simpering sort. "Oh, *mon Dieu*, these beautiful children are too thin. Get them into the house for some wild strawberry pie!"

Gilbert kissed me sheepishly and led us into the house, where the coolness of its stonework lent a pleasant air. The thirteenth-century ground floor was dark like a cave, light filtering through rounded, almost nautical peek-holes. But upstairs, tall windows afforded a bright sunlit view of the forested mountains.

And I began to feel a strange, heady freedom . . .

I had never been any place like this. Here at Chavaniac, there would be no glittering salons at which I must watch every word for political import. No galas at which I must wear hoops, headdress, and tight laces. No stink of summer heat in the city. No army of liveried servants bustling about. It was so quiet, I thought, *This is a place one can hear God . . .*

Our supper was served on humble white plates, but the food was plentiful—thick cuts of ham with lentils, finished with a delicious confection. And the conversation with Gilbert's widowed aunt Charlotte was lively and entertaining. She plainly worshipped the ground my husband walked on, tearfully saying that when she sent him to Paris as a boy, she never believed she'd live long enough to see him again.

After we put our three exhausted children to bed, Gilbert brought me to his round tower bedroom—the same place he was born. "My study is below," he explained. "If I wake in the wee hours of the night, it is easy enough to slip down the stairs and up again without disturbing anyone."

How many sleepless nights did you spend writing your letter to Aglaé?

I did not ask. I did not want to know. I pushed aside that poisoned chalice of jealousy, wanting to put it in the past. Here at Chavaniac, I believed that we could.

Later, I slipped my hand into his. "I think this place explains you."

He had come of age here, the little lord of these lands, raised on tales of chivalry, his days spent exploring these forests, these mountains, the streams, in perfect innocence. Now he was a grown man determined to live up to those tales. And again, I wanted to help him do it.

In the days that followed, I found I did not mind that there were not enough servants to see to our creature comforts. I did not mind that food sometimes came cold from the old giant oven. I did not mind the creaky floors or old-fashioned torches that left soot on the walls. I liked knowing that the king, the queen, and the royal court were far away. That the Noailles were not here to tell us what to do. And that even though General George Washington smiled down benevolently upon us from a portrait on the wall, he had no authority here either.

Gilbert was sole master of this place, and I was its mistress.

The reality of which became real to me on the day the bailiff explained that my husband's tenants were on the verge of starvation. I had heard this already and sent monies ahead, but *seeing* the wretched state of the peasants in the village was an entirely different thing. Children crying, trembling with hunger, their bellies distended, little ones rasping with coughs. Their parents gaunt, ill clad, terrified to be evicted from their homes . . .

"It is like this everywhere in France," said our agent. "Peasants are hurting for lack of bread. Under the circumstances, we can sell your grain for such a profit you may be able to recoup all your war expenses."

Aghast, my husband said, "Now is not the time to *sell* grain. Now is the time to give it to these peasants!"

Then Gilbert peered at me cautiously, as if unsure of his footing. "Adrienne, you have worked so diligently with my accounting books; I fear to ruin your careful financial plans in one stroke. Yet I cannot rest when people who depend on me are suffering."

"Nor can I," I said, reassured of it by the cross I wore round my neck.

So we opened our granaries. The curé in the village rang a bell, alerting the local peasantry. And when they came to take sacks of wheat away, they shouted, "*Vive Lafayette!*"

The next morning we were awakened by songs at our gate, where our poor villagers knelt, begging to kiss the hem of my skirts in thanks, and offering token gifts in fealty. My eyes welled to understand that we held the very lives of these people in our hands. Gilbert was moved, but also unhappy. He hated nothing so much as to see anyone prostrate in the dirt. Hated more taking gifts from people who had nothing.

"Look," he told me, an edge of anger in his voice as he showed me a basket of trinkets collected from the villagers. Little crucifixes carved from wood, bundles of herbs—the most humble gifts, but all they had to give. "I am shamed to take these things from them."

"You dare not give insult by refusing," I said. "Even starving people have pride."

"They *should* have pride," he said. "They should have their humanity. I did not risk my life and fortune helping colonists stand up against their king an ocean away only to see my own countrymen groveling in the dirt outside my gates. I would see all this—feudalism—changed."

I agreed. Change should start here. For it was easy to think here, without the distractions of Paris and Versailles. Moreover, I could think of grander things. At Chavaniac, I could dream, and in those dreams I found the very core of myself, as if I had been boiled down to my essence. I was a woman of twenty-three, a wife who wanted love, and a mother who wished to raise a family, but also . . . I wanted a sacred mission. To take all the advantages with which I was born, and what talents God had given me, to dedicate to a more enlightened way of being. This castle might be an unpolished mirror of a bygone age, but glimpsed from the right angle, I saw a reflection of an age yet to come. One in which people did not live or die at the whim of nobles. One in which people could wor- ship freely—*live* freely.

To begin with, I was glad to give our grain, but that would last only a season. I had a more permanent solution in mind. "Their crops failed, but they still have sheep. What if they could spin and weave? They could make lace to sell in the lean times."

Gilbert rubbed the back of his neck. "You are suggesting a new way of life for them."

"*Why not?*" I asked tartly, echoing the motto of the Lafayettes. "We could start a school for lace-making. I could petition for funds . . ."

Lafayette laughed, reaching to stroke my cheek. "You are burdened with motherhood and—"

"I already convinced the curé."

My husband appraised me with new appreciation. "I begin to suspect the curé must be in love with you. As am I."

Gilbert is still in love with me, I thought, heart filling with relief. Perhaps I could no longer be everything to him. Perhaps I could never again—without risk to my life—give my body with *complete* abandon. But we still had physical love between us, and our minds and hearts too.

I WENT EVERY DAY WITH THE PEASANTS TO THE ANCIENT STONE church in the village. I made plans for some manner of hospital. I bought new spinning wheels. Lafayette started construction on new roads to the village, establishing a weekly market in the square. And our agent was particularly pleased that I applied for and received a grant of nearly six thousand livres for all these endeavors.

Gilbert was even more impressed. "The officials would never have given *me* the money," he told his aunt. "It was accomplished by these letters of my wife that only she knows how to write. Adrienne does a great service to this countryside."

I basked in his praise. I basked in his presence too. I felt happier at Chavaniac than I had ever felt anywhere. The children loved it just as much—especially Anastasie, who, at now almost six years of age, wanted to know stories about the castle dungeon. "Are there skeletons like in the Bastille?"

"I am sure there are only bats and spiders in our dungeon!" I said.

Meanwhile, Gilbert grabbed Anastasie and hoisted her over one shoulder. And while she shrieked with laughter, he said, "I am going to go liberate those bats and spiders, then seal that dungeon up."

What a good heart he had. I wished we could both share a Catholic faith, but in matters of religion he was a doubter. I took some consolation, however, that he had been initiated into a secret society of Freemasonry by George Washington—a society that professed to believe in a higher being. In any case, his values were entirely Christian. Here in the countryside of Chavaniac, he was thinking about the changes he had wrought—helping to bring about one democratic republic in a world of monarchies—and wondering what more he could do. His mind was now on the slave trade. He had been told that, having been broken and degraded, and come of age on plantations, these enslaved people could never prosper as free people. My husband did not believe it, and neither did I. Our black brethren were human beings who could prosper if they were taught the knowledge that had been withheld from them—how to read, and write, and keep accounting books . . .

We decided to prove it. We would purchase a plantation in Cayenne whose black workers would be paid for their labors and educated to run the plantation themselves, with the ultimate goal of ownership and profits to be divided among them. This project, along with so many others, served as the new moral center of our marriage, and every plan we made together felt like the renewal of vows.

IF WE WISHED TO CHANGE THE WORLD, WE COULD NOT REMAIN long away from Paris. Thus, in time we renovated a modest town house on the Rue de Bourbon. We had a finely equipped kitchen and an oval salon with curved glass doors that drenched the room in sunlight.

We could have afforded something grander but wanted our guests to feel welcome and at ease. Thus, we instituted regular Monday-evening dinners to welcome Americans in Paris.

I did this even in Lafayette's absence, for now he was visiting Mount Vernon—the place to which George Washington had retired after the war. To celebrate that occasion, we arranged for him to be sent a gift of seven Grand Bleu de Gascogne French hounds, and I wrote:

As a French and American woman, as the wife of Lafayette, I feel the public joy in your peaceful retirement after so many dangers and so much glory. I am always sensible to how happy my husband was to learn from such a master and to have found such a friend.

In reply, Washington praised my charm and the beauty of my mind, promising that my children and I held a claim on his affections. He hoped we would visit, but Virginie was not yet two—too young for ocean travel. As much as I wanted to see America, I could not leave my child behind when so much needed to be done here in France.

And that included welcoming the new American envoy, Thomas Jefferson, who now bowed at the waist in courtly fashion and said, "I have always believed that the tender breasts of ladies were not formed for political convulsions. Yet in your husband's absence, madame, you've transformed his home into a veritable embassy, and are a most perfect hostess of liberty."

It was a lovely compliment. Especially coming as it did from the tall, freckled Mr. Jefferson, who would soon replace Dr. Franklin as ambassador. "I bid you welcome, then, sir," I said. "From one sort of ambassador to another."

I was, after all, my husband's representative more now than ever. There was no American who set foot in Paris without calling upon me. If an American gentleman lost money to pickpockets, or if an American lady wished for admission to Notre-Dame or simply advice on sights to see, they came here. However, Lafayette had asked me especially to befriend the Jeffersons, writing, *I beg you to take them under your wing.* Thus I took a special interest in twelve-year-old Patsy Jefferson, whose keen intelligence shone behind her eyes.

My seven-year-old Anastasie very much wished to befriend her because they both had auburn hair. To encourage this, I allowed both girls to attend a ladies' tea party in my airy oval salon the next week. Also in attendance was Abigail Adams—a sharp-nosed, sharp-tongued woman from Massachusetts whose husband had been a moving spirit of the Revolution. My other American guest was the beautiful and witty Angelica Church of New York, wife of a dealer in armaments who had supplied French soldiers during the war. I liked them both, and when conversation turned to our townhome, I explained my efforts to furnish the place. "The marquis de Lafayette says he must have a barometer for his study, and you will laugh when I tell you that he says, *A carpet will do no harm.*"

"Any carpet?" Abigail Adams sniffed. "He doesn't suggest a price?"

"Or a color?" Angelica Church bubbled with laughter. "Oh, men!"

Hoping to draw Miss Jefferson into the conversation, I mentioned, "My husband also wants a copy of the Declaration of Independence in his study."

That document was very dear to me. I could never think of my lost little angel, Henriette, without remembering Gilbert reading those words to her. Words which had soothed her tears and enlightened my soul.

Patsy Jefferson, whose father was the primary drafter of that famous document, turned pink with pride at the mention. I wondered if she understood how sacred it was.

I believed that even as a Protestant girl, she could.

Here in France, Protestants were no longer burned as heretics, but they suffered what my husband called a civil death. French Protestants could not avail themselves of the law or even be decently buried. Their marriages were not recognized, and their children were deemed bastards. They were even barred from the pursuit of certain vocations. I wondered how I had lived so long without comprehending the horror of this, for such religious persecution stained my faith and turned people away from salvation. And the more fervently I believed in God, the more I abhorred coercion in his name.

This was on my mind when saying farewell to Benjamin Franklin, whose long service, age, and gout merited reprieve. With fond remembrances, he entrusted to me a signet ring by which we should remember him. I took the ring, promising to treasure it, then kissed his cheek. "What good fortune it has been to have you as a friend, sir. All those years, when my husband was across the sea, you were a comfort and a conspirator."

"Oh, I remember, my dear. Your unwavering faith renewed my own, reminding me that rebellion against tyranny is obedience to God."

As my eyes began to mist, he said, "Now, madame, I must go home, because guests, like fish, begin to stink after three days, and I have been here *eight years!*"

I laughed. "You are no stinking fish, and are always welcome back."

Yet it would be the last time I ever saw him.

EVEN AFTER THE DEPARTURE OF DR. FRANKLIN IN 1785, I WAS KEPT busy as la femme Lafayette. My husband was still very much on the rise. He had returned from his visit to Mount Vernon with a gift of dueling pistols from George Washington and a renewed sense of personal mission and public importance.

But with Gilbert so often gone to consult with the king's ministers at Versailles, people in Paris wishing to recruit my husband's influence often appealed to me. The marquis de Condorcet had me read treatises on how to improve the nation's economy with free trade and a new tax structure. In 1786, his betrothed, Sophie de Grouchy, persuaded me to visit prisons to bear witness to the instruments of torture and the poor prisoners left to rot. And witnessing these abuses, I encouraged Lafayette to lend his name and reputation to the cause of judicial reform.

It was both wearying and exhilarating to be the wife of such an important man. If at times it went to my head, how much more dangerous might that be for my children? To keep my son away from fawners disguised as friends, I arranged for seven-year-old Georges to stay most days with his tutor. He was not the only boy for whom I arranged an education. There were also the two young men my husband brought home from America. One a young Protestant, the other an Oneida Indian. We took them both as wards, arranging for both an education. Then there were the black workers on the plantations, who must have an education to defend themselves and to support themselves as free men. I tended to these details on behalf of my husband, and now, as Gilbert and I walked the shops of the Palais-Royal, newly opened to the public, he asked one favor more. "You must go in my place, dear heart, to see the unveiling of my bust at the Hôtel de Ville . . ."

Looking up from a display of cravats, I cried, "But it is such a great honor!" In fact, it was an honor reserved for dead legends and living monarchs. However, Mr. Jefferson had prevailed upon the king to allow his home state of Virginia to gift us with this bust in honor of my husband's good service, and the king agreed to allow it. "Why would you wish to be absent from its unveiling?"

Gilbert's cheeks reddened. "Jefferson jests that I have a canine appetite for public laudits, but there are limits to my vanity."

This tiny bit of humility made me want to kiss him, but we were in public, so I held a black taffeta cravat against his throat, imagining how handsome he would look in it. "I know you are kept busy enough with your own affairs," Gilbert continued. "Not to mention all my business. Yet I beg you to go to this ceremony for me. I cannot applaud my own face in marble . . ."

How charmed I was by his pleading. "Oh, I would not miss seeing you put up on a pedestal where you belong. Besides, I find Mr. Jefferson's company to be quite amiable."

Alas, on the day of the presentation, Mr. Jefferson fell prey to a monstrous ache in the head, and his secretary Mr. Short took his place. Short was a sandy-haired Virginian of impeccable manners, dry wit, and clear-eyed idealism. He made a lovely introduction and dedication before revealing the marble bust to the assembled crowd. And after the ceremony, Mr. Short and I strolled together on the Place de Grève, where a swirl of autumn leaves trailed in our wake. "Madame, I regret your husband the marquis could not attend, yet I am delighted by the company of his substitute."

I found myself delighted by the company of Mr. Jefferson's substitute as well. Like me, Short would later become a member of the Society of the Friends of the Blacks, founded by the journalist Brissot to help abolish the slave trade. But even then, Short shared a sympathy in the cause and asked about our plantations. "When emancipated, will not these people be simply recaptured and sold back into slavery by unscrupulous planters?"

"That is why they must have property of their own, an education, and an accepting community to protect them! I am arranging for teachers and spiritual guidance and writing letters of instructions to the caretakers, forbidding harsh punishments or the sale of any human being."

I invited him to discuss it further that night, where, lit by candelabras and silvered mirrors, our dinner guests gossiped about the queen, whose love of gambling they blamed for the sorry state of the nation's finances.

The truth was that a system of monopolies and unfair taxation was bankrupting the nation. The weight of tradition and greed was strangling economic progress and throwing away economic opportunities that had been purchased with French blood.

To solve the nation's problems, the king called an Assembly of Notables. As one of those notables, my husband argued that barriers to trade must come down. That peasants should not be forced to work without pay to repair roads and bridges. That we must have elections and fair taxation on *all* citizens. That the *ancien régime*, with its feudal privileges, not only violated human rights, but amounted to financial folly.

All this angered the king and his brothers and their royal faction, but my husband had angered the king before . . . and he had been *right* to.

I did not worry overmuch about the increasing coolness to me at court. Or the rumors about my husband's infidelity, or the smears to his honor. But Lafayette had remained so long the most beloved man in France that he was no longer accustomed to the vicious sniping and petty politics of court.

The fierce resistance to reform by some of our fellow nobles—the ones who believed in their unearned superiority over their fellow human beings—did not take us by surprise. Yet the virulence of their attacks against my husband's reputation, his loyalty, and his patriotism struck so deep that Gilbert began to complain of pains in his chest.

I found him some days alone in a darkened room, sitting at the edge of the bed, struggling to catch his breath. He had always been, from the first moment of our match, entirely vigorous. But on the day that an anonymous note of false accusations began circulating, he raged, "What is the morality of an anonymous letter? The author strikes at me—but without the courage to sign a name!"

His anger did no good for the pains in his chest. He retreated to his study, where he clasped a warm poultice against his breast. I followed. "Have you sought my father's advice?"

"Your family advises silence," he said, closing his eyes.

It was tempting, but I said, "You are needed at Versailles, where no one else dares tell the king what he needs to hear."

Gilbert gave a bitter laugh. "If I continue to speak, I will squander all that is left of my fame and glory . . ."

"What value have fame and glory if they cannot be spent for good?"

"You are right," he murmured, as if taking strength from me. "You are *always* right."

So Gilbert set aside his poultices. He caught his breath. He returned to Versailles. And there, he rose in the assembly to rain down thunder. He protested corruption and wasteful spending. He supported reforms in the judicial system to prevent torture and unjust convictions. And perhaps most controversial of all, he argued for a motion to grant civil rights to Protestants and Jews.

Gilbert rose again and again, like a colossus.

To punish him, the royals divested him of his rank as field marshal. And in response, he defiantly signed his name on the last record of the session without any noble title or military rank at all.

Lafayette.

The name we shared.

A name that would, henceforth, speak for itself.

TWENTY-SIX

BEATRICE
Paris
July 1915

IT WAS TIME FOR THE ANNUAL INDEPENDENCE DAY PILGRIMAGE TO Lafayette's grave, and my nephew was coming to Paris.

I may have had some small part in convincing the ambassador to convince the French government to give all Americans fighting with the French leave for the holiday. And now Emily and I were decorating the embassy tables with red poppy centerpieces to make things cheerful for Victor's arrival.

Having returned from Switzerland, the Chapmans were overjoyed at the prospect of seeing their boy again. But neither was keen to talk to me about their visit with Willie, during which he must have revealed my desire for a divorce. Ever observant, Emily noticed. "I don't believe Mrs. Chapman has said more than ten words to you. Has there been a spat?"

"Of course not." My sister-in-law was far too well-bred for that. But if she was distraught about the state of my marriage, she should take it up with her brother, who apparently had nothing better to do than soak in a Swiss spa. Since I'd decided to get on with my life with or without my husband's consent, my anger had cooled, but resentment remained. Such that I didn't even bother to ask whether or not the specialist in Switzerland had got Willie back *in fighting trim.*

It was good practice to consider it none of my affair, and to focus on what I came to France to do. Not that the Woman's Peace Party was making it any easier. They'd come to Paris, fresh off their failed conference at The Hague. It had gone the way I predicted, and Clara Simon was complaining about it, which validated my good opinion of her. "What self-respecting Frenchwoman would attend a peace conference when it conveys weakness at the very time our men are fighting for their lives in the trenches? We feminists are to what—tell them to throw down their guns, let the Germans take us, our homes, our livelihood, and all our rights?"

Her tone dripped with scorn, and I didn't blame her. Anything short of humiliating defeat would still profit the kaiser. Marie-Louise LeVerrier added, "It pains me to think otherwise intelligent suffragettes have soiled their reputations with this foolishness."

It pained me too, because it played into the caricature of women being too sentimental to understand politics—or their audience. I thought politics was rather like an art, the realities of which could be studied, the expression of which could be perfected in the right setting. And Independence Day was just the right backdrop for my performance. For I was on hand to ensure that, for the first time in history, the French government would take part in the annual pilgrimage to Lafayette's grave—which would serve as a reminder of the alliance between our two nations.

An alliance President Wilson had thus far seen fit to ignore.

This would make another statement; one loud enough, I hoped, to be heard in Washington, DC.

"Aunt Bea!" Victor dropped his bag to lift me off the ground.

I fended him off with an outstretched hand. "Careful of my hat!" It was, after all, a dainty white straw bonnet with a ribbon of blue stars and scarlet stripes that delighted his fellow legionnaires—American volunteers all, including three black men.

Victor introduced them all with easy camaraderie. Fighting together, it seemed, made them a sort of family, without distinction to race, religion, or class—as democratic as anyone could hope. "We've quite a feast for you gentlemen," I promised. "But first, just a little more standing on ceremony."

Thereupon, I had the honor of introducing my nephew to Madame Kohn, the French wife of Corporal Kohn, a brilliant Polish mathematician, Victor's dearly departed brother-at-arms.

She had with her now their fatherless son, a boy named Uriah—a sight that rendered poor Victor nearly mute with emotion. "Your husband was my very good friend," my nephew finally managed to say to Madame

Kohn, his voice unsteady. "A genius too. He proved to me that a lovable softy can also be a very brave soldier . . ."

Little Uriah stared up at Victor, mesmerized. "Papa was brave?"

Victor stooped down to meet the boy's eyes. "The bravest."

"As brave as pilots that go up in the sky?"

"Braver, because he spent his time down in the trenches with bullets whizzing by his nose, and he couldn't fly away." My nephew's throat bobbed. "Here, there's something I want to give you. Something he'd want you to have so you can be as brave as he was."

The lights popped nearby as a photographer captured Victor removing his tricolor pin off his jacket and putting it into the boy's hand. "If you're ever feeling scared without your father, you just hold this tight and know he'll be watching over you. And I'll watch over you too, if I can."

MY NEPHEW WAS QUIET ON THE WAY TO PICPUS CEMETERY—A strangely hallowed place—a private burial ground far from the ordinary bustle of Paris. Three hundred of us passed through the plain wooden door, passed a small chapel, and walked a tree-lined path to place flower wreaths and drape an American flag where Lafayette was buried beside his wife.

The engraved stone slabs that marked the site were mantled in metal wreaths, weathered to a patina of verdigris. This was, I thought, a remarkably humble resting place for General Lafayette and his wife. Something the ambassador made note of in his speech. "No tall shafts rise toward the clouds to perpetuate their memories. Their monuments are in the loving, grateful hearts of their fellow men. In fact, I see all around me figures patterned on his model—a thousand Lafayettes."

I felt buoyed by the applause. Strengthened and cheered. Then a speaker said, "As we honor Lafayette today, let us not forget his wife, whose steadfast devotion during the American Revolution made this day possible. All her life, she dedicated herself to the cause of liberty— running great risks and making great sacrifices. Women here with us today continue her glorious tradition."

The speaker motioned to me, where I was standing with my lady friends. Emily made a little hiccup of surprise, while Marie-Louise and

Clara squeezed hands. These things we did, small symbolic gestures . . . perhaps they mattered as much as I hoped they did.

Later, at the embassy, after Victor and his fellows demolished a five-course meal, they smoked the cigars Mr. Chapman gave them and readied for a night out. My nephew hung back, wrapping leftovers in newsprint.

"I can get you another portion of steak if you're still hungry," I said.

"I just want the bone for a puppy back at the front," Victor said. "A true war dog. Born in the trenches. He's not big enough yet to keep the rats away, but he sleeps near me at night. Hate to think of something happening to him without me."

His voice broke and he was nearly in tears over a puppy . . . I realized it was more than that. "You're thinking about leaving the legion."

"I promised you I would," he said, hanging his head. "After meeting Kohn's boy, I think maybe it might mean something for me to join the aviators. I can die in the sky for the cause as easy as I can in a hole, but be more visible when I do. A thousand Lafayettes and all that . . ."

"Victor, I don't want to hear any talk about dying for your cause. Better, as the saying goes, that you make a few of those German blighters die for theirs!"

He chuckled. "I'll try to make you proud."

I ruffled his hair. "I'm already bursting with pride in you, silly boy!"

"I guess I'd better tell my folks to pull strings."

Spying the Chapmans across the banquet hall, I said, "Well, I'll let you get on with it, since I don't seem to be their favorite person at present."

Victor gulped in the way he used to as a young boy, trying to cover up for the mischief of his siblings. "They just don't want to tell you about Uncle Willie's plans."

In exasperation, I played a guessing game. I supposed my husband was going to join the French Foreign Legion. Then again, he didn't like anyone in authority over him. More likely he was going to gin up a gun-running scheme or start a spy ring, as he'd done in times of old. *Whatever Willie has planned, it's no longer your concern*, I told myself. I'd moved on to omelettes with a man who kissed me like he worshipped me. "Your uncle is free to live his life as he sees fit, and I intend to do the same."

"He's going to have his leg lopped off," my nephew said.

The air around me seemed to bend, and I couldn't catch a breath. "Pardon?"

"I'm sorry, Aunt Bea. Uncle Willie's leg has been paralyzed since the surgery . . ."

How was that possible? I'd just seen Willie a few months ago. He'd looked better. Much recovered. Then I remembered that he hadn't stood to greet me when I came to the table. Nor had he chased me when I stormed away. Realizing he *couldn't* stand up, my temples began to throb, and I felt a wave of sickness.

"He didn't want you to know," Victor explained. "Not until he was sure the leg couldn't be saved. That's why he was in such a hurry to get to Switzerland. He hoped the specialist at the clinic would have better news. Unfortunately, the medical consensus is that the leg has to go."

My hands went to my face in shock. The loss of a leg would be a terrible thing for any person, but for someone like Willie, someone who loved athletics and feats of daring—

I sank down into a chair, bereft. So obvious was my distress that Victor had to get me a drink. Meanwhile the Chapmans rushed to my side, guessing their son had broken the news. "Oh, Beatrice, darling, we had no idea until we saw him."

Victor was abashed. "Uncle Willie made me keep it from everyone."

Jack Chapman, who had himself undergone an amputation, patted his boy's shoulder with his remaining hand. "Water under the bridge now. We mustn't worry overmuch. The operation is serious, but your uncle Willie is filled with courage. He scheduled the amputation for this week."

I all but screeched with panic. "This *week*? I need to go to the train station. I—I need to be with him. I'll send for my bags."

"Beatrice," Jack said gently. "He doesn't want you there."

Smote to the heart, I was no longer willing to take that as an answer.

"HOW THE DEVIL DID YOU GET A CONNECTION THROUGH?"

Just hearing Willie's voice on the other end of the telephone line made my hand shake. "You're not the only one who can call in favors, and the ambassador couldn't bear to see me cry."

Willie didn't reply. He was probably trying to guess what I knew. The jig was up, and all I could do was replay our last horrible fight in my mind. My husband had somehow got himself to a luncheon on a paralyzed leg, and before he could tell me about the possibility of an amputation, I'd asked him for a divorce.

What a cruel harpy I must have seemed!

And what was it he'd said?

I'm afraid it simply would not be in your best interests to divorce me at this time. Perhaps, in a short time, you'll find that things have changed.

He'd been thinking he might die. That I'd be better off as a wealthy widow instead of a divorcée. Realizing this, I wanted to heave up the lavish embassy meal into the wastebin. "Why didn't you tell me about your leg?"

"Because I can't bear to see you cry either."

I smeared my tears with the back of my hand. "If you'd told me, I'd have gone with you to Switzerland. I'd have tended you until—"

"Exactly what I feared you'd do."

So he'd quarreled with me instead. Now, since I couldn't reach for him through the line, my fingers gripped the oak base of the telephone with its engraved eagle. "This is why you sent me and the boys away last autumn . . . you knew you might have to have your leg amputated."

"There was also a war going on. Regardless, the last thing I wanted was my boys to see me as an invalid. I hoped I'd heal. I didn't. Now I've just got to have the leg off and be done with it."

My heart ached for him in this hour of anguish. Trying to steady myself, I blew out a breath. I'd expected to sail home soon with Emily, but I couldn't abandon him now. "I'll take the first train to Switzerland."

"Beatrice, if I'm to bear this with courage, I can't have any of you here. That's why I sent Jack and Elizabeth away."

At least the Chapmans could say they'd visited my husband's sickbed, whereas I'd been kissing a handsome French officer, and now I hated myself for it. "Just what do you expect me to do, Willie? I ought to at least *be* there when you wake up, to hold your hand and—"

"Hold my hand after I'm up and walking again, home with the boys."

I swallowed in surprise. "You're coming home to New York after the surgery?"

"It's about time, don't you think? With Freddy Vanderbilt's death, there's the hotel to think about. And I imagine you'll still want your divorce . . ."

My eyes squeezed shut. He must have thought I was the worst kind of ingrate! After all he'd done for me . . . and he didn't even know I was a *jezebel*. Emotions ajumble, I was certain of only one thing. "Even when I was so angry at you I could spit, I told you I'd do anything for you. That's still true, Willie. Please tell me what I can do."

The pause on the other end of the line went on so long I feared we'd lost our connection. Finally, he said, "Give me a reason to get well. When this is all over, promise me I'll have a wife waiting for me at home."

I forgot the war, I forgot Max Furlaud, I forgot everything but Willie. "Of course you will. That's a promise!"

TWENTY-SEVEN

ADRIENNE
Versailles
May 1789

SINCE THE DAY LAFAYETTE SIGNED HIS NAME IN A DEFIANT FLOUR-
ish two years earlier, he had been agitating across the countryside for a
government that represented the people.

Now the king had given in and summoned the Estates-General.

The Noailles had come, en masse, to bear witness, because my family
could never be far from the center of great events, and no one had seen
anything like this for two hundred years. But at the family home in Versailles, battle lines were drawn with sighs over the silver and pouts between poached eggs. It was Grand-mère who brought the schism into the
open.

"You and Gilbert will *both* find yourselves imprisoned in the Bastille
for treason," she warned, in poor temper after having salted her breakfast
chocolate and sugared her omelette. "You must cease these commotions
for dangerous innovations."

My younger sister Pauline agreed. "Grand-mère is right. This *is* a
dangerous innovation."

Patiently, I asked, "How can it be an *innovation*, when the Estates-
General is one of France's oldest traditions?"

"Because your husband forced the king to it by threat of civil war!"

Gilbert *did* light the spark that was now burning its way across our
hungry country, but he never raised arms against the king. "That is not
true."

"It is nearly true," Pauline countered. "Your husband wrote, *To throw
off the yoke of despotism, I have tried everything short of civil war, which I
could have accomplished except that I feared its horrors.*"

Our older sister, Louise, was prone to mediate quarrels, but now took my side. "Lafayette is not the only member of the family to participate in the reform of France—"

Pauline slammed down her fork. "Your husband is just as much to blame. Marc truly wishes to abolish noble titles? It would dismantle hundreds of years of French history—and dissolve the prestige of our family!"

"Titles earned only by virtue of birth divide us from our fellow human beings," Louise said softly.

In this, Louise and I were in complete agreement, and I had no patience for those who did not see the need for momentous change. France had suffered a severe drought followed by a hailstorm so violent it beggared description. Livestock and game animals knocked dead to the ground. Olive and citrus groves smashed to bits. Wheat and barley fields decimated. All this followed by the most bitter winter in living memory—so cold it killed what remained of vineyards and orchards. Mountains of snow buried Paris, and the river froze solid, locking out shipments of grain. Flour was now so precious that even wealthy hostesses submitted to the indignity of asking guests to bring their own bread. Famine had us in her jaws, sending impoverished peasants into the streets, begging for charity. Yet here my family sat at our beautiful table in Versailles, eating off gilt-edged plates and drinking from porcelain cups, complaining that Gilbert was doing *too much* to help.

Even Maman was unnerved. "I do not like how the people treat the queen these days."

I did not like it either. In Paris, they called her *Madame Déficit* and hissed at her in the opera. The country's finances weren't in ruin because of the queen. Still, I knew that her every diamond, gilded carriage, and silver-dusted cake was paid for by crippling taxes on starving peasantry. Taxes from which nobles and clergy were exempt.

The people resented this, and who could blame them? The only remedy was good democratic reform. But when I said so, Pauline scoffed. "Mr. Jefferson and his soaring words have filled your head with *dreams*."

"It is not only Americans who dream of a better future," I said. For I had hosted some of the finest thinkers in France, from Turgot to Condorcet to Brissot and more. They all believed in liberty, and so did I. The convocation of the Estates-General was the natural step to bring it about. "You will all soon see that with reforms, we can enjoy a kinder standard of humanity for rich and poor alike."

To provoke me, Grand-mère drew up a list of proposals for the deputies on how to make non-Catholics suffer, each idea more terrible than the next. She loathed Protestants, claiming, *Nothing short of castration for heretics!* She had even worse plans for Jews. I chose to believe she did not really wish such evil on her fellow human beings, but merely wished to prove a point to me about the dangers and excesses of self-government. Yet I burned with faith. On the day of the convocation, I intruded upon my husband's toilette as his valet dressed him in the costume dictated by court protocol.

Gilbert scowled at the silly plume, but I was overcome. "What a picture you make, husband . . ." At thirty-two, Gilbert's once–fiery red hair had darkened to chestnut, but his years sat well on him; he had never been so masculine nor desirable. Yet he flipped the end of his cloth-of-gold cape with disdain. "I should wear black and march with the common people in sympathy."

Fastening his glittering diamond pin through the lace of his cravat, I said, "Everyone knows none of this would be happening if not for you."

"They should know it would not be happening but for *you*," he replied, touching his forehead to mine. "For standing by me when no one else would. For seeing through what I start . . ."

How happy he made me feel. How loved and appreciated . . . It moved me more than the trumpets heralding the pageantry of that glorious spring day when every budding tree seemed to strain with the nation to blossom into being. First in the procession came the king, resplendent in gold, his cap ornamented by the largest diamond in the realm. "*Vive le roi!*" people cried, waving from curbsides, windows, and rooftops. Then came the queen in silver. "*Vive la reine!*" was heard, though not as warmly.

From a balcony, pressed between my sisters all straining to see, I added my voice to the cries of rejoicing, for there was no holding back the tides of change now . . .

A month and a half later, while rain poured down upon Versailles in buckets, the deputies found their hall locked, and the defiant reformers splashed their way to the royal tennis court to vow *never to separate, and to meet wherever circumstances demand, until a constitution of the kingdom is established and affirmed on solid foundations.*

A week later, the king gave in.

France would at last have a constitutional monarchy. A government by and for the people with a declaration of rights—and my husband was determined to write that declaration. I cannot describe the mood that night. I lost count of toasts, and with the American delegation, I became giddy as a girl on champagne. Alone amongst them, only the peg-legged Gouverneur Morris refused to join in our jubilation.

Mr. Morris had written the preamble to the new Constitution of the United States and was, therefore, worthy of the hospitality always afforded to him. But he was also a sybaritic fellow, better known for furtive love affairs in the shadows of the Louvre than he was for enlightened ideals. And that night he warned we were plunging *headlong into destruction*, adding that *the history and character of the French does not mold itself so easily to liberty*.

This was too much to bear in silence, and with a rather overfilled glass of wine, I said, "Surely you do not mean to say that we French are somehow inferior in character to you Americans . . ."

Morris drank deeply of his red claret. "I don't think you understand the forces you are toying with, or the sorts of people waiting to take advantage."

It astonished me to think a man who had lived in France less than a year might consider himself such an expert. "Sir, the alternative to reform is letting our people freeze and starve . . ."

Morris laughed. "None of the beggars I've seen complain to me of cold. They all ask for a morsel of bread, and by *bread* they mean wine, and by *wine* they mean liquor."

His lack of compassion startled me; perhaps he had not seen the true suffering I had witnessed in visiting prisons and almshouses, or in the countryside near Chavaniac. Or perhaps he did not wish to see it. As so many in my class did not wish to see. "You are an aristocrat, sir."

Morris laughed again. "If *I* am the aristocrat here, Madame Lafayette, what does that make you?"

"I suppose it makes me the American."

Lafayette guffawed at that, eyes shining with pride.

"Touché!" Morris refilled his glass. "Forgive me. My opinions are drawn only from human nature and ought not therefore to have much respect in this *age of refinement*."

I did not like how he mocked us. And it vexed me to learn he was being considered as the replacement for the inspiring Minister Jefferson, who, after years of service in France, was now keen to return with his daughters to Virginia. We would be sorry to see the Jeffersons go, something I expressed with emotion on the Fourth of July celebration at the American embassy.

There Jefferson kissed my hand. "How sorry we are to quit your country, madame, but after five years, I sorely miss mine."

He invited me, with all sincerity, to visit Monticello, his mountaintop estate in Virginia, and left us with silhouettes of his image to remember him by. "I hope I will be remembered as having been of some service to your husband in drafting a declaration of rights for France."

Gilbert smiled with as much modesty as he could muster. A French declaration of rights had been his desire from the start—from the first moment he hung the American Declaration of Independence in a double-paned frame, determined to fill the empty half with its match.

My husband had already fought tyranny with a sword; it would be to his greater glory if he could fight with ink. Every night now, Gilbert was working over a writing table—scratching out words, putting them back, adopting suggestions, debating clauses. Some believed it impious folly to declare all of mankind deserving of equal and fair treatment of the laws, entitled to free expression and exercise of religion. Yet I believed it was the wish of a loving God for his children. It is certainly what I wished for mine.

I was warned by friends in the queen's circle that my husband was a marked man. Yet I could see no reason the royals would wish to punish Lafayette for spelling out the rights of every citizen, unless the king's agreement to a constitutional monarchy was insincere. Was the king himself—a king for whom I had much affection—dishonorable? And if he were so dishonorable as to lie to his entire nation, would he stoop to arrest my husband . . . or kill him?

Lafayette did not seem frightened. "This is not my first warning," he told me. "Philippe sent an emissary to tell me the king intends to strike out at us both. He proposes that I join forces with him."

The suggestion startled me. "You and Philippe, join forces?"

Gilbert snorted at the absurd idea. "Truthfully, I believe that since he inherited his father's title as the duc d'Orléans, Philippe has been scheming to take the throne for himself . . . and I will never help him do it."

What a knave Philippe was. I knew he now styled himself a champion of the people, and had curried favor by opening up his Palais-Royale to the public. As a prince of the blood and a cousin to the king, he had some distant claim to the throne, but did he dare make a play for it? Or did he simply intend to embroil my husband in treason?

"You must not fear, my dear heart. If I am taken up by the king's guards, Jefferson will claim me as an American citizen." Lafayette said this mostly in jest, but it was all very serious now. Jefferson had been courageous to pen the American Declaration of Independence in defiance of his English king. *That* king had been across the ocean. Our king's palace gate was no more than a hundred steps from where my husband slept at Versailles. Our defiance was more dangerous in every way, but who else had the stature and moral standing to take the risk?

Gilbert said, "To give France a declaration of rights, Adrienne, will be the greatest day of my life, even if I am dragged to the dungeon for it."

Which is why I would not dissuade him. He feared for the children and me to see him shackled by the king's soldiers and hauled away to the Bastille, so we were trundled off to Paris, where I was left to read in the gazettes how my husband rose to read his Declaration of the Rights of Man and of the Citizen.

They said he was resolute and cool, but that his words set the chamber aflame. Royalists said this was a dangerous document. An insult. That it was too American. That above all, this declaration must not be circulated, lest it incite the public. But it was already far too late.

The French Revolution was begun . . .

TWENTY-EIGHT

MARTHE
Chavaniac-Lafayette
May 1942

OPEN RESISTANCE AT THE PREVENTORIUM BEGAN WITH BOYS throwing shit at the baron's convertible. With the welcome sun of springtime, I was outside with a class of girls when our acting president screeched into the drive, then slammed noisily out of his vehicle, red-faced and shouting as messy brown slop dripped from the hood.

I sent some of the girls for buckets of water to rinse it clean while Anna and the baroness came out to see what the matter was. And now the baron's voice booms with fury. "It happened not far from the boys' dormitory. A group of the older ones threw manure! They didn't even have the decency to run."

Serves you right, I think, and not just because the boys have been more rebellious than ever, stealing bicycles and riding into town, where they're forbidden to go.

The baroness has complained about this, but the disappointment on her face now isn't for the boys; it's for the baron. "Leave it alone, Amaury. You made your choice."

The coolness between the baroness and her husband started with Madame Simon's departure, but it has since become an icy chill, and it's left to Anna to calm her father's temper. "It's all right, Papa. You're too busy to be running errands in Paulhaguet anyway. I'll go!"

Once the car is cleaned, the baron surrenders the keys, and Anna gets behind the wheel and lowers the top down. "You're brave," I say, hanging over the window. "What makes you so sure they won't throw shit at you too?"

"My chances would be better if you came with me. Get in. I'll buy you lunch."

Always tempted to get away from the castle—and having finished my classes for the day—I hop into the leather passenger seat and hold on to my red beret, laughing as she peels out. We haven't even left the village before she asks, "So do you know which of the boys is responsible for pelting Papa's car?"

"Afraid not."

She gives me a sideways glance. "I thought you said you know all the castle's secrets."

"I could guess," I say, feeling a little exhilarated as Anna takes the hairpin turns like a daredevil.

Exhilarated just to be with her.

"I'm guessing it's Oscar," she says.

It's definitely Oscar. The younger boys recovering at the preventorium listen to him; admire him, even. "It's the Riom Trial," I explain. "It has a lot of people mad at your father for testifying."

It's not a subject Anna likes to talk about, so it isn't until after we've had lunch, haggled with shopkeepers, and are loading supplies into the car that she confides, "Maman is furious that he testified."

"I don't blame her," I say.

Anna turns to me in surprise. "My father is a decorated war hero. Who is Maman to question him?"

"His wife? Anna, it was a show trial meant to blame France for the war."

"My father didn't blame France," she says a little heatedly. "He blamed the ministers who didn't prepare for war. When he served in the senate, he warned about Hitler's Luftwaffe. He argued again and again for defense funding to buy planes. It's why he started his airplane academy; he knew we'd need pilots to defend us, but he was dismissed by these weak politicians who—"

"Who led France," I snap. "They were our elected officials. Our former prime ministers and cabinet members. The Marshal put the *republic* on trial."

"Since when do you care about the republic?"

I pause, taken aback. "I actually have no idea. I guess I should've cared long before now. It wasn't perfect. But at least we had the right to say so under the republic, and—"

"Papa didn't do any harm. If anything, the trial only made everyone more sympathetic to the defendants." At least she's right about that. It caused such an outcry that the Marshal called the trial off and shipped the defendants to concentration camps. "You have to understand, Marthe, my father had no choice."

"Your father is trying to play it both ways!"

Anna's tone is sharp as a needle as she opens the car door. "We're all trying to play it both ways."

"Not all of us," I shoot back.

"So you didn't sign a loyalty oath?"

It hits me square in the conscience but feels unfair. I'm angry that we're arguing about politics—that we're arguing at all. "Whatever compromises I've made, at least mine can't get anybody executed."

Anybody but me, anyway.

"They're all dead men already, Marthe. Don't you understand?"

The way she says this—without obvious disgust—absolutely infuriates me. Maybe I *don't* understand. Maybe I'm being naive and self-righteous. All I know is that I feel real pain to realize we really don't think alike at all . . .

Instead of getting in the car, I say, "I'll walk."

"Be serious, Marthe. It's almost a two-hour walk back."

"I don't care. I'd rather not be in the same car with you right now."

IN A TERRIBLE TEMPER, I CUT THROUGH THE WOODS, MY STOMPERS crunching on twigs and desiccated leaves. I've been walking about an hour when I hear rustling in the foliage and peer between pine boughs, looking for a rabbit, or even a snake. I'd be happy to make either into a stew, but the rustling stops, so I keep going, tucking my hands in my coat pockets as I trudge on.

It's the hammering of a woodpecker's beak on a tree trunk that startles me. I turn, and when I do, I glimpse an encampment with a dying fire. I back up, wary, but I'm not alarmed until something—*someone*—grabs me.

Blackened fingers wrap tight around my arm, and as I try to wrench free, we both fall to the ground. I scream bloody murder all the way down—but my scream is cut off by a dirty hand clamping over my mouth.

Then I'm left to struggle under the bearded stranger's weight, terrified of what he might do. Even before the war, desperate men fled to the French countryside. This one might be a Spanish revolutionary who can't go home without Franco lining him up against a wall. Maybe a communist on the run from the law, or a hidden foreign Jew, or a dangerous highwayman. I don't know which, but I bite like a rabid animal, sinking my teeth deep.

The taste of iron blood fills my mouth, and my attacker cries out, yanking his hand away.

"Get off, you bastard!" I fight like crazy, kicking and slugging.

Then other men emerge, rifles slung over their shoulders, and I think I'm done for.

"Let her go," one of them shouts. "She's harmless."

Heaving stinking breaths in my face, the man who grabbed me finally sits up on his haunches, releasing me. And that's when I realize that the man who told him to let me go is Gabriella's father. I'm shocked to see Uriah Kohn's familiar face, and almost wouldn't have recognized him now that he's grown a mustache. I want to ask what the hell he's doing out here with dangerous-looking men, but I don't want to stay and find out.

Scrambling to my feet in a shower of pine needles, I bolt away.

"*Arrêtez!*" he calls after me, but I don't stop. A branch whips my face and tears the hat from my head, but I don't stop for that either. I just keep running, slipping on wet earth as I go. Christ, I must've been out of my head to come this way alone, even if I have been tromping in these woods all my life.

"*S'il vous plaît, mademoiselle!*"

Panting and breathless, my coat covered with brambles, I gasp, "What do you want?"

"To explain," he says, catching up with me. "To apologize. These days, for people like me, it's safer in the forest. Do you understand?"

Given what's happening in the Occupied Zone, who can blame him for going into hiding? But the men he's with have *guns*. Bolt-action rifles and revolvers—there's no way they have permits for them. "Does Madame Pinton know you're armed?"

He grimaces. "Mademoiselle, I made my career in the army. They may say I can't serve because I'm a Jew. But mark my words, when the time comes, I'm not going to go meekly."

I don't know what he means by *when the time comes.*

"My daughter. She's well?"

I nod. "She's made a pet of the castle's meanest old tomcat. You should visit Chavaniac to see her."

"I can't," he says. "Someone in the village might recognize me. I went to school at the castle, you see."

I blink. I had no idea. He must have been in one of the first graduating classes. I would have been too young to know or remember him. But Madame Simon would; no wonder she changed her mind about helping him. And of course now I understand why he brought his family to Auvergne; he knows that a deep, dark wood that is cold even in springtime makes for a good place to hide.

He offers back my red beret. "Here, I'm sorry. No one meant to hurt or frighten you."

"Just keep it," I say, still a little angry with Anna, and knowing he needs a warm hat more than I do.

By the time I limp back to the road, my nerves are so shot that when a car sputters up next to me, I nearly duck back behind a tree. Then I recognize the gendarme in the driver's seat.

"*Mademoiselle?*" Sergeant Travert calls from the open window of his black-and-white, steering to the side of the road, tires crunching on gravel. I try to tuck my hair back into bobby pins that have come loose. It's hopeless, and his voice lowers in concern. "Is something wrong?"

I shake my head. I feel a bruise welling on my knee and my pant leg is cut up, but no real harm has come to me; I've just taken a fright.

Travert asks, "You're hurt?"

We're supposed to report things like armed men hiding in the woods, but I say, "I stumbled over a log."

The gendarme glances to the woods, then back to me. "You seem shaken."

If he's suspicious, he might go looking. And if he goes looking, someone's going to get hurt, so I try to be more convincing. "I just . . . I had an argument with a friend, and wanted to clear my head. I lost track of where I was."

His bushy eyebrow lifts a fraction. "You came out to walk these woods alone, without a hat?"

"I—I lost it."

"Ah, we can retrace your steps. I'll help you find it."

"I mean that I lost it somewhere in the castle. I had to go without it today. I'm sure it will turn up."

I don't think he believes me. "You can't be too careful these days, you know. If someone attacked you—"

"No one attacked me." I just blundered onto a hiding spot, and they didn't want me to go blabbing about it. I must have surprised and frightened the man who grabbed me as much as he and his comrades surprised and frightened me.

Now the gendarme reaches across to open the side door. "Get in. I'll take you back to the castle."

"Thanks." I slide into the passenger seat. "Sorry to be a bother."

"A pretty girl like you is worth the bother." Travert takes a pack of cigarettes from the pocket of his uniform. Lucky Strikes. An American brand. Which means they must be dry and stale, because it's been years since the American exodus from the preventorium. "Here. Even nice girls smoke these days. It's the damned war; we all need something to put in our mouths."

I'm not sure if he's insinuating something vulgar, but I tuck them into my coat pocket. At the start of the war, Travert was a blimp of a man who patrolled the streets with a stick instead of a pistol. I liked him better then. Now he's become lean like everyone else, too impressed with the effect his new physique has on the village girls. How else can I explain the way he drapes a muscular arm over the back of the seat, like I'm meant to admire it? "Mademoiselle, for you, I can keep a secret."

"I'm not interesting enough to have secrets."

It's meant to discourage him, but he only chuckles. "You've always been the most interesting girl in these mountains. Even so, we all have to be careful and know who our friends are. The gendarmes need to know who lurks in our forests—but we can look the other way. We leave good, respectable people alone. No one wants to see them in the refugee camps."

I relax a little to hear that. We've seen reports from the Red Cross about the deplorable conditions at Gurs, Rieucros, and Rivesaltes. I'm glad he doesn't want to send anyone to those camps, but then he says, "Of course, not everyone in hiding is a good, respectable person. Since last month we've had to inspect the bags of everyone who comes into the prefecture, looking for stolen explosives. Now that the communists have started throwing bombs into swanky cafés . . . maybe you heard the news?"

It was a café where Nazi officers liked to go, so I can't really blame the communists. In fact, I'm starting to admire their daring. There's an underground Resistance now, though Faustine Xavier claims the only people who have joined it are madmen, nobodies, and ne'er-do-wells. She might be right, but still my heart feels a pang of pea-brained pride that any Frenchmen still want to fight! So I don't say anything to Travert about the men in the woods. "Not many swanky cafés up here in these mountains. Maybe you shouldn't worry."

He actually laughs. "*Touché.* Maybe I'm just hoping to do something more important than keep watch on the preventorium, the way my supervisor wants me to. We're supposed to keep Jews out, that sort of thing."

I feel sick. He doesn't mean Jewish children, does he? I pretend he's talking about the staff. "You know every teacher is Catholic. We're at Mass every Sunday."

Even if some of us mouth our prayers by rote . . .

Travert's cheeks redden. "We get denunciations, though. Mostly petty nonsense. It seems Madame LeVerrier was a rabble-rouser in her day."

It's impossible for me to imagine our stooped, lace-making doyenne as ever having been a *rabble-rouser*, but it infuriates me that someone denounced her. "Madame LeVerrier is almost *seventy*. No threat to anyone."

"All right," Travert says, holding up his hands in surrender. "Just make sure everyone at the castle has their papers in order in case someone higher up pays a visit. We have to be careful these days, especially someone like you."

"Someone like me?"

He gives a pointed glance at my torn trousers. "You're a walking legal infraction. The new prefect doesn't want women wearing pants."

Of all the stupidity. We're supposed to be *getting back to the land*, hiking and biking through nature—but heaven forbid we do it in trousers. We can't wear skirts either, because it's considered immodest to go without stockings, but nobody can get stockings except on the black market, so we're all painting black lines down the backs of our legs. "Maybe the new prefect should try walking through the woods in a skirt and heels, and see how he likes it."

The gendarme chuckles. "That's what I mean, mademoiselle—you've got a mouth. You stand out. People talk."

"About my pants, apparently."

He wags his bushy brows. "About your pants, your artwork, your friend—the baron's daughter. The two of you always together . . . together too much, some say." Sudden heat sears up the back of my neck at his implication that I'm a degenerate, and a wave of shame nearly drowns out what he's saying. "Such talk is dangerous these days."

"Then I guess you'd better stop the damned car," I rasp, finally finding my voice. "I wouldn't want to start gossip by being seen in your passenger seat."

"*D'accord*," he says, chuckling. "Suit yourself."

The gendarme lets me out just before we get to the village, and I slam his door. From there, I rush up the cobbled street past the fountain and the old statue of Lady Liberty. I break into a run at the castle gates, making a beeline for the square tower, taking the stairs two at a time. I want to warn Anna—I want to tell her everything, but when I burst into the records room, her dark lashes are glistening with tears. "Oh, Marthe. I'm so sorry . . ."

Remembering how we left it, I'm sorry too. I start to say that I don't want to fight about anything ever again, when I realize that she's clutching an official letter with a Nazi stamp. My heart sinks, thinking it must be about her husband.

Then she gives me the letter, and I see it's for me.

"The censors already opened it," she says tearfully. "It's Henri . . ."

TWENTY-NINE

BEATRICE
Newport, Rhode Island
August 1915

I TOOK THE COWARD'S WAY OUT WITH MAX FURLAUD, NOT TRUST-
ing myself to explain face-to-face that Willie's amputation changed nothing and everything. It's true that our marriage had been broken long
before the surgery, but somehow the broken pieces still *were* a marriage,
weren't they?

My letter to Max was not tender, for the shock and guilt had cured
me of that stage of my disease. I merely spelled out the bare facts, then
added, *As my affection for you cannot ripen into more, I think it best to break
off relations that might prove too fond. In any case, you would have learned
something of the real Beatrice as time went on. And I'm afraid she is a creature
far different than your imagination painted her.*

A creature far different than my own imagination painted me too, for
I was no longer an intrepid lady adventurer in a war zone, but back in the
bosom of high society, playing my old part.

"Steady, darling," I told my son Ashley, supporting his arm at the
elbow to help line up his tennis racket. On the other side of the net was
some Vanderbilt or Belmont boy, as Newport was positively *infested* with
the cream of society for the summer, all keen for parties and sporting
events as if there weren't any war at all across the sea.

Here at the Chanler villa we were waiting on tenterhooks for news of
Willie's amputation—which had been rescheduled several times now as
the doctors consulted. To keep our minds off it, I encouraged my boys to
take part in all the sports and games. Would their father—once such an
avid sportsman—ever be able to teach them to play tennis now?

Of course, it wasn't *all* fun and games in Newport. Clara Simon and

Marie-Louise LeVerrier had returned with us to America, carrying nearly one hundred thousand dollars' worth of French dolls that had been manufactured by wounded soldiers, widows, and refugee children. We were going to auction them off under the aegis of the Lafayette Fund at our next gala, the seating arrangements for which were driving poor Emily Sloane to distraction. "Disaster!" she called, approaching from the veranda. "The Reginald Vanderbilts have *both* decided to attend."

The married couple despised each other. Like most estranged couples in our set, they took turns each summer—one in Newport, the other in Europe—so as to avoid unpleasantness. With the war, everyone was now forced into proximity. "I'm afraid they'll just have to find a way to get along," I said. "Sacrifices must be made."

Emily squared her shoulders. "Yes. And in keeping with that theme, I need to tell you something." Her tone made me think I needed to sit down for this, so I followed her to a sunny bench.

"I have to resign as secretary of the Lafayette Fund," she said.

"Whyever would you do that?"

"Because I saw my mother last night," Emily said, so stiffly I thought she might snap. "I was dancing with my father, he accidentally trod on a woman's shoe, and when he turned to apologize, there she was. This woman who abandoned us both so many years ago . . ."

"Oh, Emily," I said, reaching for her hands.

She wore a fractured, watery smile. "After all these years, she didn't even recognize me."

How ghastly. What kind of woman doesn't know her own child? My heart broke for my dear friend, though I didn't understand what this could possibly have to do with her resigning. "I realize that seeing your mother must have given you—"

"Perfect clarity, actually. All these years, she's lived entirely for herself without a care for those she left behind. I'm not sure she even knows what love *is*. I finally do. That's why I have to go back to France for the man I love."

"What could you do for Amaury de LaGrange that you can't do here?"

"I could marry him." *Now, before he's killed in the war,* she meant. "It can't wait. Not even for my father's permission—if he doesn't give it, I'll elope. I don't care if we're the only two people in the chapel. I have to go back straightaway on the first ship that will take me."

She's leaving me, I thought with a selfish pang, and came up with a way to change her mind. Emily was filled with fire, but I knew how to douse it. I'd remind her of the needs of her aging father, who was no doubt smarting from this encounter with his estranged wife too. I'd remind Emily of all the work she'd be abandoning at the Lafayette Fund! If I had to, I'd even remind her of her commitment to help me sell all those dolls, without which maimed French soldiers and their children would freeze this winter, and possibly starve.

Did she want that on her conscience?

Unfortunately, the irritating truth about abiding friendship is that it fills you with an overwhelming desire to be worthy of it. I couldn't be the one to hold Emily back. "The *Espagne* sails from New York on September fifth . . ."

Emily's tears finally did come, and she sniffled into a handkerchief. "I'll make it up to you someday. Somehow. I'd have wanted to ask you to be my maid of honor, but I know you'll be with me in spirit . . . I thought you might ask Mrs. Chapman to take my place at the Lafayette Fund."

"A wonderful idea," I said, a little weepy too. "Elizabeth needs something to take her mind off her worries for Victor."

My nephew had finally joined the elite American flying unit that would come to be known as the Lafayette Escadrille—and had already written to us in poetic terms about his first bombing raids.

You can't imagine what it's like to see the forest below with its edges as though cut by a scissors—

—seeing our faint shadow on the filmy veil of moving clouds surrounded by sometimes one, often two, rainbows.

One gets such an enormous feeling of space—

So many of my loved ones were at risk now, in the zone of danger without me. On the day Emily was to set sail, the Germans torpedoed another civilian passenger liner, and I knew my heart was going to be in my throat until I learned of her safe arrival. Still she insisted on going. In parting, she gave me a dizzying report specifying the number of kits, ambulances, knitted goods, rain ponchos, and arctic shoes for the troops that we'd sent in the past year. Seeing it all itemized gave us both an enormous sense of accomplishment. From a fly-wisp idea shared by two high-society ladies aboard a steamship, we'd forged the Lafayette Fund into a fine-tuned enterprise that was making a real difference.

"I'll still work on the other side of the ocean," she promised, but of course, I knew it wouldn't be the same. She also promised to visit Victor now that he and Lieutenant LaGrange were both pilots. "Since I'm taking my nurse's training, I'll visit Mr. Chanler as well—perhaps I'll patch him up after the amputation and ship him back to you." I laughed, imagining that if anyone could manage Willie, she could. "And if—well—if I should happen to cross paths with Captain Furlaud, is there anything you should wish me to say?"

What could I possibly say to Max? He'd given me a few weeks of joy. Now that was gone, and in its place, guilt had seeped past my brave mask like chlorine gas. I'd asked him not to write, and he'd honored my request. Perhaps he didn't even think of me now, and that would be for the better. But I still worried about him every day. "Tell him only that *Marthe* prays for his safety."

Thereupon I presented Emily with a hatbox. "Wear it on your honeymoon. Or your wedding. Something borrowed *and* something blue . . ."

She hugged me. "I'll wear it with pride at the wedding, which is to be a small affair at the Ritz. Nothing to write home about."

"Write anyway," I commanded.

Before we exchanged our final embrace, she said, "And *you* must write and tell me of your next mad plan."

MY NEXT MAD PLAN WAS A NATIONAL LAFAYETTE DAY. I ANnounced it at the annual meeting of the Lafayette Fund in New York. "We observe Columbus Day, Washington's Birthday, and Lincoln's Birthday. Is it not equally appropriate that we should commemorate Lafayette, who gave so much that we might be free?"

I made up fifty thousand souvenir buttons for the children to sell. My little brigade of patriotic youngsters called themselves the Children of

1915 and adopted Roosevelt's motto as their own: *Never be neutral between right and wrong.*

I had plenty to keep me busy in the course of the next year. But as time passed, only one question occupied my mind. *Where was Willie?*

Was it all a cruel joke . . . just a ruse to make me go back to America? Last summer, I was sitting at the edge of the ambassador's desk in tears, promising my husband that after his amputation, he'd have a wife waiting for him at home. Since then, Willie had come safely through his surgery—and I'd told the reporters camped outside my door that Mr. Chanler was regaining his strength and would be home by Christmas. But the holiday had come and gone. Here the children and I were in Newport for yet another summer, and their father was still absent. At first, his doctors said Willie wasn't well enough for travel. Then, of course, there were the usual worries about crossing a mine-laden sea. Maybe I was simply impatient and resentful, because I'd given up my war relief work in France, and I'd given up Max Furlaud and Emily Sloane, and I was feeling terribly alone.

I tried to sculpt, but I could not find life within clay or stone while the war was extinguishing so many real lives made of flesh and blood. Not even attending the presidential conventions in Chicago, where ten thousand women in white marched to demand the vote, had lifted my mood. I'd cheered Theodore Roosevelt for ninety-three minutes on the convention floor, knowing he was the only one who could oust President Wilson and defeat his policy of American neutrality. Still, in the end, Roosevelt declined the nomination, and I was beside myself. Was the old Rough Rider fading?

Perhaps all the giants were.

"Willie's a proud man," said Elizabeth Chapman, unpacking a picnic lunch on the beach while the children ran in the surf. "I've limped all my life, and he's seen me as an object of pity. He's having a hard time working out how he sees himself without a leg, and he probably doesn't want an audience while he does the reckoning."

Then he should tell me so, I thought. "He's written you?"

She smiled, unwrapping Mr. Chapman's sandwich for him. "No, but Victor has, and we read between the lines."

I couldn't resent Willie for confiding in our nephew. Especially now that Victor had become a national hero. His exploits had captured the attention of the public, all of whom were riveted by vivid newspaper descriptions of diving and firing through the clouds over France. My boys pored over headlines, in which their cousin was prominently featured, most recently for having fought off six German planes all by himself.

And to think I once thought my favorite nephew didn't have the temperament for war . . .

"They say a bullet grazed his head," Billy boasted with boyish wonder one morning in mid-June. "Victor just got bandaged up and got back in the fight."

I took the newspaper, determined not to let the Chapmans see it—as any pride they felt would certainly be matched by terror. Meanwhile, my freckled little Ashley made figure eights in the air with his toy plane. "I hope the war won't be over before we get our chance!"

I hope it is, I thought.

Later, their uncle Jack said, "We'd better be prepared for it to go on for some time . . ." The Chapmans were preparing for America to enter the war with or without Woodrow Wilson's say-so. My sister-in-law was particularly active in the National Security League, serving alongside the Roosevelts, including the former president's niece Eleanor. And at the Lafayette Fund, she was helping me prepare for the first annual Lafayette Day.

I'd arm-twisted half the nation into paying tribute.

We'd planned celebratory banquets in New York, statue dedications in New Orleans, and a memorial service in Boston. And that's to say nothing of my forthcoming Allied Bazaar, during which I intended to raise a million dollars for the cause. I *was* good at this, but it wasn't the same without Emily Sloane.

She wrote frequently—of her hurried wedding, her husband's heroics over the skies of France, and her work as a nurse in the hospitals. She wrote too, very recently, that she was expecting a child. She knew, of course, that I wanted to be with her for the birth, but understood why I couldn't be.

I wished I understood it half as well. Feeling as if I were in exile, having left people I loved to fend for themselves, I was rambling around in my husband's family summer cottage . . . still *waiting* for him, as promised. Which is why, when his cable came at the end of June, I tore it open with irritation, suspecting that Willie was going to postpone his trip home yet again.

Instead, his cable brought me to my knees. I sank down, obliterated, reading the letters again and again, hoping somehow to make them spell out something else. Still, they always said the same thing.

OUR DEAR VICTOR IS GONE

SHOT DOWN AND KILLED IN ACTION

I AM RETURNING TO NEW YORK ON NEXT SHIP

There on my knees, one hand over my mouth, I rocked, absorbing this until the shock gave way to sobs. Oh, I'd never deceived myself about the danger. Never let my high-minded talk blind me to the blood price. Nor did I suppose, even for a moment, that my nephew would be safe because he had a good name, a good nature, and was so adored. Still, my sense of loss was so profound I couldn't get off the floor.

My darling nephew would never stir up hornets' nests again, would never paint a watercolor or design a building, would never have a sweet-heart or a child. I would never see his wide toothy grin again . . .

Do you realize fully what you're doing, you vociferous criers-out in the cause of humanity, you members of the Lafayette League and other mushy beldames who make themselves a party to murder?

The words of that long-ago leaflet billowed up inside me until I tasted ashes. I wasn't one of those society ladies in England handing out white feathers to shame men into the fight. But I was trying to shame a whole nation into war, and if I got my way, how many more American boys like Victor would die?

PART

THREE

THIRTY

MARTHE
Chavaniac-Lafayette
Summer 1942

GRIEF IS LIKE THICK MORNING FOG.

You breathe it, swim in it, drown in it—or at least you *want* to drown, but for some damned reason, you keep living, breathing, walking. One foot in front of the other even though you can't see the path ahead. You tiptoe, and so does everybody else . . .

—poor thing. Fiancé died in a German prison camp. Typhus.
Without Henri Pinton, she's got nobody now.
—why didn't she marry him before he went?

Good question. Why didn't I? I could've given Henri, and myself, a few weeks of wedded bliss before he got called up to his regiment. We wouldn't have even had time to know if it was a mistake. We could've rented a little house in the village and enjoyed playful mornings in bed— Henri was always like a kid in a candy store when I let him touch me, like he thought he was getting away with something, even though he was always the one to stop. Since the rationing hadn't started yet, we could've had coffee at the village café with a warm pastry, and when I came home from teaching, he'd be studying by the fire with a baguette, a crock of butter, and maybe a little salted ham.

Hey, blondie, he'd have said, and then we could've listened to the radio and argued about dirtied dishes in the sink. It wasn't the life I'd dreamed of, but we could've been happy for all the time we had left. All the time we'd ever have, and I wasted it.

I could've had his baby. Now there'll never be another little gap-toothed boy with Henri's dark eyes and dark hair. He died, not in battle, but of some disease that he was probably trying to help others fight, and now he is gone like he never existed—he's left nothing behind but a few photographs and a brokenhearted mother. And me . . . whoever I really am.

Just a nobody from Chavaniac.

"Drink up, Marthe," Anna says, popping off the cap of a bottle of cold soda pop and trying to coax me to drink by the castle's pool, where we supervise kids splashing and swimming on a hot day. I can't figure out where she got the bottle of soda, but she's been like a persistent herding dog since Henri's death, nipping at my heels.

You have to eat, Marthe.

—get just a little sleep. Just close your eyes for a few minutes.

—sunshine is just the thing. Dr. Anglade says so!

Well, Dr. Anglade might be shocked to hear it, but sunshine isn't a cure for grief. The sun just blinds me and sets off that strange buzzing in my ears that makes the sound of the children laughing and playing all seem very far away. Even the soda is tasteless as it slips down my parched throat. What I need is a *real* drink. The baron keeps a hidden stash of liquor in the cellar—quite a collection of top-shelf hooch—and I've been nipping from it on a nightly basis.

As I've said, I know all the castle's secret places.

"Maîtresse!" calls little Gabriella, in a striped swimsuit, waving her arms at me before doing a cannonball into the pool. She's not a little mouse anymore; she's made friends other than the mean tomcat. She's a good student too. If she were living in the Occupied Zone, she'd be wearing a yellow star, but here at the Lafayette Preventorium, she's just a child like any other.

Her father still doesn't think it's safe to visit—not with Sergeant Travert and his gendarmes making spot patrols—so Gabriella comes to church every Sunday and mimics all the prayers. It's the same church where the curé had a small service for Henri, putting a photo of him on the wall with other fallen villagers of other wars, and everyone lit candles in Henri's honor.

We don't know where he's really buried.

Probably some pig-shit hole, Madame Pinton had shouted the day she learned of Henri's death. Then she let out a wail that still echoes in my ears all these months later. After her first burst of anguish, she didn't seem to want to say another word to me. And I don't blame her.

Now Gabriella comes up out of the pool, grinning, her hair soaked and water dripping down her nose. "Was it good, Maîtresse? Did I make a big splash?"

I clap. "Very good, little squirt! Now try the diving board."

I've discovered that I can just *do* that. Put on a happy mask and go through the motions, pretending everything's fine. *Of course I can keep teaching. I'm better now. Right as rain!*

Acting like a person is like squeezing into some old dress that doesn't fit anymore—I can breathe shallowly for a few hours, but then the seams start ripping and I need to claw it off and gulp in air. Even here, out in the open summer sky, with the vision of the castle towers on the horizon, I feel that suffocating sensation. So I get up and walk to the church to be alone.

I come here a lot since Henri died; the big wooden doors are never locked. The curé has a note on the door warning against letting in the roaming cats so they don't knock over any candles. On my knees in the empty pews, I don't talk to God, because he clearly doesn't care about me or anyone else—but I like the quiet, which is why I'm annoyed to hear someone come in.

Anna has followed me. She makes the sign of the cross, kneels beside me, and clasps her hands beneath her chin. But she doesn't speak to God either. "I wish it wasn't me who told you Henri died."

"Someone would have."

"You'll always remember it was me . . . it's tainted our friendship."

Is that what she thinks—that I blame her for telling me? No. I'm the one who tainted our friendship with sinful thoughts . . . that didn't even feel sinful. But they were disloyal to Henri, and I don't know how to forgive myself for that. I let her get too close, and now I want to put distance between us.

We can't be friends like before.

"I have some news," she says.

It's going to be bad. There's been nothing *but* bad news all summer.

The shortages are worse than ever. Flour. Sugar. Petrol. The Vichy-controlled newspapers blame it on Jews. They're supposedly hoarding for profit. We all know better. It's the Nazis who are starving us.

On May Day, the Nazis lined up and shot French boys for painting anti-German graffiti. On Bastille Day, defiant crowds came out shouting for liberty, equality, and brotherhood. People were again shot dead for it. At least in nearby Clermont-Ferrand, protestors managed to sing the "Marseillaise" without being stopped by the gendarmes, because of a band of armed men from the nearby forests.

They fought back.

Remembering what Monsieur Kohn said, some part of me wonders—hopes, even—that the armed men I stumbled over in the forest were the ones who fought back in Clermont-Ferrand.

There are now open reports of death camps—some say more than a million Jews have been murdered already in the east. And here in France, thirteen thousand Jews in the Occupied Zone—fathers, mothers, and children—were shoved into Vélodrome d'Hiver, the indoor bicycle stadium, to await internment at Drancy, and then deportation. Even knowing what that might mean, our own policemen in Paris helped the Nazis do it. So when I ask Anna, "What news?" I'm half wondering if the British RAF is going to bomb us into hell, and if we deserve it.

But what she says is, "I've been thinking about the Relève." She means the new program through which French people can now volunteer to work for Hitler in Germany. In return, they'll release some French prisoners of war. It's a grotesque idea—Sam's been ranting on about it, and everywhere in the village we hear people cursing it, so I just stare at Anna.

"Don't look at me that way," she says. "The Nazis are executing French officers in retaliation—just pulling them out of prison camps and shooting them. My husband wasn't shot for these latest incidents, but he could've been. Next time, he might be."

She's not wrong. The Nazis love to shoot people they think will make big news—and a French nobleman will send a message that we're all just sheep to them, no matter what airs we put on. Even so, I can't believe what she's considering. "You think they'll set your husband free if you go to Germany in his place? You've lost your mind! He's a high-value hostage; they're not going to make that trade. Even if they would, you'd be helping the enemy."

"But the chief of the government says—"

"To hell with him!" I don't care that I've said it in the middle of a church. "And to hell with you if you're going to—what—work in one of their factories making guns for the Nazis? Your husband would never be able to look you in the eye again, and neither would I."

She slides back on the bench and puts her face in her hands. "I don't know what to do, Marthe! I feel so guilty."

"For what?"

She's quiet so long that I begin to wonder—or maybe even hope, in spite of my anger and distrust—that she's felt about me the way I feel about her. But in the end she says, "For being alive, when your Henri is dead. For being free, when my husband is in a cage. For not being able to do anything that could make the least bit of difference to the world."

That's not what we were taught here at Chavaniac. It's not what Adrienne Lafayette believed when she lived here. It's not what Madame Beatrice believed when she made this place a haven for desperate children. And I don't believe it either. I want to make a difference. More of one, anyway. I'm just not yet sure how.

I retreat to my turret. To my escape at the bottom of a bottle, where I won't feel anything. But once I'm good and *drunk*, I stare at the block of translucent marble the baroness procured for me. I've been studying it for days, thinking about the veins. Studying my sketches, deciding which one best captures Adrienne Lafayette. Wishing I could bring her to life again. I should make a clay model first, but tonight I just want to *hit* something, so I grab a hammer and point chisel to rough it out even though it will get grit, dust, and chunks of stone everywhere. I should be doing this outside; it's messy and hard work. Hard on my arms, shoulders, and back. It hurts . . . but I find that I want it to.

THIRTY-ONE

ADRIENNE
Paris
July 15, 1789

"WE NEED A LEADER, MADAME DE LAFAYETTE."

Having been roused from my bed, I now stood in the Hôtel de Ville with the city's elders, who cloistered around my husband's bust—the one I helped dedicate years ago. Then, as now, I was asked to stand in Lafayette's place. To answer in his name.

The king had refused to accept my husband's declaration of rights and set foreign mercenaries against Paris. And now the citizenry was in rebellion and had dismantled the ancient fortress of the Bastille stone by stone. For the first time in my life, I had awakened to a Paris sky no longer dominated by the eight fortress towers that had for so long reminded us of the king's absolute power. And I thought it an important lesson that though it takes many hands to build a prison, many hands can also take one apart . . .

But righteous fury was swiftly becoming disordered anarchy. Frightened and angry people, egged on by Philippe's mischief-makers, had a wax head of the duc d'Orléans and were proclaiming him the new and rightful king. *Was there no crisis Philippe would not try to turn to his advantage?*

If my husband were here in Paris, he would put a stop to it. But he was still at Versailles. And now the city's leaders were looking to me. "The people need a commander, Madame la marquise. Your husband turned citizens into soldiers in America; can he do it here? We have elected him in absentia to be commander of the new National Guard, but we cannot calm the people unless they know he will accept the appointment. You must tell us, if he can get to Paris, will Lafayette defend a sovereign people and restore public order?"

I put a hand to my mouth. I understood what was being asked. They wished to know if my husband would lead a new nation. They wished to know if he would be France's George Washington. Yet they posed the question, by necessity, to me. And for Lafayette's honor, whatever answer I gave must be true. I trembled at the responsibility. This was a mantle not easily taken up, and much harder to set down again. Still, everything Gilbert and I had done had led us to this point. And if I only quieted my own breath, I could hear the truth of his heart as my blood thrummed through it.

Resolving to uphold my husband's principles—and my own—I said, "He will accept."

I said this with a certainty only God could have granted me.

Oh, the joy I felt when, not long after, my husband led a procession of deputies into Paris! I clung to him in gratitude when he took me into his strong embrace. We strode together into the Hôtel de Ville, where he took command of the National Guard as I had pledged he would, and there he swore on his sword of honor—the one given to him by Dr. Franklin—that he would die to defend the liberty of the French nation.

An oath that bound us both.

Within the hour, the first floor of our townhome was an officers' mess where I fed hungry guardsmen. I doled out soup and porridge—emptying out our larder. Meanwhile, I heard dreadful stories of murders, heads being carried on pikes. The soldiers said the duc d'Orléans was behind it. I knew Philippe thrived on mayhem, but I blamed the king too. If he had agreed to a declaration of rights, he would have been the most beloved of monarchs, the enlightened king who gave up absolute power for the good of the nation.

Instead, he had sent soldiers.

Now Paris was in violent paroxysms. Never had I felt in such danger. Every morning Gilbert mounted his white horse to ride out in the name of restoring law and order, and, heart in my throat, I tried to banish the thought that I might never see him alive again.

While he quelled the mob's fury, I was on my feet, overseeing the kitchen and turning our house into a barracks. In the evenings, Gilbert returned drained and dispirited, hunched from the weight of our world upon his shoulders. "Today I stopped six people from being hanged by the mob. I do not know what will happen tomorrow."

What happened is that the king came to Paris.

King Louis rolled up to the gates in a small coach, almost entirely alone. Gilbert met him there, atop his now-famous white horse. To the king he said, "Sire, if you oppose a constitution, I am here to fight you. Otherwise, I will defend you with every last drop of my blood."

In response, the king surrendered himself into my husband's power.

Nothing else could have won our hearts more than this gesture. To everyone's joy, the king accepted a Revolutionary cockade in the colors of Paris—red and blue. Touched, my husband combined it with the white ribbon of the monarchy and held it aloft to the cheers of the crowd.

What a moment. One eclipsed only by our joy when the king wore it. The symbol my husband gave him became the tricolor—and soon every patriot in France wore one. It became our banner, and our flag.

And I hoped, this time, the king had come in good faith.

If so, then *liberty is accomplished*. God should smile upon us now. Certainly the people did, as every shop in Paris now hawked trinkets and leaflets celebrating my husband's role. Everyone declared themselves Fayettists, which greatly amused Mr. Morris, who stopped by to report on food shipments from America. "Well, Lafayette, it seems you are now the King of Paris . . ."

My husband shook this off with the dust on his boots. "If so, I reign over a city filled with enraged people who cannot seem to be calmed or reasoned with by anyone but me."

Hungry people found it hard to hear reason. Flour was still more precious than gold. Yes, people honored my husband above all men, but I believed their bloodlust would not stop until their bellies were full.

Near the end of July, I myself was forced to intervene on behalf of the commander of the Swiss Guard, who had fired on the crowd. I was so frightened they would tear the man to pieces that I cannot remember what I said on his behalf. I know only that he was spared on my say-so because, as one woman put it, "You are the Mother of the New Nation."

I might have taken more pride in this title if, the next day, a mob whipped up by the duc d'Orléans had not stormed the Hôtel de Ville in an attempt to kill a grain profiteer. To the enraged masses, my husband shouted, "I will not permit you to execute a man without a trial. It would dishonor us all. I could not support a revolution that employed such injustice."

In answer, Philippe's men swarmed the prisoner, ripping him quite literally from my husband's custody. The prisoner was swinging from a lamppost by the time my husband's men battled their way to him. Then the victim's head was sawed off, mounted on a pike, and carried to his horrified son-in-law, who was taunted to *kiss Papa*.

After telling me this story, Lafayette shook in my arms, sickened and distraught. "I saw the horrors of war in America, Adrienne. Scalping, smallpox—more death and disease than you can imagine. *But this* . . . what would Washington do?"

"From what you say of him, George Washington would never lend his name and reputation to these crimes."

"You are right," he said. "As always."

My husband announced that he would resign if these abuses continued. Within hours, it seemed as if every important person in Paris was in my parlor, begging us to reconsider. And Mr. Morris thumped his wooden leg to make his point. "Now is not the time to resign! Seize power, *rule* France, and bring an iron fist down over the country."

I gaped to realize the American was not jesting. And my husband made a sound of disgust. "One taste of power, sir, and I have eaten my fill."

Mr. Morris was not easily dissuaded. "You cannot resign. You cannot leave people to fend for themselves. I tell you frankly, sir, it is *not* what George Washington would do."

He had invoked Washington too. And as Gilbert pinched at the bridge of his nose, I knew he would rescind his resignation.

I STARTLED AWAKE AT THE CLANG OF THE TOCSIN BELLS, WONDERing if we were under attack. The king's brothers had fled to Austria; perhaps they had returned with a foreign army to put down the Revolution.

"What is it?" I asked as my husband received a missive from an aide-de-camp at our bedroom door.

"Fishwives," Lafayette replied, his reddish hair askew. "They've captured cannons and dragged them to the Hôtel de Ville."

I went to the window overlooking the river, where I saw apron-clad market women on the bridges carrying butcher knives, pitchforks, and rolling pins. "*Bread, bread, bread!*" they chanted.

"Keep the children inside." My husband pulled on his boots, then was out the door. By noon, he had not returned, and an endless stream of peasant women poured into every street, shouting for a march to Versailles.

Could this be spontaneous? The chants for bread were sincere, but ordinary women do not steal out of their houses before dawn to steal cannons, do they? I did not wish to think women incapable of protest, but to steal arms . . .

Were they taking advantage of the fact that my husband would never open fire upon ladies?

I fed our children a humble breakfast and, unable to eat a bite, gave my portion to the servants. Meanwhile, storm clouds darkened the sky. I prayed for rain. Rain would send people inside—give them time to reconsider violence, I thought. In this I was wrong. Even a cold wet wind did not disperse them.

I could not determine the mob's purpose in wishing to march on Versailles. Was it to plead with the king, overthrow him, or kill him? Later, I would learn that my husband refused, again and again, to allow a march. He was threatened with the lamppost. He was threatened with muskets. He was threatened hour after hour until at last he knew he would either die here or die defending the king. He chose the latter.

He was now a veritable hostage to the women—and to some of his own rebellious guardsmen whose pockets were filled with Philippe's gold. Thus, with rainfall battering against my windows, I watched my husband lead a long march he did not approve.

I stood desolate and in despair, my hand pressed to the glass, long after the sound of the drums faded. It would be seven hours, plodding in mud to reach Versailles. Long enough, I hoped, for the royal family to flee. For myself, I took the children to the Hôtel de Noailles, where

Grand-mère and my sister Pauline had determined our family should leave the country.

"Adrienne," Pauline said fiercely. "We cannot allow you to be here when the mob brings Lafayette's head back on a pike for you to kiss!"

I shuddered, realizing my family had given him up for dead. Even my own mind played evil tricks, imagining my husband beheaded. But I would not leave Paris. I would not leave France. I would not leave *him*. I prayed more feverishly than ever before, and my faith was rewarded, for the next morning my husband returned, leading a royal procession, installing the king and queen safely in the Tuileries Palace.

"God save the poor king," Grand-mère said, weeping. "He is overthrown!"

"He is *alive*," I said, realizing what a miracle that truly was.

I hurried home to the Rue de Bourbon to find Gilbert at the foot of our bed, head in hands. "I warned the royals," he said. "I sent word ahead. I sent drummers to make noise. I slowed the march by pacing the horses. I did everything to buy the royals time to flee, and nearly bought that time with my life; but the king was still somehow inexplicably *there* when the mob reached the palace."

Whether the king was brave or foolish, I could not decide. Of my husband's courage, I had no doubt, even though he trembled to tell the tale. "I made my men commit again to their oath to serve the law, the nation, and their king. We received word from the palace that the declaration of rights had been accepted, and the people shouted in triumph. This should have ended it, Adrienne. *This should have ended it.*"

But it did not.

"I went myself at midnight to the palace gates. My most loyal officers tried to stop me, grasping my hands and uniform to keep me from what they presumed would be certain execution. I went inside anyway, passing royal courtiers on the stairs who hissed that I was a *Cromwell.* As if I had come to murder them."

Cromwell, the English regicide! Shocked at the insult and the danger my husband had exposed himself to—with the angry mob on one side and the resentful royals on the other—I said, "Cromwell would never have had the courage to go alone into the palace."

"Just what I said," Gilbert replied, with a joyless smile. "I explained myself to the king—who allowed me to add my own men to his defense. With the mob quieted, I put my head on a pillow at three in the morning. An hour later, all hell was unleashed . . . the women had stormed the gates. A few wanted the queen's head. To quiet them, I had to take Marie Antoinette out onto the balcony, kiss her hand, and give her a Revolutionary cockade."

The tricolor, he meant. That symbol that was my husband's gift and my nation's unifying talisman. To give it to the queen was quick thinking and gallantry besides; my husband's trademark. Still, I felt faint to imagine Marie Antoinette's fear in such a moment. "But I do not understand why the king and queen are here in Paris."

"The mob demanded it. I managed that we returned with our lives, but only by a hair." My husband now was in a hot rage. "This is Philippe, again! I recognized his henchmen sprinkled amidst the women, egging them on. Every time the honest fishwives would see reason, his agitators would rile them again. And Philippe *himself* was seen breaking into the palace and giving direction to the mob, to the queen's rooms. There must be consequences."

I was present on the day my husband's guardsmen dragged Philippe to our home. He arrived, sweaty with resentment, and when I started to go, he called, "No, stay, madame. I want your husband to admit he is uncouth enough to *summon* the duc d'Orléans, a prince of the blood."

"Do you not proclaim yourself to be a man of the people now?" Gilbert asked coolly. "I did not think you would stand upon protocol of rank."

Philippe lifted his chin. "What do you want, General Redhead?"

"To warn that Paris is no longer safe for you."

Philippe laughed. "I am safer in Paris than *you*."

More than fifteen years of enmity between the two men had finally brought them to this reckoning, and I saw murder in my husband's eyes. "Understand, sir, that you are not safe anywhere I am."

Philippe stopped laughing. "You are threatening me."

Lafayette's expression was cold, like frigid mountain air. "My wife tells me you have friends in England. Visit them."

Philippe was not accustomed to taking orders. "Or *what*?"

In answer, Lafayette put his hand upon the pommel of his sword. The one carved with his great deeds in America. And I realized there might very well be bloodshed in my parlor. Philippe must have realized it too. He glanced at me, but I kept my eyes hard.

For once in his life, Philippe gauged us properly. "I will apply for a passport."

My husband nodded. "It will be granted."

Infuriated, Philippe turned to go, but before he had taken two steps, Lafayette called after him. "Philippe, if you return before the end of the Revolution, I will challenge you to a duel the same morning you arrive, and I will shoot you dead."

"HOW STRANGE THAT *YOU* CURTSY BEFORE ME," SAID MARIE ANTOI-nette, petting her little spaniel from her place of repose in the Tuileries Palace. "Since Lafayette is now the so-called King of Paris, you must be queen here . . ."

The mischief in the city had abated since Philippe's banishment. The newspapers ran for pages in praise of my husband's management of the crisis and his stewardship of a new democratic nation. With a renewed sense of hope, I took it upon myself to pay respects at my queen's levee. I still harbored much affection for Marie Antoinette, but I supposed I could not have been surprised by the cold reception. "Who has been tell-ing you such things, Your Majesty? My husband is about the business of finding men to fill important posts in the new government—not putting himself at the head of it."

"Then perhaps he should not have led a mob to Versailles."

"It was against his will."

She laughed. "Only you could possibly believe it, when here I sit, languishing in his jail!"

I worried for the common guardsmen to hear her compare a sumptu-ous royal palace to a jail, when we all knew of the rats, starvation, cold, and other horrors of actual prisons under the *ancien régime*. "He saved your life."

"Perhaps, but I would rather die than be in his debt."

I hoped, for her sake, that she did not mean this. I left her chambers praying she could find it within herself to relinquish ideas of absolute power and be the gracious queen of a free nation—a nation we would soon celebrate on the Champ de Mars, where a giant stadium was being constructed to celebrate the constitution.

Everyone was joining to help erect a triumphal arch and an altar of liberty; both my husband and the king wielded shovels to assist—a touching sight. Instead of wielding weapons in violence, my husband led the citizenry in carrying away carts of earth, slinging buckets of mortar, and driving poles for pavilions into the ground.

We would have music, entertainments, and a grand ball. Illuminations too, as in the happier days. Lafayette insisted our son, Georges, be with him to mark the passing of the torch of liberty from our generation to that of our children. So I told my boy, "You must be very well behaved and set the best example."

Our home was still overrun, every day, with officials and visitors; I fed sometimes three hundred in my parlor, courtyard, and hall. Anywhere there might be room for a table or a bedroll, men wearing the tricolor wedged themselves in. Some of them gifted us with keepsakes from the recent struggles, including a stone and a cannonball from the Bastille. Others were in desperate need of our charity.

I enlisted my daughters to serve and make our guests comfortable, wondering if even our considerable finances could withstand the increasing expense. Lafayette was right to decline a salary—the royalists would portray him as self-interested if he took a single assignat—but our coffers drained quickly.

We had scarcely any time alone, yet in stolen moments we risked making love, because with the coming Fête de la Fédération to celebrate the constitution, everything felt as if it were new.

Only storm clouds threatened our grand occasion. "Damn this rain," Gilbert said the morning of the spectacle. "It will keep the crowds away."

"It did not keep them from marching to Versailles," I reminded him.

And it did not keep them away this time either. Despite the weather, the procession through the magnificent arches went on, hour after hour.

The army, the officials, the veterans, circus performers—it was a magnificent, if wet, parade. At long last, the crucial moment arrived, and drums beat wildly to hurry my husband's footsteps. Maybe even God himself was a Fayettist, because as my husband prepared to make his oath with our boy at his side, the rain stopped and the sun broke through!

Lafayette put his golden-hilted sword upon the altar. Then all of us—hundreds of thousands—together mouthed the words of the oath of allegiance to the constitution, its king, and the nation in which we would all have a part. Even the king, without crown or scepter, made his oath before God. My faith had been shaken, but now it was restored.

The Revolution was over.

The Revolution was won.

If I was the Mother of the Nation, then this day of liberation was everything I hoped for my children. All the millions of them alive now, and yet to come . . .

THIRTY-TWO

BEATRICE
New York City
July 1916

THE WAR THAT KILLED MY NEPHEW HAD NOW COME TO OUR shores. Walking the streets of New York, I surveyed the damage, glass shards glittering like diamonds on the pavement. There'd been an explosion the night before. The Statue of Liberty had been hit. Her torch was severely damaged by shrapnel, and if that wasn't a metaphor for the current standing of America in the world, I didn't know what was . . .

The boys and I had only just returned from Newport, still disoriented by grief. Awakened in our suite at the Vanderbilt by a blast in the night, I'd half believed myself to be back in war-torn Paris, thinking one of the kaiser's zeppelins must have gotten through the air defenses and dropped a bomb on the city. Now, in the light of dawn, I saw the reality. This was New York.

As I would learn from bleary-eyed hotel guests in robes and pajamas who were reading the headlines, the munitions depot had exploded. The barges were still burning in the harbor. Two known dead. Scores more hurt. A sneak attack by the kaiser—*I knew it in my bones.*

No one knew if we should expect another explosion. Windows had shattered everywhere in lower Manhattan, to say nothing of the stained glass windows in Saint Patrick's. Another national humiliation; how many more were we to endure?

The smell of the smoke from the inferno lasted long after the firemen contained the blaze, and we were still choking on the ashes the day my husband's ship finally came in.

"Now, remember what I told you," I said to my boys, straightening little Ashley's tie. "You've seen men on crutches before, so you mustn't stare."

"Are people on the dock going to think he's a pirate with his peg leg?"

"A pirate? No. They'll think he's an injured soldier." It had, after all, been misreported in the papers that my husband had lost a leg fighting in the French lines, and I knew this false story would give Willie embarrassment every time he had to correct the record.

When I stood up, there Willie was, hobbling down the gangplank, his well-tailored pant leg covering the false limb. To prevent undue attention, I held the boys by their collars to make them wait for him—a seeming eternity for two children who hadn't seen their father in nearly two years. Leaning on one crutch, Willie gave me a tip of his hat. "Beatrice. Boys."

My husband was a formal man, unsure of how to show his affections, but I'd raised our boys to be free and frank with theirs, and they flew at him. "Careful!" I cried, worried they might topple him in their embrace.

My admonishment embarrassed Willie. "Not to worry! I've spent all these months strengthening my arms and remaining leg. I'm steady as a rock."

Perhaps he was, but he was also pale, and the effort it took him to get into the car drenched him in sweat, though he insisted it was only the summer heat. And his obvious exhaustion vindicated my decision to have separate rooms readied for him at the Vanderbilt. Of course, there was another reason too. Namely that I wasn't sure upon which footing we stood. I promised he'd have a wife waiting for him, but he never promised I'd have a husband . . .

Once Willie was settled on the divan, the boys tried to disguise their interest in their father's peg leg. "I don't suppose there's anything to drink?" Willie asked, and I understood he needed a little liquid courage to indulge their curiosity. By the time I returned with a crystal decanter of scotch and a bucket of ice, he had his pant leg up and was knocking on the wooden prosthetic. "I tried everything else, but in the end, the peg worked best. It was good enough for our ancestor, old Peter Stuyvesant, when he built New York. So it'll be good enough for me."

I smiled, relieved by his old bravado. The boys seemed reassured too. For the next hour, they chattered excitedly at their father about everything from their toys to their lessons and marks in school. "I'm r-rotten in arithmetic," Billy complained.

It was his speech that most worried his father, as I learned when we sent the boys to bed with a promise of an outing in the morning. "Billy's stutter hasn't improved."

"It certainly has. You just don't remember how bad it used to be."

My husband poured himself a glass of liquor, and one for me too. If we were about to quarrel about our sons, our marriage, or the past and future, I might need it. I took a gulp, only to see my husband's shoulders round with defeat. "I saw Victor, you know, the week before he died."

"That's—" Familiar grief rose up at the mention of my nephew's name and made it difficult to speak. I'd put the picture up—the one we took in Amiens when Victor was mourning his friend Kohn and wanted so badly to make his life count for something. "I'm so glad you saw him . . ."

Willie nodded, rolling the crystal glass between his hands. "He'd been wounded. His head was still bandaged; I told him no one would blame him if he took time to recover. He said it didn't matter. He said, *Of course, I shall never come out of this alive, Uncle Willie.*"

My hand fluttered to my lips, my throat a painful knot. I tried to think of words of comfort, but nothing came. Then I reached for my husband, because I realized it wasn't only the amputation of his leg that had left him exhausted, pale, and unwell. It was grief too. We'd both loved Victor, but my husband had loved him like a son. "I shouldn't have let him go out on another mission thinking that way," Willie said, his hand gripping mine. "You can't go into battle deciding to die, or you will."

I had no place to argue with him about war, but by now, the details of Victor's flight had made all the papers. "That's not how it was. Victor had a basket of oranges with him. He was going to deliver them to a wounded friend after the sortie. You don't make plans for the future if you've decided to die, Willie. But none of us can cheat death when our hour comes."

"I have." Willie lowered his head and made a sound I'd never heard before. It took me a moment to realize he was sobbing. Not as an ordinary person might. He was sobbing like a man who had never wept before—

like an *animal* in pain. He dropped the glass, splashing us both. I ignored it, reaching to comfort him, but he recoiled, curling in on himself, struggling to regain his composure. "Goddammit."

"Oh, Willie," I whispered softly. He'd never shed a tear in my presence before. He'd brazened out every difficulty, bearing up under any danger, whether it was rhinos charging in a blistering African sun or political opponents ripping him to shreds. There never was a moment Willie ever let anyone see him low.

Until now.

And I felt strangely moved and privileged to bear witness.

"*Goddammit!*" he roared, ripping his hand from mine as if horrified to show a weakness. "You should go."

"Now? No. I'm not leaving you like this."

"I don't want you thinking I'm a wreck of a man."

I knew better than to offer him soft, soothing words. "I'm touched you still care what I think about you."

He glowered with bloodshot eyes. "Of course I do. You're the mother of my sons." I was his wife too, though he didn't mention it. "This isn't how I meant our reunion to be. I don't want to be so beastly."

"It's always been part of your charm." My smirk pricked the balloon of his gathering belligerence, and I stroked his cheek. "You're *not* a wreck of a man."

He turned his head, as if to escape my words, but in so doing, his mouth pressed into my palm. Then he kissed it. "Do you know, I still remember the first time I saw you. The night was hot, the theater chairs insufferable. I'd already decided to slip out at intermission. Then I heard you sing."

He closed his eyes, as if hearing it anew.

Rhoda, Rhoda ran a Pagoda . . .

It was a song about a girl who clawed her way to the top of the heap, finding love and forgetting her humble past. Remembering it, an ember of the old fire sparked between us.

All at once, he tugged me into an intimate embrace. I wasn't ready; wasn't expecting it. *We ought to have a conversation,* I thought, trying not to surrender to his familiar touch, even though I craved it more than anything. *We ought to have a real conversation about our marriage and if we intend to keep it . . .*

Instead, our bodies did the talking. Willie needed to prove he was still a whole man, and he was. I needed to know he wanted me, and he had no difficulty demonstrating that either. We undressed hurriedly, as if we might think better of this if we had time to think. Perhaps he feared that I'd recoil from the sight of his missing leg.

Truthfully, I feared it too.

Afterward, damp with spilled whiskey, sweat, and tears, I mustered the courage to touch the puckered scar where his knee used to be. And I found it was infinitely dear to me. I softly kissed the red, raised flesh, for time was a cruel and greedy thief, stealing off with our hopes, our dreams, our bodies, our love.

All the more reason to treasure what remained.

If we were normal people, I thought, *we'd now exchange tender sentiments.*

Unfortunately, if I searched my heart to ask what our conjugal relations portended, I might not like the answer. And if I pressed him, he might very well swim back to Europe. So I affected insouciance. "What kind of family scandal shall we create? The one where I anger your saintly sister Elizabeth by leaving you to fend for yourself, or the one where I outrage your sanctimonious sister Margaret by staying the night without pajamas?"

He eyed me with a slow grin. "I've always taken a perverse pleasure in irritating Margaret . . ."

CONDOLENCES FOR MY NEPHEW'S DEATH POURED IN. HIS BODY hadn't been found yet, but funeral services were held at the American Church in Paris, flags of both France and the United States upon the altar. Here in New York, my long-planned Lafayette Day celebration turned into one long funeral procession. At every banquet and parade, Victor's name was invoked, his eternally young smile on posters for all to see. His spotless life and brave death served to reproach the Wilson administration and tugged hard at patriotic sympathies.

I'd persuaded my nephew to become a pilot by telling him he could become a hero to millions. What I hadn't told him was that if he *died* in the skies, he'd become an even more potent symbol of the cause. But he'd known . . .

He'd told me as much the last time I saw him.

Victor would have been content with the sacrifice of his life, I thought, which made it even more difficult not to sob at the sight of his parents, thrust into the public spotlight. Poor Jack and Elizabeth—both of them putting on a brave face. I couldn't have done so with half as much grace, and my husband seemed capable of uttering the necessary platitudes only if he drank half a bottle of brandy before every memorial service.

We needed to get away. We decided on a trip to Bar Harbor, but before we left, Willie insisted on dressing for a formal dinner in the hotel, and asked me to bring the boys, wearing their finest. Once seated, he downed his liquor in one gulp. "You see this dining room, boys? This was your mother's creation. She put her beautiful mark on this place."

I smiled at this long-overdue recognition, even if it told me he was half-sauced. Then Willie flagged the waiter and called for champagne.

"Are we celebrating something?" I knew all too well that pain and joy can coexist side by side, but we were dining in public at a time our family was in mourning, and the public was both judgmental and unforgiving.

With a glint in his eye, Willie said, "I've bought out Freddy Vanderbilt's interest in the hotel—his widow has no use for it. We own this place now, boys, and your mother and I hope to pass it down to you one day."

Your mother and I. Did I imagine that he'd stressed the words? He hadn't consulted me, but I'd have told him to buy it. Now he'd both surprised and delighted me, all while emphasizing to our children that we were still a family. That made it easier to say, "How wonderful!"

It also made it easier not to mind that my husband drank most of the bottle of champagne, and then called for several rounds of daiquiris—a drink he had discovered in Cuba and popularized in New York—which meant that he needed help from the staff in getting back to his room.

It even made it easier for me not to mind his bullheaded insistence on *driving* to Bar Harbor instead of taking the train. He was eager to prove to the boys that, with some minor mechanical modifications, he could work an automobile with his remaining leg. Halfway into the drive, while the boys boasted about being old enough to attend Saint Paul's boarding school, like Astor and Vanderbilt scions, Willie cheerfully announced, "And when you boys are away at school, I'm going to learn how to fly an aeroplane."

I stewed on this revelation for hours on the harrowing drive, practicing a diplomatic way of dissuading him. Unfortunately, the moment that our bags were unpacked, my emotions got the better of me. Facing the windows to watch the boys playing on the beach, I said, "You must promise me you've no intention of flying in the war."

"Must I?" Having fallen back into old marital habits, he came up behind me and grazed my bared shoulder with a kiss. "As I recall, you've always liked a man in uniform."

I enjoyed our renewed intimacy. I also knew that it was, for both of us, about more than enjoyment. For Willie, it was—like his idea to fly aeroplanes—a way of reclaiming his manhood, so I tried to be gentle. "You're now past the age that even the French would wish any man to volunteer."

"That's the beauty of aeroplanes," Willie murmured against my hair. "Flying isn't just a young man's game."

Flying in *war* must be. War pilots like Victor needed the physical agility to leap into a plane at a moment's notice, to say nothing of what it took to control the machine in the air. But Willie took my silence for agreement, adding, "I'm still the sharpest shooter on either side of the Atlantic."

I closed my eyes at this boast, and inhaled. I'd always loved the scent of expensive liquor on a man's breath, but Willie had been drinking so heavily, it now seemed to emanate from his pores. "Well, you'll have to sober up if you mean to hit a target. You've been drunk every day since you returned from France."

He didn't deny it. "Drinking is better than the alternative."

"Which is?"

He pressed his forehead to the back of my head. I wanted to turn and look him in the eye, but he might not speak if I did. "You haven't any idea about the drugs the doctors gave me for the pain. I had to get off them somehow."

I *didn't* have any idea, and I hadn't asked. I'd assumed that after the surgery, all he had to do was get stronger. Aghast, I asked, "You still have pain?"

More silence. Oh, I should've known better than to expect him to admit it. He'd have to be forced to it. So I turned and took his face in my hands. "I don't understand, darling. Where does it hurt if not—"

"It's the damnedest thing." He rubbed at the back of his neck. "You won't believe me if I told you. You'll think I'm a lunatic."

"I've thought you were a lunatic since the day we met, so that ship has sailed. You might as well tell me."

"I can still sometimes feel the missing leg, and it hurts like the devil." That *did* sound like lunacy, but he'd never admit to it if it wasn't true. While I tried to form a response, he continued, in a rush, "When it's not the missing leg, it's the stump chafing against the prosthetic, or the bruises from the crutches under my arms, or the ache in my back from swinging my body like a chimpanzee."

He said all this angrily. As if it were a personal affront that his once-perfect body should betray him this way. "Oh, Willie . . ." I reached for him again, trying not to be *too* gentle, lest he shrink from my pity. "If you're in pain, why won't you take the medicine?"

"It's morphine," he said. "They need it at the front."

Unaware of shortages, I wondered if—well, if he were somehow punishing himself. "Don't be prideful when it can keep you from getting well."

Willie sighed. "I don't want to end up like some opium-addicted sultan, wasting my days away."

An unbidden memory returned to me of my childhood. Of men stumbling out of opium dens in a glassy-eyed trance. In a choice of vices, perhaps my husband was right that liquor was the better one. Certainly it was the more socially acceptable. "We'll have to see what else can be done for you," I said, running my thumb against the harsh line of his lips to soften it. "Wholesome food, good rest, ocean air . . . and perhaps a little restorative amusement."

Willie smirked. "Are you going to sing for me?"

I did more than sing for him, but even in love, he wasn't a tender man, and I hadn't the faintest idea how to pull down the wall between us. I would've nursed him if he'd allowed it, but for now I decided simply to *indulge* him, even if it meant his drinking got worse.

And it did get worse.

A few days into our trip, he was drunk before noon, which made him short-tempered. He was particularly hard on Billy and his stutter, making him repeat himself at the lunch table until he got it right.

"You're embarrassing him," I snapped.

"A little embarrassment never hurt anybody. He's got to practice his diction if he means to become a leader of men." At which point, my husband attracted the stares of passersby with a boorish ten-minute lecture about the way children were disciplined in the tribes of deepest Africa. I bit back a comment about what sort of discipline he might exert over *himself*, since he was so drunk he couldn't have stood up even on two legs. I'd said that he wasn't a wreck of a man, and I'd be damned if I let him become one. Still, I wanted to be understanding. It was just hard to do when my boys were both wary of setting their father off like a powder keg. And especially when I didn't have Emily to confide in.

Oh, how I missed her! She was married and with child, so much in love, and so devoted to her husband, that perhaps she'd have counseled me to be patient with Willie. Or perhaps she'd have advised me to push him into the sea.

I wrote her a letter, but letters were no substitute. Certainly, I couldn't write down everything I felt. The knowledge that she was making a real contribution as a nurse, while I was soaking up the sun, made me restless and discontent. Maybe Willie and I weren't so different after all. We both wanted to be in the action but had children who needed us. That's what made me think that perhaps we should team up to do something at home for the war.

On the morning we went out on the yacht, Willie made the boys laugh by hobbling with a pirate's shout. His mood was good, and once his fishing line was off the side, I took advantage. "I'd like your help opening a toy shop in New York."

Willie eyed me. "A toy shop?"

He thought it a frivolous endeavor, so I challenged him. "Marie-Louise LeVerrier and Clara Simon have come up with an ingenious way of funding refugees and giving work to maimed soldiers. They have the wounded creating French dolls, and the Lafayette Fund has been selling them. Ask me how much money I raised selling French dolls at the Knick."

He grunted, waving a hand. "A small fortune, I don't wonder, but you have enough projects already. Fundraising is all well and good, but—"

"I'm also doing my part to undermine the German economy, a large part of which is toy manufacture." This remark stopped him short, and he scratched the back of his head. Since it was so rare to catch him speechless, I hurried forth with, "The kaiser needs *money* to buy bullets, doesn't he? . . . There are other ways to *fight*, Willie, even from this side of the ocean. And don't you remember what a good team we made?"

He scowled. "Beatrice—"

"If the toy shop doesn't interest you, I'm also planning a costume ball at Madison Square Garden in honor of the ten allied nations . . . do you think you could get me an elephant to represent India?"

My husband was, in fact, the only man I knew who could produce an elephant on short notice, and I could see that he was tempted to prove it—or to lecture me on why the floor at Madison Square Garden would never hold up said elephant. I'd have welcomed either discussion, but he seemed to guess exactly what I was about. "Don't be one of those silly, mollycoddled women who think that do-gooding is the same as stopping poison gas."

"My *do-gooding* has sent over plenty of gas masks to soldiers in the trenches, thank you very much."

"And that's more than I've managed to do—is that what you're saying?"

"Not at all. I just thought that we could do something together to take your mind off—"

"I'm not one of your damned charity projects!"

As his shout carried on the sea spray, I stood up. I retrieved my towel and a pair of aviator sunglasses I'd been gifted in Paris by a grateful soldier. "Have it your way, then . . ."

A little rueful now, he called after me as I walked away, "Where are you going, my darling hellcat?"

"This boat isn't big enough for me, you, and your temper, so I'm going to tell your hired captain to take us back to shore."

Willie took a long drink from the bottle. "The devil you are. This is *my* yacht."

My hands went to my hips. "I see. This is your yacht, and I'm your wife, and those are your children belowdecks . . ."

"Exactly," he said, sinking smugly back into his sun-drenched chair.

I stood there a moment, taking in the scene. "This tackle box is also yours, isn't it?"

Without waiting for an answer, I heaved it over the side.

The entire box splashed, and the blue sea swallowed it up.

"Beatrice!" my husband roared in impotent rage.

"That was childish, I know, but I'm making a point. Anything that's yours, Willie, is something you can lose, including me. So take me home before I find something else to throw overboard."

He took me home.

We were silent as the boat docked. We were silent as Willie drunkenly teetered on his crutches on the gangplank. Even the boys didn't say a word. I wanted to tell my husband not to get behind the wheel, but his mood was so dark now, I didn't dare.

While the motorcar jerked and lurched around every curve, I started to regret my behavior. What had Willie done, after all, but snap at me? He was in pain, he didn't want to face his own limitations, and he'd been home only a few short weeks. I'd pined for his attention for so long—and now that I had it, why was I threatening to ruin it all? Willie could've died on that operating table and left me a widow. I needed to appreciate how lucky I was.

That was, in fact, my very last thought before the car crashed.

THIRTY-THREE

MARTHE
Chavaniac-Lafayette
August 1942

"THESE ROUNDUPS REPRESENT A CONTEMPT FOR HUMAN DIGNITY," the curé says on Sunday to a packed church, everyone in the village squeezed into the pews. He's quoting the archbishop of Toulouse and the bishop of Montauban, who've written letters of protest against the dawn raids that are now spreading terror in both the Occupied and Free Zones. Jews, communists, Freemasons, and people who help them are being deported en masse; to where, we don't know, but the Germans claim they are being *resettled*. "Remember," the curé continues, reading from the letters of his colleagues, "that Jews and foreigners are real men and women. Everything is not permitted against them, against these fathers and mothers. They are part of the human species. Our sisters and our brothers. A Christian may not forget this."

The church is silent as these words echo. Not a whisper, not a breath, not even a sputter of candles on the altar. The entire village seems to be remembering how, just a year ago, Catholics seemed united in wanting to get rid of the Jews. Since then, Radio Vichy has made it sound as if all Christians support the anti-Semitic policies that are tearing families and communities apart, driving the innocent to suicide. But now everything has changed. Even the curé of little Saint-Roch is no longer too afraid to say, "The idea that we must protect religious liberty is at the center of our faith. It is also at the center of our history in Chavaniac. It was here, in this church, that Madame Lafayette"—my head jerks up—"once prayed for strength to speak God's truth when it was forbidden. She risked her life to save the persecuted. Now I ask you, what would we do, in her place?"

I inhale sharply—a little shaken, because we *are* in Adrienne's place—in every sense of the word. And I feel like an idiot. I've been try-ing to embody her in stone when I should be trying to embody her in my own skin. And this is the closest thing to an epiphany I've ever experi-enced in a church.

That afternoon Sam says they're rounding up children in our area. They say only foreign Jews, but this is a lie. "I heard it from my girl in Langeac," he confides. "Her father works at the gendarmerie in Brioude. Trucks are lining up."

I feel a cold rage that this could be true. And rage is almost a relief from the grief since Henri's death. It hurts in a new way, and I embrace it, like the boys in the dormitories who punch their legs to give them something else to feel besides growing pains. I'm worried for Gabriella, but her secret is safe in the preventorium. It's her father and her siblings and Madame Pinton I have to worry about now. And for once, I know just what to do about it.

MADAME PINTON LOOKS PAINED TO SEE ME, AS IF MY APPEARANCE alone dredges up memories of Henri, and her eyes fall upon the ring dan-gling from my neck. *Her* ring. Now that he's gone, it's never going to be mine, and in these past few months of drunken grief, I haven't been wor-thy of it—so without a word, I return it to her, pressing it into her palm. She holds it—studying my face—and I can't tell what she's thinking.

But this isn't the reason I've come. "Where are the kids?"

"Hiding," she replies. "Their father has them practice in case a stranger comes or they hear dogs bark in the night. They sleep in their clothes, climb down the drainpipe, then hide in the root cellar. Maybe that's the first place the police would look—I don't know."

I swallow at the shame of it. "Monsieur Kohn is here?"

She shakes her head. "In the woods. He visits when he can."

He's written letters and sent packages with treats for his children, but given that he's running with an armed band now, he's probably right to stay away.

Madame Pinton thinks I've come to give a progress report on Gabri-ella, who loves camping trips, catching fish in the stream, and telling ghost stories under the stars. But that's not why I'm here either. "I want to place all the Kohn children in the preventorium. Can you get Dr. Boulagnon to say they're sick? If so, I'll try to get them in under the name *Beaufort*, like their sister."

"It's too dangerous," Madame Pinton says. "You've already done too much."

"I haven't done anything," I say flatly. And it's true. The women who lived in Lafayette's castle before me did important things—things that would outlast them. Hell, they saved *me*, and for what? Right now, the only thing I'm proud about is getting Gabriella Kohn into the preventorium, so I'm going to help her siblings too.

Madame Pinton warns, "It's different than before." She rummages in her drawers and shows me Josephine's identity card—which is stamped with the word *Juif* in red. Then she shows me an older one, without the stamp. It should've been confiscated, but Madame Pinton explains, "My cousin works at the town hall in Paulhaguet. She quietly gave back the old identity cards, but someone might notice the date . . . unless you can remove the word *Juif*, it's no use."

I've got no idea how it could be washed away, but I could get blank identity cards, because they're sold in various shops. Then I'd need photos and fingerprints. Real stamps leave different impressions based on the position they're placed and pressure used. There's no reliable way I can duplicate that *unless I carve my own stamp* . . .

That could get me jailed as an antinational—or worse than jailed. I'd be an idiot to risk it. And I'd want to chew a cyanide pill if I made a mistake, which, given the fact that I've gotten blackout drunk a few times these past months, seems like a real possibility.

But I have to try.

In the frantic weeks that follow, whenever I disappear into my tower room, everyone thinks I'm sculpting. And I am—just not a bust. I've got a bright lamp overhead illuminating the delicate work of carving a stamp. Wood was easy to find—pine is soft enough to carve easily—but tracing paper I had to steal from Anna's desk, along with the key to her files so I could grab an example of a document with an impression clear enough to trace.

Even so, I'm not sure it's going to work. It's one thing to slip a school certificate under the nose of the preventorium's staff. Something else to make identity cards that have to get past gendarmes. This should give me pause, but it doesn't. I only work harder, faster, obsessively.

The first stamp I make is wrong. The impression is hazy around the edges. Maybe I need harder wood. Hickory, mahogany—what's the hardest I can get? I spend a few days helping Sam down near the boys' preventorium, where he's now working as a scoutmaster. "Almost like old times," I say, following in his boot prints on the trail with a troop of boys on a botany walk.

"*Almost* like old times," Sam echoes, "but without Henri . . ."

His words, tight and strained, remind me that I'm not the only one who's grieving. Not the only one who feels restless. Here in the Free Zone we've been waiting for someone to save us, for the world to come to its senses. Well, I'm done waiting. There's nobody but us. "Help me find some maple."

"What for?" Sam asks.

I want to tell him the truth, but the fewer people who know, the better, and the lie rolls off my tongue. "An art project."

"Ah." Sam stops to wipe sweat from his brow, and there's sympathy in his nut-brown eyes. "I'm glad you're getting back to your art. Henri would want that."

It's one of those things we say to help the living. Henri didn't care about art, but he cared about helping children, so I know he'd approve. Meanwhile, Sam hacks a nice-sized piece of maple from a fallen tree, and I take it back to my tower lair, where I whittle out too large a chunk and ruin the stamp.

Merde. It's the sixth of September and time is running out. The police are posting signs at the side of the road saying that anyone caught giving refuge to foreign Jews will be fined, interned at a concentration camp, or sent to jail for up to five years. They don't admit it, but they're arresting French Jews too, so I need to get the Kohn children off Madame Pinton's farm and into the preventorium as soon as possible.

If I can't get them admitted by the fifteenth, they'll have to wait another month, and the urgency makes me aggravated with every interruption—even the impromptu celebration for Lafayette's birthday that's an annual tradition here at the castle. When I was a kid, we used to perform a little costume play. I have a memory of being stuffed into a miniature hoopskirt and powdered wig. We don't have anything ostentatious planned this year, but Madame LeVerrier insists we mark the hero's day.

The doyenne is herself now wrapped in a lace shawl in the English garden, where she's arranged a special luncheon of apples, cheese, and a vegetable pie. How many ration coupons must have been spent for this, I can't guess. I just make a plate of food and hoist myself up on the stone balustrade, wondering how quickly I can finish eating and get back to making illegal papers.

The mood on our impromptu Lafayette Day is anything but festive, but no one can say we're not honoring the renegade hero, because we're all complaining about the government. Sam's voice is loud and frustrated as he argues, "You don't think it's a coincidence that the French National Assembly is officially abolished the same week—"

"If people had volunteered to go to Germany, these new measures wouldn't be necessary," Faustine Xavier interrupts, primly slicing her apple into wedges.

And I want to slap her. Since only a few Frenchmen volunteered to make munitions for Hitler's war machine, the rest of us are now being conscripted. Under the so-called Service du Travail Obligatoire, the first group—young Frenchmen between the ages of twenty and twenty-three—have already been called up. With many more to follow, to *be subject to do any work that the Government deems necessary.*

"It's slavery, is what it is," argues Sam, his eyes fiercely defiant as he scarfs down his vegetable pie. "I didn't get shot at by Nazis before the armistice only to now help them shoot at someone else. If they go through with this, I won't go to Germany. I won't collaborate."

"You have no choice," says Faustine. "It's the law."

"Let them try to arrest me, then," Sam spits. "Just try rounding up every able-bodied Frenchman between the ages of eighteen and fifty. They'll regret it."

"They're going to register women too," Anna says from the patio table, glancing at me warily. She must be remembering our conversation in the church. Maybe she still thinks that if she'd gone to Germany she could've freed her husband, and saved fellows like Sam besides.

I think she's wrong.

"Let's not exaggerate," Faustine scolds, readjusting her Victorian collar as if she were getting a little hot under it. "Only unmarried women like Marthe will be subject to the labor draft. There's nothing to worry about."

I snort. "There's plenty to worry about." And I *am* worried. I can't go to Germany, and not just because I'm afraid to get bombed by the Allies. *Your papers are in order,* Madame Simon said, but what if they're not? What if the Germans find out something about me that I don't even know myself? They're making people undergo medical examinations for Jewish lineage, using calipers on noses. And I've caught myself staring in the mirror, looking for signs—if there really are such things.

But while the rest of us are afraid, Faustine Xavier laughs it off. "Marthe, if you don't want to go, just get married. It's high time you found a man to make an honest woman of you."

I don't know what comes over me. Maybe it's her smug expression, or the fact that I slugged back four shots of the baron's whiskey in secret before coming out here. But before I can stop myself, I pitch my half-eaten apple like a baseball at Faustine's face. It bounces off her cheek—and after that, it's pandemonium, and I'm shouting, "If you want me to be honest, you won't like what I have to say!"

Faustine hops up in red-faced fury, wiping apple pulp from her nose. "You mongrel!"

"Don't call her that," Anna says, stepping between us. "Don't you dare. Marthe just lost the man she loved, and what you said was cruel."

Faustine's eyes narrow to slits. "I might have known you'd take her side, madame. There is something between you two. Something unnatural."

"Hey," Sam barks, shouldering forward, ready to defend my honor. But the word is already in the air.

Unnatural. There it is, bald and ugly . . . all it would take is someone like Faustine Xavier to denounce us for sexual deviance, and we could end up in jail or worse. I'm frozen in fear, my throat constricting in panic as Faustine says, "I intend to report this to your father, madame."

Anna doesn't flinch. "It's countess to you. Or Madame Secretary-General—your superior either way. Remember *that* when you make your report."

Leaving the bitch sputtering in our wake, Anna hurries me toward the stone stairway into the castle. Once inside, I follow her into the privacy of the dark wood-paneled breakfast room, and I'm so exultant I want to grab her and kiss her on the mouth. Anna stood up for herself, she stood up for me, maybe she even stood up for *us*. "You were amazing—"

"You have to tell her you're sorry!"

"I'm only sorry I didn't knock her on her ass."

Anna takes me by the arms. "You have to get hold of yourself, Marthe. You shouldn't have to. If I lost my husband the way you lost Henri, I'd want to scream and burn down the world, but—"

"But that's just my personality on a good day," I say with a jaunty grin.

She frowns. "I can smell the alcohol on your breath, you know. Papa knows someone's been taking bottles from his liquor stash. I told him it was me. We've agreed to keep it our little secret, but if you keep acting this way, so distant, crazy, and angry, you're going to get denounced. It's not bad enough people spread these ridiculous, disgusting rumors about us? You have to give Faustine Xavier another excuse!"

I pull back and stand there blinking. *Disgusting.* That word brings me back to the painful reality. The reality in which there's no *us* to defend. The reality that I have a crush on a married woman who loves her husband. I need to accept that we can't ever be together. *Really* accept it this time. Even if I have to walk away from this castle and leave her behind . . .

"Are you trying to get fired?" Anna asks, and that's another slap of reality. Because I can't walk away from the castle, even if I could afford to. I promised Henri that I'd *hold down the fort* and I promised Madame Simon that I'd look after Gabriella Kohn, and now I need to get her siblings admitted too.

"Okay," I say in resignation. "I'll—I'll keep out of sight for a while and not antagonize Madame Xavier."

This gives me an excuse to go back upstairs and get back to work on the forged identity cards. Fortunately, the third time is the charm. The impression my new stamp leaves is the crisp round mark of the prefecture in Haute-Garonne. I chose it because the stamp is simple—no stars, no wreaths, no coats of arms, no fascist hatchets. Certainly no Lady Liberty, like the one from the prefecture of the Haute-Savoie that some hapless official has probably been forced to retire in a drawer for fear it might remind us what we used to stand for.

I glue photographs of Monsieur Kohn and his children onto the cards and stamp them. *Voilà.* Monsieur Uriah Beaufort and his little Beauforts, French nationals, every one. Now I need to get their fingerprints. I get the opportunity on Thursday—the usual day Sam drives the *camion* to either Le Puy or Paulhaguet to get supplies. But there have been officials already sniffing around these parts lately to recruit young men for the Service du Travail Obligatoire—the labor draft for Hitler we're now calling the STO—so the baron has advised Sam to go into hiding for a week or two with the village butcher and a few local farm boys. The baron, of all people! A year ago he was such a stickler for the rules when it came to Madame Simon, but now, after the Riom Trial, maybe he's learned his lesson. In any case, *somebody* needs to go for supplies, and the baroness is fretting. "We need vitamins, flour rations . . ."

She has a long list, and asks Faustine Xavier to take on the errand, but I volunteer to go in her place.

"Isn't it your day off?" Faustine asks, suspicious.

"Yes, but I'd like to make up for . . . well."

It's as much of an apology as she's going to get from me, and as I hoped, Faustine nods, like it's the least I can do. "Take one of the big boys to help," the baroness says, even though this is technically against the rules of the preventorium. Fortunately, I know just the boy I want to take.

Oscar hasn't been too keen on me since I caught him chalking a *V for Victory*, but his little band of followers in the boys' dormitory makes less mischief without him. Besides, Oscar isn't bad company. Especially when I promise the kid a few hours on his own. Parking the *camion* in front of the grain store, I give him money and some of my ration coupons. "I have to pay a visit to the Pinton farm; why don't you treat yourself at one of the cafés?"

"*Oui*, Maîtresse." He grins, holding his hand out for an extra coupon. This is highway robbery, but I give it to him so he'll keep his mouth shut.

At Madame Pinton's farm, I notice the picture of the Marshal is gone from its place over the old stove. I also notice that Madame Pinton has cut down some of Henri's old clothes to fit the Kohn children. If I didn't know her to be such an unsentimental woman, I'd think she'd taken to these kids.

I help the Kohns press their fingerprints onto the cards, and wary Josephine asks, "As easy as that?"

Remembering my failed attempts, I say, "If only you knew!"

Since I saw them last, Josephine has developed a twitch. Daniel, who still hasn't grown into his ears, is thin and somber. To cheer them, I say, "Once you're out of isolation at the lazaret, you'll get to see your little sister on the playground every day."

Josephine asks, "Will anyone else know who we are?"

"It's better no one knows."

She nods thoughtfully, tugging at her braid like she wants to chop it off again. "We were happy in Paris before the war, you know. Our neighbors accepted us. No one ever made us feel like dirty Jews and criminals."

"You aren't dirty, and you haven't done anything wrong."

"Then why do we have to hide?"

I don't have an answer, and the way she looks at me with haunted eyes is a punch to the gut. I want to blame the Nazis, but even before the war, French people complained about immigrants, and shouted, *France is for the French!* On the other hand, we elected a Jewish prime minister . . . though maybe that's why the democratic republic we've been so proud of is no longer French enough for us.

When I return to the castle, I decide I should probably burn the forged stamp . . . but what if I need it again? On impulse, I go to stash it inside one of Madame Beatrice's old hatboxes under the bed, in which she's stored old letters and trinkets. And that's when I find a photo of a middle-aged man wearing a baggy Edwardian suit and a boater.

And on the back of the photograph is written the name *Furlaud* . . .

THIRTY-FOUR

ADRIENNE
Paris
June 1791

I CRUMPLED THE PAMPHLET, WHICH FEATURED A DRAWING OF MY husband kneeling before the queen, stroking her exposed genitalia. In another pamphlet, he gave himself over to a ménage à trois. I crumpled this one too, but they were all over Paris—and I knew who was to blame.

With the new constitution on secure footing, in a high-minded flourish, Gilbert had allowed the duc d'Orléans to come home—and the moment that depraved schemer set foot on French soil, vile rumors erupted about my husband and Marie Antoinette, who would sooner spit in my husband's face than kiss it.

These pornographic drawings both entertained and outraged the mob. Royalists and traditionalists barked that my husband was the king's jailer. Radicals and reformers snarled that my husband was the king's apologist. Our abolitionist friend Brissot believed my husband too hard on the mob; our relations believed him too soft. And rising politicians like Maximilien Robespierre demanded inquiries . . .

It was endless and exhausting.

Caught between scoundrels on both sides, Lafayette complained, "In America I saw attacks on George Washington too. Admittedly, none so vile. Yet I must endure with as much grace as possible these slings and arrows to my reputation, so long as everyone keeps faith with the new French government."

These words were no sooner out of his mouth than young Jean-Louis Romeuf, my husband's aide-de-camp, marched into the parlor to announce, "The king is missing!"

"What can you mean, *missing*?" Lafayette snapped. "I just saw him last night near midnight."

"He's gone, sir," reported Romeuf. "The entire royal family. We've searched the Tuileries Palace from courtyard to rooftop; they aren't there."

My husband's face went white to the tip of his nose. And I sputtered, "The duc d'Orléans should be brought in for questioning."

If our old enemy had designs on the throne, was it too far-fetched to think that he had kidnapped or murdered the royals with the help of British agents? The same thing must have occurred to my husband, who ordered, "Put out the word that the king has been abducted. We must prevent the kidnappers from harming him or removing him from the city."

Only once his officers scattered in different directions did my husband reveal to me that he did not truly believe the king had been abducted. Rather, he believed the king had run off to raise an army against us. My husband had a well-deserved reputation for keeping his wits about him in a crisis, but his hands now shook as he buttoned his coat with its military braids, his expression torn between disillusionment and dishonor. "To think King Louis gave his oath upon a field with hundreds of thousands of witnesses . . ."

It was Lafayette's responsibility to defend the king from the people. But it was also his responsibility to defend the people from the king. My heart ached to see the fear in his eyes that he had failed at one duty or the other—and would be blamed for both.

Crowds were already gathering outside, shouting that my husband must have helped his lover, the queen, escape to Austria to lead a counterrevolution. "Traitors pay with their heads!"

With the alarm of the tocsin bells ringing, I tried to keep calm, sending our girls upstairs and advising my husband that he needed to go before the National Assembly at once. But to do it, he had to *fight* his way out of our house. I watched him go, the crowd kicking and punching some of his officers. My heart was in my throat as I wondered if I dared to follow. He might need my support, perhaps even my witness as to his whereabouts last evening. I had determined to join him when a bruised and battered aide-de-camp stumbled into my toilette, carrying news—a statement by the king himself.

I read the missive, so startled by its contents that I accidentally knocked little bottles of perfumes and pots of cosmetics from my dressing table. I read it again. A statement by the king *denouncing* the constitution. King Louis groused that the Tuileries Palace was not as comfortable as Versailles. He bemoaned the privileges he had lost. He expressed fury that he should be accountable for his expenditures, even to the nation who paid for them.

This sounded like the king—his cadence and word choice. Still, I did not want to believe that he would write such a thing unless a pistol had been pressed to his temple. Surely he knew this would embolden his enemies and mortify his friends. Few but the most staunch royalist left in the country would defend such a petulant manifesto!

Meanwhile, the people raged outside. *What competent commander lets an entire royal family disappear into the night? Lafayette is either a traitor or unfit to lead!*

And I began to fear that if my husband did not find the king and drag him back, we would all be torn to pieces.

Thank God for young Romeuf. The king had been recognized on the road by an ordinary citizen who compared his profile to the portrait of the king on an assignat in his pocket. Led by Romeuf, my husband's forces fetched the royal family and escorted their caravan back to Paris—an ignominious return filled with shame for all of us.

Badly shaken by the king's betrayal, Lafayette received the king outside the Tuileries Palace with the words, "Your Majesty, I have always said that if you made me choose between you and the people, I would choose the people . . ."

"That is true," the king admitted.

Not knowing what else to do, Lafayette reverted to ancient protocol. "Does Your Majesty have any orders?"

King Louis barked with bitter laughter. "It seems I take your orders now."

That bitter laughter unraveled my remaining love for the king. I realized now that he had always been insincere, and that he had sworn falsely before God and the nation. However personable and well-intentioned he might seem, King Louis was no longer seeking the good of his people, if ever he was before. His actions were meant only to assure his own personal power. He truly was a despot, and this realization broke my heart.

That night I told Gilbert, "I fear for his life if people should believe he was going to raise a foreign army against us . . ."

Gilbert agreed. "They will tear him to pieces."

Many would say we should let them. King Louis liked to think of himself as a merciful and enlightened king, but his bad governance had killed hundreds of thousands—some through starvation, others through torture. He might say that was ignorance, or that he was badly advised, but his determination to reinstate an absolute monarchy at the point of a gun was with knowledge aforethought and with no consideration of mercy to those he left behind. Those like my family and me . . .

Perhaps he deserved to be torn limb from limb, but as a Christian, I did not believe justice could be served through murder. I wanted mercy for the king, but more than that, I wanted mercy for the nation, and to my profound shame, the only way to achieve both was through deception.

My husband, whose oaths and principles and sympathies also stood in opposition to one another, now admitted, "Some excuse will have to be made for the king's escape."

The official story put out by the National Assembly was that the royal family had been kidnapped. This was the first time my husband put his reputation behind a lie. As a woman of scruple, I should have abhorred it, but it was the only way, unless we wished to throw our lot in with the bloodthirsty zealots wishing to murder all the royals.

Our friends warned, *In running a middle course, you run the risk of being hated by both sides . . .*

And my family was wavering. My younger sisters Pauline and Rosalie left for the countryside. My father fled the country with his mistress to Switzerland. Even Maman sided now with the royals, for radicals in the new assembly were bent upon destroying the Catholic Church.

All the clergy were now required to swear a civic oath breaking their allegiance to the pope and promising to hold the laws of the nation as more sacrosanct than those of God. I didn't understand how a movement for religious liberty could devolve into persecutions of priests. I would not support that, and was glad to take Communion with my sister Louise at Saint-Sulpice when the curé announced his refusal to take the oath.

As a result, I found myself denounced in the papers for treason.

"This hurts us," Gilbert said, throwing the paper into the fire. "Your support for *nonjuring* priests."

He did not share my faith, but believed always in the right of every person to freedom of religion. I had sacrificed much to support him as a champion of that idea, but I would not sacrifice this. "Do not ask me."

"I ask only discretion," Gilbert said.

"Do not ask that either." It pained me to distress him, and yet in this, I had to. "I have stood by you, every moment of our marriage, every moment you have expressed controversial beliefs, no matter the danger. Now we come to my own principles and you must stand by me."

Gilbert stared as if I had grown two heads. Never before had I asserted myself this way. So accustomed to our being in accord in every particular, he did not seem to know what to do or say. So he said nothing—wordlessly slamming out the door in haste to some appointment.

My heart physically ached. I had chosen now, of all times, when he was in the most precarious position, to stake out ground that could ruin us, but how could I give way?

Gilbert scarcely uttered a word to me in the days that followed. And when I refused to play hostess to the new bishop of Paris, who was persecuting nonjuring priests, I feared Lafayette would never forgive me. *We are going to become like my parents, alienated and cold.*

Even so, I would not change my mind—this was a matter of faith; I had not fought and sacrificed for a revolution that would, in turn, oppress others. What I *could* do—I decided at the last moment—was explain myself to the bishop. Thus, I dressed and went down to the dining room. I had not yet entered, however, when I heard the bishop say, "Your wife sets a bad example, and it reflects poorly on you that you cannot control her. You must *crush* this spirit of dissent in your own house, just as I will crush it on the streets of Paris."

I trembled, there at the threshold, wanting to turn back but too upset to move. Especially as the silence dragged on, and I began to worry for what Lafayette would say. At long last, I heard my husband's voice rise up over the clank of his fork settling on the dinner plate.

"Sir," Lafayette began, "I do not share my wife's religious beliefs, but if you knew my marriage, you would realize that she is not my *subject*, nor would I wish her to be. She is a woman of high-minded principle and the model of kindness; of a character we would all do well to emulate. I would no more crush my wife's spirit than I would persecute any other citizen for matters of conscience. And I promise that if *you* try to crush her spirit, you will find me in your way, sword in hand."

Oh, the nameless satisfaction I took in his defense of me! I would not have minded even if my husband stayed away that evening, but he came to our bedchamber and wrapped me in his embrace, murmuring apologies. "I will always stand by you, my dear heart."

The next morning, he was awake early, and furious. "Someone has been in the locked compartment of my desk . . ." Our children knew better than to touch their papa's papers, much less unlatch the chambers he kept fastened. My heart sank to think we might have in our house a spy. Truly, so many people came and went, it could be anyone, and I said so.

"Have the locks changed. All of them," Lafayette said.

We had enemies, and because of me, we would now have more.

Let us go away to Chavaniac, I wanted to say. Yet I knew if we left Paris now, our carriage too might be dragged back to the city while people spat upon it and pelted it with rocks. And I also knew the first person to throw a stone would be Philippe Égalité—which was the name that the duc d'Orléans now went by to please the mob.

I heard it said everywhere now in the Palais-Royale that King Louis was an untrustworthy despot, but Philippe Égalité would be a faithful king of the Free French. Thus, Philippe started a petition to demand an investigation into the king's treachery. His supporters intended to gather to sign this petition on the Champ de Mars upon the same altar where my husband led our oath to the constitution. Even our friends the Condorcets intended to sign. Not because they wished Philippe to be king, but because they asked, "What kind of constitutional monarchy can exist when the monarch so obviously despises it? We now have the opportunity to form the government we should have had in the first place. A republic without any king at all."

They make a fair point, I thought. I did not say so, because I saw the danger of upending what we had accomplished so far. It had been difficult enough to achieve a constitutional monarchy. The last thing we needed was to start over and return to days of anarchy and violence.

Yet anarchy and violence are what we got . . .

On the day people went to the Champ de Mars to sign Philippe's petition, my husband and his National Guard were on hand to keep order. I was at home with the girls, carrying a tray with tea, when I heard the crack of musket fire in the streets. Glancing out of my windows, I saw a mass of people racing down the Rue de Bourbon for my house. I backed away, somehow managing to set the tray down without spilling anything as I retreated, but as the guardsman sprang to action, flying out of the house, ready for battle, I was spotted by an angry brute whose face pressed against my glass. "There she is! Kill her!"

I stumbled back as someone else screamed, "Let's make Lafayette a present of his wife's head!"

"Get out of sight, madame," said Romeuf, my husband's aide-de-camp, pulling me behind him. I had fed these men with my own hands and had faith in them; if they could defend us, they would. And so it was with an eerie sense of composure that I withdrew, setting about bolting the shutters and gathering my tearful children.

Hearing the shake of leaves against the side of the house, I realized the mob was trying to come in through the garden. "Up the stairs," I told the children. "Quickly!" Not wishing for them to be afraid, I added, "Praise God these marauders are here and not at the Champ de Mars. If they have come for me, it is because they cannot get to your father, and he will be safe and come to our rescue."

"Madame," a blue-and-white-clad guardsman called after me. "We will die before we let them take you."

"God preserve you, sir!" I cried.

The sounds of fighting echoed. Punching, kicking, shouting. Then galloping horses as my husband and his guardsmen rounded the house to drive away our attackers. No one was killed at our home that day, but on the Champ de Mars, corpses littered the ground. The number, we did not know. It was being called a *massacre*. And that night, Gilbert leaned against the door of my chamber and closed his eyes.

"Two drunkards were caught sleeping beneath the altar," he explained. "The mob accused them of trying to set off explosives to prevent people from signing the petition. I fired warning shots, but it did no good. I was left with the choice of complicity with murder or firing on the people . . . so I fired. Nevertheless, the unfortunates were torn to pieces."

"You did all you could."

He put his head in his hands. "Adrienne, in the melee someone aimed a pistol in my face and pulled the trigger." My heart stopped. "The gun misfired, but now I wonder if this near-death angered me so much that I did the wrong thing."

"No," I said, my heart thumping wildly with gratitude that God had spared my husband's life. It made me more firm in my conviction. "You are no butcher, Gilbert."

Surely he knew it, and yet this self-doubt broke something in him.

In September, the king ratified the new constitution. After he forswore his oath to a constitutional monarchy, I would never trust the honor of King Louis again. I did, however, think he could not possibly be foolish enough to risk all our lives a second time. Thanks to Lafayette, he had survived the turmoil, remained one of the richest men in the world, and kept his crown. He could now rule in the same way the British king did.

All he had to do was keep his word.

Nevertheless, the royal family made clear that they did not wish for my husband's help or protection any longer. The royals resentfully celebrated every dent in my husband's armor—even as he shielded them with it. Though he had saved their lives, they scorned him. Now they believed they were in better hands, and I hoped they were.

I wished no ill on the queen's family even though she wished much ill upon mine. The royals said Lafayette was now welcome to leave public life altogether. Perhaps they thought to test his integrity. Some people still accused Lafayette of wanting to be king. Others *wanted* him to be king.

Yet I knew he wanted to be George Washington.

Which is why, with peace restored, my husband twined his fingers in mine and asked, "Will you steal away with me to Chavaniac—the only place we can be free?"

THIRTY-FIVE

BEATRICE
New York City
November 1916

AMERICA MIGHT STILL BE NEUTRAL, BUT NEW YORK CITY DECID-
edly was not. After the explosion, no one with a modicum of good sense
was willing to repeat President Wilson's inane mantra that America was
too proud to fight. And even without an elephant, I was able to lure more
than fifteen thousand people to the Allied Ball.

From the hoity-toity of Manhattan to jazz musicians from Harlem,
everyone turned out, and I encouraged the audience's applause for the
uniformed Gurkhas and sepoys. It was a world war, after all. Men from
India fought alongside the French, Belgian, English, Scottish, Irish, Ca-
nadian, Russian, Italian, Japanese, Portuguese, and more. They all deserved our praise. And I hoped the roar of the crowd could be heard all
the way from Madison Square Garden to the White House.

After the pageantry followed an evening of dancing, and I awarded
an automobile to the lady with the best costume. (I took my dazzling
ensemble of Indian sari silk out of the running, because who could com-
pete with me?) I'd raised piles of money, and now my dressing room was
filled with bouquets. Bitter-scented marigolds from the reporter Mitzi
Miller . . . well, now this was war. I'd be forced to retaliate by penning
an ebullient handwritten note of thanks accompanied by a bone-dry
fruitcake.

The red roses were from Willie.

I threw them in the trash.

I hadn't returned his calls since the car accident. I had, in fact, spent
the better part of the past two months avoiding him.

You're all right, sweetheart, you're all right, it's just a little glass . . .

I closed my eyes, forcing away the memories of the summer, the screams, the crash. Had it all been a terrifying rush that way for Victor before his plane hit the ground? Killed instantly, they said, but now I wondered. Perhaps that's what Willie had been wondering, just before he drove us into that tree.

I shook my head, pulling jeweled combs from my hair. As long as I kept busy, I could keep bad memories at bay. Fortunately, I had plenty to keep me occupied. I'd moved out of the hotel. My new doll shop on Madison Avenue was doing brisk business as Christmas shoppers readied for the holidays, and I was sending the proceeds overseas for Emily, Clara, and Marie-Louise to use for the benefit of refugee children. I'd also recently received formal thanks from French generals on the front lines, to whom we'd sent more than seventy thousand more Lafayette kits. With the success of the Allied Ball, I'd be sending more.

I certainly had more important things to do than listen to Willie fail to apologize for the hundredth time. Yet when I returned to my town house that night, I found him there, just where I least wanted him to be. Somehow he'd managed, with his crutches, to get to the top of the stairs. Now he sat waiting for me by the fire. "The boys are asleep," he said.

"I should hope so, given the hour."

Willie cleared his throat.

You're just a little banged up, darling, nothing serious . . .

I closed my eyes, reminding myself that though the car was damaged, and Ashley's toy plane was smashed to pieces, the boys had come away from the crash with nary a scrape. My cuts were minor too. And by some miracle, my husband hadn't been hurt at all.

I'd have to be an ogre to wish more pain upon the man, which is why I hadn't told him that it wasn't just cuts that bled after the accident . . . I'd awakened to cramping, spotting, and a devastating sadness. The doctor later told me that it was impossible to know if I'd been pregnant, but he doubted it very much due to my age, and that in any case, it might be better to avoid pregnancy given my declining health. *Thyroid and cardiovascular abnormalities*, he said. Something about how unusual such a condition was in a woman of my wealth and status—such ailments sometimes being the product of childhood starvation.

Well, I wasn't shocked.

He insisted that I get rest or my life might be cut short. But I could sleep when I was dead. As Victor said, *We have so short a time to make our lives mean anything.* Besides, when you grow up as I did, you don't expect to live long. Still, something struck me about the diagnosis.

Cardiovascular abnormalities?

Well, I did have a broken heart. I found myself wondering if another child would have brought Willie and me closer together. He was hard on our boys, but a little girl with my blue eyes might have melted him. Now we'd never know. And I couldn't even bring myself to share with him the pain of it.

Tonight he was clean-shaven, tie neat. His smart appearance was meant to prove he wasn't drunk. "You're looking well, Bea," he said, reaching for my hand as if to examine it for lingering bruises.

I could've told him there weren't any. None of the physical variety. "It's late, Willie." My voice was frosty. I didn't like to be this way. And I didn't feel like I had a right to be. Yes, he'd crashed the car, but he'd been drunk. What was my excuse? I got into that car with him. I let my children get in that car. Looking at Willie now reminded me of every bad decision I'd ever made in my life—every opportunity I'd wasted or taken for granted.

"I know it's late . . ." Willie said quietly. "If I could wait until morning to say what I've come to say, I would."

My heart seized as I realized that he might have bad news. "My God, is it Emily?"

"It's Lafayette's birthplace. I'm going to buy it for you."

Having braced for horror, I was entirely unprepared for joy. *"What?"*

"It's a castle in the mountains of Auvergne—"

"The castle at Chavaniac is for sale?"

Willie nodded. "I've made inquiries. With the war, the descendants can't maintain it. They're reluctant to sell to someone outside the family, but they're looking for a reason to part with it. They're aware of your work at the Lafayette Fund and—"

"You want to buy me a castle," I said. *"Lafayette's* castle."

Willie stared at his hands. "It's no more than you deserve. I know how you grew up. How it left you feeling like you were on the wrong side of the gate, clamoring to get in. When we married, I really did want to fix that for you . . ." He risked a glance at me. "I still do."

My heart filled with more emotions than I could name. He wasn't the sort of man who knew how to apologize, but he was making a grand gesture. This was his way. And as far as grand gestures went . . . this was the grandest.

I was an illegitimate child of a bog Irish mother who started with nothing. And though Willie was American royalty, he hadn't cared about that. He'd given me a new start. He'd helped me support my mother and half brothers—the ones I scarcely knew. He'd given me *everything*. And now he wanted to make me the fairy-tale princess of a castle.

Not just any castle either. The legacy of the Lafayettes had come to mean a great deal to me, and he wanted to give me a real, tangible connection to it. It was a terribly foolish, expensive, and impractical idea that could not have been better calculated to soften my heart! But what would I do with an old French chateau in the midst of a war? I couldn't accept.

How to break it to him gently? "Willie, do you mean for us to live at Chavaniac? Because otherwise, it'd seem somehow disrespectful to transform it into just another place to throw parties."

He leaned back like a man rejected. "Make it into a museum, for all I care."

A *museum*? That too seemed like an impractical thing to think about during a war, but maybe if people had learned the lessons of the past, the war wouldn't have come about in the first place. I knew monuments to kings and conquerors veritably littered the French countryside, but I was aware of only a few memorials for Lafayette—the hero who set the French on a path to becoming the republic they were now dying in trenches to defend.

I gripped Willie's arm. "A museum is a marvelous idea."

My husband's expression warred between confusion, irritation, and surprise. He hadn't made the suggestion with any seriousness, but seemed happy that I was happy. "A museum?"

"Yes!" I felt something growing in the hollow place inside me—a new creation we might conceive together. Something other than our children that might outlive us both. "It could be a museum to *the alliance of democracies*. Even if France, Britain, and America don't always agree, we share a history of ideals worth fighting for."

And perhaps it wasn't the only alliance that could be reinvigorated . . .

Willie squinted, and I could almost think his thoughts. It was one thing to buy me real estate. An investment. Something he could sell if times got hard. I was suggesting the wholesale donation to charity, which made it all the more touching that he didn't dismiss the idea out of hand. Just to please me, he was actually considering the monumental folly of buying this chateau with his own money only to turn it into a public museum. So I let him off the hook. "We'll start an international subscription. Create a foundation. Recruit contributors. No need to bankrupt our children."

My husband exhaled in relief before his sense of competitiveness kicked in. "We'll have to move swiftly and bargain in person before someone buys it out from under us. I'll go to France to arrange it before the winter makes a crossing even more dangerous than it already is."

This was a rare and important opportunity that might never come again—too exciting for me to quibble about any ulterior motives. It was worth the risk, which is why I said, "I'm going with you."

ON A COLD BLUSTERY DAY, AS OUR TRUNKS WERE BEING LOADED into our ship bound for France, our son Billy asked, "Why c-can't we come with you to see Lafayette's castle?"

"It's not safe," my husband barked, unsteady with his crutch. I shot him a warning look, for we'd been quarreling about this for days, but he was too drunk to heed me. "The sea is riddled with mines, not to mention submarines waiting to torpedo ships, and yet your mother insists on risking her life."

Until recently, Willie had somehow convinced himself that I didn't *really* mean to go. For the past few weeks, we'd worked together to raise, almost overnight, a veritable fortune to buy Lafayette's birthplace. We'd thrown ourselves into the venture, enjoying every minute of it. It had been quite like the old days—a reminder that we could move *mountains* together if we tried. But when Willie learned I'd booked passage with him to France, he'd lapsed into drunken fury, telling me it was a mother's place to stay with her children.

I might've excused his behavior as romantic chivalry if only he'd refrained from mentioning mines and torpedoes in front of the boys. Now he'd frightened our children, and I felt consumed by a fury of my own. "Oh, you mustn't worry about us," I hastened to reassure the boys. "We'll be gone only a few weeks, and by then you'll be back at your boarding school with all your friends, having too much fun to miss us. In the meantime, the governess will spoil you with every sort of candy, and I shall not be any the wiser!"

Unfortunately, my boys were both too old now to be distracted this way. They knew Mr. Vanderbilt had died making this same crossing, which is why we now owned the hotel. The dangers of war had become painfully real when their cousin Victor had been shot down. Now Ashley quietly sobbed against my side, and Billy pleaded with us not to go.

Since there was no way to convince my sons there was no danger, I decided it was wrong to try. Like Minnie, they would have to face, sooner or later, that life was full of partings, and that none of us was ever truly safe. "You must be very brave, my darlings. Your father and I are doing something important that we hope you may one day be quite proud of."

I didn't want to teach my children that safety was more important than duty or honor, so we left our boys on that dock, my heart breaking to see them wiping away tears. Only once we were under way did I whirl on Willie. "You frightened them. Worse, I suspect you did it on purpose." My husband had never made me so angry. "You're drunk, but that doesn't excuse you from terrifying our children just to try to force me to stay behind."

Willie punched a frustrated fist against the crutch that reminded him of his incapacity. "I'd have locked you in a bloody closet if I could have. A father has a right to want to prevent his children from becoming orphans."

The loss of his parents shaped his life—just as being fatherless had shaped mine. That pain once drew us together, and remembering it should've softened me, but I was too angry. "Then maybe *you* should've stayed behind."

After all, since the amputation of his leg, I was now the more physically capable, though I wasn't cruel enough to point it out.

"The boys can do without me," he said. "They can't do without a mother. Even one so reckless as you."

"Willie, when we quarrel like this, you make me wonder if our loss at sea would be no great loss at all to our boys or to the world. And you nearly make me wish for oblivion."

He grimaced, then positioned his crutch on the stairway to the upper deck. "I'm going up to see Forts Hamilton and Lafayette. Good view from up top."

He's going to fall, I thought, half wishing it in spite. I didn't want to be around to pick him up, so I went belowdecks where, like worms, Willie's words wriggled themselves into my mind and made me feel rotten. Maybe my presence in France wasn't necessary, but I couldn't be satisfied at the sidelines anymore, longing for Emily and trying not to pine for Maxime Furlaud. Especially knowing there was something wrong with my ticker, and that there might be fewer years left to me than anyone supposed. Resentful that my husband had made me face this unattractive inner truth, I kept away from him the first dark days of our voyage. Eventually, I found Willie in his stateroom, bathed in sweat and vomiting into a trash bin. "It's nothing but seasickness," he rasped.

"*Seasickness?* That's rich." The man who ran gunboats and took our yacht into a storm on our honeymoon had never been seasick a day in his life. Suspicious, I poured a glass of brandy. He refused it, which was the proof I was looking for. I knew things were bad between Willie and the bottle, but a perilous sea voyage was scarcely the time to go sober, and I told him so.

But with Willie, it was all or nothing. "I shouldn't have frightened the boys. I didn't mean to. So for you and for them, I'm giving up my life of drink and dissipation. I shall not touch a drop for a year."

It should've made me happy, but I knew why he'd started drinking so heavily in the first place. What else could he take for the pain? "This journey is going to be difficult even without the well-meaning bravado of sobriety . . ."

"Damn you, woman, won't you let me do anything to prove your happiness means more to me than my own?"

He spit this loving sentiment in my face with such cantankerousness that I didn't know whether to press a pillow to his face or a kiss to his brow. "Oh, Willie," I said, laughing at the absurdity of it all. And in that moment, I loved him, hated him, and everything in between.

I didn't think he'd keep to his resolution not to drink, but for the rest of the trip, his force of will was something to behold. By the time we approached port, he emerged from his stateroom sober but limp as a noodle. "France at last," I said, hardly believing it possible. It was painful to think that Victor would not be here. That he was forever young and gallant . . . and gone.

"We got past the Boche anyway," Willie said with grim satisfaction.

"Don't tempt fate." The *Lusitania*, after all, had been sunk within sight of shore.

As it happened, our luck held with regard to submarines. In the matter of hats, I wasn't so fortunate. "I'm sure they're here somewhere," I said, forcing the porters to search every nook and cranny of the steamer for my missing hatbox. I needed my ostrich cartwheel, my peacock tricorne, and my lacy sleeping caps! Surely it was bad luck to go ashore without them. How could I possibly entreat with the descendants of Lafayette to sell me Chavaniac while wearing a pedestrian straw peach basket?

Willie didn't want to wait. "If we don't get through customs quickly, we'll miss the last train to Paris tonight. I'll pay someone to keep looking for your hats. In the meantime, I imagine you're eager to see your friends, and I'm rather anxious to meet them myself."

He'd never been much interested in my friends before; to the contrary, he tended to be jealous of my relationship with any person of truly interesting character, male or female. So this was a campaign, I realized. *The chateau, the sobriety, the bonhomie.* Willie was trying to win me back the way he'd once won a seat in Congress: by sheer force of will.

And I was willing to let him try.

EMILY WAS OUT OF HER HEAD WITH JOY TO SEE ME IN PARIS. SHE embraced me so tightly that I felt her baby kick, and I scolded her distended belly, "Is that any way to greet your aunt Beatrice?"

Inside Emily's well-furnished flat, Marie-Louise LeVerrier was pouring tea, and Clara Simon lit a cigarette with a sigh of exhaustion. She didn't look well; none of them did. Especially not Emily, who ought to have been glowing with the fullness of motherhood, but while I'd been fishing in Bar Harbor, she'd been up to her elbows in blood nursing soldiers, and worrying about her husband's fantastically dangerous night flying missions. I felt keenly guilty for not being here with her.

"The war has taken a toll," Marie-Louise said, explaining they'd already used the proceeds from my toy store. "Widows and spinsters and lost children all are in desperate straits. We do our best for one, then ten more appear."

I hadn't done enough in New York. Maybe I never *could* do enough . . . still, I was determined to try.

Emily said, "I made up the guest room. Please promise you'll stay with me until the baby is born. I hope my child has good sense enough to wait on his father. The baron is trying to get leave for the holidays. Wouldn't it be wonderful if he could be home for the birth of his son? At least I hope it will be a boy."

Clara rolled her eyes. "There are reasons to be happy for a girl too . . ."

I agreed, but I wouldn't have said so while blowing a contemptuous ring of smoke. Yet that was Clara's way. With a disagreeable harrumph, Emily stirred her tea. "I should hate to be so American that I disregard my husband's desire for a boy to inherit his title." The baron seemed modern enough to welcome a healthy child, whatever its sex, but one never knew when it came to the French. "Besides, Clara, aren't you always saying French wives will do *anything* to please their men?"

Clara smirked. "I never said it was a good thing!"

Marie-Louise asked about my plans to buy Lafayette's birthplace, which I explained in great detail, holding them in my thrall. "The current marquis de Lafayette—or at least, the man who styles himself so—descends from the female line. He's heard of the Lafayette Fund and is interested in selling the castle, but doesn't want to sell over the objections of the rest of the family—most especially the Chambruns, one of whom is serving now at the front as a commandant in the artillery."

"I know him," said Clara.

"Well, I need to convince him. I don't suppose you could help?"

Clara shook her head, then reminded me, "But you know someone else who can . . ."

Which is why, despite all my better judgment, I sent a cable to the front lines, for the eyes of Maxime Furlaud.

THIRTY-SIX

MARTHE
Chavaniac-Lafayette
September 7, 1942

THE BARONESS IS FROWNING. I'VE CAUGHT HER ON ROUNDS AT THE preventorium. She's inspecting the dormitory, where boys perform their daily calisthenic drills in the yard just outside, while on the veranda, the more fragile boys sleep fitfully on a long row of beds—some coughing, others wheezing. She probably expects me to update her on my progress with the sculpture I'm supposed to be making, but I shove the photograph I found in Madame Beatrice's old hatbox under her nose.

"Where did you get this?" she demands to know. I don't have to ask if she recognizes the man. I can see from the way her mouth turns down at the corners that she does. I can't very well tell her that I found the picture while trying to hide my forged stamp. And I can't tell her that I've since snooped in all Madame Beatrice's things, reading a stash of love letters from Maxime Furlaud, and that some of these letters mention a girl named Marthe. Instead, I tell the baroness, "I was looking for paper in the desk upstairs and found this instead. Do you know this man?"

"Yes," the baroness says, ostentatiously returning her attention to her clipboard. "Monsieur Furlaud was Beatrice's friend—a banker, as I recall."

My breath catches. "But when I showed you my birth record you said you didn't recognize that name!"

"I said I didn't know anyone named Minerva Furlaud, which is true."

You shouldn't shake this tree, I tell myself for the thousandth time. I might find out something I don't want to know. Something that might endanger me with the authorities. The baroness didn't want Madame Simon to leave the preventorium, but she didn't put a stop to it either, and they were friends. If I was in trouble, would the baroness help me, or would I too be on my own? I don't know who I can trust or what's safe to ask, but having found this photograph, I just can't help myself. "You don't think there's a connection between *this* Furlaud and the one on my birth record?"

"If there is a connection worth mentioning . . . well, Beatrice would've told you."

The baroness is usually a very direct person, but she's avoiding my gaze. And though I'm afraid if I press her too hard, she'll clam up, I say, "Do you know what I think? I think he was more than a banker and more to Madame Beatrice than just a friend. I think he was a French officer. In fact, I think he's the same French officer pictured with a little pigtailed girl in a photograph hanging in the tower room where I sleep every night. And I think that little girl might be me. So what's the story?"

Her lips purse. "One that's not mine to tell."

I press my own lips together, knowing my timing couldn't be worse. There's an epidemic of scarlet fever afflicting the older boys right now, and she's preoccupied with it. Still, I have to know. "But there *is* a story?"

She whirls on me. "Marthe, my heart goes out to you, truly it does—"

"Does it?" I snap, sure she's holding back.

"Yes, my heart truly *does*," she says, voice softening. "I won't pretend to know what you're going through, but I have some notion of what it's like to grow up without a mother—to wonder where she might be, or if she ever cared, or—"

"*What?*" I nearly stammer with surprise.

She drops her eyes and clears her throat, like she's embarrassed. "My own mother left me when I was six, and I spent my youth wondering what was wrong with me that she could have done such a thing. It took me a long time to learn that though the people who bring us into being are important, and it's natural to want to know them, we all become people of our own making. That's all Beatrice ever wanted for you . . ."

I'm still absorbing her words when a policeman's car pulls up in front of the dormitory. Sergeant Travert and another gendarme step out. *Merde.* They're probably here because of the STO. And they're probably looking for Sam and others who have gone into hiding rather than be sent to Germany.

But the baroness grumbles, "What trouble do you suppose our boys have gotten into now?"

I bite my lip, worrying that Oscar has been caught drawing anti-Nazi graffiti again. I've warned him repeatedly that boys can be *shot* for that, and my belly fills with dread as Sergeant Travert climbs the steps, pistol at his hip. Before he can get to the veranda, the baroness marches straight up to him and blocks his path, hands on her hips. "What brings you to the preventorium, Sergeant?"

I glance at the yard where Oscar and his mischief-makers were doing jumping jacks before the gendarmes arrived, and I want to shout, *Run, Oscar, Run!*

But as it turns out, the gendarmes aren't here for Oscar.

They're not here for Sam either.

They're here for me.

THIRTY-SEVEN

ADRIENNE

Paris

September 1791

MY HUSBAND'S GUARDSMEN, LIKE YOUNG CAPTAIN ROMEUF, pleaded with us to stay in Paris, but Lafayette wished to be a victorious general who gave power back to the people before retiring to the life of a gentleman farmer. He wanted to be the George Washington of France.

For my part, I was eager to leave for Chavaniac without delay. I threw everything into trunks, arranging for two coaches to take us up into the mountains. On the day of our departure, the National Guard presented my husband with his second sword of honor—this one made from the iron bolts of the Bastille and carved with his motto, *Cur Non?*

On our way to Chavaniac, I attempted to visit my sister Pauline, but she refused to receive us for fear of her royalist father-in-law's wrath. Instead, she met us on the road, and there confessed in the privacy of the coach, "I am leaving France."

Desperately, I grasped her hands. "No, Pauline. Not now when things have finally been put right."

Gilbert also tried to persuade her against this course of action, which so many were now calling treason, but she would not hear him. "Royalists think *you* are the traitor, Gilbert. Worse, your Revolutionary friends think so too. They wanted to cut off Adrienne's head!"

Memories of that terrible day flooded back, and Lafayette reached for my hand as if to reassure himself that I was alive and well. "How can you think people who behaved that way are my friends?"

Pauline clenched her teeth. "Just tell me I wasn't wrong to confide my plans. Say you will not arrest me for trying to leave the country."

Gilbert threw himself back into the carriage seat, indignant. "I am no longer commander of the guard, and if liberty means anything, it must mean the freedom to go where you please."

"*Liberty*," Pauline sneered, and kicked his boot. "How can you still speak of liberty, Gilbert? Admit it. The common people you have spent half your fortune to champion are *animals*, less capable of ruling themselves than a flock of sheep, and more dangerous than a pack of wolves. They need a king to inspire terror, noble boots on their necks to keep them working, and hunger to keep them too weak to devour civilization."

"*Pauline!*" I cried. "May God forgive you."

She was unchastened. "The king is going to be restored; his brothers will see to it with the backing of Austria."

"That would be *utter* calamity," Gilbert warned. "A war with Austria and a civil war besides will destroy everything we have suffered for in France."

"The king has accepted the constitution," I argued. "Why can't you?"

"The king is a hostage," she snapped.

"Let me tell you something," Gilbert replied, lifting a finger to make his point. "The king is not the only man who has had to make choices with a gun pointed at his head. He has had his guns pointed at all our heads since the day he was crowned. If he is a hostage, then so were we all. We all decide for ourselves how best to spend our honor. And he has chosen his course."

Still, Pauline was firm in her decision to leave France.

"When do you go?" I asked.

"By Christmas." Pauline twisted her kerchief. "We should all go. When King Louis is a *true* monarch again, you may beg his pardon, Gilbert, and if you fight on his side—"

"If the king stands with liberty, I fight for the king," Gilbert said. "If he betrays it, I fight against him."

Pauline put her face in her hands. "At least take my sister to America, where you may yet survive."

I realized it was neither fear nor fancy that drove my sister to say these things. The royalists in exile really *were* planning to invade . . . and the thought filled me with indignant anger. Were our choices in France truly between corrupt aristocrats on one side and fanatic mobs on the other? I could never count myself amongst either faction.

Pauline pressed kisses to our hands. "In spite of our disagreements, I love you both and your children. I need you to know this in case . . ." She trailed off, but my mind supplied the rest. *In case we end up on opposite sides of a war. In case we never see each other again.*

It was only my faith that our farewell was not forever that allowed me to part with my younger sister. I stared after her coach long after it rolled away, my emotions such a jumble that the next sight I remember was the twin white towers of Chavaniac, shining like a welcoming beacon.

Aunt Charlotte hobbled out, overjoyed to have us, insisting we were all too thin. Inside, she had the servants pile plates for us of cheese and stored preserves. But like the feudal matriarch she was, even Aunt Charlotte argued, "I do not approve these changes in France. Promise me, Gilbert, that you are still loyal to the king."

My husband kissed his aunt's gnarled hand. "I am precisely as loyal to the king as he is to the constitution."

The next morning, watching my children take turns riding a donkey in the yard while sheep grazed in the field beyond, it eased me to hear Anastasie and Virginie laughing together. I hoped my daughters would never find themselves on opposite sides of a political divide, but had faith that they would love each other, just as I still loved my sisters—each and every one.

In the next few days, I slipped into a near-drunken happiness to finally, after nearly fifteen years of public life, have my family to myself again. To concern myself with making a new home for them here in the mountains. It was true that we had spent nearly half of everything we had in the cause of charity and two revolutions—yet there was enough for me to contemplate fabrics for freshening up the old chateau, which was in need of renovation.

Gilbert had been gifted with a stone from the Bastille and thought to have it carved into a liberty cap to be a capstone over our door. Red toile for Gilbert's room, I decided. I had seen a print with American farmers and Indians that I knew would please him. For my own chambers, colorful tapestries with peacocks; nothing extravagant. I would insist upon a game table for my children to amuse themselves with in my chambers; I never wished to be far from them now.

"We must test the soil for the best crops," Gilbert said, thumbing through a book of agriculture. I was not convinced that he would exchange his sword for a plow, but he was determined to try. And soon he was debating with neighboring farmers about whether or not we should keep our weather vane.

My weaving and lace-making school had helped to enrich and sustain the village, which was now thriving, and by the time the fruit in the orchards was ripening, my mother and sister Louise joined us.

I boasted, "You must see Gilbert's treasure room in the tower."

We had transformed the round chamber into a modest display of artifacts from both revolutions. I hoped my husband's swords of honor would remain here, forever sheathed.

"Pretty," Maman said, admiring the silver stencil work. "But you cannot mean to settle here. This room alone is chilly and so dark—just the one window."

"It makes it more difficult to assault," I said, flashes of my tall airy windows on the Rue de Bourbon in my mind, angry faces pressed against the glass. Our home in Paris was more beautiful and filled with pretty trinkets, but Chavaniac was a haven. "And the mountain air does wonders for your health, Maman. I look forward to you and Louise visiting more often. We shall all be very happy here . . ."

BY CHRISTMAS, MY HUSBAND WAS ORDERED TO TAKE COMMAND OF fifty thousand troops and defend France against counterrevolutionary forces gathered at the border—forces that included many of our old friends and relations.

Below stairs, where a ham roasted in the giant kitchen oven, destined for a table I had set with garlands of evergreen, I watched Gilbert dig out his uniform and spurs. I could not banish the unworthy thought: *The mob in Paris called you a butcher, but now beg you to protect them . . .*

Meanwhile Gilbert stared at his portrait of Washington. "I said I fight for liberty or not at all. Is it truly liberty that I am now defending? The Jacobin Clubs are terrorizing the elected government . . ."

"I know," I said, and reminded him that though we had seen wickedness in the Revolution, we had also seen grace. French Protestants and Jews had been granted full civil status with the right to worship as they wished. And every French citizen from peasant to aristocrat had a stake and a say in his own government now. That was an accomplishment to protect. Slipping my arm into his, I said, "Let me come with you. You have told me Martha Washington went with her husband to tend to his soldiers . . ."

He stroked my cheek tenderly. "My dear heart, I know of no instance when *that* great lady was in so much peril as you have been with me. It would be easier knowing you and the children are here, far from the battles."

I had no right to be far from the battles; I too had brought about this revolution. I must also be willing to defend it. When I said as much, he pressed his forehead to mine. "Then I do not command you as a husband. As your general, I charge you to stay here and defend everything that is precious to me, especially yourself. For Chavaniac is for me a temple which gathers the sacred objects of my heart. And you are the lady of my dream castle. May you guard each other well."

INSTEAD OF WAITING FOR THE ROYALISTS TO ATTACK, THE NEW government of France declared war on Austria, and promptly suffered a humiliating defeat. A defeat the common people blamed on their officers, many of whom were nobles like my husband. The soldiers began butchering their own commanders, accusing them of treason. Facing the mutiny of his own troops because of his aristocratic blood, my brother-in-law, the vicomte de Noailles, was forced to flee for his life.

I do not understand, Louise confided in a letter sent by trusted courier. *My husband was the first to call for an end to noble titles. It beggars belief his soldiers might condemn him as a royalist. Now he summons me to join him in exile in America.*

So I was to lose another sister. Louise, my best beloved sister. I despaired of it and its cause. I despaired too of how it would reflect upon us. Already, Pauline's emigration had been taken in the worst possible light. Worse, my father had returned to his post as the king's captain of the guard, an office that had been abolished by current law. My father took it under his own authority to show that men of prominence—even men who had once supported the Revolution—had no faith in the constitutional government.

For Louise to fly to her husband in America now would be taken as further proof that all the Noailles were traitors. And perhaps the Lafayettes too.

This weighed on me when my husband changed his mind and invited me and the children to join him at Metz. My heart filled with tender emotions to read how much he longed for us; how he wanted us near. Still, I could hear the evil gossip. *There Lafayette is, at the border waiting to smuggle his family out of the country before he goes over to the enemy and takes fifty thousand troops with him!*

If our constitution was to survive, we had to instill trust. Thus, I decided to remain at Chavaniac.

And that was among the most fateful choices of my life.

THIRTY-EIGHT

MARTHE
Chavaniac-Lafayette
September 1942

SERGEANT TRAVERT USHERS ME INTO THE EMPTY BOYS' DINING hall and closes the door, while another gendarme waits outside to prevent my escape. Then Travert drops his visored policeman's cap onto the table. "Why don't we sit down like friends, mademoiselle?"

I try to hide my fright behind insolence. "When did we become friends?"

In answer, with the toe of his boot, the gendarme kicks a chair out for me. Glaring as if my insides weren't going to jelly, I slide into the wooden chair, keeping my back straight. "What can I do for you?"

"It's what I'm going to do for you, mademoiselle! Let me start by telling you a story about an armed man I arrested in the woods this morning. Goes by the name of *Beaufort*. Are you acquainted with the monsieur?"

I stiffen. My first instinct is to lie—to say I don't know any Monsieur Beaufort—but Travert wouldn't be here questioning me if he didn't know something. "Maybe. The name sounds familiar. I can't be sure."

"Perhaps this will refresh your memory," says Travert, pulling some papers from his coat pocket, laying them on the table between us. He unfolds them, very carefully, revealing the papers I forged for the Kohn family.

And I go from stiff to rigid.

I'd say that everything is quiet as Travert watches me for a reaction, but the sound of my own breath roars past my ears as I struggle to keep it steady.

"These are false papers," Travert says conversationally, as I wonder how he got hold of them. "We see them every day at the gendarmerie these days. Artists are the usual culprits—we have to take a second look at every cartoonist or painter in the Haute-Loire, because they can make remarkably convincing forgeries. But these? No. These were done by an amateur."

Despite the steady ticktock of the clock on the mantelpiece, time itself slows. Do I confess and throw myself on his mercy or try to bluff? In the end, bravado wins out. "How can you tell?"

Travert actually smiles. "Glad you asked. According to these papers, Monsieur Beaufort was born in this little town," he says, pointing to my improvised stamp. "Probably the forger believed an obscure birthplace would make it difficult to confirm. In fact, it is as easy as a phone call to the mayor's office there to cross-check birth records."

What an idiot I am! Even as I think this, I force myself to feign a yawn. "Interesting."

Travert arches one bushy brow. "It's the kind of mistake a small-town person makes; someone who hasn't seen much. And then the name, of course. *Beaufort.* It made me think."

It's making me think too. I'm thinking: *I'm going to jail.*

I won't do well in jail. I hate feeling trapped more than anything.

In the face of my panicked silence, Travert continues, "What are the chances, I wonder, that I would arrest a man who has forged papers that evoke a pretty castle, and that he'd be wearing the missing red hat of an artist I know. An artist who also just happens to live in a pretty castle?"

Merde! That damned red beret. A lump of fear for Monsieur Kohn and loathing for Sergeant Travert makes it almost impossible to speak, so my voice comes out as a rasp. "Are you accusing me—did this Beaufort fellow say I had something to do with this?"

"He refuses to say anything." Travert takes out his cigarette lighter and holds the flame between us. "I don't think his silence will last, do you? Our new German friends say it's easy to make people talk if you hurt them . . ."

I watch his lighter flicker and go cold and clammy. Travert wouldn't burn me, would he? Not here, where children might hear me scream . . .

If he does, can I keep quiet? I just don't know! Even Saint Joan cried when they burned her, and I'm no saint.

Travert leans forward, and by instinct, I bolt for the door, but he grabs me by the wrist and yanks me back into the chair. Between clenched teeth he says, "It occurs to me I could burn these, mademoiselle, and erase all evidence of the crime."

So he's offering a way out, and my heart leaps at the possibility, but nothing is free in this world. I remember the way he touched me when he caught me with contraband in my bicycle. The way he gave me cigarettes after finding me at the side of the road and drove me home, telling me, *A pretty girl like you is worth the bother.* So it's going to be blackmail.

Unable to keep the disgust out of my voice, I ask, "What do you want?"

He brings his face close, dark eyes boring into mine. "What I want, mademoiselle, is your promise that if you do something like this again, you won't be so stupid."

I blink as he lets go of my wrist and sets the forged identity cards on fire. Tears of confusion spring to my eyes, and my every limb goes weak with relief as the paper curls and burns to ash.

"Don't be cute, Marthe," he says. "If you're making false papers, don't use birthplaces that can be verified. Don't let people know who you are—protect your identity so no one can give you away. Do you understand?"

I nod dumbly. But then I have to ask, "Without papers, what's going to happen to the man you arrested?"

"They'll check if he's circumcised. He had an unauthorized weapon. They'll want to send him to Drancy and then some place called Auschwitz."

Not wanting to reveal Monsieur Kohn's name, but still wanting to protect him, I blurt, "But he's French."

"Good. Then I'll charge him with being part of a thieving ring, and it'll take time to get through the court system. Maybe time enough to arrange it so he's sent somewhere else. It's the best I can do."

Poor Monsieur Kohn! It's a terrible solution, but I can't think of a better one. "Thank you . . . but I have to know why you're helping . . ."

"You think I like rounding up people like cattle? Up until now, we knew the camps were harsh—bad conditions. But they were French camps, not Nazi death camps . . ."

"So it's true." I almost choke on the words. "They're killing deportees."

His expression is bleak. "The Germans claim they're resettling Jews in the east—but it's not all Jews they're taking, and no one hears from these people again once they board those trains. You tell me what I should think."

I can't wrap my mind around it. "I don't know."

"All *I* know is that if I quit, they'll put some gendarme in my place who won't look the other way. And even I can't look the other way every time, because if I'm fired, they'll send me to jail or to Germany. It's a box. There's no way out but small acts of defiance."

I understand the dilemma. Blowing out a breath, I admit, "You scared me half to death!"

"I was trying to. Being scared will keep you from being stupid."

If I were smart, I'd wash my hands of this whole forgery business now—but with Monsieur Kohn under arrest, getting his children admitted to the preventorium with new papers is more important than ever. I have to start again. New cards, new photographs, new stamps, with only days to spare. Maybe I should ask Anna to help, but then she'd be in danger too. Maybe she would help me, *or maybe she would tell* . . .

That thought has a venomous bite, and I squash it like a stinging insect. "The baroness is going to have questions. How am I going to explain your coming here? Am I supposed to tell everyone I know something about a thieving ring?"

"No." Travert clears his throat. "As it happens, there's a simpler explanation for my visit."

"Which is?"

"I've come to make you an offer of marriage."

I give him a look that should wither his balls. "Just when I was beginning to think you were a hero . . ."

"You're too smart to think that." Travert lights his cigarette. "The age of heroes is over, even if their castles still stand. Nowadays, we're all just savages willing to do terrible things to get what we want."

"And you're saying you want me?" When he nods, my fists clench. "So this is a bargain for your silence . . ."

"*Mon Dieu*, what does a man have to do to earn your trust? I'm offering a free choice! At least take a little time to think it over."

I laugh. "You think I need time?"

He winces like my laughter hurts his feelings.

On the off chance he might be sincere, I say, "I'm sorry, but you've got to admit, this is out of the blue."

His dark brown eyes meet my blue ones. "Is it really, mademoiselle?"

I think back.

You've always been the most interesting girl in these mountains . . .

Mademoiselle, for you, I can keep a secret . . .

Now he stiffens like a man trying to hold on to his pride. "I have a house. A steady paycheck. Marry me and you don't have to register for the Service du Travail Obligatoire. What's more, I admire you and what you're doing, and if you want to keep doing it—well . . ."

"Well, what?"

"No one suspects the gendarme's wife."

THIRTY-NINE

BEATRICE
Amiens
December 1916

"YOU'RE A MADWOMAN TO COME HERE." CAPTAIN FURLAUD'S BLUE eyes burned despite the snow that dusted the dark wool of his officer's coat and frosted his mustache. "And I'm a madman for helping you."

A year and a half had passed since last we laid eyes upon each other, and seeing him again was a bittersweet pain. "Yes, well, madness is part of my charm," I replied, still stinging from a marital argument with Willie, who insisted it would be dangerous to travel without him, and from my efforts not to state the obvious—that because of his lameness, my trip would be safer and swifter if I went to Amiens on my own.

None of that did I wish to share with Captain Furlaud, especially not with so much else still left unsaid between us, so I settled instead upon, "I don't fancy that I can be in much danger here at a hospital."

"It's illness and exposure that's killing us here," he said, motioning to the rows of beds and staff nurses bustling to attend them in the ward behind us.

When arranging this visit, it had seemed prudent to meet him somewhere public. I'd hoped it would make it impossible to speak with any degree of intimacy, but Max dug his hands down into the pockets of his coat and said, "I was grieved to hear about your nephew's death. I know how much he meant to you."

"Thank you," I said, staring at my feet.

"How is Mr. Chanler?"

I didn't hear a note of bitterness, only honorable concern. What a sincere man he was . . .

"Mr. Chanler is regaining his strength," I said, which was more hopefulness than fact. "Thank you for helping me find Lafayette's great-grandson. Is Monsieur de Chambrun's artillery unit nearby?"

Under the visor of his officer's cap, Max raised a well-groomed brow. "Surely you don't think I'd bring you to the trenches. No. I convinced the commandant to stop in Amiens to visit wounded friends on his way home for Christmas leave. He can spare you a few moments, but wonders why you must speak to him in person . . ."

"Because my person is more persuasive than my pen."

The corner of his mouth tilted into an unbidden smirk, which he tried to smother. "Yes, well, I might agree, but I have too few letters from you by which to judge."

I didn't know if it was a rebuke or a plea to resume a correspondence, and I dared not ask. Thankfully, in that moment, a staff nurse approached us, a baby in her arms. "I'm sorry to disturb you, Captain Furlaud, but the Red Cross can't take this one yet."

I watched in astonishment as Max took the child from the nurse. "Ah, poor little *jolie fille*, this war is no place for you!"

The nurse smiled. I smiled too, with a pang, for the sight of a baby in Max's strong arms was like a glimpse of a life I'd never have. I'd chosen Willie. Even if Max understood and forgave that, I wasn't sure I could forgive myself. Was my heart really so fickle? Thankfully, I was distracted from these thoughts by the little pink creature in Max's arms, who looked about with such curiosity. She could be no more than a year old, but it was difficult to tell, with all the children in France being so small and starved. "Who is she?"

He gave a sad shrug. "One of my soldiers found her abandoned in a bombed-out village. He tried to find her parents but was shot dead in the attempt. I brought her here, but the ambulances and Red Cross are too busy with urgent cases to take her somewhere better."

My heart lurched to think some mother might be wandering the rubble searching for her daughter. "Which village? Maybe—"

"There was no one left alive," he said, as if divining my thoughts. "Those who could flee did so. Those rest are corpses in the rubble. Sadly, not so rare an occurrence." It was a desolate statement for what it said about the fate of the village, of this fair little babe, and for others just like her. Her cherub cheeks drew me close enough to tickle under her chin. Then she reached for me. I laughed as her fingers grasped my pearls, and to keep her from tugging them, Max released her into my arms.

"That's right, darling," I said, kissing her forehead. "Reach for what you want in life and never let go . . ." I stole a glance up at Maxime. "Does she have a name?"

Suddenly, he couldn't find his tongue. It was the staff nurse who answered, "The captain told us to call her *Marthe* . . ." My heart snagged upon this name, for Max had, in some way, made this child my namesake. The bittersweet ache of it must have shown on my face, for the staff nurse said, "Sorry for interrupting. I'll take her now."

But the milk scent of the child pulled at something inside me, and I didn't want to let her go. "Where will the Red Cross take her when they *can* take her?"

"To Paris," Max said. "Probably hand her over to Clara Simon's operation."

I made the decision all at once. "Then don't trouble the Red Cross! I'm an officer of ARCH now, so when I return to Paris, I'll take her to Madame Simon myself. This way, even if I fail in my other ambition, at least I'll have done something useful here."

Max smiled wistfully, and said by way of farewell, "Madame, I cannot imagine you might fail at anything you set your mind to."

It was a sentiment I took with me to meet Commandant Chambrun.

I couldn't help but stare, for the resemblance to the man's famous great-grandfather Lafayette was subtle but obvious in the forehead, the brows, and the regal nose. Rarely in my adult life have I been at a loss for words, but the emotions I felt in the man's presence took me by surprise. Looking at his face was so much different from studying portraits of Lafayette. The blue blood of nobility and heroism that changed the world ran through his veins. Still, here I stood in my borrowed hat, wondering at my own audacity, acutely aware that I was nothing but a bastard brat. He was part of a family legacy I admired; would he think me presumptuous to want to become a part of it? Chambrun was an officer short on time and temper, having learned that a friend he'd come to visit at the hospital had perished in the night. "My friend had three children. What will they do now, orphans all three?"

I feared this was an inopportune time to discuss business, and despite having come all this way, I offered to postpone our talk in deference to his grief. But he waved this off. "There are millions dying—if we stopped to grieve, we should never stop."

He motioned for me to speak, and I felt as if I ought to be quick about it. "Sir, I hope to make you understand that mine is an honorable offer for Chavaniac. I've started a charitable foundation, and among the sponsors are descendants of your great-grandfather's friends and comrades in the Revolutionary War."

"So I've heard," replied the commandant.

As we walked the hospital hall, I said, "I've no intention of wresting away from your family their ancestral home. To the contrary, I invite you and all Lafayette's descendants to be on the board of the foundation that will preserve it as a museum. Together, we can make a Mount Vernon of France . . ."

He stopped walking. "You mustn't have visited Chavaniac before, madame, if you think it can be made into a genteel tourist destination. It is a forgotten castle in the remote wilds. It's not like the old days, when such houses were fortresses to hold the king's territories. When the tenants all paid rents to the lord and the lord provided from inherited wealth . . . It cannot be made profitable. The economy is nothing but cheese and cabbages and lace."

Was he trying to discourage me, or excuse the family for having to let the place go? I wasn't sure which, but I did know one thing. "This is a very dark hour for the world. I believe this forgotten castle can give us hope. Hope that in this war, humanistic ideals will prevail. Hope that after the war is done, there will never be another one."

He snorted. "If history teaches us anything, madame, it is that there is *always* another war."

"There has never been a war before like this one."

"That is true, but does it matter?"

I realized I'd taken the wrong approach. In a world consumed by a struggle for survival, concerns about preserving history might seem trivial. I was talking about museums while this man was faced with the pressing and practical challenges of defending liberty in the present. As Lafayette would have done if he were alive now . . .

In an instant, it swirled together. My own desperate childhood. The wounded children I'd seen on the train platform at the start of the war. The orphaned son of Victor's fallen friend. The baby Maxime rescued from a bombed-out village. The fact that we were standing in a hospital where men left behind orphans every day. And then I knew what should be done. "I'll make Chavaniac into more than a tourist destination. Not just a collection of dusty old relics, but a *living* monument." I had Chambrun's attention now, and he waited for me to go on. Breathlessly, I did. "Why hold it only for the dead, when there are living to be cared for? The country is overrun with unfortunates with nowhere to go. Why not open the chateau as a sanctuary for displaced children and the orphans of French heroes like your poor perished friend?"

I could see this appealed to Chambrun's old-fashioned notions of *noblesse oblige*. What, after all, was a castle good for if not to offer shelter? Then my gift for ideas on a grand scale came to the fore. "Chavaniac can be a school for these children," I continued. "The war is swallowing up an entire generation of young men. Once we've won— and we *must* win—a new generation will have to follow. One ready to make the world over with new and better ideals. What better ideals than those of Lafayette?"

Chambrun's gaze drifted to the windows as they rattled with the biting cold wind. "Ambitious."

"Yes, but *why not*? We can train these children into distinguished careers . . . and with my husband's connections, secure them internships in American companies, so that they can return to France and rebuild. The chateau can foster diplomatic relations, and the Franco-American alliance of sister republics shall be renewed."

As he stared down at horses in the street, snorting steam as they pulled wagons filled with munitions, his expression revealed a sentimental crack in the hard facade. And at length, he said, "Well, madame, if that is your aim . . . you have my blessing to try."

I RETURNED TO PARIS WITH THREE THINGS THAT WOULD CHANGE my life. The first, an option for the purchase of Lafayette's chateau. The second, a baby girl named *Marthe* with fair hair and eyes as steely blue as the winter sky. The third, concealed within my coat, a sealed letter that Max had asked me not to open until Christmas.

The last burned like a guilty secret as I found myself torn between the impulse to tear it open or tear it to pieces. Especially when my husband's relief at my safe return was so evident, and his praise so unstinting. "Your plan is marvelous," Willie declared. "By George, it could make a real difference in this world."

Together we worked the phones, dashed off cables, and applied ourselves to the necessary paperwork. My friends greeted the news with equal zeal, and philanthropist John Moffat agreed to be the primary financier. Given the heavy snow, it would be quite impossible for us to journey into the mountains of Auvergne until spring. But we didn't wait—we purchased it right away for four thousand pounds, which included both the house and the ancient grounds. "Just think," Marie-Louise said, bouncing baby Marthe on her knee. "This little girl might be the first to find a home on Lafayette's mountain."

"If only she were a boy," said Clara sarcastically, flicking ash from the end of her cigarette and giving Emily an amused look that recalled their earlier dispute. "Just today I had to listen to important men talking of the uselessness of educating girls. The war has made men so resentful, as if it was *our* idea. They seem to fear women will take their place in everything from the bedroom to the factory and beyond."

"We might have to, if the war keeps on," I said, tucking a cushion behind Emily's back, which obviously pained her. "You needn't be such a stoic about your pregnancy, Emily."

"To the contrary, I think we all must be stoic," she replied. "Whenever I'm of a mind to grouse, I think of the poor shivering soldiers, or of

Amaury—he says the air is very cold in the sky. I don't think he'll get leave for Christmas."

"We shall make it a merry Christmas for you anyway," I resolved.

We tried, decorating a tree and making a spare holiday feast. Coal was incredibly scarce. The midnight mass for Catholics was rescheduled to conserve fuel, and even pagan souls prayed for another Christmas truce . . .

I worried Willie would resent my devotion to Emily, but he declared himself anxious to celebrate with us. And he remained on his best behavior, rising to Clara's bait only a few times. She loved to poke the bear, and in days of old he would have engaged her in brilliant debate, but I scarcely recognized this man who suddenly stared aimlessly into the distance, almost as dull as he was dazed.

Our fevered work in purchasing the castle must have taken a toll, but Willie roused himself for the holiday gift giving, pronouncing the tie I had given him the very thing he wanted most in the world. For me, Willie had somehow procured a fur hat in the Russian style. "Since your hatbox cannot be found . . . I wonder who is responsible for that stupidity?"

Rather than blame a servant, I said, "Someone who gave you an excuse for a very nice present. With this new hat, I can now retire the other, which has become a veritable landmark in Paris."

I kissed his cheek, knowing it must have cost him a pretty penny, as it was nearly impossible to find a reasonably priced coat, blanket, shawl, or warm *anything* anywhere in the city. More frivolous luxuries were affordable. Thus, I'd purchased a beaded handbag for Emily, lace for Marie-Louise, and for Clara, an ingenious trench lighter embossed with an owl. I also gave a doll to Marthe, since Emily felt it best to keep the little urchin with us for the holiday. "I have a nursery ready, after all."

Watching the little girl, I felt a terrible longing for my boys, imagining them tearing open gifts. The way Willie's mood dropped by evening made me think he was feeling the same way. In the hall, awaiting his coat and thinking that no one was watching him, he leaned on his crutch, pressing his head to the paneled door in exhaustion.

I realized, belatedly, that the day's celebration had been too much for him without liquor to take the edge off it. He shouldn't have come. "You ought to see if a doctor can do *something* for your pain."

"It's just the grippe. This weather. After a few days' rest, I'll be good as new, and we can start planning our trip to Chavaniac."

I couldn't imagine him making the trip. If physical exertion didn't kill him, the effort to be pleasant surely would! It seemed so strange, in a way, that after spending so much of our marriage apart, now he wanted to be together every day. *He's trying so hard*, I thought.

Wanting to feel close to my boys, I turned my attentions to a newly arrived letter from New York. I settled in to find little drawings from my sons, and news from the governess that stopped my heart.

> *Your friend Captain Furlaud stopped by to reassure the boys you were safe. They were taken with this handsome man in uniform and peppered him with questions about the war, but he told them that you were doing all the important work. I cannot tell you what good it did them to hear of their mother's heroism. Billy didn't stutter in conversation even once. Afterward, your charming friend said we must call upon him if in need of anything while he's in New York.*

I clutched the pages, confounded. What the devil was Max Furlaud doing in New York? How could I be *here*, so far from home, and he be *there*? I would've known the answer, of course, if I'd opened his letter this morning.

I opened it now, slitting the envelope to find he'd been sent on a mission to the United States. He wrote that, while there, he'd take the liberty of checking on my children. He also wrote a few lines more.

> *I never had the opportunity to tell you that our short weeks of happiness saved my life. And that I love you. So never hesitate to call upon me for help, no matter how mad the scheme.*

My hand fluttered to my throat, where I felt my heartbeat pound beneath my pearls. *No*, I warned myself. It couldn't be true. My relationship with Max had been too fleeting to give rise to real love. And in any case, romance was a malady I must never allow myself to fall sick with again. It had been the ruin of Minnie, after all . . .

Perhaps if it were only honeyed words, I might've been able to keep that door closed, but he'd provided comfort to my children. *That* was a flame in the bleak winter landscape of my emotions that I couldn't bear to stamp out. And so I burned.

I shouldn't have gone to see Max in Amiens. Not even for a favor. Not even when that favor had turned out so well. I should've found some other way. Perhaps it was a blessing, then, that we were an ocean apart. Now I wanted to go even farther than that.

How desperately I wanted to see the birthplace of Lafayette—to bring all my grand plans for it to fruition. I would have taken a train that very night, but the weather would not allow it. And in any case, I had promised to stay with Emily through her ordeal.

"You mustn't be unduly afraid of childbirth," I said, sitting beside her one blustery evening. "If I got through it twice, anyone can."

"I'm not afraid of giving birth," Emily replied. "Only motherhood. Here I am, about to meet my child, wondering if I will be an unnatural mother . . ."

"You're not unnatural!"

Voice suddenly quavering, she said, "I don't know why I thought I could do this. Amaury is made so happy by the idea of fatherhood, but then he loves all children, whereas I am impatient with all but a chosen few. Your Ashley and Billy, I adore. But what if my own child doesn't charm me? Will I simply—"

"Walk away like your mother did? You won't. Put these disordered thoughts out of your head."

"I fear a daughter because a boy would be better able to weather whatever comes."

"Which tells you precisely how disordered your thoughts are. Little girls are stronger than little boys; they have to be." I knew that better than anyone. "In case it *is* a girl, you must have a name picked. You don't want to saddle a child with her grandmother's name. *Clémentine* is far too old-fashioned."

"I've always been partial to *Anna*," she mused.

"Well, if *Beatrice* isn't in the running, I suppose *Anna* will do."

Emily gave birth in the New Year, precisely when the physicians predicted, and I was there wiping her brow and letting her squeeze my hand. "Just a few more pushes and you shall have your heart's desire."

Emily was close now, panting. "If only the baron were here."

"Trust me, you don't want him to see you like this. Your hair is an ungodly fright."

Emily groaned. "You're a monster . . ."

She didn't think so when, not long after, I held the swaddled bundle, feeling a now-familiar maternal longing. But this was Emily's child, not mine, so I put the bundle in her arms and said, "A perfect babe, fine and strong, with brown eyes just like yours. But better fashion sense, I hope."

Emily laughed, melting all at once with the sentiments she had so feared she wouldn't feel.

Later, we had lucky timing—the father himself came home on leave!

"I came as soon as I could," LaGrange said breathlessly, having run from the train station. "Is Emily—"

"She's doing well, and the baby too. Congratulations, Amaury. You have a daughter."

He looked down, stamping snow off his boots until he could hide his disappointment at the sex of the child. *At least he* would *hide it*, I thought. "It is not ours to argue with nature," I said, then led him into Emily's bedchamber. "Now I'll leave your little family to get acquainted . . ."

"You are part of our little family," she said, warming my heart. It was wonderful to feel cherished. We were all so sentimental, but the baron had only two days' leave from the fighting, and when it came to pilots, I was acutely aware of how precious such moments were. It still seemed some manner of miracle that he'd lived long enough to see his child, and I didn't wish to intrude. I checked on Marthe, fast asleep in her cradle, and wondered why she couldn't be mine. There were thousands of children in need—hundreds of thousands, in truth—but Max had placed this one into my arms, and maybe . . .

It was foolish. I wasn't even doing right by my own boys. My husband would be of no help in caring for a baby, and I doubted very much he'd be willing to bring a foundling into his distinguished family line. Still, Willie did love to surprise me. So that night, my blood thrumming with hope, I decided to surprise him by visiting his house. I found him in bed earlier than he normally retired. Worse, he was unable to rise, his eyes dazed and blank as I had never seen them in all our years together or apart. This man, so full of vim and vigor, seemed suddenly *vacant*. I was terribly alarmed. Was it the months of drinking so hard that did this to him? I could almost wish him to be a raging drunk again . . .

"We must ring up a doctor," I told his pretty secretary, whose name I didn't bother to learn. "Something is wrong with Mr. Chanler."

"The doctor has already been here, madame."

And I followed her eyes to the bedside table, where I saw the vial and needle.

FORTY

ADRIENNE

Chavaniac

August 1792

"MAMAN!" ANASTASIE'S SLIPPERS SKIDDED ACROSS THE POLISHED parquet floor, her auburn hair sweat-damp. "There are soldiers in the village."

I'd been studying our plantation books to see where our lands could be parceled out and given to freed slaves, if only I could assure that their manumission papers would be honored. Now I closed the books and stood as a clatter of horse hooves on the cobbles echoed into my open window. "Which soldiers?"

Anastasie raised her hands in a helpless gesture. "National Guard, I think. They wear the tricolor . . ."

That was a relief. Or at least it should have been, but splintered shouts began to filter through the window.

"Burn the chateau!"

"—at least every aristo inside."

I grabbed up my quill and parchment. "Tell the cook to prepare a feast. I'm going to invite the officers to dine. Meanwhile, have your sister and brother make up their beds for them."

"Where will *we* sleep?"

"In my chambers," I said.

Though Anastasie was more prone to argue than most children, she obeyed me at once. It was Aunt Charlotte who resisted. "I will not dine with the rabble!"

"You must," I insisted with all the authority I could muster. "And for the love you bear your nephew, madame, adopt an egalitarian tone."

Aunt Charlotte sucked her teeth, and the cook went pale at the notion of what must be prepared on short notice. Thankfully the commotion beyond our gates was powerful motivation to see it done. I arranged a wagon to bring jugs of milk, wheels of cheese, crates of cabbages, and sacks of potatoes from our stores. All this I sent out with a note of thanks on behalf of General Lafayette to all the brave gentlemen defending the nation. Then I dressed—no wig, no hoops, no jewels. A blue riding coat with buttons gave the best impression of a general's wife, and this I wore over simple white. No rouge or powder either; the tricolor alone would serve for ornamentation. Truthfully, I dressed much the same before the Revolution, but was now conscious of it as a choice born of fear rather than pride.

There *was* pride, though, in Chavaniac, with its liberty capstone over the door. This chateau wasn't an intimidating palatial edifice. And I was pleased to show the officers the treasure room, where, in the place of honor, was my husband's copy of the Declaration of the Rights of Man and of the Citizen. Letters from Washington. Keepsakes from Dr. Franklin. All the reminders that my husband was, and had always been, a champion of liberty.

Over wine and pork stew, the officers explained they no longer trusted the king, and they wanted a republic instead of a constitutional monarchy. Given the king's likely conspiracy with the army at our borders, I could no longer blame *anyone* for preferring a republic, yet I restricted my comments to learning their names and asking after their families, and talking about my hopes for France, which were hopes we all shared.

They explained they were on their way to the border to join the fight against our enemies. And when the wineglasses were drained and plates scraped clean, I said, "On behalf of General Lafayette, I invite you to billet here for the night."

The ranking officer kissed my hand. "Madame, after what you have shown us today, I consider it an honor to sleep under the same roof where Lafayette was born. And even more an honor to have dined with the Mother of the Nation."

The next day, as I watched them march off, I felt a flicker of hope in my breast that the Revolution might still defend itself and prove its own worth.

It was a short-lived hope, for in Paris, it was now civil war.

For while my husband was battling at the border to defend France, his enemies in Paris went to war with his *bust* in the Hôtel de Ville. They chopped to pieces the gift from Jefferson that I had dedicated, the same bust near which my husband swore upon his sword to protect the people. Only after they destroyed my husband's imitation did they find the courage to storm the gates of the Tuileries Palace—destroying everything in their path, slaughtering the Swiss Guard, and arresting the king.

The Jacobins took power with the same cruel tyranny they condemned. This was not a revolution, but a *coup d'état* led by corrupt demagogues like Danton and ascetic fanatics like Robespierre.

They had overthrown the monarchy and the constitution. And I was now in more terror for my family than I had ever been. I knew that back in Paris the Hôtel de Noailles was caught betwixt the Jacobin Club on the one side and the Tuileries Palace on the other. Had Papa, as the king's guard, been slaughtered at the Tuileries? What about the rest of my loved ones? I felt a thousand regrets and was desperate for news. "Does my husband know what these scoundrels have done in Paris?" I asked the local curé.

The priest swallowed, pressing the latest reports into my hand. "He does, madame. He denounced this uprising and summoned his troops . . . but they are in mutiny. And now there is a bounty on your husband's capture, dead or alive."

I sank down into an armchair, in despair. These wicked men would slaughter my husband without trial. The Jacobins spoke of rights, but honored none. So everything was undone . . .

Where was Lafayette now? He might be captured. He might be in hiding. He might even be dead—murdered by his mutinous soldiers. I had to know. I sent to Brioude for news, then gathered the children into my chambers. Georges and Virginie had been playing shuttlecock, having little notion of the catastrophe. Yet my eldest stood at the window, staring at the mountains all mantled in green foliage. At fifteen, Anastasie was now older than I was the day I married her father, and she understood our situation all too well.

The church bell rang for vespers, and still no news. I paced, feeling more faint with every chime of the clock. Then a cannon boomed from the direction of Paulhaguet, and we all startled. At last came a missive from my sister Louise, who had decided against leaving for America to join her husband.

My eyes raced over my sister's elegant script, savoring her reassurance that everyone I loved in Paris was alive. How my father escaped alive from the Tuileries, I will never know, because the mob butchered even the servants in their fury, leaving bloody red gore smeared upon the walls. Then my sister dared to add the postscript that would change everything.

Gilbert has made it across the border.

I dissolved in tearful joy to learn my husband had fled into neutral Belgium with his loyal officers. Aunt Charlotte dissolved into a different emotion. "Left France? No! He cannot have done it."

I tried to explain he had escaped certain execution. Still Aunt Charlotte keened, stumbling into the corner as she plucked at her cap, wailing that she would never see her nephew again. It was her age, I thought. She did not understand this was the best possible news under the circumstances. Then again, was I any more sensible? I had wasted hours waiting for news when there was much to be done. If our enemies could not capture my husband, they would come here. They would seize his papers. His property. His—

I glanced at Georges and Virginie. Were these Jacobins vile enough to punish Lafayette's children? I would not gamble on the decency of such men. We had to flee. An offer of shelter had been made to us by a little parish deep in my husband's mountains, where the tangled woods still echoed with his legend. Now we would hasten there . . .

"Anastasie, take your sister and gather up the valuables. Rings and watches and jewels—the silver too."

My girls raced to do as I asked, and though the sun was setting, I called for the carriage to be brought round. That was when doubts assailed me. When the royals stole away from Paris, they went together and traveled too slowly. That is how they were captured. It would be safer to scatter my children, even though it was an affront to my mother's instinct . . .

Though it rent my heart, I sent my wailing daughters away in the carriage to Langeac, ignoring their tearful pleas to stay at my side. The monsters might not think to look for the girls, at least not right away. But

Lafayette's only son and heir—they would hunt. "You are going to have an adventure," I said, helping Georges into peasant's clothing we had borrowed from a servant. "Just like the kind your father used to have."

I pressed into his hand a dagger, telling him it must be used to defend himself against any wild dogs or wolves he might encounter, but I worried more about the beasts who walked on two legs. Thus, I led my boy and his companions—a tutor and a lad from a nearby village who would serve as guide—to the secret passages in the castle walls, now cobwebbed with age and neglect.

How I thanked God for them! They would lead away from the castle, to the darkened woods, and if we were being watched, no one would be the wiser. If my son were to be caught and questioned, he would give a false name. Jacques, Jean, Pierre . . . it did not matter. He must not admit he was the young Lafayette.

I kissed my son in hurried farewell, trying not to let him see my terror. Oh, my mother's heart *bled* to send my darlings off in such distress and haste, with kisses that might be the last they ever received from my lips. Yet I remembered all too vividly the shouts of the mob in Paris.

Kill her! Let's make Lafayette a present of his wife's head!

My children were safer without me, and I did not want them to bear witness to my death, should it come. With my children dispatched, all that remained now was for me to steal away with Aunt Charlotte. I planned to flee deeper into the mountains, where the Protestants who lived there might remember us favorably as champions of religious freedom. If not to the Protestants, I would flee into the wilds near Mont Mouchet. In trying to decide, I went to my husband's treasure room, grabbing up George Washington's dueling pistols and personal tokens; I even took down my husband's swords of honor from their case on the wall.

I should've sent these with Georges, I thought. As my fingertips slipped over the gold hilt of the one from America—a gift from a grateful new nation—I wished to stand and fight, wielding it in protection of everything and everyone I loved. Alas, I was no soldier.

Heartsick, I went to fetch Aunt Charlotte. I nearly got her over the threshold and out into the evening air when she stopped. "*Non.* I will not be rousted from my home by brigands."

"Then you may be burned out of it!"

She tightened her lips. "I am a Lafayette. I was born here and will die here . . ."

Was I less a Lafayette than she was? I remembered my husband's words: *Chavaniac is for me a temple which gathers the sacred objects of my heart. You are the lady of my dream castle. May you guard each other well.*

I had no cannon or army. I didn't know how to guard this place. Still, now I realized I couldn't abandon it. So as the sun finally set in scarlet splendor over the mountain peaks, I sat sweating by a blazing fire in August, burning papers our enemies might twist to their purposes. Invitations and calling cards might lead to our friends, so they went into the fire. Letters too. I worked feverishly to erase intimacies I could bear for no one to abuse.

Watching our innocent correspondence burn felt like some kind of death, but there was no choice but to entrust these memories to God for approbation or forgiveness. What I could not bear to burn, I hid. I stashed papers behind loose stones. I broke into the old dungeon chamber that Gilbert had sealed off and concealed valuables there too. I hid everything I could in the house.

Except for the swords.

Whatever should come to pass, I resolved not to let these swords fall into the hands of the desecrators of our revolution. Thus, outside into the moonlight I went, kneeling in the dew of the rose garden.

These swords, like Chavaniac, were only symbols; a symbol was nothing. And yet, everything. Thus, with the moon as my witness, I dug with my bare hands into the cold earth. I hid the blades deep in volcanic soil that served to remind me that the precious things we bury, like fire in the heart of the world, must one day rise up again. And that our voices would not be silenced forever, but echo through the ages for those who are willing to listen.

At daybreak, Aunt Charlotte stared at me in confusion when I told her my idea. "Put Chavaniac under seal? What does that mean?"

I forced myself to calm. "It means we surrender the castle and everything in it to the civic authorities. Gilbert's enemies are calling him an émigré and consider all he owns forfeit, so they will not want it stolen by pillagers before they can take it for themselves."

Aunt Charlotte laughed like a hyena. "You want bourgeois brigands to protect us from peasant pillagers?"

It was our only hope. Aunt Charlotte believed there was no lawful government but the king's, yet she did not stop me from writing the letter that invited the tribunal in Brioude to vouchsafe our castle and all its belongings. The Revolutionary officials came straightaway to affix the seal on our door, and though Aunt Charlotte took this for the greatest indignity, it would keep looters away.

The officials then advised that I go before a tribunal in Brioude to answer a warrant that had been issued for my arrest.

"*Non*, Adrienne," Aunt Charlotte said. "You must not go. Here at Chavaniac, you can hide in these woods. They will keep you safe."

"But amongst the officials in Brioude, we have Fayettist friends," I argued. "If I go now and prevail upon them before the Jacobins can remove them from power, we stand a better chance."

I was dressed and ready with a small traveling valise when the curé, waving a missive, came from the village. "Madame! You will want to read this."

My breath caught at the sight of my husband's handwriting. The letter both comforted me and put me in torment, for Gilbert, in crossing over the frontier as a noncombatant, invoking the right of safe passage to a neutral country, had nevertheless been detained—not by the Jacobins, but by our Austrian enemies.

> *When I am released, I wish for my family to join me in America, where we will find the freedom that no longer exists in France. And I will try, with all my love and tenderness, to console you for all you've lost.*

I did not know when he might be released, or when we could go with him to America, but he was alive. We were *all* still alive, and I meant for us to stay that way. "Guard this letter," I said to Aunt Charlotte, surrendering the precious pages to her.

"With my last breath." She tucked it into her bodice, near her heart.

In Brioude I was surprised to find an atmosphere of carnival. Every person was in the streets for the elections. Only one man shouted, "For shame! There is a warrant for the wife of Lafayette and yet no one dares lay a hand on her?"

Thankfully, he was alone in his ranting. I was welcomed. Friendly officials came to console me. "No one here would hold against an innocent wife the transgressions of her husband. You will not be arrested."

The grandee of the town meant to imply it would be easier for me if I denounced my husband, and this gave me the deepest insult. "Monsieur Lafayette has not transgressed. He's been captured by our enemies, sir. He's not one of them."

"He is lucky to have so loyal a wife, madame. Many still love your husband and remember all the good you have done. For your own sake, though, at least refuse to take Mass from a nonjuring priest."

It seemed so simple a request, yet the pain of my conscience burned. "Is the violation of my religious principle the price of my safety?"

He was not base enough to force me, but when I announced my determination to take Mass with a nonjuring priest, he said, "To give so little care for pragmatic concerns, madame, I fear you have been infected by the heady air of Chavaniac."

Perhaps I had been. And perhaps I would have been more circumspect if I had known of the atrocities committed that terrible day. For throughout France the Orléanists and the Jacobins embarked upon a killing spree. They went first for the priests, killing hundreds of them, and bishops too. Then they killed common prisoners, the surviving king's guards, aristocrats, or any noble they found.

Princesse de Lamballe was raped, beaten, and dismembered—her head paraded through the streets. When I heard this, I nearly howled with sorrow, and went straight to see my daughters at Langeac—both of whom had also heard about the massacres. Virginie was in a terrible fright, flying into my arms, but Anastasie was furious. "How can God forgive such crimes?"

Both my daughters wanted to come home to Chavaniac. Anastasie argued, "We've been warned a contingent of soldiers will pass through in the morning, and how much joy they would take in violating Lafayette's daughters. At Chavaniac, Virginie and I know to hide in the fireplace, in the attic, in the passages and little chambers behind the stairs. Let us come home with you, Maman."

Though I wished to shelter her from the world's horrors, she was too much her father's daughter to be held back. I was also reassured by my reception in Brioude, and by the friendly villagers who now wanted to accompany us safely back to Chavaniac. That night, before we slept under our own castle roof, I demanded of Anastasie, "Assure me again that if soldiers come in the night, you know what to do."

She nodded. "You will get torches and send for the field hands to carry Aunt Charlotte away in a sedan chair. I will take Virginie upon my shoulders and bear her away through the tunnels, then into the forest."

"That's right," I said.

But the soldiers didn't come in the night; they came in the morning.

"*Mon Dieu!*" screamed the housekeeper, rushing to wake us, keys jingling from her belt. "They are at the gate."

I bolted from my bed to the window—praying not to see an armed mob. What I saw was nearly a hundred armed men. Why should they possibly need so many? *The girls know where to hide*, I reassured myself. So long as I kept these men out of the house, the girls could get free.

I threw on a robe—issuing orders to the servants, praying Aunt Charlotte would stay in her room. Already I heard angry voices echoing in the grand salon, and flinging the door of my chambers open, I came face-to-face with a hard-looking man, a pistol on his belt.

Too late. I was too late to keep them from the house. But Anastasie was clever; she would've already taken her sister to a secret place. I could at least take solace in that. From amidst the soldiers emerged their leader, a man from Le Puy—famed for having recently killed a prisoner in cold blood.

"La femme Lafayette," he sneered.

Meanwhile, a commissioner presented me with a warrant for the arrest of me and my children.

I always feared they would come for my children, but somehow I had not imagined they would be shameless enough to put it in writing, under color of law, as if without fear of the judgment of humanity. "I will go with you straightaway, sir," I said, wanting nothing so much as to get these men out of the chateau. Let them center all their rage upon me.

But the leader persisted. "And the children of Lafayette?"

I opened my mouth to say my children were gone to the countryside, but at that very moment, Anastasie swept in, auburn hair cascading over slender porcelain shoulders. "I am the daughter of Lafayette, monsieur, and I intend to accompany my mother if you take her."

Oh, Anastasie, what have you done? I could scarcely breathe for the terror of what they might do. "My daughter oversteps! She will remain behind. Pray call for horses, sir. I am ready—nay, *eager*, to surrender myself to you."

Already uncouth men flooded my chambers, smashing open the drawer where I kept my husband's most recent letter. "What do we have here?" said the one who boasted of murder.

"Letters my husband would be happy to submit to a court for examination, for no action of his life could incriminate him in the eyes of true patriots."

"Madame," the commissioner snapped, "these days there is only the court of public opinion."

Hearing that, I knew the sooner they took me away, the better. Outside my apartment, the soldiers had hold of the housekeeper, making sport of her, and pointed their sabers at portraits. "Wench, who are these aristocrats on the wall in gilded frames?"

"Good people long since dead," the housekeeper replied, her countenance awash in scorn. "If they were still alive, things would not be going on as badly as they are now."

The men smashed vases and pocketed trinkets. Then they saw a portrait of my husband and stabbed it through the heart. It was this, I think, that roused Aunt Charlotte from her hiding place. "For shame!" she cried, wagging her finger.

"Go back to bed, old hag, and we will leave you unmolested."

Yes, I thought. *Go back to bed, Aunt Charlotte.*

Instead, she lifted her walking stick like a bat. "Young man, I will not be kept apart from my niece. If you take Adrienne, you must take me too. Even to Paris, if need be."

All I wanted was to keep my loved ones from danger, yet they insisted upon flinging themselves into its jaws! Should I throttle them or weep with gratitude? All that kept me from sobbing was the thought that Virginie and Georges were safely hidden.

The men who had come to seize me had to lift Aunt Charlotte into the carriage, and she made it as difficult for them as possible. Meanwhile, one of the well-meaning men in the village rushed to me. "Should I watch over young Georges whilst you are gone?"

Mon Dieu, would the soldiers realize he was speaking of my son? I nodded quickly, pleading with the good villager to be silent. One of the marauders glared in our direction. I feared he would ask after Georges— instead, he snarled at the villager, "Stop groveling before this aristocrat."

The villager ran off, looking back only once as if to promise my son's safety. In the chaos and upset, though, all the men of Chavaniac seemed to have lost their senses. I had just stepped inside the carriage when *another* servant came to see me off, fretting, "Mademoiselle Virginie is to stay behind?"

It was too much. Nearly faint with distress, I cried, "Oh, please, monsieur!"

Was everything to go wrong? The commissioner narrowed his eyes and approached. Officiously, he read the warrant again. It called for the arrest of my children, but did not name them.

A small mercy.

In the carriage, Aunt Charlotte made the sign of the cross over herself; God must have seen, because the commissioner slammed the carriage door shut, and then we were off. Anastasie reached for my hand. "Don't be angry, Maman. I could not allow you to be taken without anyone to defend you. Papa would never allow it, so how could I?"

"Oh, my sweet," I said, pressing my lips to her hair. "Your father would be so worried if he knew, but, like me, so proud."

FORTY-ONE

BEATRICE

Paris

February 1917

MORPHINE. THE PAIN HAD FINALLY BECOME TOO MUCH FOR WILLIE. Having sworn off booze for my sake, he submitted to the needle. And that needle became the center of my husband's world, though he convinced himself that I was. He did not want me to join him at his house— and Emily needed me anyway. So while I set up the Lafayette Memorial Foundation and recruited our executive board, Willie came for tea with me every afternoon at Emily's house.

There, he only sipped at his cup and had nothing to say. Not even when explosive news reached us that the Germans had sunk another American cargo ship. I expected Willie to rage at Woodrow Wilson's weak response. I expected him to call Wilson a craven jackass, a pompous professor, a lickspittle . . .

Instead, he just nodded. He didn't even open the newspaper. Perhaps current events were too black a subject for his already-black mood. I tried to interest him in books, but he was too tired to read; too drugged to want to debate, or discuss, or even recount old stories of his glory days. He just sat and stared.

Under the influence of morphine, his brilliance was all gone.

Was my larger-than-life Willie to become an old man, addlebrained before his time? "Perhaps this summer," he finally mused, "we shall go fishing at Buzzards Bay."

Buzzards Bay! Of all the dreary holes. I would die there, and so would he. He was no longer steady enough to walk on land, much less the deck of his yacht. A traitorous part of me wondered if this would be our future together, and I dared not bring up the subject of adopting Marthe, for it seemed to me as if my husband himself might soon need more care than a babe.

Instead, day after day, week after week, I was as kind to him as I knew how to be, and polite. *Achingly polite.* For when he left each afternoon, I knew that he'd go directly to bed and stay there, writhing in pain, or drooling on morphine, and though he still refused to let me tend to him, I was consumed with pity.

"*Pity* is the death of romance," Clara said, on her third cigarette in an hour. "Let him keep you at a distance if he wants. You weren't destined to spend the rest of your life as a nursemaid."

She knew, of course, about Max's letter. I'd confided in her, fearing Emily might judge me more harshly. Now Clara stubbed out her cigarette viciously. "You need to read Nietzsche! Trample down all feelings of pity and live for yourself alone!"

This from the woman who had become a chain-smoking scarecrow under the stress of trying to find housing for refugees. The truth was, I *had* read Nietzsche. More recently, I'd been reading the letters donated to our foundation. Priceless letters from Lafayette to his wife, Adrienne, and hers to him, filled with archaic devotion. Letters of honor and un- selfishness and sacrifice. With their example in mind, I shook my head against the bleakness in my heart. "As admirably suited to our era as the rules of Nietzsche may be, I cannot live by them. I married William As- tor Chanler for better or for worse."

"And now things are worse," Clara said. "Where was Monsieur Chanler when you were at home raising children? When you needed him, he was adventuring. He wanted a separation then. Now that it's worse *for him*, he wants a wife again . . ."

I winced at the way she laid it out so coldly. It didn't capture the whole truth, but neither was it a lie. Perhaps if Willie had allowed me to help him, to live with him, to tend to him—if he'd let me get closer than skin upon skin—things would be different. Hell, even fighting would be better than this disconnected existence, this half marriage . . . it was in- tolerable.

And I didn't want to think about any of it.

What I wanted was to bury myself in work. I hoped to recruit the most important men in France to serve on the board that would oversee the work at Chavaniac. I also wanted to visit the chateau—the sooner, the better. And all my friends wished to go with me.

Marie-Louise LeVerrier was to help with the school. Clara Simon with the orphanage. And the ever-practical Emily with reconstruction. It wasn't until the end of February that we were finally able to go, which was fortuitous, because it meant that Emily was out of childbed and could bring along little Anna on our journey.

It was, of course, impossible for Willie to accompany us. And as the reality of his condition set in, I did my best to detach myself from baby Marthe, surrendering her into Clara's lap for the trip.

The road to Chavaniac ran all the way to Brioude—a trip so arduous that we'd been advised to take the train. It provided an excellent distraction for Emily, who had bade her husband farewell with a stiff upper lip, but sobbed when he was gone back to his duties in the air corps. Now, as five-week-old Anna slept in her lap, Emily marveled at the passing scenery. "What a wild country. Are we sure it will be a good place for children?"

Clara shrugged. "Better than living in rubble and poison gas."

Marie-Louise chirped, "They say pine forests exude a health-giving air."

"Let's take a deep breath, then," I said, watching a farmer drive oxen along the road. This was old France—as steeped in her essence as Paris, but in her raw unchanging state. Something untamed, and perhaps untamable. "It was probably little different in the time of the Gauls, when Vercingetorix resisted the Romans, and we must do all we can not to be seen as invaders here."

I'd already decided to make a donation to the locals for a monument they wished to erect to their war dead.

We disembarked at Saint-Georges-d'Aurac, then piled into a *camion* for the rest of the trip, and as we sputtered up into the little village of drab stone houses with red tile roofs, I caught sight of an old church, the curé of which stepped out to wave. I was struck by the pastoral nature of the place—sheep in the grazing land beyond, and an angry donkey at the side of the road that brayed as we passed. How did I never realize Lafayette had been a *country bumpkin*?

Something flashed white at the summit—surrounded by sparse trees denuded of their leaves by winter—one of the twin towers of the chateau. "Stop!" I told our driver, and threw the door of the *camion* open before he applied the brakes. Here it was. Here *I* was. Where Lafayette had played as a child, where he'd ridden his horse, where people doffed caps to him. The towers didn't gleam so white as they must have in Lafayette's time, but in my mind's eye, I could see them as he must have seen them. What a home this would make for lost children. *Why, if Minnie had been able to grow up in a place like this . . .*

Not wishing to wait on the groundskeeper, I unwound the iron gate's rusty chain, which fell to my feet. Then we made our way up the bramble-covered walk to the heavy wooden door, so old and weathered I worried it might fall from its hinges. Dirt stained the white walls, and upon closer inspection, I felt dismay at the shabbiness of it all.

"Look!" Emily cried, pointing to the Phrygian cap embedded over the door. "That must be the stone from the Bastille." We left the babies under the supervision of Emily's lady's maid, and I took another invigo-rating breath before approaching the house. I opened the door, squinting in the dim light. Clara had thought to bring a lantern, but it wasn't bright enough to fill the space, so I reached to draw back one of the dusty old curtains.

It was then that I felt a swoop near my hat and a flutter by my ear, into which some creature emitted a squeak. Naturally, I screamed. But when I screamed, so did my lady friends, all of us creating a comical jam in the doorway in our retreat, dropping pocketbooks and losing hats to the wind until our screams turned to shrieks of laughter.

That is how our guide found us after parking the motor and finding the concierge, who, upon introduction, made a sweeping bow to Emily. "*Bonjour*, Baroness . . ." Emily was now above me in social station by vir-tue of noble title, and that was going to take some getting used to.

The groundskeeper spoke with accented French that I couldn't make out. "*Bats*," Clara translated. "There's a colony of them in the attic. Some come down through a crack in the ceiling. That will have to be repaired straightaway . . ."

Emily dutifully added that to our list of planned renovations. We would also need to add electricity and running water. Meanwhile, I was eager to explore, bats or no. Brandishing my parasol, I said, "Into the breach . . ."

Entering the chateau, we found that despite the family's attempts to buy back many of their belongings after looting during the French Revolution, the whole house still remained sparsely furnished.

I was charmed to find, in the apartments that had belonged to the hero's wife, several game tables by the fireplace, where I imagined Adrienne must have played with her children. Would she be pleased to see children play here again? I hoped so. There was much to explore, from the kitchen where guardsmen and servants used to take their meals to the little blue-painted chamber where Lafayette sat at his desk and did his writing. That was to say nothing of the secret tunnels . . .

"There is a rumor they lead out to the village; another that they lead to the water's edge," Clara translated.

"*Goodness*," I said. "What an adventure!"

However, I didn't have a hat suitable for spelunking.

The library was a shambles—the floors rotted away and the walls crumbling. But the philosopher's hall with busts of the thinkers Lafayette admired was intact, and a charming room at the top of one of the towers where a chandelier now hung was perfectly habitable.

Lafayette's bedchamber had been kept pristine.

The wood floor creaked under my feet as I took in the faded red toile. Did the Revolutionary general choose this himself? Pictures and portraits still hung upon the wall, little items on the mantelpiece that might have amused the great man. The room having been kept as a veritable shrine by the family, the chamberlain explained that he had made it ready for the baroness with fresh linens.

"*Oh, no*," Emily said, embarrassed. "The honor should go to Mrs. Chanler."

"The bed is big enough for two," I said. "It isn't the Ritz, but what romantic dreams we'll have!"

This was going to be a greater enterprise than I had ever dreamed. We'd need a staff—a housekeeper, housemaid, and gardener at the very least—to put the house back to rights, and a curator for the museum. For the orphanage, we'd need a school, a headmaster, teachers for the children, a physician to tend them, seamstresses to sew their clothes, and farmers to tend the sheep and perhaps raise crops to keep them fed.

First, however, we'd need to hire architects, because the chateau would have to be repaired and reinforced. Of course, that would take time. Time that homeless children like Marthe did not have . . .

Clara blew out a long stream of cigarette smoke. "It would be faster to build something new."

"You're right." I lit upon an idea. "You're *exactly* right. Which is why we're going to build a new addition."

The chamberlain winced as if I intended a desecration, but I was convinced this was nothing Lafayette would have opposed. He was, after all—like me—a person for progress. And I felt certain this was work I was born to do.

FORTY-TWO

MARTHE
Chavaniac-Lafayette
November 1942

"DO YOU, MARTHE SIMONE, TAKE YVES JÉRÔME TRAVERT . . ."

The mayor is droning on, dragging out the civil ceremony like it's a love match.

Anna has been trying to talk me out of this wedding for weeks, but the only way she could stop me is to say she's jealous, or that she wants me for herself, and that's just a fantasy. This morning, zipping me into the white gown I wore to the gala all those years ago—still the prettiest dress I own—she said, "Don't marry someone just to get out of being conscripted into the STO! The Vichy government isn't going to force women to go to work for Germany—Papa says it would turn the whole country against them."

"The whole country is already turning against them."

I couldn't tell her that I have better reasons to marry Travert. For one thing, he helped me make an entirely new set of false documents for the Kohn children to keep them from being rounded up with foreign Jews. He suggested a new place of birth—some town where a fire had wiped out the records. To make the whole thing more authentic, I used a second stamp to show a change in domicile. The more stamps, the more convincing, Travert said; police assume the papers have been checked by numerous authorities. I kept the name *Beaufort*, because everyone at the preventorium already knows Gabriella, and Travert said my work would fool most gendarmes.

It fooled Anna, anyway. She admitted Josephine and Daniel a month ago. Now I've got to get their father out of prison, because it was my stupidity that got him arrested. I need Travert's help to do that . . .

Then again, he said he'd help whether I agreed to his marriage proposal or not. *So why am I marrying him?*

The question keeps echoing in my mind, and my answers keep changing. I'm marrying him because he can help me with forged paperwork; because his name can protect me if I get caught. Because I'm reckless and destructive and wanting to punish myself. Because Henri is never coming back; because I am lonely and tired of longing for what I can't have. Because I'm almost twenty-seven, and not likely to get another offer. Maybe most of all because respectable married women don't get denounced as sapphists.

Then there's the simple fact that someone wants me, and I haven't felt wanted by anybody in a long time . . .

I don't want a ring. I don't think of it as a real marriage—whatever that's supposed to be. Just an alliance of sorts. But for the wedding, Travert is freshly barbered, eyebrows trimmed, and he's wearing aftershave, the spicy scent of which fills the mayor's office.

When we're done saying our vows, our marriage certificate is duly filed by the clerk. She gives me my new identity card and stamps it with the authority of the village of Chavaniac.

I don't want a celebration—no wedding feast or church service—so for our wedding night, Travert takes me to a nice hotel in Le Puy, a cradle of terra-cotta rooftops watched over by dramatic religious statues atop volcanic outcroppings. I want to climb the summits and study the sculptures, but it's getting late by the time we check into the hotel room, and I tuck my borrowed suitcase under the bed, wondering what the hell I've gotten myself into.

Didn't I always say I wasn't the marrying kind?

Travert has arranged for supper and a bottle of iced champagne. He tips the porter too much. Then he surprises me with a small radio concealed in his own suitcase. The Germans confiscate radios now, but maybe there are exceptions made for the gendarmes. Whatever the case, he sets it up and tunes in music, and lifts the silver domes, revealing our meal. It's quite a spread. Cassoulet, bread, a week's ration of butter. "Hungry?"

My mouth should be watering, but it's like I've swallowed cotton balls. "Not yet, but don't let me stop you."

Travert quietly covers the food again, then joins me at the window, digging his hands into his pockets. "Ah, a view of the big city. You might have trouble getting used to my house in the little hamlet after this . . ."

"I won't be at your house much," I remind him, because he knows I'm not a girl to cook, sew, or darn socks. We've agreed I can keep my job teaching at the preventorium—and that I'll stay at the castle five nights a week.

Now he points out a bronze statue of Lafayette standing near the tramway, a Revolutionary tricolor cockade in hand. "Your favorite general."

"Can't seem to get away from him . . ."

"Be nice. I think he's here to give away the bride!"

I snap the curtains shut. Meanwhile, the groom tugs open his black tie. "Should I pour you a glass of champagne, Madame Travert?"

"I'd rather guzzle the whole bottle," I reply—because it's the first time anyone has ever called me *Madame Travert*, and it's starting to sink in that I've really gone through with it.

"You're having second thoughts."

Second thoughts, third, fourth—I've lost count. But Travert didn't force me into this marriage, and it's not fair to treat him like he did. "Just jitters."

"It's normal." He pops the cork, then starts to pour. "We don't know each other well, but a little mystery is good, no?"

Travert hands me a glass of champagne, and I'm reminded of Henri and the night he proposed. I'm even wearing the same dress, and it is bringing back painful memories . . .

Travert clinks his glass against mine. "Getting to know each other better gives us something to talk about."

I don't want to talk. I don't want to be in this dress. And I *definitely* don't want to remember. So I knock back the champagne, then reach behind me and yank the zipper. The gown falls to my feet in a heap, and then I'm standing in a strapless longline brassiere and panty girdle.

Youthful fumblings with Henri were always in the dark. I'd have been too nervous to get undressed with the lights—too worried he wouldn't like my figure or the pale peach fuzz on my thighs. Happily, I don't care much what Travert thinks.

It's freeing, really. For me, anyway. Travert stares like he can't decide what to do, his brow knitted in consternation. "I didn't expect—"

"It's our wedding night, isn't it?"

Travert drains his champagne, his gaze traveling the length of me. I let him look, almost like I'm daring him to find fault and call the whole thing off. Like I hope he will. The problem is, he's not looking like some cool-eyed art critic appraising a painting. No, there's a tender expression, and when he lights a cigarette I worry this is going to take a while. "Don't people usually smoke *after*, Sergeant Travert?"

"It's Yves."

"I know your name."

He exhales a plume of smoke. "I like to hear you say it."

I sit on the edge of the bed. "All right . . . *Yves*."

"I need the cigarette to calm my nerves," he explains. "I thought we wouldn't do this until we both feel . . ."

As he searches for the words, I'm afraid he'll get sentimental, and I go prickly as a cactus. "Let's not try to make this into something it's not."

I promised him marriage; I didn't promise him love.

Now he watches his cigarette burn. "People speak well of your betrothed. Was he good to you?"

What kind of question is that? Henri was good to me, good for me, perfect in every way . . . and even if he wasn't, I'll always say he was, because he's forever young and forever dead.

Like he can read my mind, Travert asks, "So he was a saint? Whereas you and me, we're just made of flesh and blood."

"I don't want to talk about Henri."

Travert drops the ashes of his cigarette into a crystal tray. "Okay. But I have to say this much . . . I know I can't be him. I wouldn't try . . . And I can't be her either."

I try to guard my eyes, but too late. If he didn't know about my feelings for Anna before, he does now. He's a good detective. Maybe he guessed when he interrogated me about the graffiti and Anna put her arm around me in a hug. Maybe I'm more transparent than I think. Now he's caught me at a vulnerable moment, shocked me by guessing those feelings I'm too depraved even to count as sins. And my mouth is too dry to deny it.

He's stripped me bare with six words. Now he tries to absolve me with four more. "Who can explain love?" He shrugs like it doesn't matter. But it does. I want to say so. I want to say something, *anything*, even if just to deny it, but I can't get the words out.

"We want who we want, Marthe."

"*Shut up*," I finally hiss.

"You can't have either of them, but you can have me. It doesn't have to be love, but we can still make it something."

This marriage is a mistake. I want an annulment, but as I try to get up off the bed to get dressed, he catches my wrist. He knows he's gone too far. That he's upset me. "I'm sorry."

I just glare, but when he lets go of me, I don't move and neither does he. The music swells on the radio. We're silent for a long time. Eventually he asks, "Do you want me to go?"

How bitter I am to realize that the answer is *no*. I don't love Yves Travert—I don't even like him. At least, I don't want to like him. I tell myself he's not funny or dashing or sophisticated, and he's older than me by a decade. He's just a burly village gendarme. A plodder trying to get by.

But somehow he's also the only person in my whole life I don't have to lie to, and that makes me say, "Stay."

He nods, stubs out his cigarette, climbs into bed in shorts and a sleeveless white undershirt. He's all brawny shoulders and hairy arms, and I want to feel revulsion when he reaches for me. I want to feel violated. He's got muscles like stone, and I want to hammer against them until I provoke him to do something terrible to me.

Then he hugs me, which is the most terrible thing of all . . .

I actually gasp when he pulls me close. His big arms tighten around me, not in lust, but to give comfort—and I burst into tears. I've never liked anyone to see me cry, not ever. My whole life, I've held back the flood . . . only for the dam to burst on the shoulder of a man whose middle name I just learned today.

And now I cling to him, sobbing in the crook of his neck. I can't seem to stop. I'm crying all the tears I haven't felt like I deserved to shed for Henri. All the tears I'm not entitled to cry over Anna. All the tears I've been holding back for every kind of reason, as petty as my stalled ambitions and as big as my nation's shame.

Travert strokes my hair until I'm spent, all dried out. Then he gets me a handkerchief and watches me blow my nose. I reach for my pocketbook, take out a mirror, and try to fix my makeup, but it's no use. I'm a red-eyed, red-nosed ruin.

I glance back at him, realizing that I've soaked his undershirt with my tears and he's watching my every move. I find it unbelievable that he could possibly still want me, but he's got a pillow in his lap, and it's easy to guess what he's struggling to hide. I start to feel a little sorry for him. *What a pathetic pair we are . . .*

I dry my eyes and say, "Let's have sex, then. Let's just get it over with."

"You're upset. You don't really want to."

"Don't ask me why, but right now, I really do."

His brows lift. "Then should we talk about—"

I kiss him, hard, before I can change my mind. I try to get the upper hand, but he's already fisting my pin-curled hair as he draws me down. He returns my wet kisses like he's dying of thirst. Then we're rolling in the bedsheets, wrestling to be on top. I don't like to let anyone get the better of me, but he's stronger, and when he pins me to keep me from scratching, he whispers, "You can't make me that person."

"What person?"

"The one who hurts you," he says.

I stare into his earthy brown eyes, chastened. Quiet. Confused that he seems to know what I'm doing even before I do. "Okay?" he asks.

"Okay," I whisper.

We kiss gently this time and I like the weight of him pressing down. He's solid, and heavy, and *here*. And when he reaches for a rubber I go soft in spite of myself, because I know there are laws against contraceptives under the current regime, and that abortion is punishable by death. My mood has been too bleak to even think about that before now, but Travert thought about it. And it says something good about him that he doesn't want to bring a child into the world at a time like this. That he doesn't just want to knock me up and leave a kid behind if he dies. *Because I know what it's like to be a kid left behind . . .*

When he puts himself inside me, the pain isn't terrible. Then the sensation of heat and the friction of skin-to-skin in urgent need becomes a mindless pleasure. There's only this breath, and the next, this moment and the one after, my first cry of pleasure against his mouth and his throatier groan.

When it's finished, he sits at the edge of the bed and smokes a cigarette. I wrap myself in the sheet, strangely satisfied, and offer my confession to his back. "You should know I've never . . ."

He turns, and the cigarette nearly falls from his lips. "Never?"

"Don't look so surprised!"

He still looks shocked, and also amused. "Okay."

I whack his arm. "Now I'm sorry I told you."

He shrugs apologetically. "I'd have done it differently if I knew."

I pause, surprisingly curious. "There are different ways?"

"I would've . . ." His neck flushes. "I could've—"

"Shut up."

He frowns. "*Merde.* We're back to this again?"

"I mean, shut up and listen to the radio!" I bolt to my knees, straining to hear now that music has given way to an announcement that strikes like a thunderclap from the sky:

"The Americans have landed in North Africa."

FORTY-THREE

BEATRICE
Paris
Spring 1917

AMERICA WAS FINALLY IN THE WAR.

While I'd been in the mountains at Chavaniac with architects and electricians, trying to restore Lafayette's chateau, President Wilson went before Congress and finally said, *The world must be made safe for democracy.*

What eventful days were these!

By the time I returned to Paris, Willie—nearly falling in the entryway when his crutch caught on the stair—brought the newspapers to Emily's house, and after I read President Wilson's words, they echoed in my mind.

> **We desire no conquest, no dominion, no compensation. It is fearful to lead this great peaceful people into the most disastrous of all wars. But we shall dedicate everything we are and everything we have, knowing America is privileged to spend her blood for the principles that gave her birth.**

I fished through my purse for a handkerchief to dab my misty eyes. That old flubdub mollycoddle somehow found precisely the right words, and I complained, "*Damn Woodrow Wilson.* I made it this far through the war without blubbering like a sentimental fool . . ."

I wept that American boys would soon die in trenches. I wept in anger that it had taken so long for us to save other boys from that fate. I wept too with thanksgiving, for this must bring an end to the savagery. For three long years I'd done everything a woman could do to convince a nation to take up arms. I'd begged funds, left my children, risked my life, harmed my health, and hectored an American president.

Now we had, at last, thrown down the gauntlet. "I believe this is the noblest thing we have ever done . . ."

Willie's hand closed over my shoulder. "Victor didn't die in vain."

I clasped his hand, hoping that was true. Glad too to see my husband peeking past the shroud of morphine. "Beatrice, what say Saturday I take you to lunch? I've got a surprise."

I readily agreed.

After a busy week of setting up a Paris office for the newly formed Lafayette Memorial Foundation, I joined my husband at the restaurant where I'd first suggested divorce. "We don't have the best track record in this place," I jested, and when I looked askance at the glass of liquor in his hand, he shrugged.

"It's either liquor or the needle, and morphine makes me a drug-addled half-wit. So which would you prefer?"

I didn't want to answer. He'd promised me a year of sobriety; he hadn't made it six months. I'd never before seen him fail at anything he put his mind to, but was addiction his fault? "I'm sorry you're not feeling better . . ."

"I'm not sure one can ever feel better after losing a leg."

I nodded with sympathy, hoping he'd finally open up to me about it. "Are you ever going to tell me how you hurt it in the first place?"

"And ruin the romance?" he snapped.

I sighed, realizing that we had, both of us, always kept secrets, but not from each other. At least I hadn't thought so. But he was never going to tell me the truth; in fact, he enjoyed keeping it from me. He was the only man I'd ever let see past all my masks to my naked soul—but now I wondered if I'd ever seen the real Willie at all. If, in the end, he was the better actor by far.

I sighed again, a dreadful headache descending. "What does the doctor say about your condition?"

Willie grimaced. "He says another trip this year will kill me."

I breathed a sigh of relief that I hadn't been the one to have to tell him. "I'll explain to the boys. I'll take back all the photos and newspaper articles about our work here."

Willie frowned, trying to flag down the waiter to refill his glass. "You can't return to New York without me."

I wanted desperately to go home to my boys and hold them tight now that New York was likely to be a target of submarine warfare. I needed to go back for the sake of my work too. With America in the war, most charity efforts would go toward supporting the troops now, and in the aftermath of the war, no one would want to give to the Lafayette Memorial. I had a very narrow window during which I could secure an adequate endowment to keep Lafayette's chateau open for generations to come.

Still, I didn't want to abandon Willie. Guilt-ridden, I suggested, "We'll get better care for you round the clock. I can have friends look in on you every day. The end of the war cannot be far off, and—"

"The Germans are *trying* to sink American ships now. There is no safe route, and your life is worth too much to be risked. You cannot possibly think of traveling alone."

I softened at his protective, if illogical, drunken sentiment. "Willie, even in your younger days, you couldn't have defended me from a torpedo."

Willie waved again to the waiter. "In any case, your presence here is, for at least a few weeks, necessary."

I imagined he was worried I'd leave the whole Chavaniac business in his hands, so I reassured him, "All the committees have been formed, with capable persons at the helm. The work at the castle itself is now under the supervision of Marie-Louise LeVerrier." I had, reluctantly but with great fortitude, surrendered little Marthe into her care, and I didn't want time to think better of it. "I've already stayed longer in France than I should have."

Willie leaned back. "Won't your special friend mind you going?"

"Emily will understand."

"I meant Captain Furlaud."

The candle on the white-cloth-covered table between us flickered as he studied my face for a reaction. And blood rushed past my ears as I tried to guess whether or not I'd be better off pretending ignorance or candidly admitting everything. What, after all, did I have to hide? Max was in the past, and I doubted Willie had lived our years of separation as a monk. "I don't know that Captain Furlaud and I are friends at all anymore, much less special friends."

"He got the Lafayettes to sell the chateau, didn't he?"

I took umbrage that anyone else should get the credit. "He only arranged a meeting."

Willie smirked. "Is that all he's done for you?"

I didn't bother to ask what he knew, or how. My husband had contacts and informants on every continent; I'd be naive to think he'd never ask them to spy on me. The only thing I wondered was how *long* he'd known about Furlaud. In any case, I refused to justify myself. In loyalty to Willie, I'd broken things off; I'd be damned if I paid a second price for it. "Captain Furlaud wouldn't presume to tell me what to do or where to go. Whereas you presume too much."

Willie thumped his empty glass on the table, perhaps hoping to catch the attention of our inattentive waiter. "You're worried I'll cause a scene, aren't you? Fly into a jealous rage. Truthfully, I'm quite amused." He did not look amused. "In fact, I feel sorry for the old chap."

"*Willie*," I warned.

"A banker, of all things." He laughed in mockery. "You can toy with him if you like; you have my blessing. Because if a man like that thinks he has a chance, he doesn't understand you at all. You'll chew him up and spit him out and leave his heart bleeding on the floor."

I glared. "Is that what you think I've done to you?"

Willie's gaze dropped to his empty glass. "No. I haven't a heart for you to chew up, which is why you married me in the first place."

"That's not why I married you."

"Why the devil did you marry me, then?"

Because I loved him. Because he told me that if I married him, I could become someone new. But now I wanted desperately to be more than *Mrs. William Astor Chanler*. I almost said it aloud, but managed to keep it caged behind clenched teeth. "I don't intend to sit here and trade insults."

"I'm not insulting you, my dear, not at all. You've always lived a big life. Who knows? One day, maybe your life will be bigger than mine. I simply know that no matter how big it gets, there'll never be room in it for a man who does nothing but move piles of money from one account to another."

He does more than that, I wanted to say. Max was an officer, and a gentleman. Still, there wasn't any point in defending him, because this was a childish conversation. "I don't enjoy bickering in public."

"Really? I've missed it," Willie said, fiddling with his new prosthesis under the table as if it were giving him pain. "In all these months of inactivity due to the morphine, I've worked up a thirst for conflict, not to mention an *actual* thirst, if the damned waiter could be bothered to refill my glass."

I turned to catch the attention of the headwaiter, who was facing away from our table. That's when my husband's artificial leg, with its sock and garter, sailed past me and struck the waiter in the middle of his back. I gasped as the poor man dropped and Willie's prosthesis clattered to the floor. The whole restaurant hushed to a tinkle of forks dropping on plates and cups upon saucers. Then my husband shouted, "Do I have your attention now, sir?"

I was paralyzed with mortification as waiters rushed to help their felled companion, who, fortunately, was not hurt. Then Willie's dark, drunken laughter was the last straw.

The last straw!

God knows, I'd tried to make this marriage work! I'd weathered years of his wanderlust, abandonment, and neglect. I'd forgiven and excused his failings as a father. I'd turned a blind eye to likely infidelities and refrained from prying into his secrets. I'd tried to care for him even when he wouldn't let me. I'd been understanding about his addictions to alcohol and morphine. And I'd put up with casual cruelties. But in that moment I knew, deep down, his dark laughter wasn't only at the expense of the poor waiter. He was laughing at me too.

I took my napkin and flung it on the table. Then I rose with all the dignity I could muster. "As it happens, I *do* prefer you as a drug-addled half-wit!"

I was done feeling sorry for him; if he could find the strength to hurl an artificial leg across a restaurant, then he didn't need or deserve my pity. Certainly not my company or my marital devotion. I was sick to death of trying to make this work. I was determined to get on the first ship home I could find, but when I turned to go, Willie blocked me with his crutch. "We haven't had our salad."

"Don't make me tell you where you can stuff your salad!"

"Come now, I told you that I had a surprise," he said, taking a letter out of his breast pocket with the seal of the United States embassy on it. "A little gift for you."

I RETURNED TO EMILY'S APARTMENT IN A STATE OF STUPEFACTION and found her perched over the baby's cradle. In a hushed tone so as not to wake the child, I murmured, "The American ambassador wants to send me north. I've been asked to do some work in the war zone of the British Army—near your husband's chateau."

As angry as I was at Willie, my skin prickled with excitement as I explained the mission. On the pretext of business for the Lafayette Fund, I was to go near the front, earn the confidence of the British officers, and report back a great many things about our new allies.

Willie had been doing this kind of thing for years, using his personal charm and his fortune to keep his thumb on the pulse of global politics, reporting back to his contacts at the highest echelons of government. Now he was giving me the opportunity to do the same. Even if it was just Willie's way of keeping me from getting on a ship, could I refuse?

"I don't suppose you'd like to come," I teased Emily.

"I can't," she murmured distractedly.

"Of course not, you have the baby and—" She turned to me, and the look on her face stopped the words in my throat. "What's wrong? Has Amaury been hurt?"

She shook her head. "He's been chosen for a mission to the United States to coordinate French and American air forces. It's been suggested that I go with him."

"Wonderful!" It would do her good to see her family after nearly two years' separation. More importantly, Emily knew precisely which captains of industry to press for help in equipping aviators and coordinating this new mode of warfare. Amaury's command of English was excellent, but his wife's connections would prove most valuable. *New Money* or not, she could open doors for a French delegation, to say nothing of the way she could shift public sentiment with the lantern slides of the destruction here in France that she'd been preparing.

How gratifying that after having both tried so hard to be useful, we were both now *needed*. How ironic that we should both be called upon in the same moment, flung in opposite directions. "Well, you must go, of course." Alarmed to see her tremble, I quickly added, "They'll send you by military ship. You won't be as defenseless as on a passenger vessel."

Her gaze dropped to her sleeping child, and I realized it wasn't fear that made her tremble. "I can't abandon Anna, and I couldn't possibly take a four-month-old baby across the sea."

No, she couldn't. Quite apart from the risk of submarine warfare, there was the potential for illness in the company of so many travelers, against which infants had so little defense. I knew what a sacrifice it was to be parted from one's children, even in the care of a trusted nurse. I was painfully tempted to tell her to refuse on the grounds of motherhood. That's what everyone else would tell her. But she relied upon me to remind her that no father would be excused from duty. We had, from the start, believed ourselves just as capable as men, and she'd never forgive herself if motherhood took that belief away from her. "Emily, you mustn't think you're abandoning your child. You're answering a call to make the world better for her."

"Do you think that's how Anna will remember it?"

Watching the babe curl her little pink fists under her chin, I thought of Marthe and how I'd left her behind at Chavaniac. "She won't remember it at all," I said, as much to convince myself as Emily. "She's too young for it to leave the slightest impression."

"What if . . ." Emily trailed off, as if calculating the odds. "Last spring when Amaury's plane was hit by shrapnel, I realized that one day soon he might not be so lucky and my daughter would grow up without a father. I've reassured myself that she'd have me, but if we're both lost at sea, she'll have no one."

"Anna would have her grandparents and her aunts, and of course she'd have *me*."

Emily smiled gratefully. "But *you* are going close to the front lines . . ."

"Not too close, but it would comfort me to know, if the worst should happen, my children would have *you*, wouldn't they?"

"Of course!" Emily wrapped her arms around herself in a torment of indecision. "Amaury's mother has agreed to watch over the baby, but if I leave, what kind of mother will people say I am?"

"You're a baroness. You don't have to care what the little people say."

She stifled a teary laugh, and I was glad to put her in better humor. "Emily, you aren't sacrificing your child's happiness to run off with a lover. Every courageous thing you do will bring Anna pride one day."

The baby gave a wail of irritation, and Emily lifted her up, whispering, "I'm sorry, darling, I'm so sorry."

Her regret was not, I knew, for awakening the child.

She'd made the decision to go, and so had I.

FORTY-FOUR

BEATRICE
The Chateau at Motte-aux-bois
Hazebrouck, France
Spring 1917

MY TRIP ON BEHALF OF THE EMBASSY HAD BEEN, UNTIL NOW, UN-
eventful. On my way north, only occasional patches of trees and winding
canals relieved the eye of the dreary and flat muddy plains. At least the
Spanish-influenced houses and neat little farms were picturesque, and
under normal conditions must have given the impression of quiet peace,
but this had been a battlefield for centuries.

Never more so than now.

The LaGranges' ancestral home was now a military headquarters of
the British Army, and the drive of the baron's chateau was crowded with
every sort of conveyance, from carts to wagons to motorcars and ambulances. British Tommies engaged in a fierce football game in the field
against some Australian soldiers and a few from India. And the grand
manor house bustled with more than twenty British officers, to say nothing of orderlies and hunting dogs, all of them banished from the kitchens
by the fastidious cook.

Yet, in a sea of khaki uniforms, the very first soldier fate flung in
my path was a blue-clad Frenchman with whom I'd once drunk enough
tea to swamp a battleship. And here I was again with a baby in my
arms.

"What brings you here?" Max wanted to know.

"I'm here to deliver my friend's infant to her grandmother. I should
rather ask what brings *you* here."

The captain was droll. "Did I neglect to mention I'm a liaison officer
between French and British commanders?"

He was remarkably sarcastic for a man who had penned me a letter saying, *Our short weeks of happiness saved my life.* Of course, I had not answered that letter, and perhaps he resented it.

"Meet Anna de LaGrange." I made the child wave her pink pudgy hand. "I learned just this morning that her parents have come ashore safely in America, from whence I imagine you've recently returned." Gratitude warmed me. "I should thank you for seeing my children in New York—for reassuring them."

"It was nothing." Furlaud smiled down at his boots. "They're wonderful boys. You raised them well."

"I like to think so, but it nearly broke me to leave them in tears, and you put them at ease . . ."

Just then, Emily's mother-in-law swooped in to take up her grandchild. "I hope this little one will be able to sleep tonight," she said. "The Brits keep the place lit up like a casino. Bombs rarely hit their targets, so it actually serves as some protection, though our neighbors are not so fortunate."

"*Goodness.*" And to think I brought a child here.

The honorable old lady gave a courageous shrug. "When one thinks of the cost of a zeppelin or bomb, it seems a poor investment for the Boche, but he continues his evil ways."

I realized how well Emily must fit in with this stouthearted family. Meanwhile, my task was to charm the British generals, though I daresay pretty little Anna outshone me in this. The gruff General Godley professed himself smitten, promising to marry her when she grew up. I regained my footing only when one of the officers recounted having seen me on Broadway and offered to play the piano if I'd sing after supper.

Emily's mother-in-law scoffed. "It's not right to ask Mrs. Chanler to sing for her supper like a cabaret girl."

Thankfully, I never found it beneath my dignity to perform. I sang that night, I made the officers laugh, and before the clock struck midnight, I had them in the palm of my hand. I observed their temperaments, opinions about the progress of the war and the morale of the soldiers, not to mention attitudes toward Americans in general. And by breakfast, General Godley—who had a reputation for being a cold-tempered, rigid, and officious general—agreed to break the rules and take me closer to the front at Ypres, or what remained of it . . .

"How did you convince him?" Max wanted to know.

The French captain had come upon me where I labored over a type-writer, and I looked up to reply, "Oh, I praised Godley's heroism and asked if he might be willing to donate his uniform to my new museum at Chavaniac."

"Ah, flattery . . ." Hands behind his back, Max bounced on his heels. "What are you working on now?"

I glanced proudly at the page. "A letter to procure a *doctoresse* for the children at Chavaniac—one Dr. Alice Barlow-Brown, who has just been refused for the American military medical corps on account of her gender."

Max leaned against the doorway. "I begin to suspect you're a suf-fragette."

"You're only now beginning to suspect?" I asked, grinning.

I liked the relaxed slant of his shoulders and the softness of his blue eyes when he asked, "What else don't I know about you?"

"What you don't know about me could fill a book."

We were flirting. This was dangerous. Unfortunately, it seemed I now loved to live dangerously. And I was tempted to find that our connection was still a very live thing, growing in strength.

"Did you always admire Lafayette?" Max asked. "I cannot decide if you've given yourself over like a nun to the religious order of his memory, or if you simply decided his name was the most obvious one to invoke for your charity."

"It can't be both? Though I daresay no one has ever compared me to a nun before!"

It was so good to laugh together again. To feel appreciated and ad-mired, and not always on my guard for a barbed comment or flare of temper. How nice to converse with a gentleman who wasn't drunk or drugged or hurling artificial legs across a restaurant. How nice to know we were *on the same side.*

I somehow found myself telling Max about one of the few happy memories of my childhood: climbing the rooftops on Tremont Street to watch fancy ladies in their fancy hats promenading down the row of stately elms that led to Lafayette Mall at the Boston Common. "Those hats, I thought, were the difference between people that mattered and people like me. On hot days, I'd splash in the frog pond near all those Revolutionary monuments, and they seemed to whisper, *Even if you're a hungry urchin now, you could be a person of significance someday.*"

"So then, you're the very embodiment of the American dream."

"It shouldn't just be an American dream," I said, altogether too earnestly. "After all, Lafayette was a chivalrous knight-errant like you, who spent his life trying to secure that dream for everyone."

"Oh, you mistake me. I've no taste for chivalrous adventure. I was *drafted* into this war, and after three years of being shelled, I want nothing more than to return to the peace and quiet of office life."

I couldn't blame him. I'd noticed the way his knuckles went white around the handle of his coffee cup at every far-off rumble of the guns, and I remembered how he'd once said, *You've rescued me from the despair of this war.*

A despair I was soon to experience firsthand.

In Ypres, the hospital had been deliberately targeted. Bombs had blown out buildings in such a way as to leave walls standing, and I walked through the rubble of what seemed like dollhouses, paintings still hung, toys in cribs, plates set out on tables for abandoned meals. What happened to the inhabitants here—gassed, buried, shot—I didn't want to guess. The wind whistled and howled through these haunting structures. Guns thundered not too far off, battle fire lighting the sky like bolts thrown from the hands of Zeus. And my mind reeled to think, *Little Marthe was found in a place like this . . .*

The next day I saw a tank for the first time, and great guns painted in harlequin colors. I plucked out of the rubble two helmets—one British battle bowler and one piked German *Pickelhelm*—to preserve in our museum after the war. After we'd won.

The busy officers deposited me in the relative safety of Poperinge, less than three kilometers from the fighting, where I made careful note of the men returning from the trenches worn and bedraggled, others sitting out with the smoking kitchen on wheels, carts filled with provisions and tents. All this gave me an idea of what organization was necessary to carry on a great war, though I felt a frisson of fear to see a long line of lorries with munitions, realizing that a single bomb dropped from an aeroplane might send us all up in a fiery apocalypse.

I didn't know if any of these details would prove useful to the embassy or to American commanders, but I recorded them dutifully and tried not to get in the way. This was especially so when warning of a new bombardment came—and the sirens went off with warnings that the entire hospital must be removed. Never would I take up space in an ambulance meant for one of the wounded, so I was left stranded.

Let me send my motor for you, wrote Maxime. And when the tires of his Rolls-Royce came to a crunching stop beside me, he was himself in the driver's seat.

"Have you been demoted to chauffeur duty?" I asked.

"I consider it a promotion to drive your staff car, *Madame General*," he teased. "As I told my commanding officer, no one in the French army can allow you to come to harm; you're too valuable to the nation."

"He bought that?" I asked, trying to disguise both my relief at being rescued and the mix of emotions Max's presence always stirred up.

"Your country coming into the war has created amongst my countrymen the greatest love for Americans."

I didn't imagine his emphasis on the word *love*. *I still love you*, his eyes said. After he'd loaded my luggage, I climbed into the front seat and straightened my skirts over my knees. "It's very thoughtful of you to have put your automobile at my disposal."

I clutched my hat, because Willie always liked to test the engine by pushing it as hard as it would go. But Max eased carefully onto the pockmarked road as if carrying precious cargo.

I cleared my throat. "I'm sorry to have troubled you. I'm sure you have more important things to do."

"As it happens, there's nothing more important. I've been given a few days' leave to see you back to Paris."

Did he mean to say there was nothing more important to him than me? I tried not to wonder if he'd forgiven me for going back to Willie. If he meant what he'd written at Christmas. And I hoped going back to Paris together wouldn't be more temptation than I could withstand. I still found this man alarmingly sympathetic—a danger to my impregnable heart.

What would we speak about on the journey? I couldn't tell him I was here at the behest of the embassy. I also couldn't allow conversation to drift to our past, so I chattered on about my work.

"And how is our little cherub?" he asked. "Marthe."

My breath caught as I wondered whether it meant something that he called the baby he once put into my arms *ours*. "She's thriving in the mountain air, safe in Lafayette's ancestral home. She owes her happiness to you."

Being alone with him again reminded me of how we had been before Willie's amputation. Before the drinking. Before the morphine. Before the ugly scenes. I wasn't sure I could abandon my husband now that he was crippled, but I knew, without a doubt, that we'd never be happy again. That our marriage was over in every sense of the word but one. Perhaps that's why I'd thrown myself into work. It was a way to keep from thinking about the lonely marital road ahead of me . . .

On the road *actually* ahead of me, the earth suddenly roared, spitting up black smoke and soil and stones that hailed down upon us. The car shook with the blast, and my hat fell over my face, blinding me as Max slammed the brakes. I was thrown into the dashboard and crumpled onto the floor, where I crouched wordless with shock.

Another shell exploded in front of us and shattered the windshield. I shrieked at the spray of glass while, with wrenching speed, Max backed up, turned the car, and careened away. I clutched the seat for balance as the automobile jumped and bumped down a smoke-filled road I hoped would lead us to safety. Instead, our front wheels hit a crater where some previous shell had landed, and our car fell half in it, coming to a dead and painful stop.

There was near-silence a long time after that.

No more shelling. No birds chirping. Only a high-pitched screech in both my ears. A man was standing over me, face bloodied, reaching down for me. Was he shouting my name? I didn't know. I couldn't even remember where I was. Had we been in a car crash?

If the boys were hurt, I'll never forgive Willie. Never.

But it wasn't Willie calling to me. It was Max's voice that finally penetrated the fog of my mind, reminding me that this was war. Clutching my hat, I tried to push myself up. Max grabbed my wrist, dragging me out of the wrecked car. Only then did I come to my senses.

We ran through the field, grasses whipping at our ankles as we fled the range of the guns. We didn't stop until we reached an old orchard tree, where Max took hold of my arms. "Are you hurt?"

"I don't know," I said, gasping a painful breath. "I don't think so."

Blood dripped from his forehead, mingling with his sweat. Somehow I had the presence of mind to take a kerchief from my pocket, dabbing at what was, thankfully, only a cut over his brow where his forehead must have smashed into the wheel.

"Thank you," Max said. He stood, bent over me, staring into my eyes with tenderness. "There is a farmhouse not far. We must try to locate a telephone, and I'll find us a way back."

I nodded, but didn't move. Instead, I held up my hat to show him that shrapnel or sparks from the explosion had burned holes in the brim. "I might have been blinded . . ."

Instead, I felt I was seeing clearly for the first time in a long while.

I'd just been reminded what little beings we are—so ill matched against destiny. My tomorrows were not promised, but I desperately wanted today. "Kiss me, Maxime."

A flicker of surprise behind his eyes sparked with an unspoken question. He'd want to know what this meant, where it would lead, what decisions must be made. I wanted to answer none of these questions, and to stop him from asking, my mouth closed upon his in reckless joy.

How long we clasped each other under that tree, I couldn't say, for the clock of the universe now ticked to the time of our beating hearts. And I knew there would be no struggle against this hour of happiness, however long it might last.

FORTY-FIVE

ADRIENNE
Le Puy
September 1792

IT WAS TOO GENEROUS TO CALL THE ASSEMBLAGE OF ARMED MEN who arrested me *soldiers*, but they wore the tricolor cockades my husband had popularized at the start of the Revolution. There were some amongst them, at least, who still gave a care to duty, offering courteous hands to help me, my daughter, and Aunt Charlotte in and out of the carriage at our stops along the journey. "It's the women of Chavaniac!" someone cried when we rolled into Le Puy. A mob formed around us, and a rock cracked against the glass window, causing my daughter to jolt. I squeezed her hand to keep her calm. And Anastasie did the same for Aunt Charlotte.

Not wanting either of them to see my fear, I stared straight ahead. Alas, this only inflamed the *sans-culottes*. Wearing red Phrygian caps, wielding pitchforks and pikes, they shouted, "Look at the aristocrats. Still so arrogant!"

My cheeks burned, because I'd never been called *arrogant* before. My gown was modest, bosom covered in a fichu made for me by local lacemakers from the school I had established. I wore no jewelry but my wedding ring and a small holy cross dangling from my neck—which I supposed would be counted against me in godless Paris, where blood flowed in the streets.

Another volley of stones slammed into the carriage, causing a shrill whinny from the agitated horses, and when the glass shattered, I yelped, hastily brushing shards away, even as they opened little cuts in my hands. I couldn't understand how this could be happening. Not so long ago, the people of France called my husband *the Hero of Two Worlds*, the father of our new nation, and some called me its mother. Now people I didn't know spewed torrents of abuse against me.

"If Lafayette were here, we'd tear out his bowels, so let his bitch be his substitute!"

My daughter's hand tightened upon mine, and I felt the slick sweat of her fear. Seated across from us was a tenderhearted guardsman I'd known since his youth, and I saw his jaw was so tight he might crack his teeth. "My child is with me, sir," I said, as if he could restore decency.

And he tried. He shouted at the mob out the shattered window to have a care for innocent ears. It made no difference. "*Citizen*," they called back. "Her children are only parasites nurtured at her bosom."

I should have prayed for the souls of anyone depraved enough to say such a thing, but indignation filled my heart. It's barbarism to take vengeance upon the women, children, and elderly relations of public men. But barbarity had been unleashed in France by Philippe and the Jacobins. The sacrifices we made for *liberté, égalité, fraternité* were now wasted by these lawless criminals. Everything we honored was desecrated, every dream corrupted, every ideal defiled . . .

I gasped with relief when the soldiers somehow beat back the crowd, and our damaged carriage clacked its way down the stone road. It was not the end, by far, of the danger. A trembling worked its way into my knees, my mind scrambling for some way out of this situation. I tried to think what my husband would do. "Sir," I whispered to the guardsman whose eyes brimmed with sympathy, "do you think it is possible I should find the means of escaping?"

Blanching, he could not meet my eyes. "It would not be possible for a person bearing your name . . ."

I knew what he was suggesting. The hope he was holding out. Half the aristocratic women I knew—amongst them even loving and religious wives—had divorced to keep their property or save their lives. Some renounced or even denounced their husbands. If I did the same, maybe I too could go free.

My heart beat wilder with hope that my family might one day be reunited if I made this concession. What was a name in these days when divorce, forbidden under the *ancien régime*, was now so prevalent, and titles meant nothing? I was born with my father's name—of the house of Noailles. Then I exchanged it for my husband's name. Why not change my name again for survival? Perhaps, like Philippe, I could simply choose a new one.

These thoughts buzzed like stinging insects in my poor brain until, at last, the carriage stopped before the department in Le Puy. This was the crucial moment. If they took me all the way to Paris, I would be murdered, but if I could convince *these* men to set me free, here in this friendlier, faraway province, there was a chance.

My daughter and her aunt insisted upon going with me into the room where I wrote a petition protesting the injustice of my arrest. They looked to me for guidance, because Lafayette couldn't give it. He was a prisoner. *Lafayette, the Hero of Two Worlds*, the invincible soldier who never raised a sword to conquer, only to liberate. Nevertheless, he had conquered my heart, and now I feared I would never see him again. So what did it matter now if I put more distance between us?

If I gave up his name . . .

As I reached the place on the page where I was to sign, the tender-hearted guardsman stared intently as if *willing* me to choose expediency. My pen hesitated. The quill pen shook in my fingers, one of which bled from the glass. That was but a trifle considering the amount of blood they said gushes from the neck when the guillotine falls.

Yes, it is but a trifle, the guardsman's eyes seemed to say. *A name means nothing. Honor means nothing anymore either.*

I glanced at Anastasie, so like her father, with an intrepid spirit and the heart of a lion. I was already in agony that my children might soon be orphans, and blinked away tears to think of them shamed by the one thing their father and I could still leave them. Our name.

Already, *Lafayette* was a name people had died for. A name that meant everything to me, but also a name that didn't belong only to me. It belonged to the ages, where I hoped it might yet inspire great deeds. So I signed in large letters and bold ink what might be my death sentence: *la femme Lafayette.*

FORTY-SIX

BEATRICE
Paris
May 1917

HOW GLAD I WAS TO LEAVE THE BARREN LANDSCAPE BEHIND, BOTH the one at the war front and the one that had been my fidelity to an empty marriage. These last days with Max had been glorious, and the time flew by too quickly. It is always so when one is happy in the paradise reserved for lovers . . .

In Paris I purchased an apartment—a private bungalow tucked away behind the Monnaie de Paris, where the Condorcets hosted salons for Lafayette and Americans like Jefferson and Paine. When I explained this, Max grinned. "So we're walking in the footsteps of freedom . . ."

In truth, we were only free inside the apartment with the curtains drawn, shielded from the judgment of the world. There, drinking rations of bad wine and eating candlelit suppers of cold duck, I didn't want to think of anything, or anyone, else.

For the world played no part in this new life of mine.

Why, then, did the world insist upon intruding?

Thanks to Clara and her connections, our work at Chavaniac had received government recognition as a public utility, which meant we had access to labor and raw materials in preference to civilians. As secretary-general, she would help preside over a Paris school for boys like Uriah Kohn who needed not immediately travel to Chavaniac. And thanks to Emily's accounting, I now realized that I was managing almost two million dollars of public works.

Chavaniac was set to open for forty orphans by the first of June, so I spent my days purchasing and shipping furnishings, dishes, linens, bedding—everything they might need. My nights, however, were spent with Max by the fire. One night, he whispered, "I have to return to duty soon."

In a dreamy haze, I murmured, "I'd rather you stayed. What a lack of discernment in the powers that be that so valuable a man should be wasted thus at the front!"

He chuckled. "Wasted? I'm at least a *little* useful, if not necessary."

Whether he was necessary to my happiness was a burning question. I was in love, and that love was now the compass that guided my thoughts, my desires, and without which I felt certain I would founder. I traced his shirt button. "But if you go back to the front now, you'll miss my birthday."

I shouldn't have said it; after all, the last thing I wanted was for this man to think of me as a creature who aged. I wanted him to think of me like Paris—a timeless beauty dressing for romance with an evening visitor, her lights enveloped in a mantle or shade. Unfortunately, the visitors who came to Paris at night were unfriendly, and our idyll was interrupted by the blare of horns as military motors zoomed below my windows.

Pulling on boots, Max said, "Another air raid. The Boche are in a hurry to blow us to smithereens before American troops can come to our rescue."

I slid my feet into satin mules, and Max held my jacket so I could slip it over my pale pink *robe d'intérieur*. This he did with great tenderness, and hearing the familiar rumble of the guns, we stared out my windows to see flashes and sparks of antiaircraft fire light up the sky. Sometimes the kaiser's dark birds of night didn't get to the heart of Paris—instead dropping bombs on the outskirts before mounting higher in the skies and sailing back to their cruel nest. Still, Max insisted we descend the stairs to the cellar for shelter.

These air raids, night after night, were hard on us all, but no one complained. More often, people would sigh and say, "*C'est la guerre!*" Still, my heart went out to the little boys and girls hastened from their beds each night, blinking and terrified. I was grateful my own boys lived relatively charmed lives, and after five months apart, I missed them unbearably. In a dark corner of the musty cellar, Max lit a candle, made a place for us on a pile of sandbags, and opened his arms. I wanted to melt into his embrace and fall asleep there, but I murmured, "I have to go home."

In the dim light, he rubbed his chin. "If you wait a little longer, I'll have more than a month's leave."

It was too delirious a thing to contemplate. I imagined a string of long days with him. Taking a newspaper over coffee in the balcony window, strolling the shopping arcades in the afternoons, opera in the evening. I wanted more of Max, but my faults as a mother were not boundless. "I should have gone back already."

"What if I came with you?"

"What a lovely dream . . ."

As the air raid sirens wailed, he explained, "Your friend LaGrange mentioned I could be of assistance in wrapping up the mission in New York. It would only be a short assignment, but I could volunteer to go."

Could it be possible to bring happiness home with me? I thought of leaving Willie behind and sailing off with my cavalier, but instead of feeling overcome with guilt, or even a need to say good-bye, I felt relief. Beset with the memory of my husband at our last luncheon with the sneering and pitching of prosthetic legs, I knew that Max would never do such a thing. They were, in fact, such different men, I no longer believed my heart could be divided.

I wondered what the future had in store for me with regard to this last actor to appear on the scene.

Well, I would take Max home with me and let the Fates decide . . .

IN THE PRIVACY OF MY STATEROOM AS OUR SHIP CAME INTO THE harbor, Maxime wrapped his arms around me and asked, "Will you be jealous if I love her?"

"Yes," I replied, gazing up with him at the towering Lady Liberty. "She's too beautiful, even if scarred and under repair."

"These days I think we're all scarred and in need of repair."

Except for fear of mines and submarines, our journey had been idyllic. We'd been able to dine together every night without causing a sensation. We'd listened to a musical concert together. We'd stood on deck and stared at the stars. On the seas, far from the sound of the guns, far from my husband, far from responsibilities, we had been suspended in a bubble.

But now we had to contend with the needle of reality.

Within hours of coming ashore, Max reported for duty at the French consulate in lower Manhattan. Meanwhile, I went directly to the Vanderbilt Hotel, where the overjoyed desk staff told me I could find my boys in the old offices of the Lafayette Fund.

"Billy! Ashley!" I smothered them with kisses until both boys squirmed with embarrassment. How was it possible for them to grow so big in only six months? "I've missed you beyond the power of expression."

"Where is Daddy?" Billy asked.

"In Paris, darling. A sea voyage would be too difficult for him just now."

Ashley's eyes welled. "We wrote him a letter. He hasn't written back yet."

I kissed his freckled nose. "Your father is busy just now. Still, he cherishes all of your missives! He asked me to tell you to keep writing, and once the war is done, he wants you to come for a visit." Such lies were a kindness. "Whatever are you doing in the office on such a beautiful summer day?"

"You're early," Emily chirped from the back of the office, where she sat toiling over a typewriter, like old times. "I told your boys that as soon as I finished this letter, I would take them for ices."

Happy but bewildered, I asked, "What are you doing in New York?"

"I heard your ship would come later this afternoon and meant to take your boys to meet you at the docks!"

"But last I heard Amaury was in Washington training American pilots."

"I took the train up," she explained. "Now, tell me, how is my baby?"

"Anna is thriving in the care of her grandmother," I said.

Ashley tugged at my sleeve. "*Mumsie.* Aren't we going for ices?"

I laughed. "You little rogue. Let's all go to Coney Island!"

That afternoon we stood in lines for the Helter Skelter and Shoot-the-Chutes rides. We went in a gondola too, which was no competition for Venice, but had its charms. I enjoyed the sound of children's laughter—children who were, by and large, untroubled by war.

On a shady park bench where we watched my boys play, Emily explained that she'd not been idle—she'd arranged an art exhibition that would be called *The Sky Fighters of France*. The monies collected would go to the children of French aviators killed in action to be cared for at Chavaniac.

"We must invite the Chapmans to take part." My nephew had been the first American aviator to die at war, and it would not be right to leave him—or his family—out of such an exhibition.

Emily nodded her understanding and sympathy. "Speaking of, there has been some music composed in your nephew's honor. A string quartet. It would be nice to play it at the exhibition, and of course our Lafayette work seems to take on a grander scope every day."

"That's true," I said, for I dreamed of transforming Chavaniac into an international school. "Clara and Marie-Louise send their regards."

"And Mr. Chanler?" she asked. "How does he fare? There's a rumor going round—something about a nasty altercation in a Parisian restaurant."

The story apparently traveled faster than I did. "How he hurled his wooden leg at the headwaiter like a spear? Oh, yes, it's true. I was there."

Appalled, Emily's jaw dropped. "I never knew he had a violent temper."

It was my instinct to defend Willie. To explain it was the pain. The alcohol. Still, the excuses had worn thin. The Chanlers had explosive tempers. I'd once seen Willie stab a knife into the table while spatting with his brothers. He'd always been a man of self-proclaimed *medieval* temperament; it's only that he used to curb it for my sake, so the kindest thing I could think to say was, "Mr. Chanler means well, but age and habit have conquered. I fear the day has passed where a change might be expected."

How grateful I was for Max—a man who never got drunk in public, never lost his temper, never let his manners slip. "Furlaud is here."

Emily's eyes narrowed. I waited for questions or accusations. She hadn't approved of our romance before Willie's amputation; she'd approve even less now. At least she knew me too well to suppose I'd done this lightly. "You're on a dangerous path. Is it too late to warn you off it?"

"I'm afraid so. I know you have misgivings, but please don't darken my skies. Rejoice in this hour of happiness with me."

"Is he at least a decent man?"

"More than decent! He's a most attaching person. A remarkable person, truly. His devotion is enough to inspire love, and added to this a charming personality, the effect becomes irresistible."

Emily took a breath. "It's one thing to find love in the crucible of war, quite another for it to flourish in everyday life. This might be your chance to know if this man is worth upending your life for after the war."

Must it upend my life? The war had ingrained a habit in me of living hour by hour, rarely thinking about what would come. "I see you've regained your pragmatic footing. Has daily life with your baron knocked the stars from your eyes?"

"No." Her eyes still burned with love. I imagined mine did too. So then, we were both in love and in America with our soldiers. Surely that was a thing to celebrate!

And I *meant* to celebrate, if only there hadn't been so much to do. From the office, I sent countless letters recruiting coal industrialists and newspaper magnates and college presidents to provide internships for the boys who would graduate from the school at Chavaniac. Still, the most important priority was the orphanage. Accordingly, I made phone calls to every prominent writer I knew in an effort to collect essays, poems, and stories for an anthology to be published, the proceeds going to fund my work there. When Max learned that I'd convinced Theodore Roosevelt to write the foreword, he teased, "Now you have presidents at your beck and call!"

"I *am* a rather prominent woman."

And I knew I was doing important work in New York, but I hated to know that I'd missed our American general Pershing's flower-strewn entrance to Paris. I hated more to have missed the iconic words uttered when the general and his staff visited Picpus Cemetery and paid tribute.

Lafayette, we are here!

I knew, even then, that these words would live forever in the history books, and I wanted to weep with frustration that I'd not been there to hear them. Fortunately, I had Max to comfort me, and he asked, "Why not bask in the satisfaction of knowing those words might never have been spoken but for you?"

PARTIES. SOCIAL CALLS. AFTERNOON TEAS. I MADE CERTAIN FUR-laud met everyone who was anyone. The Chapmans remembered him fondly as the French officer who had helped facilitate their visit with Victor. My society friends received him warmly because Allied officers were especially praised. When he walked the streets in uniform, complete strangers approached, offering encouragement. After a few weeks, I jested, "You're such a celebrity, I dare not be seen with you in public."

But he knew the real reason I must be at least a little circumspect about our appearances together. This was not France, after all. An open love affair was still a scandal in New York City. "Why don't we go some-where else? Your boys want to see Fort Ticonderoga. We can make a weekend of it."

On a warm summer day, Max pulled up in a brand-new Ford Model T touring car, and my children piled in the backseat for a leisurely drive. They showed off their Lafayette buttons, and Max indulged them with the greatest patience. Later, when my little rogues played on the battle-ments, he said, "I really do think they're wonderful children."

I stretched on the picnic blanket. "I like to think so. Though I sup-pose every mother does."

Max stretched his legs next to mine. "You've brought them up to be interested in the world."

I was risking my place in that world to be with him, but I didn't want to care. I didn't want to care about anything but the way I felt when we were together. "I think it's a good thing for children to have a mother who is interested in something other than tatting and tangoing. How can a mother influence her children in good things if she doesn't know them?"

Max nodded. "But you've also instilled them with character."

I liked that he spoke of my boys' knowledge and character, rather than looking for deficiencies. He said nothing of Billy's stammer, nor Ashley's rambunctious nature.

"You're a good mother, Beatrice." He plucked at a blade of grass. "In my youth, all I wanted was to escape family expectation. There would be time enough for children later, I thought." His blue eyes glistened with intense feeling. "Now, here I am, a man of nearly forty, in love for the first time."

I startled. No, that couldn't be true. "For the first time?"

He nodded. "Whatever I thought was love before you, was nothing."

Oh, be still my heart. I wished I could tell him that he was the first man I ever loved, but that would be a lie. Instead I said, "I'm deeply honored. I love you too. I love your generosity, your pertinacity and charming personality. I love that you're so calm and steady."

He squeezed my hand. "With you, my darling girl, I could be happy to buy the first little white house I saw—like that one there, over the bluff—and devote myself to you and make your family mine."

Make your family mine . . .

It was too soon to make such plans, but he was so earnest, so tender, so loving . . . and I could not discourage a soldier from the dreams that might comfort him at the front. "And what would we do there in that sleepy little house?"

"Put a few logs in the grate, read stories to the children, sleep in a feather bed, safe and sound. I could build you a trellis for your garden or shelves for your kitchen pantry, and you could cook me a cassoulet like my *grand-mère*'s."

I laughed, amused by this portrait in which I decidedly did not fit. "I don't cook; I have people for that."

"And I don't know any carpentry. For you, I'd learn."

"Why, I had no idea you were so enterprising . . ."

But just as I worried that in such future plans as these, I would feel like a firefly imprisoned in a mason jar, he stood, then pulled me to my feet, guiding me to the automobile. "This is yours, you know. I bought it for you."

"*What?*" I cried. "This isn't the sort of gift—"

"It's to remind you that you aren't trapped," Max said. "Whatever is mine is yours. You can go whichever direction you like. If you don't like it, I'll sell it before I go back."

Even as he urged me behind the wheel, I protested, "I couldn't accept. This is ostentatious!"

"I can afford it." *I can afford you*, he meant. He didn't want me to cling to my marriage for financial reasons, and I was unutterably grateful. "Beatrice, I'm not a secretive man by nature. I tire of hiding our relationship . . ."

"I know," I said, aching to reassure him. "I'm not free. Not yet. Not only because I'm still married, but because . . ." I feared to sound vain, but then decided I must express it. "The work I do for the war—it has relied upon my husband's name and, just as importantly, my good reputation." Max winced, so I hastened to add, "Not that I consider our relationship to be any stain on my character. It's only that—"

"You were young and naive when you married Mr. Chanler. Under such circumstances, a divorce shouldn't be held so much against you."

I'd been neither as young nor as naive as he wished to believe, and I was suddenly too ashamed to tell him otherwise. "People can be petty."

"If so, what do we care? After the war, we will be living our quiet private life in our sleepy white house . . ."

Did I want to live a quiet private life? "The war isn't over yet," I said.

He chuckled a little, ruefully. "We need even petty people to win this war. Is that what you're saying? That until you have gilded Lafayette's old domain, it's our patriotic duty to keep our love a secret."

My cheeks warmed at what I took for mockery. "I feel a weight of responsibility. Especially with orphaned children like Marthe depending on me."

His smile fell away. "I'm sorry. It's only that I want to be with you, and a man at war is desperate to make plans for the future."

Yes, of course I could understand that. At the start of the war, I had despaired that I might never feel loved again. Now I did. What sort of woman would turn it away? "Of course I want to be with you too."

He kissed me, again with absolute adoration. "That is settled, then. I have to go back to France now. My mission here is over. But when I go back, I'll know I'm fighting to keep you and your boys safe, and to end this war, so we can be together."

"Oh, Maxime . . ."

Very seriously, he pressed a photo of himself into my hands. One from before the war, when he was a civilian in an elegant Edwardian suit. "Keep it by your bed, won't you?"

When I clutched it gratefully to my heart, he added, "No more crossings until after the war, madame. You've done your part. You've no idea the anxiety it gives me every time you step on a ship. I don't want you to even think about seawater. When I'm being deafened by the guns, I want to know you're safe here on dry land. The minute the shooting is over, I'll rush to you, even if I have to row the boat myself."

I laughed at the image. "Then I'll see you after the war, Captain."

"After the war," he promised.

FORTY-SEVEN

MARTHE
Chavaniac-Lafayette
November 11, 1942

ALL FRANCE IS OCCUPIED NOW.

It's Armistice Day, and Nazi soldiers are everywhere; even here in the mountains, where every tree by the side of the road is covered with red and black swastikas and tacked-up posters of the new rules we're forced to obey under penalty of death.

The threat of American invasion scared the Germans into crossing the demarcation line. So much for the Marshal and his Vichy government. I'd say good riddance, but now all France is at the mercy of soldiers who shout *Heil Hitler*, change our clocks to keep German time, seize even our hunting weapons, and requisition buildings and supplies.

There are whispers some fat Wehrmacht general wants Lafayette's castle for his headquarters, and I'm sick to my stomach when the baron calls a staff meeting. It's the baroness who rises to speak, and she gets directly to the point. "All contact with the United States has been cut off. We can't get word to the foundation in New York at all." Which means we won't be getting any more help from Madame Beatrice or the American Red Cross. "Given these circumstances, we've been advised to close down the preventorium, and I know many of you wish to return to your homes and look after your families."

A few heads are nodding.

"We understand, of course," she continues. "But we're going to try to continue on here. This castle has stood in defiance of dark times before. With your help, we mean to follow the example of those who came before us."

"We can't defy the Wehrmacht," one of the nurses says.

"No," replies the baroness coolly. "That's true. Still, we can try to discourage them. For those willing to stay, it's not going to be easy, but we have to try for the sake of the children."

None of us really knows what this means. I don't know if there will be money enough to pay my salary, much less to purchase the rest of my sketches—and the sculpture, if I ever finish it.

I don't have to stay, I realize. I'm respectably married now, to a gendarme. I could probably get a teaching job in Paulhaguet, Le Puy, Brioude, or even Clermont-Ferrand. I always thought I'd jump at the first real chance to leave, but even if I didn't have the Kohn children to look after, this is the only home I've ever known . . . and I'll be damned if I let the Nazis take it.

So I'm the first to ask, "What's the plan?"

The baroness and Madame LeVerrier have thought it out. We start by boarding everything up. We create false walls with sheets of paneling to hide the valuable tall gilt mirrors and paintings—ostensibly to keep the children's sticky fingers off them, but more importantly, to make the whole thing look shabby. Then we start moving the girls from the dormitory into the castle proper.

The Nazis probably wouldn't think twice about kicking sick kids out of hospital beds, but a building filled with tuberculosis, measles, and scarlet fever shouldn't be too inviting, even for a fat German general.

Faustine Xavier calls our plan *germ warfare of low cunning*. Unfortunately, she doesn't disapprove enough to quit in protest, which means I have to listen to her yammering while Madame LeVerrier hands nails up to me where I stand on a ladder with a hammer. "The German soldiers are so *young*," Faustine is saying. "I saw some in a café in Paulhaguet. Very handsome, very correct. Their uniforms are quite smart. If only we could teach our French boys to be so mannerly and well dressed."

I give her a look, the kind the Italians call the *evil eye*. "So you're saying they've sent kids to invade us. They're sending *men* to fight the Russians, but they think they need only boys to keep hold of France's leash?"

"Because we're cooperating," Faustine says. "As we should."

Before I throw my hammer at her, Madame LeVerrier intervenes. "I feel sorry for these German boys. How pitiful. What a shame to throw such youngsters into such awful business!"

Well, I don't feel sorry for them. Not all of us do what we're told. Our boys—boys like Oscar—paint rebellious graffiti and ride bicycles around to deliver pamphlets for the Resistance. So to hell with these German boys, no matter how young they are!

The children I feel sorry for are the ones I've hidden in this pre-ventorium. Josephine and Daniel have been out of quarantine now for almost a month and spend recess with their little sister, who chatters all about her new Girl Guide badges. Daniel has learned Morse code, and the boys have stopped teasing him about his elephant ears. Josephine complains about the hours she spends in the gymnasium doing corrective exercises for her spine, but she's already leading a Girl Guide troop. But with the German invasion, they're now terrified for their father, and dur-ing recess on Wednesday, Josephine whispers, "Why isn't Papa sending letters?"

She and her brother and sister all look up at me, and I don't have the heart to tell them that their father has been sent to Rivesaltes, an intern-ment camp only slightly less dangerous than Drancy. Any letter he sends might lead the police here, so he's been silent, but I tell Daniel, Josephine, and Gabriella, "I'm sure he'll write soon."

That's when Daniel shows me the pin that his father gave him when they last saw him. A tricolor—old and faded. "He said he got it from a superhero, and that it always made him feel brave, and watched over. That it would make me feel brave too. So why am I still scared?"

God knows I'm scared too, so I hug him close. "Daniel, it's not brav-ery unless you're scared."

He sounds dubious. "You think Lafayette got scared sometimes?"

"Yes."

Daniel, who, like the rest of the boys, collects old American comics, asks, "What about Captain Marvel?"

"As sure as you can say *Shazam*."

On Thursday, I see Travert. It's supposed to be my day off, and I'm supposed to spend it with him at his house. It's the arrangement I agreed to before German tanks rolled into the Free Zone—now there's too much to do at the chateau. I expect an argument, but he doesn't give me one. He only asks how he can help.

Meanwhile, his fingers tentatively brush my shoulder. It's a question. One he doesn't voice, but he doesn't need to. I know what he wants, and I want it too, so before returning to the castle, we settle for a few minutes' diversion in the front seat of his police car on a deserted road.

It's better this time because we don't talk or try to examine our feelings. I've already learned hard lessons about how dangerous feelings can be during a war, but sex is like getting blackout drunk without the headache or hangover. And thankfully Travert doesn't make it more complicated than that.

After, we roll down the windows because we've fogged them, and pulling my sweater back down, I ask, "Do you think I should tell Mr. Kohn's children that he's been sent to an internment camp?"

Travert grinds his jaw. "Not yet. With the German invasion, no one knows who is in charge of the camp. Now might be the time to take advantage. Maybe we can get him out before they ever have to know."

"How?"

"If you falsify a permit of travel from the prefect in Nice, the French guards are in no mood to question. If I can get the permit to Monsieur Kohn, we might get lucky."

I don't hesitate. "I just need tracing paper, ink, and an example of the permit with the stamp of the prefect."

Travert doesn't hesitate either. "I'll get one from a friend at the gendarmerie in Brioude. I'll have to buy him lunch, so I'll take you on Sunday morning to buy supplies and send you back on the train with what you need."

It's a thirty-minute drive to Brioude, which means that on Sunday morning, I have at least thirty minutes alone with Travert that won't involve taking my clothes off. We've been married for exactly seven days, during which time what remains of my country has been invaded by two different armies, so we should have a lot to say. For some reason, we're quiet almost the whole way—maybe because we both know the risk we're taking now. The stakes are higher; if it goes wrong, it's not the French authorities we'll have to deal with, but the Gestapo.

I find everything I need at the stationery store, and Travert meets me outside the train station near a poster of Hitler someone has tacked up under the arched green doorway. Travert gives me an old document with the stamp and signature. I put the document in my purse and ask, "You're not going to invite me to lunch with your friend?"

He looks surprised and a little pleased. "You want to meet my friends?"

I smirk. "Maybe I just want lunch."

Travert is the hard-boiled type, but he almost laughs. "Better you don't meet him."

He's right. If his friend is questioned, he shouldn't connect me to this.

In saying farewell, I'm not sure if Travert and I are supposed to hug or kiss. Sex is one thing—the easiest thing. The marital peck he gives me on the cheek is somehow more intimate. I'm not used to it, and I don't know that I'll ever be, so I'm relieved when he leaves me alone on the train station platform.

At least, that is, until I notice all the German soldiers. Down the tracks, they're shoveling coal into a railway car—looting us, loading everything valuable we have onto trains for Germany. Coal, food, lumber, art, *people* . . .

Well, I hope they'll get one person less because of me and the piece of paper in my handbag. That's what I'm thinking when one of the young Germans puts down his shovel and, with an impish smile, approaches me.

"*Guten Tag,*" he says, leaning against one of the posts and offering me a chocolate bar from his pocket.

He's shockingly young. Under that uniform is a kid no older than the boys in the preventorium. I'm so incredulous that I sputter, "How old are you?"

"Sixteen for my Führer!" the kid boasts, pushing out his chest.

I'll eat my handbag if he's sixteen. He's no more than fourteen if he's a day. I'm tempted to tell him so and snatch that chocolate for good measure, but someone barks something at the boy in German and he stiffens to attention.

I turn to see an officer in polished boots, black leather trench coat snapping at the hem as he makes his way to us on the concrete platform. "*Hallo, Fräulein,*" says the officer, greeting me by touching the visor of his cap, its silvered imperial eagle and swastika glinting in the light. "I see this soldier is bothering you."

"No, sir," I murmur, all too aware of people watching us on the platform as they wait for the train. Not only don't I want to speak to German soldiers—I don't want to be *seen* speaking to them, so I turn away.

The officer blocks my path with a chilly smile. "I see what attracted the boy's notice, *Fräulein*. Your fair hair, blue eyes . . . you are very pretty."

Trying not to glare, I stare at his inverted widow's peak, which seems to point, like an arrow, at the skull and crossbones on his visored cap. What kind of brutes would wear that? When the silence drags on, the officer squints his glacial eyes. "Where are my manners? Obersturmführer Konrad Wolff, at your service. May I see your papers, please?"

I don't want him to search my handbag, where he might find the document Travert gave me, so I quickly fish out my new identity card.

"Congratulations, Madame Travert," Wolff says, examining the card closely while the younger soldier remains at attention. "I see you're a newly-wed." Then he narrows his eyes. "You're missing something, aren't you?"

I feel a spark of fear, though it's an authentic document. "Missing something?"

"A father," he says with a chuckle. "*Father unknown.* A blond and blue-eyed Frenchwoman born in the last war? It could be your mother opened her legs for a German soldier. Bad for her reputation, but maybe good for you. Maybe you are *Volksdeutsche*." Of German ethnicity, he means. Someone who might be given special favors. The officer hands me back my identity card, turns to the boy, and says, "Give her the chocolate."

Though my stomach is growling, I don't want to take chocolate from Nazis. "I don't care for it."

"Nonsense; everyone loves chocolate! Besides, this soldier won't be needing it. He must be punished for his incorrect behavior; he allowed your loveliness to distract him and forgot to return his shovel to the stationmaster."

The child-soldier gulps, then the officer pulls from his boot some sort of collapsible baton. "I could report him for disciplinary action, but I'm not a patient man. I believe in the power of immediate lessons."

Neither of us has time to react before the officer swings the truncheon against the boy's jaw, then does it a second time, sending a spatter of blood and saliva to my feet. I skitter back with a cry of surprise and horror as Wolff shouts in German, lashing at the boy again and again. The pathetic young soldier tries to stay at attention, but another vicious crack to the skull breaks him. He whimpers, shielding his face as I scream, "Stop!"

But it doesn't stop. I've seen boys brawl on the playground, but I've never witnessed violence like this. It's a brutal beating that goes on and on until I think I hear teeth crack.

Mon Dieu, is the officer trying to beat the boy's brains out?

Obersturmführer Wolff keeps hitting and hitting, and I want to snatch that bloody baton and drive it like a stake through his heart, but I'm frozen in shock and terror. None of the other soldiers intervene, but an angry crowd of French people all drop their luggage and begin to surge closer. Too late . . .

As it turns out, a skull doesn't shatter like a marble bust. It makes a sickening sound, wet and hollow. That's what I hear when the boy collapses to the ground at my feet. I don't know how or why, but somehow I'm on my knees on the cold concrete platform, cradling the young soldier's head—now a bloody mass of red oozing wounds. I scream again as his hot blood soaks my skirt. "Please get a doctor!"

Obersturmführer Wolff only wipes off the baton and slides it back into his boot. *"Guten Tag, Fräulein."*

Then he walks away, bloodred boot prints in his wake.

I try to hold the boy together, try to mold his broken jaw back into shape with my fingertips. But there's so much blood pooling underneath me. Sticky, and steaming into the air with the boy's increasingly shallow breaths.

AT THE HOSPITAL IN BRIOUDE, A NURSE GIVES ME A WASHBASIN, A sponge, and the privacy to wash. I scrub my skin clean . . . but there's nothing to be done for my skirt or my shoes. And I let out a shaky breath because I can't get the iron scent of blood out of my nostrils.

French people at the train station carried the young soldier to the hospital. We carried him here because we're not *savages*, and I held his brains in his head the whole way. Now I don't want to leave until I know . . .

Travert knocks lightly, then steps into the room, offering me his leather coat. "In case you wanted to change."

His expression makes my knees wobble. "He's dead?"

Travert nods. "There was never a chance."

"But I held him together," I whisper.

"There was never any chance, Marthe."

To hell with these German boys, I'd thought. If the boy had been blown up by RAF planes, or riddled by American bullets, or crushed under Allied tanks, what could be the difference?

The difference is that I've never seen anyone murdered before . . .

"I want to report that officer. I thought Germans prized correctness!"

"Only in the Wehrmacht. Wolff is Gestapo. Reporting him won't do any good." Travert puts a heavy hand on my shoulder. "Let's go. Try to put this out of your mind. I'll rent a hotel room; we'll stay the night."

He's being thoughtful, but I pull away. "I want to go home."

He nods. "Okay. I have a little bread at my house, some tea."

That's his home, not mine. "I mean Chavaniac."

It's still daylight when we set out for the castle, and in the front seat of Travert's police car, I open my handbag to inspect the signature I'll have to copy to save Monsieur Kohn. Instead, I find myself fingering a photograph. Travert turns the steering wheel as we pull onto the road home, and asks, "What's that?"

"A picture of Maxime Furlaud."

"Furlaud? Like the brand of cognac?"

Cognac. Not my drink, but that's where I recognized the name from. "The baroness tells me he was a banker, but I don't know much about him."

"Then why do you have his picture?"

"Because he might be my father."

It's the first time I've voiced that suspicion, and Travert slants me a glance. But my attention is now riveted on the smooth texture of the snapshot. The way Madame Beatrice wrote *Furlaud* on the back, first in smudged pen, then in pencil as she realized the ink would take too long to dry on the coated paper. *Photography paper.* Why didn't I think of it before? "I might have just figured out how to duplicate a stamp without having to carve one . . ."

When we get to the castle—which is now crowded with beds—I leave it to Travert to explain to everyone why my clothes are stained with blood, and Anna rushes to me in sympathy. *"Mon Dieu.* You must be so shaken. Let me put you to bed."

"I can't sleep," I murmur.

She nods sympathetically. "I'll sit with you. I'll read to you until you nod off, if you like."

What I mean is that I *won't* sleep. Not yet. She's already tugging me gently to the stairs, and I want to go with her. I want to put my head on her shoulder, and curl up in bed nose to nose, and be lulled to sleep by her voice. So it's hard for me to pull away, but I do. "Travert can stay with me."

Anna looks as if I've slapped her. I wish it were jealousy, but I know it's just the natural hurt when a close friendship must make way for marriage, and because I need to accept a deeper hurt and get over it, I let Travert lead me upstairs. While I strip off my bloodstained clothes, Travert doesn't seem to know what to do with himself in this frilly, feminine tower room with its crystal chandelier.

"I just need you to keep everyone away." I explain that as long as he's here, I'll have privacy, because no one will want to walk in on a married couple. "I have to make Monsieur Kohn's permit. We may be running out of time."

At first, Travert sits in Madame Beatrice's armchair, laces his fingers, and holds them between his knees. I know he's thinking Uriah Kohn could already be on his way to Auschwitz. Still, we have to try. I turn away, wrap myself in a bathrobe, and switch on the desk light. To test my theory, I quickly trace the stamp with a little pencil. Then I turn the tracing paper over to transfer it onto the back of Maxime Furlaud's photograph and fill it in with ink. A different sort of paper would lose shape and ruin the impression, but photography paper might just be firm enough.

Please work. I don't even breathe as I press the still-damp ink onto a piece of paper, but I can hear Travert breathing over my shoulder as he watches. With the side of the pencil, I gently rub the impression, then check my work.

"*Sacrebleu,*" Travert mutters. "It's perfect."

"A little blotting paper and it will be!" I want to throw both my fists in the air with triumph. This is an amazing discovery. I can forge stamps this way in a fraction of the time, without the incriminating evidence of a wood carving.

I explain this to Travert, who is wry. "You're becoming a better criminal."

"I have to stay one step ahead of your ilk," I say, riffling through the desk, scattering old sketches of Adrienne Lafayette, looking for anything that will work as blotting paper. "Can you hand me that newspaper on the kindling pile?"

He reaches for it, then stops at the photograph of the girl in pigtails. "Him again . . . the man you said might be your father."

I turn over the photograph of Furlaud I've been using to forge a stamp. This is a clean-shaven man in a suit, whereas the French officer has a thin mustache, but with my artist's eye, I knew they were the same man. "So you see it too . . ."

"I'm good with faces," Travert says. "Lineups. Wanted posters. That's the same man in both photographs."

I nod. "The baroness has been avoiding me ever since I asked about him and what I think was his love affair with Madame Beatrice."

"I'm not surprised," Travert replies. "The women here are devoted to Madame Beatrice. They'd want to protect her reputation. Back in their day, a love affair was still a scandal."

"Maybe if I could find him, I could ask."

"I'll do some digging," he says, meeting my eyes. "But right now, you need rest, Marthe."

I can't rest. I can't think about Furlaud either. "Right now, I need to *work.*"

Because it's one thing to hear of the terrible things Nazis do; another to have held a kid's cracked skull in my hands. That's what they're willing to do to their *own* children. If we don't stop them, they're going to desolate the whole earth . . .

FORTY-EIGHT

ADRIENNE
Le Puy
September 1792

I CURTSIED BEFORE THE OFFICIALS OF THE REVOLUTIONARY GOV-ernment in Le Puy as if before royalty. These were not the rabid Jacobins of Paris. I might still be spared if I could convince these men not to send me there. "Gentlemen, it is with great respect for representatives of the people that I entrust myself to you. You may feel bound by orders from Paris, but I consider myself *your* prisoner and will be honored to take orders from you."

My remarks seemed to sober them to their responsibility, and the mayor, who in previous years had been my frequent guest at Chavaniac, thought of a way to protect me. "Instead of sending you to Paris, we have decided to send your husband's letters ahead of you to be inspected for treason."

It would buy me a few more days, but it was plain the gentlemen believed the letters would condemn my husband—and me. Knowing our enemies weren't above forgery, I took a gamble. "I should like to read them to you before they are sent."

Pitying looks betrayed that the councilmen thought me the greatest fool. "Madame," said the mayor, "that is not necessary. We would not wish to cause you further humiliation."

"Nothing my husband has written brings me anything but pride for his elevated sentiments."

A hush fell over the assemblage as I read Gilbert's words: "*You know my heart would have been republican if my fidelity to my oaths and to the national will had not rendered me a defender of the constitutional rights of the king.*"

Gilbert had written this knowing it would be seen by his enemies. Thus, I added to it the inflections of my voice, and a crowd gathered just outside the doorway of the municipal building as I explained my husband's conduct. When I finished, the room erupted with sympathy. Now was the time to make my plea. "You know what I face in Paris, where massacres are the rule, and I trust you will protect me. No one has charged me with a crime; thus I beg you to let me remain under house arrest at Chavaniac. I give my word not to leave without your consent."

It would be easier for these gentlemen to pack me off to Paris. They would take a risk to harbor la femme Lafayette. I was again reminded that divorce was now legal, and that I should perhaps avail myself of it, but when they saw I would not bend—that I would not abandon my husband or his name—the mayor announced, "We will submit your request to remain under house arrest to Minister Roland."

Roland. Not a rabid man. I began to hope when several National Guardsmen loyal to my husband volunteered themselves to watch over us until we had Roland's reply. I did not sleep, but called for pen and paper, racking my poor brain to remember everyone who might have sway over Roland.

I decided upon Brissot, with whom we had helped found the Society of the Friends of the Blacks. We had, after all, many times discussed over dinner at my home the abuses of the *ancien régime*, which denied prisoners impartial hearings. A reformer like Brissot must see the injustice in my situation.

Two weeks of imprisonment passed, during which I learned that the Americans had not yet secured my husband's release and may not have tried. Lafayette and I were *both* still prisoners. Then, finally, good news. Roland agreed to place me under house arrest. "Yet, madame," the mayor cautioned, "Brissot showed a letter to Minister Roland, who now rebukes you for the high aristocratic manner with which you still write."

I reeled to know my confidential correspondence had been betrayed, but a rebuke was preferable to a prison cell.

CHAVANIAC WAS CHANGED SINCE MY ARREST, BUT NOT DESTROYED. Beyond slashed portraits and shards of pottery, the brigands had taken things I hadn't thought to hide. Gone were paintings of the American Revolution, artwork dedicated to the storming of the Bastille. All things that should have proved our patriotism. At least Lafayette's swords were still buried . . .

The villagers welcomed us back in joyous thanksgiving, delivering unto me Virginie, whom they had sheltered these long weeks. My youngest sobbed as I stroked her hair. And that night, under cover of darkness, Georges's tutor slipped into the chateau to reassure me of my son's safety.

Praise God for this castle, these people, and the wooded mountains that kept all my secrets!

How sweet it would be to embrace my boy again, but I pleaded with Georges's tutor, "Take him to England, I beg you. Go to the American ambassador there."

After all, I knew three of the American ministers in Europe, having entertained them for years at my table. Mr. Pinckney in London, Mr. Short in the Netherlands, and Mr. Morris in Paris. Between the three of them, they could see my entire family to safety.

To hasten matters, I wrote President Washington.

> *In my abyss of grief, you are my only hope. I ask an American envoy to claim Lafayette and emancipate him from his captivity. It would be sweeter if his wife and children could be comprised in this happy mission, but if this would delay its success, we defer the happiness of a reunion, and, when he shall be near you, we will bear the separation with more courage.*

While I was writing letters, Aunt Charlotte took inventory. "They emptied the larder, but left the copper cooking pots."

Anastasie fretted, "With winter coming, we may regret more the loss of the larder than the pots."

Anastasie is no longer a child, I thought. Our ordeal had forced her to maturity, and though I regretted this, she might well need that maturity in days to come. Mr. Morris wrote that I should *be of good courage, for sooner or later the present clouds will be dissipated. All human things are liable to change.*

This did not console me. According to the new French government, everything my husband owned was forfeit—even, to my horror, the faraway plantations and all the persons that remained on them. The beautiful promise of that experiment—our attempt to end slavery—was now a nightmare. The full legal emancipation of the people on those plantations had not yet been achieved. Frantically, I wrote pleas to the Revolutionary government not to sell these people. Certainly the ideals which the Jacobins professed should have induced them to set them free. Unfortunately, the Jacobins were too depraved to act upon the sentiments they professed . . .

I had taken upon myself the fate of sixty-three souls, and I had failed them. The weight of this was too heavy to bear. "How can they do this?" I asked the solicitor I had summoned to Chavaniac. "How can they seize these people, who have been working for a wage, and auction them like cattle? The only reason we purchased plantations was to free them. These people were promised liberty. Isn't that one of the principles of this Revolution?"

"These days the only principle is *property*, madame," the solicitor said.

"Then I must buy them back at once and set them free. Sell anything. Sell *everything*!"

"You have nothing to sell, madame. Your husband is deemed an émigré."

"Lafayette only left France under duress. They have no right to his property, and even if they did—"

"Madame! You are fortunate to have this roof over your head. Lucky too that your enemies are too busy murdering others to come for you. You risk doing great mischief. There are those in the government who resented your agitation against the slave trade in the first place, and if you persist, they may revenge themselves not only upon you, but upon these enslaved persons. Do not doom them with any more well-meaning gestures."

Shock and despair warred in my breast. I had never before faced such helplessness. The fear that I could help no one—not even myself. I had never before faced impoverishment, much less powerlessness and isolation.

On a bitingly cold winter's day, my daughters and I went to collect firewood. We came upon two filthy peasants in the woods—a man and a youth, both of them covered in nettles.

"Maman?" cried the boy.

Georges. Oh, again I was reminded how intimately joy could twine with dismay.

"I tried to get him out of the country," his tutor explained. "It was too dangerous. *Mon Dieu*, they've even put the king on trial!"

As I clutched my child, my heart ached at this news. I believed King Louis was guilty of having plotted against the constitution, yet it was the Jacobin coup that had destroyed it. By what right did they judge him?

"I thought better to bring your son home for a Christmas visit," the tutor explained.

Christmas. Only a year before, we had been celebrating our son's birthday, a ham had been roasting in the oven, and my husband had been whispering tender words against my ear. There was no ham to feast upon now, no husband to embrace, and our son was in terrible danger. It was safe neither to keep him here at Chavaniac nor to send him away. I could count on only the secret passages if he needed to make another narrow escape.

In the meantime, I filled my days by reading to my children from their father's books in the library. The grand salon required too many logs to heat, so we took our meals bundled against the cold in my chambers. Food was scarce, but on Christmas Day, a dairy farmer gave us a large wheel of sharp-veined cheese. A shepherd offered a parcel of tripe that we boiled into a spicy stew. A farmer delivered a sack of green lentils, which we simmered with bits of pork sausage. We were grateful for every bite.

As the winter deepened, howling winds carried terrifying whispers.

Lafayette is dead, eaten by rats in a dungeon.

Lafayette has gone mad, scratching out his eyes.

Lafayette is starved in his prison cell.

I prayed for my husband. I prayed too for the king. According to the gazettes, thirty-three charges were put against him. More moderate men like Roland and Brissot might not *want* the king dead, but would commit murder to save themselves from the radicals. Robespierre was the first to vote for the king's death. Philippe too voted for his own kinsman's execution. And on a cold and rainy morning in January, the king was driven in a green coach through Paris for the last time. Mounting the scaffold to the guillotine, he cried, *My people, I die innocent! I forgive my enemies and pray my blood will make you happy.*

Then the blade fell.

Reading this, I wanted to beat my fists against the stone walls of Chavaniac. Somehow, in my heart, I had expected my husband to escape his prison, mount his white horse, and put a stop to the killing. It seemed that without him, there was no brave hero left anywhere in the world. Even the man my husband had called his adoptive father had turned a blind eye.

I confess, I wrote more pointedly to George Washington, *your abandonment of M. de Lafayette and your silence during the last six months is inexplicable to me. If there is any hope I am to see his face again, it still rests upon your goodness and that of the country he helped to found.*

Meanwhile, my sister was active on our behalf in Paris—Louise went to Mr. Morris again and again until he was finally prodded to send money. Yet I worried for her to bind herself so closely to our cause. Through a trusted courier, I begged Louise to either join her husband in America or join me at Chavaniac. In the rugged isolation of winter, I'd been at least a little forgotten by my husband's enemies. My relations would be more easily forgotten here in the mountains too.

It would be safer for my family here than in Paris. Alas, Louise refused. *Grand-mère cannot travel, and needs my care. Besides, I am more useful to you in Paris.*

I feared for my loved ones remaining in the center of the bloodletting. I was praying for their safety in the village church when horsemen arrived. "Madame," said the curé in dismay. "Escape out the back way—"

There was no time.

Swaggering thugs threw open the carved wooden doors and lay hold of the curé. "You are under arrest."

"On what charge?" I demanded.

"This papist parasite is a traitor to France, madame." He had done nothing but minister to the good people of Chavaniac. Nevertheless, the toughs menaced him with a sword. "You know the penalty for clergy who refused to take the oath."

"The oath was to put the laws of France above the laws of God, was it not?" I asked, driven to fury by violence in a church. "Gentlemen, I beg to know how the curé can be seized for refusing an oath to the earthly laws your masters have violated, rejected, and invalidated."

They had no answer. So puzzled were their expressions that, for a moment, I hoped they might be dissuaded from their business. Then the one with the long mustache snarled, "He can ask that of the jury in Brioude." With that, they dragged him out of the church.

They're going to kill him, I thought. *Oh, Merciful God, please save your faithful servant!*

By nightfall, the village women came to me in tears.

"They are drowning priests in Lyon by the hundreds!"

"—priests thrown into prison or deported to be worked to death."

"All Catholics will be next."

I felt sick to the marrow of my bones at our terror and helplessness. We needed our faith now more than ever, but Mass was forbidden in the church, which was now guarded and chained shut.

What would Lafayette wish me to do? What would God ask of me? The answer came to me clear as glass. I invited the religious women of the village into the castle as if for tea, then took them into the dark passage through which I had once sent Georges to safety. It let out by a beautiful stream with a spectacular view of what my children and I called our charming mountains. There we knelt in prayer, and though I was not ordained, I led our little congregation, reading to them the prayers of the Mass.

This was right. There must still be goodness in the world . . .

That night I learned that though the jury had acquitted the curé, they wouldn't release him, because they feared officials in Brioude would punish them for showing clemency. This was without law or decency. The priest had hurt no one—he was merely of a different faith than those in power. For that, he must die?

I staggered outside and got only as far as the garden before sinking down in the dirt, near to where my husband's swords of honor were buried. There, I held my head in my hands in helpless despair. My husband was in prison. My father had, once again, fled to Switzerland, leaving Maman behind. My brother-in-law was gone to America. George Washington was indifferent to us, and the king was dead.

Not one man in my life could fight this wickedness and injustice. There was no cavalry riding to the rescue; no one to set things right.

There was only me. What would Lafayette do in my place? What would he have me do? In the madness of the moment, I imagined that I heard the white towers of Chavaniac call to me.

Cur non?

Had I taken leave of my senses? Gilbert had once told me the ancients believed in a *genius loci*. A protective, guiding spirit of a place. He dismissed it as fable, and I dismissed it as heresy, but I couldn't deny the feeling now welling in my breast.

Cur non?

The motto of the Lafayettes. Why not? Why not me? Why not now? Why not here? No one else could answer the call to protect this place and the principles it enshrined. In all of France, there might be no other true temple to liberty. And it had no other defender.

Only me, only here, only now.

"You are mad to even *think* of going to Brioude." Aunt Charlotte clutched my hand. "You are under house arrest!"

"Minister Roland gave me permission to travel within the department," I told her, though I did not add that Roland warned it would be perilous to travel anywhere in France with my husband's name.

Aunt Charlotte warned, "You will draw dangerous attention to yourself and the family."

That was true. I dreaded it. Perhaps I would not do it if I were not la femme Lafayette. "No one else will argue for the poor curé. If I don't go, it is as good as signing his death warrant."

"You may be signing yours!"

This was true, but I went anyway. In Brioude, I found townspeople pleading with the curé to take what they called a meaningless oath. If he renounced his religious beliefs, they could let him live. In the meantime, a message was sent to higher-ups. No one wanted to do the right thing upon their own authority. Fortunately, I knew the young man who was to carry this message to Le Puy, and had educated his sister in our weaving school.

"Sir," I pleaded. "I only ask that you delay your departure. Just long enough for me to speak to the authorities." I'd taken only enough coin with me to pay for my lodging and meals, but I gave it to the messenger.

"These are hungry times, young man. You will want a good meal before you travel. Bread and wine. If you should feel sleepy with a full belly after so long, who could blame you for resting?"

It would buy me crucial hours; long enough, I hoped, to argue for the curé's life. I was known in Brioude, where I sought out each official. And to each one, I said, "I have taken from its place of honor at Chavaniac this document. It is the Declaration of the Rights of Man and of the Citizen. Words as sacred to me as the Bible. Words that inspired patriots to tear down the Bastille. This document declares we are born equal and free. That we have the right to liberty, property, security, and to resist oppression. It guarantees religious freedom."

They all listened. Some coldly; others with emotion. But they *listened*. "This was the reason for our revolution," I explained. "The curé has disturbed no one. So by what authority does anyone threaten his life?"

"The same authority that allowed you to remain under house arrest," one answered. "Now you will renew calls to throw you in jail."

My voice shook, but still I spoke. "I ask to be left with my children in the only situation which can be bearable to me so long as their father remains the captive of France's enemies. Yet, if that will not suffice, I beg of you, good patriots—put me in jail and send the curé home."

It was this offer to give up my freedom in exchange for his that moved them. "You have expressed feelings worthy of you," one of the officials said in announcing that the curé would be spared.

With grateful relief and an emboldened heart, I met the man's eyes. "I wish only to be worthy of him that I love."

IN JUNE, I HAD A REPLY FROM GEORGE WASHINGTON, AND WHEN I read it, I wished it hadn't come at all. *I feel sincere sympathy in your afflictions on account of Lafayette*, it began. *I can only add my most ardent prayers that you may again be united. With sentiments of sincere attachment to yourself and your dear offspring, George Washington.*

So the Americans would do nothing as our bloody red summer gave way to an autumn of crimson gore. Slicing heads off was now the favorite pastime of Robespierre's minions and their new policy of *terror*. It was not enough to have murdered the king; the queen's blood was also sacrificed to the thirst of the mob. It was the death of Marie Antoinette—for whom I grieved—that made me fear the national bloodlust was a thirst that might never be slaked. After the queen's execution, Philippe was dragged to his death. Minister Roland was proscribed, then Roland's wife went under the blade. In the end, Brissot, Condorcet, our old friends all, were—as Mr. Morris might say—*crushed under the same wheel* of revolution that we put in motion.

Catholics were drowned and burned. The Jacobins changed even the calendar, banning saints' days and the word for the sabbath. All those stories Maman used to read about martyrs had always seemed to belong to a long-forgotten age.

Now I knew the torments of cruelty were with us in every age.

On a clear November day, a representative of the Revolutionary Committee came to Chavaniac with a new warrant for my arrest. I had delayed this moment for more than a year. Now there was no escaping. As my whole world became a buzz of bees, only my daughter's voice broke through. "Citizen, are daughters forbidden to go with their mothers?"

"*Anastasie,*" I snapped.

The commissioner shook his head. "Mademoiselle, be still . . ."

Anastasie would not be still. "I am sixteen; I am the daughter of Lafayette. I should be arrested too."

"*Non,*" I insisted. These were different times. This time they would kill her too. Even Aunt Charlotte knew it, because she grasped Anastasie's arm, holding her fast. With my eyes, I pleaded with the commissioner, *Don't take my daughter.*

As this drama of love and loyalty played out, the commissioner found some decency and ignored my daughter's outburst. Kissing her lovely face, I surrendered to her all that I loved in the world but my wedding ring. "If I should not return—"

"You will!" Anastasie cried.

"*Courage.*" I smoothed her tears from her cheeks. "Whatever happens to me, protect your siblings and try to get to your father free . . ."

All three were crying now as I took Georges's hands in mine, whispering to him the secret of where his father's swords were buried. "You will know when the time is right to take them up again . . ."

A soldier crowed from the courtyard, "Look what we found in the barn!" He held a marble bust of King Louis aloft. Aunt Charlotte had stashed it away. It went into a wagon with the papers and titles and deeds the Lafayettes had held for centuries. Then I was led out of the gates.

Parading me in the town center, the soldiers shouted, "Come see us burn the king in effigy!"

Wasn't it enough that King Louis was already dead? He had caused us all much pain, but his soul should be left to rest.

When none of our villagers came out, my tormentors shouted, "Don't be afraid of nobles anymore. You are liberated from the aristocrats. Come celebrate the fall of la femme Lafayette."

Not a single door opened. Every shutter remained latched. No one in Chavaniac wished to see me shamed. There was, perhaps, still goodness in this village, if not this world.

I was dragged first to the jail in Brioude, filled with noblewomen who blamed me for their imprisonment. One crowed, "At last, the Revolution bites the mother that rocked its cradle!"

"This is not the child I nourished," I whispered.

I slept that night on a bale of straw with a baker's wife who was imprisoned for her faith, then took upon myself the duties of cooking for everyone and serving the ladies who had rejoiced to see me brought low. My daughters saw to it that my linens were laundered, sewing secret messages to me into the hems. Then one night, Anastasie arranged to have herself smuggled into the prison for a visit.

I marveled at her audacity, even as she cried bitter tears. "I rode alone at night, then hid during the day. I had to see you, I had tell you . . . it is terrible news . . ."

Maman, Louise, and Grand-mère had all been arrested.

And by morning I would be sent to Paris to die.

FORTY-NINE

MARTHE
Chavaniac-Lafayette
June 1943

"I WAS *HOURS* FROM BEING LOADED ONTO A GERMAN TRAIN BOUND for Auschwitz," rasps a rail-thin Uriah Kohn, sitting by Madame Pinton's hearth and eating soup. He's been fighting with the Jewish militant resistance since his release, but now he's taken the risk to come back and check on his children. "How did you get me out of the camp?"

"I can't tell you," I say.

"I didn't give you up," he assures me. "I would die first, after what you've done for my children."

I believe him, but I still can't risk telling him the role Travert played in getting the permit I forged to camp authorities.

People can't talk if they don't know, Marthe, Travert said. *Catch a refugee, the Nazis have nothing. If they catch* you, *they can catch everyone you help, because forgers know all the real names . . .*

Travert fears I'd break under torture, and I fear that he knows what he's talking about. The Germans are furious with the French police for failing to meet their quotas in rounding up Jews, so I never ask how Travert decides who to warn or when to look the other way. I don't want to know about the people he arrests, interrogates, or gives over to the Gestapo.

But I know it's destroying him . . .

Last night I stayed at Travert's house—a well-kept place with a deep farm sink and flower boxes and a feather bed in the loft. In the middle of the night, he cried out, cold sweat glistening on the hair of his arms. And when he caught his breath, he whispered, "I'm going to hell."

Now I shake that memory away and take the letters Monsieur Kohn has written to the kids. In exchange, I give him a thick envelope. I've made him two different identities, complete with birth certificates and travel permits. It took less than ten minutes to make each stamp using my new method. How I want to slap myself for all the hours I wasted carving wood! "Here. Now you're a whole new man."

He thanks me and puts down his bowl on the hearth to inspect the papers. "These might be good enough to get to Switzerland . . ."

"Your children might be safer where they are. Gabriella has been with us since '41, but Dr. Anglade is willing to say she's had a relapse, or find some other medical reason to keep her longer."

"There are other children in need of help," Monsieur Kohn says, and I realize he wants something more. "Organizations like the Œuvre de Secours aux Enfants are smuggling them out of France. The OSE has doctors, passers, and forgers, but they need more."

"I'll do it."

He startles, not having expected me to agree so easily. What he doesn't know is that I've spent the past few months making papers for men who joined the Resistance to escape the STO. The Resistance is not just communists, Spaniards, and refugees in the woods anymore. Not just boys like Oscar with chalk. The Resistance is now everywhere in Auvergne. From the castle, we can actually hear the maquis training with heavy munitions in the forest, and two months ago, when it was my turn to go with the kids on their camping trip, I saw men in clogs and berets drilling—and one of those men was Sam.

Since then, I've made papers for him and his friends on the condition that Sam be the sole courier and the only person to know my identity. Now we exchange messages by stuffing them in the old stone mailbox of the house in the village that Madame Simon used to occupy. It's not just the rightness of the cause or the cloak-and-dagger adrenaline of it all that keeps me going; it's the addictive feeling of solving problems and doing something that matters for a change.

Travert has probably figured out that I'm working with the Resistance now—he's not stupid—but he doesn't ask questions. Now I explain my conditions to Monsieur Kohn. "You give me the children's names and photographs from the OSE, and I'll give you the papers. No one else should know I'm involved."

Except Madame Pinton, who has been silent in her rocking chair all this time. She's still quiet after he leaves, grim-faced as she makes lace, weaving bobbins and pinning threads on a pillow in the ancient way once taught at Adrienne Lafayette's school. It's been a little over a year since we learned Henri was dead, and I know we're both thinking it. "I don't see you much anymore since you married the gendarme."

I want to defend myself by saying it's not a real marriage—that even as I've come to know and like Travert, I've kept my emotional distance—but I know how it must look. She's been mourning her dead husband for nearly three decades. I married Travert just months after learning of Henri's death. If she's disgusted with me, I can't blame her. "I had to marry him."

It isn't true in one way, but it is in all the others.

"You didn't ask my blessing," she says.

I tell her what I've been telling myself. "I knew you'd take it as an insult to Henri's memory, and I was too depressed to stomach your perpetual disapproval without wanting to slit my wrists."

Her head jerks up. "I don't disapprove of you."

I cross my arms over myself. "I know you never wanted me to marry Henri."

"That's true." She puts down her lace-making. "Since you were a girl, you were like a feral cat, prone to hiss and scratch. You never trusted anyone or let anyone get too close. Not even my Henri."

Her words are so painful, I actually have to take a few breaths to recover. "Well, you sure have my number . . ."

"Now I know you're not a feral cat, but a lioness, and that not even Henri knew how brave you really are."

A sudden sob catches in my throat. I try to hold it back by pressing the back of my hand to my lips, but tears spill over. I have to turn away until I get hold of myself. When did I get so weepy—and why is Madame Pinton, of all people, being kind? "You're the one who took in Jewish boarders."

"I wanted my roof thatched."

I manage a teary, wobbly smile.

"Marthe, I've lost a husband and a son. I can't lose you too. If the gendarme protects you, then you have my blessing, and you were right to marry him."

I'M NOT SO SURE I WAS RIGHT TO MARRY HIM THE NEXT NIGHT, when Travert shouts, "Tell me you won't have anything to do with this!"

"Keep your voice down," I hiss. We're in the old vaulted kitchen that I don't think has been redecorated since Lafayette's time. Since the dorms were moved into the castle proper, little girls are always wandering in and out until nurses chase them back to their hospital beds, so the walls have ears.

Travert quiets down, but slaps a flyer onto the wooden table—a flyer we've all seen. "Well?"

"We always celebrate Bastille Day in Chavaniac. The castle's keystone is a stone from the Bastille, and—"

"You want to piss in the eye of the Nazis to celebrate a glorified jailbreak?"

"Spoken like a gendarme . . ."

He looms over me. It used to be that he treated me like some skittish animal he cornered who might bolt if he made a wrong move. But we're more accustomed to each other now, and I've come to like the scent of him, all leather and pine. "I don't argue with you about much, Marthe. But to march on Bastille Day is a stupid risk to take for a stupid symbol."

I should agree. I'm annoyed that I don't. But on the illicit radio we listen to in secret, we're hearing that de Gaulle's Free French are going to swathe Algiers in the tricolor for the holiday. And the Resistance has put up flyers asking us to show our solidarity. It isn't just a stupid symbol for them, so how can it be for us? "Chavaniac's a small village," I argue. "The Germans have forgotten we exist. It's a small risk to take when other people are doing more."

"Like who?" he snaps.

"Like Jean Moulin." Everyone is talking about the Resistance leader recently captured and tortured in Lyon. Especially the boys in the preventorium. To keep from betraying others, Moulin ate papers before he was captured. The Gestapo beat him to death with chair legs, and he never gave up a single name. Not one.

At the mention of Moulin, Travert lowers his head. "And you want these maquisards hiding in the woods to share his fate? They need guns, bombs, planes, and tanks. Not a damned parade. Maybe you'll make a few boys brave, but it won't matter when the Gestapo lines them up against a wall."

"Yves." I say his name softly. "It'll matter especially then."

Besides, I don't think it's so risky. Even the baroness plans to take part. Since the Riom Trial, many people in the village think her husband is a collaborator, and she probably wants to redeem his name, but I don't mention that to Travert, because he might remind me that I've told him Anna always takes her father's side . . . and that's salt in the wound.

On Wednesday at the appointed hour, I go down to the village, at the center of which is a Lady Liberty statue. We aren't as stupid as Travert thinks. None of us wears a tricolor cockade or waves a French flag. No, old Madame LeVerrier sits at the edge of the fountain wearing an all-suffragette white lace shirt over white skirt. I'm in a red dress—one of the few I own. And the baroness is wearing a sensible suit of blue. I grin when Anna strides over to join us in a smart red-checkered skirt and white blouse. And women of the village emerge from their stone houses wearing red scarves in their hair, or blue shoes, or white turbans. Separately, we're nothing to look at, but standing together we're a defiant flag of red, white, and blue!

For fear of the Nazis, we can't light fireworks or sing our national anthem, but we parade in the streets around the church. Children in every window look down as we march, and men in every rough-hewn wooden doorway watch us pass, tears shining on their faces. It feels like *hope.* I look up at the castle and think each of us is just a stone, but mortared together in common purpose, we might just be a fortress that can't be ripped down.

I'm still buzzing with good feelings when Travert and his gendarmes roll through on patrol, stopping in front of the *mairie,* where I happen to be sitting with my sketchbook.

"Everything okay?" Travert asks the mayor. "No excitement today?"

The mayor looks like he doesn't know what to say with the gendarme's own wife nearby. Scowling, he tells Travert, "Everything is fine."

I know Travert waited to patrol until dusk for my sake, and that he's not happy about it, so that night in his bed, I try to soothe his temper. It never takes much to satisfy him, and he's more willing to experiment with pleasurable acts than a man of the law probably should be. "Are you happy with yourself?" he asks.

"*Oui*," I say, tangled in the sheets. "You were too, just a minute ago."

He doesn't crack a smile. "You know what I mean."

"And you know they're making us take banned books out of the castle library. That they want us to take the kids to see an anti-Semitic exhibit about 'racial characteristics.' And that I had to initial the damned notice to prove that I received it! So I just wanted to be a part of something *good* on Bastille Day. To remember when French people fought for their freedom. And I felt like I heard their voices today. I remembered that when she was teaching me to sculpt, Madame Beatrice used to tell me, *There's life in the stones . . .*"

Travert growls in frustration, grabbing my hand and pushing my palm flat against his chest. "*This* is life." Then he pulls me into a kiss. "*This* is life." He strokes my bared abdomen. "We could make life, after the war. We could go someplace nice. Travel the world—or what's left of it. Make a baby. Who knows? Maybe you fall in love with me someday. Or maybe you leave me for someone else. *That's* life. But we have to survive to live it."

FIFTY

ADRIENNE
Paris
Summer 1794

THE NAMES OF TWENTY CONDEMNED PERSONS WERE CALLED EACH morning in the prison courtyard. Upon hearing their names marked for death, some would gasp, faint, or cry. Some even laughed, knowing we would all meet Madame Guillotine eventually.

On two separate mornings I thought I heard my name. I stepped forward both times, cold with fear, but made no sound at all. For death would be a release from the torment of guilt under which I suffocated to know that my mother, sister, and grandmother were imprisoned.

They had been charged with having conspired with Lafayette to massacre citizens that terrible day at the Champ de Mars. It was the flimsiest, most absurd pretext. I was kept in the prison at Le Plessis. The school at which my husband received his education and formed ideas about liberty was now a makeshift jail, with male prisoners packed in the basement and female prisoners stuffed in the attic. In my lonely cell, I struggled to think how I might get a message to my sister, my mother, or even Grand-mère.

Mon Dieu, how frightened they must be. How they must blame me. Perhaps it was better to keep apart. Here with me was Marc's sister, my cousin the duchesse de Duras. A staunch royalist, she might have rained down curses upon my head, but instead she embraced me. Even when it fell to me to deliver the worst possible news. "Your parents . . ." How could I say more? After all my quarrels with Aunt Claude, it did not seem possible she could be gone from this world. Butchered. Murdered. I wondered, as they led Madame Etiquette to the scaffold, did she spit at the rabble? No. I believed my aunt would have preserved good form to the end.

Would I be brave when my turn came? There were rumors I would be called to the guillotine in the morning. Then a priest I passed in the courtyard confirmed it, whispering, "I saw your name on the list. You will be called in the morning, child. Prepare yourself."

I thanked him for helping ready me to meet my fate. I prayed only that God spare the rest of my loved ones. Yes, I still prayed. One might be excused for thinking Madame Guillotine was the thirsty goddess to which we now paid tribute, but faith in my husband and my God was the only thing the murderous Jacobins could not take from me.

Oh, Lord, thou hast been my help and my strength; do not forsake me, and I shall fear nothing even in the shadow of death.

At sunrise I washed my face; it would not do to meet God in a state of dishabille. They said the blade was humane—death came swiftly, and painlessly, despite the blood. It was only terror one felt in having one's hands bound, in having one's gown opened to expose the neck, in being laid down upon the plank . . . I imagined these things vividly so they might be familiar and less frightening when my time came.

Then I was led to the courtyard to hear my name—a name that was precious to me. A name through which I would find the courage to meet my death. But when I reached the courtyard, someone was saying, "Robespierre is dead . . ."

That hardly seemed possible, but now everything was in confusion. No names were called, and I felt a faint flicker of hope. I began to breathe air again and like its taste. A few precious gulps filled my lungs before I began to dream this nightmare could be over. That soon I could be reunited with my husband and our family. The mere thought of holding our children in the circle of our embrace made me smile at my fellow prisoners and even my guards . . . until I realized that no one would meet my eyes.

If I were not to die today, then why would no one look at me?

A numb horror came over me as I asked, "What's happened—is it my husband?"

"Your mother," someone finally had the mercy to say. "She was guillotined."

These words hit the center of my chest and I curled inward. "Maman?" I gasped, then could not catch my breath. I nearly swooned again before pleading desperately, "What of my sister? What of Grand-mère?"

Silence was answer enough.

No. No. No! Not Maman. Not Louise. Not Grand-mère. I would have fallen prostrate with grief, but someone might try to help me, and I could not bear the slightest human comfort. For in my howling despair I did not feel human—I felt like a creature in the jaws of a predator. I fled, taking the stairs back to my prison cell as swiftly as I was able, collapsing to my knees there, where I screamed at God, demanding to know why. *Why* was I still alive when they were dead? Why would our enemies kill my grandmother, whose mind was enfeebled? Why kill my mother, who had never taken part in politics? And Louise . . . *Louise* . . . who had been a finer patriot and daughter and sister than me. Dutiful Louise had stayed in France for her family when she could have fled to America with her husband. In her place, to be with Gilbert again, I would have gone. So how could she be dead whilst I lived?

The injustice could not be borne. It was so much more than my mind could withstand that my sobs cut off abruptly. Then I rose, almost like a marionette, drawn inexorably to my window, which hovered five stories above the pavement. And there I felt a powerfully seductive impulse.

It is the only escape from your shame, said some voice, unbidden. *The only justice. The best way to protect your children. They will be safer when you're dead . . .*

I would not be the first person to jump—to deprive the mob of satisfaction. The Bible taught it was a sin to take one's own life, but my God was forgiving. If I leapt from this window, he would surely reunite me with my loved ones in a world less wicked than this one.

My fingertips found the cold latch. My hand gripped the wooden frame. My foot found the ledge. One push is all it would take. Let it be done swiftly before fear stopped me.

I am coming, Maman!

Good-bye, my beloved children. Good-bye, Gilbert . . .

It was the thought of Gilbert that stopped me. My children might be safer when I was dead, but not Gilbert. The rumors that he had gone mad in his prison cell, torn out his own eyes . . . I had not believed them. But if I stopped my heart, would it stop his too? Perhaps I was the only hope he had of survival.

Don't think, Adrienne. Just jump. The temptation was stronger than I could have ever fathomed. Stronger than almost any other urge of my life. Stronger than thirst, hunger, or lust. Shame and grief are more powerful than anything . . . but love.

It was love that made me step back from the window. Perhaps tomorrow I would fling myself into the sweet freedom of the hereafter, but not today. Instead, I passed my days in blackness. I did not eat. I did not drink. I did not sleep. Nor did I wish to speak to those who came to offer comfort. I was scarcely interested when a guard said I had a visitor. I was only curious when he said, "It's *la belle Américaine*."

I emerged from my prison cell dazed and blinking, not knowing what day it was, much less the identity of the mysterious visitor who could have charmed Paris into giving her this sobriquet. A waiting carriage behind her, the dark-haired beauty stood at the gates in splendor—a beautiful topaz cross glittering from her neck. How shabby I felt in my unlaundered garment, my hair a nest of straw. Yet without the slightest hesitation, this stranger reached for my dirty hands and grasped them warmly. She introduced herself as Elizabeth Kortright Monroe, wife of the new American ambassador. "It is my great honor to meet the wife of Lafayette, a hero who shed his blood in the cause of liberty . . ."

She said this in such a manner to be overheard by the guards and passersby. And terrified that even one more person should endanger themselves by uttering the word *Lafayette*, I whispered, "You shouldn't have come."

"Yet I did," said Mrs. Monroe with a kind expression. She explained that with Robespierre dead, there was some chance now of a legitimate government. "Can I bring you food, a blanket, or some means of comfort?"

"Oh, madame," I said, my throat swelling with emotion. "Bring me news of my children and my husband. That is all I need."

My visitor's dark eyes glistened. "I will make inquiries about your children. Your husband's situation is unchanged, but I have hope of changing yours. Though forbidden from making any official plea on your behalf, Mr. Morris hinted to the Committee of Public Safety that your death would greatly offend American sentiment and might put our alliance into peril."

So it was to Mr. Morris that I owed my life. The prickly peg-legged debauchee had gone as far as he dared, possibly in contradiction of his orders. Now his successor was prepared to go further. "Mr. Monroe intends to publicize that he has a personal sympathy in your cause, as he fought with Lafayette at the Battle of the Brandywine."

Monroe. The name came back to me from all those years ago, when Gilbert boasted of his comrades-at-arms. The brave young Virginian who stayed with him when he'd been wounded—without God, could fortune have turned in such a way that the very same soldier was now here in France?

"Mr. Monroe is tireless in his advocacy," she was saying. "So I beg you to have courage."

He should not risk it, I thought, still longing for oblivion. How would I ever again be fit for life when my every thought was poisoned? *You were the death of your family, Adrienne. Your affections, your ideals, your opinions, fatal to those who had the misfortune to love you . . .*

I did not speak these words, and yet I believe Mrs. Monroe somehow saw them upon my countenance, for she brought her face close to the bars. "Madame, do not forget the obligations that still bind you to this world."

The next day I was sent to a new prison. Then another. And another. I did not know if this was done to save me or punish me. Having no fire, I shivered violently beneath a pile of rags, my breath frosting the air, little crystals of ice glistening on the wall. The cold was so painful I welcomed the slow creep of numb sleep over my senses.

For when I closed my eyes, I saw Chavaniac.

There, beneath the frost-capped towers, my children might be playing games in the snow, free to laugh, to worship as they wished, to speak according to their consciences. There the little church bell might be ringing to summon the faithful, there might be a blazing fire by which I could read, surrounded by my husband's books and busts of his favorite thinkers. A ham would be roasting in the oven, and I would find Gilbert in his treasure room, working on plans to improve the place, working on new ideas to improve the world. He would take me into his strong arms and—

"Madame! Awaken, *s'il vous plaît!*" I did not want to be awakened, torn away from my dream castle. Yet the stranger persisted. "Have my coat, you poor shivering woman," he said, wrapping me in the warmth of wool.

I took him for a carpenter sent to patch the holes in the roof. He was, in fact, a priest in disguise, having contrived this excuse to be alone with me. "Madame, I must speak swiftly. I don't have long. I am the man who gave last rites to your mother, sister, and grandmother."

The mention of them made me groan as if run through, and I again curled in on myself with fresh pain.

"In their final moments, they commended their love to you, and I have come to deliver it," he said.

Could it be true? That they might have felt love for me in such a moment was both grace and a torment.

He told me how he walked beside their tumbril as it rattled through the streets in a rainstorm. How my angelic sister Louise, all dressed in white, comforted Maman. How the executioner tore Grand-mère's black taffeta gown to expose her pale neck to the blade. How Maman, in blue and white stripes, said she was grateful to die before her child. How the executioner yanked her cap, forgetting to unpin it, causing her to flinch in pain. How courageous Louise stopped upon the bloody stairs to ask God's forgiveness for a man in the crowd who tormented her. Then Louise too suffered the pain of her cap being torn from her head before the blade severed her neck, spraying the jeering crowd with crimson.

It was a long time before I could speak. Into the abyss of my dark silence, the priest whispered, "They were shorn before their executions. Louise sent her hair for her children. She would like for them to join their father in America."

My eyes closed at the reminder that Marc was by now across the sea, pleading our cause with the Americans, quite probably ignorant to the fate of his wife and parents. When he learned this, he would feel he had abandoned them. He would feel as if they had been murdered in his name. He would never recover from it. The self-reproach would surely kill him as it was killing me . . .

All I wanted was to know the final resting place of my butchered family, but the priest said they had been carried away in secret to prevent proper burial. *What spite and savagery!* The intolerable horror of this made me wish to beat my head against the stone wall.

And when the priest left, I would have begged for beheading.

Instead, I learned I was to be set free.

On a blustery winter day—after more than a year of imprisonment—I limped through the cobbled streets like a beggar, unrecognized and unmolested in my reduced state.

Not knowing where else to go, I walked to the American embassy. There, Mrs. Monroe hastened to wrap me in a blanket, sending her servants to fetch biscuits, jam, and hot tea. What a fright I looked; how wretched I felt, trembling when the warm porcelain cup with its dainty flowers was put into my dirty hands. Minister Monroe appeared at the threshold, and I put my cup down to kneel in gratitude before him.

"Please, madame," he drawled, trying to keep me upright. "It was and remains my honor to render any service to the wife of my dear friend. My countrymen owe Lafayette a sacred debt. It is the only thing upon which all factions agree."

How sweet to hear these words. I remembered the cagey Franklin. The prickly Adams. The dashing Laurens. The eloquent Jefferson. The earnest Short. The witty Morris. All those American envoys had expressed appreciation for my husband. But the unguarded zeal in Monroe's gray eyes gave me courage for what I must do next. My fourteen-year-old son was still especially vulnerable. They had guillotined boys his age, and at present, there was no place for a boy with the name *Lafayette* but America. So by Monroe's special envoys, I sent another letter.

To President Washington:

Sir, I send you my son. Although I have not had the consolation of being listened to nor of obtaining from you those good offices likely to bring about his father's delivery from the hands of our enemies, it is with sincere confidence that I put my dear child under the protection of the United States.

I have nurtured in my son a love of country where his father is disowned and persecuted, and where his mother was sixteen months confined in prison. But he has been taught to regard America as his second country. I shall not say anything of my own position, nor of the one which interests me still more than mine. I will only cherish the hope that my son should lead a secluded life in America, resume his studies, and become fit to fulfill the duties of a citizen of the United States.

To send my boy away tore my withered heart and made me remember I still had one. I closed my eyes, remembering every freckle upon my boy's nose, reassuring myself that Washington would not, *could not*, turn away his namesake. Yet I would not wait upon the Americans. I had learned I could not wait on anyone. *Cur non?* It was now my motto too. I must use my freedom while I had it. I had rescued a priest from certain death.

Now I must rescue my husband too.

FIFTY-ONE

WHEN THE NEWSPAPERS SENT MITZI MILLER TO INTERVIEW ME, I decided I could afford to be magnanimous. After all, the years had proved me so right and her so wrong! I took the greatest satisfaction in answering her polite questions about my war relief work.

Thoroughly chastened, she asked, "Are you going to accept the government's invitation?"

"Of course."

I'd spent ten months at the home front, gnashing my teeth at newspaper headlines about how the Germans were taking advantage of our delay in transporting American troops. I still thought President Wilson was a jackass who should have better prepared for this war, but now that he was committed to winning, his muleheadedness was turning out to be a real asset. No matter how much it stuck in my craw, it was important for patriots to be loyal to our commander in chief, which is why, when called upon to lead a mission of American labor leaders across a war-torn sea, I had no choice but to agree. "I hope to be of real service."

And truthfully, I was honored that my government believed I could be. I'd come a long way from the days when people whispered, *She's just an empty-headed actress who should stick to what she knows.* "There's so little one can do to help our brave allies that if the opportunity does come, one must be quick to embrace it."

I was also pining for my friends and loved ones on the other side of the ocean. Emily—having returned to France with her husband—had worked miracles at Chavaniac with Clara and Marie-Louise, but I was increasingly convinced that I was needed there myself.

Is it really necessary for you to risk yourself this way again? Max complained in a letter. *I begin to think that after your time in France, no party in Manhattan could be exciting enough for you unless it ends with artillery fire!*

I ignored this not entirely lighthearted teasing and packed my bags, bracing myself against the pain of leaving my boys again. But of course, I reminded myself that they'd be at boarding school, so we'd be parted anyway. For my journey, I wore a black velvet tam with a gold tassel instead of my fur Cossack hat, because after all, this journey was partly Russia's fault.

Oh, we'd all applauded the February Revolution to topple the czar and install a democratic republic, but the October Revolution by the Bolsheviks was a despotic Soviet dictatorship. Now Lenin's Russia was neutral, out of the war just as the kaiser wished. Naturally, the Germans hoped the same trick might work twice. Thus, their Bolshevik agitators fanned throughout Europe to wreak the same havoc in remaining Allied nations, dividing patriotic common working people and socialists from disloyal pacifists, anarchists, and other misguided idiots. The Soviets called for an international conference of labor organizations to *force* a peace before the United States could send enough troops to turn the tide.

A rather ingenious villainy, I thought. All eyes had turned to the 2.5 million American skilled workers represented by Samuel Gompers's American Federation of Labor. Would American workers undermine the war effort? The answer was a resounding *no*. And to give that answer, a delegation of patriotic labor leaders trooped aboard a ship bound for Europe in order to reassure our war-weary allies to hold out against Germany a little bit longer. Of course, most of the delegates had never traveled overseas before—necessitating an experienced leader. And because I was an officer for ARCH with several sea crossings to my name, I was chosen as chairwoman, presumably to prevent pandemonium on the gangplank.

I led the delegation aboard a refitted and armed luxury liner in a convoy with troop ships, a battle cruiser, and six torpedo boats—more protection than I'd ever had in making the trip before. Among the male delegates of the mission were the president of the Pattern Makers'

League, the executive officer of the Molders' Union, the president of the International Association of Machinists, and the president of the Brotherhood of Railroad Trainmen. Lady leaders joined us too, including the presidentress of the Straw Hat Trimmers' Union and the vice presidentress of the Glove Makers' Union.

Working people, every last one.

When I tried to tell a gentleman where to put his portmanteaux, he said, "I suppose we'll be a trial to you, Mrs. Chanler. I don't guess millionaires like you rub elbows too often with the wage-earning riffraff."

Before I could make a diplomatic reply, the presidentress of the Straw Hat Trimmers' Union whacked his arm. "Stuff and nonsense! She's one of us. Even former chorus girls know what it's like to go hungry."

Had it really come to pass that after a lifetime of hiding them, my humble beginnings might be a badge of honor in these strange days? As chairwoman, I did my best to reassure and amuse the delegates on a journey that promised to be long, and full of incident! I expected some rivalries between our socialist delegates and the more conservative members, but after mediating a heated late-night quarrel about the merits of Marxism, I was nursing a headache.

Thus, as we passed from the Atlantic into the Irish Sea, I retreated to my cabin and submerged in a hot bath, reading *Kubla Khan*. I was fully immersed both in bubbles and Xanadu when a hard knock came at the door. "Madame, a U-boat has been spotted! Come on deck with your life preserver. There's no time to dress."

No time to dress? Surely the stewardess didn't mean for me to come out in my birthday suit. Just then, I heard the boom of our cannons. *Damn.* I imagined leaping out of the tub to find a robe and thrusting my shivering body into a life preserver only to be blown to smithereens.

Well, stuff and nonsense, indeed! If I was going to drown, I'd much rather do it in this warm tub. It was with a strange calmness that I simply turned the page of my book, only to be splashed in the face with both the reality of my situation and a tidal wave of tub water.

The captain, it seemed, had ordered full speed ahead.

My bath and book both ruined, I climbed out of the tub, cursing the kaiser, and threw on a fur coat and my gold-tasseled velvet tam so my corpse could be identified if I were to be found floating facedown in the Irish Sea.

Bedraggled and bad-tempered, I came on deck to find the delegation in a tizzy, all of them struggling to get into life preservers, several trembling as they told me a torpedo had missed the bow of our ship by no more than twelve feet. "That can't be—"

A deafening sound cut me off like a storm summoned by ancient sea gods. I turned, amazed to see a plume of water. A torpedo had hit a cruiser in our convoy. People screamed and scurried for cover, but I stood at the rail, staring, wondering what other predators lurked beneath us even as our destroyers raced hither and yon, dropping bombs to flush them out. I watched this dread scene until I realized that the whole delegation had gathered around me, some crying—even one of the men. "Mrs. Chanler, you're not wearing your life preserver."

Little did he know, I wasn't even wearing underthings.

They were all frightened and looking to me for guidance. Whatever our political differences, I realized that fear and duty had forged us into one cohesive group. Courage was the only option. But how to inspire it? "The work ahead of us is so big that in the vastness of the war and this ocean, I feel small and insignificant. The length of our days is in the hands of fate. And we must all come to the same night . . ."

I was remembering Victor, still grieving him bitterly, but that sounded like resignation, and I was anything but resigned. What had Willie used to say to encourage his Rough Riders? Probably something bombastic. Thinking of Lafayette, I found better words. "What happens to us as individuals doesn't matter much in the larger scheme of things. We must win this war. Our cause is just, and righteousness must prevail. If we must perish to see that it does, it will be to our everlasting glory, even if no one remembers our names."

"MADAME CHAIRWOMAN, WELCOME TO OUR ISLAND," SAID THE balding Winston Churchill. "I understand you escaped a torpedo, then got rained on by a shower of German bombs as you came into port. Bad luck, that."

Bad luck indeed. We were shaken, having slept not at all while bombs dropped around us, leaving us with a choice of risking a watery death belowdecks or a fiery one above. Now, on behalf of our exhausted delegation, I smiled brightly and said, "I'm just happy to come ashore safe and sound."

Churchill smiled as if we'd met before. In truth, I only knew the gentleman had once been first lord of the Admiralty and was still somewhat in disgrace after failures at the Dardanelles and Gallipoli. Now he had another chance to prove himself as minister of munitions, and I hoped to help him do it. For purposes of enabling us to report back the morale, organization, and efficiency of our allies, he arranged to give us tours of hospitals, shipyards, and ammunition factories—and I was permitted to ride in a tank.

In England, Scotland, and Ireland, we vouched for America's ability to win this war. We lunched with mayors, presented at clubs, chatted over ladies' teas, and bickered with British radicals in pubs, one of whom argued, "All this war has done is reveal the rot of the class system. Who cares if the kaiser walks away with half of France?"

"If the kaiser walks away with half of France," I argued, "he'll come back for a chunk of Britain too. He'll take your home, culture, and livelihood—to say nothing of your freedom to spout off like that. Real reform for the workers of the world requires a complete repudiation of this barbarism. Not indifference to it."

I was forceful—perhaps even unladylike—but I felt that I was right.

From bars, we went to the East End of London to comfort victims of the latest air raid and to promise that America was with them now, through thick and thin. We even received an invitation for an audience with the king.

How strange to realize that however many doors in my life had been opened because of my husband's fame and fortune, the great doors of Buckingham Palace opened for me because of my war work. I took a fierce pride in that as the red carpet fanned out beneath me. I pinched myself, wanting to reach back in time and tell Minnie, *One day I'll be presented to a king and queen.*

But of course, royals were just people like any others.

The king said, "I hope especially the lady representatives from America may give a satisfactory report of the manner in which women have come forward to replace men called from various national industries to the fighting ranks, and how efficiently they are carrying out the work entrusted them."

Yes, I thought, *because it's our war too, and it's about time someone noticed.*

The king seemed desperately hopeful that America could give his war-weary people some relief. It was the same impression I took away from Mr. Lloyd George at 10 Downing Street. Yet everyone we spoke to—hotel owners and hotel chambermaids, motorcar aficionados and taxicab drivers, shopkeepers and doormen—all showed the same qualities. They were suffering and had sustained terrible bereavements; they were enduring privations, but not one complained. All showed calm courage and wonderful steadiness. Which is why I said in the papers: *No one can ever beat a people like this, not if the war goes on one year or ten years.*

From England we went to France to meet the exiled government of Belgium, Marshal Joffre, and the president of the French Republic—the latter of whom gave us a reception at the Hôtel de Ville, where so much French history had been made. I looked to where I expected a bust of Lafayette, but of course, that had been destroyed during the French Revolution.

I'd just have to take inspiration from walking in his footsteps.

Though even he, I daresay, would have been stunned by the unimaginable destruction on the battlefields, the rubble of Verdun, not far from where my nephew had died. I had wanted to go, in part because we had no grave site for Victor, and to pay respects, Verdun was as close as I could get.

It was also there that I was reunited with Max Furlaud.

At the first sight of his officer's cap, I wanted to run into his embrace, but we had to pretend to be only acquaintances. It took all my thespian talent to disguise my relief that he was alive and well, whereas he could not hide his concern for me. "Don't scold me for coming," I said when we finally stole away for privacy in one of the underground galleries beneath the citadel. "I'm doing important work."

"More than you realize," Max admitted.

"Is it true there's been mutiny on the French line?"

He hesitated for a long moment. *"Non."*

"You're lying," I said gently.

"I'm sorry you think so."

"Do you worry I'm Mata Hari?" I asked, referring to the infamous double agent who had recently been captured and shot by firing squad. "That I am prying state secrets out of you with my feminine wiles? In the first place, I was a better dancer in my day, and in the second place, I'm asking on behalf of an allied nation."

He stiffened, his breath puffing in the cold air. "And I'm answering in my capacity as a French officer."

It didn't seem right that French mutinies should be kept secret from American generals, and it pained me that there seemed always something between Maxime and me. If it wasn't my husband, or the war, it was separate duties. I would learn later—much later—that nearly half of French infantry divisions had been hobbled by mutinies—exhausted men despairing the Americans would ever come. Thousands of secret court-martials had been held, but all Max would admit was, "Russian propaganda flyers encourage soldiers to desert, and workers to abandon our munitions factories. If not for Pétain, the Germans would this moment be marching under the Arc de Triomphe."

He meant Philippe Pétain, the Lion of Verdun, who had, two years earlier, beaten back the German assault and was now commander in chief of the French army. He'd made reforms to relieve exhausted troops, promising to hold the line until more Americans were in the fight. Now Max complained, "It is one thing to visit Lafayette's grave and say, *Lafayette, we are here.* But that was last summer . . . Where are the Americans?"

Our first wave of doughboys were giving the kaiser some grief, but the bulk of our forces weren't in Europe yet. "We're coming," I promised, fighting the desire to kiss him. "I'm a harbinger of that."

"How are your children? They must have been as frightened as I was to learn you would cross the ocean again."

"Oh, they're so big and brave now they wanted to come with me and fight!"

454 · STEPHANIE DRAY

Max chuckled softly. "Well, I shall do my best to end this war before either of them is big enough to take part."

"I love you for that."

"I love you too." He took my hands. "In fact, I've been thinking about where we should live after the war. New York is the best place for our children to have a fine education and develop character. We shall want one or two more, don't you think?"

My smile wavered. He'd already dreamed up our white house on the bluff, with cassoulet in the oven—a vision about which I was dubious—and now he wanted to add one or two more children at our feet. I ought to tell him that at my age, and with the complications of my health, I was unlikely ever to have more, but now, with the thunder of the guns so near, was no time to shatter such dreams.

His hands still shook with the roar of the guns. He was *beyond* exhausted and dispirited waiting on American troops. My entire mission here in Europe was to inspirit our allies, and this wonderful man was mine. So I let him have fantasies—it could all be ironed out after the war.

Then I dared to kiss him, right there in the bunker.

"How long will you stay in Verdun?" he whispered.

"Just until morning. Can you get leave to see me in Paris?"

"I'll try. It depends if there is a big push at the front."

I buried my worry of what could happen to him and plastered on a bright smile. "Well, then, we shan't wait for romance. We'll make it here and now."

In the dim light of the subterranean passages, I pulled a little table beneath the lantern and used my shawl for a tablecloth. There, we shared what he deemed a shameful pinard from his canteen and a sparse picnic of tinned beef, hardtack biscuits, and chicken noodle soup that he heated up for us on a makeshift olive oil burner. "I've been waiting for an occasion," he said, adding to it a bit of saffron he'd been saving in an envelope.

I was delighted that despite the intermittent shower of dust that rained down upon us with the shelling, he was getting into the spirit of things. "Fine dining," I said. "A dimly lit table. What next? Poetry?"

"Beshrew your eyes, / They have o'erlook'd me and divided me; / One half

of me is yours, the other half yours, / Mine own, I would say; but if mine, then yours, / And so all yours!"

It was Shakespeare's *Merchant of Venice*, which I had sent him with perfumed letters, using our private code, wary of the censors he said liked to gloat over a man's correspondence in camp.

"I memorize the passages you mark," he explained.

Taking a spoonful of soup from his mess tin, I said, "You are really a very romantic spirit, which is rather surprising for a man who appears at first glance so matter-of-fact!"

He laughed. "Between the two of us, Beatrice, I'm not the one filled with surprises. When are you going to tell me some of those things I don't know about you that you claim could fill a book?"

I peered at him cautiously, wondering what might be safe to confide. If we were to have a future, we ought to start on an honest footing. "To begin with, my name isn't *Beatrice*."

"Not Beatrice?" he asked with a tilt of his head. "What is it, then?"

"Minnie Ashley." And there she was again, in the room with us, the waifish girl I was—that hungry girl I left behind. The one with the Boston accent who smiled when she wanted to cry, who learned to make people laugh to survive, who wanted more than anything to be *somebody*. Now her big blue eyes met mine, and this time I didn't look away. *"Minnie Ashley* was a fine name for the stage, but it wasn't the sort of name with which one could rise above one's circumstances."

"So you changed it to marry Mr. Chanler?"

I nodded. "And to leave behind my past."

"You say *my past* as if there is something shameful in it."

"A divorce," I admitted, telling him of the actor I married at sixteen.

He dismissed this. "You were a veritable child."

I didn't think he'd be as dismissive of the rest, for which I was not much older. "There were also cigarette cards . . ." These were glamorous celebrity photographs, collected by gentlemen. Sometimes wholesome. Sometimes . . . *risqué*. Now I struck a sultry pose. "For a time, I was the pretty face of Ogden's Guinea Gold cigarettes, wearing not much more than a straw cowboy hat!"

I said this boldly, but from beneath my lashes, I glanced up to gauge his reaction. Unfortunately, his shadowed expression gave away little. "Mr. Chanler knew of this?"

"Oh, yes. I daresay he was quite the collector in his day . . . though, with so many Minnie Ashley photographs in currency, it seemed wiser to take a new name than to try to buy them up and burn them."

Wiser to discard my old self like a costume, slip into a new one, and hope everyone would forget . . .

Max took a gulp of the pinard from his canteen, then steepled his hands beneath his chin. At length he shook his head in what seemed like bewilderment. "What Puritans you Americans are to worry about a thing like that . . ."

I blew out a nervous breath, sputtered a relieved laugh.

"Is *Beatrice* a family name, then?" he asked.

"Oh, no. It's only . . . well, I've never really had a name of my own. I wasn't entitled to the Ashley surname, or to my natural father's, and Minnie became a persona upon a stage who would do anything for laughs. So in marrying Willie and starting fresh, I just chose a name of my own. Beatrice."

He tilted his head as if this were a great curiosity. "It's an apt name in any case. For me, you've been like Dante's Beatrice, the spirit who leads him from Purgatory to Paradise. Is that where you got it?"

"I plucked it from *Much Ado About Nothing.*"

He grinned. "Shakespeare's *pleasant-spirited* Beatrice?"

Shakespeare's orphaned Beatrice. The one who scorned conventional love, fearing to give up her freedom. The one wooed by a stubborn, infernal bachelor, who spit at her, *I love thee against my will.* And to whom she returned much the same sentiment. That was the way of it with Willie and me from the start . . . but to Max, I said, "I liked the posh sound of it."

"Well, between us, *Mrs. Minnie Furlaud* will do nicely . . ."

Dear God, no, it wouldn't. Minnie sang for her supper. Minnie was a climber. I wasn't that girl anymore. Besides, the atrocity of *Minnie and Maxime* was not to be borne. "Maybe Minerva," I said cheekily.

"My battle goddess." Max laughed, noting our surroundings and my fashionable military-style coat—one I'd chosen because it looked very much like something Lafayette would have worn in his day.

Suddenly, Max's expression sobered. "When you go to Paris . . . will you see Mr. Chanler?"

I schooled my features carefully. "Yes. I've left him alone and sick for too long, and his sons will wish me to check on him. You understand, don't you?"

He nodded like a man who wasn't happy about it. Good. A little jealousy was healthy, but like most everything, the point was not to take it to extremes. For better or worse, Willie was a part of my life and always would be. Perhaps Max understood. "He has my best wishes for his good health."

I think he meant it. Still, I teased, "I don't suppose you'd like me to convey those wishes."

Max's smile turned a little feral. "Actually, I would. At some point, my love, there must be a frank conversation about—"

"You don't need to say it." I knew our relationship must be explained to the children, and to my husband.

And I shouldn't want to put it off any longer.

FIFTY-TWO

BEATRICE
Paris
May 1918

IN RETURNING TO PARIS, MY FIRST PRIORITY WAS TO MEET THE CRI-
sis of a new wave of child refugees. I helped make a refuge of the old
dilapidated seminary complex of the Church of Saint-Sulpice, where
Adrienne Lafayette had once been a parishioner. And I felt certain she'd
approve, for it was there, with Emily and Clara, that we fed more than
two thousand refugees, more than a quarter of them children—mostly
orphans—in need of food, clothing, and medical treatment at our makeshift hospital ward.

We couldn't send them all to Chavaniac, but we could save some, and
it meant all hands on deck. Thus, I spent my mornings in a battle with
lice, stripping children of louse-ridden clothes and shearing them like
lambs. I spent my afternoons bathing ragamuffins until the tub water
turned black. In the evenings I spooned broth into the mouths of children too weak to do it themselves.

All of this should have exhausted me, but I felt gloriously awake, and
I resolved to confront Willie.

"I fear for you to go alone to see him," said Emily. "I had Amaury pay
Mr. Chanler a visit when you were gone. He found your husband in an
agitated state, whistling, snapping his fingers, imagining conspiracies
everywhere . . ."

"Yes, well, Willie does have a mind for international intrigue," I admitted. On the other hand, morphine and alcohol also caused irrational
whirling in his tempestuous brain. "But I'm not in the least concerned."

I'd survived *bombs*; I could certainly survive Willie, and I meant to.
So I went to his house and found him enthroned upon an armchair, sur-

rounded by a clutter of books, letters, and various scribblings in piles on the floor. He didn't seem drunk, but the day was young. No, the most alarming thing was that between portraits of prizefighters and race-horses, someone had nailed Willie's rejected prosthetics to the wall of his home.

Had he decorated his home with plaster feet and aluminum peg legs to remind himself of his resilience, or to set a foreboding aesthetic for visitors? Whatever the purpose, the overall impression was that of an imbalanced mind. "Couldn't stay away, could you?" Willie asked.

I cleared a stack of newspapers from the only available chair. "Who could pass up the opportunity to enjoy such a welcoming atmosphere?"

Willie smirked. "I meant you couldn't stay away from the war. By my count, it's your seventh war-crossing, and I can't think of any relief worker, man or woman, who has taken the risk as many times as you."

Now was plainly not the time to tell him I'd nearly been torpedoed in a bathtub! Instead, in a vain attempt to soothe myself, I tried to conjure up images of Max building bookshelves in a little white house and myself in an apron, learning to make cassoulet. "This will be my last great adventure—a relief to your mind, I'm sure."

"Your last great adventure?" He lit up a cigar. "I don't believe that for a minute. You won't give it up now that you've become a real player. Truthfully, my lameness has made me pretty useless, and you're the only one in this family keeping up its end in the war. I'm rather proud of you."

Willie was *proud* of me? I didn't think I still cared what he thought, so I was shocked to find myself moved. "Why, I think that might be the nicest thing you've ever said to me."

"Then your memory is failing you." He snapped open his newspaper. "How are the boys?"

"Billy has been learning to play the bugle," I reported. "And Ashley dreams of aviation . . . They miss you—it really would delight them if you'd write more often. And when you do, I think it'd help if you could sign your letters as *Daddy* and not *Your Father, William Astor Chanler.*"

"I'll take that under advisement," he said. "How's Billy's speech?"

"Much better. He's out of short pants, growing like a weed."

"Good. Perhaps he can wear some of my old clothes."

I crossed my legs, settling in for a longer discussion. "Are you hurting for money?"

"Everyone is hurting for money. The idiot ranters think the war was fought to line industrialists' pockets, but it's impossible to calculate the damage it's done to wealth. Trade is disrupted. Factories bombed. Capital gone up in smoke. A whole generation of workers wiped out."

He knew more about economics than I did, but I'd learned a great deal recently. "I suppose labor will have the upper hand after the war."

"Who told you that? The communist agitators on your labor mission?"

"They're socialists," I protested. "And patriots."

"Rabble-rousers," he shot back.

"Well, I got on with them like a breeze. Strange, but true. I'm sorry you couldn't be a spectator—you'd have had much to tickle your sense of humor!"

It was oddly comforting to argue with him again, until he burst forth with, "They're all conspiring. Labor leaders. Bolsheviks. Catholics. Especially Jews—"

"You sound mad as a hatter," I interrupted, having no patience for this. "You're just looking for someone to blame for the state of the world!"

"Someone *is* to blame, aren't they?"

I didn't have any intention of getting drawn into a quarrel about his increasingly prejudiced thinking. Especially not when I'd come with another purpose altogether. There would never be an easy time to broach it, so I took a deep breath and blurted, "I'm leaving for Chavaniac at the end of the week, but before I go, I'd like to talk to you about Captain Furlaud . . ."

Willie peered over the top of the newspaper. "Tiring of him yet?"

I decided to be patient. Gentle, even. "He's quite devoted to me and the boys. It isn't some tawdry—"

"Oh, spare me. You're not going to give up everything for a man like that."

"I don't want to argue, Willie. You and I have tried to make each other happy, but we haven't managed it. I know you're capable of great generosity of spirit, so let's not wreck each other."

Somewhere in the house, the telephone was ringing, but Willie's attention was entirely on me. "You're wrestling with your conscience, my dear," he said, leaning forward. "If you knew the right thing to do, you'd do it. When the right thing isn't obvious, you do any damned thing you please and make no apologies. Yet you didn't file for a divorce when you were in New York, did you?"

"I didn't wish to be cruel."

He puffed his cigar thoughtfully. "To me or to your banker? Between me, him, and the war, your life is a three-ring circus, and maybe you like it that way. You're not going to settle down and become someone else's little missus."

My temper flared. *"Willie—"*

A knock interrupted. It was my husband's manservant. "Sir, there's a call for you from Mr. Chapman."

"Not now," Willie barked.

"They think they've found your nephew, sir."

A thick silence descended, every other thought driven away. I knew Victor was dead; still, I let myself imagine. Perhaps there'd been some manner of confusion. Perhaps my nephew had been a prisoner of war all this time. Perhaps he'd—

"I'll take the call," Willie said, and I had to bring him the phone. After a brief conversation, clipped and flat, I knew my imaginations were cruel hopes. Hanging up the receiver, Willie explained, "The Chapmans want me to identify the corpse. A pilot's body in a shallow grave somewhere not far from Verdun. They've got him in a pine box now and shipped him behind the fighting lines. Some of Victor's old comrades in the Lafayette Escadrille—the few still alive—went to take a look, but the body is so badly decomposed they can't be sure it's him."

Naturally, Victor's parents wanted someone who knew him longer to look upon the remains. They wanted Willie to do it, and I knew he would, though it would put his heart to torture. It was a heavy responsibility, and I found myself asking, "Do you want me to go with you?"

Willie dropped his gaze. "You needn't. It's an ugly business."

I wasn't going to make him beg. Going didn't change anything, after all. It was an act of simple humanity. And I too needed to know the truth about what happened to my nephew.

Willie remained sober during the long trip, which made him more cross than usual, of course, but I didn't mind so very much. When it was time for American soldiers to pry open the pine coffin, he asked me to wait outside. "Bea, I can't imagine I'll ever be able to wipe what I see from my memory after today, and I want one of us to remember the face of that boy as it actually was."

I wanted to argue, but in the end, I waited outside, holding a wreath of flowers I'd hoped to lay on the coffin. Then I waited some more. Never good at waiting, even with a book, I wondered if I ought to write a letter to Max explaining what I was doing here with my husband, but decided against it.

On crutches, Willie returned to the car, glassy-eyed and shaken. "It doesn't *look* like Victor, but he had letters in his pocket he might've been delivering to a friend."

"He's been a long time in the ground," I said gently. "He's not likely to look like himself."

Willie rubbed the back of his neck. "You remember his smile, those perfect teeth . . . well, this poor fellow had fillings."

I recoiled to think how close Willie must have come to the corpse to discover fillings. Then I inhaled sharply, remembering something. "When I saw him at Amiens he mentioned having found some holes in his teeth. Said he had them looked at by a Romanian comrade-in-arms who studied dentistry . . ."

"Ah, well, then maybe." Willie dropped his face into his hands. "What am I going to say to the Chapmans?"

There wasn't any right answer. There wasn't any wrong one either. Even if those were Victor's bones, *he* wasn't in that pine box. He was somewhere else now. The only people for whom it mattered were still alive. "What does your instinct say?"

Willie looked up and stared at me. "It's not him."

"Then it's not Victor."

Willie's hard gaze melted into a pool of gratitude for my faith in his judgment. He blew out a breath. Then another. "I'm sorry, Beatrice."

Had Willie just apologized for something? I was so shocked it took me a moment to recover. I wanted to ask what he was sorry about, but he wet his lips and stared straight ahead. "I've made you late for your visit to Chavaniac . . ."

"I'm the president; they have to wait for me."

He put his hand on my knee. "Your work there seems to have made you happy. Happier anyway."

"I owe you for that and much more."

"Less than you suppose," he said. "As it happens, there's nothing I've ever given you that you haven't transformed. I buy a house, you make it a home. I buy a hotel, and you make it the showpiece of New York. I give you a chateau, and now it's an international charity with an impressive budget."

My heart swelled, feeling this was very fine praise. "You've always known I was a good investment."

"I've always known you were more than that."

I love thee against my will, I thought. Our marriage was dead, but love survived. Unfortunately, it didn't change that we could never live together again. And it didn't change that our marriage was broken beyond repair. He must have known it, because his shoulders rounded in defeat. "I regret . . . well, I try never to regret, but I won't fight you about the banker if that's what you really want."

"Thank you," I whispered, and kissed his cheek.

We were silent a long time after, just sitting together reflecting on all that had passed. Then he drew me into a companionable embrace. "We had a good run, didn't we?"

And my smile was bittersweet. "That we did."

FIFTY-THREE

MARTHE
Chavaniac-Lafayette
August 1943

A BLACK MERCEDES-BENZ, POLISHED TO A MIRROR FINISH, ROLLS into the castle drive, and two Gestapo officers step out.

It's morning and the sun is already scorching hot, but I go cold with dread. I'm supervising the girls, who are having their breakfasts, sipping from bowls of café au lait in the castle's dining hall, which no longer boasts of checkered tablecloths, for these have long since been torn up for bandages or washrags. The littlest girls are swinging their feet, because they're not tall enough for their chairs. Some of the older girls are gossiping or reading books at the table, and Josephine is braiding her sister's unruly hair.

They're all so innocent of the evil at our door. And I don't want to scare them, but I'm already panicked. With sweaty palms, I remind myself there could be simple reasons for the Gestapo's visit. Maybe they want to requisition the castle for that fat German general after all. I feel a little flare of anger to realize they might even be here at the baron's invitation, since he's chummy with some Germans—maybe they want advice.

Still, when the occupying officers at the castle's door bang loudly with the brass knocker, I jolt, because I know they could be here for the Jewish children. Josephine's eyes dart to me, then to the window, and I see her struggle to hide her fear. Should I grab her and Gabriella and hurry them out? We'd be noticed—maybe even chased—and we'd have to leave Daniel behind in the boys' dormitory, because it's half a mile away.

It might be better to brazen it out.

Of course, the Gestapo might be here for *me*, but nothing I use to forge papers now can't be explained away; teachers and artists need ink, pens, compasses, and glue. It's only the papers themselves that are incriminating. If they search and find the identity cards I've been making for the OSE and hiding in Madame Beatrice's old hatboxes, they'll not only guess that I'm a forger—they'll have pictures of exactly which children to hunt down.

If they catch you, they can catch everyone you help, because forgers know all the real names . . .

I should've had a better plan for this. I need to get the documents *and* the kids out of the castle, so I hastily reassure the girls, "I'll be right back." Then I race up the back spiral staircase, taking the old wooden steps two at a time. I grab the identity cards—four in all—and stuff them into my girdle. As I race back down the stairway, I'm sure I haven't been seen, but as soon as the sole of my saddle shoe hits the stone landing, someone calls to me.

"*Guten Tag*, Madame Travert!" The Gestapo officer touches the visor of his cap with its skull, and I recognize him. A slither of loathing slips through my veins as Obersturmführer Wolff looks me up and down, his gaze as cold as the day I watched him beat a boy to death.

"What a surprise to see you again," he says. *Is* it a surprise, or did he come to arrest me? "Surely you remember me . . ."

The fact I want to spit in his eye makes me reckless. "I don't know. We see so many Germans in France these days . . ."

He laughs. "Well, *you* are unforgettable. And I have come to know your husband. A good policeman—excellent detective. Very helpful."

He can't begin to fathom how sick that makes me to hear.

He's introducing me to his partner when Anna appears in the corridor, her expression inscrutable. "Gentlemen," she says, with a tone I've never heard before—somehow both softly feminine and absolutely authoritative. "My father will be with you shortly. Would you care to wait upstairs in the library? Madame Travert and I can arrange refreshments."

I'd like to arrange rat poison in their wine.

Then Wolff says, "Actually, I was hoping for a tour of the facility—

466 · STEPHANIE DRAY

particularly your little museum of Americana that I've heard so much about."

I blink. Don't tell me the bloody Gestapo are here as sightseers!

"I'm afraid it's locked for renovations," Anna replies smoothly.

It doesn't put him off. "I'm sure someone has a key."

"It's really not worth the trouble," she says with a charming little laugh that only I would know is all artifice. "Nothing of real value to interest you."

"Nothing of real value, she says!" Wolff slaps the other officer on the back. "That's what my friend says too, but he's not a civilized man. As for me, I spent a summer in the States. I can't say much for American beer, but I love their writers. Edgar Allan Poe. Such bone-chilling tales. Who could forget the 'The Cask of Amontillado'?" Wolff pretends to shiver. "To have such patience to take the revenge of burying someone alive . . . As Madame Travert perhaps recalls, I myself don't like to put off the satisfaction of doling out punishment!"

My shiver is real, because he says this with the barely suppressed glee of a boy who burns ants with a magnifying glass. Then he continues, "But to return to a more genteel subject, I heard you keep certain American valuables here—possessions that once belonged to George Washington, Dr. Franklin, and so on. Some Great War trinkets from the fabled Lafayette Escadrille. I'm eager to see them. I'm a collector of sorts."

"Those belongings aren't on the premises anymore." Anna delivers this bald-faced lie in a shockingly convincing way. "Renovations, as I said."

"How disappointing!" says Wolff, coming closer. "I was told the people at this chateau consider themselves guardians of such objects; unlikely to let them out of their sight. I hoped to use this quaint affinity for history to explain to my superiors why the women of this village marched on Bastille Day."

At this, Anna and I both take a breath, drawing closer together. Despite the brave face, this rattles her. It's up to me to say, "It wasn't anything political; only a historical tradition because this is the birthplace of Lafayette."

"Ah, another great French general," he says with an edge of mockery. "Remind me of the lands he conquered."

"He wasn't a conqueror," I admit. "He was a liberator."

Liberator is a dangerous word right now, and Anna gives me an incredulous look. She must think I'm an idiot. And I am, because I am taunting a Gestapo agent while hiding false papers in my underwear. They ought to shoot me for stupidity, but before they can, Madame LeVerrier shuffles into the corridor, eyeing the two officers like they're dirt tracked in by a careless gardener. "Gentlemen, the baron will see you now."

With crisp farewells, both Gestapo officers go upstairs. Anna and I both collapse against the locked museum door in relief, and she hisses, "I was afraid he'd find the guns."

Now it's my turn to be incredulous. "What guns?"

"George Washington's dueling pistols."

It's laughable that the Germans could be afraid of flintlock pistols from more than a century ago—but they've been confiscating everything from hunting rifles to old bayonets. I assumed the baron had a permit for these antiques, but I don't know what the laws are now in what used to be the Free Zone, and I'm equally sure people have been shot for less.

Anna checks the door to make sure it's locked, then asks, "Why do you think the Gestapo is here?"

I shrug. I've heard German soldiers visit French doctors for treatment so their commanding officers don't find out they've got a venereal disease. If that's why Wolff's here, I hope his prick rots off. The important thing is that he doesn't seem to be here for me or the kids. "I have to get to class . . ." Anna was so poised a moment ago, but now she's shaking, so I add, "It's going to be *fine*."

In that, I couldn't be more wrong.

LONG AFTER THE GESTAPO OFFICERS DRAG AMAURY DE LAGRANGE out of the castle, the baroness stands at the window with her hands over her face. The baron went with dignity, everyone agreed—angrily yanking his arm from the Gestapo officers so he could straighten his jacket and don his fedora. Then he stooped to fold his tall frame into the backseat of the Mercedes-Benz, and with a little wave, he was gone.

"I don't understand why they didn't arrest me," the baroness says again, as we all try to comfort her. "*I'm* the American. I'm the one who helped found this place and marched on Bastille Day . . ."

I marched too, and now my stomach is in knots.

Before he was taken, the baron assured everyone that it was a simple misunderstanding and that he'd be back in a few hours. But a few hours have already come and gone.

I stay with Anna and her mother that night—though I'm not sure how much comfort I am. And by the next morning, when we wait in the library by the silent telephone, the baroness has circles under her eyes. She starts pacing, then suddenly stops by the walnut desk where her husband's pipe is still where he left it. Then she throws open the desk drawer and fishes out a set of keys.

Anna's head jerks up from the sofa. "What are you doing, Maman?"

I think I know exactly what the baroness intends to do—something we should have done at the first whisper of the occupation. "Let me do it," I say. "My husband is a gendarme. If the pistols are registered, he'll know. If not, he'll know that too. I'll get rid of them."

The baroness takes the measure of me, then confesses, "I don't want to *get rid* of George Washington's dueling pistols. I want to hide them."

Anna blanches, and maybe she's right to. We see lists in the newspapers of people who have been executed for hiding weapons every day, or just failing to denounce those who do. Maybe this is why Anna says, "Better to turn them in, Maman. There have been amnesties . . ."

"The Germans don't always honor them," I say. "You'd be handing them evidence to use against your father. If they needed any." Then I turn my attention back to the baroness. "Which is another reason to let me do it. If I'm caught, I'm not so closely associated with him."

Anna's eyes mist over in both gratitude and shock. Two years ago, I felt like she was the only person left in my life who really knew me at all. Maybe she did. Two years ago I wouldn't have risked my neck for stupid flintlocks that belonged to George Washington.

I wouldn't have done it to protect the baron either, but here we are . . .

Anna wraps her arms around me in thanks—and I let her. Her closeness and her perfume still dizzy me, even though my feelings for her are all twisted up because of my guilt over Henri and my marriage to Travert. My longing still exists, even if we're not as close as we used to be. Even as I've tried to push her away. "Marthe, we can't let you take such an awful risk for us."

"Better me than you," I say. Besides, though she doesn't know it, I'm already hiding children and forging documents, so what's one more secret? After all, the Germans can only kill me once . . .

I roll the pistols into an old dirtied rag. I take them into the secret passages and dig out a stone from the wall to make a pocket, which I cover with a shallower stone and seal with dirt. The Germans aren't going to find them, and even if they do, they might think the pistols have been hidden here for years. I'm feeling pretty proud of myself.

Almost proud enough to tell Travert, but that night he has news for me. "I wasn't able to find a current address for Maxime Furlaud. But an old neighbor said he moved to New York sometime after 1918 and married an American sculptress."

That's curious, and more than anybody has been able to tell me before. I'm so grateful to Travert, and I wish I had time to think about it, but what I really need now is for him to find the baron.

Unfortunately, the Gestapo doesn't even try to respect the jurisdiction of French police anymore.

Another day passes. Another day without word. Finally, the baroness comes down from her room with a suitcase, and announces, "I'm going to Clermont-Ferrand."

Anna darts in front of her mother and tries to block her path. "What can you do there, Maman? We don't even know why Papa was arrested. You're only going to put yourself in danger too!"

"I'm not going to let your father be disappeared," she says, kissing Anna's cheek with surprising tenderness. "I'm so sorry, my darling. I thought our family did enough in the last war. In this war, all I wanted was to keep quiet, but look where it's gotten us."

"Don't be crazy." Anna looks to me, desperate. "Tell her she's lucky the Germans didn't arrest her too. She might not get so lucky this time."

Anna's right, but I don't argue with the baroness. I think she knows her money and title aren't going to protect her. For the first time in a long time, I think she's remembered exactly who she is and knows exactly what she's doing. I think she's going to try to save her husband, because she loves him.

And maybe even because we're all living in the house of a woman who did the same.

PART

FOUR

FIFTY-FOUR

ADRIENNE
Paris
March 1795

IT WAS AN IMPOSSIBLE PLAN, BUT I WAS DETERMINED TO SEE IT through. "I need an American passport," I said to James Monroe. "If you would be so kind as to provide me with one."

"You are optimistic to think it will be honored; the name *Lafayette* is known throughout the world . . ."

This was a sticking point, for even in my darkest moments, I had clung to my husband's name. I had even made myself content to *die* for that name. I did not wish to deny it now or ever. Yet I remembered that when my husband made his own daring escape from France at the age of nineteen, he too went in disguise.

Few people would suspect me if I traveled now as *Mrs. Motier*, a simple housewife of Hartford, Connecticut.

As I explained my plans, Monroe pinched the bridge of his nose. "My dear lady, I cannot believe Lafayette would wish me to give his wife the means with which to throw herself back into danger."

"Yet I sincerely believe, sir, that unless your president intervenes, I am the only one both willing and able to save him."

That I did not know *precisely* how was of secondary concern.

The cruelties visited upon my family whilst I myself was at the foot of the scaffold would poison the rest of my days, but they had killed my illusions too. There was nowhere safe in this world; death was always waiting. My husband and my children were the most precious consolation left to me. Thus, having secured a loan and the necessary papers from Monroe, I made the long journey by foot to Chavaniac to buy it back.

The roof now leaked in ten places, the Italian plaster was chipped, but still the place was a shelter for Aunt Charlotte and my girls, both of whom came running to embrace me. That they never thought to see me alive again was attested to by their sobs as I stroked their backs, kissed their hair, and inhaled the scent of them as if they were babes again.

At nearly eighteen, tall, auburn-haired Anastasie was now the same age I was when I gave birth to her. Though Virginie, at twelve, was not yet a woman grown, she had lost all traces of childish fancy. Both girls—whose survival had been assured by the kindness and courage of our villagers during my imprisonment—declared, "We will go wherever you go, Maman."

Thus, when the leaves turned in September, we traveled like peasants, with only a single satchel of belongings among us. Then, under cover of darkness, my daughters and I slipped quietly aboard an American ship with our papers and left France. Oh, the twisted pangs of relief and grief at leaving my country for the first time, and possibly forever. Yet as the dark water opened a chasm between my past and my future, I was filled with a single-minded purpose: to rescue the man I loved.

OUR SHIP'S CAPTAIN CARRIED US WITHOUT INCIDENT TO HAMBURG. It was rumored my aunt Madame de Tessé was now living there. Weary from travel, the girls and I found our way to an inn, but no sooner had we set down our bag than did my venerable old aunt come rushing into the establishment, throwing her arms around us. "Oh, my sweet girls!"

I startled to see my sister in her wake. *Mon Dieu*, Pauline. The grief on her face told me she knew everything about the guillotining of our mother, grandmother, and sister. I was at once assaulted by love and lashed by guilt and regret. I sank down to the floor in sobs. Pauline did the same, clasping me, both of us wailing for our murdered family.

It was some time before we could get up—all of us swept into my aunt's entourage as she ushered us to her new home, a veritable encampment of émigrés. I could not expect these aristocrats to have kindly feelings toward me. Still, I gave them news of their loved ones whenever I could, and in return secured a valuable prize.

"Letters of introduction," said Anastasie, who had become my accomplice. "We are to carry this to the comtesse de Rumbeck. She does not have the means of introducing us at court in Vienna, but she knows those who might . . ."

Pauline warned against this. "You cannot go on to Vienna. What can you do for Lafayette there except offer yourself again as a hostage?"

"I will argue for my husband's release."

"Adrienne, the Viennese authorities will laugh in your face."

"I have endured worse than laughter," I replied softly, stroking Virginie's dark hair, wondering if I ought to leave her with my relations, but already my family was too scattered . . .

Pauline warned, "If they know you are French, they will arrest you the moment you step foot there!"

"We will speak only English," I said, grateful that my children had learned the language from the earliest age. "And I will employ a German-speaking servant to do the talking."

Oh, the anxiety of coming to the first post at the Austrian border. I could *hear* Anastasie's stalwart heart beating as she battled her own fears. How strange it was to walk the streets of Vienna—like some kind of rewinding of time, where a monarch still reigned supreme and a palace rose up shining, powerful nobles in brilliant dress bustling in and out with scarcely a glance for the downtrodden peasantry, all of whom removed their hats and averted their eyes.

It brought to mind my youth at Versailles, both the arrogance and splendor.

The comtesse received us, her curiosity winning out over caution at Americans presenting themselves at her door. When, in the privacy of her toilette, I revealed my true identity, her hand fluttered to her pearls. "Oh, goodness me. You are the wife of that *fanatic*!"

"Monsieur Lafayette is a fanatic for liberty and all that is good. If I had hours, I could not recite his virtues, so I beg you not to betray a loving wife who wishes to set him free if she can, or join his imprisonment if she cannot."

It was this last part that caught her attention. "Join him? My dear, even a fanatic cannot wish for his wife to escape the clutches of one jailer only to deliver herself to another."

"Yet, if he knew all we have suffered without him, he would consent. Lafayette is our strength, and I flatter myself to believe we are his . . . I will beg the mercy of the emperor upon my knees if need be."

"Oh, my." She dabbed her eyes. Was it possible there were still enough decent people in the world to be moved by our plight? "Dear me. I am afraid I cannot be of use to you." Then, perhaps broken by my dismay, she finally said, "However, I happen to be acquainted with the grand chamberlain. He would never see you if he knew your name or purpose, but perhaps . . ."

Perhaps. One of the sweetest words!

Much sweeter than the word uttered by the grand chamberlain. *"Nein!"*

Hard of hearing, the old man had at first squinted. "Motier?" He'd flicked a bit of lint from his embroidered robes. "At least bother to tell me why I should know this name."

"I am better known as Adrienne de Noailles-Lafayette," I whispered.

Hearing this, he seemed ready to eject me by force of arms. "Your husband is a notorious traitor, madame!"

"I cannot agree. My husband saved his king's life on more than one occasion, sir. It was, in fact, his determination to *rescue* the king that occasioned his fall. It was my husband's enemies who put King Louis to death, and yet several of those who voted to guillotine him have passed through Austria unmolested. Why should my husband pay the price for their villainy?"

The chamberlain scowled and rose to walk away. He stopped, though, at the gilded chamber door. "You come from fine stock. The Noailles. I knew your uncle. A good soldier. I once danced with your grandmother at a ball." He scratched his chin. "To this day, I believe she stole from me a little silver cross . . . and yet I was quite charmed by her."

A knot swelled in my throat at the memory of Grand-mère. "Sir, I will never again know another breath that is not mingled with grief. Which is why I beg an audience with the emperor. The only person who can restore my heart."

The chamberlain ground his teeth, then made a sound almost pained. "Come tomorrow. You will have ten minutes with the emperor—no more."

I stifled a cry of triumph. Then, in the hours that followed, the clock could not turn fast enough. As I contemplated all I would say to the emperor, I was interrupted by my daughters. "Teach us to curtsy in obeisance."

As the children of Lafayette, they had never learned to humble themselves before any monarch. Yet I believed that the beauty of their souls would plead eloquently for their father. We owned nothing suitable to the occasion of visiting the winter palace in Vienna. Our jewels had been long since confiscated or sold, so we donned borrowed gowns and simple ribbons of scarlet round our necks.

The chamberlain arranged the most secret of meetings in a small chamber without audience; none of the ministers had been informed. In white hose, Emperor Francis II received us politely but came directly to the point. "I cannot grant Lafayette's liberty. My hands are tied."

How could that be? He was a champion of authoritarian rule and the divine right of kings to do as they pleased. Yet something constrained him. At war with France, he did not wish to free the most famous, or infamous, Frenchman of all. If I had learned anything in my years in public life, it was that public opinion could be both manipulated for evil and swayed for good. My husband had changed minds with his courage, and my Lord Jesus Christ had transformed the hearts of humanity with his sacrifice. I wished to be worthy of them both. "Sire, if you will not release my husband from your dungeon, I ask permission to share his fate, as I vowed in marriage to do. You will make me happy if you grant this."

The emperor swallowed, shifted in his chair, started to say something—perhaps to refuse me, and my heart sank. It would have been worse, in that moment, to be sent away than to be clasped in chains.

Then the emperor's flinty eyes softened. "I grant it to you, madame."

"Merci!" How perverse to be made so happy by the prospect of imprisonment! Yet I felt on the cusp of life again. After all these long years, to set eyes on my beloved . . .

I would have flown to Gilbert that instant, but time grew short and

I must not waste it. "Sire, there are rumors about Prussian prisons . . . if I should encounter troubles in your dungeons, I would like your permission to address you with requests."

"We consent," he replied, with the royal *we*. "You will find Lafayette well fed and well treated. You will be pleased with the commanding officers. The prisoners are distinguished only by number, but of course, your husband's name is known and he is given privileges accordingly."

This eased my worries, and as our audience came to an end, I was resolved to join my husband in prison. My daughters were too. Anastasie said, "We will never consent to be parted from you again, Maman."

"*Never*," Virginie echoed.

As if to prove she harbored in her breast not only the sincerity of a Lafayette but the courtier's instinct of the Noailles, Anastasie argued, "It will shame the emperor more to lock up my father's children. Our going with you will draw the eyes of the world and soften hearts to a little family, already so wretched, reduced to this by our devotion to one another."

It was upon this hope we staked everything.

AS MY DAUGHTERS BOTH PREPARED THEMSELVES TO BE CAGED, I knew that if I had done nothing else well in my life, I had done well with my children. For them, if for no other reason, I would do *this* in a manner befitting, even though a horror came over me at the sight of the redbrick fortifications at Olmütz in which my husband had been left to rot. I felt the need to gasp fresh air, not knowing the next time we might have the opportunity. Yet I was determined to show no fear, even when given warnings from the guardsmen. "Think carefully what you are doing, madame. It is a harsh life inside these dungeon walls. You will suffer."

"I have been assured by the emperor that prisoners are well cared for, sir." Of course, King Louis once believed his prisoners were well treated in the Bastille too. But our captors should know we *expected* humane treatment. "Surely he is not mistaken to put his faith in you. He granted me permission to write him if I found anything amiss."

The guard had nothing to say to that. Instead, he inspected our satchels. "No knives, forks, or spoons allowed. Prisoners tend to use them for suicide."

"How do you expect us to take our meals?"

"With your hands," he said, turning the key in the first door, to lead us through a maze of dark, fetid hallways. We discovered my husband had been kept alone, in a chamber closed off by an iron door with locks and chains, and a wood door behind it—all this, as if to imprison a dragon.

As the guard rattled the key ring, my heart pounded. *Brace yourself for whatever you find*, I told myself. My husband might have lost his senses. It might be true, as the rumors went, that in a fit of insanity he had scratched out his eyes. I dared not imagine the torments he had suffered in this terrible place.

The door creaked open and a noxious smell wafted out as my daughters and I peered into the darkened cell, our eyes racing over the chains upon the wall, a little wood bench, and there—a scarecrow of a man curled upon a mattress of dirty straw.

"Gilbert!" I cried, hurrying to him. The pale lifeless figure turned and blinked in confusion. I nearly sobbed in relief that he *did* have eyes—those beautiful hazel eyes, in which I had lost myself as a girl and found myself as a woman. Though, were it not for those eyes, I should scarcely have recognized him. He had grown a mustache and bushy beard. No spark of life animated his expression. He did not speak or move. He only stared until I feared his tongue was cut out or his mind gone. Surely he must know me. I held my breath, fearful. Perhaps no one could withstand such abuse for so many years and remain the same . . .

Then his parched lips cracked open and he rasped, "My dear heart."

"Yes, yes, I am here."

"I am dead then, or we both are?"

I took his withered hand. "No, we are here together, reunited in life."

It was only my tears splashing upon his cheeks that seemed to convince him. With some effort, he pushed himself upright on spindly arms. *Mon Dieu.* What had they done to those strong arms that had been so often my pleasure and solace? Half-starved, his clothes hanging upon him, he was in a frightful state. He glanced from me, to his weeping daughters, and to me again. Had no one told him we were coming?

"Villains!" He gave a ragged shout, like a man readying for battle. "Who is responsible for imprisoning my family?"

"I am responsible," I said, reassuring my general, who was still ready to fight injustice even when he could barely stand.

Praise God, he was not broken.

"Oh, Papa!" Virginie threw herself into his arms, and he winced at the impact but pulled Anastasie to him too, and a moment later we were all in one sobbing embrace.

When our tears were finally spent, the girls and I set straightaway to cleaning. We asked for a broom, a bucket of water, and washrags—only to be refused. The noxious smell came from some manner of sewage ditch just under the barred window. Gilbert told us, with a hint of pride, the reason for all the locks and chains and his solitary confinement in this dreadful part of the dungeon was that he had attempted an escape—and might have got away too, if he had been willing, or strong enough, to kill the guardsman with whom he had wrestled. He had somehow got upon a horse and galloped away before being captured in a village not far hence.

Now he was not trusted outside for more than a few moments. Beyond this small boast, he avoided my gaze, explaining that the people who had tried to help him escape were now in prison too—a thing that weighed heavily on his conscience, as did the fate of the people on the plantations that had been seized.

I reassured him that our son was in America, which pleased him, but not once did Gilbert ask after our loved ones. It was only after our daughters were taken to their adjoining cell for the night that he dared to look at me. "Adrienne, people have risked so much for me. Some have smuggled news. I learned of the atrocities against the king and queen; I have heard . . . of the terror . . . the bloodletting, which left me in fear you were dead."

He broke off here with such a shudder that I feared to tell him how near I had come. He took my hands, kissing each finger in worship. "It seems a miracle to find you and my children unharmed, but I do not know the names of the victims, and I tremble to ask . . ."

I will not dwell upon the way he shattered when I named loved ones, all sacrificed to the guillotine. I will not dwell upon it because it shattered me too. Let it suffice to say that we were both cut by the shards of guilt and grief in the recitations of those names, in the vows to find their remains. In the violent emotion of our reunion, we knew these wounds would never heal. That we were, now, for each other, the only salve.

And freedom, our one remaining hope.

FIFTY-FIVE

MARTHE
Le Puy
December 24, 1943

A FROSTY MORNING WIND SWEEPS OVER THE STATUE OF LAFA-
yette, around which ropes are tied like nooses. Despite the cold, a small
crowd gathers in the square to watch—with clenched teeth—as the Germans unbolt the statue from its pedestal. They're pulling Lafayette down
to melt for ammunition.

I had no idea this was happening when I volunteered to drive Madame
LeVerrier to Le Puy to stock up on supplies before the snows make the
roads too treacherous. Now I wish I hadn't come, but I have a secret errand
of my own that can't wait. Monsieur Kohn gave me a packet of passport
photos from the OSE for endangered children who need falsified identity
cards. I need to affix photos onto the forged documents, and I'm out of glue.
I also need more ink and tracing paper. I've already been seen buying these
things in Paulhaguet and Brioude, and Travert says it's safer not to buy
supplies from the same shop twice.

So I park the car, then Madame LeVerrier and I go our separate
ways, and all the while people are muttering darkly on the street.

"The Nazis may do to us what they want—but to take our general!"

"We can't let them get away with it. No, they won't have him."

"But what can be done?"

By the time I've made my purchases, a German band has begun playing a Christmas concert for an empty square; no one wants to listen. And
the statue of Lafayette is lying in a gutter to await transport. A bronze
figure with a sheathed sword, hat in one hand, patriotic tricolor in the
other, lifted to the heavens. It's a beautiful piece—dramatic and lifelike. Maybe that's why the Nazis wrapped the hero of old in ropes so

he looks like he's bound and gagged. I stare with a bellyful of bile until I can finally tear myself away to meet Madame LeVerrier at a nearby café.

But as I make my way to meet her, I get a prickly sensation that I'm being followed. I pick up my pace, passing military vehicles and ducking under a snow-dusted awning before risking a glance over my shoulder.

"Sam?" I hiss in surprise, not having seen him for weeks.

"Keep walking," my old friend says, taking my arm. I fall into step, passing frosted shop windows as his voice drops low, muffled by the winter air. "Do you trust your husband? Do you *really* trust him, Marthe?"

Travert and I have been married a year now. I should have a quick and easy answer, but trust has never come quick or easy to me. "Why?"

"The truck the Germans brought to haul Lafayette's statue to the forge isn't big enough. They've called in help from the gendarmerie in Brioude and Paulhaguet to come pick it up after dusk."

Clever bastards. The Nazis want to make French police do the dirty work when it's dark and there aren't so many angry people milling about.

Sam takes a deep breath as if he isn't sure if he should say more, but then he does. "There's a plan afoot. No one wants to see gendarmes caught in the crossfire, but we're not going to let them take Lafayette. He belongs to us . . ."

I come to a sudden halt on the sidewalk, realizing that he's trying to tell me Travert is in danger. "What plan?"

"Keep walking," he says, tugging me forward so we don't draw attention. "I'm only telling you because . . . I don't want you to lose someone again. Not after Henri. So if you trust your husband, tell him to convince the gendarmes not to show up on time. If they do, they'll be ambushed on the road. If you don't trust him, but want to keep him out of danger, think of some lie to make him late." Sam glances at his watch. "Whatever you do, just do it fast."

I TAKE THE SLIPPERY HAIRPIN TURNS FROM LE PUY LIKE A MAD-woman, terrifying Madame LeVerrier in the backseat. "I'd ask if you were drunk, Marthe, but there's nothing left in France now to drink!"

"Just trying to get back early," I say, pushing the motor hard. "It's a busy Christmas season!"

It can be nearly an hour's drive from Le Puy to Chavaniac in winter conditions, but I make it in nearly half the time. I help Madame LeVerrier unload the packages, but instead of parking in the carriage house, I peel out of the castle drive and head straight for Travert's house, where he's plucking a chicken for our holiday dinner. Last Christmas, our marriage, and the occupation, was too new to celebrate. But this time he insisted on a tree and trimmings, and he's in a jolly mood when he says, "I didn't expect you—"

There's no time for pleasantries. "Are you on duty tonight?"

"*Oui*," he says, watching me stomp snow off my feet. "I have to go to Le Puy for a few hours, but don't worry, I'll be back in time for midnight mass."

"And do you know what the Germans are doing in Le Puy?"

His smile falls away, and he keeps plucking feathers. "It's just a hunk of metal, Marthe."

I don't want to fight again like we did about Bastille Day. Could I just lie to keep him safe? Maybe. I could pretend to be sick and beg him to care for me. I could seduce him and make him late. I could lie to him and keep secrets from him like I've learned to keep them from Anna . . .

But I don't want to, and I hope I don't have to. So I take a risk and tell him the truth.

When I'm done delivering Sam's warning about the ambush, Travert throws the chicken down on the wood table. Then he lets out a string of curse words that would scandalize a whole brothel.

"The last thing we need is Frenchmen fighting Frenchmen," I say.

"Tell that to your maquisard friends!"

Travert shakes his head, teeth gritted. Then he grabs his policeman's coat and cap.

I grab his arm. "What are you going to do?"

"I'll let you know when I decide," he says, slamming out the door.

I'm not sure if I should stay or go. At a loss, I sit down and finish plucking the dead chicken, a morbid task for my hands while watching the clock. Then I peel the precious potatoes he's saved for the occasion, tensing up at every chime, waiting, waiting . . .

For all I know, he's gone off to make arrests. Travert is willing to take risks for people—not for things. He's made that clear. Telling him the truth might have been a big mistake, and I should be worrying about Sam. But deep in my gut, I'm worried most for Travert. It's strange to feel fear like this again—I didn't think it was possible after Henri.

Travert is nothing like Henri, of course. He'd rather be gulping wine in some bistro or playing cards in a smoke-filled hall than going on a camping trip, hayride, or midnight swim. He doesn't know anything about medicine or baseball or Hollywood movies. And Travert is nothing like Anna either. He's not fashionable or sophisticated or brimming with perky new ideas and good cheer. But he's good at repairing things. Automobiles, sinks, leaky roofs. I look around his neat little house, with its patched-up stonework, and think that Travert's a simple man in the best possible way.

And all I ever do is complicate things for him.

It's long after dark—almost midnight—when the door bangs open. Travert's cheeks are pink from the cold and he thunks down a heavy black box. "Merry Christmas."

It looks like an automobile battery, and I gasp. "You sabotaged the transport truck?"

He nods. "It was the best I could come up with on short notice. It's one thing to ask subordinates to look the other way. Another to make them accomplices. This way everybody but me can be an honest man."

I feel a twinge of guilt, but still ask, "Did it work?"

He puffs up, affronted. "*Of course.* It was more than two hours before a replacement battery could be found, so we were late to pick up the statue . . . and by the time we got to Le Puy, it was already gone."

My blood rushes with triumph. "Gone?"

He shrugs. "A band of men in police uniforms claiming to be from my gendarmerie had already come to get the statue and made off with it. Now I have to worry how the Resistance came by police uniforms."

"Who cares?" I go and throw my arms around Travert's neck. *"Merci!"*

"Don't thank me," he says, still scowling and grumpy. "I only did it to protect my gendarmes . . . and because I'm a sentimental idiot about that statue because of our wedding night."

I grin and try to kiss him, but he gruffly fends me off. "We have to go to midnight mass now. We can't do anything different—anything that might cause remark."

Reluctantly, I agree. He's helped make me a better criminal, and I almost regret that I'm making him into a better criminal too. I also want to go to midnight mass for Anna. Since the baron's arrest in the summer, we learned he was sent to Buchenwald concentration camp; the baroness is traveling across France, working her contacts to see if she can at least get him transferred to a different prison. Without any of her family, it's going to be a lonely Christmas for Anna.

By the time we get to the Church of Saint-Roch in Chavaniac, today's news is on everyone's lips. About how the area's Resistance, now calling themselves the Secret Army of Lafayette, spirited the statue away. The Germans are reportedly furious—spending their Christmas Eve in the cold forests, searching for a statue, with threats that they'll be searching every home and building.

But here in the village, the mood is exultant, like it's a Christmas miracle. The curé risks saying a blessing for *our maquisards*, and for the first time in a long time, people are willing to say aloud what they really think. At least a little bit. After the service, Anna draws me into a warm hug. "Merry Christmas, Marthe," she breathes into my ear, quietly confiding that after the late-night *réveillon*, she and Madame LeVerrier are going to hide Lafayette's letters and trinkets and other valuables in the museum, in case the Germans come to seize it as punishment for the stolen statue.

Fortunately, hiding rings and snuffboxes and historical papers isn't illegal; it's not dangerous like hiding pistols. It's still *something*, though, so I hug her tight, proud of her, smiling at the familiar scent of her perfume.

But I don't return to the castle with her for the *réveillon*. I know she wants me to go with her, but for once I'd rather go with Travert, even if he's sour-tempered and surly with me. As soon as we've latched the wooden door, I kiss him, and instead of cooking our dinner, I keep kissing him until the heat of our bodies overtakes the heat of his anger. Then I draw him to the quilted bed, where so many of our silent conversations take place.

Afterward, he asks, "Do you think of her, when we're together like this?"

Normally I'd bristle at a question like that, but tonight I tease. "Why—do you want to know if you fixed me? That's what men think, isn't it? That a good romp between the sheets sets a woman straight."

But Yves says, "I don't think it works that way."

"It doesn't. But no, I don't think of her when we're together like this."

I don't think of much of anything when we're together like this. It's easy to be with him. For a year now, his body—thick neck, broad shoulders, wide back—has been a fallow field of forgetting where I bury everything I don't want to feel. But I think maybe now something is growing in that soil.

FIFTY-SIX

BEATRICE
Chavaniac
July 1918

HAVING PARTED WITH WILLIE, I WAS NOW A FREE WOMAN, BUT while the war raged on, where better to enjoy my liberty than Chavaniac? "Welcome back, Madame President," said the castle's steward, taking my luggage. Already I could see that the changes wrought since my last visit were nothing short of miraculous. Paved roads now led to the castle, where an entirely new wing had been constructed for the children and employees while restoration work continued in the castle proper.

A new school and medical facility could now boast of electricity and indoor plumbing . . . and though the library remained a scene of disaster, with rotted floorboards and a collapsed fireplace, the walls had been re-inforced and the roof repaired. All this was accomplished in record time.

Some work had been performed by German prisoners of war—which seemed fair under the circumstances—but we were also aided by passing American soldiers, an entire company of whom were, even now, at work with shovels and pickaxes. The sight of these sturdy doughboys stirred my heart, as I imagined it might stir Lafayette's heart too were he here to see it. These were the great-grandsons of the generation of Americans he fought beside, here to rescue Europe and restore his home to glory . . .

As a black cat wound itself around her ankles like a familiar, Clara said, "We've adopted some feline friends to help with our bats."

A welcome solution. Inside the castle, the historic furniture and fac-similes thereof that I'd managed to acquire were kept free of dust by the housekeeper and six housemaids. We also had three gardeners, four teachers, and two cooks to feed the eighty-five children who now slept peacefully beneath our terra-cotta rooftops. Among them darling Marthe, who was, according to the staff, a two-and-a-half-year-old terror in flaxen pigtails.

"She has much to say," reported Marie-Louise LeVerrier, who had dedicated her life to this place in the past year. "She's a very bright girl and quite the mistress of this domain."

"Is that so?"

By way of example, Clara Simon explained that on the Fourth of July holiday there'd been a scuffle between the children who had been living here and those newly arrived. *We're the real children of Lafayette*, taunted the former. Which sent the latter crying to the staff to see if this were true. That's when precocious Marthe told them they were *all* Lafayette kids.

Oh, how I loved this story! Eager for a reunion, I found little Marthe sitting at a picnic table in the courtyard, drawing with wax crayons under the supervision of Marie-Louise. The girl blinked up with those steel blue eyes, and as I slid into the bench beside her, I was astonished at how she'd grown. "I don't suppose you remember me."

The girl shook her head, cautiously.

"Well, I remember *you*, and hope we'll be special friends."

Marthe's nose wrinkled as if she was uncertain she *wanted* a friend, much less a special one.

"Be nice to Madame Chanler," scolded Marie-Louise.

But I waved this away and leaned closer to the girl. "What is it you're drawing?"

"You can't tell?"

I squinted, admiring the zeal of her scribbles. "Hmm, well, let me see . . ."

With one quirked brow, the little girl asked, "Is it a kitten?"

"Ah, yes, of course. I see it now. A pretty kitty!"

My enthusiasm was rewarded with a sigh that seemed to come from the center of the little girl's very soul. "No, it's not. It's a piggy."

Having been tested and bested by a little girl, I laughed until my sides hurt—as did all my friends, with whom I was so glad to be reunited. Marie-Louise had prepared a magnificent tower chamber for me with a view of the garden, where a gaggle of children played—clean, clothed, rosy-cheeked, and thriving after having escaped bombed-out towns in gas masks or having scavenged for food in the streets of Paris. Their bright laughter told me the horrors of war were beginning to fade away here in the volcanic mountains, where I could almost feel the earth's fire warming the very soil beneath which these orphaned children would start anew. Here, after all, was a place that instilled the heart with courage and reinvigorated the spirit.

Certainly it was reinvigorating mine.

I liked my tower sanctuary. I could work here, I could sculpt here. What a peaceful studio it would make with all the light filtering in. Maybe I could even teach little Marthe how to draw a better pig. But of course, I could not stay forever . . .

"We must cherish Beatrice while we have her," Emily warned when we took a light supper in the ancient kitchen. "She insists this is her last great adventure."

Emily wasn't happy about my determination to make a future with Furlaud in New York after the war, though she pretended otherwise. She was still, after all, a very stouthearted girl.

Clara, perched by the casement window, chewing licorice in an effort to give up cigarettes, guessed what Emily was getting at. "So you mean to go through with it, Beatrice? Tell me you're not going to leave Mr. Chanler and marry your French cavalier. That's hard to believe after the news article . . ."

"What news article?"

Clara, who devoured newspapers, fished one out of a copper vase. She'd been saving it just for me. Then she leaned back, propping her feet up until Marie-Louise gave her a harsh look as if to say, *Not on Lafayette's table!* I supposed Clara had got hold of Mitzi Miller's latest column about my labor mission. Or maybe even some feature about our work here in Chavaniac. Still, my stomach churned at the thought it might be gossip about my relationship with Maxime Furlaud . . .

"It seems you've been held up as an example of marital bliss!" Clara explained, spreading the pages onto the rustic table so we could read the headline in the *Buffalo Times*: *Why the Home-Loving and Maternal Instinct in a Good Woman Is More Powerful Than Any Desire for a Career . . .*

A photograph of me from another era graced the article, from which

Clara read aloud, "*No more practical husband lives than William Astor Chanler, explorer, author, soldier, politician, and game hunter. Mr. Chanler flung riches at his lady's feet, but something else moved the starlet to become Mrs. Chanler and fade forever from public view—*"

"Fade forever?" I tried to snatch up the pages. "I've never faded from anything in my life, much less public view!"

Clara kept the paper out of my grasp, her voice lilting with amusement. "*Mrs. Chanler has never spoken of the happiness which is hers, but it is mutely expressed in the perfect life that has marked the union.*"

Having just ended things with Willie, I was actually pained by this, but Clara unwittingly plunged on. "*Minnie Ashley had eight years of public worship, when along comes the practical husband offering nothing but home and himself. And with a smile she pushed aside the wreath of fame and took instead the veil, which spells happiness and all things worthwhile.*"

"What a silly article," I said. It vexed me. And not only because it dredged up my stage name. Or at least what I claimed was a stage name. The more upsetting matter was that I was very much not a woman for whom marriage had spelled happiness *and all things worthwhile*. Though I hoped for happiness, at least, with Max, and I was angry that an article like that should make me doubt it. I wondered what sorts of hats I would wear as the wife of a French banker. I didn't think any of the ones I owned would suit!

Still, all this was to think about after the war . . .

Of course, I'd given up guessing how much longer the war would last, now that the Allies were beating the Huns in the trenches, crippling their naval yards, and smashing their air force. Since the arrival of the bulk of American troops, Maxime wrote, *The advance is now so swift I sometimes sleep uncovered on the cold ground, there being no time to pitch a tent and take it down again.*

He was predicting the war really could be over by year's end.

In the meantime, we were overrun by displaced children—starving, wounded, diseased, seemingly from all corners of the earth. Unable to build fast enough, we'd rented space in structurally sound but abandoned buildings not too far from Chavaniac. We delivered ten little girls to a nunnery in Le Puy before taking four boys back with us to Chavaniac.

All sons of fallen soldiers. Among them a brown-skinned French-

Algerian boy named Samir Bensaïd, who couldn't sleep without his gas mask. A roguish little Auvergnat named Henri, whose widowed mother was too sick to care for him. And a pale, freckle-faced English boy named Victor, who had fallen ill on the journey, coughing up blood.

Tuberculosis, the *doctoresse* said, warning me away. The Red Cross personnel should have caught such an infectious disease and prevented him from coming here, where we had only rudimentary medical care. Now it was too late to send him back, and soon we despaired of his life.

I couldn't bear that *this* little Victor should suffer the way my nephew had, without comforting arms around him. I couldn't bear to lose another Victor to this war. Thus, in our makeshift hospital, I sat by his bedside in the days that followed.

With gasping breaths—before it became too difficult to speak—the boy told me how the Germans had forced him to drive cattle for them, making him sleep in the stable without a blanket and promising to shoot him if he ran away. But he ran away anyway, and said he was happier to die in Lafayette's castle.

Which is what he did not long after.

I held his body for a long time, sobbing, and Emily had to gently coax me away. "He needed you before, but now he must be buried . . ."

He needed me. But I couldn't save him. And now other children needed me too. It was the worst time to find myself overcome with exhaustion, unable to rise from bed. Sick and sad like a blackness had descended over my soul. Emily feared I'd contracted tuberculosis from the dying boy. But when I complained of aching joints, weakness, and lost appetite, our *doctoresse* feared it was the deadly Spanish flu, which was now sweeping across continents, heaping more misery and grief upon a world already filled with it.

It was only when she discovered my lowered heart rate that I revealed my lingering illness, the thyroid and cardiovascular abnormalities. Ailments that reminded me of my mortality and how much I still wanted to accomplish in a life that might meet an early close.

IT WAS EMILY WHO TENDED ME UNTIL I WAS WELL ENOUGH TO sketch again in my turret. I drew the dead boy because I felt that some memorial ought to be made for him. Meanwhile, Emily was trying to soothe her eighteen-month-old daughter, who wailed inconsolably in her mother's arms. "I'm afraid Anna is happier with her nurse than with me. Either that, or she's determined to make me pay such a price for my neglect that I never leave her again."

Emily said this in a humorous vein, but it was true that Anna was as sunny a child as ever lived *except* in her mother's arms. Why, I'd even seen her playing happily in the courtyard with pigtailed Marthe, who tugged her around in a red wagon. Still, Emily's sigh was so disconsolate that I hurried forth to reassure her, "That just goes to show you that you're going to have a spirited daughter—the only kind any mother should want."

Emily only sighed again. "I missed Anna's first words. Her first steps. We know now that gas from the trenches leaked into Motte-aux-bois—my mother-in-law is being treated. What if Anna has poison in her lungs too?"

"Then she wouldn't be wailing with such vigor," I said, wishing to put a halt to this litany of self-recrimination. "No more of this. Last year, we both did what we felt must be done."

It was a good thing too. Thanks to Emily and Amaury de LaGrange, America now had an incipient air force that was bombing the Germans to bits. Still, my friend simply could not reconcile her good service with the fact that she'd left her infant daughter. I'd seen Emily hold up in blood-soaked infirmaries, in air raids and hard winters. She'd never complained of being a pilot's wife or the hardship of leaving her family and country behind. No adversity of this war had broken her, but guilt at having left her baby was smashing her stout heart to pieces.

And her anxieties for her husband—like mine for Max—were keen. It would be tragedy enough to lose a loved one to war; nearly unbearable to lose a loved one in a war's closing hours, when the illusion of freedom is so tantalizingly near.

FIFTY-SEVEN

MARTHE
Chavaniac-Lafayette
April 1944

WE HEAR OF ANOTHER GESTAPO RAID NOT SO VERY FAR AWAY. Klaus Barbie—the so-called Butcher of Lyon—and Konrad Wolff captured children from a safe house, snatching little Jewish boys and girls from the breakfast table where they were drinking chocolate. More than forty children were dragged kicking and screaming, pulled out from hiding places in closets and under beds and bushes. They are likely all murdered now.

Gone is my feeling of triumph on Christmas Eve when the whole village celebrated the spiriting away of Lafayette's statue. We've managed to keep it from the Germans, while somehow letting them take little children instead . . . and I'm sick over it. As I toss and turn, Travert pulls me under one arm, his hand in my hair, heavy as his breathing in the night. He doesn't like to stay in my room at the castle. He thinks a man should bed his wife under his own roof. But since he likes bedding me more than he likes being right, he's here on a Thursday night.

"Can you find out their names?" I whisper in the dark.

"Why do you want their names?"

I squeeze my eyes tight. "Because it might have been my fault . . ."

In recent months, my new technique with photographic paper led me to an even greater discovery—namely that the hectograph tablet I used to copy spelling tests can, with the right ink, print almost any kind of official form. I've been reproducing stamps by the dozens. Mostly for adults—maquisards, nurses, teachers, and passers who smuggle kids into Switzerland. But in working with Monsieur Kohn and the OSE, I've made some for children too. I remember the photos I've so carefully glued onto identity cards. *Twelve-year-old Otto and his dimpled chin. Ten-year-old Hans and his big round eyes. Five-year-old Lucie and her beautiful curly hair . . .*

Maybe I made a mistake that gave them away. "If the authorities are onto my tricks—"

"It was an informant," Travert says.

I sit up to face him in the moonlight. "How do you know? Did you—you weren't part of the raid, were you?"

"I'd eat a bullet before I was part of that."

I believe him, but that makes me feel sicker, because he might be faced with that choice. The littlest child taken was only four years old. Younger than any of our Lafayette kids. When I try to sleep, I picture lorries pulling through our gate—jackboots banging on Lafayette's door—Josephine, Gabriella, and Daniel screaming.

It's too easy to imagine.

Maybe that's why Travert whispers, "I want to quit. Maybe go work in a factory or a repair shop . . ."

Last week he spent an hour and drops of precious glue putting back together a broken flowerpot. I told him I could make him a new one, but he said he liked the cracks. Now I tell him, "They'll send you to Germany."

"What's the difference these days?" he asks, rolling away from me. There is a long pause before he adds, "You know, I was soft and tubby as a boy—I used to get beaten in the schoolyard . . ."

There's not much that's soft about him now, and as I stroke the strong muscles of his back, I think that if I ever carved him, I'd use a hard wood, with rough cuts, leaving some bark to show the texture of the soul.

"I wanted to be a gendarme to protect people," he continues. "Now I feel disgust every time I button my uniform. Can you understand?"

I do, but say, "You still have to stay—to protect people, to warn us, to help the Resistance."

He blows out a long breath, because he knows I'm right. "Well, if *I* can't quit, you have to. You need to stop forging papers. It's not like before when I could protect you. When the Gestapo seized those children, they took their caretakers and put them on that train to Auschwitz."

I've heard that. The rumor too, that one of the children's protectors—

a young woman with convincing false papers—revealed her own true identity so she could stay with the children. I can't imagine making that choice, and I don't want to. But I also can't stop forging, which has become more important to me than sculpting, because it's an art that's saving lives. So I swallow, sink back down, and pretend to sleep.

Travert isn't fooled. "Marthe. If you're caught, you'd be on your own."

So what else is new? I don't feel bitter about it. I'm grateful for everything he's done. I realize now more than ever all the ways people have cared for me and about me. And all the ways in which I've been ungrateful and held them at arm's length—even Yves, who makes it hard to do. But maybe there was a reason for my prickliness in the grand scheme of things. Maybe it's so that when I'm taken down, I don't drag anyone I care about with me . . .

I'M BLEARY-EYED AND RUNNING LATE THE NEXT MORNING, WHEN Madame LeVerrier tells me Anna wants to see me in the library. I find her sitting behind the big walnut desk that used to be her father's. The baron's pipe is just where he left it, as if she wants to pretend he isn't gone and her mother with him. We think it was the efforts of the baroness that got him transferred to the less horrific prison at Tyrol, where he's locked up with defendants he testified against in the Riom Trial. The baroness believes they're all being held as hostages—more valuable alive than dead for the moment.

She won't rest until they're free. In fact, Anna and I both believe the baroness might be making clandestine trips to Algeria, where we have reason to believe her son-in-law, Henry Hyde, is now operating as an American intelligence officer.

"Madame Travert," Anna says in greeting, hanging up the phone. Then she gives a harried shake of her head. "I'm sorry—I don't mean to be formal, Marthe. I really don't know *how* to act these days . . ."

I can't blame her. We've both changed so much since we smoked together in the attic listening to music on Madame Beatrice's old windup gramophone. I remember giving her a bouquet and curling up with her under the blankets, and comforting each other through the loneliness and cold. It's only a memory now, though.

In the end, I couldn't tell her about my feelings or forgeries. And maybe closeness can't survive so many secrets . . .

"People still see me as an upstart," she's saying, and I realize Anna isn't struggling to know how to act around *me*. She's wondering how to make people respect her authority as the new interim president of the preventorium. Madame LeVerrier was too old, and we'd have rioted under the leadership of Faustine Xavier, so of those of us left, Anna was the natural choice. Now she confides, "I think the Germans have taken Dr. Anglade."

My guts turn to water. "What—why?"

If they suspect him of hiding Jewish kids, if they interrogate him—

"He went to consult on a case and sent back a worried note that there was a chance he might be . . . more or less conscripted into service to tend the wounded at the front. He was due back last night, but he hasn't returned."

Merde! I don't know what to do for poor Dr. Anglade. How much more of this are we supposed to take? I try to stay calm. We're losing our managing physician, but I'm also losing a coconspirator. Thanks to Dr. Anglade, Gabriella Kohn has been with us since '41. A different physician might send her away. Should I have advised Monsieur Kohn to smuggle his kids out through Switzerland when the border was safer?

"I don't know how to hold the preventorium together without Dr. Anglade," Anna says plaintively.

"You'll find a way," I say, as if I'm not anxious too.

She touches the cross she wears. "Maybe I'll buy a donkey cart and go from farm to farm to buy food. Maybe raise some pigs to sell them for medicine or have the boys boil clothes in the courtyard to save on laundry costs."

"There, you see? You've always got a new idea, so we'll muddle through," I say, as much to convince myself as her. "We have so far, haven't we? Between frigid winters and food shortages and running low on medicines and bandages, blankets, and everything else . . ."

Anna brightens a little. "You know, my relationship with Maman has never been easy. I've always thought of my father as the only war hero in the family, but I'm starting to realize my mother's work was important too. And she's trusting me to keep this place running, so I want to make her proud."

"Well, if it matters what I think, you're doing a good job."

Anna gives me a grateful, but pained, smile. "Will you still think so if I tell you some of our boys are climbing out of their sickbeds to join the maquis?"

I know this already. Oscar has been teaching boys to fight with sticks in the yard and to pretend they're maquisards robbing collaborators for supplies. The other day he and Daniel stole the truck and drove off with a merry band of boys to join the Resistance. But they were all back by supper because they didn't want to miss another meal. They could've been captured or killed for such a stunt, but there's not much we can do to stop it. *"C'est la guerre."*

She nods and squares her shoulders. "Would you consider taking on more? Watching over the boys' dormitory, leading camping trips, that sort of thing. I know you're already busy with sculpting, and I can't pay as much as you deserve, but—"

"Yes, I'll do it," I say, feeling a little guilty at how little sculpting I've really been doing.

"Sergeant Travert won't mind?"

"Travert doesn't tell me what to do." *Or at least, I don't listen when he does.*

"Well, that's good," Anna says, picking up her pen like she means to get back to work, but then she bites her lower lip. "What's it like with him?"

Years ago, she'd have meant, *What's he like in bed?* Or she'd have meant, *Are you still grieving for Henri? Does it hurt to be married to a different man?*

I don't know what she means now. "It's fine."

Anna looks at me like I'm holding out. "Only fine?"

"He loves me." Travert has never told me he loves me, but he says it with his body when we touch. Personally, I don't trust love—inside me it's been a confusing and slippery emotion, taking on too many forms to recognize. And I've apparently been so starved of it that I've developed feelings for everybody who ever showed a real interest. But whatever it is that I feel for Yves, I enjoy his company, and I'm happy to know he wants more from life than what's in the hills of Auvergne. Sometimes we talk about what we'll do *after the war* if we live to see it. So I shrug and say, "I trust him."

Hearing the word *trust*, she crosses her arms over herself. And there it is, what really came between us, and my heartbreak exposed. All these years, I've told myself I couldn't confide in her because I wanted to protect her, but that was only half of the truth. I've wanted to protect myself *from* her. Until the occupation—even up until her father's arrest—I couldn't be *sure* what side she was on. I'm not even entirely sure I know now.

Oh, she hates the Germans. She wants the liberation of France. And she never said anything in favor of Pétain's backward revolution. She never said anything against Jews or Freemasons or so-called sexual deviants . . . but I never heard her defend them either. It's not fair to blame her for things nobody wants to talk about; it's not like I make defiant speeches in the town square. But I never thought about volunteering to go work for the Nazis. Not once. Not ever. Maybe it's as simple as that. Of course, it's *not* that simple—because my husband actually *does* work for the Nazis, and I just convinced him not to quit. But Travert is risking his life for what's right, and that makes all the difference. "Things are fine with Travert. In fact, they're really good."

At the boys' dormitory they're all talking about the maquisards. Young Daniel excitedly tells me there's been a meeting of the Resistance in Paulhaguet, and that thousands of fighters are coming to the area. Of course, the boys always have as many stories about the Resistance as they do about comic books, so it's easy to discount. But they also have a *verboten* radio, and the BBC broadcast is warning French people to take shelter in anticipation of an Allied bombing. We all know there's going to be an American invasion with a bloody battle fought on French soil. It's just a matter of when.

One afternoon in mid-May, I get a message in the mailbox from Sam to meet him by the rotting old tree house we used to play in when we were kids together. When I finally slip away from my duties at the preventorium, I find him sitting in the branches of a wild cherry tree. The same one where I first kissed Henri.

There was a time when seeing that tree would've sent me to the bottom of a bottle. The edges of grief aren't so sharp now, and I can almost smile at the memory. Almost. Sam jumps down, looking like a real warrior now. His dark skin is weather-beaten. And he's wearing a black beret, a rifle slung over his shoulder, and grenades on his belt.

"Where'd you get those?" I ask.

"A woman commander, if you can believe it. Australian. Parachuted in."

I wince, knowing I shouldn't have asked. Meanwhile, Sam plucks some ripening cherries from the tree and uses his shirt like a basket to hold them. "You should meet her."

"No. I deal only with you."

"And if I get shot?"

I press my lips together, not wanting to admit that possibility.

He gives me some cherries. "We need safe caches of weapons."

I tilt my head. "I can't help you with that."

"Yes you can," he replies. "We're already storing guns at the preventorium."

I almost choke on a cherry, then slug him in the shoulder.

"It wasn't my idea," he protests, holding up his hands. "It was the boys'. Oscar, Daniel, some of the others—they're hiding weapons for us under the floorboards in the solarium of the boys' dormitory. When the nurses are asleep, our night patrols come, we get the weapons, then put them back before morning."

"You're entrusting weapons to kids?"

"Only because the Germans are *killing* kids, Marthe."

I sigh, because he doesn't have to tell me that. Nor does he have to explain that French militia—the leaders of which have sworn allegiance to Hitler—are recruiting boys and girls to be part of their so-called Avant-Garde. Kids are victims and soldiers in this war whether I like it or not. "Just tell me what you want me to do."

"Make sure the boys don't touch the guns unless they need them."

Unless they need them . . .

I grimace. "How long? You can't keep guns in the preventorium forever."

"Hopefully the Americans invade soon and we won't have to. Almost the whole village is for the Resistance now but the mayor. Even the gendarmes are on our side."

Travert's gendarmes, he means, and I feel a flare of pride.

"We have sixty fighters, maybe more. And you . . ."

"I'm not—"

"Oh, put a sock in it. You're part of the club, like it or not." Sam leans against the tree trunk. "Speaking of . . . don't use Madame Simon's old mailbox to pass messages anymore. I kept watch, and I think the mayor saw you. Now that something big is happening, let's not take chances. To get word to me, leave a message under the floorboards at the boys' dormitory, and leave a chalk mark on the floor. I'll do the same."

Something big is happening. After I walk away from Sam, I can't stop thinking about those words.

Especially when, on the twelfth of the month, I hear from Monsieur Kohn. "The OSE is desperate this time," he says, telling me about fifteen Jewish girls they're evacuating from a Catholic convent where they've been hiding. "The Gestapo is planning a raid any day now."

The girls need not only new papers, but also false school and medical records that can get all fifteen admitted to the preventorium. And they need it on two days' notice. "*Fifteen girls.* In two days? It's too much."

"You're their only hope, Marthe. They have nowhere else to go. If you don't do this, they'll be killed."

I stare at Monsieur Kohn, a once-respected soldier who now lives mostly in the woods as an outlaw, hunted like an animal. I don't know where he's getting the strength to go on, but I can't complain to a man like him that my nerves are shot—even if it's true, and it is. "All right, I'll do it."

To protect these Jewish girls, it might be safest to steal the identities of Catholic children. Travert could get me a list of names; he's done it before. In the end, though, I don't want to ask my husband for help, because he'd try to stop me. He'd say it's become too dangerous. But who else will do it if I don't? In my tower room, I spread the passport-sized pictures out under the light and try to think up new identities. Fourteen-year-old Rachel will become Renée. Twelve-year-old Esther will be Édith. Ten-year-old Sarah will become Stéphanie. For the younger girls, to keep it simple, I'll change only their surnames.

What's not simple for me is that these girls can't all be from the same place, or it will trigger suspicion. I make one from French Algiers, where the Americans are now. Another from the Italian border, where things remain confused. I give another girl a British father, because the Nazis bloody well can't cross-check references across the English Channel, can they?

Then it's a matter of using French towns without records or with town hall clerks willing to lie. Sam has been wooing a mademoiselle from Langeac—a sympathetic clerk at the mayor's office—so I make twin sisters from there. The OSE provided me with a few notes on plausible medical conditions, but I need more details. What if the girl I made half-English has a Polish accent? There are a thousand mistakes I can make, especially working this quickly . . . and with so little sleep. Up all night hunched over the table in my tower studio, I pray Anna doesn't see the light on and knock on the locked door. By the time the rooster crows in the pasture, I'm sick with exhaustion. Parched. Hungry. Badly in need of a break.

But it's life and death for these kids, so there's no time to stop.

I make a big show of sneezing, then plead illness to get out of teaching class. I'm convincing because my eyes are bloodshot, running, and blurry. My neck aches. My shoulders throb with fatigue. Even my fingers are stiff. I keep going, and by the time I'm done, I've been awake for more than forty-eight hours.

I ask Travert to take me to Paulhaguet, because it's the easiest way to bypass a Gestapo checkpoint and because I think I'll faint if I try to walk. I've told him I want to visit Madame Pinton. I don't say why, and he doesn't ask. But after the trip, when he takes me back to his house and I nearly fall asleep in a bowl of soup, he figures it out, and the jig is up. "I told you to stop forging. Didn't I forbid it?"

"*Forbid* . . . who are you, the Führer?"

I don't want to argue. I just want to sleep. I have to be back at the castle in the morning. A Haitian nun from a nearby order will bring the girls to the preventorium, and I should be there to make sure nothing goes wrong. So I remind him, "After Bastille Day, you wanted to tell me what life is. Well, let me tell you. It's hard. We lose people we love. Our dreams fall to shit. Then we die. It happens to everyone. But at least we can go down fighting."

He leans against the doorway, shaking his head. "So it's contagious. Whatever madness is in that damned castle that makes people forget good sense, you've caught it."

I suppose I have. On Monday, the nun pulls a rusted, mud-spattered red truck into the drive just before two in the afternoon. Perfect timing, because the village is overrun by parents either checking their children into the preventorium or checking them out. The lines are long, winding into the village, and the hope is that our fifteen Jewish girls will blend in.

I watch from the castle window and tell myself I don't have any reason to worry. The girls are just girls—not the ugly cartoon the newspapers make Jews out to be. I go down to help usher the newcomers into the lazaret for quarantine and get them undressed for examinations and vaccinations. Some will need ultraviolet ray treatment, others will need radiography and radioscopy. Some will need blood tests or dental treatment. None of the fifteen has any condition serious enough to attract special notice.

A few have rosary beads, so I'm guessing they've been taught to fake being Catholic. They've likely also been instructed that no one knows their secret and that they should keep it from everyone, but wanting to make them feel safe, I say, "Hello, girls. I'm Madame Travert. I grew up here, so I know it may seem a little lonely at first, but in a few weeks you're going to get to play outside with all the other children. Even better, you'll get to go into the castle, where you'll get special slippers and can pretend to be little princesses . . ."

Rachel, the eldest, meets my eyes and manages a wobbly smile. She's terrified, but I think maybe she *does* know I'm a friend. Or that I will be.

The examinations go quickly. I hold my breath the whole time, wondering if Dr. Anglade's replacement will realize that while some of the girls really *are* so malnourished as to belong here, some aren't. Fortunately, my forgeries are excellent, and he seems happy to accept the girls and their paperwork.

The nurses get them into bed and bring bowls of broth, and I breathe a sigh of relief to think that it's been a perfectly ordinary admissions day. I almost float back to the castle, ready to collapse in triumph and exhaustion, but as I pass the library, I catch a glimpse of Madame Xavier on a telephone call.

"I recognized a Jewish girl from another town," she's saying. I freeze, peering through the crack of the partially opened door to see her talking into the receiver. "She arrived with about a dozen others from a convent. I called the local gendarmerie, but they say they can't come till tomorrow."

You bitch.

"Thank you, Obersturmführer," she continues. "I won't say anything to anyone. Just get here soon."

You hateful, rancid bitch. As she hangs up the phone, I want to storm into the library, grab Faustine Xavier by her bun, and break her neck.

Unfortunately, there isn't time. The Gestapo usually prefers dawn raids, but Wolff isn't a man to wait. If he's coming from Brioude, it will take him no more than twenty-five minutes, and then, *my God, what will he do?*

FIFTY-EIGHT

ADRIENNE
The Prison of Olmütz
Austria
December 1795

IT WAS THE SAME EVERY DAY IN THIS PRISON, THIS AUSTRIAN BAS-tille. My daughters were permitted to come to us each morning at eight o'clock for a breakfast of bitter coffee or weak chocolate. At noon, the Prussian guards delivered food upon dirtied plates swarmed by flies. A thin soup, braised meat of indeterminate animal, and a slop of vegetables, usually garnished with little bits of tobacco and ash from someone's pipe. Even the most bloodthirsty French Jacobin jailer had more pride than to abuse cuisine this way!

We were obliged to scoop up food with filthy hands and wash it down with our ration of Hungarian wine. "Not the best vintage," Gilbert observed. "But more healthful than water."

After our meals, he read to us, delighting Virginie by imitating voices like a stage actor. Alas, our little joys were interrupted by the screams of prisoners being lashed in the courtyard. These Prussians were as cruel as Jacobins were arbitrary and capricious. Yet they seemed to take to the task of tormenting prisoners with rigid exactness.

With jingling keys, a round guardsman would fetch the girls back to their cage in the evening. During these transfers, seemingly every guard in the compound gathered to watch, a great show being made of checking locks and chains, my girls being obliged to pass under crossed sabers to prevent their escape. This ludicrous show of force was too much. Every day, Virginie would flush with indignant anger. Anastasie, however, be-gan to make faces at the guards, sometimes with the haughty bearing of a Noailles and sometimes in silly mockery.

"They bear up so well," Lafayette whispered.

I worried imprisonment would become more difficult for them over time. How had my husband endured this, alone, for so long? Despite the misery of our conditions, I found myself content to see my husband eat, to see his health improve, to know our presence was a balm. I felt a guilty happiness too, to have him to myself.

We had years of conversation to catch up on, and I told him everything I had done in his absence. How gratifying to know he approved of my decisions with pleasure and pride. And sometimes a little amazement. "What noble imprudence to be the only woman in France endangered by the name she bore, but who always refused to change it! You could have divorced me." I was overpaid by his tender words, but he wasn't finished, his eyes now lowered in humility. "I have always known I loved and needed you, Adrienne, but did not always appreciate how *incomparable* a woman I had the good fortune to marry."

I gave him a melting smile, feeling that it was God who had given us to each other, not fickle fortune, but how blessed we were for it. That night, nestled in the crook of his arm upon a fetid bed, I mused, "What a novelty it is to wake up with you each morning without having to watch you dash off on your horse to save someone's life—I don't know that we've had so many uninterrupted hours together since the king made you my prisoner . . ."

A sliver of moonlight through prison bars allowed me to see him grin. "That was a far more pleasant confinement than this."

"Yes, but perhaps if we close our eyes, we can remember the softness of our feather bed."

"The softness of the bed left less impression upon me than the softness of the girl upon it," he said, stroking my hair. "I counted myself so fortunate to have a feminine little wife. I loved the silk of your lips and the tenderness of your gaze. I did not yet know your gentleness is a velvet drape over steel . . ."

"Is this a compliment, sir, or a reproach?"

He kissed me. "The highest compliment, but a reproach to me every day I do not find the firmness in my own character to command the guards to eject you from this terrible place."

"It is not so terrible," I said.

He snorted, twining his fingers with mine. "Look how swollen your hands are. It will get worse with the vapors rising from the moat of sewage outside."

"Gilbert, I am happier with you in a prison than I could be anywhere in the world without you."

I'm uncertain he believed me; nevertheless, it was true. And I did not yet despair of regaining our freedom. Gilbert was allowed no contact with the outside world, but the same restriction did not apply to me. I obtained with bribery some paper and ink. I was forbidden to write our son in America because our captors were uneasy about news of Lafayette reaching the United States. I was warned not to reveal the conditions of our imprisonment or to write anything that might embarrass them. Yet, I hoped my sharp-eyed friends would divine enough from what I did not say to shout it to the world.

DESPITE THE WINTER'S FROST, I BURNED WITH FEVER. "*MORBUS sanguinis*," said the physician, where I lay plagued with headaches and swollen extremities.

"Blood infection," Gilbert translated from Latin, as it was the language he shared in common with the doctor. "He wants to send you to Vienna for treatment."

"No. If I go, I will never see you again."

Gilbert pressed a cloth to my brow. "That is your fever talking."

My daughters sat near to the stove, warming their hands, both frowning. "We will stay with Papa whilst you are gone," Anastasie insisted. "You need not worry. I will do exactly as you would in my place."

I believed my courageous girl. She understood how necessary our presence had been to saving her father's life. Still, the thought of being separated again was too terrifying. I did not realize I said this aloud until Gilbert thumped the wooden table in frustration. "You may well be separated from us by the grave if you do not go. Petition the emperor." I started to shake my head, but he resorted to his general's bark. "Obey me, Adrienne. As my wife it is your duty."

He had seldom commanded me in anything—and had told the bishop of Paris that I was not his subject. I nearly rebelled, but remembering it was a mutiny of his soldiers that brought us all to this place, I relented, writing my petition to the emperor even though I suspected his reply would be precisely what it was: *You will be allowed to go to Vienna for treatment, madame, but if you leave the prison, you will not be permitted to return.*

"Accept at once," said Gilbert.

My daughters understood why I did not, but I alone seemed to understand the triumph when the emperor demanded a written answer. "He wants evidence," I said with the greatest satisfaction. "No monarch needs evidence of anything unless he fears the judgment of humanity. He regrets letting us join you. The censorious eyes of the world are now upon him, and the only way he can justify keeping you here is if we abandon you."

Lafayette seemed not to care, shaking his louse-ridden head as if he thought the fever was robbing me of good sense. "I cannot stand by and watch you expose your life to a struggle with a tyrant."

"Why not?" I asked softly. "You asked it of me every day of our marriage since you first stole off to America. Day after day, year after year, I was obliged to swallow my fears whilst you risked life and limb. Now you will simply have to do the same."

My husband flung his hands up. *"Mon Dieu,* Adrienne, you are not a soldier, and it is not the cause of humanity at stake. It is only me."

"You're mistaken. Glory is a bittersweet wreath of both flowers and thorns. Your name, your house, your wife, your story—we are all now inextricably woven together with the cause of humanity. Your officers rode across the border with you for this reason; some of them are rotting in this prison too. That is to say nothing of simple patriots who tried to help you escape. Many people who are not soldiers have lost their lives for our causes. I cannot dishonor these sacrifices."

"Adrienne," he groaned, hiding his face in his hands. "How much guilt do you think I can bear?"

I stroked his beard. "Have faith in me, my dear heart . . ."

All I had to do was endure.

Already my spirits were bolstered knowing I had, in the eyes of the emperor, become a troublesome woman and a thorn in his royal side. *Your terms can never be acceptable to me*, I replied. *I remember how, when my husband and I were both near death—I because of Robespierre's tyranny and Lafayette because of the torments of his captivity—I was neither able to hear news of him nor to send word that his children and I were still alive. I will not willingly expose myself to the horrors of another such separation.*

To bear up under a red prickly rash, I remembered the patience of my dear martyred mother. I had no paper, but the wide margins of a book became my parchment as I scratched out her biography with a toothpick dipped in ink, for my pen had been seized. I wanted this keepsake, these memories, for my children.

Eventually, though, my hands became too swollen to write. My arms too heavy to lift. When my legs pained me too much to sit upon the wooden bench, I requested to purchase an armchair to ease my discomfort. When this was denied, I felt more satisfaction. "How frightened the emperor is of a little suffering woman that he denies me the comforts of a *chair*. He is trying to force me out; he is testing my resolve."

"And you are testing mine," Gilbert growled.

Why was it, I wondered in my fevered state, that every damsel sighs in gratitude to be rescued by a knight, but the knight himself hates to find his fate in the hands of the damsel?

Well, he would simply have to endure it too.

FIFTY-NINE

MARTHE
Chavaniac-Lafayette
May 15, 1944

IMAGINING THAT GESTAPO OFFICERS WILL SOON SEARCH THE PRE-ventorium building by building, room by room—I'm grateful that Gabriella, Josephine, and Daniel are all safe in the woods, camped with their scout troops not far from where maquisards train.

But now I have the fifteen Jewish girls from the convent to think of. If I can get them in the *camion*, I'll drive south like a bat out of hell, but then I find that the old truck is out of petrol again.

Merde, merde, merde!

For a crazed moment I think about stealing a car from the village or trying to siphon its fuel. Any solution I think of takes time I don't have, or involves people I'm not sure I can trust. Five minutes have already passed since the phone call to the authorities. I might have only twenty minutes more to hide these kids.

An imperfect, panicked solution comes to me, and I run all the way to the girls' lazaret, bursting in with a clipboard. "The doctor is asking for the follow-up examinations of a few of the girls," I tell the nurse, and before she can question me, I pretend to read off the fifteen names, trying to hurry the Jewish girls out of bed and into their shoes without creating a panic. When they're dressed, I pick up the littlest, and the others follow me like ducklings.

I don't take them to the examination room, though. Instead, I violate every rule about keeping newcomers in isolation, and sneak them into the side entrance of the mostly empty castle. "Let's be quiet as we pass the kitchen . . ."

Fortunately the cook's back is to us as she tends the hearth, and I usher the girls quickly past, leading them to the oldest part of the castle, with its trapdoors and hidden passages. How many people left on staff know about them?

The baroness knows, but she's gone. Madame Simon is gone too. Madame LeVerrier would keep quiet. But I'm the idiot who told Anna about them, and now I'm having to bet my life that she won't tell the Gestapo. As I lead these fugitive girls into the dank passages carved between the walls, I think they might be safe here even *if* the Gestapo searches building by building and room by room. But I don't want to chance it.

Taking a flashlight from where it hangs on the wall, I turn off the electric lights and plunge us all into darkness. "Let's play follow-the-leader and see how quiet we can be."

"The Nazis are coming, aren't they?" Rachel asks, having been through too much to believe it's a game.

Reluctantly, I nod. "But they won't know to look here." *Probably.* Germans are horrifically thorough. "And we're going to be gone before they know it." We're not trapped, after all. These aren't just passages. They're *tunnels*. One leads to where Adrienne Lafayette used to read the Bible to the village women when Catholic services were banned. If I can get the girls away from the castle, without anyone seeing—if I can get them into the woods and upstream . . .

"*Allez allez allez!*" I say to hurry them.

As the girls follow, I hear their panicked breaths. They're holding each other's hands, making a human chain, and I lead them through the dark using the stone wall as my guide. I remember the old stories we used to scare one another with, about getting trapped in the tunnels and turning to a pile of bones, and my breath quickens too.

Eventually, we come to a door. It's meant to keep people out, not to keep people in, so there's got to be a key here somewhere. We start searching—looking for loose stones it might be hidden behind. Am I going to have to go back and search Anna's desk in the library?

For Chrissakes, I have no idea what I'm doing. I wanted to be an artist, not a child rescuer. Did I think I was brave enough and smart enough just because I live in a hero's castle?

I'm no Lafayette.

I blow out a breath, asking myself what he'd do. Probably something reckless. Adrienne was the clearheaded one. When the soldiers came to arrest her, she hid the valuables and sent the kids fleeing into the woods. But there wasn't a door in her way. I can't find the key, and time is running out. Could the Gestapo be pulling trucks into the drive already? They might even be in the castle, their jackboots thundering on the parquet wood floor. On the other side of these stone walls, they might be throwing doors open, smashing valuables, interrogating Anna and everyone else in the house . . .

I've endangered everyone.

Are they going to be punished for what I've done? I remember Travert's warning as the walls close in on me. And I press my forehead to the cool stone to fend off panic. Madame Beatrice used to say there are voices in the stones and that we can hear them if we listen. I strain to hear them now. Adrienne. Beatrice. The baroness, Madame Simon, Madame LeVerrier, and every other person who made themself a part of this place.

One of them needs to tell me what to do!

Damn it! I kick the door twice in a fury of frustration, feeling as if I could batter it down, and that's when something metallic clinks to the stone floor. The key must've been resting on the wooden door ledge. I'm so giddy with relief I nearly laugh, though we're not out of trouble yet. I've wasted so much time, the girls will have almost no head start. *Unless I give them one . . .*

Even as I unlock the door, I know I can't go with them. I know, because I remember that at every opportunity Adrienne Lafayette risked herself so others could get away. And she had more to lose than I do . . .

"When you get to the stream," I tell the girls, "follow it east. In a few miles, you're going to stumble on a campsite with a couple hundred Lafayette kids. Find a girl named Josephine Beaufort. You can trust her. Tell her to take you deeper into the woods to Mandaix, where we saw the maquisards training. They'll know what to do."

With that, I kiss each of their heads like a sacrament, knowing that beyond this door is a different kind of tunnel. One that's older, abandoned, and primordial. They'll have to run through cobwebs and deeper darkness, pinching their noses against the ammonia scent of bat droppings and dead rodents, but then mottled daylight will break through where the tunnel lets out, and they'll be free.

Even if I can never be . . .

SIXTY

ADRIENNE
The Prison of Olmütz
July 1797

ANASTASIE USED HER THUMBNAIL TO DRAW A PORTRAIT OF THE cruelest guard and flirted with the friendly ones, which vexed her father. "Do not draw their attentions," Gilbert said, swishing away flies. "You are too beautiful to put yourself at their mercy."

"Perhaps my beauty puts them at *my* mercy," Anastasie argued. "The guard who passes beneath our window every night has a hungry look. I teased I would give him our ration if he smuggled messages, and he did not flinch."

It amused me to see Gilbert fuss and fume at a daughter who was so like him in daring and ingenuity. In the weeks that followed, she not only charmed guards into sneaking letters, she also transformed herself into a veritable cobbler, making new shoes out of leather strips she finagled off a young guardsman. She took dictation using my little toothpick and ink. And due to her efforts, we soon had news from the outside.

"We are being talked about everywhere!" our eldest cried. "In America they clamor for our release, and in the English Parliament ministers have been moved to tears. Someone has even written a play called *The Prisoner of Olmütz*."

I smiled to think we had not been forgotten! We'd also learned a French Revolutionary army was marching across the Alps toward Austria. The emperor was not so secure in his power now, was he? Did I dare hope the Republic of France had come to free my husband—who was rotting in jail for having started the Revolution in the first place? I had been too long in this prison to know whether France was now led by good or wicked men. Yet I promised my family, "It will not be long now until we are free."

I believed this, even if our freedom would come too late for me. My blood infection had lately left my arms red and raw, exposed by peeling skin. I could no longer close my hands, and my entire nervous system was afflicted by spasms. Yet in some perverse way I welcomed the pain as a manner of expiation, and knew that the sharper my suffering, the better my weapon. For above all, the emperor did not want me to die in his prison . . .

Not with public sentiment running in our favor on both sides of the ocean. Americans finally bestirred themselves to push for our release. French persons too, including friends and my surviving family. Our most unexpected champion was a young military commander named Napoléon Bonaparte, who was sent by the Directoire to negotiate our release.

One morning, my husband and the loyal officers who had been arrested with him were suddenly reunited in our cell. To lay eyes upon one another for the first time after such long confinement was a sweet torment, and the men burst into tears to see how wretched they had become. They were told, "You may be set at liberty, under the condition that Lafayette promises never again to set foot in Austria."

But for me, my husband would have refused this offer. For five years he had been caged unjustly, and his honor should not allow him to be treated as if he had committed a crime. However, for once in his life, Lafayette seemed ready to compromise.

Yet I did not want him to give an inch. We were a headache the emperor did not need. This was still my battle with the tyrant—one I meant to win. Like all despots, the emperor had thought to break us. Because of who we were, because of the causes to which we had devoted our lives, it would matter a great deal *how* we left this jail—dead or alive.

The next offer came. We could be free if we would blame our illtreatment upon the lowest-ranked guards and absolve the emperor of guilt. This too we refused. The emperor finally negotiated our release directly with Bonaparte, who took matters out of our hands. In mid-September, the doors of our prison swung open. We were to be taken directly to Hamburg, then handed over to the American consul.

Gilbert and I held each other upright, blinking against the sunlight, which had never seemed so bright. Scattered groups of curious onlookers lined the roads, silently watching us go. At the frontier, noisier crowds awaited. Fayettists cheering our carriage, calling out, *"Vive Lafayette!"*

What a glorious sound.

We stopped briefly at an inn. I had to be carried inside for food and water, but our entire party was giddy. My daughters claimed to have forgotten how to use knives and forks after having so long been forced to eat with their hands. Next we went to the American consulate, which was so crowded with well-wishers, they had to be held back. My husband's speech faltered, both because he was overcome and because after five years in captivity, his English was a little forgotten.

Everyone wanted to shake his hand, to bring him news, curry favor. Various political factions urged him to champion them. In the group of men who encircled us, I saw Mr. Morris, my savior and sometime nemesis. With customary dryness, he explained that Monroe had been recalled by the president and that tensions between France and the United States were quite high. Before I could think what this might mean for us, I was approached by a young man who dropped to his knees in worshipful ecstasy.

"Thou art the goddess of liberty," he said, trying to kiss the hem of my skirt.

I snatched it away, admonishing, "I am no goddess."

Then I saw that I had wounded this admirer, who was sincere. So I invited him to sit beside me in the hopes of smoothing his feelings, and Gilbert bent to whisper, "Savor your victory, my love."

It did feel like victory, never more than when we were reunited with our son, who now, at nearly eighteen years old, had his father's auburn hair and big brown eyes like mine. What happy thanksgiving to have Georges safe in my arms again. How right I had been to send him to America! He had returned at the first news of our release, gone straight to Chavaniac, and now presented the swords he'd dug up from the earth where I'd buried them in safekeeping. The blade on the American sword had rusted away, but Gilbert thought to combine them into one sword, using the blade made of iron taken from the Bastille with the golden hilt of the American masterpiece.

Lafayette recovered his strength quickly; for him, freedom itself was nourishment. As for me, my legs were a mass of open sores. He and Georges had to carry me from bed to couch. They had to feed me soft bites of food because my teeth ached, and I could barely keep down what I ate. And the doctors said the marks of my captivity would last the rest of my life.

I counted it a fair price for what I'd gained.

I had freed my family by force of will. Not only my family, but those who had been arrested for our sake. I had done it without sacrificing any principle or doing violence. It was not the sort of victory for which people built stone monuments, but I hoped it might still, someday, be remembered.

SIXTY-ONE

MARTHE
Chavaniac-Lafayette
May 15, 1944

"MARTHE," ANNA SAYS, AGOG AT MY DISHEVELED APPEARANCE. "What's happened to you?"

I've lied to her so many times before, but I can't do it now. "The Gestapo is coming."

On the stairway, where I've caught her, she grips the rail and pales. *"What?"*

I already think I hear the screech of tires at the gate. I don't want her to be terrified that they've come for her, so I quickly explain, "I overheard Madame Xavier reporting Jewish children at the preventorium."

Anna blinks. "That's absurd."

I shake my head. "It's not."

"Are you telling me—" Anna grasps the situation quickly. "How do you know we have Jewish children here?"

I don't answer. I don't need to. In this moment I can't disguise a single thing.

"My God, Marthe. How could you do this?"

"Someone had to!"

"You kept it secret—even from me?"

"I was trying to protect you." That's not the whole of it, though, and I see from the pain in her eyes that she understands the ugliest and most painful truth. That I didn't trust her. That I *couldn't* trust her.

"What did you think, Marthe—that I'd turn over children?"

The question cracks my heart. "Honestly, I don't know *what* you'll do."

But I'm about to find out, because the Gestapo are hammering at the door. We peek out the curtains to see them below with shepherd dogs at the end of taut leashes. Anna and I go down together as Obersturmführer Wolff bursts into the entryway with three of his agents, guns at the ready. "Hands up! Hands up!"

While their dogs bark, the Gestapo lines up nurses and doctors against the wall, where my sketches of Adrienne Lafayette look on. Madame LeVerrier yelps when a Gestapo officer forces her arthritic arms over her head. And Anna draws herself up to her full height, gloriously beautiful in anger. "Gentlemen! I demand to know the meaning of this."

Wolff's lips quirk, and he comes close enough to kiss her. "My apologies, Countess, did I neglect to mention this is a raid?" He reaches for her cheek, but she flinches. Then he pulls out handcuffs to bind her. "You're all under arrest. We'll sort out the guilty and innocent later."

It's how they protect informants—they arrest everyone. Children, their doctors, their caretakers. As they start handcuffing everyone I know—people I care about—my stomach roils. Old Madame LeVerrier won't survive a camp, and I can't let everyone suffer for what I did. There has to be some other way . . . but I'm too tired to think of it. Hands laced behind my head, I shout, "I'm the only guilty one! I can tell you everything you want to know."

Wolff turns from Anna and grabs my collar. "You?"

I stare into those icy eyes and my teeth begin to chatter.

"Where are the Jewish girls?" he asks, shaking me.

"I'll show you if you let everyone else go. I brought the Jewish girls here, no one else."

My words have everyone gasping. I don't dare look at my colleagues. I don't know if they'll understand or be furious. At first, Wolff doesn't even seem to believe me. I'm the wife of a gendarme, after all. It's only after I confess that the girls came from a convent that Wolff's eyes take on the gleam of a predator who has scented prey.

I tell him, "When I overheard Madame Xavier call you, I knew I'd made a terrible mistake bringing them here."

Another gasp echoes as every eye turns to Faustine Xavier—and she is visibly shaken to be exposed. *You didn't think you'd get away with it, did you?* Whatever happens to me now, at least I'll have the satisfaction of everyone knowing what a poisonous collaborator she is.

She reddens, sputtering, then admits everything. "You made a terrible mistake, indeed, Madame Travert. Yes, it's true, I made the call. I wouldn't want the authorities to think any of us at the castle harbor criminals. I'm sure Madame Travert is exactly right, that she took this upon herself and no one else was involved."

Wolff shakes me again. "Where are they?"

I clench my chattering teeth. "First, promise—"

"You'll find them in the girls' lazaret," Faustine interrupts with a lift of her chin.

"Wait," I say, to buy more time. "Let someone go to the records room. You can compare the list against whoever you're looking for, so that you don't frighten the rest of the children."

Anna is nodding, but Faustine says, "There's no need. The lazaret is just a few minutes' walk. I can point out the girls who came together if Madame Travert refuses."

Wolff nods, then yanks my arms back. Handcuffs bite into my wrists. He drags me to the door—but not before I see Madame LeVerrier spit in Faustine Xavier's face.

I'll break if I look at Anna, so I stare straight ahead as the Gestapo officer frog-marches me out. He grabs the back of my neck, fingers digging hard, pistol jabbing the small of my back, propelling me out onto the drive, where I'm actually a little surprised not to see more Gestapo agents.

They must not have realized how big the castle really is and how difficult it can be to keep children under control. Or maybe these are all the men Wolff could round up on short notice. They must have called the gendarmerie to help, because Travert is now here. As he gets out of his car, our eyes lock, and he blanches. I know what he's thinking. He warned me. He starts to say, "My wife—"

A Gestapo officer barks something at him in German and shoves Travert back, threatening him. *It's all right*, I try to say with a nearly imperceptible shake of my head. *There's nothing you can do.*

But Travert shouts, "Where are you taking her?"

"If you wish to appeal her arrest, do it in Brioude," Wolff says as his officers force Travert back into his patrol car at gunpoint. Travert looks furious and hopeless all at once, and I'm sorrier than I could've imagined to know this is the last look I'll ever see on his surly face. Because, of course, I'll never be taken to Brioude alive.

I watch Yves drive off in a cloud of dust.

If you're caught, you'd be on your own . . .

I'll go down alone, and it's better that way. By now, the girls are likely out of the tunnels. I can almost see them, in my mind's eye, helping one another hop from stone to stone in crossing the stream. It's a pretty thought . . .

When we crash into the lazaret, there are only three girls present, and Wolff barks at Madame Xavier, "You said at least a dozen Israelites?"

The nurse on duty, confused, looks to me, then to the Gestapo officers. Before she can lie or betray me, I say, "These girls aren't Israelites. I hid the Jewish girls away. You should have listened when I said I'd show you."

A sudden blow to the cheek knocks me back, and because my hands are handcuffed, I lose balance, crashing into a medical tray, syringes and medical equipment scattering to the floor. It takes me a minute to realize that Wolff has hit me, and now his face is in mine. "Where are the Jews?"

"At the boys' dormitory." I choke out the lie. "Not far."

I think Wolff realizes he's being drawn away from his quarry. Nevertheless, we take a short ride to the boys' dormitory, and he marches the length of the empty open-air solarium in fury, boots thumping on the loose floorboards. "You think you're clever, do you?"

"I don't know about *clever*," I say, because I know I'm not going to survive what comes next, and that's freeing in a way. "But I did make you look like a *nitwit*, and that's good enough for me."

It's dusk now. The girls have probably found the campsite. Gestapo officers won't risk going into maquisard-infested forests after dark. He seems to know what I'm thinking as he pushes me down the stairs, into the empty yard where the shepherd dogs are still barking. "We'll hunt them down eventually."

"Have you ever wondered if maybe you picked on people your own size, you wouldn't be losing the war? All the man-hours you've wasted hunting down kids . . ."

His smile glints like a blade, but he pulls a baton from his boot, and the memory of that baton kills my bravado.

"I don't enjoy this, Madame Travert. These tedious roundups. Forcing children into trucks and trains." For a split second, I dare to hope for a sliver of humanity, but then he says, "It would be easier to shoot them. Of course, I've always hated the ugliness of shooting a beautiful woman, though. It's impersonal. Nothing intimate about it." He draws closer, and I shudder. "I once killed a woman by drowning her in a lake. She looked like an angel as she sank and her hair fanned out in the water. Just *beautiful*. But there's no lake here . . ."

I want to think of a smart remark but my mouth is bone-dry. I want to be brave and defiant, but I can smell my own fear-sweat. I'm so frightened that I feel almost outside of myself, watching it all from a distance.

"Perhaps your husband is not the upright policeman we supposed. Did he involve you in this? Perhaps you did it to please him. A wife must obey . . ."

He's holding out false hope, and my voice, when I find it, is no more than a scrape. "Travert knows nothing."

The baton blow hits me in the ribs, knocking the wind out of me. I bend at the waist, and while I'm gasping for breath, he pokes at the sore spot. "Why did you do it?"

I'm so scared I can sputter only a tearful, terrified laugh. *"Why not?"*

He has no idea why that's funny, and grabs my hair. "Are you a secret Jew?"

I laugh harder. I can't help it, even though it shoots pain through my abused ribs. The truth is, I don't know.

I don't know who my father was, I don't know who my mother was, I don't know if they were rich or poor, if they had a noble title, or if they were of peasant stock. I don't know if my parents were French or German or Catholic or Protestant or Jewish. And I'll die without knowing . . .

"It doesn't matter," I choke out.

We're all equally human. All deserving of compassion and justice. All capable of love and courage . . .

He hits me in the same spot, and I crumple to the ground, where little boys in shorts were doing jumping jacks and calisthenics only yesterday. As Wolff stands over me, I know he's going to beat my brains out, and I almost wish he'd just get it over with, but he pauses to say, "What a waste. To throw away your life for vermin—for nothing that matters."

I'm in too much pain to speak, but I want to tell him that he's wrong. It matters. Even if we lose this war, even if the Reich lasts a thousand years, then a thousand years from now, someone will need to know that we stood up against the darkest forces of humanity. And that we did it here at Chavaniac, just like those who came before us.

It'll make them stronger to know it.

It'll make it easier for them to rise up again if our ideals survive us . . .

Wolff hits me again, and this time something cracks. I can't scream or even draw a breath without agony. The next blow hammers my head by my ear. Things go bright, then black, and when I come back to myself, my thoughts are confused. Disordered. A high-pitched wail is screeching through my brain.

Nearly blinded by my own blood, I think I'm hallucinating moving tires and boots on the ground. Dogs barking at the woods, barking at the road. I drag my head from the dirt, and through red-hued tears, I see a blurry police car. *Mon Dieu, is it Yves?*

Has that idiot come back to see me murdered?

The tires screech, and I see my husband leaning out the window, his pistol leveled as shots ring out. One of the Gestapo officers falls backward, slumping next to the van. It's a moment before I realize he's been shot. I hear shouting, and my eyes are caked with blood and dust, but I catch a glimpse of Yves scrambling out of the car to take cover, gun drawn.

Wolff drops his baton in the dirt and yanks his pistol from its holster, his draw lightning-fast.

A moment later, Travert drops, falls backward, clutching his chest, his mouth open in silent agony and his legs splayed. *"Yves!"* I twist, trying to pull myself up, trying to crawl to him on my belly in the dirt. I call his name again and again as he writhes, red blood flowing from his stained uniform out over his fingers.

Then my screams are silenced by the *rat-tat-tat* of submachine-gun fire cutting through the air from the direction of the solarium. I turn in time to see Wolff's cap fly off his head. Then his face explodes in a gory crimson spray. Everything goes quiet. Everything but the dogs and Travert's groaning. I am bloody and disoriented, but through the blur of my tears, I'm sure I see boys in scout uniforms. Young Daniel and Oscar on the solarium porch with submachine guns on their shoulders, the pried-up floorboards scattered, and maquisards melting out of the woods to help us.

SIXTY-TWO

BEATRICE
Chavaniac
November 1918

THE WAR WAS OVER.

My dearest, Max wrote.

> *I'll never be able to paint a picture of the ecstatic joy of our soldiers,*
> *of the cheers of ragged civilians as we came to liberate them. Never*
> *mind the rubble, the fly-bedeviled corpses, the rotting horses, the*
> *smoke from still-smoldering fires—there has never been any place*
> *I've been happier to be, save in your arms. Soon I will be free to come*
> *to you; that is my one constant thought.*

It was my one constant thought too, and I was equal parts eager and anxious. Everyone around me was jubilant. I too felt palpable joy. Relief at an end to the carnage. Pride in victory for my country and cause. Hope we'd all have a part in shaping a better future.

Still, I felt sadness too. Particularly for Emily, whose husband had been in a near-fatal crash. One that broke his ribs, his collarbone, and pierced his lung. She'd gone straightaway to his hospital in Bordeaux, praising God he was alive, but with such injuries—and an operation performed without the benefit of chloroform—the recovery would be difficult, and who could guess if the baron might ever be himself again?

In some ways, I didn't know if *Emily* would ever be herself again. She was done with war. Wanted nothing but private life now, with her husband and daughter. So I dared not share my petty and private grief to know that with the war over . . . I would never again do such important work. In a world where men returned to their usual positions of authority in the workplace and in home life, I would never again be seen as someone who could be useful to her country.

And I feared that I would never again be so much *myself.*

It was a winter day when Max was finally released from his military duties, the weather crisp, clear, and cold. I'd had no warning of his visit to Chavaniac, and startled to see him stride through the gate past a white-clad nurse and a tall stack of Red Cross crates, to find me kneeling in the yard, tying the bootlaces of a little rogue who had lately been pestering the *doctoresse* to play with her bag of instruments. A nearby rooster crowed at my cavalier's approach, then flapped its wings when Max wordlessly pulled me to my feet and into his embrace. He didn't say my name. He didn't mutter platitudes. He just held me, squeezing so tight I could scarcely breathe. We stood that way for such a long time, just holding each other and breathing in the healing pine-scented air, until I finally took Max's face in my hands and whispered a tearful, "Is the war over?"

He nodded, eyes shining, as if he too marveled that we'd both survived it all somehow. "For me it is. One of my superiors suggested I might be part of a force to occupy Germany for the next two years; but I'd have shot myself in the leg before I'd let them keep me away from you another hour."

I wanted desperately to kiss him, but in nursing apron and cloth forager cap, I was in no state for romance, and we had an audience. When the little gap-toothed boy whose bootlaces I'd been tying tugged at my sleeve, I disentangled myself from Max, who stooped down to eye level with the boy and asked, "Who might this be?"

"Henri Pinton," I said, ruffling the boy's hair. "Son of a fallen hero. His mother is too ill to care for him . . . and I suspect when she is better, she won't have the money to see to his education, so we've taken him in."

"Can I try on your cap, monsieur?" Henri asked.

Max surrendered his captain's visor to the boy without a hint of regret. "Keep it. I've no intention of wearing it again."

Then he stood and surveyed Lafayette's domain—the castle, the pastoral grounds where the children were playing, the ambulance, and the improvised cantina on crates we'd made to entertain American dough-boys. All that of which I was so proud . . .

"I thought you said the castle was white?"

I smiled. "It was. But as it turns out, white walls are devilishly expensive and time-consuming to maintain. And now that the years are taking their toll on my own facade, I feel happier with my decision to remove the plaster and let these stones reveal themselves *au naturel*."

He laughed, bringing my hand to his lips. "Madame, both you and your castle are magnificent *au naturel* . . . Now, tell me, where is our little cherub?"

I smiled tenderly, shielding my eyes from the sun. "I'm not sure *where* Marthe is just this moment . . ."

"She's not with the other children?"

"She's an odd duckling. There are days she prefers her own company."

"I know where she is," said our gap-toothed interloper, leading us to a nearby covered passage where the pigtailed terror was watching frogs hop about.

"Marthe!" I called to her. "There's someone I'd like you to meet."

She let Max pluck her right up into his arms.

One of the doughboys was taking pictures to send back home, and just then he snapped one of the three of us together; I asked him if he would be kind enough to take another and send it to me. I knew we should both like to have it. And all this attention put the little girl in a fine, cooperative mood.

She let Max carry her on a tour of the castle. Only once Marthe was asleep, thumb in her mouth and golden curls damp on her brow, did I pry her from his arms and give her over to Marie-Louise. Then we continued on to the museum room, where I showed him our treasures.

"Are the rumors true, Beatrice, that you're soon to be knighted?"

I grinned with a warm rush of pleasure, for I was soon to be awarded the Legion of Honor—the highest civil merit in France. Whatever else I had ever been, I would now also be a chevalier of that order, a rank and title not conferred by birth, but earned, and by a woman at that!

"Congratulations, darling girl." Max took me into his arms. "I know how much this must mean to you."

"I shall try not to let it go to my head."

"I suspect you're already planning occasions to which you might wear your decoration."

"I've been wondering if it can be worn as a hatpin!" Then, with a laugh, I stole away with him up the tower staircase to my chambers, where we might have true privacy.

It was there, beneath the chandelier in the turret, that he kissed me with an air of sanctity. "Do you know that I'd marry you right here, right now, if I could?"

If I could . . .

There was still, of course, the little matter of my divorce, a thing Max wished to dispense with straightaway. "I'm taking you home to New York, to your boys. I've booked passage for us on a steamer from Bordeaux, and we can leave in the morning."

My head spun with pleasure at the idea and distress at the suddenness of it. "In the morning? I can't just leave on a whim . . ."

"Oh, don't fret about so much as packing a bag. I'll buy you anything you need and send later for the rest."

"It isn't that—I meant I couldn't possibly leave France while Emily sits vigil at her husband's bedside. And not while there's still so much to do here at Chavaniac."

"There will always be more to do here, *ma chère*, but you have people to do it. The one place you are indispensable is in my arms, and if I've learned anything slogging through mud and hails of bullets, it's not to waste a single moment."

I understood the sentiment. More than ever, since the recurrence of my illness.

These weren't wasted moments at Chavaniac, though. Now that the guns had stopped booming, there was the peace to attend to. The rebuilding of the world. It couldn't wait. I was still part of that fight . . .

My cavalier tried to pull me into another kiss, but a heaviness descended in my limbs. "Max, the operations you've seen here are only a fraction of what I'm responsible for. We're beginning a preventorium to treat tuberculosis, and there's the Paris office too. I'm needed awhile longer, if only to set things on the right track."

Max rubbed at the back of his neck. "How long—a week—a month?"

"I don't know."

"A few months?"

He was trying to be reasonable. He *was* being reasonable. So why did I prickle with frustration? "I didn't expect you today, and while it's a lovely surprise, I . . . well, as I said, I didn't expect you."

Max sat on the edge of the bed, hands clasped. "You're right. I beg your pardon. Like a brute, I've invaded your fortress intent on carrying you off."

"You're just eager to start a new life," I said, caressing his cheek.

He took my hands. "Yes. As soon as possible, I want you to become Mrs. Maxime Furlaud."

Mrs. Maxime Furlaud. It should've made me delirious with happiness to hear it spoken aloud. But it would be another name that wasn't my own. Another role to play in a production not of my own direction.

What was wrong with me? I loved Max. I admired him. He'd be good to me and my children, patient and kind. Still, I had already failed at being a wife twice before . . .

As a chasm of silence opened between us, Max squinted. "You *do* want to be my wife, don't you?"

His question turned me into a rigid statue. To answer, I had to carve words out of my own heart. "You don't know me . . ."

"I know you as well as you let me know you."

With a shaky voice I admitted, "And I've only let you see the side you needed to see."

He paled. "Not again, Beatrice. Don't do this to me again." I let out a sudden sob, bringing my hand to my lips to silence it. And he stared, devastated but finally comprehending. "How long have you known?"

All along, I thought. *Also, somehow, not until just this moment . . .*

Every time a doubt crept in, I remembered he was a soldier at war and that I must do nothing to dispirit him. Now the curtain on the war had fallen, so I started with the easiest truth; the one he had a right to know. "I can't have more children, or at least I shouldn't. The doctors have told me so."

His eyes brightened, hopeful. "Is that all? Doctors can be wrong!"

"They're not wrong." I was, after all, nearly thirty-nine, older than he supposed, with an allegedly frail heart.

"Then we'll adopt," he said. "Marthe needs a mother and father, doesn't she?"

I could so easily see this lovely future in my mind's eye. Pigtailed

Marthe, the daughter I'd always wanted, a precious child I'd taken to my heart the first moment Max put her into my arms . . . but I'd already lived the life of a new bride and mother to small children. Already bought and furnished nurseries and picked schools and shopped for back-to-school clothes. Already gauged my every move by how it might reflect upon a husband. And all this besides the fact that as much as I loved that little girl, I now had hundreds like her to love and provide for.

As my silence lengthened, Max frowned, staring down at his clasped hands. "I've already taken your boys into my heart. It can be enough if I have you and the future we dreamed."

"You are a dear, sweet man," I whispered, knowing I was breaking him. Wishing I knew how to stop. *You'll chew him up and spit him out and leave his heart bleeding on the floor.* That's what Willie had said. Had he known me better than I knew myself? "Maxime," I said, sitting beside him. "I want you to have everything. New York. The white house, the cassoulet, and quiet evenings by the fire . . ."

He swallowed, not missing my meaning. "But you want to stay in France."

I nodded. "Once the peace accords are signed, I want to send for my boys. I need them to see what kept me away all this time. I want them to understand Chavaniac." There was so much I wanted to show them. So many places I wanted to visit myself. My hands positively ached with the longing to sculpt and create again. To make art, to write books, and to enjoy the freedoms that victory had secured. But maybe I could learn to make the damned cassoulet. "Would you build a different kind of life with me, here, in France?"

He started to nod, but I saw the exhaustion and disillusionment in his face. And all at once, his resolve crumbled. "I—I know you've seen the front, Beatrice, but you haven't lived it the way I have, day after day, year after year. You haven't done what I've had to do. *Everywhere* in France I look now, I see the men I buried." His hands were shaking again when he admitted, "I can't stay. I don't even know if I can stay even one more day."

I'd seen shell-shocked men, and I'd known for quite some time he lived with torments. It was natural that Max should wish to cross the ocean to where he last felt safe and happy.

"Then you must go," I said, even though I felt our future together unraveling.

He felt it too. "What then? Me in New York. You in France with your children and your husband . . . What should I think? I think you are a loyal Adrienne, in the end, willing to sacrifice your whole life to the prison of your marriage."

"No," I said softly. I knew Willie's faults. He knew mine too. I'd been unable to domesticate him, and he'd never again domesticate me. I was free. We both understood that.

The truth was, I never wanted to do to Max what Willie had done to me. I could never be content in a private, quiet life. I would always venture forth to put my mark on this world until my last breath. And where would that leave him? "If I may be permitted the vanity, I think I may be more like her adventurer husband, always on crusade."

Max laughed bitterly, and he had a right to be angry. It was ending between us on what should have been the happiest of days. It was ending even though we loved each other. It was ending so that my life could have yet another beginning. One I never expected, but which I knew was right for me. "I'm sorry, Maxime. I'm so sorry."

Stricken, he hung his head. Then, at length, he said, "Well, I'm not sorry. I've no regrets, because until you, I lost myself in this war. I simply lost myself."

But I'd found myself in this war, and for me it wasn't over.

We stood and embraced, exchanging a chaste kiss that I knew would be our last—one that tasted of poignant sorrow. The next morning, I walked him to the gate and watched him go.

Wiping away tears, I walked back to the castle, where Marthe pedaled her tricycle near my feet.

"Why are you crying, Madame Chanler?" she asked, blinking those steel blue eyes.

"Oh, we're all sad from time to time, darling, but I shall soon be better." I took a deep breath. "And from now on . . . why don't you call me *Beatrice*?"

It was, after all, at long last, a name of my own.

SIXTY-THREE

MARTHE
Paulhaguet
June 1944

"YOU'RE A TERRIBLE NURSE," TRAVERT GROUSES, DABBING HIS BAN-daged chest where I've spilled broth.

He's a worse patient, but I can't complain, because my battered face still hurts when I talk. I try giving Travert another spoonful. He holds up a hand to say he's not hungry. It's a good sign that his Frenchman's pride is more severe than his wound, but my bruised lower lip wobbles to remember him writhing on the ground in front of the boys' dormitory, a bullet in his gut. And all for my sake . . .

He'd have died if Sam's maquisards hadn't carried him to the nearby preventorium hospital, where doctors rushed him to a surgical room. Now we're in hiding at Madame Pinton's farm, dependent on Dr. Boulagnon, who comes to change Travert's bandages, check the stitches, and give him something for the pain.

It's a miracle the bullet hit nothing vital, but Yves still can't walk on his own. It won't be long before the German authorities connect the dots between us, fifteen missing Jewish girls, and three missing Gestapo officers. So Travert wants me to go without him—flee to Marseilles or a village in the mountains—but I could never abandon him after he came back for me.

No one's ever done that before.

To keep him from arguing, I say I'm not strong enough to go on my own. With a broken rib, that's not far from the truth. I also have crushing headaches and lingering dizziness. I move very slowly around Madame Pinton's house in helping to care for him. I'm ashamed to be putting her at risk, but she says she isn't worried. "You think I'm afraid to leave this lousy world? And anyway, the Nazis have bigger problems than an old woman in an isolated farmhouse."

With grim satisfaction, she tells us about the battle raging between the Germans and our maquisards at nearby Mont Mouchet. Then, just as my purple-black bruises are yellowing, the Allies land at Normandy and fight their way from the beachheads. British, Canadians, Free French, and fresh-faced Americans, well fed, well supplied, and motored by that quintessential spirit of get-up-and-go.

We celebrate the D-Day landings with a bottle of wine Madame Pinton has been hiding. And later, in the quiet of the loft bed, Travert asks, "Are you crying?"

"Maybe a little," I whisper. "I'm teary these days for no reason."

"Getting beaten with a truncheon will do that to you."

He traces his thumb gently on my still-swollen jaw and broken lip. And I finally find the courage to ask, "Why did you come back for me?"

"You know why." He winces as he tries to sit up against the pillow. "Don't insult me by making me say it."

The last thing I want is to insult him. I know he loves me. Even if he doesn't want to say it. For him, it's simple. You bed a woman you desire. You marry a woman you both desire and honor. The marriage and the desire came first with us, but now, little as I deserve it—he loves me and honors me too. I haven't been very good to him, but I want to be good to him now, and I hope it's not too late. "Thank you for saving me."

He snorts. "I didn't save you. I only got shot for you. We'd both be dead if it weren't for two brats barely out of short pants."

Oscar and Daniel, he means; two boys who should have been with their scout troop, building fires and baking beans and telling ghost stories. They're children I was supposed to protect, not the other way around. Having joined the Resistance, they'd been posted to guard the cache of weapons at the preventorium, and when the moment came, they crept out of their hiding places and used them. Last I heard, they were fighting with Sam's band on Mont Mouchet. And it's a bloody, bloody summer.

The Resistance blows up trains, roads, cuts phone lines—and the German retaliation is horrific. We hear about maquisard boys being murdered at the side of the road. They'd been eating wild cherries when a Red Cross ambulance drove by and they waved it over, hoping to get help for their wounded comrades. When the back doors opened—German soldiers were waiting inside with machine guns and mowed them down.

I learn this from Josephine and Gabriella, who come to the farmhouse to tell us that Oscar and Daniel were among the dead left on that bullet-riddled road. When I hear all this, I grieve with rage-laced tears. I want to break things. I want to pull Madame Pinton's pots down from where they're hanging over the stove and smash porcelain into pieces. Me, who never likes to see anything broken . . .

Those boys saved my life, and now what justice will there be for them?

It's a crime to use an ambulance that way; there's no other word for it.

Instead of raging, I comfort the girls who have lost their brother— and their father too. Monsieur Kohn was gunned down in a firefight on Mont Mouchet—a soldier, a father, a hero for France. I can still hear him saying he wouldn't *go meekly* . . .

It's fitting, I think, that Josephine is now wearing his old tricolor pin. She says she's been learning about Victor Chapman and the Lafayette Escadrille. And now she asks, "Madame Travert, do you think a girl could ever become a pilot?"

Very seriously, I say, "I think a girl can become anything she wants."

She and Gabriella will never get back their loved ones or childhood innocence. I hope, at the very least, they can get back their names, their freedom, and their faith. Josephine remembers how to say the mourner's kaddish. She says it's an orphan's prayer, and invites us to gather round the hearth as she recites it. Haltingly, hauntingly, her little sister Gabriella repeats her words in honor of their dead. I don't know this ritual or this prayer, and I don't understand the words, but they are for me a symphony of comfort and gathering strength.

After the reciting of the kaddish, we share a meal of tapioca soup with dried rosemary and sage. Madame Pinton has saved a few slices of fruit-peel cake for the girls, which she wraps in a checkered napkin when Josephine prods her sister and says, "We better go. We have to walk back to the preventorium before anybody realizes we're gone."

My mind works slower than it did before I was beaten with a baton, but I still remember the rules. "You walked by yourselves? You're not supposed to leave without a guardian. How—"

"We slipped out the tunnels," Josephine explains.

The Jewish girls told her about them, and now she knows the castle's secrets too. It was Josephine who helped lead all fifteen high up into the mountains, where the maquisards saw them to safety. Then Josephine found her own way back to the preventorium, where the staff was too agitated to ask questions. What a little heroine she is.

I'm worried for everyone at the castle now—for the girls, for Anna, the staff, and anyone else who might still be held to account for what I did. It's already a miracle the Gestapo hasn't tracked us down here, so I don't dare go back . . .

It isn't until August, when the Germans start abandoning their checkpoints under the pressure of a rapidly advancing Allied front, that it seems safe enough to go into Paulhaguet for foodstuffs. There, I have the good luck to run into Anna, who is dropping off a package for her husband, in the hope it'll reach him in his prison camp.

We sit together in the back of a little bistro by the post office, where we have privacy. Over a lunch of salmon and tomato in a vinaigrette, I say, "I'm sorry."

I can't say more, but I don't need to. "No one blames you."

"Not even Madame Xavier?"

"You didn't hear?" Anna makes the sign of the cross over herself. "A farmer found her in a field with her throat cut. No one knows what happened, but you can guess. These days, we're finding bodies everywhere. In ditches, wells, and barns . . . resisters, collaborators, who knows?"

I still have enough humanity in me not to dance a jig that someone slit Faustine Xavier's throat, but not so much I'm sorry she's dead. One day, I might find it in myself to pray for her soul. Today I'm just glad there's one less person the kids need to fear, and one less stain to be washed off the castle walls.

From what we hear on the BBC, Hitler can't win—even his henchmen have to realize it. Travert says that at this point the Germans must be idiots not to negotiate for peace. They've lost Italy as an ally. The Russians are crushing German forces on the Eastern Front. And the Americans are driving them out of France. But, according to Anna, they're doing as much damage as they can in retreat. Nearby villages have been burned and looted, men lined up and shot. I wince at the word *shot*, and she asks, "How is he?"

She's smart enough not to say Travert's name aloud. "Better, but still in pain. And I'm chewing again."

She reaches for my hand and squeezes it. "You were nuts to give yourself up like that. Positively *certifiable*."

"I know," I admit, and she doesn't know the half of it. On the other hand, maybe she's guessed.

She shakes her head, big brown eyes downcast. "I wish I was even half as nuts as you . . ."

"You're crazy enough to stay," I tell Anna. "You should go to your *maman* in Marseilles in case the Germans return to the castle and try to hold you responsible for what I did."

"I'm not going anywhere until after the war," she says, looking very much like her mother in that moment. "And it's almost over."

As it happens, she's right.

On August 18, the Secret Army of Lafayette attacks Germans in the streets of Le Puy. The Germans surrender there and evacuate from Brioude the next day. At Chavaniac, we're liberated even before Paris. Sam and his maquisards march through town singing the "Marseillaise," and it's got even me all choked up . . .

Travert is out of hiding and back in uniform, wearing an armband with the tricolor. He and his gendarmes aren't precisely sure who is in charge of France now, but what else is new? Probably General de Gaulle.

Travert holds me against his waist, and together we watch the fearless parade of red, white, and blue. The castle gates are flung open for parents who want to tell their children the joyous news. I see Josephine wearing her tricolor pin, and Gabriella with old Scratch purring in her arms. And, reunited with the girls, I kiss them and hug them a thousand times.

"Careful," says Travert, "or someone might mistake you for a woman who wants a few babies underfoot."

I laugh because I'm feeling happy enough to pull him into an alleyway and risk it, but I don't say that in front of the girls, who are keen to visit Madame Pinton. It's against the rules of the preventorium—but who cares?

I promise to take them the next morning.

Meanwhile, I'm awash in bittersweet memories, allowing myself to think of Henri without feeling like a traitor for doing so. Guilty for being alive, but relieved that the war and suffering are over. Exhausted and happy and sad all at the same time. I can't seem to get it together until later that night, when Travert turns on the radio and pulls me into his embrace.

"So where are you going to take me?" I ask.

He chuckles. "There isn't a café in miles where every table won't be occupied tonight."

I wrap my arms around him. "I meant where are you taking me after the war. You said we could go someplace nice. Travel the world—or what's left of it . . ."

He meets my eyes. How did I never notice before that his are as dark as fertile volcanic soil? Now they glisten, because he remembers the rest of what he said that night. *We could make life, after the war. We could go someplace nice. Travel the world—or what's left of it. Make a baby. Who knows? Maybe you fall in love with me someday. Or maybe you leave me for someone else. That's life. But we have to survive to live it.*

Somehow, we survived. Now I want to live.

Yves holds me close. "I'll take you anywhere you want to go."

And these are the words I've been waiting to hear all my life . . .

SIXTY-FOUR

ADRIENNE
December 24, 1807

IT IS CHRISTMAS EVE AGAIN AT CHAVANIAC, AND A GLAZED HAM IS destined for a table I've set with garlands of evergreen. My surviving sisters Pauline and Rosalie, and Lafayette's elderly aunt Charlotte, join us at the table, where we take turns lighting a candle over the brioche. Gathered too are our best beloved children. Tall, upright Georges, who looks so like his father that strangers on the street know him at once for Lafayette's son. Courageous Anastasie, now a mother and loving wife. Virginie, who has been my devoted aide-de-camp in the battles fought to regain our lost fortunes. On the slope of our forested hills, my grandchildren are sledding, and I smile to hear their laughter, knowing we have at last made a home where happy children can laugh and play without fear of man or beast . . .

I don't know how much of this is true, for I am in delirium. Beset with illness, I have a makeshift head on a mortifying body, so I don't know exactly *where* I am now. Yet I prefer to think it is Chavaniac. That's where we were going, anyway, when I was afflicted. The doctors treated me with tinctures of lead, and since then hallucinations have transported me to biblical times and back again.

"I've gone mad, have I not?" I whisper, certain only of Lafayette at my bedside, hand in mine. "Tell me if I've lost my reason."

With kindly eyes he says, "My dear heart, I would be very distressed if I thought all your charming words of love to me were absurdities."

In recent days, I have told him I love him in every way possible. As a Christian, a human, passionately, even voluptuously, or I would if I still had any senses left. "But I have said strange things too, and you are pretending otherwise," I accuse. "Here I am, married to the most sincere of men, yet I cannot get the truth. Tell me and I will resign myself to the shame of being mad!"

He kisses my fingers as if we were still at Versailles. "You are only sick, my dear heart. And we will care for you. Be comforted that you are highly regarded and loved."

"I care less to be highly regarded so long as I am still loved . . . but I cannot remember now these years since our liberation. Help me find myself again. It is ten years we've had together since Olmütz, is it not?"

He nods. "Ten years of freedom, and every one of them precious. Years of watching you crusade for the restoration of our friends and family, years in which I have had to accustom myself to the novelty of thinking of *you* as my commanding officer."

Despite his teary smile, I am tremulous to ask the next question. "And in that time, did I become . . . I am not empress, am I?"

How relieved I am to hear Lafayette chuckle. "No. That was a fevered nightmare."

"I thought so, because if I was empress, then you would be emperor, and that would weigh heavy on your conscience!"

"Indeed. But you did battle an emperor," he reminds me. "Two of them, actually. If you had not won Napoléon Bonaparte's admiration, I would have remained forever in exile."

Ah, yes! I remember now. General Bonaparte's pretty round face, in which I should have seen a devil in an angel's guise. When I thanked him for negotiating our release, I found him quite cold. We were too dangerous, he believed, to return to France. Equally dangerous, according to the Americans, for us to go there. And when I pleaded with Bonaparte that it would do much for his reputation to let a champion of freedom come home, he told me I understood *nothing* of politics.

Yet I knew enough to arrange for a false passport for Gilbert and to summon my husband home at the precise moment it was too politically inconvenient for Bonaparte to send him away again. Thus we have lived together with our children and grandchildren in France.

"Ten years of freedom," I say.

"And thirty-four precious years of marriage, during which you have charmed, blessed, and honored my life."

He is worried. He wants for me to rest and get well. He barks at anyone who disturbs me. When next I wake, I am certain that I must be in childbed, for Gilbert is giving me spoonfuls of warmed wine and getting ready to light the candle for our Christmas Eve tradition. *Christmas Eve*, I think. Our son's birthday. "I've finally given you a boy," I say, wanting to hold our baby in my arms.

Then I realize Georges is a grown man now . . .

And that I am dying.

I say as much to Lafayette, who will not hear of it.

But Christmas Eve is a good day to die. I don't fear it; I know a heavenly reunion awaits. Today I will see Maman, Louise, Grand-mère . . .

I spent nearly four years traversing France, often on foot, to reclaim our inheritances, settle debts, and negotiate for friends and loved ones to be removed from the list of banished émigrés. All the while, I searched for the remains of my family. And with the help of Pauline and Rosalie, I finally found where their guillotined bodies had been dumped during the Revolution. Men, women, children, priests, nuns, nobles, and peasants . . .

There, on the spot, my sisters and I founded Picpus Cemetery, where they might be venerated perpetually. And I—who contributed to the circumstances that led to their deaths—wish to reside eternally by their side.

I am not in pain as my life ebbs away, and I tell my husband so. I despair only to be parted from my loved ones. I am enough a heretic that even heaven will not console me for leaving Gilbert. I sense he has more yet to do for the cause of mankind in this world, but I want desperately for us to be together again in the next.

"You're not a Christian, are you?" I ask it softly, and seeing he is tempted to lie, I am ashamed, for freedom of religious scruple is sacred. "Ah, but I know what you are. You are a Fayettist!"

He puffs in mock indignation, wiping tears. "You must think me quite vain." Then, for my sake, a glint of the old mischief enters his countenance. "But are you not something of a Fayettist yourself, my dear?"

"Oh, indeed, sir," I say. "With all my soul, that is a sect for which I would gladly die."

These words break him, and he pleads with me, repressing sobs. "Say no more of death. Stay with me. Think only of how much I love you. That you are fused into my life such that I cannot distinguish you from my own existence."

Then I will live on, with him here, even after I die. There is no part of me I withhold from him anymore. No old grudge or pain, no wish or hope to have lived any other life. For ours, together, was glorious. "And I am all yours," I whisper, finding the last of my strength to raise my arms, draw his head to mine, and press him against my heart, where between us, I feel a single pulse.

EPILOGUE

MARTHE
New York City
March 1945

MY FIRST PLANE RIDE.

My first trip to America.

My first semester at Parsons School of Design, courtesy of an art scholarship awarded on the basis of my wartime portfolio—not only sketches, but sculptures combining styles and eras.

My first days in New York are spent dodging taxicabs and getting neck strain from staring up at skyscrapers like a rube. Having lived my whole life in rural France, the noise, the lights, and the hustle of New York streets make it hard to think.

Madame Beatrice says that might be part of the charm . . .

She lured me here with both the art scholarship and an ulterior motive. Now, leaning on her cane in the entryway of a stylish Manhattan shop, she says, "Darling, when going to war, one should begin with a new hat!"

She has me try on a black satin pillbox with dotted veil, but when I choose a beret, she pats my cheek with an age-spotted hand and says, "How *French*, darling. Very fitting. I do believe the committee will hang on your every word."

She's now vice chairperson of the National Citizens Committee in Aid of the United Nations War Crimes Commission. She's pressuring President Franklin Delano Roosevelt to maintain serious cooperation with the Allied war crimes commission in bringing Nazi war criminals to justice.

Eleanor's husband is sympathetic, she explained. *But like all presidents, he needs to be prodded!*

She always calls the president *Eleanor's husband* and rattles off the first names of congressmen and ambassadors who are personal friends.

As she does so, I'm all nerves. I'm having second thoughts about appearing before her committee, and I tell her so.

"Oh, for goodness' sake, Marthe, after facing down the Gestapo, you've nothing to fear from my little committee!"

Of course, nothing Madame Beatrice ever does is *little*. Trapped on this side of the ocean during the war, she ginned up her rusty old war relief machinery despite being laid up with various ailments. She's due for a second decoration, and even now, she's preparing to send almost fifty cases of children's clothing, surgical supplies, and other provisions to the preventorium. So when I see her open her pocketbook, I tell her, "I can buy my own hat! I'm not a penniless urchin anymore."

"Oh, I know you're a married woman now with a nickel or two to rub together, but buying you a hat is the least I can do after all the trouble I caused. I'm really very sorry, you know . . ."

She's been apologizing for my birth record almost from the moment I set foot on American shores. *It seemed simpler to say you were born in Paris*, she explained, telling me the whole story. *I didn't know what the rules might be for foreign children after the war, and I didn't want anyone questioning your citizenship or your right to be cared for at Chateau Lafayette.*

Not so different, really, from what I did in forging all those documents for Jewish children. But today she says, "I've fibbed so often on my own official records, I can scarcely remember what's true anymore. If I'd chosen another life, another marriage, I might have been *Minerva Furlaud*. Writing that name down was my way of saying good-bye to what might have been . . . with Max, and with you. I never dreamed it could harm you, but I should have. I hope you can forgive me, darling."

"There's nothing to forgive," I say, and I mean it. I'm more grateful for her than I can ever express, and it pains me to see how frail she's become. I take her shaking hands and say, "But I do wonder . . ."

"Argentina," she says.

"What?"

"You're going to ask what happened to Maxime. He married an American woman. A sculptress, actually, isn't that an interesting coincidence? A relation of the Chapman family, in fact. They have two boys who must be grown now . . ."

She turns her head wistfully, and I catch the scent of her perfume. She still wears L'Heure Bleue, and knowing how much she loved Maxime, I say, "I'm sorry."

"Oh, I'm not, darling," she says, squeezing my hands. "I lived the life I wanted to live. I had the wonderful good fortune to watch my sons become men and see children like you grow up and thrive. And though Willie and I remained on good terms until he died, men have *never* stopped wooing me. In fact, I'm spending this summer with the distinguished Saint-John Perse . . ."

That's the *nom de plume* of a Nobel Prize–winning poet the world knows better as Alexis Leger—a French diplomat who opposed the Vichy regime. "You cradle-snatcher, you . . ."

Her bright blue eyes gleam. "Stuff and nonsense! Alexis and I are precisely the same age, give or take a year or seven. As for Max, maybe we can get word to him and see if there's *anything* he remembers that could help reveal your true identity."

"Maybe," I say, having long since returned to her the man's pictures and love letters. "On the other hand, I think I've finally got a pretty good idea of who I am. Anything else I discover isn't going to change that."

"There's the spirit," she says.

That night I tell the committee about my experiences in war-torn France; I'm ashamed to say the crimes weren't committed only by Germans, that French people were complicit. And I can't think back on the past five years without believing that we're all at least a little guilty. For remaining neutral, for appeasing, for turning a blind eye, for refusing to help.

For looking out for me, myself, and I . . .

After the applause dies down, Madame Beatrice says, "Our values must be defended in partnership with our democratic allies—not just here, but everywhere. It's a lesson that's taken us at least three wars to learn; I hope it's not a lesson we ever need to learn again."

We lunch the next afternoon at the Vanderbilt Hotel—a scene of faded elegance. Madame Beatrice lost the hotel, and most everything else, during the Great Depression, but she wants to show off her bas-relief frieze. I study it, admiring what must have been backbreaking work, even in her prime.

"I couldn't even attempt it today," she says with a sigh. "My hands aren't steady enough. That's why I took up writing books about interesting women. But not even my shaky hands show more clearly the passing of time than the fact that I've already conditioned my mind to taking orders from Anna about the preventorium. What a shock to hear it has become her calling! And yet, quite fitting in a way, as she is a child of both America and France."

I never imagined Anna would want to stay on as president of the preventorium, even now that her husband has been released. But she's dedicated herself to the place, and I truly admire her for it. Keen for gossip, Beatrice asks, "I'm sure I'll hear it from Emily when she comes to visit for our long-awaited reunion—but I must know, what's he like, this son-in-law of hers?"

I laugh. "Nothing I would have expected. Anna's husband is a bit of a philosopher—quite religious. After five cold winters in a German POW camp, he now dreams of starting an orange grove in sunny Morocco."

Truthfully, I've never seen Anna so happy. One night soon after he returned, I saw him bend to light her cigarette with the glowing tip of his, and I was struck by the memory of her doing the same for me all those years ago in the attic. She'd pulled me into an intimate moment, and I was caught there for five years.

But I realize now, it was a moment too crowded . . . her husband was always there.

I don't long for her anymore. I've let that go. I'm happy for her.

I'm happy too for Sam, who is now running for mayor of Chavaniac. For Madame Pinton, who has started official proceedings to adopt Josephine and Gabriella Kohn. I'm happy for Madame Simon, whose newspaper articles helped expose the Vichy regime, and whose son-in-law miraculously survived the concentration camps. The baroness is soon to be decorated for her own work in two world wars. I'm even happy for the baron—who will be released any day now.

I'm happy for myself too. My life in New York is everything I ever wanted. Swank parties in fashionable neighborhoods. Rides on ferries and elevated trains. Hot dogs and soft drinks in Coney Island. Museums and musicals, and art house cinema.

It's all a bit much for Yves, but he doesn't complain.

One warm night, when we're smoking cigarettes on our apartment's iron fire escape, listening to the traffic below, I ask, "You don't miss your little house in France?"

"It's good to be somewhere different for a while."

While I've been working on a series of sculptures made out of black volcanic stone—a child carving herself out of the rock, then that same child helping to carve another out, and then another—he's been working at a private detective firm to help Jewish families in New York locate missing persons from the war. There are millions of shattered families he wants to put back together. He says he *needs* to put them back together, as if in penance.

He also needs somebody like me—somebody to slug his arm and muss his hair and push him into new and uncomfortable adventures. And I need him because he's no saint; he's something solid to hold on to, someone who feels like home. Someone who loves me, cracks and all . . .

Maybe it's because we fought a war together. Because we know things about each other no other person on earth, man or woman, would ever understand. That's an unbreakable bond.

It doesn't have to be love, Yves once said.

But it is.

And *why not*?

I daydream sometimes about having a kid with his soulful brown eyes and my spunk. I don't know how that would work, but Yves says we've got time to figure it out . . .

At the end of the war, we're in Times Square with everybody else. Bells are ringing; sailors flood the streets and kiss nurses. Colorful confetti rains down on us as more than half a million people of every complexion pour out into the streets, holding up newspapers with victory headlines, waving hats and flags, lifting one another in the air, and breaking open bottles of wine and beer.

Thanks to General de Gaulle, we French can say this is our victory too. And Yves hoists me on one shoulder so I can see over the crowd. Exhilarated, I want to laugh and cheer that it's over. But of course, it never is. It's an eternal battle, fought generation after generation, and maybe all we can ever do is keep fighting, which takes more courage by far.

I BEGAN THIS PROJECT BECAUSE I WANTED TO TELL THE STORY OF America's French Founding Mother, Adrienne Lafayette—wife of the immensely likable marquis de Lafayette, without whom the United States would not have won her independence. But when I learned that the Lafayettes' castle at Chavaniac served as a sanctuary for Jewish children during the Holocaust, having been purchased, renovated, and repurposed by Americans, I knew this really was a story about the Lafayette legacy. How the torch was passed to new generations who made Chavaniac a sanctuary for orphaned children and orphaned ideals that lit the way for humanity through three of history's darkest hours.

Telling that story required not only Adrienne, but two additional heroines, and I'd like to explain the choices and changes I made in fitting their narratives together.

ADRIENNE

In the lyrics of *Hamilton: An American Musical*, Lafayette is called "America's favorite fighting Frenchman." While Laura Kamoie and I were writing *America's First Daughter* and *My Dear Hamilton*, Lafayette certainly became a favorite of ours.

As a grieving widower, Lafayette wrote a letter extolling Adrienne's virtues, giving her credit for his honorable life, and describing their union as so close that he "could not draw a line of distinction between her existence and [his] own." I had to know more about the woman whose death the buoyant French hero characterized as the first misfortune of his life that he wouldn't be able to recover from. As it happens, Adrienne's good works, unassuming self-sacrifice, and raw courage helped carve out a world-changing democratic legacy that is still playing out in our lives today. She was a founding mother of not one but two nations: America and France. And quite a bit of historical evidence survives in Adrienne's own hand, which made her a perfect heroine for a novel.

With biographies, letters, and accounts by her husband and daughter, I had such an abundance of information, I didn't have room for her many family members, friends, and acquaintances—important persons almost every one. Another challenge was that Adrienne was almost *too* perfect a heroine. So rarely did she complain, she didn't mention a miscarriage she suffered early in her marriage. (And because she omitted it, I chose to leave it out too.)

Her contemporaries described her as lacking all jealousy or pettiness, though she had ample excuse for both. When Lafayette returned triumphant from America, his tragic affair with Aglaé inspired ballads, and the crowd at the opera really did encourage him to kiss the queen's lady-in-waiting. What I left out of the story is that the lady he was encouraged to kiss was Diane, the comtesse de Simiane, with whom he enjoyed a love affair that transformed into a friendship of many decades. I was able to infer Adrienne's unhappiness about Lafayette's affair with Aglaé because her powerful family raised a fuss, but I found no evidence of her distress about his relationship with Diane. In fact, Adrienne seems to have liked this mistress. So much so that she encouraged her children to call Diane *aunt*, and often met with her socially without Lafayette. Perhaps Adrienne felt pity for Diane, whose homosexual husband died under mysterious circumstances. The subsequent scandal put a dent in Lafayette's reputation, but Adrienne stood by both Lafayette and his mistress. All this begged for a more in-depth exploration than I could provide in a novel that is primarily about the legacy at Chavaniac. Thus, it seemed better to omit this otherwise fascinating drama, to portray Adrienne as having already come to terms with her husband's youthful affairs, and to assume that the comtesse de Simiane was "the charming sort with whom a wife enjoys taking tea."

Perhaps Adrienne simply banished jealousy as un-Christian. After all, surviving portraits describe her as a deeply religious woman who risked her life in service of her faith. But that faith was hard-won. According to her daughter, young Adrienne was "tormented" by religious doubts; she declined to take her first Communion until after she was married. Her husband would later say Adrienne's religious beliefs were "amiable heresies," fervently entwined with his revolutionary ideals. Maybe that's why, as she lay dying, she jested that they were both Fayettists, a sect for which she would willingly give her life.

Adrienne's spirituality is fascinating, but I wanted to explore the way she navigated the world politically. She understood finances and took command of them. She joined abolitionist organizations and personally managed the project of purchasing plantations to emancipate the people working them. She took in wards and transformed the economy of Chavaniac. She cared for National Guardsmen and saved the lives of at least two people we know about—not even counting her husband. She had the temerity to poke at Washington's conscience, then travel to a foreign country under an assumed name to join her husband in a dungeon . . .

As in all my historical novels, the most outrageous bits are true. Adrienne's grandmother really did have a habit of stealing holy relics—and was nearly excommunicated for it. Adrienne had personal relationships with many famous Americans of the founding generation, including Benjamin Franklin, John and Abigail Adams, John Jay and Sarah Livingston Jay, Angelica Church, Thomas Jefferson and his daughter Patsy, William Short, and James and Elizabeth Monroe. It's even true that her relationship with Gouverneur Morris was testy and that she verbally jousted with two emperors. And Adrienne did die on Christmas Eve, hallucinating, likely due to lead poisoning.

But of course, in every historical novel, a few things must be altered for the sake of brevity. For example, Lafayette wasn't given the cross of Saint Louis until after the American war, but I put it sooner. The duc d'Ayen didn't entirely oppose the idea of his son-in-law, the vicomte de Noailles, going to fight in America, but he didn't think Lafayette could handle himself. The duc might not have been quite as terrible a father as I've portrayed him to be, but Adrienne's tactfully expressed frustrations with him are evident in the historical record. As Laura Auricchio makes clear in *The Marquis*, Lafayette's meetings with his coconspirator, the Baron de Kalb, took place in Adrienne's home, so perhaps Adrienne wasn't as much in the dark as she portrayed to the world, and her easy forgiveness of Lafayette, as well as her steadfast support, was because she already knew of his plans.

Finally, while the incident with John Laurens at Versailles is based on historical fact, how great a role Adrienne took in his argument with the minister and audience with the king is unknown. However, since Lafayette asked Adrienne to introduce Laurens around court and help him at Versailles, it seemed fair to assume she did so.

BEATRICE

While Adrienne was the starting point, this novel was swiftly overtaken by the formidable personality of Beatrice Chanler—a founding mother of a different sort. Like most people, I surrendered to Beatrice's charms, never guessing the journey ahead!

As a celebrity, Beatrice was frequently mentioned and photographed in old digitized newspapers. Yet her amusingly casual relationship with the truth on official documents became the bane of my research existence. She did, in fact, put "See *Who's Who*" on a passport application in March 1918. And this was only part of a pattern of obfuscation. She frequently changed her middle name as well as her date and place of birth. I was stymied until, shortly after my return from a research trip to Chavaniac, I stumbled upon a wonderful article in *The Gazette of the American Friends of Lafayette* written by Beatrice's grandson, William A. Chanler.

I took a chance and reached out to him, and a heartwarming correspondence commenced. Bill—who, like his grandmother, is a generous soul and an author in his own right—shared family letters with me, and together we tried to guess the identities of people Beatrice mentioned, like the mysterious Pierre and the even more mysterious Kate. On the surface, the letters painted a deceptively simple picture of a well-heeled society maven whose troubled marriage somehow survived the Great War and gave way to remarkable philanthropy at Lafayette's castle in Auvergne.

Though dazzling Beatrice and her colorful husband Willie had separated on amicable terms before the First World War, reconciliations were attempted. Unfortunately, according to her letters, her brilliant but boorish husband sometimes aggravated her to exhaustion. They often bickered—sometimes about the children, with Beatrice comparing Willie to a stern Roman father. Beatrice admitted to having black moods when she considered the future of their marriage, saying in one letter that Willie was "mad as a hatter" and that others feared for her safety, though she wasn't in the least concerned.

In the wake of her husband's leg injury in 1913 (the exact cause of which remains a mystery), Beatrice sat at her husband's hospital bedside. But by springtime of 1915, they seem to have been so estranged that she mentions not having heard from Willie, and even being unsure of his whereabouts. In fact, the newspapers appear to have been better informed, since they'd already printed where he was.

Other family letters confirm Beatrice's frustration with her husband's alcoholism. This would get worse in the wake of amputation and a morphine addiction. Beatrice implied in one letter that Willie was "unbalanced." She may have been referring to his conspiracy theories and anti-Semitic beliefs—beliefs that would become more virulent before he died in 1934. Fortunately, his wife appears never to have shared his views. Beatrice seems to have taken in Jewish children at the chateau, but I found a correspondence with John Moffat in which she agreed it should be kept quiet, presumably lest it scare off bigoted donors. Moreover, Beatrice would ultimately go on to serve as vice chairwoman of the National Citizens Committee in Aid of the United Nations War Crimes Commission after World War II, advocating a strong response to Nazi crimes against Jews, and she championed Jewish congressman Emanuel Celler, a critic of America's insufficient response to the Holocaust.

So why did Beatrice stay married to a man like Willie?

That she loved him and his garrulous extended family is beyond question. "Operatic" Chanler family dramas—described in both *The Astor Orphans: A Pride of Lions* by Lately Thomas and *Sargent's Women* by Donna M. Lucey—no doubt entertained Beatrice. But, having come from a fractured family herself (more on that later), Beatrice perhaps welcomed being a part of a close-knit group, and it might've pained her to lose those family connections by pursuing a divorce. Certainly she wouldn't have wished to fall afoul of her starchy sister-in-law Margaret, who ostracized divorced family members. Another possibility is that Beatrice had Catholic sympathies that made divorce, for her, out of the question. If so, these sympathies weren't ones that she would've easily shared with her anti-Catholic husband or anti-Catholic brother-in-law, Jack Chapman. But Beatrice once described herself as being "too pagan" for the spirit to descend upon her, so I searched for other clues.

I found them among twenty-six unsorted boxes of papers at the New-York Historical Society.

When I first discovered a sheaf of unaddressed letters tucked into a Valentine's Day folder, I wasn't sure what I'd found. Love letters, to be sure, but they weren't from Willie. Beatrice's eldest son had labeled these "Maxime Furlaud & other letters from Front in France 1918," but I didn't remember having come across the name Furlaud before. The author of these love letters openly worried about the prying eyes of the censors, expressing love for someone called Marthe while seeming to refer to himself as Catherine.

And I began to wonder if Catherine could be the mysterious Kate of Beatrice's private letters.

To find out, I cataloged and transcribed the private family letters, putting them into correct historical order and lining them up with this new correspondence. They fit together like two sides of a zipper! Had I uncovered a century-old secret love affair? To confirm my suspicions, I dug into immigration records. As it happens, Beatrice mentions Kate visiting her children at the same time Maxime Furlaud was visiting New York. I also found a ship's manifest for 1917 in which Beatrice and Maxime Furlaud later traveled to America together. And of course, every now and then, Beatrice would drop the code and call him *F* or Furlaud.

That Beatrice apparently had a romantic attachment to this French officer did not shock me; after all, in our first interview, Bill Chanler told me he assumed both his grandparents likely had companions or relationships outside their ruined marriage. (Certainly Beatrice's letters evidenced admirers such as Pierre and the vicomte de Breteuil, the latter of whom she said "worship[ped] at [her] shrine.") What *did* shock me was that the romance with Furlaud was so serious—serious enough that he loaned her money, may have given her a car, and seems to have suggested marriage, children, and a future together.

That Beatrice stayed married to Willie anyway raised more questions than it answered.

I set about rewriting Beatrice's narrative as a doomed wartime love affair when the story changed *yet again* in an even more dramatic way. In January of 2019, Bill Chanler let me know about a discovery he'd made upon reviewing photos I sent of his grandmother's papers from the NYHS. Bill had dived down the rabbit hole of genealogical discovery. The rabbit he found was extraordinary.

It seems Beatrice was born Minnie Collins in 1880, illegitimate daughter of an Irish immigrant line. Growing up, she went by Minnie Ashley, either in honor of the Boston butcher with whom her mother was living, or in the probably mistaken belief that she was his child. (She would later claim this was just a stage name.)

Beatrice wasn't born in Charlottesville, as she so often said; her childhood address was in Boston's Chinatown—not far from Lafayette Mall. And she was older than she wanted people to believe. She was six years old when the Statue of Liberty—a gift from France—was dedicated in New York Harbor. She was eight when the butcher died, and nine when a kindly French instructor took pity on her reduced circumstances and gave her free dance lessons. She attended a charity school for impoverished children, and while other kids her age worked in factories, twelve-year-old Minnie found a job on the stage.

That this flamboyant polymath had such humble beginnings was, for me, a deeply moving discovery. The genesis of Beatrice's generosity—her single-minded devotion to war relief work, and how much she wanted to think herself "capable of great deeds"—came into stark focus. I understood for the first time that Beatrice wasn't merely an *agent* of the Lafayette legacy; she was an *embodiment* of it. She was his American dream in living flesh.

In all the desperate children she helped, she likely saw herself. And to the husband who helped her leave those humble beginnings behind, she likely felt a gratitude and loyalty that made divorcing him impossible.

Because I wanted this book to honor Beatrice's truth—the one she felt she had to hide—I incorporated as many of her own words from her letters as I could, and as many authentic historical details as were available to me. In Paris, Beatrice really *did* stay at the St. James & D'Albany—the remnants of Adrienne Lafayette's childhood home. She did lose a personal friend on the *Lusitania*, and of course she also lost her nephew Victor Chapman, with whom she said she used to talk about love, marriage, and philosophy. If she was Victor's champion before the war, I don't know; but after, she certainly was. And it seems fitting that he was a founding member of the Lafayette Escadrille.

Beatrice really was asked to do work by the embassy, in addition to being sent on a dangerous labor mission before the end of the First World War. The story of how she was nearly torpedoed and refused to get out of her bath comes from an unpublished biography written by her son, and is corroborated by other accounts. She braved the front at least three times and crossed a war-torn sea at least seven times; for having risked this trip more than any other war relief worker, she was made a chevalier in the Legion of Honor. After the First World War, Beatrice would undergo surgery and hospitalization for an illness having to do with her thyroid. Her husband and friends make reference to her ill health and to their certainty that she was overworking herself. Yet she survived until just after the Second World War, dying of a heart attack on a train at the relatively young age of sixty-six. It is likely that when she died, she was on her way to be reunited with the Baroness de LaGrange, who was en route to America, but the two friends never saw each other again in this life. Her companion on that last journey was the Nobel Prize–winning poet Saint-John Perse, aka prominent French diplomat Alexis Leger. (When an interviewer asked about this relationship, Beatrice's eldest son confined his remarks to his late mother's admiration for Leger's work, but confirmed that they spent every summer together for a decade.)

I was thrilled to bring the facts of Beatrice's large life to the page, but of course, a few liberties were taken. For example, though Beatrice's oldest son went by Willie, like his father—or Blue Willie, because he had his mother's eyes—the novel calls him Billy to distinguish. To keep the cast list manageable, I had to omit people like Tebby Dearborn née Evans, who served as Beatrice's secretary and de facto governess. I also couldn't explore the deeply important contributions made by Beatrice's friend and philanthropist John Moffat, but he deserves much of the credit for keeping Lafayette's legacy alive.

It also pained me to all but leave out mention of Valentine Thomson, an irrepressible magazine editor who befriended Beatrice, found homes for thousands of displaced refugees, and dedicated a large part of her life to Lafayette's chateau. I attributed many of her attitudes and accomplishments, including her brainchild about French dolls, to the equally important Clara Simon, who served as secretary for the Lafayette Memorial Fund from its foundation until she was denounced in an anti-Semitic newspaper and dismissed by the Baron de LaGrange in 1941.

I also combined, condensed, or moved historical events—for example, Victor Chapman saw his parents to safety in London before deciding to enlist, but to streamline the story, I had him decide in Amiens. In fact, Beatrice and her boys stayed as guests of the Baron de LaGrange's sister at Hardelot until the German offensive came straight at them. Beatrice's husband had already left for Switzerland when she returned to France in the spring of 1915, but she did find out about his impending amputation from the Chapmans. Woodrow Wilson did make a speech declaring war that asserted America's role as a defender of democracy, but I condensed his powerful words. And Willie really did throw his prosthetic across the restaurant, and he did examine what were probably Victor Chapman's exhumed remains, but both incidents happened later than this novel posits. The baron's mother, Clémentine de LaGrange, mentioned Beatrice's visit in her memoirs, *Open House in Flanders*; but Clémentine had already fetched her granddaughter, and if Maxime Furlaud was present, we have no record of it.

Also, it was Emily's daughter Amicie who was born 1917, not Anne, but Beatrice was present for both births, so I combined them.

Other times, I had to make educated guesses, like how Beatrice Chanler became such a knowledgeable person or what rank Maxime Furlaud held at the end of his service. And occasionally, I had to invent things entirely. For example, Mitzi Miller is a fictional character based on a number of similarly situated members of the Woman's Peace Party.

And since I had no idea how Beatrice met Furlaud and I wanted to show how relationships could blossom quickly in wartime, I was inspired by an interview with Beatrice's good friend Valentine, in which an incident was recounted about having been lost in the dark after the opera and being helped home by a stranger.

As for Beatrice's name, her grandson suggested she might've plucked it from literature or the stage, so I went with Shakespeare's *Much Ado About Nothing*, which was remarkably applicable. The historic Victor Chapman had a Jewish comrade and good friend who died in his arms—a Polish mathematician named Kohn. And Victor did ask his family to be in touch with "Madame Kohn." Because this relationship helped illustrate the continuing thread of France's struggle with religious liberty, I included the Kohns at the Picpus ceremony in 1915 and invented descendants among those who suffered under the Nazi regime in the next generation.

Beatrice Chanler might have been involved in a car crash with her mother in 1909, but I turned that into a drunken wreck with Willie years later and combined the several bombardments Beatrice endured with the shelling at Poperinge, where Furlaud did offer the services of his car. It seemed like the easiest explanation for what drove a new intensity in Beatrice's relationship with the French officer, as evidenced by her letters. Which brings me to my most important invention in this novel . . . *Marthe*.

Though Beatrice was directly responsible for saving thousands of children in her lifetime, and indirectly responsible for saving tens of thousands more after, I did not find evidence of a special relationship with any of them. That doesn't mean such relationships didn't exist; having worked on a book about another orphanage founder, Eliza Hamilton, I found it unlikely that Beatrice didn't form an attachment to any child she rescued . . . so I decided to give her one.

MARTHE

When I first learned that Jewish children were saved at Chavaniac during the Holocaust, I was deeply moved. French Resistance fighter Charles Boissier testified that almost the whole village was pledged to the cause of opposing the Nazis. Chavaniac is a very small village, and yet maquisard Aimé Monteil—a valet at the castle who was the inspiration behind Samir Bensaïd—testified that almost sixty of these villagers fought alongside him. And in apparent defiance of Nazi occupation, the chateau issued a pamphlet saying they did not discriminate on the basis of religion.

In light of all this, I was excited to show how the work of Adrienne and Beatrice culminated in heroism at Chavaniac. Imagine my surprise, then, to discover that this most modern period at the castle was the one about which the least is discoverable. Though communications between the Free Zone and America were possible before 1942, my research uncovered complaints from the chateau's American benefactors that they weren't even sure the Lafayette Preventorium was still operating. There wasn't much more information to be gleaned on the other side of the ocean. When I visited Chavaniac, guides told me castle records for the Second World War no longer exist. This was later confirmed by Myriam Waze, founder of Le Club Lafayette. Thus I was forced to rely on other sources—like Gisèle Naichouler Feldman's touching memoir, entitled *Saved by the Spirit of Lafayette*.

Gisèle and her brother were hidden and protected at the chateau—and she recounts that an additional fifteen Jewish children were brought to the preventorium, betrayed by a supervisor, and escaped high into the mountains with the help of staff and resistance fighters. Unfortunately, this recollection does not name the persons involved in orchestrating the escape. Ms. Feldman also asserts that her brother witnessed resistance fighters storing weapons under the floorboards in the boys' dormitory of the preventorium, but again does not say which staff members aided or abetted them. The Resistance had a friend in the aging Marie-Louise LeVerrier, whose carefully worded letters, reprinted in *The Gazette of the American Friends of Lafayette*, tell us about the young German soldier who was beaten to death at the train station. In another issue, Clara Greenleaf Perry reported from her correspondence with those at the chateau that the castle's museum collection, including George Washington's dueling pistols, were hidden from the Nazis. Yet she doesn't say where or by whom. Resistants praised the women of Chavaniac for marching on Bastille Day in defiance of the Nazis, but didn't name which women of the

558 · AUTHOR'S NOTE

castle took part. Charles Boissier tells us a fifteen-year-old boy from the preventorium joined the Resistance, but not which one. These mysteries presented a real challenge. I had overwhelming evidence that heroic acts took place at and around Chavaniac—often by women and often in Lafayette's name, as the true story of Lafayette's stolen statue and the Secret Army of Lafayette attests—but I couldn't know *who* the heroes and heroines were.

I did know that after the Fall of France, the Baron de LaGrange served as interim president of the preventorium, and his twenty-five-year-old daughter, Anne, took over as acting president after her father's arrest by the Gestapo in 1943. Yet there are questions surrounding his arrest, which is commemorated by a brass plaque across from the Church of Saint-Roch. Discussions with modern-day residents of Chavaniac indicate that the baron's reputation is complicated. It's likely that he was not arrested for heroic resistance, but simply because he could serve as a high-status hostage. Yet in *Témoignages de résistants: 1940–1945*, a collection of firsthand recollections from the French Resistance—excerpts of which were generously provided to me by the United States Holocaust Memorial Museum—one resistance fighter went out of his way to say that Amaury de LaGrange was arrested by the Nazis *because he refused to collaborate* in connection with his aviation training school.

Given that the baron was the president of the influential Aéro-Club de France, that's certainly possible, and because of his honorable and heroic service in the First World War—not to mention his generally favorable view of Western democratic ideals—I would very much like to believe it. Unfortunately, the evidence is mixed. LaGrange seems to have been on good terms with the Vichy puppet government of France, and in a letter to his son, he praised Marshal Pétain for his negotiating skills. On the other hand, the baron also praised the Marshal for trying to be rid of Pierre Laval, who was seen as a far more malevolent collaborator. (Coincidentally, Laval's daughter and fierce defender married Lafayette's direct descendant René de Chambrun, son of Aldebert de Chambrun, whom I have Beatrice meet with in this novel. The loyalty of the Chambruns to the Vichy regime is beyond the scope of this novel because, of course, the Lafayette legacy was never about heredity.) Amaury de LaGrange's sympathies are difficult to unravel. LaGrange himself corresponded with the German Baron von Sichart, who wanted his opinion on how to gauge Americans entering the war. Yet far more damning is the fact that the baron testified for the collaborationist prosecution at the Riom Trial.

To paraphrase LaGrange biographer André Vignon: In the darkest hour of his country's moral need, LaGrange gave his support not to the forces of moderation, democracy, and progress, for which he had fought most of his life, but to a fascist regime. To put it mildly, taking part in a show trial was not the baron's finest hour, and though it's easy to judge from a distance of more than fifty years, it remains difficult to make sense of the family position on these matters. I don't know what Emily thought about the Riom Trial, but chose to portray her as disapproving, simply because I hope she was.

How the baron's daughter and successor felt can only be surmised. Anne, who was actually a young mother raising a baby in the village during the war, left behind little for me to unearth. In letters, Beatrice described Anne as being very beautiful but seemingly unaware of it. She also described Anne as being athletic and having knitted for the orphans when she was herself a young person. Unfortunately, I was unable to get much more of a picture from Anne's descendants. How much about Anne's political opinions could I infer from her husband, who became a conservative Catholic newspaperman in the aftermath of his release from a German prison camp? Did Anne know Jewish children were being sheltered at the preventorium—and if so, did she approve? Given her family's long-standing public service, I think it likely she would shelter Jewish children, but given her father's casual anti-Semitism, I couldn't be sure. Did Anne know guns were being hidden under the floorboards in the boys' dormitory? Again, I think it highly likely, since her brother-in-law, American spymaster Henry Hyde, was arming the French Resistance. (Fun fact: Henry Hyde was the son of James Hazen Hyde, who first took Beatrice Chanler to see Chavaniac.)

Given the instrumental role that Anne and her mother, Emily, played at the castle, it would have been *unconscionable* to leave their valiance out of a story about its history. But without more information, I couldn't make either of them the heroines of the novel. I love to write biographical fiction, but when the history is fraught and relatively recent, I'm wary of lionizing real historical figures who might not deserve credit, or demonizing any real person who might not be guilty.

That's where fiction came to the rescue. I decided to put a little distance between the historical Anne and her fictitious counterpart, Anna, by looking for a different heroine around which to center the story.

I noticed that in the 1918 yearbook for the preventorium, a bishop in Amiens refers to the plight of thousands of so-called children of the frontier: orphans and refugees, many of whom had unknown origins, and who were saved by the women of Chateau Lafayette. Then I found a picture from the castle—a child with flaxen braids, a lone girl sitting in a classroom of boys, looking straight at the camera with challenge in her eyes, as if demanding to be noticed.

I see you, I thought. And thus Marthe was born.

Historical fiction authors look for patterns and omissions in the records, and what I found was a Marthe-shaped hole. I made Marthe a teacher, because Pétain's National Revolution was first directed at educators. They were endlessly lectured against the French Revolution and Lafayettist notions of liberty, and they were coerced into spreading the Vichy regime's propaganda. I also made Marthe an artist as a tribute to Chavaniac artist-in-residence Clara Greenleaf Perry and the nearly 150 known forgers working in occupied France.

In fact, according to Peter Grose's *A Good Place to Hide*, while some forgers laboriously carved stamps modeled on the official versions, others made clever use of the primitive copying tablets used by schoolteachers. One of the actual resistance fighters from Chavaniac, Eugène Laurent, describes having been helped to go into hiding by a teacher at Chavaniac, so I decided that would be Marthe.

Marthe's method of using photograph paper to forge official documents comes from Marian Pretzel's *Portrait of a Young Forger*. And the method by which I had Marthe spring Monsieur Kohn from Rivesaltes prison camp, including the confusion of the German invasion, was the same means used by forger Oscar Rosowsky. Dr. Anglade and Dr. Boulagnon were true-life heroes, as was the Pinton family, who helped protect Jews in Paulhaguet, but Henri Pinton and his mother specifically are my own inventions. Meanwhile, I based Oscar on the historical figure of Madame Foch's son and the unknown fifteen-year-old resistance fighter from the preventorium. (The tragic anecdote of the boys, the cherries, and the ambulance comes straight from Madame LeVerrier's letters.)

As for Yves Travert, he was inspired by local police officer Marcel Fachaux, who was in charge of arresting Jews, but he and his wife, Marcelle, gave them forged papers instead. And Madame Xavier is representative of many Pétainist collaborators in France.

As for outright liberties, I made the fifteen Jewish children all girls to ease the logistics of getting them in and out of the castle through the historic secret tunnels. (The boys were housed separately.) How their escape was actually managed, we don't know. The stamping of French identity cards with the word *Juif* was not required in the Free Zone until a little after I posit in the novel. What happened to the foreign children Beatrice saved at the castle—if they were sent home after the war or allowed to remain as French citizens—is unclear except in the instance of Sétrak Simonian, who went on to become the village shoemaker. As for Washington's dueling pistols, they are now missing. Some stories say they were stolen from the chateau in the lifetime of Gilbert Bureaux de Pusy Du Motier de Lafayette, and others say they went missing later, but I like to believe that they're still there in the tunnels where I had Marthe hide them.

Finally, I have mentioned the French tricolor and the American flag flying side by side in 1939, but this might not have been a convention until after the war. You can see them flying at Chavaniac at the time of this writing, and I encourage you to visit this inspiring historic place if you're at all able.

For more information about my choices and changes in this novel, please see StephanieDray.com.

ACKNOWLEDGMENTS

This project is the most consuming I've ever undertaken, and I couldn't have done it without "my own dear heart," my incredible husband, who lived in the dungeon with me, fed and watered me like a houseplant, and pulled me back from the brink on more occasions than I care to recall. In addition to my wonderful sister and the rest of my family, there are so many other people to whom I am endlessly grateful, including especially William A. Chanler, whose dedication to his grandmother's memory was so touching and who granted me permission to incorporate Beatrice's own words into the novel and bring her story to life. I will miss our adventures together as historical detectives, but I know that we only uncovered the tip of the iceberg when it comes to Beatrice, and I'm hoping we can eventually explore another project about her beginnings!

In the meantime, I'd like to thank my long-suffering agent, Kevan Lyon, and my whip-smart and whip-cracking editor, Amanda Bergeron, without whom this would have never come to fruition. Thanks to the whole wonderful, scrappy team at Berkley, but especially Jin Yu, Bridget O'Toole, Lauren Burnstein, Loren Jaggers, Craig Burke, Jeanne-Marie Hudson, Claire Zion, Sareer Khader, Lindsey Tulloch, and Emily Osborne. Thanks also go to Richard Furlaud, Jr., who offered some insight into his grandfather Maxime; LaGrange descendants, including Jean Nicolay and Lorna Graev, who shed light on their family's accomplishments in and out of Chavaniac; Chuck Schwam and the American Friends of Lafayette; and Myriam Waze for all her knowledge about Chavaniac and the many theories we bounced back and forth across the ocean, as well as for the footwork she did asking current and former residents of the village for information. Thank you to Jean Masse for her recollections; the United States Holocaust Memorial Museum for testimonies of French Resistance fighters; and Odette Begon, Marjolaine Lacaze, and particularly Claire Pratviel for leading me on the tour at Chavaniac and answering my many questions.

I'm grateful to Annalori Ferrell and Karenna Sarney for research assistance; SarahScott Brett Dietz, MD, for consulting with me on medical questions; Megan Brett, Heather Webb, Janet Oakley, Melanie Meadors, Erin Bartie Krueger, Gérard Gotte, Jane Lee, Jason Jorgenson, Keith Massey, Erin Ahlstrom, Craig Hooker, and Jane Lee for help with French translations; Aimie Trumbly Runyan for help with telephone protocol; Stephen Wycoff for help with ships; Donna Lucey and Carol Rigolot for advice on research materials; Keith Massey, Jr., for help with legal questions; Andrew Cooper, Evan Singleton, David Passmore, Dave D'Alessio, and especially Christopher Otero and George William Claxton, for questions about weapons; Julia Faye Smith, Jennifer Hartley, Caroline Zarzar, Angie McCain, Kathy Wasserlein, and Jennifer Hartley, who gave early feedback; my mom, who put her eagle editor eye to work and helped me with some research to boot; and Kate Quinn, Lea Nolan, Laura Kamoie, Cara Kamoie, Michelle Moran, and Stephanie Thornton for brilliant time-sensitive critiquing—and all of them plus Christi Barth, Misty Waters, and Eliza Knight for being my writer besties, for years' worth of listening to me agonize over story problems, and for offering brilliant solutions and help whenever I asked.

For scenes with the duc d'Ayen, I was inspired by Charles Dance's performance in HBO's *Game of Thrones*. And for Adrienne's grandmother, I injected a little bit of my own great-grandmother, who was crazy like a fox.

Other books not previously cited in the Author's Note that were especially helpful sources include *Outwitting the Gestapo* by Lucie Aubrac; *Adrienne: The Life of the Marquise de La Fayette* by André Maurois; Jason Lane's *General and Madame de Lafayette: Partners in Liberty's Cause in the American and French Revolutions*; Stephen Halbrook's *Gun Control in Nazi-Occupied France: Tyranny and Resistance*; *Victor Chapman's Letters from France, with Memoir by John Jay Chapman*; Gérard M. Hunt's *Ram-*

bling on Saint Martin: A Witnessing; Charles Inman Barnard's *Paris War Days: Diary of an American*; and Constance Wright's *Madame de Lafayette*, the last of which served as an important resource for details about Adrienne's harrowing flight from Chavaniac.

Finally, I would like to credit Lafayette College for their interpretation of the motto *Cur non* as a rallying cry for service, leadership, and bold living—an interpretation that the Lafayettes would assuredly have approved: *Why not you? Why not here? Why not now?*